FORGOTTEN REFLECTIONS

———

A Novel

YOUNG-IM LEE

ISBN-10: 1684113822
ISBN-13: 978-1684113828

Dedicated to Oh Hak-Sun and Lee Young-Im,

my beloved grandmothers

PROLOGUE

"Do you believe our time will ever come?" An old lady said, lying on a hospice bed by the window that overlooked the bright night lights of Seoul.

She was not alone—no. She was in the city that never sleeps where a thousand lights stood witness to her passing with eyes that never blinked. They stood at an arm's length away, so close yet so far.

Mother. She said to herself. *Father.*

She was beneath the evergreen tree whose branches stood guard of their graves. *I'm coming...*

An incense-like scent wafted into the room, a mixture of medicine, antiseptic and dying flowers.

She had been searching for years, no decades even, for those warm dark brown eyes she vaguely recollected from a time that had long passed. *Yeong-Hoon,* she called.

There was nothing there but an old cracked guitar, an empty sofa and a TV that incessantly told her she did not belong in this world anymore. The lights outside blurred into a haze of colorful dots.

She knew he would never come back to her. She knew...she knew. She held on to that fact for as long as her train of thought would last. She had proof for when she would forget. Where was it again? She had hidden it somewhere safe, somewhere easily accessible.

A confetti of bleached white paper poured so heavily she thought she might drown in it. A tiger roared somewhere in the distance, and the world was crumbling around her. Had the war begun again?

She needed to be reminded of something—a truth of some sort that had kept her at the shores of an ocean fast disappearing. She was tempted to step in, her feet sinking into the sand as if it were ready to swallow her alive.

What was it?

Yeong-Hoon, she called again. She must remember him. No one else would.

Part 1

CHAPTER 1

[Present Day]

I live in Seoul, South Korea on the 35th floor in an apartment complex near City Hall. *Prime real estate.*

They say there was once a time when the only bright lights that filled the night sky came from another bomb falling to level this city. But times have changed. Instead, the stars have all but disappeared replaced with the unrelenting night lights of Seoul, flicking in colorful hues.

Throughout my adolescent years, I remember spending most mornings immobilized by the window, watching as dawn descended upon my city to reveal skyscrapers that paint the skies. I'd stand there overlooking cars and buses that rolled by in bright blue and green like toys on display. Office workers would trickle into bus stops as the sun finally peeked past the nearest high-rise to blind me awake. It would be another minute or two before I'd force my feet towards the drawer to get into my school uniform.

Thinking back, it was certainly a strange habit—one that had my mother puzzled as she directed a glare towards the back of my head. I'd like to think there was some reason behind my strange behavior. It probably had something to do with the bed that kept enticing me to come back. At least that's what I thought at the time, though it seems clearer to me now: It was the ultimate reminder that I too will be standing right there by the bus stop in a few minutes, if not in a few years when I must fend for myself in the world beyond my glass orb.

I'd always found it strange that some of the most mundane conversations remain vividly etched in my memory. It was one of those rare occasions our entire family gathered around the dinner table, spooning granny's kimchi-stew as we discussed some topic I'm sure I found amusing at the time. I remember thinking to myself that I should probably learn how to make it before granny dies (to this day, I regret never having asked). Perhaps my morbid thoughts had some genesis in the vivid dream I had the night before: A roar of an engine filled the sky before planes loomed over the highrises to hurl bombs at us.

"And so, what happened?" my dad asked.

I shrugged. "I think we were trying to run away, but it was too late. We were all blown to smithereens."

They held a moment of silence, wondering how to respond before bursting out into laughter. I don't know why they found it funny, but I laughed along too. Despite the oddity of that situation, frankly, it had been so long since we last had a decent family conversation that the moment just felt right.

When the laughter died down, granny took on a grave tone as she proceeded to say, "Don't run when the bombs drop. It's better to die comfortably in your own bed."

I wasn't quite sure if she was serious, but she had a point and I took it to heart. My parents would likely never know war before they die. Granny knew all too well, and I had a feeling war may not elude my generation altogether.

The rest of that evening centered around stories granny told about her time during the war—about how she had fed rice to refugees fleeing south, and sang us some Japanese song she had forgotten the meaning to. She told us about her cousin who was raped by a Japanese, Chinese or an American. She couldn't quite remember which one it was; those were turbulent times.

As with most stories my granny told, her tales seemed to be as tall as her voice was loud, though she was always adamant that they were one-hundred percent true.

So it goes.

Never mind the war that happened two generations ago or the possible one that might happen in the near future. North Korea has called wolf too many times for any of us to be seriously bothered, except maybe America that seems to need a reminder every so often that their almighty dollar is well spent on foreign soil. As far as technicality is concerned, Korea is still at war but just at a standstill.

That night passed in stellar normality though the memory of it mulled and struck a few years later sometime during my senior year of high school. One routine morning as I stood staring outside of my window half asleep, my mind drifted to my grandmother and that haunting dream I once had of the bombs as I shuddered awake with an epiphany: We were still at war—one that my very own rambunctious grandmother was a part of! I felt a strange affinity to the state of our nation since it was not unlike how I felt at eighteen—at a standstill, looking out of my glass orb into the real world I would soon join.

The alarm on my phone went off again and with it, all thoughts of war and my future were relegated to that space between dreams and reality.

I am Kim Jia, one insignificant student among a million others who are taught to stick our heads into the square confines of a book and stuff its contents in our minds so that when we emerge from the two-by-two, we will suddenly become massive successes in the three-dimensional world.

I am not here to moan about my situation in life. Many outside this orb have it a lot worse, stuck in a smaller, dirtier orb.

Or so I'm told.

This, in fact, is the story of my grandmother Ji Iseul, who passed at the age of eighty-four with Alzheimer's. I had never been curious about my grandmother nor her past. Perhaps this was because she repeated the same five stories as if her life could be summarized in bullet points:

1. How she had married my grandfather after the war
2. Relocated to Seoul
3. Set up one of the most successful businesses selling hand-crafted guitars all around the world
4. Had her first son
5. And had her second son

My mother is the only daughter, the rough that got stuck between two diamonds, and I, the daughter and only child to my mother. Needless to say, I rank quite low in this family. I never dream of inheriting a part of granny's business; that would be taken care of by my male cousins.

And so, my mother made it a point to drill into me that "time is of the essence" and that I must either become smart or beautiful to secure my future.

That was true. In fact, everything she said was true.

But the truth of the matter is, I got sick and tired of my mother repeating the same nagging remark of how great my future would be if only I would study harder. All the while, I witnessed my granny disintegrate into a catatonic state as I watched a perpetually numb look replace her once feisty temperament. I had turned sixteen when we figured out something was wrong with her, growing into the cusp of adulthood as my granny raced towards death. At eighteen, nearing my national exam and at the brink of breaking my glass orb, I was met with the sudden realization that the old woman I called granny might just be me, born two generations earlier and stuck in a body that refused to work.

And so, I did what every teenager would do—procrastinate, perhaps even live in denial of the upcoming exam. *Rebel*, as mother would say. But really, who could blame us? We were all just passing the time until our lives would presumably begin. It just so happened that for me, a chance event had set me on a very particular path that led down the road to my grandmother's past.

***

It was early in May and granny sat in her wheelchair staring blankly at the TV. She wasn't in a hurry to go anywhere, at least not until she was startled by mom.

"Jia, could you please check your granny's room to see if we forgot anything?" Mom shouted from the other end of our apartment. Granny was sure to sense an unease in her voice; she may even remember today was an important day, though she probably couldn't quite recall the exact details.

I grunted, ruffling the pages of my textbook as I stomped out of my room.

"Honey, I don't see why it has to be tonight," dad said as mom ran around the kitchen wrapping kimchi-stained china in newspaper so they wouldn't break during the move.

Mom sighed. "I doubt there is another hospice center that's on the top floor of a skyscraper and I don't see how we'll find another place she'll like. We should go before she forgets she ever liked it."

It seemed granny had gotten used to living so high up in the sky. She had barely left our apartment the past two years as she slowly lost her mind. I could see how the lights at night kept her company, just as they often kept me company most nights as I fought drowsiness to memorize an extra page of my textbook.

But there was one thing my dad and I could agree on: Why would granny need china at an old person's home? God knows we were already paying a fortune!

"If we take it, she'll use it one way or another it," mom would say.

Earlier that afternoon, the owner of the hospice center reassured mother, "Not to worry! Everything will be well taken care of," he had said, and with those magical words, my mom's hand reached for her credit card. I was there too. If you ask me, the man's voice was a tad too high-pitched as his eyes too heavily fixed on my mom's hand.

It was all granny's money anyway and she had finally chosen a place. Frankly, our entire extended family was more relieved than anything. All of us knew mom was too busy taking care of granny's old instrument business to be properly taking care of a woman with late-stage Alzheimer's.

A strange feeling washed over me as I stepped into her room. It was almost as if the same doorway I had walked through a thousand times before somehow resisted my intrusion now that granny would no longer be living with us. It seemed as though it was in the process of being haunted. In time, I could pinpoint that strange feeling I had as I walked past the threshold of her room. It was the feeling of breaking free from shackles I never knew I had— finally free from her heavily supervised stories that had been told with the exclusivity of her own perspective.

They would still be granny's stuff no matter how much time would pass; but strangely, in those first few moments, I began to see them as mere objects. I imagine it is the same feeling detectives have when they walk into a crime scene for the first time.

I pulled open a stubborn drawer to find pictures of family, weddings, trips abroad, and of course, the one that swept my imagination in a whirlwind of curiosity.

It was an old black and white polaroid that seemed to have been taken in a hurry. The two soldiers stood too far from the camera that their faces were barely recognizable. I knew my grandfather had fought in the war so it must be him and one of his buddies. Surrounded by white soldiers, the two Korean soldiers stood in the middle of what looked like a warehouse full of crates.

In between them was an object wrapped in one of those old rice sacks. The curvature was distinct: a body arched in the middle with a stick poking out of the top. *A guitar.* There was something tantalizingly curious about the silhouette of something so common in our family. In fact, a guitar sat in the corner of granny's room just as it always had for as long as I could remember, collecting dust. I squinted at the picture, hoping it would help resolve the strangeness I felt.

I had always known granny came from a long line of carpenters and founded the first guitar manufacturing company in South Korea. But what was my grandfather doing with the instrument during the war? As far as I knew, he hadn't even met grandma until after the war.

I picked up the dusty guitar to look at the manufacturing information. Every guitar had one stuck on the inside where light reached through the sound hole. I held it close to my face, almost as if I knew a thing or two about handling guitars.

"Established 1953, Ji-Iseul Instruments, Co. Seoul, Kr. Date produced: March 1954"

I was right. The war ended in 1953 and she had established her company soon after.

"Jia, hurry up! We'll wait in the car okay?" My mom yelled.

I finally remembered what I was there for. Looking around, I saw nothing out of ordinary as the room stood just as it had been for years, full of granny's junk that consisted of wooden pieces, miniature instruments, scratches on her counter top, and pictures of her instruments taken with famous musicians nailed along the walls. Surely, mom didn't expect me to load all of it, did she?

Outside, I heard soft chatter from mom and dad as the elevator dinged open. I lunged to grab the guitar along with the photo. I figured, if this particular guitar was important enough to collect dust in granny's room for decades, it can keep collecting dust in her new room.

***

Granny's new home was aptly named "Sky Nursing Home,"

overlooking the entire northern side of Seoul. It was around 8 PM when I saw her looking out the glass window down onto the busy streets where cars passed by with their pretty lights. I placed the guitar against the wall and the picture on her bed stand as I settled in a chair close by, ready to unpack my books and set up a make-shift studying station for the evening.

My granny had always been the talkative type, at least up until Mr. Alzheimer set up shop in her brain. These days, she babbles.

"What is it, granny?" I asked. "Water? Your glasses?"

I followed her eyes to the guitar that leaned against the wall. It was as if she had seen a long-lost friend, her hands grappling towards it as her mouth and legs failed to follow the spark in her eyes. I brought it to her, but her hand kept flailing until it caught in the sound hole.

"Granny, no!" I said as I gently guided her calloused hand out. She was a child now—beyond all of us and it had taken us nearly two years to accept the reality of her situation.

Barely visible, a wrinkly brown slip of paper peeped out from the sound hole. Granny's eyes were still fixed on it. Was this what she was looking for? How had I not seen it before when I looked inside the sound hole?

I unfolded the delicate page. "October 12, 1949."

The date was written neatly, but the rest of the note was scribbled in boxy letters. Whoever wrote the letter was in a hurry, but it was undoubtedly written in a hand that was common amongst old well-educated men. It took a while to decipher but I finally made sense of it:

"My dearest Ji Iseul, I am sorry. I wish I had something better to say. If this letter doesn't reach you, it saddens me to think that you'll remember me as a traitor."

Was that it? I flipped it backward and sideways. So much of the page had been left unused and the words were written in the top margin of the page as if the writer had so much more to say, but hadn't gotten to writing it.

Granny's hand still stiffened towards the letter, her gaze fixed on me. Perhaps she wanted me to read it. She leaned back into her pillow as I cleared my throat.

I read the letter. Once, and then twice, and whenever I tried to stop, granny grew restless again. She clamored for the guitar as if I hadn't just found the letter in it minutes ago. Perhaps there was another. I brought the guitar close to us again, rattled it to listen for any loose pieces, but there was no indication of any foreign objects within.

I sighed. "Sorry, granny. There's just this one."

There was something about the letter, no, something about the combination of that night that kept my mind churning. Perhaps it was the way the guitar had animated my granny from her stupor. I couldn't deny that some part of me envied how she still had something worth getting excited over at her age. Perhaps it was the mounting stress of my upcoming exam—the lure of examining a life-lived, hoping it would lighten the weight of my own uncertain future.

Who really knows?

In the weeks after, my mother clarified that night for me: "What's the use in trying to unravel the mind of an Alzheimer's patient?"

And so, the story begins. But before we delve into this tale, perhaps it might be worthwhile to clarify the facts:

1. My granny was born March 15, 1927. She was seventeen when the mysterious letter was written, the same age I was when I discovered it that night.
2. My granny lived through the War. The rest of the world would know it as "The Forgotten War," but who really remembers? It was fought between June 1950 - July 1953. 1.2 million soldiers died. They say more than twice as many civilians perished.
3. Three clues fueled my investigations: the photograph, the guitar, and of course the letter.

Disclaimer:

1. This is not meant to be a war story, though a war is fought in it. It's all well and good since wars mostly look the same all around the world. Different machinery, same outcome.
2. This is not meant to be a story about Korea. You'll see people in an unfamiliar location, but it is home to them.
3. This, in fact, is a story about growing up and preparing to die all too soon.

CHAPTER 2

[Autumn, 1946]

"Turn it off! Turn that damn radio off!"

The driver could barely understand thirteen-year-old Jung-Soo who heaved with his head hanging out of the car window.

"I'm sorry, sir!"

The rocky gravel road paved into dust as Jung-Soo's car approached his new school. He could almost hear the whispers from the students who crowded the windows as they shouted, "He's here! The new prince of the Golden Palace is here!"

"Wow, take a look at that car!" another student added.

If there was one thing Jung-Soo hated more than motion sickness, it was the prying eye he thought he would escape when he left the big city. He swore that day that cars were meant for cities and not for some remote rice farming village in Yeoju. He never much liked the car anyway, particularly because it had his father's mark all over it, engineered and made with his own two hands to have the latest modern conveniences.

"To the back!" Jung-Soo screamed to his driver.

"Sir?"

"Park behind the school, you idiot! Do you expect me to show up to my first day of school looking like this?"

The car lurched to a stop next to a giant grandfather tree whose branches hung like an umbrella above the school building. Jung-Soo jumped out of the car, held onto the trunk of the tree and gave another heave. He could still feel the prickly heat of curious eyes trying to peer past the branches.

"You okay there?" It was the voice of a girl. Before he could turn around to see who it was, she had placed her hand on his back.

A warmth rushed through his body like the times his mother had given him a pat on the back for being such a good boy. It was the same warmth he felt rush out of her as she died in his arms, blood oozing from her bowels where a Japanese sword had punctured.

He hated them—the coldness of men with guns and swords and most of all, the warmth that reminded him of his mother.

"Get your dirty hands off me." Jung-Soo swatted the hand away. He scanned the girl from head to toe. Her filthy hands mopped against the rag-like dress of her hanbok as she held a wooden bowl of water with leaves that floated atop the surface.

It then dawned on him. "You're here to win my favor," he touted. He knocked the bowl out of her hand and snapped his fingers at the driver. "Get her out of my sight. She's nauseating."

What Jung-Soo didn't realize was that this little girl, who seemed timid enough at first, could possibly be the feistiest girl in the village. Most knew not to bully her, perhaps because they knew whose daughter she was. The girl's father was the carpenter who lived at the foot of the mountain, and everyone knew carpenters harbored ghosts, so unless they wanted one to tag along with their next table, chair, cabinet, or paper delivery, they knew to keep out of the girl's way.

"What utter nonsense!" the girl said under her breath as she returned to the well, crouching as she let out her anger on the rags. She scrubbed so hard that the dust unsettled under her, clinging back onto the wet rag.

She hadn't realized how loud she had spoken. She peered back to a silent figure who glared at her as the entire school watched on. She rolled her eyes and decided she didn't care.

Jung-Soo couldn't back down now. "What did you just say?"

"You heard me, you little rascal!"

"Are you unaware of who my father is?" He stomped across the dusty ground and towered above the girl. "You just wait! I'll see that you never step foot in this school and I'll kick your entire family out of this good-for-nothing village!"

The girl had had enough. She threw the rags back into the dust and stood up. As short as she was, she had no problem staring him down with her signature glare.

"WHAT. UTTER. NONSENSE," she enunciated. "I'd love to see you try because I don't go to school and I don't even live in this village."

She gathered her belongings as Jung-Soo stood there, stunned. His nausea seemed to be coming back as the whispers from the school windows traveled with the light breeze straight into his ears. Backing down now would be a dishonor, the boy was convinced of it.

"You!"

She ignored him.

"Who do you think you are?" he yelled out.

The girl lifted her hefty wooden backpack onto her shoulders and walked up to Jung-Soo.

"Iseul. I'm Ji Iseul," she said.

With a glint of a smile that smeared across her satisfied face, she walked straight past him towards a line of shocked faces peering out of the window.

She was almost tempted to look back.

***

The birds in the surrounding mountains stirred as if they too heard Iseul declare her name, fluttering out of the trees in unison with her footsteps. With the wooden back-carrier, *chige* filled to the brim with firewood and hand-crafted paper, Iseul glanced at the sun making its final descent towards the tip of the mountains.

Her steps quickened; she had three more houses to go.

At the village restaurant, Mi-Jung's mother peered out of the kitchen welcoming Iseul who stacked the firewood by the outdoor stove.

"Iseul, is that you? Just in time, my dear. Are you hungry?"

Mi-Jung's mother always had a stern but warm air about her. Perhaps it was because she felt Iseul would be a good friend to her daughter, who like Iseul, was raised by a single parent. They all wore worn out hanbok dresses where the cuffs were less than crisp and the colors faded almost beyond recognition. Iseul looked down at her own dress for the first time in many months. She sighed as she saw that the bottom hem rose above her ankles and was stained with mud.

"I'm fine, thank you," Iseul said, ready to leave as quickly as she had come. She nearly bumped into Mi-Jung stumbling around with a sack of rice. They quickly diverted eye-contact. The two had already decided to steer clear of each other so as not draw any more attention to their pitiful predicament.

Mi-Jung's mother handed Iseul a piece of cinnamon hotcake left from the night before and although it wasn't hot or even warm, it reminded Iseul of the rare occasion her mother had made some for her. With a mouth full of ironically cold hotcakes and her shoulders somewhat lightened from the delivery, she stepped back onto the dusty road. She collected the sum of money, bowed to say goodbye and went on her merry way.

Funny how coincidences work in a small village. Just around the corner stood Jung-Soo, venturing his new village alone. They held a momentary look of surprise, diverted and went on their respective ways again.

Next stop was the home of the village's oldest grandmother. Placing a stack of wood right by the fireplace, Iseul left in a flurry, though she knew it was rude.

"Iseul... Iseul," the grandmother's voice quivered as she tried to project. "Promise me you'll collect your money next time, okay?"

The old woman stood by the entrance of her home, holding a handful of home-grown peppers she had saved for her all week. Now the old lady had no choice but to eat them herself.

There he was again, Jung-Soo at the end of that street that led to the Golden Palace. They shared another sneer, trying their best to ignore each other. In all honesty, Iseul had been replaying the earlier events of that day with some regret. She had, after all, insulted the son to the most powerful man in the village.

She watched helplessly as the sun disappeared into the mountains, waiting for Jung-Soo to walk ahead of her. When she couldn't loiter any longer, she headed to her final stop of the day.

It was a thing of beauty under the right circumstances. The "Golden Palace" wasn't actually made of gold nor was it a proper palace, but it was called so because of the lights that never ceased to spill from the only infrastructure in the small village that completely ran on electricity. They say it was grand and some envied the maids and even Iseul who were some of the few who had witnessed the insides of the palace. Iseul had never made it past the gardens, but if the insides were as grand and as the neatly kept as the garden outside, she could just imagine how extravagant it was bound to be on the inside.

She had seen it many times before when she had delivered firewood to the Yamamoto family who had built the premises as the Imperial Japanese headquarters for the 'export' of rice to Japan. It was colonial tax to put it gently, and stealing to be precise. All the while, the people who farmed the rice were starving. Yet, it was the beacon that taught all those who saw it to bow to the superiority of the Japanese.

She remembered it like it was yesterday—the elders in the village celebrating when the Palace was finally emptied of the stench of the Japanese while the children, who were taught to idolize their colonizers, cried that their Japanese guardians had abandoned them.

Iseul had never liked these men who spoke in a smooth tongue, which was just another reason she didn't get along with the other kids in the village. Now, it seemed another idiot would be replacing the Japanese.

Iseul took a deep breath as she walked into the dimly lit garden. She was already late which meant the two men waiting for her at home would go hungry for a little while longer. She held her stomach that growled at the thought of food.

"What are you doing here?" someone said.

Iseul stopped in her tracks, tracing the voice to a vague figure that laid watching the night sky with arms wide open. In our language, we call such a person, 'one born with a golden spoon in one's mouth.'

"I'm here to deliver your firewood," Iseul replied.

"Get out."

The words spilled out of Jung-Soo so naturally that it became quite clear that such a tone was part of his routine demeanor. Iseul seemed to have come to her senses and decided it was best to keep quiet. She did what she was paid to do, though she couldn't completely erase her brazen nature. She lifted the pile of wood and plopped it right next to Jung-Soo's face, close enough that he could feel the breeze as the pile landed. Iseul stomped towards the gate.

"Wait…" Naturally, he was curious. Who did this girl think she was? *Iseul,* he remembered. "Take your trash with you," he said, waving at the pile.

She was ready to burst—waiting to give him a lesson or two on the repercussions of *not* having firewood and how he would freeze his precious toes off and die of hunger in the winter months ahead. The ever-reserved voice of her father reminding her to keep her mouth shut barely registered and she had long forgotten her painful troubles with the Japanese.

"Sure thing!" Iseul answered, at first. But mind you, my dear readers, this is my granny Iseul we're talking about and so she went right ahead and said exactly what was on her mind.

Jung-Soo was intrigued more than anything. The precise concoction of raging hormones and a tinge of teenage rebellion got him wondering who would break first.

"Alright. Just leave it there." Jung-Soo finally stood up and smiled. This girl called Iseul was growing on him. He held his hand out for her to shake. "It's nice to meet you, Ji Iseul. Next time, if you're going to annoy me, address me by my name. I'm Ham Jung-Soo."

Strange, she thought. She watched Jung-Soo's hand hang in the air, her eyes meeting his firm resolve. She couldn't bring herself to extend her calloused hands, too small, ugly and too heavy with stubborn pride to meet his.

Jung-Soo saw her hands lingering unsure around her skirt as he found himself drawn to her right hand as he reached to grab a hold of it. He had seen the callouses that covered every inch of her palm earlier that day, but his disgust was oddly displaced with a calmness that came with encasing her small but sturdy hand in his own. He shook it with such enthusiasm that Iseul, for a fleeting moment, believed her heart skipped a beat. It must be her anger. Yes, she was angry—very angry.

It was too dark to know for sure if they were gazing into each other's eyes, or for how long they stood there shaking hands, but it was Jung-Soo who walked away first.

"See you again," he said, as he took his spot in same the patch of grass, star-gazing.

Iseul left the premises in a haze and when she passed the bounds of the Golden Palace, she leaned against its metal gates and let the cool summer breeze bring her back to her senses.

"What utter nonsense," she whispered under her breath.

Jung-Soo heard those signature words as he let out a smile he knew no one would see in the dark. A strange sense of familiarity rose from the pit of his stomach—a warm feeling he had tried so hard to quell over the years but was now gushing forth.

Somehow, this time around, it didn't feel so bad to hear those words.

It almost felt like home.

CHAPTER 3

[August 1948]

Exactly three years after ousting the Japanese from the Korean Peninsula, history records that on August 15, 1948, two separate Korean governments were established, the North championing communism as the South established itself as a democratic nation.

Despite the division, the day was marked with hope, of the endless possibilities ahead, and of the blissful ignorance of the years of bloodshed and war that would soon come.

Jung-Soo and Iseul are now seventeen.

***

Yeoju, also known as the rice capital of Korea, is situated southeast of Seoul, central to the entire Korean Peninsula. Flat plains meet rocky peaks as the Han river runs thick through its center, flowing down from the heart of Seoul. The region is known for crops other than rice, as the natural irrigation of the river provides a rich bed for a wide array of produce to be grown. Sweet potatoes were sweeter than in any other place in the Peninsula, as were the yellow melons that grew crisper and brighter.

But further down south, straddled on the southern mountains of Yeoju was a small farming village. There was nothing special about this village nor will it be remembered once all is said and done. It was in every sense of the word, plain—bland even, only useful for its mediocre harvesting potential of the nation's staple, rice, averaging far lower yields than the villages of northern Yeoju. In fact, the village had no name other than its nickname, "the Wasteland" for its dusty gravel plains that lay at the foot of two mountain ridges that came together from the East and the West, blocking all road that led to the south of the peninsula.

The days were long and hard as both men and women, boys and girls, hunched back in the rows of muddy green rice paddies. And when the sun rose to its peak and beat down too hard to endure, they would gather by the river underneath the shade of pavilions and persimmon trees that were beginning to bud. The sound of men and boys wrestling would fill the air as masked men and women danced to the sound of buk drums. Kites fluttered by the narrow riverbed where women kept watermelon steeped in the chilly water as the children gathered, each awaiting his or her turn for a slice to quench their thirst.

While the rest of the village was busy planting and harvesting rice throughout the year, Iseul roamed the mountains southeast of the Wasteland, harvesting from the trees that fed her appetite for instrument crafting.

The haegeum was her current muse. It was the first instrument her father taught her how to make, though for a while, Iseul didn't much like the sound since she thought the stringed instrument could barely hold a note long enough to convey what it meant. It sounds like a crow's caw, muted and extended in various notes as if it had heard a song bird and cried in envy. As odd as it may sound at first, the cries of the haegeum eventually grew on her and soon enough, Iseul was out and about her mountain, looking for just the right tree to cut down.

Father usually used oak to make furniture and the rarer birch tree to decorate in contrast with the darker oak. But Iseul's favorite was the pine that sprinkled across the entire mountain range. She loved them for their softness and lightness, which perfectly suited her coarse temperament. Hammering away at chunks and pieces of wood, pinewood would indulge her stubbornness to bend and twist to her will. Even when winter came and left the fields and hills covered in dreary white snow and the leafless tree trunks boasted of their uniform color, the pine tree's green bristles always reminded her that spring would come soon enough.

August was the month of harvest and while most of the

villagers were busy lending a helping hand before the frosts arrived, three kids roamed the mountains of Yeoju.

"Yeong-Hoon oppa! I don't know why it isn't working." Iseul called her fiancé as she banged the side of the radio.

"I told you it'll be easier if I just do it." He took Iseul's spot as the radio mechanic.

Though a cripple whose left leg limped a step behind the right, Yeong-Hoon was a man among men—a responsible fellow whose past had always struck Iseul as mysterious, confusing and perhaps even amusing. He was a man of the sea. He could feel the strength of the ocean coarse through his veins, harnessing the power of the waves to travel here and there. He had shown up one day at Iseul's family home and long before Iseul knew what the word 'daeril-fiancé' meant, her parents had decided she was to be engaged to this fine young gentleman.

Like all things, Iseul protested when she found out. But when the village kids bullied Yeong-Hoon for being a cripple and criticized her parents for upholding such old traditions, Iseul found herself seriously conflicted as to which of the two sides deserved greater protest. Sentiment had never been an issue—she really couldn't care less who she married at that age. But eventually, by means of rote calculations, she conceded. With many more voices to protest against in the village, and with the sudden passing of Iseul's mother, the village voices vastly outnumbered the ones at home so soon, she became amenable to the idea of a traditional marriage.

Besides, the villagers didn't know Yeong-Hoon like she did. He had always had a special gift: a heart so big, ears wide open and eyes that pierced through the most hardened exterior and peered into souls. It was a difficult gift to notice at first, but anyone who would give him the time of day would quickly be blind to his crippled state. Iseul was certain of it!

Since that fateful day, Iseul and Yeong-Hoon grew up as siblings-fiancés and with the addition of Jung-Soo, the three became inseparable.

"What'll you do for me if I win this round?" Jung-Soo beckoned Iseul with her favorite 'ja-chi-gi' stick.

"What will *you* do for me if I win?" Iseul ran towards Jung-Soo who was already practicing batting the 'baby stick' with the larger one.

"Quiet down a bit, will you? I can't hear the radio," Yeong-Hoon said.

"Sorry, hyung," Jung-Soo said, turning to Iseul. "I'll make a radio for you."

"Really? You can do that?" Iseul naively said, then looked at Jung-Soo suspiciously. "Then why do you always steal the village radio if you can make your own?"

He grunted. "Fine! What do you want?"

"Teach me how to read."

"Read? And what will a simple girl like you do once you learn?"

"Well," she began thinking. "I haven't thought that far ahead yet." Jung-Soo had that smug look again which only meant she was being made a fool of. "After all the things I've done for you, you should be glad I still hang around such a snobby rich kid! That's the least you can do for me!"

Jung-Soo had long outgrown his childish egoism, but who could resist teasing this girl? "Alright, alright," he pretended to concede. "Reading isn't hard at all. I'm sure I can get someone as simple as you reading in no time!" Jung-Soo boasted. "But if I win, you have to teach me as well."

"Teach you?" Iseul couldn't possibly conceive of a single thing Jung-Soo could learn from her.

"Carpentry!" he said.

"Oh…"

"I want to learn how to work with wood!"

"And what's a rich boy like you going to do with that? Why don't you ask Yeong-Hoon since he's the real expert? Oppa," she called to Yeong-Hoon, "Jung-Soo wants to learn…"

But before Iseul could finish her sentence, Jung-Soo leaped to cover Iseul's mouth.

"Owww! What's wrong with you?" she said.

"Sorry, it's just that… you see…" Jung-Soo hesitated. "Maybe it's better if he doesn't find out, you know, with him spending so much time with your father and all."

"What do you mean?"

Iseul hadn't always been the brightest when it came to these things. We call it "noon-chi," meaning wit or sense.

"Seriously, work on your noon-chi," Jung-Soo said.

Iseul stopped to think for a moment. "What's noon-chi got to do with anything?" she said, eyeing him suspiciously. "I see what you're doing here! You're trying to get me distracted so that you'll win the game. You sly little brat!"

Jung-Soo gave up. He stuck his tongue out at her. "You go first. On the count of three. Hurry or you'll be disqualified!"

With all sense of initial mistrust gone, Iseul yanked the stick from Jung-Soo's hand and scurried to her place. "Wait, I'm not ready yet!"

Jung-Soo began his count. "One… two…"

She readied herself to swing the batting stick.

"Three!"

Three things happened at once, only one of which caught Iseul's attention. With all her might, Iseul swung her stick just as Yeong-Hoon yelled, "Got it!" as the radio came roaring alive.

Buried beneath the sound of the blaring radio was Jung-Soo's painful "Owwww!" as Iseul swung at a rather tender spot.

"Turn it up!" Iseul said as the lyrics wistfully sang the classic, "Tears for my hometown village, Mokpo," completely oblivious to the fact that she had almost emasculated Jung-Soo.

Yeong-Hoon chortled under his breath, watching Jung-Soo cradle his crotch.

"Turn the channel! I hate that song!" Jung-Soo whimpered, limping towards the other two.

The jachi-gi game was quickly forgotten as the three huddled around the radio. It had become a sort of ritual of theirs, 'chasing radio channels like fireflies,' as Iseul would often say. Jung-Soo and Iseul would tug the radio back and forth, run after each other up and down the hill to find the perfect spot where the trees didn't block out too much of the sound coming through. At times, they would listen to the classics or what Jung-Soo called old-fashioned, and at other times, they would get lost in the stories of adventure, friendship, love and even loss through the sound waves that briefly came and fluttered away with the wind.

The sound of music sizzled away as a man's voice replaced it, cutting through with a sense urgency: "We interrupt your regularly scheduled broadcast to bring you this public service announcement: The election results are finally in! Today, August 15th, 1948 marks a historic day for our nation, the Republic of Korea. Yes, it is official, we are finally a democratic nation! The United Nations has announced…."

The three listened on, petrified.

"We're in so much trouble..." Iseul's voice lingered.

The entire the village would have heard the news by now and would be making their way one-by-one to Mi-Jung's restaurant to celebrate their independence, looking forward to the Presidential address. Iseul could imagine Mi-Jung's mother panicking as she opened the cabinet in the restaurant to find the radio missing.

The three shuffled like deer being hunted. Yeong-Hoon packed the radio, placing it back into the make-shift rice sack. "Jung-Soo, we're depending on you!" he said.

Jung-Soo let out a little groan. "Why do I always have to do all the running?"

Iseul shot a look at him. "You should have thought of that before you went ahead and 'borrowed' the village's only emergency radio."

Jung-Soo begrudgingly put the knapsack on and began his descent, first limping and when his crotch finally eased up, he ran and disappeared into the trees.

"What's wrong with him? Did he hurt his leg on the way up?" Iseul said, noticing Jung-Soo's limp.

Yeong-Hoon smirked. "He'll be fine."

With a worried look on her face, Iseul and Yeong-Hoon also made their way towards the village, Yeong-Hoon shuffling a step behind her quickening pace.

***

Rarely did the village come alive as it did in times of celebration. Children populated the edges of the restaurant, skipping stones to a song they didn't know wasn't in their own language as farmers and their sons drifted inside in batches of three and four.

To add to the festivities, women gathered together bringing in root vegetables they had cultivated in the patches of land around their homes, bartering with each other to be part of the merriments. Mi-Jung's mother took them gratefully, putting the women to work, and bringing out larger mats to accommodate the sudden influx.

"A bit more rice wine here!" the village scholar roared. Mi-Jung, who was serving bone broth to Mr. Park, heard the call and ran back towards the kitchen.

Jung-Soo approached the restaurant from the side, closing in on the little girls playing hopscotch, nearly tripping over them as he barely hung on to the knapsack. He could see the village leaders gathered inside the restaurant where the radio belonged, the dusty yard quickly filling with farmers. It was clear Jung-Soo needed a stealthy plan to place the radio back, and a quick one at that.

Out of the corner of his eye, he saw his father seated amongst the leaders, his silhouette sipping rice wine and nodding at the others. *So, he was finally back in the village,* Jung-Soo thought. *How long till he would disappear again?*

"Ah my dear Jung-Soo," a familiar voice approached from behind, as a sturdy pat landed on his shoulder. Jung-Soo froze in place. He turned around to find Mr. Lim, the local farmer and one of his father's loyal dogs.

"I see you've come to hear the presidential address! Look at you, a real Korean patriot! Your father must be so proud."

Jung-Soo politely nodded, as Iseul taught him was proper etiquette.

"You must know my son, Byung-Guk," Mr. Lim said, pulling his son in next to him.

Byung-Guk was drenched in sweat, the white fabric of his work clothes clinging onto his skin. He shot Jung-Soo a look of such blatant disgust that it got Jung-Soo thinking...

"Of course, I do, Mr. Lim! We're best buddies at school!" Jung-Soo replied in a sickeningly superficial tone, putting his arm around Byung-Guk as he let out an involuntary sigh of disgust. He was acutely aware that it would now be impossible to complete his task without being noticed.

Another farmer from across the yard yelled towards Mr. Lim. "Why don't you let your son loose for a while and come spend time with someone your own age!"

For that brief moment Mr. Lim's attention had been diverted, Jung-Soo took the opportunity to make his case. Tightening his grip on Byung-Guk in a head lock, he whispered, "Do me a favor this one time! If you do this, I promise I won't tell your father that you skipped school to spy on Mi-Jung."

"Who told you that?" Byung-Guk wrestled, attempting to free himself, but it was useless. His attention shot towards Mi-Jung who was wiping a bead of sweat off her forehead as she ran back and forth from the kitchen to the farmers in the yard.

"I'll be right there!" Mr. Lim yelled and when he faced the boys again, Byung-Guk already had a crooked smile on and had stopped trying to wriggle out. "Two strong and sturdy Korean boys! Here," Mr. Lim forced a Jeon coin into Jung-Soo's hand. "You two grab yourselves a hearty bowl of bone broth as you listen to the broadcast."

Before Jung-Soo could refuse the money, as was proper etiquette, Mr. Lim was already on his way to his friends. Jung-Soo unclasped his headlock and looked down at the Japanese coin.

"What? What is it you want from me?" Byung-Guk said, suspiciously.

"It really is the simplest favor," he said, passing along the rice sack covering the radio within. "You see that large wooden cabinet next to where the men are sitting?"

"Yeah…" Byung-Guk said.

"All you have to do is get this bag in there! Simple, isn't it?"

Byung-Guk took a long look at the knapsack, curious as to what was inside. He didn't want to know. Taking another look at Mi-Jung, the knapsack and the room full of men, he tore it out of Jung-Soo's arm and grunted.

"Fine, but if this goes wrong, I'm taking you down with me." Byung-Guk's voice shook as he whispered, "Don't think I don't know what you and your *commie* friends are up to when you skip school."

It was a fearless threat—one a mere farmer's boy wouldn't dare do to the Prince of the Golden Palace without any real proof. Jung-Soo deserved it; it was a threat for a threat.

"Thanks, my friend," Jung-Soo said nonchalantly as he flicked the Japanese coin towards Byung-Guk who barely caught it mid-air. With nothing to hide anymore, Jung-Soo trotted amongst the farmers in the yard towards the entrance where he saw two distant figures approaching.

Byung-Guk fumed, one arm embracing the knapsack and in the other hand, holding his own father's money.

Iseul ran up to Jung-Soo. "What happened? Did you get in trouble?"

"Who do you think you're talking to? Of course not! I'm Jung-Soo and the situation is under control," he said, smugly.

"What did you do now?" Yeong-Hoon said with a disconcerting look, and as if he had recited a chant, a familiar voice projected from within the restaurant loud enough for the three to hear.

"Who are you, boy?" a man sternly said.

Jung-Soo jerked his head towards the voice he immediately recognized. His father's Captain was wrestling Byung-Guk in the restaurant, the radio spilling from the knapsack with a thud on the wooden floor.

"Oh no…" Jung-Soo mumbled.

"I said who are you, boy?" The Captain's voice grew louder as the festivities in the yard turned into murmurs of concern.

"I'm Byung-Guk, sir."

One of the leaders seemed to have recognized the boy. "Oh yes, Byung-Guk. That's the Lim's boy." He let out a chuckle, failing to lighten the mood.

Half-way through delivering the next bowl of soup, Mi-Jung had also noticed the commotion as well.

The guards surrounded the boy, holding and patting him down, but Byung-Guk wasn't having any of it, elbowing and fidgeting as much as possible as he yelled, "Get off me! I didn't do anything wrong! I said get off me!"

"Where did you get this radio?" the Captain said.

Mr. Lim's head turned from his chess game at a familiar voice, his face pale white as he ran and knelt in front of a man who sat sipping rice wine. It was Jung-Soo's father, Ham Young-Nam.

"I'm so sorry sir, I apologize," Mr. Lim said to Jung-Soo's father who still remained reticent. Jung-Soo's father turned his head ever so slightly towards the entrance as Jung-Soo's eyes flickered in recognition, struggling to keep eye contact with the man.

"Oh no, Jung-Soo," Iseul said, "tell me you're not responsible for this."

He didn't blink as the standoff continued. Of all the people in this world, Jung-Soo promised he would not back down to his father. The leader broke first, turning away as he spoke to his Captain. The entire village, even the little girls who had been singing, were acutely aware of the man who owned the Golden Palace as they listened on.

"Let go of him," he commanded in his soft-spoken tone that did nothing to take the edge off his words. "Can't you see he is a wise boy? He used the eastern entrance since the western one was occupied."

Jung-Soo knew all too well about his father and the games he played. His father had always loved riddles and numbers as if being a good father meant that he should confuse his children with useless proverbs.

The Captain let the boy go as Mr. Lim profusely thanked Mr. Ham for his graciousness. One at a time, the leaders held their cups up. "Nothing to worry about," an older man said. "Drink! Let's drink to our new country!"

The festivities continued as Jung-Soo turned and began walking away from the restaurant.

"Aren't you going to clear that up?" Yeong-Hoon said, following behind Jung-Soo and Iseul who seemed happy to be on their way again.

Jung-Soo scoffed. "There is nothing to clear up. I did nothing wrong."

"Do you think your father knows?" Iseul said, concerned.

Jung-Soo could only smile at the girl. He ruffled her hair as he would to a little child and said, "No, he's clueless about it all. That's why he kept looking at me." He looked at Yeong-Hoon who was clearly thinking the same endearing thoughts of this girl with no 'noon-chi'.

"So what's next? What should we do now?" Jung-Soo said, the mischievous tone already back in his voice. But before any more conniving could ensue, a hand grabbed and pulled Jung-Soo back. It was the Captain.

"Sir," he said formally. "Your father would like to see you tonight."

Jung-Soo hesitated. There was always something going on, and whatever it was, he didn't want to know. He looked up into the Captain's stoic face to read for more but before Jung-Soo could pry, the Captain bowed once again and began walking away. "Please don't be late this time."

Jung-Soo sighed and glanced at his Western-made watch, hoping dinner would be postponed indefinitely but instead noticed the hour hand had ticked past five.

"Hyung! It's already five-thirty," he said to Yeong-Hoon.

Both Iseul and Yeong-Hoon looked to the mountains where they saw the sun quickly disappearing, imagining their father waiting for them as he crafted the most recent cabinet order.

"What?" Iseul said, grabbing Yeong-Hoon by the hand and pulling him into a jog towards the hills. "Gotta run, Jung-Soo. Good luck with your father tonight. Bye!"

Yeong-Hoon could tell Jung-Soo wanted to say more, but the

opportunity had passed. Jung-Soo kept his hand waving long after the two had gone as he looked down at his watch again. It was the only watch that existed in the small village—a reminder that he would soon have to leave his haven and step into the real world.

But in the meantime, he took a deep breath and dragged his feet towards his temporary home. He was going to the Golden Palace.

CHAPTER 4

The sun had set long before Iseul and Yeong-Hoon reached the foot of the hills where their traditional hanok house stood. Built by Iseul's great great grandfather with his bare hands, the L-shaped home was constructed with the most intimate understanding of the distinct seasons that boasted of bitterly cold winters and hot summer where the house made with soil, rock, and timber breathed as one with nature. Oil-treated hanji paper lined the windows and doors that made the modest home breathe with life. Yet, years of use and the lack of upkeep had rendered the place ridden with hole and crevices that were constant reminders of the run-down legacy Iseul's father toiled so hard to maintain.

But to most who ventured into the mountain, Iseul's home was a house to be avoided, as myths perpetuated amongst children who recounted stories of a haunted figure roaming the area. The older ones would often coerce their younger siblings to do more of the chores, threatening that a ghost just might attach itself to them the next time they went into the hills if they did not oblige. Though oddly, parents didn't seem to mind the folklore too much.

Iseul's mother loved ghost stories. Maybe that's why she had fallen in love with her father. No one else in their right minds would let their daughter marry a carpenter, let alone a paper-maker for as the saying goes, "I would rather eat sand than let my son become a papermaker."

Try being married to one.

Next to the family home stood the carpentry workshop that was nearly three times the size of the quaint home. It was also where Iseul's father spent the majority of his time carving, sanding, repairing furniture, and making the odd instrument for the modest population of the Wasteland.

"Wait." Iseul stopped Yeong-Hoon in his tracks as the two buildings came into view. "Shouldn't we have some sort of plan before we go in? You go keep father busy while I cook as fast as I can. Got it? Good!"

"Same old, same old." Yeong-Hoon nodded.

Iseul lit the lantern and headed towards the kitchen shed next to their home as Yeong-Hoon peeked through the hefty wooden doors of the workshop.

"Father," Yeong-Hoon said, as he walked towards Iseul's father whose silhouette flickered with the dying lantern. Mr. Ji looked around, startled by Yeong-Hoon.

"You two are back early tonight," Mr. Ji said as his hands fumbled with a piece of wood as if he were trying to hide it. "Ah," he sighed, "it seems there is no point in hiding it anymore."

Yeong-Hoon hadn't a clue about what his father meant, then he looked towards his anxious hands. It was the family heirloom carving knife. Mr. Ji rubbed the freshly carved wooden handle and gave it a final inspection, blowing on it to get rid of the dust before handing it to Yeong-Hoon.

Yeong-Hoon knew what this meant. "I couldn't father… really." He tried to push it back into Mr. Ji's hands. Their eyes met and it became clear that Mr. Ji wouldn't take no for an answer. It was a small but meaningful dowry exchange.

"I hope you like the new addition," Mr. Ji awkwardly added.

The last time Yeong-Hoon had seen the carving knife, the handle had been so worn by daily use that the decorative carvings were virtually gone. Now, it displayed inlays and miniature lacquer paintings of swirls and simple lines. The knife handle glistened ever so slightly against the lantern. How much had the knife witnessed, from generation to generation and how much will the ancestors grieve to know that it had been handed down to a stranger, instead of a legitimate son?

"I'm sorry this is all I have to give you two," Mr. Ji continued. "Of course, the house and the workshop is yours to keep once I'm gone and I'll teach you everything I know so you can carry on making a living," he said as if needing to make known the obvious.

Yes, he was poor. Yeong-Hoon knew that. But hadn't he proven he was here to stay, after all these years being his apprentice? Didn't he know that he too had grown to care deeply for Iseul too?

"Father. Thank you," Yeong-Hoon managed to say as he took the carving knife. He didn't quite know where to put it or whether he was allowed to use it. The two idled around the workshop as they tried to figure out what to do next when it hit them both simultaneously—a loud hungry rumble.

"You reckon Iseul put the rice on the stove yet?" Mr. Ji said, holding his stomach.

A clatter sounded outside the workshop. "Probably just getting the kimchi out," Yeong-Hoon said. He could picture Iseul stumbling in the dark as she dug her hands into the underground clay jar of fermented goodness.

Mr. Ji nodded. "Perhaps another fifteen-minutes will do."

The meal was finally set on the table as the three gathered around it. It was simple like all the other days with plain brown rice, a few pieces of kimchi and some dwenjang soup to wash it all down. The soup looked bland, which is something the whole family had become immune to as Iseul often forgot to add salt. They dug in as if it were the same deliciously seasoned soup Iseul's mother had made before she passed. Iseul looked up at the only black and white photograph of her mother, hoping it might speak some revelation to her.

Father took a spoonful and avoided eye contact. Yeong-Hoon dug into the soup a second time and gave an overreacted, "Umm, good."

Even Iseul, with as little noon-chi as she had, could tell something wasn't quite right. She took a spoonful, suppressed a gag as she led her spoon straight to the salt container, dumping a heaping spoonful into the steaming soup. She hoped it would taste better, but the darkness of night disguised their reactions as did their hunger.

***

Deep within the labyrinth of the Golden Palace, Jung-Soo sat in the dining hall as the food lay before him in colorful varieties. Kimchi was the furthest from the table as Jung-Soo found it to be quite rudimentary for his more developed tastes. He had often ordered the chef to create dishes that weren't strictly Korean, so to speak, and so began the hunt for delicacies rumored from faraway lands and of course, the firing and hiring of countless chefs.

Jung-Soo's favorite, other than the spiciness of Korean food, was the soothing and savory Japanese cuisine which he had acquired from the numerous parties his father hosted to the Japanese elite during the occupation. And so, with his exile into a remote village, Jung-Soo, who had once been a stickler for new foods, learned to be content with Korean and the occasional Japanese food in a small village where the chef too had to be imported from the city.

Just as he was about to dig his silver chopsticks into the soba noodles, the captain of the guards entered, taking a deferential bow as he approached the dinner table. The maid followed soon after, bringing in a platter of freshly baked wheat cookies, a delicacy of the west.

"I hope the meal was delicious, master." His gestured to Jung-Soo with a look he had seen so many times before: he had news for only his ears to hear. The Captain had already headed towards the door, assuming the boy would follow. Jung-Soo's head turned towards the cookies as the smell of import butter wafted into his nostrils.

"Ah…" he sighed as his stomach growled, still empty. He turned towards the door where the Captain vanished through, but with a single lunge, Jung-Soo tailed the maid with the cookies and grabbed a few to stuff in his mouth. His stomach ached for more as the first bite hit it. With a crazed look, he jumped back to grab as many cookies as his hands could hold and then sprinted to catch up with the Captain.

The night was still and the garden's green was barely visible under the sliver of the crescent moon. The two made their way through the garden and approached the foot of a small hill where two rocks laid in a set. Since its discovery the first few weeks in Yeoju, it had become the place where Jung-Soo and the Captain set aside their status and age and talked almost as equals.

"You want some, old man?" Jung-Soo spoke with the buttery goodness still in his mouth as he held out the hand with the fewer cookies. The Captain picked one and took a curious bite.

"Sometimes I wonder what kind of peculiar fate I have, sitting here eating this thing that doesn't even look like food." The Captain took another bite and grabbed another cookie from Jung-Soo's other hand. "Your father had to leave for Seoul again," the Captain said through his chews. "It seems your brothers have been imprisoned."

Jung-Soo didn't quite know what to say. It had been a possibility—a likelihood that they had all been preparing for.

"When is the execution date?" Jung-Soo said, as he swallowed the last bite.

"Boy, you don't have to worry about it. Your father won't let it come to that."

It was a tone of voice Jung-Soo had become used to, almost fatherly he had always thought. But where was his real father? What was the next scheme too important that he had to be so far-removed from his family? Where was he when it really mattered—when his mother's blood spilled on the yard of their own home because his father couldn't, no wasn't there?

Father always said mother could protect herself…that she was a strong woman. The Captain later told Jung-Soo that his father had been away, negotiating promising roles for his two older brothers with the Japanese, and introducing the toys he had engineered to the highest bidder.

Jung-Soo's stomach twisted at the thought, the cookies churning within. His mind drifted to his father's warehouse next to the Golden Palace The last time he had gone in, he had been so angry that he tried to burn one of his toys. Needless to say, he could not muster up the courage to be so defiant.

"In any case, you should prepare yourself," the Captain continued. "It won't be long till you'll be part of this world."

Jung-Soo doubted it. If anything, he was certain his father disliked him. Why else would he exile him to the countryside? He had overheard his father one day saying Jung-Soo had a frivolous mind, not practical like his brothers. 'A dreamer with no purpose…' In one occasion, his father had whipped his two older brothers with no apparent cause.

"Injustice has no reason," he used to say. "You are mere animals to them, you hear! Not even a woman in their eyes. Remember my sons, dignity is only afforded to the victors."

His father then handed Jung-Soo the flimsy stick and had forced him to wield it against his own brothers, leaving bloody and deep ridges on their calves.

"After all," the Captain said. "You are your father's son."

Jung-Soo emerged from his memories. "Well then," he said as he shoved the last cookie into the Captain's mouth to shut him up, "if you're done reporting to me, why don't we go for the old night hike!"

Jung-Soo saw the look of innocent excitement in the Captain's eyes. He jumped from his stone bench and steadied himself for a sprint.

"Ready..." Jung-Soo said with that all too familiar smug look, "steady...start!"

He tripped the Captain with his left foot as the Captain fell face first into the soil and leaves with cookies crumbs all over his face. It was a sight worth glimpsing even under the dimmed moonlight.

"Ah you little rascal!" the Captain groaned.

Jung-Soo stuck his tongue out like he used to do when he was young and said, "Nothing you haven't taught me before, old man," as he disappeared into the trees.

The Captain chuckled as his heavy shoulders pushed him back up, sprinting towards the darkness. Taking in heavy breaths of fresh air, he felt reinvigorated. He had always known something burned within the boy, a fire perhaps greater than his own father's. It worried him, though his father urged him to kindle it. What would he grow up to be? He sighed. Such times could not afford looking too far ahead.

When the Captain left to attend to some urgent matter, leaving Jung-Soo at the edge of his garden again, Jung-Soo felt the blood coursing through him, hot and tempered with the urge to do something—anything. It was in such nights that he allowed himself to wander the Golden Palace with prying eyes now safely indoors and nearly asleep.

The warehouse would be locked, but he had found a way in months ago. The glint of the glass window caught his attention as it did whenever he walked past it at night. *There.* He walked stealthily to it, and pried it open. The servants would hear, but wouldn't think much of it. The occasional hedgehog, fox and dog roamed the gardens at night when it was left unattended.

The window was small and he was getting much too big to squeeze comfortably in. The lantern sat near the entrance. Jung-Soo stumbled through items covered in tarp, loose wires and metal to get to it. He fumbled for a match as he finally lit the lantern, revealing a cavern so deep that the light did not reach the ends of the room.

Jung-Soo had ventured the entire space once before. There wasn't much to see: trucks, cars and car parts, wires and tires, and an old sofa that reeked of leather father boasted as Italian-made. There were boxes with screens known as the television, but nothing ever came out of them other than a screeching noise and a grey background. And as for the odd camera in the mix, Jung-Soo could never think of anything interesting enough to capture in the Wasteland where rock and more rock was all there was to see.

Jung-Soo deliberately walked towards a table hidden in a dark patch of the room. He needed wires, thin and long ones for the radio he hid deep within his bedroom closet, tucked under a pile of books. In truth, he had been having problems lately. With two mountain ridges blocking a straight path for any radio wave to arrive, reception had always been a problem. He needed a second power source to the amplifier to boost the incoming signals, perhaps even a spare battery to figure out a way to remotely power the radio.

Jung-Soo pulled two different types of electrical wiring. He wasn't sure which one he would need so he cut an arm's length of each, rolled them up in a neat circular pattern and pocketed them. He remembered seeing the batteries somewhere, perhaps near the trucks. He uncovered a tarp further down the room as he noticed an old typewriter covered in a thick layer of dust. It was one his father deemed important enough to bring from Seoul for reasons unfathomable to him. He moved on.

Here. Underneath a thinner tarp were rows and rows of batteries of all shapes and sizes laid neatly on the table. Jung-Soo grabbed the smaller one, circular and barely the size of his palm. No one would notice such a small object missing. He rearranged the batteries to cover up the spot left missing.

Outside, Jung-Soo could hear men nearing the warehouse. They were the truck drivers, here just in time as they usually did in the cloak of night.

"You think we'll get back home by the weekend?" One said. Jung-Soo placed the battery into his pocket and blew out the lantern.

The two men walked closer towards the window where Jung-Soo had come in from.

"All the way to Mokpo? Likely not," the other said. "They'll need us to take the next load south, and it looks like it'll rain tomorrow."

"A man can hope," the first driver said, disappointed. "We wouldn't want to drive too fast on the slippery mountainside roads anyway."

A waft of cigarette smoke entered through the small window and reached Jung-Soo as he held a cough in. He never understood why men smoked them. Jung-Soo held his breath a little longer as he heard the same two footsteps dissipate into the garden.

CHAPTER 5

[Present Day]

I had been running late for school that morning, though I still found myself standing by the window half asleep, watching as the day began in the world outside. It didn't take long for me to come to my senses as I made a mad dash towards the door, when I noticed granny's weekly supply of Chinese herbal medicine by the door. Mom must have forgotten to take it to the hospice center before she headed to the factory. It would've been easy to ignore; I could imagine how much more my arms would hurt with the extra load alongside my growing book bag.

I grabbed the oriental medicine, slipped into my flats and made my way to the bus stop. I really wasn't quite sure what I was thinking that morning as I took bus number 526 instead of the 521. It was a relief when the nice lady in the recording announced, "Sky Hospice Center."

The elevator wasn't crowded, though it took a good while for me to reach the top floor as I noticed my ears pop on the way up. The place was clean and bright, which was to be expected as the whole floor seemed to have glass windows as walls, revealing the miniature world that continued down below. It was a quiet place— a place where rich people came to die, or as I'd like to believe, where old people came to practice being angels floating in the sky.

A familiar song trickled down the hallway.

"One, two, three, four. Two, two, three four." A voice rang in shrills much too loud for the early hours of the day. I went down the hallway and stopped in front of the door where the sound came from. From between the cracks of his door, a grandfather stood in front of his bed, flailing his arms in the motion of the national physical exercise, providing his own beat to go with it: "One, two, three, four...."

Next to him was an old woman with a frail stature, her back facing me.

"Come on, lady!" the grandfather said, grabbing the woman's arms and forcing them in the motion of the national physical exercise. Just then, the nurse burst through the doors and walked right past me.

"Grandpa, you can't keep doing that!" she said, as she gently took the woman's hand and turned towards the door. "Why can't you wait till after breakfast to do some exercise, am I right, granny Iseul?"

I looked closer, and lo and behold, it was none other than my very own grandmother! I walked in, amused at the scene that seemed to have been occurring quite regularly here.

"I can't understand why you have to remind me every morning!" the grandpa said to the nurse. "I've got cancer, I'm not deaf and my memory is just fine, thank you very much! Isn't that right, Miss Iseul?" he said, with the most exuberant voice that a senile grandpa could muster. "See you after breakfast, my dear!" he added, "I'll be sure to pick you up!"

"You must be the granddaughter," the nurse said as we headed next door to my grandmother's room. The old man's voice continued to ring from a distance.

"It must feel great, granny, to have so many people looking after you! And look at that, you even have a nice bachelor still chasing you!" the nurse said, as her voice trailed on with an unspoken note of melancholy.

"Well, what do you think?" the nurse said as she looked at me. "Do you approve of your grandmother's suitor?"

I let out a chuckle, and she followed suit. "He is a bit too old to be considered a bachelor, I think," I said, as we led my stoic granny to her bed.

Through the corridor, the grandpa's voice grew louder. "Like I said, I'm not deaf!" He then began singing the nationally-loved anthem, "Age Is Just a Number."

"Alright, alright, grandpa! We get your point!" the nurse said. "Wait here, I'll be right back with your granny's breakfast."

Granny's eyes remained fixed on the door as if waiting for someone. Perhaps she had understood what the grandpa next door was saying and hoped he would come to pick her up as he had promised. Perhaps she was waiting for my mother as she would regularly visit in the mornings.

"Mom's not here today," I said. "Look! I came to give you this!" I raised the box of oriental medicine for her to see, but her eyes were still fixed on the bed stand where the guitar leaned against just as I had left it, still collecting dust.

A faint murmur left granny's mouth the moment my eyes landed on the guitar. It had been ruled out as an impossibility at this late stage of Alzheimer's, yet I was sure I heard my granny's voice break through.

"Yeong-Hoon..." she said.

"Granny, is that you? Did you really speak?" I said in a flurry of disbelief and excitement. It was surely a name, a common one at that, but who was Yeong-Hoon?

The nurse came in with a steaming bowl of rice, a healthy selection of stir-fried vegetables and a bowl of dwenjang soup.

"Do you happen to know someone called Yeong-Hoon here?" I asked.

"Not that I'm aware of." The nurse shook her head as she left me to help feed my granny. I brought the guitar closer towards the bed, following her eyes that remained on it. I could remember all the years the guitar laid motionless in the corner of granny's room. To me, it had always been one of many instruments that came and went in a house where a luthier lived.

I watched on for a few moments, hoping that she would repeat herself. Nothing happened; I had probably imagined the whole thing. I sighed, pulling up a chair next to her bed as I spooned rice and vegetables into her mouth. Once she refused to eat anymore, I reached towards the drawer for the letter that was once inside the sound hole of the guitar.

I read again: "My dearest Ji Iseul..." My granny's ears seemed to perk up at those three words.

Could it be? "Granny, is Yeong-Hoon the person who wrote this to you?"

I waited. We stared at each other like that for a moment, until granny's hands reached towards the letter and grasped it tight.

"No, it's going to rip!" I said, knowing she no longer had the sense of how strong her grip was. I let it go as the old paper barely held together, wrinkling even more in my granny's rough hands. I winced, but it was, after all, her letter so I let it be.

She took the page and laid it on the sliding table where a drop of the soup seeped through, dampening the page. It would surely rip. She dabbed the drops on the page with the sleeve of her night gown. It was as if she knew exactly what to do, a second nature of sorts that came from years of experience as if she understood the intricate properties of paper.

It then dawned on me. I had seen this paper before! The same brown and worn textured paper hung in a glass frame hidden amongst the photos that lined the walls of our apartment.

"Granny, I'm so sorry, but I'm going to need to borrow this," I said, as I gently pulled the page away from her grip. My mind was racing, trying to piece together what little I knew about my grandmother's past, this letter and the mysterious person called Yeong-Hoon.

Granny's eyes whined as I placed a bag of lukewarm oriental medicine in her hand instead, but she would not be pacified.

"I promise, I'll bring it back to you and read the whole letter to you a hundred times!"

Afraid to look back, I grabbed my book bag, glanced at the clock and jogged out the door towards the elevator.

I was already twenty minutes late for school. I would surely get detention for this, but I couldn't care less. The 521-local bus dropped me off right in front of my school, and the day went on as if nothing had happened. While I had expected the assistant principal to be waiting by the gates of our school to check for late students, the time had long passed since the gates had opened and he had long since retired his post. Even as I slipped into my seat in classroom 3-2, only my friend Mi-Na seem to notice I had been missing.

"Where were you?" Mi-Na whispered.

"Did the teacher take attendance?"

She nodded. "I answered for you." She looked at me, waiting for an answer.

I watched as the teacher's eyes darted back and forth from the textbook to the chalkboard. Any second now, the teacher would look towards us and the last thing I wanted was to draw attention to myself.

"I'll tell you later," I said as I opened the history textbook, looking as though I were focused. When it finally became clear that not a soul knew or even cared that I was over an hour late to school, my mind drifted back to the worn piece of paper in my pocket. Before I knew it, the bell notified that the school day was over, and the real studying would soon begin as most of us would be on our way to our specialized academies.

"What was that all about?" Mi-Na asked as we walked out of the school gates.

"Oh, nothing really," I said.

As much as Mi-Na had been a good friend to me, I wondered if she would understand. I had always been the odd one out—the one who couldn't stop questioning and had once been dubbed as the "difficult one" by my head teachers. Mi-Na had been the one to help me through the years of wondering and feeling trapped. There was a simple way about her that calmed me, a child-like acceptance that life in high school was meant to be this way; the life that we had always dreamed of, though we didn't know what this looked like, was just around the corner once we passed the national exam and went to university.

So I answered in the only way she could understand. "It's a family matter, nothing really to worry about, but thanks for covering for me this morning." I managed a wide smile for my only friend in school, gave her a big hug and ran the other way.

"Where are you going?" she said. I could hear the frustration in her voice. "Aren't you going to the academy with me?"

"Gotta go! See you tomorrow!" I yelled and headed straight home.

With my foot barely out of my shoe, I ran towards granny's empty room and stood in front of it. It was a framed piece of paper next to the clock that read, "*Ji Iseul Instruments Inc.*" I had walked past it thousands of times, yet, here it was, finally holding my full attention.

My hands fumbled as I gently took the back of the picture frame off to release the relic page. I touched the letter from the guitar, and then the framed page, letting both pages glide through my fingertips. Though I wasn't an expert, there was no denying they were nearly identical, or at the very least made around the same time period.

The instrument company headquarters was just a few kilometers away. I could go to my uncle and probe him about the paper, but I had a sense he had nothing more to offer me than the rags-to-riches story my own mother had once told me about granny. I knew I had to go further back.

I glanced at the dated letter. *October 12, 1949*. My grandmother would have still been in Yeoju. That was it! I needed to go there. I took out a random book from my bag, placed the two artifacts between the sheets of my textbook and dumped the rest of my books on granny's empty bed.

All throughout dinner, mom noticed I was preoccupied with something, though she was relieved when I excused myself to head straight to my desk as I flipped my history textbook open to where the twin pages were wedged.

At first light the next morning when dad's snore still rang throughout the apartment, I placed that single textbook back into my bag, flung it over my shoulder and headed out the door. I barely even noticed that I hadn't stood in front of the window to watch the sun rise over the busy bus stop that morning, all my focus funneling into the twin pages as I headed towards granny's hometown.

I was going to Yeoju.

CHAPTER 6

[Early Spring, 1949]

Dawn rose in the quaint village of Yeoju as Jung-Soo began descending that final hill towards Iseul's home. For the past few months, he had been spending his nights in a valley between two mountains, chopping, sawing and laying slabs of wood down, hoping it would amount to a cabin.

Most nights, he would pass by Iseul's home either on his way up or down from the valley. It was not his intention to spy on her, though he had his excuses, one of which was that he had most certainly beat Iseul in the jachigi game and that meant he was entitled to a few carpentry lessons!

Jung-Soo hid in his usual spot next to the bushes where a gaping hole on the hanji-lined window let him peep into Iseul's workshop, though he did feel a bit guilty for having played some role in expanding the hole to bring Iseul's entire figure in view. Iseul went about her usual routine, nodding off on her father's stool as she occasionally let loose a snore in between her frantic realizations that she had fallen asleep.

On the countertop was a slab of stone Iseul was using to weigh down a pile of paper. He remembered the first time he saw her covered in sawdust and runny amuck the workshop. Surely this couldn't be the daughter of the genteel carpenter Mr. Ji, could it?

As the weeks passed, Jung-Soo began to recognize the method to the madness. First, she dipped the bamboo filter into the fibrous bark solution, moving it from side-to-side, before layering the fibers atop each other until it was thick enough to resemble a wet sheet of paper. They would be laid to dry until the entire workshop counter tops were strewn with wet paper. Some of the dryer ones required slabs of stone to be placed on top of them to smooth and squeeze out the excess water until they were left to dry on lines under the sun for another day.

She didn't seem particularly talented at the task, yet he couldn't help but remember that old saying about how one would rather eat sand than become a papermaker. At least, it was something along those lines. He had often witnessed Iseul's frustrations at having moved the rock away too soon that the side of the page would rip. *Impatient and stubborn.* He smirked at her attempts, bemused though also terrified to be around her when she swung her carving knife.

Mostly though, he found himself coming back for Iseul's idiosyncrasies.

Like clockwork, she reached for the haegeum that leaned against the main counter top. Jung-Soo held his breath as she prepared herself to play. Surely this time, the entire woods would wake at the distinctive cries of the instrument. She then cleared her throat.

"Hmmm….Ummm…" Iseul hummed a tune to go with the haegeum. "Hmm, no wait, is it ummm?… I think," she hummed again, changing the notes as she pleased as each day, the tune of her hums transformed minutely and indefinitely.

Iseul and the haegeum sang together for a while longer, as Jung-Soo was surprised that neither Yeong-Hoon, her father, nor the animals in the vicinity seemed to bat an eye at the noise. It had become, like to Jung-Soo himself, a lullaby of sorts. As irksome as it was, it signaled it was just another night in the mountains of Yeoju.

Iseul had fallen asleep again with the bow of the instrument in her hand. She woke herself up when her own music stopped.

"Oh no! The paper!" she said, leaving her stool again to lift the bamboo filter.

Jung-Soo couldn't help but smile. "What a dork." He muffled his laughter as he rose from the bushes to head back home before daybreak. The last thing he wanted was to reveal his own midnight adventures and give the villagers even more gossip fodder. He knew not to cut through the middle of the village for this very reason so his morning hikes lead him around the village's northeastern boundaries where golden rice fields began and stretched out towards the rising sun.

It was hard to believe that the village had always struggled to have enough to eat, verging on starvation just a few years ago when the Japanese took every last grain of rice they could with them before being pushed out for good.

In the distance, a truck rolled towards a barn. For a moment, the scene felt familiar, as if the Japanese were still here, making their routine runs to collect rice. But the barn was too familiar, and so was the truck. He had seen deliveries on those same trucks in his father's warehouse in Seoul, but this time, it was parked in front of Byung-Guk's home. His pace quickened towards the barn where he could see men loading large sacks of rice.

He squinted. It was his father's men and there stood Mr. Lim. What was Mr. Lim doing, just standing there? Why wasn't he fighting for his rice, as he had always done when the Japanese came by? Surely, he couldn't be giving away his winter supply so easily?

Jung-Soo remembered that year before the Japanese had been forced out. How many had died—children, grandfathers and grandmothers, fathers and mothers? He remembered the bodies found each week covered in colorful hanboks in the river. They were mothers who had gone to the river to wash clothes never to return home again. He could feel the rage burning, the same way it had so many times when the Japanese men came and slapped his father around for failing to reach the quota for rice and valuable collections. Jung-Soo had stood by for years, watching helplessly as the scene repeated itself over and over again. How could his father do this to his own people after finally being released from the Japanese?

Jung-Soo wanted to run and tell his father's men to stop, command them to obey their master...that he wasn't the helpless boy he used to be anymore.

One of his father's guard bowed to Mr. Lim as the men closed the door to the truck. Mr. Lim bowed back. Byung-Guk had finally woken and joined his father in the barn to find it empty, his arms flailing in rage at his father, and at the truck that had left a cloud of dust on the road. Byung-Guk kicked the door of the barn in so hard that the chickens jumped and squawked in the pen nearby as he finally stormed back inside.

Jung-Soo stood still on the dusty road, overlooking the entire scene. Mr. Lim followed his distressed son towards the house when his gaze stopped at Jung-Soo. Strange, Jung-Soo thought. Mr. Lim gave no indication that there was anything wrong. Instead, he exuded a sense of tranquility that said he knew exactly what was happening. He gave Jung-Soo a look of stern reserve he had never seen in his usually spirited exterior.

Mr. Lim turned away as if he hadn't seen Jung-Soo and closed the door of his home behind him.

***

A few days had passed since Jung-Soo noticed suspicious activities in Byung-Guk's home. It was, in fact, an eventuality Jung-Soo had foreseen for a while, despite his great efforts to ignore the fact that his father had always been a man of many secrets.

While Jung-Soo had turned a blind eye to what occurred at home, life outside the Golden Palace seemed to continue on as usual as he had more than once embarrassed himself at school by falling asleep and banging his head on his wooden desk. It seemed he had something in common with Iseul.

Iseul's wooden *chige* backpack was filled with the usual supply of paper and firewood as she squatted to lift the load off the ground.

"See you in the evening!" she called out to Yeong-Hoon and her father through the open door of the workshop. She had taken two steps when she remembered she had forgotten something important—very important. She stood in place and began thinking.

"What is it?" Yeong-Hoon asked from inside the workshop.

"Oh right!" she said as the finger on her chin pointed straight in the air in delight for having remembered. She ran back towards the kitchen shed and grabbed another set of chopsticks and shoved it between the stacks of paper on her chige. It was hard to tell that there were now two pairs of chopsticks protruding from her backpack along with all the firewood, but she somehow felt complete and finally made her descent into the village.

Iseul made her regular rounds, first starting with Mi-Jung's restaurant where her mother always appreciated the extra fire wood to get the soup started for the early customers. The village granny would always be in her front yard tending to her green peppers and yellow melons, hobbling around with her weak hips.

"Hold on there, my dear," she would say as she shuffled over to Iseul unloading the firewood. "Wait till you have eight kids, you'll know how to appreciate strong hips."

It was her subtle way of telling her she should be marrying soon. At seventeen, Iseul was on the descent from her prime, even verging on becoming an old maid if you asked the older generation.

She laughed the matter off. Didn't they know she was as good as married? She took the peppers from the granny as payment, though she was always perplexed as to what to cook with them, and usually ended up dumping them in a stew with some kimchi.

Next stop was the local butcher's in the north side of the village. He had always been an odd fellow. Iseul's father and the butcher had gotten along quite well over the years, often trading sheets of cow skin with tailor-made knife handles the butcher required for his ever-increasing collection of knives. The two would often be found in the village restaurant bonding over the latest steel, sharing their trade secrets on how to best carve meat or wood for their respective expertise.

This time, the butcher handed Iseul a hefty coin and added, "Get yourself a treat too, don't just hand it all over to your father." His toothless grin was always a warm welcome to her.

"Thanks, mister!" Iseul said.

Her back felt lighter, and she had just one more stop to go. Within minutes, Iseul stood in the front yard of the school with just a few stacks of paper to deliver and four individual chopsticks still sticking out of the bag.

The school was rugged, as Jung-Soo would often say, since he was a city boy used to larger schools with bigger classrooms, desks, and even a larger field to run around in. The corridors were usually long and wide, housing multiple sliding doors and classrooms. Yet, the narrow hallway of Jung-Soo's new school had just three rooms where the floor was unkempt and perpetually dusty.

Going to school was a luxury, a hobby designated for the rich or scholarly boys who had nothing better to do than to sit amongst themselves and stare down at words on paper. Or so Iseul's father had always commented. He had always said Iseul was better than a son, certainly ate more than one and was grateful that all that food rendered useful because she had always managed to get more done than any son he could have ever dreamed of.

Yet, it was only in these narrow halls of school that Iseul was acutely aware of her place—she was a girl, and even a poor one at that. Though it was the last place Jung-Soo wanted to be, for Iseul, every time she walked the halls of the school, it was as if she were infringing on holy ground she wished to be worthy of.

Classes seemed to have been in progress since the sliding doors of the teacher's office opened to an empty room. Iseul slipped the stacks of paper in the storage cabinet as she usually did and made her way to the corridors and back towards the gate. She felt the nudge of the extra pair of chopsticks against her back, as she grunted and turned back towards the school to find Jung-Soo.

Stepping into the corridors again, the sliding doors of the classroom opened as a flood of boys passed Iseul as if she were invisible. She stood looking for Jung-Soo in the crowd, wondering if the whole thing was a terrible idea. And just when she decided it was best to leave, she felt a tap on her shoulders and shuddered.

"What are you doing here?" Jung-Soo said with a concerned look on his face.

"Jung-Soo!" Iseul said, a little too excitedly. "I mean, I came to drop off paper, you know, like I always do."

"I know. But what are you *still* doing here," he emphasized. "I was looking out the window and saw you leave and then come back in. Did you forget something?"

In the classroom next door, Jung-Soo and Iseul could hear a familiar, boisterous voice. It was Byung-Guk with two of his rowdiest friends running down the corridor. Jung-Soo instinctively pulled Iseul back behind him, as if to hide her from Byung-Guk's view. The two shot a look of contempt towards each other as Byung-Guk sneered and exited the corridor.

"What was that all about?" Iseul asked.

"Never mind," he said, as he realized he had been grasping Iseul's hand a little too tightly. He let go of her and began a brisk walk towards the exit. "Follow me," he whispered.

Iseul was nearly jogging, trying to keep up with Jung-Soo who led the two towards the back of the school building where they had first met and where Iseul had often snuck in to rest and drink water from the well before hiking back home. He looked side-to-side, making a round around the lonesome grandfather tree in the yard before taking her hand again and leading her towards the side of the building.

"Where are we going?" she asked.

"Shhh..." He placed a finger to his lips.

She had walked past both sides of the building many times

before. "There's nothing here, except for the storage room," she said.

Jung-Soo led the way down a short flight of stairs and pushed open the creaky doors of a dingy room. "Exactly," he said, "I found this place a few days ago and guess what?" He turned the lantern on and walked over to the desk in the corner. "There's a radio in here!"

"Radio?" Iseul said. "I thought the only radio in the village was at Mi-Jung's restaurant?

"That's what I thought too, but apparently not," he said. He set the lantern on the table as he reached for the electric cord. "This must be one of the first radios in Yeoju by the looks of it." In the dimly lit room, Jung-Soo bent and felt for the cord attached to an oversized battery. A concerned look crossed his face. "That's strange, I was here just yesterday and the cord wasn't plugged in then."

Iseul shrugged, fascinated by the slightly damp but cozy room. "Maybe someone's been here between then and now."

From behind, the door suddenly creaked closed, plunging the room into darkness as a sinister laugh followed.

"No!" Jung-Soo sprinted towards the door as it closed shut right in front of him. "Who is that out there?" he yelled. "I heard you laughing, you coward! Who are you?"

A few sniggers following a familiar voice.

"So what if I'm a coward? What are you going to do about it, oh Prince of the Golden Palace? Are you going to come beat me up with your guards?"

"Byung-Guk, is that you?" Jung-Soo said.

The boy behind the door didn't answer as the two others next to him seemed to shift in place.

"Okay, he gets the point, let him out now," one said.

"Oh no, we should have thought about this before," the other added, as Jung-Soo heard footsteps scurrying away.

Iseul banged on the door and tried to yank it open. "Jung-Soo, what's going on? Let us out, you little rascals, let us out!"

Jung-Soo could hear the panic rising in Iseul's voice. He knew as fearless and strong as she seemed to be, being trapped was one fear Iseul never quite overcame.

"Byung-Guk, listen, I know it's you. Is this because of rice you saw my father take from your barn?" Jung-Soo asked, looking towards Iseul who crouched against the door, her face turning paler

By the second.

"So what if it's me! You know what, I don't care anymore! We're already starving as it is, so I might as well take you with the rest of us!" Byung-Guk said.

"Byung-Guk, listen! I'm sorry about what happened," he said, looking at Iseul who was only focused on breathing in and out, "Byung-Guk?" He waited. "Byung-Guk!" Still, no answer came. "I'm not my father you know!" He let out in a roar, as he collapsed next to Iseul. He took a few calming breaths himself and reached to pat Iseul on the back to help soothe her.

"Unbelievable!" he said. But as he turned to look at Iseul, she was fast asleep under the line of light that made it through the side of the door. He nudged her a little, then shook her by the shoulders, worried she may have lost consciousness, but with the last jolt to the shoulders, Iseul let out a gentle snore and slid down to lay comfortable on Jung-Soo's lap.

It seemed like an eternity for Jung-Soo whose leg had long since fallen asleep as he too dozed off. When she finally roused from her nap, stretched and yawned, a jolt of blood rushed through him.

"Owww!" he groaned.

"Well, aren't you a little grumpy mister?" Iseul said, as she slowly began to remember her predicament. "Please tell me we're not still stuck in the shed."

"You're unbelievable, you know, falling asleep just like that!" He half giggled and let out another groan, holding his leg. "And by the way, what's in that head of yours! It's heavier than a whole watermelon!"

Iseul was now rubbing her head where her hair stuck out from laying on it. "I can't help it! It's the only way I know how to... well, calm myself."

"I'll keep that in mind the next time we're trapped somewhere." Jung-Soo limped towards the table again and switched the radio on, tuning it to the same channel he had been enjoying lately. From the old speakers of the radio, music filtered through and with it, a calmness washed over. He brought the lantern to where Iseul was sitting.

"Aren't we going to try and find a way to escape?" she asked.

"What for?" Jung-Soo banged his fist against one of the walls. "Reinforced cement with military grade locks. I was here a few days ago and noticed this place was built just like the bunkers we had up

58

in Seoul."

"Odd, isn't it, in a school of all places?"

"Very odd indeed."

Iseul shot a suspicious look at him. Jung-Soo tensed up. "Is that the only thing you have to say?" she said. "You know I don't like to pry, but what's really going on between you and Byung-Guk?"

"I didn't do anything, I swear," he said.

She wanted to believe him.

He hesitated, mainly because he did not want to explain what he was doing out and about at that ungodly hour and the inevitable lies he had to tell to cover up the fact that he had been spying on her.

Iseul had her arms crossed, waiting for an answer. He sighed and gave in. "Fine. A few days ago, I saw some of my father's men taking sacks of rice from Byung-Guk's barn."

"And so, will you investigate the incident? Find out what your father is up to?"

"I don't want to know," he said too quickly, as he did every time his father was brought up. The little he did know about his father assured him of one thing—he was up to no good.

"Be nice to Byung-Guk," she said.

"He's the one who's bullying me!" Jung-Soo protested.

She scoffed. "I doubt that."

"What? Don't you believe me?

"Of course, I do. All I'm saying is, try to be nice. He's a lot like us, all things considered..." her voice trailed as if she meant more.

"Why? Because his mother's dead?" he said, indifferently. "We're hardly the only ones."

Iseul gave him a stern look. "No. Actually, his mother left the family."

"Oh..." Only someone as naive as Iseul would be so forgiving, though Jung-Soo felt something akin to pity. He never thought he'd feel the way he did about the boy.

"How long do you reckon it'll take the Captain to find us here?" she asked.

"Give it another hour. He's always got a tail on me and I have a feeling he already knows this place exists." Jung-Soo got up towards the radio again, this time to turn up the volume.

"I love this song," he said with that carefree look that made Iseul wonder if getting locked up in this shed was his idea all along.

Iseul knew it was one of the songs Jung-Soo had been waiting for on the radio ever since he first heard it months ago. The song fizzled through damp air, despite the sound breaking up.

It was one of those songs from America. At least that's what Iseul assumed since she couldn't understand a single word.

She smirked. "Do you even know what they're singing about?"

"Of course, I do."

"Liar."

"Okay, you got me. But who cares? I still get the point of the song and that's all there is to it." He spoke with a genuine enthusiasm that he rarely displayed.

Both were lost in their own thoughts for a moment before Iseul let out a soft chuckle.

"What?"

"Nothing, it's just that I find the radio kind of," she said, searching for the right word, "funny." He looked on, wondering what she meant. "Think about it! No one's let them in the room, yet there are voices coming out from a box. Isn't that a bit odd?"

"No, nothing funny to me at all. The concept of the radio is quite simple, actually. Just as long as you find the right frequency, the radio will transmit." Come to think of it, he hadn't yet questioned how these particular sound waves cut through the cement-reinforced walls and still remained relatively clear.

"I guess you're right," Iseul said, still her mind captured by the thought. "The wind must take it here and there, wandering until it briefly finds a home, and then leaves without notice."

Jung-Soo sniggered. What a naïve girl.

"Are you mocking me, mister?" she said, breaking her trance.

"Of course not! Just in awe of your proverbial statement of wisdom," he said, in a deferential tone.

"There you go again you little rascal, with all your utter nonsense!"

"Yes, *utter nonsense!*" Jung-Soo repeated, laughing nearly to tears at those words he had heard from her countless times. "Utter nonsense, that's all there is to life!"

The two sat there, giggling like little children again. The radio played the next song, this time at a slower beat that swayed and echoed in melancholy within the confines of the shed, dimly lit by a dying lantern between the two. It was another one of those American tunes.

"Do you know?" Jung-Soo broke through the music. "Out there in the world, people perform on stage with thousands and thousands of people watching with nothing but a single guitar?"

"A guitar?" Iseul said, mouthing the unfamiliar word.

"You know, a guitar," he said, matter-of-factly. "Don't you know what a guitar is?" he said, now stunned. Iseul shook her head.

"Listen. Do you hear that beat in the background? One, two, three, four…" He tapped his hand to the beat on her lap, as her head nodded ever so slightly in unison.

Jung-Soo was on his feet again, frantically walking towards the table and cabinets nearby. They were all locked, as Jung-Soo expected from his previous visits. But between the crevice of a drawer on the desk, a single white sheet of paper poked through. He yanked it and grabbed a pencil lying on the desk.

"Let's see," he began drawing on the page, "it's an instrument that looks like this." He squinted and it looked roughly like a guitar, accentuated with curves and knobs at the end of the guitar's neck.

"Wow," Iseul held the piece of paper in complete awe.

"Amazing instrument, isn't it?"

"The instrument? Oh yeah, that too, but look at this paper!"

Jung-Soo face-palmed. "Spoken like a true country girl," he said, nodding his head from side to side in disapproval.

"Look at it, Jung-Soo! This paper is so… white!" she said, letting the crisp page run through her fingers. "I don't know why my paper never turns out this way. I've tried washing and washing it but I can't seem to get the pages quite so… well… nice!" She had a hunch about why it was the case, but it was a technical issue: the fibers of the bark needed a glue, and she had always found a tiny bit of dust and soil helped the fibers stick together. She wondered what the alternative would be.

"And the guitar?" he asked, wondering if she even noticed at all. The acoustic music still played on in the background.

"This isn't a very good drawing." Iseul looked on confused with crooked eyes. "How am I supposed to know how deep the body of the instrument is, or how thick the wood planks are, let alone the type of wood used, if it is wood at all?" she said.

There was no doubt she was an instrument-maker, though still an aspiring one at that.

"Well, sorry for trying to help you visualize the instrument." He yanked the page out of her hands. He looked down at the pitiful drowing that was now barely visible under the dying lantern.

Beneath the shadow of fading embers, a marking on the page caught Jung-Soo's attention. He pulled the page closer, then flipped it over. On what Jung-Soo believed to be a blank piece of paper, were writings and markings. He had seen it years ago when his father was still working with the Japanese and before Jung-Soo knew how to read, but the symbol was undeniably identical. In bold red, a hammer and a sickle were printed on the corner of the page, an evident symbol of the communist party.

Jung-Soo's skimmed through the page, reading the first few words.

"What is it?" Iseul looked on with concern. He realized he had been lost in thought, and gave a weak laugh to brush it off. He folded the page and tucked it into one of his pockets, keeping it safe until he could properly examine it on his own time.

For a moment, he wondered if Iseul had also read the page or recognized the red markings on it, but one quick look at her blank face reminded him that there was nothing to worry about. Besides, she didn't know how to read quite yet, and for once, he was relieved that he had neglected their reading lessons.

"So, you think you can start making one?" Jung-Soo said, changing the topic.

"Are you kidding me? With that drawing?"

"That bad?" he asked.

She nodded.

"I'll draw you a better one next time. Better yet, I'll try to get one from Seoul the next time my father makes a trip."

"I know what you're doing here," Iseul said suspiciously.

Panic rose in him. *Maybe she knew…about his father,* he thought.

"You're trying to get me to agree to make an instrument for you! Don't think I'll do it for free! You'll have to pay for my services!"

Jung-Soo sighed in relief. "Not to worry, money's all I've got!" he said, as the two bickered on with the rising moonlight that barely spilled within.

"What's with your fascination with the guitar anyway?" Iseul could almost hear Jung-Soo thinking in the dark.

"I'm not sure. Like I said, imagine the roar of a thousand, no ten thousand people in a crowd, and they've all come to see you— that is, you and just your guitar! And think of all the beautiful women in the crowd singing along!"

Iseul gave a disapproving look. "Beautiful women?" she said, mocking him. "Now I know exactly what you mean."

"What? No, that's not what I meant," he shook his head. "I mean... I mean," he said trying to find the right words. "I'm just saying, there are people out there who live that life. Amazing, courageous people, free to do what they love, learn an instrument, make songs and travel the world, all with just a single guitar!"

Iseul nodded along with his fantasies.

"And what about you?" he said. "Have you ever thought about what you wanted in life?"

Iseul didn't need to think too hard. "Well, I'll likely have to keep up with the deliveries, at least until father and Yeong-Hoon get a footing on their carpentry work."

Jung-Soo found himself shaking his head again. "Not what you *have* to do, silly, what you *want* to do."

It took a while for the question to really sink in. "Quite honestly, I'm not too sure, but if I had the choice, I'd love to continue making instruments, you know, starting with the haegeum, and then the gayageom and so on."

"Really, you want to keep doing carpentry? Aren't you tired of it yet?"

"It's not carpentry!" she protested. "This is completely different from what my father does. I don't want to just make cabinets and doors. We're talking about instruments that make sound and seem almost... well, alive! Although, father used to be an instrument-maker too..." Her voice trailed, somewhat dismayed at the realities her father had to face too. Hadn't he once dreamt of being an instrument-maker too?

Jung-Soo dwelled on the idea for a moment longer, then his brows furrowed. "Where am I in this life plan of yours? "

She had never thought about it in that way. Jung-Soo had become a close friend in the past few years, but she had always figured he would soon go on to do bigger and better things in the city—in Seoul.

He saw it in her blank face. *That's what I thought.*

"Close your eyes," Jung-Soo said.

"Why?"

"Couldn't you do just one thing without questioning me every time?"

"Okay, okay! I mean, what's the point, the lantern's almost out anyway," she said no one obliged

"Imagine we are in the middle of mountains in a cabin that no one can find. All around the cabin, we'll plant your favorite trees like cedar, oak--"

"It's pine," she interrupted, opening her eyes. "My favorite tree is pine, not cedar or oak."

"That's not my point," Jung-Soo said, frustrated. "And of all the trees you could choose from, why pine? The mountains are already full of them! We wouldn't even need to plant new trees!"

"So? I don't care. I want to plant more pine trees," she said, adamantly.

"Alright, we'll plant more pine trees," Jung-Soo said as he moved on to the bit he liked. "But the best part is, inside the cabin is the most spacious workshop you could ever dream of with all the special tools to make instruments. While you're making instruments, I'll..." His voice suddenly deflated. "I'll be your radio mechanic, turning the channel for you..."

Iseul opened her eyes to find Jung-Soo in silent contemplation and gave him a pat on the back. "Oh, don't worry! We'll figure something for you to do! You can help me chop wood and find customers to buy my instruments!"

Jung-Soo's spirits lifted again. "I promise, Iseul, that day is coming! The world is changing as we speak and soon, you and I can dream all we want!"

Iseul let out a little giggle and then slapped Jung-Soo on the back.

"Oww! What was that for?"

"I'm slapping the nonsense out of you," she said, laughing. "But whatever nonsense that is, sign me up!"

The last light of the lantern had long gone out as Jung-Soo and Iseul looked towards the moonlight through the crack in the door frame as their stomachs rumbled.

"Since it seems the Captain is enjoying his time away from you, perhaps we should eat before we starve to death."

"You've got food?" Jung-Soo's eyes widened trying to look for it.

Iseul hesitated for a moment, wondering if she should forget about the rice and the four chopsticks that stuck out of her bag. It had been a while since she had packed the lunch box with rice and a few pieces of kimchi on top. She didn't have to see to know that it would be an unsightly thing, and if they weren't in such a dire circumstance, she would have taken the thing straight back home.

But the night was young and the two were hungry. Iseul reached for her bag and took out the tin box. The dingy room filled with the smell of overly-fermented kimchi as Jung-Soo wondered why he hadn't it smelt it all long.

Then, it struck him. "Is that why you came back to school?" he laughed, "to have lunch with me?"

"Shut up," Iseul said as she poked Jung-Soo a bit too hard with his pair of chopsticks. "You'd better not waste any of it," she threatened.

Deep down, Iseul was relieved the moonlight was dim and the lantern useless. The music from the radio accompanied the two as they sat silent and content, filling their empty stomachs that were already half-filled with hopes of what their future might bring.

When Iseul had eaten just enough for the food coma to set in, Jung-Soo watched as her eyes fell heavy with the strange lullaby of foreign music, eventually closing shut for what he knew would be the rest of the night. Her breathing became heavy with a crescendo of snores until the steady beat of her own snores kept her under a deep sleep.

He listened to both Iseul and the sound of the radio, lulled into worry as his thoughts set in. Who would be the one to find them? What would happen when the rumor spreads of Jung-Soo and Iseul found in a communist bunker? He felt useless as he sat up all night, hoping the Captain would find them first.

Jung-Soo noticed Iseul's head had flung back into a painfully awkward position.

Silly girl, no wonder you always complain of neck pains. He adjusted her head on his shoulder and couldn't help but think it was oddly heavy for a girl who didn't seem to have a care in the world. Her snores confirmed this, and before long, Jung-Soo's own head plopped onto Iseul's.

I'll just rest my head until I hear someone outside.

Soon, the snores doubled with the sound of music.

CHAPTER 7

That night in the school shed passed with Iseul and Jung-Soo piled on top of each other, snoring till early dawn. When the Captain yanked the door open, the two, who had been leaning against the door, spilled out onto the dusty road right next to the Captain's feet.

"Comfortable?" the Captain said.

"Took you long enough." Jung-Soo stood up, still half asleep, dusting off his bottom. Without a single word of goodbye to Iseul, he took the back seat of the car and drove off. It was to be expected since Jung-Soo always struggled to be a morning person.

Iseul rubbed the side of her neck, curious as to why it ached. She too dusted herself off, and was past the school gates before realization struck her: she had spent the night out! Her father must be fuming! She sprinted as fast as her wobbly legs could take her towards the edge of the village where the dusty road met with soil and scattered trees.

But to her surprise, she burst into the workshop to find her father without a single worry; the Captain had apparently paid a visit earlier in the morning, though it was impossible to pry out from him what the Captain had said to convince her overprotective father that a night away from home was ever acceptable. It was one of the many curious things that happened when the Ham family was involved.

Autumn had lingered longer in the colors of the leaves that refused to fall. It seemed as if the long warm nights of the year 1949 refused to pass on as if to forestall the dark days that would haunt the peninsula in the coming months.

For Iseul, Jung-Soo, and Yeong-Hoon, the days were brisk with chores that seemed endless with the changing season. Stockpiling had consumed the community and had left Iseul tired as the days grew shorter and the number of wood deliveries increased. Even the village poet, who also happened to be the butcher, seemed to want a few extra stacks of paper in hopes to write his way through the bitterly cold nights ahead. And so, when it came time for Iseul to rise in the early hours of the morning to continue carving her haegeum, she found herself rising later and later and such a minor detail as a new handle on father's heirloom carving knife had gone unnoticed to her.

In fact, were it not for the carving knife that stood proof of the transaction, no one would have guessed wedding plans were underway, though rather unceremoniously, which was to be expected in a poor family who had already informally wed the two children the day Yeong-Hoon became Iseul's 'daeril' spouse ten years earlier.

It barely registered in Iseul's mind when one night her father asked, "What do you think about a summer wedding?" to which she responded, "I don't see why anyone should care when the wedding is held." Clearly, she hadn't a clue.

As for Jung-Soo, his sole goal was to be as far removed from the Golden Palace as he possibly could, escaping nearly every night into the valley to build his cabin.

It was one of those chillier nights that seemed to anticipate winter. The wind grew steadily as Jung-Soo laid shielded behind the walls he had recently finished erecting. He took out his usual bundle of ripped paper and folded sheets, rummaging through his pockets for his stubby pencil.

Out of habit, he dated the top left corner of the page. "October 12, 1949." Writing was one way Jung-Soo kept track of time in the village where everything seemed to progress at a snail's pace.

There wasn't much on his mind that he could write down on paper. Jung-Soo had never deemed his father's suspicious workings or the fact that his two brothers would soon be executed as worthy enough to waste paper on.

He had been working on a letter for Iseul for a while, though the words never seemed to come out in the right way. A letter was just a precaution, he told himself. He'd speak to her face-to-face like a man should.

A poorly white sheet had slipped out and laid on the soil next to him. It was the same one he had quickly folded out of view from Iseul in the school shed. He had forgotten or rather had ignored it while it dug itself so deep into his pockets that he thought he'd never find it again. He unfolded the sheet. The red communist logo caught his attention again. Next to it, were words typed in bold black letters: "Surrender is inconceivable. Democracy will oppress us. We must fight to be our own nation again."

The words were unabashedly militant, meant to recruit those who read it to the communist agenda. Just a few years ago, Jung-Soo was convinced that the Communists were poised to take over once the Japanese left. Now the tides seemed to have turned, at least in this small southern village of Yeoju. He had always been told he was too young to understand, to join the fight with his father and brothers; yet, now that he was old enough, he had grown to despise the very party they served.

Everyone knew about the Communists, yet were afraid to speak out as rumors of missing peoples and unauthorized police killings had spread across the entire southern half of the peninsula. It was surely the reason why his brothers would die in prison, and why each night, he secretly hoped his father would return home safe and sound while he remained in exile in a rural village whose jurisdiction was rarely covered by the police who remained vigilant in the city.

Jung-Soo broke away from his thoughts when he noticed the edges of the pearly page had tattered and ripped. Iseul would scold him for not taking care of such an excellently crafted page. He, on the other hand, wished to tear it into a million pieces, but he swallowed his momentary fit of rage. The page would come in handy at some point. He let his schemes lay to rest for a while as he shoved the page back into the deepest part of his pocket.

Jung-Soo's eyes grew heavy as the stars shimmered into a blur, eventually plunging into darkness. He was ten, underneath the same sky atop a hill where the Captain stood with a gun pointed at him.

"Hold your gun up," the Captain said with the usual calm in his voice that made him seem invincible.

Jung-Soo's skinny arms trembled, his shoulders tensing up.

"Good, now shoot."

He looked incredulously at the Captain who stood barely further than a few arm's length away. With a loud bang, the

Captain's gunshot echoed through the forest; Jung-Soo's eyes shut closed at the sound, his finger jolting the trigger as the second shot rang in unison. Blood pumped through Jung-Soo's entire body; he couldn't know for sure if he had been shot, or if he had shot the Captain.

Jung-Soo looked down at his body, sensing every inch of it to see if pain would seep through to the surface of his consciousness. He was still standing. He scanned the Captain who likewise stood as tall and broad as he was seconds ago. A smile crept up the side of Jung-Soo's lips.

"Good, but you're too late. You're already dead." The Captain stopped mid-way as if to let his words sink in. "Don't hesitate."

Don't hesitate... Don't hesitate...

In echoes, the Captain's last words rang over and over again until another shot was heard, waking Jung-Soo from his slumber. Behind the dense branches of the leaves, the first signs of dawn rose from the east as each echo from his dream was replaced by the sounds of steady hammering.

It was the Captain, beating away at a half-constructed wall. He smiled, looking down as Jung-Soo squinted up, wondering if it really was the Captain, here in the middle of the valley he thought he had successfully kept a secret.

"It's hard to believe you did all this by yourself," the Captain said, throwing another smaller hammer towards him. Jung-Soo took it as his cue and began hammering the pillar next to the Captain.

"When did you get here?" Jung-Soo asked, wondering why he had ever thought the Captain didn't know where he ran off to every night. Father would have known all along as well.

"Couldn't bear to wake you. You were snoring so peacefully," Captain said, sardonically. "Why didn't you have some of the men help you with this little project of yours?" The absurdity of the question was the Captain's way of letting Jung-Soo know that it was okay—that he had kept his mouth shut.

"So," Jung-Soo hesitated, "does that mean you'll help me?"

"Who's the lucky girl?" he asked.

Jung-Soo moaned. It was as if he were a little boy again, teased by an uncle who didn't know when to stop.

"No need to reveal your secrets quite yet. I'll make sure to visit once we've finished and find out for myself!" he said, laughing hysterically to an idea that mortified Jung-Soo who just kept hammering harder and harder. Ignoring the Captain had always been the easiest way to make him stop.

"Alright, alright, can't even make a joke anymore," the Captain said. "I'll help till your father returns."

Jung-Soo let out an innocent smile as the two men, almost equal in height, stood working in unison, one holding planks of wood against the structure while the other hammered it into place. So content, Jung-Soo barely noticed the splinter that lodge into his palm when he grazed his hand against a freshly chopped plank. It was dark enough and Jung-Soo involved enough in his own discomfort that he remained oblivious to a patch of blood that seeped out from the side of the Captain's torso, his face getting paler until he finally dropped his hammer.

"I'll be back in evening. Don't do anything foolish in the meantime," the Captain said, as he began his descent. Jung-Soo raised his hand to say goodbye to the Captain who didn't look back to acknowledge him.

***

Returning home from his night in the covert valley, Jung-Soo had an idea. He glanced over to a few servants who made their way outside towards the washing area and tiptoed towards the corner where the chicken coup was still hidden in relative darkness. The thought had occurred to him before, yet he had never been quite so hungry and quite as much in need of an excuse to visit Iseul again.

He tiptoed into the garden with just a single lantern, afraid to turn on the electric lamps to the entire garden. He knew he was sneaking around in his own home, and imagined how much easier it would be if he had one of his servants catch the chicken for him. He decided against it; he had always known getting others involved never boded well for anyone.

Eyeing the white feathered chicken near the cage entrance, Jung-Soo inched towards it as its one eye watched his hand appear into view. In an instant, the white hen cackled and flew to the other end of the pen, animating the entire coup in a frenzy that caused Jung-Soo to lose balance and fall head first into the chaotic pen.

Jung-Soo laid flat on his stomach as the men washing their faces, stopped midway to look towards the pen and then returned to their morning rituals. With a sigh of relief, Jung-Soo looked from side-to-side and towards a chicken that confidently strutted right in front of his eyes and into his hands.

"Gotcha!" Jung-Soo said as his hands clutched the brown feathers of the rooster.

Before long, with the chicken tightly clasped in both hands, Jung-Soo tip-toed back out of the gates of the Golden Palace and paced towards Iseul's home. So excited at the prospect of meeting Iseul early in the day, he barely noticed that he hadn't had a single minute of sleep.

But he still had to drop by Mi-Jung's restaurant before heading to Iseul's. If Jung-Soo's calculations were correct, Mi-Jung and her mother would now be preoccupied with chopping onions in the kitchen shed that they wouldn't even notice that he would be "borrowing" the village radio for just a little while.

The chicken's head jerked anxiously as he neared the restaurant, then seemed to ease as he tiptoed his way towards the east gate. With the chicken in one arm and a radio in another, Jung-Soo's arm began to tire. It didn't help that the once mellow rooster began twitching and cackling as if it knew that with each step Jung-Soo took, it too would soon meet its end.

Jung-Soo shoved the wooden doors of the workshop open.

"Iseul, Iseul, help me!" Jung-Soo panicked, though Yeong-Hoon, Iseul and her father didn't seem the slightest bit surprised by Jung-Soo's sudden intrusion.

"Good to see you, boy," Iseul's father said, as he kept both hands firmly gripping one side of what looked like a cabinet.

Iseul, on the other hand, jumped at the sight of the chicken, nearly dropping a block of wood onto Yeong-Hoon's infirmed left leg. Yeong-Hoon gracefully moved his leg out of the way before the block tumbled to the floor.

"A chicken for me?" Iseul said, running and grabbing the frenzied animal from Jung-Soo's arms. "You're holding it wrong. The poor thing must have been suffocating the whole way here!" She gave a quick glare at Jung-Soo as the rooster calmed in Iseul's arms.

Little did it know. With a twist and a half-yelped croak, the chicken was soon featherless on the breakfast table faster than any previous meal she'd ever prepared. Before long, the table was strewn with bones of the brown rooster that once was, and the three including Iseul's father was back in the workshop again.

It wasn't Jung Soo's intention to merely bribe Iseul and her family with chicken. He had come ready to be of service so as to spend the rest of the day down by the river before the chill would freeze it over completely. And so, Jung-Soo got to work, fighting his heavy eyelids as he swept the floors—the one and only task he was allowed to perform—to one corner of the workshop where rice-straw and sawdust were piled.

And when their daily tasks were complete, Mr. Ji shooed the three away as they proceeded towards the western face of the hill where the river flowed to a steady stream, slow enough that the fish almost seemed to swim in place against the current. The radio sang in quiet lulls in harmony with the steady stream as Iseul rolled up both her sleeves and her the bottom hem of her hanbok, fishing knee deep with her bare hands.

Jung-Soo took in the scene as much as he could. Fishing with his two best friends had been one of his most memorable pastimes. In fact, he couldn't remember a time when their summer days weren't spent to some degree in and around the river and hills, passing the days away whenever Iseul and Yeong-Hoon weren't completely overrun with work.

It was colder than expected and Jung-Soo worried for Iseul in the water. It wasn't quite the picture he had in mind as even his favorite radio channel would occasionally be interrupted by another emergency national announcement.

"As the communist regime gains strength, President Rhee urges every citizen to stand united against these forces of evil in these troubling times…"

Sitting next to Jung-Soo on a rock, Yeong-Hoon was the first to break the silence.

"Jung-Soo," he said in a grave tone. "I know it may not seem like it, but I don't want to lose Iseul."

Both of their eyes fixed on Iseul who had now grabbed a hold of a sharp stick, jabbing it into the water in futile attempts to skewer a fish.

"I know," Jung-Soo said, letting out a soft chuckle. Laughter had become a defense mechanism, and though he knew this was not the right time—that he had really meant for this conversation to be heartfelt—his habits seemed to overtake any plans he had envisioned.

Jung-Soo continued. "It may look like I'm clueless most of the time, but I know. I know that you care deeply for Iseul, just as I do."

Jung-Soo half expected a shocked expression, but none came.

"Don't hurt her," Yeong-Hoon said. "I'm not giving you my permission. It's just, she looks so happy these days."

Iseul nearly slipped but caught herself at the last second. Her hanbok was drenched up to her waist as she yelled out, "I'm okay!" and continued fishing.

"Babo," Yeong-Hoon sighed.

"Stupid," Jung-Soo repeated.

It was now or never. "Hyung," Jung-Soo addressed Yeong-Hoon. "Say, if I were to ever leave..." It seemed nothing could shock Yeong-Hoon who kept a straight face. "Never mind," Jung-Soo broke eye contact. "Where else would I go? This is my home now," he chuckled. "I just wanted to let you know how relieved I am, hyung, that Iseul has you in her life."

Iseul was now getting bored with her failed attempts to try and practice her "noon-chi" by somehow telepathically communicating to the two boys that she needed their help. She gave Jung-Soo one last intense stare to no avail and finally yelled through the sound of the stream and the radio.

"Hey, you two! What's so serious? If you're done resting, do you mind catching us some dinner?"

Jung-Soo gave Yeong-Hoon a sturdy pat on the back as he rose and quoted a proverb he had heard somewhere. "A bird rarely comes back once it leaves its nest." He flung his leather shoes off on the river bank, plunging his feet into the frigid water. "Don't think I'll let her go once I catch her," he said as he turned his back and ran towards Iseul.

Jung-Soo dipped his hand to drink from the stream, to which Iseul exclaimed, "No!" She looked to a woman washing her clothes by the edge of the stream and next to her was her little boy, naked and peeing into the river that ran downstream towards Jung-Soo. Iseul giggled, as Jung-Soo spat out the tainted water in his mouth and groaned.

Yeong-Hoon let Jung-Soo's words sink in. They rung in his ears, and then drifted away, filling instead with the laughter of the two strangers he had grown to care deeply for.

"Don't think I'll let her go either..."

CHAPTER 8

[December 1949]

The sudden arrival of winter chased autumn away, the colorful leaves of the forest finally plucked by the weight of snow on them. The skeletal branches soon poked through a thick white blanket, effectively transforming every landmark into an unrecognizable maze for everyone but a few.

Jung-Soo's daily walk to and from his secluded valley became an unbearable task in the weeks the transformation took place, forcing him to tie his beloved leather shoelaces on branches as markers to find his way home. Yet for Iseul who had experienced the unique changes each season brought throughout her seventeen years in the forests of Yeoju, winter ushered a fresh landscape that reminded her of her mother whom Iseul revived in her memories with each passing season.

There were only so many places you could go in such a small village and Iseul could often be found near the lump of grass where her mother's remains lay. The lump was as big as her father could afford as a taller, rounder, and wider grave meant a larger patch of grass would have to be maintained.

Iseul remembered the time when her father had taken the entire family out of their small village towards the bustling center of Yeoju. They were going to see the grave of Sejong the Great King of the Joseon Dynasty. The tomb was an attraction many came to see from all over the peninsula, whose rotund belly that marked the grave seemed like a hill of its own. It was surrounded by statues of his faithful servants, as engraved tablets marked his great deeds.

"Back in those days, the kings wore bright red with gold embroidered near their hearts," Yeong-Hoon had said that day.

"Really?" Iseul said with bright eyes then squinted. "How do you know that?"

He used to knock Iseul on the shoulder when she doubted him. "Oww!" she yelped.

"Listen to Yeong-Hoon," her mother always used to say. "Your fiancé is right, Iseul. Now, pay some respect."

Mother held her head down and demanded that they close their eyes, as the two children followed in a moment of silence. Iseul did as she was told, though occasionally, they would peek and scowl silently at each other.

"This is your home, Iseul," mother said with her eyes closed. "You are born in a province where the Great King is buried." Mother walked behind Iseul, held on to her shoulders and turned her around. "Look! There lies the birthplace of the last queen Empress Myeongseoung of the Joseon Dynasty." They turned back to towards the grave. "Raise your head high, and there just north of where we stand lies the mountain fortress of Pasaseong-Ji, made by King Pasa to protect his people from invaders. Be calm and courageous, my daughter," she said looking towards Yeong-Hoon too, "and my son. For you are kings and queens of this land, protected by the blood of our ancestors."

Iseul remembered that day like it was yesterday. She had tried to keep the reverent silence mother wanted, but distinctly remembered ruining the mood.

"Queen Iseul!" she said out loud but tilted her head from side-to-side. "It doesn't quite sound right, does it? Mother, maybe if you would have put the word "great" in my name, I might have had a chance of becoming a queen too!"

She had never really liked her name—it was uncommon, and just another thing the other kids in the village teased her about. Wasn't it enough that she lived in the mountains with barely any friends?

Iseul's mother shook her head. "That title, you must earn. Iseul, your name means morning dew."

"I know, I know. I was born early in the morning."

"It's not just that, my dear. Dew is water that cannot be seen. Hidden water comes together to become rain. The trees that your father cuts down to make furniture, the rice fields that stretch across our lands—all of that would not be possible without the dew that first forms before a rainstorm."

Iseul. She loved her name from that day forward.

Now, standing by her mother's grave, it looked so meager compared to King Sejong's tomb in her memories. Now that she was older, she felt she could understand her mother. She was never one to burden her husband and children, and even in her death, she had blessed them with modesty since a small grave meant the upkeep and rituals would in turn, also be modest.

She later heard that her mother had made Iseul's father promise to place her just where she was, with a grave barely recognizable to the casual hikers that walked by.

In the summer, Iseul would spend hours on end sitting underneath the pine tree next to the grave that thinly veiled the beating summer heat from her eyes, waking only as the sun disappeared into the horizon. This winter, like clockwork, Iseul brushed off the snow atop the lump of her mother's grave, leaning against it as long as her thin coat would allow. She found herself humming a tune she had been singing for as long as she could remember as if the notes of the unfinished song seeped into the grave and spilled out her unspoken cries of frustration and anger perhaps even she herself was unaware of.

***

In the garden of the Golden Palace, Jung-Soo laid on a patch of sunlight with a thick mattress underneath that insulated him from the snowy blanket on the ground. He laid there each afternoon after school at the edge of where the sunlight disappeared, basking in the sun to its maximum potential as he did his best to block out the noise of trucks, servants, and guards not so furtively entering and exiting the premises.

Just as the last strip of sunlight remained on his face, the Captain strode over to Jung-Soo who squinted up. He tossed a newspaper towards Jung-Soo's face, who blinded by the sun, raised his arms to catch the newspaper at the last second.

"Your father's coming any day now," the Captain said, his

voice tinged with gravity.

Jung-Soo quickly glanced at the headline: "Will war be inevitable in the Korean Peninsula?" He tossed the newspaper aside as if those words meant nothing to him. The Captain let the words sink in for a few seconds before he turned his back to walk away.

"Hyung," Jung-Soo called the Captain, just as he would freely call Yeong-Hoon. "Can't I just stay this way for a little bit longer?"

There was a sincerity in the boy's voice that seeped through his usually inane tone of voice. It stopped the Captain in his tracks.

Jung-Soo couldn't tell if the Captain sighed or if it was his breath condensing in the winter air. The Captain paused before he spoke.

"If it isn't this war, it'll be that war. It's too late to choose a side. As long as you are born into the Ham family, the choice has been made for you."

The Captain had always been honest with Jung-Soo, as much as Jung-Soo wanted to avoid the truth.

He continued, "Byung-Guk seems to have figured out what's happening, especially taking into account the incident at the school shed. You don't need me to tell you to be careful at school."

"Hyung," he said again with his mischievous voice signaling he had had enough of the seriousness. "Since we're in the mood for asking favors, let me ask you one too. Why don't you leave Byung-Guk and his family alone? It's no fun going up against a poor starving boy."

There was nothing left to be said between the two. Both knew the issue was greater than just Byung-Guk's family and the rice that was still being confiscated. The entire village was on the brink of starvation and if they managed to survive the winter months ahead, there will be war awaiting them on the other side.

***

[Spring, 1950]

Byung-Guk had always been a popular student, and though he was just another farmer's boy, his father was revered as one of the village counselors who was humble enough to take on the post of a farmer.

The school was in its usual uproar when the girls from the opposite building walked past the yard. They had finished their morning classes and were headed home, floating with their heads held high and legs turned in, knowing that the wealthier boys of the village would be watching them from the window.

"Hey, Byung-Guk," one of his friends teased from near the window. "Yoon-Sun is coming this way!"

Byung-Guk's popularity only seemed to grow with his blatant disinterest in the girls. In fact, this girl, Yoon-Sun had always walked past the windows of the school disappointed when she didn't find the face she was looking for. The boys were jealous and utterly confused as to why he never showed interest to any of them.

But Jung-Soo knew the real reason. He had witnessed Byung-Guk one afternoon, lurking around Mi-Jung's restaurant leaving dotori roots and sesame leaves by the kitchen, waiting behind the bushes to see her reaction as she found the mysterious ingredients.

Byung-Guk's friends would occasionally give him the stink eye for staying at his desk while the girls passed by since the girls would quickly lose interest when they didn't see Byung-Guk by the window. So that day, Byung-Guk decided he would oblige his friends and headed towards the window.

It was the moment Jung-Soo had been waiting for. He walked past Byung-Guk's desk, dropping a note before heading to the window himself as if that had been his intention all along. After a few more seconds gazing down towards the girls, he returned to his seat.

Jung-Soo watched from the corner of his eye as Byung-Guk returned moments later to discover a note on his desk. He looked around, wondering who had placed it there. He unfolded the slip of paper, as he read its contents: "Dearest Byung-Guk, please meet me by your barn at 8:00 pm tomorrow night." Byung-Guk turned the slip over, upside down and even tilted it before scanning the room to find the person who had dropped it on his desk.

"Who's it from?" Jung-Soo sheepishly asked. "From Yoon-Sun or Mi-Jung?"

Byung-Guk jumped and shoved the note into his back pocket. "That's none of your business." The last thing Byung-Guk wanted was a confrontation with Jung-Soo who had already seen too much. He got up, flustered, and walked away.

"Isn't it time that we set aside our childish bickering?" Jung-Soo said as the other boys began returning to their seats, curious about the conversation between the two boys that had been a long time coming.

"I have no idea what you're talking about," Byung-Guk touted, as he turned around to face Jung-Soo, conscious of the gaze on them.

Jung-Soo nodded. "Tit for tat, my friend," he said with his hand sticking out for a handshake. He was only beginning to realize how infuriating it was to be on the receiving end of a charade that mocked his intelligence. "Maybe it's time we call it a truce," he said, leaning forward ever so slightly to whisper, "for our families."

A look of unsettling confusion flickered in Byung-Guk's eyes before he regained composure. He glanced at Jung-Soo's hand, debating if he should take it, and in one sweeping motion, Byung-Guk clasped Jung-Soo's hand and jerked him close.

"Family?" he seethed. "Listen, you commie traitor, we're not some Japanese slaves anymore. I'd kill myself and take you with me before I bow to you and your family." Byung-Guk let go of Jung-Soo's hand, ready to turn away, but Jung-Soo's grip only grew tighter.

"Traitor, you say?" Jung-Soo sneered in a whisper. "Betraying one's country is bad enough, but can you live with betraying your own family?"

Jung-Soo let go as Byung-Guk stumbled a step back. He gave Byung-Guk a half-nod as friendly as he could muster. "Glad we cleared that up, my friend," Jung-Soo said as he walked away from Byung-Guk who still remained visibly confused.

***

Winter seemed to know no end as Jung-Soo huddled in his room, longing for the summer nights when he could star-gaze. A sudden pang hit him, realizing that perhaps, he might never spend another summer in Yeoju again.

He tried to push the grim thoughts out of his mind, instead focusing on a more present concern. Ever since that night at the school shed, he had wanted to figure out a way to turn the radio into some sort of transmitter. He began asking the Captain and some of the other guards from the city about whether or not they've ever seen a device that had both a transmitter as well as a radio. He was sure it existed somewhere, yet they only gave a wishy-washy response, one that was to be expected from the guards who rarely said anything that might offend their leader's son.

While his nightly routines had otherwise kept him occupied,

he had managed to uproot the radio from the car and had been fiddling with it for the past few months. The batteries finally worked, though the exterior of the radio was still unkempt with wires protruding in every direction.

Lying on his warm mattress, he looked out of the window where the stars grew brighter. The night was deepening and his warm bed was only making him feel more anxious and cooped up.

He looked down at his watch. It was almost time. He jumped off his mattress, walking in circles in his spacious room before making his way into the garden. He stopped for a second when he saw the two maids fanning the flames for the ondol floor heating, wondering if he should sneak out as he usually did or tell them to just go back inside since he would be out all night. But watching the embers glow in the dark, he had a better idea.

Once the maid had been sufficiently shooed away despite their adamant resolve to do their duties, Jung-Soo tiptoed to the food shed, hoping to raid it. With the dimly lit lantern, he walked towards what looked like a sack of some sort of food in the corner. To his dismay, it was just plain rice, but next to it, in a smaller sack shoved in the corner, was a sack of sweet potatoes. He grabbed a handful and proceeded to roast them over the ondol fire. And when his face was covered in soot, he poked the largest sweet potato that gave in nicely to the silver chopstick.

He wrapped the roasted sweet potatoes in a cloth that kept his hands warm on his journey towards the hills. Despite all that had been happening, his steps sprung with life with the idea that the day had finally come.

When he had reached his usual hide out behind the bush of Iseul's family workshop, he took a moment to stare. He looked on with the same expression he had when he first saw the girl. It must have been pity, or was it anger? He remembered the day he saw that little girl holding out a bowl of water for him in the school yard. He had been just a little boy too; he couldn't be sure of what he had felt that day.

Iseul was half asleep on the stool with a carving knife in her hand as her head bobbled around. She was clearly a hazard to herself. Jung-Soo moved towards the workshop door and with the sound of the creaking doors opening, Iseul jumped from her seat as her head perked up again.

"Yes, father!" she said.

She looked around to see that father was not there, realizing she had once again fallen asleep. Her shoulders shuddered in the cold, still oblivious to Jung-Soo standing behind her. She stretched her arms high up in the air and began jumping in place, humming that familiar tune she always had ready for moments between tasks. All this came as no surprise to Jung-Soo, still waiting to be noticed.

She stopped and squinted, looking through one of the crevices of the workshop and noticed a lighter shade of blue; dawn was near.

"Oh no, I must have slept all night," she said as she spun around to find a familiar face looking back at her. She jumped in place, spooked as the blood drained from her face.

Jung-Soo had his arms crossed and said, "What utter nonsense! Of course you slept there all night. You might as well just sleep on a mattress inside, you know."

Realization flooded. "How long have you been standing there?" she said, looking horrified.

"Long enough to hear you wake all the animals in the hills with your singing."

"Well, I didn't know you were there so…" Iseul tried to brush it off. "And what were you doing, just standing there! Are you trying to give me a heart attack? Do you know how startled I was… And what if…"

But before she could continue, Jung-Soo unwrapped the roasted sweet potatoes from the cloth and shoved it into her mouth with a snarky smile. "Here, just eat this."

"Hot, hot, hot!" Iseul screamed. "Well, you can't have been standing there for too long." She seemed pleased now, fully awake as sweet warmth of the potatoes soothed her chills. She took another painfully large bite out of the sweet potato as she struggled to speak past the steaming food.

"This better not be another one of your bribes, Ham Jung-Soo! I'm not about to apologize to Mr. Jung again about the stolen potatoes so if that's what this is all about," she said, waving the steaming sweet potato around, "you can take back your sweet potatoes because I'm not doing your dirty work for you again!"

With just one mouthful left, she returned the favor and shoved it into Jung-Soo's mouth. It was warm and sweet, just as he had imagined it. She looked on, waiting for him to answer who likewise couldn't talk past the food in his mouth. Frustrated, he tried to chew quickly.

"No...it's not... about," he managed to say.

"What utter nonsense!" Iseul said as she usually did with that distinct tone of voice. "Why don't you figure out what you want to do—talk or chew!"

Jung-Soo chewed and chewed, impatient as ever. He had, after all, waited months to tell her the news, yet there he was, chewing instead. With a shrug of defeat, he grabbed a hold of Iseul's hand and took her outside as they began moving away from her home. When Jung-Soo finally swallowed the last of the sweet potato, he spoke.

"I have something to show you."

The chill knocked the air out of them as Jung-Soo held onto her hand tighter. He placed the rest of the roasted sweet potatoes in her spare hand, still warm to the touch as he led her further and further away, twisting and turning around streams and boulders, hiking upwards and sideways on less-trodden ground until they reached the valley.

CHAPTER 9

The rays of moonlight hit the cabin, revealing the small but sturdy-looking building. Next to it was a river dividing the two mountains with a watermill that seemed to magically churn ice and water from the steady stream that flowed below the top layer of ice.

"What is this place?" Iseul said, as her eyes traced the cabin and watermill to the river where larger rocks peeped out of the water.

"After all these years in the mountains, you're saying that you've never once been here?"

Iseul gave Jung-Soo a disapproving look to which Jung-Soo could only look on with a sense of accomplishment. It was exactly how he had imagined it—a place so remote that only someone with an intricate knowledge of its whereabouts could reach it. Iseul traced the river as far up as she could see where the stream of water began at a familiar point on her side of the hill.

She squinted with intrigue. "Isn't that where our river starts?" Iseul asked.

Jung-Soo nodded with excitement. "Exactly!" he said, "but the river splits somewhere near the top of the hill and some of that water trickles down towards this valley."

"That explains it." She nodded.

For Jung-Soo, this was a crucial point; if anyone were to follow the river, it'd likely lead them down a different route towards the village and away from the cabin.

"Wait, did you see that?" Iseul tensed up.

Jung-Soo followed Iseul's gaze. "What is it?"

In the months he had spent building the cabin, the only movements he saw was the towering figure of the Captain emerging from the trees.

Iseul squinted. "A tiger…"

Jung-Soo rubbed his eyes. It was too dark to see what was in the mountain, but near the top where the two rivers met at a single point, two green dots appeared faintly between the trees.

"It can't be tigers," Jung-Soo said timidly. "It's been over a century since the last tiger had been spotted in the entire peninsula." He instinctively quoted a phrase he had read somewhere.

"Oh." Iseul's shoulders slouched back down as she eased up. "You're right. I've been up that mountain before."

"And?"

"Nothing but mountains, trees, and valleys for miles and miles."

"It's probably the moonlight hitting particularly green leaves in our direction," Jung-Soo said.

Somewhat relieved, Iseul looked up at the full moon that hung in the night sky and concluded Jung-Soo must be right. She closed in on one side the cabin, attempting to look inside, contemplating on whether or not she should puncture a tiny hole in the hanji-lined window to peep through. Jung-Soo watched on, soaking in every moment as he watched Iseul discover the place he had built for her. He boldly walked towards the front door and opened it.

"What are you doing?" Iseul said, looking mortified. "What if someone is inside?"

"So what?" Jung-Soo said defiantly, taking a step inside.

Iseul's head turned from side-to-side, wondering if anyone had witnessed their break in, and not so reluctantly followed close behind. The scent of freshly chopped wood wafted in the air, filling her with the same thrill she felt when she carved wood, further intensifying with every step she took inside. She stood paralyzed, fighting the urge to take her shoes off and feel the hardwood floors, all the while conscious that her mud-tainted feet might ruin the pristine room.

Jung-Soo took the lead, kicking his shoes off and striding towards the counter where a familiar object stood on top of the wooden counter. It was a radio, strangely disfigured from the one she had once seen in Jung-Soo's car. Static filled the air until voices and music rang with such clarity that Iseul wondered how they could have possibly found it difficult to find the same channel in all the other times they had gone channel hunting.

"I'm keeping my promise," Jung-Soo said, as he turned the volume up.

"What promise?"

"Remember three years ago when we were playing jachigi?"

"Which time?"

"That one time I promised I'd make you a radio and you said you'd help me learn carpentry."

"Did I really say that?" she said. "So we're breaking into someone else's cabin so that you can learn how to chop wood?"

"Well, if you put it that way..." Jung-Soo was beginning to realize his excuse was scant, even for someone as simple as Iseul.

"How I am I supposed to teach you carpentry when we don't have the right tools or planks of wood here?"

Jung-Soo raced towards the other end of the counter where below, a stack of carving knives, an axe and various types of wood planks laid stored away. Her eyes widened.

"You silly girl," he said, as he opened the door to the cabin, a gush of wind taking Iseul's breath away. "We're surrounded by all the trees we could ever dream of!"

Her eyes landed on a line of pine trees that gently waved their branches with the wind amidst the skeletal wasteland of the barren winter mountain. Yet, Iseul found it hard to shake off an odd feeling.

"So, who does it this place belong to? Your father?"

Jung-Soo shook his head. "No, I built it for you. It's yours now!"

Iseul squinted. "Something really fishy is going on here..." she said. "You don't even know how to properly cut wood! How am I supposed to believe you built an entire cabin?" she exclaimed.

"If there is a will, there is a way," Jung-Soo boasted.

"Oh, poor old Captain! You must have had him build it for you," she said with the same look of pity she had whenever she spoke of the oldest granny in the village.

"If you care so much about the Captain, you should have taught me carpentry when I asked you to!" Jung-Soo bellowed. It was understandable Iseul didn't believe he had built the cabin himself, but he had expected praise and admiration. Certainly not this!

He sighed and tried to let it go. Time was running out and he didn't want to spend what little they had left bickering over something so fickle. He rummaged through his pockets, pulling out sheets of crumpled pages before grabbing a particularly smooth one from the mix. He shoved it a little too close to Iseul's face.

"I want you to make me this," he said.

Iseul grabbed Jung-Soo's wrist and pulled it further away. The drawing came into focus; it was a sketch of a guitar much like the one he had drawn for her at the school shed, except he had added a few more details. She took the page from him, but as she did, her hands grazed his.

Strange…Iseul didn't remember Jung-Soo's hands being so rough. Layers of callous covered his palm, just as rough as her own hands. Could it be true then, that Jung-Soo had built the cabin himself? It hit an uneasy nerve in Iseul. The scent of newly chopped wood of the cabin panels and the roughness of Jung-Soo's hands painted a picture that began adding up.

"You really did build this cabin, didn't you?" Iseul said.

"So you think you can build a guitar for me then?" he asked, now hiding his hand behind his back with a warm smile she hadn't noticed before.

Iseul stood there, unsure of what to say or do. A thin layer of tears veiled her eyes; it seemed she could see Jung-Soo clearer than ever. She scanned him from head to toe, his once tall and proper frame now slouched with the weight of his growing shoulders and his hair and clothes unkempt, unlike the day they had first met at the school yard. Iseul let out a bright smile as she noticed how much Jung-Soo's facial hair had grown in.

So much had happened over the years, and they had both changed, though she looked at herself and noticed she was still wearing the same hanbok.

Jung-Soo hadn't quite imagined this part of the reveal, wondering why she stood so still with tears glistening in her eyes. She must be happy. Women cried when they were happy, didn't they?

Iseul turned around in that moment, walking towards the counter where a few slabs of wood lay. She laid the sketch on the counter, examining the wood available as she tried to concentrate. She was embarrassed. Cry, in front of Jung-Soo? It was inconceivable! The boy wouldn't know what to do!

"I don't know why you're in such a hurry with this whole guitar thing, but I suppose I might be able to manage," she said. "But this picture really won't do. Look! How am I supposed to know how long this part is, or what type of strings they use to make the sound?" She talked and talked, much like Jung-Soo did to avoid the topic. Years together did that—made two people pick up each other's mannerisms.

A warmth seeped from her back and tightly gripped her; Jung-Soo had her in a tight embrace as a calm warmth rolled over her. She sighed and eased into his body.

Jung-Soo's mind raced, the frame of a girl who had grown into a beautiful woman finally in his arms. He had been confused, yes, it did seem like confusion when he first noticed her form, yet he had made it a habit of pushing such thoughts away. She was like a sister to him, like his strong-willed and kind mother he missed so dearly. He recalled the day when he realized this, shocked at how Iseul had eased into his life like the warmth he had been craving and gave him reason to believe in something more than the cold hard facts that had always plagued him.

His rough hands laid gently around her waist, and against her slender arms, careful not to squeeze too hard. But who was he kidding? This was Iseul, his scrawny friend who often rightfully bragged about how strong she was. Hadn't he more than once witnessed her drag a log of wood twice her own weight?

They stood there, listening to the whirl of the wind outside and the music within until their breathing joined in unison. Jung-Soo slid his calloused hand down Iseul's arms to meet her small and hardened hands. He could feel her tense up as her fingers hesitated to curl into his own.

"These hands," he said, firmly gripping hers. "I never understood why, but I always felt uneasy when I saw them." She jerked her hand away, though Jung-Soo held tight enough for the both of them. Iseul sighed and gave in.

"I see now," he continued, "I made your hands the way they are. You make paper day and night, collecting dust and bark, boiling, washing, drying them, but all for what? For people like me who don't understand the value of it?"

His voice rang with anger, mingled with mixed emotions that ran deeper than the words that contained them.

"Well then," Iseul said, "it's a good thing you taught me how to read and write. In the future, I'll be making use of the paper I make!"

Jung-Soo chuckled. "What I'm trying to say is, you have

nothing to be ashamed of, especially not with me."

Iseul spun around and gazed into Jung-Soo's face, content yet curious as to what had brought on such a behavior. There was a brazenness about him today, a sternness that kept his eyes firmly fixed on Iseul. She looked away first; Jung-Soo thought he saw a tinge of red color her cheeks.

She reached out to hold both of his hands, tiptoeing upwards to meet Jung-Soo's lips with her own. For a moment, she lingered, finally coming to her senses as she pulled herself away. Her cheeks colored like ripe persimmons. Yet, when she raised her head to meet Jung-Soo's gaze, a shy but taunting smile spread across her face. It was a look that said, *'What took so long?'*

He gazed a little while longer to make sure, and though Jung-Soo knew he might regret it, the brazenness overtook him as he pulled Iseul close in his embrace and finally let loose.

And in that moment that lasted no more than a minute, Jung-Soo took everything in—every curve in her body and her lips that moved, almost frantic, unaware and unabashed. He already knew that he would spread this moment into a hundred, no a thousand other moments in the dark days to come.

Outside, the dark blue dawn turned a hue lighter. The orchestral sounds of birds reached the cabin, gladly singing along with the flowing river and the rustling of evergreen branches. Together, Jung-Soo and Iseul leaned against the counter, warming each other in an embrace with fingers intertwined. They captured each and every detail, measuring where each callous began and ended. Jung-Soo pleaded for the night to never end, though dawn had come and gone quite a while ago.

In all honesty, Jung-Soo's leg had been falling asleep from Iseul's weight yet again, his mind swimming with the possibilities of what to do next. He could ask her to move over, tell her he has to leave or perhaps finally get to the last part of his revelation he had been putting off. Yet, none was quite as appealing as Iseul's weight warming up against his chest. That is, that had been the case until a few minutes ago when the prickly pain had become a dull throb; he was quickly losing all sensation.

"I've got one last present for you," Jung-Soo finally said.

"Present?" Iseul's head turned back in anticipation.

"It's hidden somewhere in the cabin."

She leaped off of Jung-Soo and began her search, the blood

rushing back into his leg one prickly throb at a time.

"You're close," he said, as she approached the furthest counter where various types of wood were piled up.

"Where?" she said, shoving the pile aside unceremoniously, oblivious to the fact that Jung-Soo had spent hours setting each type into a neat pile.

Jung-Soo, whose leg had finally woken, got up and headed towards Iseul, stopping next to the wall where the counter ended. Leaning against the counter with one foot against the wall, Jung-Soo's sinister smile lingered and with a click, a small compartment opened where his foot had pressed into.

Iseul's eyes widened. She leaned down and pulled open the drawer, wondering what kind of present Jung-Soo had for her.

She frowned. A single hand-gun laid inside with loose bullets rolling around. The look of wonder turned into terror.

"A gun..." she muttered, looking accusingly at Jung-Soo. "Why do you have a gun in here?"

"Listen carefully," he said, pulling out the gun and the bullets. "This is how you use it. You see this part here? This is the magazine and you release it like this. The bullets go in here, like this." Jung-Soo plowed through the instructions, trying his best to sound calm and collected as he relayed the information. "Are you listening?" he said, frustrated by Iseul's stunned look.

"I asked you," she murmured sternly, "why do you have a gun in here?"

The pieces began to fit together. The cabin, the sudden kindness, and even the brazenness...the kiss. He must be in trouble. It must have something to do with his father. He had always shied away from talking about his family, yet now, Iseul was struck with horror, wondering if Jung-Soo would vanish as abruptly as he had appeared in her life.

How could Jung-Soo explain to her in a way that she would understand? So much had been left unsaid, unplanned and put off until today. Surely, even without her lack of noon-chi, Iseul would have some inkling as to who he was—who his father was, especially after that day in the school shed. He looked into her eyes, frustrated as he tried to find the right words.

Taking two strides towards the counter, Jung-Soo turned the channel of the radio where a broadcaster announced in urgency:

"The UN Secretary General has just announced that it would be sending

troops toward the Korean Peninsula, headed by the American military...As the northern forces militarize with the help of the Chinese and the Soviet Union, so too have the brave soldiers of the south. Conscription is soon to begin nationwide..."

The broadcaster's voice weaved in and out of Iseul's mind as she tried to make sense of the difficult language and piece it together with Jung-Soo's peculiar behavior.

"We're just preparing for the worst," Jung-Soo said calmly. "For you, Yeong-Hoon hyung and your father, just in case the war reaches this village."

"War? Here in this village?" Iseul said, skeptically.

Jung-Soo hoped the violence would remain outside this village. It certainly seemed likely that nothing would happen in such a remote place, yet he would err on the side of caution when it came to Iseul's safety. His father was here, and he always brought trouble with him. All the better that they evacuate south, but with Mr. Ji's failing health and Yeong-Hoon's leg, Jung-Soo knew an extended journey might not be possible.

"What about you? Aren't you going to stay with us?" she said, knowing deep down that she was just hoping.

Jung-Soo reached over and placed a reassuring hand on her shoulders. "Don't worry about me. I always find a way," he said, smiling. "Besides, I'm the Prince of the Golden House, Ham Jung-Soo! Who could touch me?" he said.

Iseul managed a weak smile. As much as Iseul wanted to grab a hold of him and never let go, she knew she could never muster up that kind of courage. She was a lowly carpenter's daughter; he seemed to have an entire army of people protecting him. Surely, he would be safer if he were away from a war-torn village. Surely, she couldn't ask him to stay.

"Read this," he said, pointing to small letters etched on the side of the gun.

"Sa-f-e-ty," she read slowly in Korean.

Iseul looked on and in one swift motion, Jung-Soo flipped the switch, placed the gun at eye level as he steadied it with both hands.

When did he learn to do that? Jung-Soo had always been that annoying brat who couldn't even behead a chicken, yet here was a stranger with a killer instinct. More importantly, where would his father's men be taking him? Watching his steady and sturdy hand hold the gun, a quiet reassurance washed over Iseul who grabbed the gun from Jung-Soo and poised it herself, imitating Jung-Soo.

Jung-Soo leaped away from the barrel of the gun and reached to guide her hands around the safety button and the trigger.

"Turn the safety off when you're ready to shoot," he said, "and remember, you shoot to kill."

CHAPTER 10

[Present Day]

It was still dark when I left the apartment in Seoul to head to Yeoju with granny's note and the once framed document that read "Ji Iseul Instruments, Inc." If it weren't for the busy time of year when the entire extended family was needed to manufacture, package, ship and manage workers for the instrument business, mom and dad would have noticed I would not be going to school this early in the morning.

The bus stopped at Central Yeoju City station where tourist information and bus routes were plastered on the walls and on pamphlets at the ticket booth. I flipped past the first few pages that displayed the tomb of King Sejong, the birthplace of the Queen Empress, and the wall that wrapped the northern bounds of the region to get to the bus routes and maps. I needed to transfer to a local bus route. I couldn't quite remember the name of the neighborhood, but I knew it was the southern-most village somewhat isolated from the rest of Yeoju. I followed the "V" formation of the mountain ridges on the East and the West with my finger and landed at the village at the southern tip. Next to it was written, "local bus 05."

When I woke up next, the sun was glaring into my eyes through the bus window as my stomach lurched with the twists and turns of the smaller country road. I had always thought the rice fields of Yeoju extended for miles and miles, but it seemed the mountains were closer together and the fields more interspersed around the mountain than what I remembered. The rocky gravel road was just big enough for the bus to pass through as rice patties spread to the right and left of the road.

It remained the same ghost village I remembered in my childhood, populated by people barely younger than my grandmother. It was a place that seemed frozen in time.

The bus stopped next to small parking lot where a ticket booth was housed in a one-story building with just a single row of public seating. As I stepped down on to the rocky cement ground, it seemed, in every sense of the word, quaint. Breathing in that distinct concoction of soil, manure, mountain and naturally fermented soybeans, I was already imagining a younger version of my grandmother, roaming the village or hiking up a nearby mountain.

The village stood in perpetual stillness where everyone seemed to be stuck looking out into the world beyond their village through their television screens, oblivious to the fact that they had been left behind. The ticket seller too joined in the community past time, his one leg propped up a table as he bit into the side of a soft served ice-cream, both eyes firmly fixed on the television screen.

I had to knock on the glass window twice before he realized I was there.

"Ajeoshi," I called him. "Do you know where the old instrument factory is?"

He jumped from his seat, his whole body shaking out of his hypnotized state. Surprisingly, the ice cream stayed intact, leveled and without a single drop to dribble over the cone.

"Hello, oh yes," he said, gathering himself. "The instrument factory… that place has been out of business for decades now. There's really no point in going."

"I know," I said, smiling at the old man. "I'm the granddaughter of the owner."

He squinted, then his eyes widened. "Ji Iseul," he laughed, pointing a finger at me. "I see the resemblance! You look just like her! So tell me, how has your grandmother been doing since, let's see, yes, it must have been about a year since I last saw her," he said.

"Granny was here a year ago?"

"Yes, yes! I thought she had forgotten all about us after her success, but it was sure nice to see her again. You know, for old time's sake," he said, chortling.

I rummaged through my bag, pulling out the two sheets of paper. "Then you must know something about these and where they were made. Perhaps somewhere near the old factory?" I said, excitement growing at the fact that already, this trip seemed to be paying off.

As if he had seen the pages before, he plucked them out of my hands and pulled them closer. "This!" he said, "I can't believe it! It's Iseul's old paper!" he said. He then looked at me, squinted and shook his head. "Don't you know? It was all one and the same—the house, the instrument factory and even the paper factory!"

It made no sense to me. He looked at me, at a loss for words, until he finally gave the pages back and said, "Follow me!" biting into the last bit of ice cream before locking down the entire bus station in mere seconds. Before long, we were taking a stroll on the dusty roads of my granny's village.

The cement roads soon turned to gravel and then soil as we walked past a worn wooden gate towards the edge of the hill. My eyes darted up and down. The trees were thick and boulders stood in all directions with a thin patch of trodden soil as our only guide up. It was hard to believe that my granny had made this trip nearly every day. The sunlight filtered through the underbrush, birds chirping as I imagine they would have done for my grandmother decades ago.

The wooden infrastructure of the home stood smaller than I had expected, the second workshop building next to it a mammoth compared to the size of the house. Sunlight was scarce with the underbrush over the two buildings. A heaviness pressed against my chest, imagining my grandmother working in such dingy conditions, carving away at chunks of wood.

The doors creaked open. This must be the workshop. A thick layer of dust covered the entire space though remnants of its original purpose scattered here and there. A rusty hoe-like knife sat on the counter with planks of wood next to it still waiting to be molded into something useful. Pages and pages of dusty brown paper were well-preserved and strewn throughout.

"Your grandmother was born here and made history in this place. You should be very proud," the bus stop manager said.

I nodded. Outside, the gravity of the hills lay heavy on my chest. To think that anyone could have made it out of this place—

to have made something out of the vast number of trees outside—seemed even more impossible the longer I stood there. I was glad she made it out of this small town, eventually found her place as a city girl and had gone on to make something of herself.

"Ajeoshi," I said. "Do you know of someone called Yeong-Hoon?"

"Yeong-Hoon?" he said, tilting his head back and forth. "I don't recall anyone by that name. You see, I'm quite a bit younger than your grandmother, but I don't remember Iseul noona having more than a handful of friends, and none by that name."

I can't say I was surprised, yet it didn't lessen the disappointing blow. I couldn't quite give up, not when I had come all this way.

"What about her friends then? Did she have any male friends, anyone rumored to have romantic feelings for her?" I said, cringing at my own words.

He stood there thinking hard, glancing back towards my desperate look. "She lived so far away from the village," he said, trying not to let me down too hard. "But I do remember a boy her age. "Umm…" he said, deep in thought. "Oh yes! His name was Byung-Guk! Lim Byung-Guk!"

I listened earnestly.

"But, I'm afraid he is long gone now. Died soon after the war began, if I'm not mistaken. The whole village was taken into conscription and only a few made it out alive."

He must have seen my deflated shoulders. My eyes wandered the premises where my feet dare not walk. Somehow, I felt I should preserve even the dust covered floor; there must be something else here for me to discover. Out of the corner of my eye, I saw a sizable and oddly square-shaped rock on top of the counter. The ajeoshi walked over, leaving footprints for me to follow as he proudly placed his hand on that rock.

"This here is one of the rocks your grandmother used to weigh down paper!" he said.

Underneath the rock, age-stained pages that looked much like the ones in my hands laid stuck where it had been left decades ago.

"I've got an idea! Follow me!" he said as if rubbing the dusty rock a few times had given him sudden inspiration.

He trotted towards the door again, making another set of footprints that I tried to tiptoe on. As he hobbled his way around rocks and boulders towards the village, I hesitated, looking back one more time at the dusty workshop, wondering if I'd ever make it back here again and whether this place would still be standing if I did. Teetering down the hill precariously, all I could think of were the footprints we had left behind, and how many months or possibly years it would take for our visit to be erased from the workshop's memory.

***

My phone exploded with texts and calls as soon as we reached the edge of the village. Funny how I thought the cell phone reception would be better higher up in the hills, but it seemed to be a logical fallacy. I looked down at my old watch. It was noon, which meant the school would have notified my parents and they would have had ample time to be worried about their missing daughter.

I sent a message, telling them not to worry and turned my phone to silent.

The bus stop manager occasionally looked back as if remembering that I had been huffing and puffing all day trying to keep up with his quick pace. What do these people eat here? There must be something in that ice cream.

The gravel road tapered into soil until it paved into cement again. Ahead, a peculiarly tall building shimmered against the midday sun, revealing a traditional Japanese-style building, showcasing a neatly tiled roof and wooden pillars. It was nothing like the modest rice straw-thatched and mud-built homes that populated the rest of the village.

The inside of the building revealed an office-like infrastructure, a small but modern collection of computers, marble-tiled floors and bright fluorescent lights that felt almost sterile. To one side, sat a woman no older than my mother and to her left, laughter and shouts of drunkenness flooded from the wooden platform where half a dozen grandfathers sat playing a game of cards and Chinese chess.

"Hyung-nim-deul!" said a grandfather, bowing in deference as he approached the platform with a tray full of disposable cups filled with steaming coffee.

He didn't seem much younger than the rest of them, yet the man with the whitest hair of them all didn't even acknowledge him, the wrinkles sculpted into his face in a permanent frown as if it had been years since he had made a different expression. The rest of them nodded as they took their cups of coffee.

"Hyung-nim-deul," the bus stop manager said, louder than the grandfather who had just preceded him.

The woman jumped in her seat as a sneer flash across the oldest grandfather. It was somehow relieving to know that I was not the only one who found the bus stop manager's behavior peculiar at best.

"I have a surprise for you!" the manager said to the grandfather. "This is Iseul noona's granddaughter... umm... what was your name again?" he faltered, whispering not so subtly.

"Jia," I said, loud enough for the rest of them to hear, "I'm Kim Jia."

A grandfather pointed at me, his eyes just as wide in recognition as the manager's had been about an hour ago. "You look just like her!"

The manager had now taken my precious artifacts and ruffled them in the air. "Then, you must recognize these as well!" he said, passing it on to the grandfathers.

"That's Iseul's old paper!" one said.

The rest of the grandfathers' heads turned, even those who had been heavily invested in their Chinese chess game. They pulled out their reading glasses and took turns with the note. Oddly enough, they were all reading it upside down, or sideways—a sight that had me hiding a giggle under my breath. Of course, reading had always been a novelty in my grandmother's generation, yet, somehow, they all seemed to think they were experts.

The manager was distracted, walking to the other side of the building.

"Miss Kim!" he said to the woman who clearly did not want to be disturbed. "Can you get me just one of those delicious ice creams in the freezer?" he ordered with a laugh that did nothing lessen the woman's annoyance. "And what about the village records of families and their histories? Can you pull those out too?"

The woman, who seemed like she would ignore the manager to the bitter end, raised her voice as she seemed to have done many times before.

"You old hag, you're going to die of some disease if you keep eating all that ice cream!" she yelled, though in a way that seemed strangely cordial. She then pointed to a single book shelf.

"Thanks, dear," the manager said with a smile that seemed to cover all wrong-doings.

The reticent white-haired grandpa spoke up. "So Jia, are you looking for the man who wrote this note?" he said with a tone that commanded respect. The hall fell silent except for the rowdy noise of the manager slurping ice cream and vigorously turning the pages of the village records.

"Yes, sir," I said.

"Got it!" the manager said from behind. "Lim Byung-Guk." His fingers traced the page towards his final fate. "Died in battle, 1950." His voice weakened. "What was the other name you mentioned?"

"Yeong-Hoon, sir," I said. "I'm afraid I don't know the family name." I felt the grandfathers' intent gaze piercing me as the manager's fingers flipped through the pages before he reached the last one and solemnly looked up and shook his head.

"No one by that name," he said.

It was the final nail in the coffin. I turned back around towards the grandfathers who were suddenly invested in their chess game again as they whispered amongst themselves. I had come all this way with a few sheets of paper and a half-muttered name, all from a senile old woman who had lost her mind. I looked down at my phone that notified me of a slew of missed calls and messages, most of them from my dad.

"Did anyone here know my grandmother before the war?' I asked.

The manager smiled the same wide smile he had given the woman, pointing his entire hand respectfully at the grandfather with the whitest hair. "Two soldiers came home alive. One died in a car accident just ten years after the war, and the other graces us with his presence here."

"Your grandmother had always been a feisty one," the white-haired grandfather said, clearing his throat. The chess had been put to one side, the coffee now lukewarm as the others listened on. "For a woman, that is," he added.

A rush of anger pumped through my body, a lump in my throat stopping me from talking back.

"How is your grandmother doing these days?" he asked, sipping his coffee. He seemed to be enjoying the fact that he was the oldest. "Did she give you that note, telling you to come and investigate?"

I held my silence. His eyes wandered the halls that echoed the silence he demanded of all of them.

"Do you know where this place is?" he asked, this time, not waiting for an answer. "This was once called the "Golden Palace," he emphasized, "home to those Japanese monsters and later to a Korean traitor."

"I had forgotten it was called that," one grandfather said.

"Yes! The Golden Palace," another said. "I remember! Who was it that lived here?"

I could hear the manager flipping through the pages again. "Ham Young-Nam," he yelled out. "He was the last owner before it was turned into public property."

"Ham Jung-Soo," the white-haired grandfather sniggered under his breath. "The Prince of the Golden Palace, as he seemed to like to call himself. If you ask me, he's the greatest traitor of them all."

"What happened to him?" I found myself asking. The word traitor had piqued my curiosity. The grandfather finally looked straight at me, as if to emphasize what he was about to say.

"They're all dead," he said definitively. He softened his gaze, perhaps recognizing his rage was misplaced decades too late. "What I'm saying is, since I'm the last one standing, he must be dead. If I'm not mistaken, he died in the 1950 massacre once we found out his whole family were communist traitors, though your grandmother was certain he wasn't. He died right here, burning down with this very building on that fateful night."

An eerie chill ran down my spine, looking around the reconstructed building, wondering how much pain and suffering its historic walls held. I couldn't help but think of the words written on the note itself. "Traitor."

The manager yelled from across the hall. "But hyeong-nim," he deferentially addressed, "I can't seem to find anyone by the name, Ham Jung-Soo."

"Well, the records must be mistaken," the grandfather said.

Ham Jung-Soo. I had never heard of that name before, yet it hit a deep nerve. *My granny—friends with a communist?* It was unthinkable, especially during that era.

"There must have been some reason why my grandmother thought he was innocent." I found myself saying, desperate for more—desperate to vindicate my grandmother. Who was this Jung-

"Reason?" he scoffed. "The evidence was stacked up against him and his family. Your grandmother probably lost her mind after the massacre and couldn't see the facts straight, just like all the other women in the village."

The white-haired grandfather was already placing his chess pieces on the board for the next round. *So nonchalant.* How could he accuse my grandmother of such treason? Here was yet another reason why I disliked the older generation of men: tactless, misogynistic, and always certain they were right! Unlike them, my grandmother could read, and she had achieved so much more than he ever would in two lifetimes! I held my tongue.

All I could do was imagine my granny here, putting this grandfather in his place. Yet, she was probably propped up on her bed, staring blankly at the city view. She probably couldn't even understand what the grandfather was saying anymore.

I was conscious of my phone again. I knew my time was coming to a close here in Yeoju. Still, I hoped for one last miracle or some sort of an epiphany that would help me make sense of my grandmother's life that seemed much more intricate than the summarized rags-to-riches story I had heard all my life. The worst part was, it didn't seem like I had a single thing to show for my trip that would alleviate the sting of my parents' reprimand that would be awaiting me.

I finally answered the phone. It was my dad.

"Jia?" he said, calm and collected. "It's your grandmother. She's in critical condition."

There was not much I said that seemed to matter to my dad other than the fact that I was coming home. As I left the place once called the Golden Palace, I was somewhat relieved. It felt almost haunted—a place that did nothing but add more questions to the riddle of my grandmother's life.

Ham Jung-Soo, who are you? I took one last look at the place that stood ablaze as it glistened under the sun, hoping it would be the last I see of it and the white-haired grandfather who guarded it.

CHAPTER 11

[Spring, 1950]

Jung-Soo tailed Iseul like a new puppy everywhere she went that day. She had hoped he would be of some help, but like all the things his hands touched, it turned into a massive joke that only he thought was funny.

Earlier that day, Iseul reached the butcher's shop to deliver a pile of paper, as she distinctively recalled taking the order from the butcher herself two days ago.

"Let me handle this," Jung-Soo said as he whispered something in the butcher's ear. She didn't know quite what he said but somehow, Jung-Soo had managed to convince the man that his order had been mixed up and that instead of paper, he would do better with an extra pile of firewood.

"Do it for the children," Jung-Soo added. He winked at Iseul and walked outside the butcher's store as she collected her payment. It was four jeon coins, a whole extra jeon than the going rate. "My fees," he said, demanding it as he held out his hand.

"Huh?"

Jung-Soo had no patience as he swooped in and plucked the extra jeon from Iseul's hand. She grunted as she followed him into the market. The butcher's wife was there, selling red bean buns amidst other women who had come to populate the weekly open market with their fresh produce.

"Two red bean buns, please," Jung-Soo said as he managed his most charming smile on the butcher's wife.

Iseul was livid. "You selfish brat! Couldn't you buy yourself a bun?"

He grabbed her wallet, counting the day's earning right in front of her. It was the exact amount, and not a single copper jeon was missing. She looked at him, confused.

"Babo. Stupid," he said. "What'll you do without me, you silly girl?" he said, ruffling her hair. "I charged a little extra at the school and at the butcher's store. Let's just say they valued what I had to offer."

Iseul couldn't possibly imagine what he could have said to convince them to pay her more, but she remembered Jung-Soo pulling the butcher aside as the two proceeded to converse about what seemed like the most intriguing topic.

Jung-Soo felt like the day had been passing as if he were a third person in his own life. He etched into memory the wrinkles on Iseul's face that came together to form a particularly angry look. He promised he wouldn't forget the look as he stuffed a hot bun into her mouth.

"Hot, hot! Oww!" Iseul complained though it pleased him that the creases on her forehead eased and the yammering stopped.

There, that's a better look. He knew just the way to make her happy.

In any case, Iseul happily munched on the hot red bean buns, only just realizing how hungry she was; it must be because the weather had changed so much lately, or perhaps because she had the extra task of babysitting Jung-Soo for the day.

It wasn't until the sun set when Jung-Soo suddenly halted in his tracks. Iseul realized they had been taking the long route back home. Just ahead, she saw a house that looked familiar, brown with a straw-thatched roof like the rest of the ones in the village, but the barn next to the home was made distinctively with ashen wood. They were at Byung-Guk's home.

"What are we doing here?" Iseul said.

"Shhh…" he cautioned Iseul to quiet down, grabbing onto her hand as he began leading the way.

"I've got one task for you," Jung-Soo whispered. "When I say 'now' I want to you say *'oppa'*, got it?"

"What's all this about?" Iseul shot a glare at Jung-Soo, tugging her wrist away from him. "You're most definitely not my 'oppa;'

we're the same age!"

"What month were you born in?"

Iseul stood silent, her arms crossed.

"Okay, I confess," Jung-Soo said. "I set up a harmless prank for Byung-Guk and I thought you might be interested."

She knew it! Of course, Jung-Soo was up to no good. "Forget it. I'm not getting involved in your feud. Shame on you, Jung-Soo! Don't you think you've done enough to torture that poor kid?"

"Kid? Technically, he was born in January so he is at least a month older than we are and…"

"Don't you dare get me started!"

But before she could begin her usual tirade, Jung-Soo had already prepared a full-blown desperate look, like a dog just before slaughter. Iseul's expression eased.

"So when I say 'now,' you say…"

"Oppa…" Iseul reluctantly said.

"Yes, your oppa is here," Jung-Soo said, trying to lighten the mood with his meager attempt at a joke. Iseul grunted and rolled her eyes. He had always wanted to hear those words from her, like the way she said it to Yeong-Hoon that signaled they were close— closer than he was to her.

"Okay, that was perfect!"

With his smile tinged with anxiety, Jung-Soo glanced down at his watch before opening the creaky barn door. From what looked like his back pocket, Jung-Soo pulled out a black wig, made with long black hair like Iseul's own.

Iseul giggled. "Where did you get that from? Is it another toy from your father's collection?"

"Of course not! My father is a mechanic. Why would he have a wig in his warehouse? I made the Captain get one for me from Seoul."

She giggled louder. "I wish I could have seen his face when he went into the store."

"Exactly," Jung-Soo laughed with her. "Two for one prank. Shh! It's almost time." Jung-Soo scanned the area for a place to hide before taking Iseul behind a stack of hay in one corner of the spacious barn. Iseul fumbled, tripping over a half-pile of obscured hay, landing comfortably on her bottom on another stack.

"Ouch," a voice squeaked in the darkness, but before Jung-Soo could help her back up, the door creaked open again and light spilled into the barn.

"Now," Jung-Soo whispered, just loud enough for Iseul to hear.

Before she could stand back up, she found herself saying, "Oppa...?" with a whiff of confusion in her voice.

The lantern turned on, illuminating Jung-Soo's equally perplexed expression. Iseul suppressed a giggle, ready to stand and see Byung-Guk's reaction, but Jung-Soo waved his hands towards her with a look of alarm that told her to stay exactly where she was.

Jung-Soo spun around to face the barn door. "Hyung?" Jung-Soo said. "What are you doing here?"

Had the prank worked? Why wasn't anyone laughing? Iseul began wondering how long she was supposed to stay hidden. She crouched next to a tall heap of hay, peeping through a small gap between two stacks.

The massive figure of the Captain stood in front of the barn door, almost blocking the entire entrance. A few steps behind him stood Byung-Guk, leaning against the door with a satisfied look on his face.

"Your father is waiting for you at home, master Jung-Soo," the Captain said.

Something wasn't quite right. Iseul fumbled for another larger hole to look through.

"Way to go, ruining the moment," Jung-Soo awkwardly chortled, "Yes, *home*," he emphasized. "We should be going back to YOUR HOME," he emphasized again. "I mean back to my house."

"Quickly now," the Captain said, as he rushed Jung-Soo out.

The situation seemed more ominous than a simple prank was supposed to be. She shifted in place, hoping Jung-Soo would reach behind and take her away with him, though it was clear he had already left. Why was she told to stay down? Was she supposed to meet him at the Golden Palace? Perhaps back at her home? She almost grunted, holding her breath in at the last second. If Jung-Soo knew she was terrible when it came to hints, why was he talking in codes?

The light of the barn dimmed again as they closed the door behind them. She waited until the footsteps faded and the sound of car tires on gravel vanished. It was pitch dark in the barn as she tiptoed towards the door.

"Ouch!" Iseul said. She had bumped into something. The

lantern turned back on and there stood Byung-Guk, in the same position he had been in minutes ago.

Iseul jumped. "What are you doing standing there in the dark?"

"Oppa," Byung-Guk said, mimicking her voice. "Not bad hearing those words coming from a girl, and not Jung-Soo." Red flooded in her face. "I've always liked girls with long hair," he said, reaching to grab a strand of hers. "Surely, you must think I'm decent, or at least better than that commie scumbag." He let out a sinister smile.

Iseul swatted Byung-Guk's hand away, "Commie?" she said. "Who are you accusing of being a commie?"

"Just as I suspected. Clueless. I always knew you weren't the brightest, but really, not even the slightest hint of suspicion?"

Her eyes flickered in doubt. *Jung-Soo?* She had known something was amiss, but a communist? She hated them, almost as much as she hated the Japanese! Iseul could sense Byung-Guk's eyes searching for any indication that she had known about Jung-Soo. She couldn't betray him, not now. *And if he really was a commie?* Her mind wandered.

Byung-Guk reached even closer and shoved a slip of paper in her hands. "You might be slow, but I trust you're not stupid," he said.

The letters on the page flickered in barely comprehensible shapes: a red hammer and sickle—the communist symbol. She couldn't read what it said under the dim lantern but the distinctly square handwriting scribbled hastily over the red symbol indicated it was indeed Jung-Soo's hand that wrote it.

"Oh no, what did you do, Byung-Guk?" Iseul muttered.

"Nothing. I just relayed the information to the appropriate government officials."

What had Jung-Soo gotten himself into? Surely, he would be okay. After all, the Captain was with him; she knew he would protect Jung-Soo with his life, if it came to that. But what if they are ambushed? *What if... what if...* There was only one way to make sure.

She could see Byung-Guk's gloating face looking on, just waiting for her to lose it. But no, she wouldn't. She couldn't. She shoved the page back into Byung-Guk's hands.

"I trust that you're not stupid either," she said with as much command as she could muster. "Don't forget, that page was found in your hands. What would the officials think if they start hearing rumors of your father joining hands with the Commies?"

She was about to leave, run across the fields, take the first left up the hills and down the other side as a short cut to the Golden Palace, but Byung-Guk blocked her way, holding the door firmly closed.

"Too late for threats now," he sniggered. "Really, you should be thanking me for keeping you here."

"Too late? Spit it out, Byung-Guk!"

"When I found this slip of paper on my desk and realized it was a hoax, I thought it was just Jung-Soo's way of paying me back for the unfortunate school shed incident. And then I saw the communist mark. I've had my suspicions about Jung-Soo for a while now but I had just hoped they were true, imagining that arrogant Japanese sell-out turning over to the Communist side for their filthy money and attention."

A tingling sensation spread across Byung-Guk's face. "You idiot!" she roared as she slapped him. Iseul looked down at her hand that had almost involuntarily done the deed. Silence resounded in that hay-filled barn, her hands stinging and pumping with blood.

She had known the rivalry between the two boys had gone on for months, maybe years, but this? This farcical story Byung-Guk created… they couldn't be true. Jung-Soo hated the Japanese, and the Communists even more!

"How could you? It's Jung-Soo we're talking about. It's Jung-Soo, not some random person!"

She didn't need to hear any more. She shoved his stunned and heavy frame away from the door and ran out. Where could Jung-Soo be? Where would the Captain take him? *Faster… faster*, she thought, the air blowing away the tears that wouldn't stop. *Home*, he had said. *The Golden Palace*. In softening echoes, Byung-Guk's voice rang with each step she took. 'It's too late…It's too late…'

Back at the dingy barn where Byung-Guk still stood in darkness, Iseul's last words rang in his ears. 'It's Jung-Soo, not some random person…'

It would remain ringing with guilt long after that fateful night.

***

The car twisted and turned faster than they had ever gone before on that narrow road as Jung-Soo tried to suppress his nausea and think....think! What had happened? This was not part of the plan. He thought he had at least a few more hours. Jung-Soo reached for the radio, hoping some news would have trickled in the air, then realized he had taken the radio out to place in Iseul's cabin.

The Captain took a sharp turn left down a bumpy road, as fog wafted in a shallow layer off the ground, the car's headlights accentuating it. An eeriness seemed to seep through the metal casing of the car and reach them to the bone. Barely keeping his eyes open, Jung-Soo peeped outside to try and find his bearings; they were on the back road past the east gate.

"What's going on?" Jung-Soo heaved. "Why are we on this road?"

The Captain's knuckles had gone white, gripping the wheel while the whole car shook with the rugged rocks that scattered beneath it.

"I'm sorry," he spoke. "The South Korean police found our records."

"Records?" Jung-Soo said. He was beginning to realize which ones they were—a list of those who supported the communist cause in their village, meant to deter anyone from betraying the others. "How?" Jung-Soo managed to say, "A rat? Byung-Guk?"

"There are no traitors amongst us," the Captain stated with absolute certainty. "It wasn't Byung-Guk either. I stopped the boy from doing too much damage with the officials."

Jung-Soo groaned. It seemed his prank had backfired. He had written the note to Byung-Guk on the page with the communist symbol as a way of warning him to keep his mouth shut. But Byung-Guk didn't seem to have a clue about his own father's involvement with the Communists, or else he wouldn't have gone to the officials with it.

"There are bigger issues now, Jung-Soo," the Captain said with urgency. "Soldiers. They are everywhere, many more than we had expected, and much sooner."

Jung-Soo listened. It wasn't anything they hadn't prepared for.

"And with the records public, our men are going up the hills."

Jung-Soo's head spun. "Up the hills?" The Captain didn't need to finish his sentence; there would be a bloodbath tonight, and he had just told Iseul to go home towards the hills.

"Stop the car," Jung-Soo said firmly. Jung-Soo only wished he hadn't said those words to Iseul. He should have told her to stay in the Dyung-Guk's barn till daybreak. The car still rocked forward, picking up the pace. He could only hope that Iseul didn't hear or hadn't understood. Yes, he knew Iseul and there is no way she could have understood him. He could bank on that, but there was only one way to be sure.

"You've done with you could, Jung-Soo," the Captain said with his fatherly tone.

"I said stop the car!"

"They would've passed Iseul's place by now, and you've kept her long enough in the barn. She should be safe," the Captain tried to reason with Jung-Soo, but he was ready to jump out of the car.

"Ham Jung-Soo," he said sternly. "Listen to me. There isn't enough time, you hear? If not for yourself, do it for your father," he sighed, wondering if he should tell him the whole truth. "Your brothers are all dead. They've been dead for a while now. "You're all he has left, and he..." the Captain hesitated. "He disowned you."

"Disown?"

"Kim Jung-Soo," the Captain said. It didn't quite sound right, but he continued. "It's official. You're no longer your father's son, no longer the son of a communist or a Japanese sympathizer. You get to have a fresh start."

It had been everything Jung-Soo had ever wanted—to be free from the chains of his father's past—of the Ham family name. But what about Iseul? He glanced over to the Captain's white knuckles that gripped the wheels. Not many knew that they chapped during the winter because they had been pummeled, cracked and broken so many times that a calloused barrier had formed. Those were just the tip of the iceberg of the injuries this man had endured. But for what? For him? For his father? For the cause? It was all in vain; Jung-Soo saw that now.

"So, you want me to leave and abandon the only place I call home while everyone here dies?" he said, helplessly.

This time, Jung-Soo didn't wait for an answer. The car door slid open and before the Captain could take his hands off of the wheels to reach for Jung-Soo, he was already on the dusty road, rolling then hobbling towards the trees, vanishing from the Captain's rear view mirror.

***

Two lefts and a right, Iseul repeated to herself. She was almost there. Straw-roofed houses were barely visible in the dark, the villagers scattered here and there as unnerved voices and barks from the neighborhood dogs filled the thickening skies.

There were soldiers—so many of them.

She should stick to the narrow roads and head towards the back entrance of the Golden Palace. But even between the dense brushes of the hills, Iseul could hear the screams of women, cries of little children and shouts of men in uproar. Could it be Mr. Lim? Mr. Park and his three little boys? And what about the grandmother who lived not too far away?

It can't be. They must be communists from a nearby village, hiding in our hills.

"Don't let him get away!" A man yelled through the thicket.

Iseul's legs pushed forward, faster and when she took the final right, ash and smoke stung her eyes and drew out tears. She blinked and she was standing in front of the Golden Palace in a blaze that rose in pillars of smoke to the sky. She scanned the front garden, but it was engulfed in flames. In the side of the road stood three servants, whimpering in the dark.

"Where's Jung-Soo?" She tugged at one who stood crying at the scene, unsure of what to say.

"We've been told to leave hours ago. No one has been allowed inside since." Another servant answered for the first.

"Are you sure Jung-Soo's not inside?" Iseul yelled at the one who answered, shaking her.

"I…I don't know," she muttered. "I thought I saw someone jump into the flames, but I couldn't say…"

"Jung-Soo!" Iseul said in a trance, her feet still trotting towards her final destination.

A hand grabbed her by the arm and pulled her back. "Have you lost your mind?" a man said, though Iseul's gaze still fixed on the blaze that reached for the skies. "Jung-Soo isn't here. How could he be? Even the servants have been told to leave hours before the soldiers arrived!"

The man seemed to make sense. She looked back and saw Mr. Lim, ashen and black with soot, standing in the streets with many other onlookers and soldiers surrounding the premises.

"He should be with the Captain of the Guards," Mr. Lim said. "He should be safe," he whispered into her ears.

How? Iseul looked at Mr. Lim whose pupils flickered with the flames. How did he know? How could he know for sure?

"Go home, Iseul." Mr. Lim nudged her towards the east gate. "Make sure they're alright."

"What do you mean?" Iseul said, confused. And then it hit her. *Father, Yeong-Hoon, the soldiers in the hills.*

"It can't be..." The soldiers were here to arrest communists, and his father wasn't one. Everyone knew that... didn't they? Surely, they wouldn't take the innocent. An image of Mr. Park and his three boys came to mind.

She nearly tripped, taking a few steps back and then turning to sprint down the same road she had just come from, plunging into the cover of night as she moved further away from the flames. Her thoughts cleared, planning the fastest route back home. She must avoid the soldiers; she must get home before they do.

Lanterns alerted Iseul of the soldiers dispersed in the hills. There were many more than the ones she had passed on the way into the village as the cries grew louder and sharper—cries of people she usually heard laughing, and of their little feet pattering on the dusty roads on a normal Saturday afternoon.

She quickened her steps, hoping her father, Yeong-Hoon and Jung-Soo would have joined together and escaped with the Captain. She was so close. She had just a minute or so until the twin peaks of her hanok home and workshop would appear in view.

A light caught her attention from behind. Iseul squatted behind a bush. Three soldiers and a silhouette of a familiar woman followed close behind. It was Mrs. Sohn, and just beside her, hidden in her shadow was her daughter Jin-Soon. Iseul had seen the little girl from when she was just a baby. Just two days ago, she stood waiting for Iseul to pass by her house just to hand her a handful of chestnuts.

"Mom, where are we going?" the little girl Jin-Soon squeaked.

"Shh," Mrs. Sohn hushed. "Don't bother the nice soldiers."

Where was Mr. Sohn? She scanned the area to no avail. *Mr. Sohn, a communist?* She doubted for a brief second. Had he escaped while his family was being taken in the middle of the night? Iseul traced their route and she was sure the group of ten or so were headed towards the river bank. She had to hurry. Her legs began to numb, anxious to get home, and when the group had disappeared into the brush, Iseul shook her legs and ran.

***

It was early in the night when Iseul's father heard the ruckus outside his normally quiet home. He looked at Yeong-Hoon then went back to work. There was much to get done before the last rays of sunlight would leave them.

It wasn't long before three soldiers barged into the workshop, each pointing a gun at Young-Hoon and Mr. Ji who held carving knives in their hands.

"What's all this?" Iseul's father said as they restrained him with his arm twisted up his back, sending a spark down his weakening spine.

"Father!" Yeong-Hoon tried to shove his way towards him, but it was no use.

"Iseul? What about Iseul?" father said, wincing.

Yeong-Hoon shook his head, looking helplessly at Mr. Ji.

***

Jung-Soo knew his way around Iseul's part of the hills. He eyed his favorite route towards the bush where he could see through the peephole into the workshop. He was near—so very near. He just had to get past the soldiers scattered just ahead. As each minute passed by, Jung-Soo's heart raced, his eyes scanning for a familiar figure.

From the outside, Jung-Soo could see that a lantern was lit in the workshop. He crouched to look through the peephole and saw a figure pacing back and forth. It was the Captain.

Jung-Soo burst through the doors.

"We're too late," the Captain said.

"What about Iseul? Was she taken too?"

"I don't know. I just got here too."

Outside, footsteps and voices neared the workshop. Jung-Soo blew out the lantern.

"Come on, we've got to go," the Captain said, taking Jung-Soo's arm.

"I can't." Jung-Soo yanked his arm away.

"I know," the Captain said. "We have to get out of here. They're closing in fast. The soldiers have set up a shelter down by the river bank. I'll check there. You go."

"Where?" Jung-Soo instinctively asked.

He could almost see the Captain's sly smile they had picked up from each other and had perfected over the years. "To the cabin, of course!" he said. "I'll meet you there."

He reached to grab the Captain's elbow at the last second. "Hyung," he said, "Thank you."

"Wait till your father hears about this," he sighed. Jung-Soo knew the Captain rolled his eyes.

And the two were off into the wood again, the heaviness still weighing on Jung-Soo's chest as he passed each tree towards that remote location.

CHAPTER 12

[Present Day]

Atop Sky Nursing Home, grandmother Iseul's head was turned towards the oversized windows where she had a direct view of the city where people roamed as specks of dust in a spiral haze of light.

While everyone else complained about the night lights in a city that never sleeps, Iseul was used to it. She had always been a night owl of sorts. The nurse had noticed that Iseul would sleep only on one side and her neck would strain all day and all night to see what was beyond the glass aperture. So the kind nurse had pulled the bed closer to the windows.

Through the stillness of the night, Iseul could hear her next-door neighbor snoring. It was somehow soothing to her, like the sound of her late husband's snore that lulled her to sleep for many decades. As her brain disintegrated, it would be the unexpected things that triggered memories and emotions, like the smell of red bean buns on a cold rainy day, or the sound of an instrument coming from a novice player.

It was October. The sweltering heat of summer would simmer down by this time of year, but inside Sky Nursing Home, the temperature remained at a steady cool twenty degrees Celsius, like spring just before summer. Fireworks lit the night sky as it did each year in October, Seoul's night sky flashing in brilliant colors to match the buildings that stood awake.

Not many would sleep that night, except for maybe her next-door neighbor who could sleep through anything. *Strange*, she thought, which was about as deep as she could think these days. The lights unnerved her. Perhaps it was because of the distant sound of blasts that accompanied the pretty lights, unlike most other nights when the sky remained a dullish gray without a single star nor a sound to light it up. Her eyes shot back and forth in the room, finally resting on the guitar next to her nightstand. She would focus on this tonight. Her hands reached for it, hoping to grasp the soothing familiarity of finished wood, but something was missing. Her eyes began wandering again. *Strange... strange...*

***

[Spring, 1950]

Jung-Soo could feel the slight tilt on the ground that told him he was nearing the valley where the cabin lay hidden. He hadn't seen a soldier for minutes, but there was no way of knowing they hadn't already found the cabin yet. Every hundred meters or so, he would make a mad dash to the next bunch of trees or bushes, catching his breath and scouring the area for any signs of life.

Ominously silent, even the animals seemed to have gone into hiding. Beads of sweat ran towards his brows and down his back. He'd feel cold if he stood there for too long. A twig broke beneath his feet, the echo traveling towards the hidden hill and back again. It startled him as he crouched and scoured again.

A voice echoed with the twig. "Sir, you don't think we'll get in trouble for wandering so far away?"

"You're with me, soldier," another soldier said, laughing as he slapped the soldier on the back, sending echoes across the hills. "We're supposed to be patrolling and that's exactly what we're doing," he said, taking a dose of his medicine in a bottle.

Good, they were drunk, at least one of them. He could outrun the drunk one, but the other? Even if he could, he couldn't outrun a bullet. They might even follow him and what was he to do—lead them straight to the cabin?

A trail of whispers ricocheted off of the rocky hills. Or was it the echoes of the first pair? He laid there immobilized, but he couldn't stay there for much longer. Time was running out.

It was the first time that night Jung-Soo had time to stop and think, forced into a state of stupor. His thoughts reached out to Iseul. Somehow, until the very end, she had a way of getting under his skin. Why couldn't she just be normal like the rest of the village girls who stayed put at home? And then he recalled what had happened earlier in the day, and realized he had been half the problem.

The drunk soldiers disappeared back up the hills, away from the valley. He sighed in relief but the whispers below had now turned into voices and footsteps. He rolled over on his back, shoving his hands into both of his pockets, feeling for something sharp.

"Ouch!" he whimpered.

He forgot he had sharpened his pencil earlier in the morning. He was sure the rustling of the pages in his pockets would sound a lot like someone stepping on autumn leaves. He pulled out a random sheet. It was the dated page he had meant to write his goodbye letter for Iseul. He regretted not having written it sooner.

"My dearest Ji Iseul," he began scribbling in his boxy handwriting. He didn't know quite what to say. He had planned for the evening with Iseul to be quiet and peaceful, savoring their last moments alone together before he would tell her goodbye, answer all of her questions and promise her that he'll be back. He had even imagined stealing a few intimate moments with her.

Blood shot through his body with the realization that this could be the only explanation he would leave her with. That is, if he was unable to find her that night.

He needed to make it down to the cabin alive. That much was certain. Words failed him as he stared at the blank page. He did not have the time to look up at the stars and wait for inspiration to strike.

Footsteps drew closer.

He'd have to think on the way down. Back on his stomach, he pushed himself up, his head ducking instinctively as his feet shuffled down the quickest route to the cabin.

***

The Captain knocked a soldier to the ground, dragging his unconscious frame away from the crowd of villagers and soldiers. He got into the soldier's uniform, shaking his shoulders, only stopping when he heard the seams rip. The soldier's uniform didn't quite fit on his broad shoulders.

The soldiers herded the villagers like cattle into a shed that had been erected that day, while the rest of the men with guns lit cigarettes on the campfire next to the river.

"When do we start cooking?" the same soldier blew a puff of smoke that dissipated into the stars above, the howls of drunk soldiers rising with it.

The Captain walked past them, his head steady and his nerves as steel as he scanned for two familiar faces. He had become inured to the cruelties of men, yet even still, he held a special place of fury in his heart for those who reveled in the pain of others.

"Captain!" a voice rang from his left.

It was Yeong-Hoon, his arms around Iseul's father as he waved towards the Captain in disguise. The soldiers urged them on, the line behind them slithering down one side of the hill. The Captain turned his head, making an innocent loop around the shed, meeting Yeong-Hoon on the other side.

"Where's Iseul?" they said in unison.

Mr. Ji's worried look said it all.

"Jung-Soo went to look for her," the Captain said. "I'm supposed to meet him at the cabin."

"What cabin?" Yeong-Hoon said anxiously. "Is that where Jung-Soo thinks Iseul is?"

The Captain had already taken a few steps back. There was no time for explanations; he needed to get to Jung-Soo, and most importantly, get him out of Yeoju. He had made promises, and he intended to keep them.

A soldier approached the three. "Is there a problem here?"

"No problem at all. Back to your station, soldier," the Captain ordered in his natural disposition.

Another group of soldiers was fast approaching, trying to keep the line in check.

Mr. Ji eyed them intently. "Promise me you'll find her. Go! I'll be here waiting."

With these last words, Mr. Ji ran into the incoming group of soldiers in a fit of rage, creating a diversion. Yeong-Hoon was already beside the Captain, limping down the hill. He looked back towards his father whose arms flailed towards the three soldiers.

"Come on, old man," Yeong-Hoon said, already two steps ahead of the Captain. "I promise I won't slow you down."

Yeong-Hoon couldn't bear to look back, hoping the shouts

that grew distant did not come from the man he called father.

***

Just a little bit further. Jung-Soo's lungs filled with the midnight forest air that reeked of sweat and damp mud that was not unlike blood. This would be his final pit stop and then he was just one sprint away from the cabin. He had to make sure he wasn't being followed. His head bopped around every few seconds to double check. Still unsure of what to write, his hands scribbled the first words that came to mind:

"I am sorry. I wish I had something better to say. If this letter doesn't reach you, it saddens me to think that you'll remember me as a traitor."

He could hear the steady flow of water running down the covert valley just beyond the boulder. His hands fumbled to fold the page as he plunged the letter deep into his right pocket. The stillness was a good sign; he knew he had found a good place to build the cabin.

Jung-Soo pushed forward into that final dash.

"Iseul," he burst through the doors of the cabin. Only echoes greeted him. "Iseul, it's me, Jung-Soo. Please...where are you?" he said, words losing their meaning, stuck in his throat like chili left in the summer heat to dry.

A rustle in the wind echoed like ghosts haunting the night. They all sounded like Iseul, resounding in cries for help. He closed the door firmly behind him, instinctively reaching for the lantern, lighting a match then blowing it out again. He mustn't be rash. He couldn't risk the slightest bit of light spilling out of the cabin.

He wondered how much longer he could stay in the cabin without a stray soldier venturing inside. He couldn't stay for long. Iseul would eventually come, if not tonight then another day when the soldiers have all left.

Lighting another match, he stumbled in the dark to the hidden compartment, then quickly blew it out. Someone was fast approaching. His fingers fumbled around the hidden compartment, clicking it open then clasping around the metal object. Huddled in the corner like a lame duck, he could only hope it was Iseul.

The door swung open; he pointed the gun at the intruder.

"Jung-Soo!" a voice said.

Jung-Soo let out a sigh of relief, his hand only then starting to tremble with the gun in it. It was the Captain and next to him was Yeong-Hoon hyung, catching his breath.

"Where's Iseul?" Jung-Soo said.

"She's not here?" Yeong-Hoon managed to say.

Outside, echoes only seem to grow louder.

"Come on, we have to get out of here," the Captain said, taking Yeong-Hoon's arm over his to shoulder his weight.

The gun. Jung-Soo only just felt the weight of it as he exited the cabin. "Hold on," he said. He ran back towards the hidden compartment, dropping in the gun and the letter he had written for Iseul. He had so much more to say…so much more to explain to help her understand, but there wasn't enough time. There was never enough time.

He clicked the secret compartment close and swung the cabin door behind him.

***

Iseul swung the cabin door open. She couldn't speak; breathing was more important. The pitch darkness seemed to suffocate her as the sound of her own breathing bounced around the wooden walls.

Outside, a single gunshot rang clear, hitting rocks, boulders, hills, and the river in all directions before landing within the walls of the cabin. A second one rang like its twin.

"No!" A man's voice agonized.

***

Those twin echoes would travel far and wide, eventually becoming one and the same. Some say they never stopped to rest, making their way around the globe in circles like an arrow shot through time, never to cease and never to pass.

Somewhere, sometime much later, those twin echoes would wake grandmother Iseul from her brief slumber. *Strange…* she would think. It would've died down by now. Yet, it rang so clear, one after another, then another…

CHAPTER 13

[Present Day]

The nurse heard it first over the sound of the fireworks, the incessant TV playing in the background and the snores of the grandpa next door.

"Grandma, wake up!" she said. Panic filled her voice. The flat line continued. This was the second time granny Iseul had flat lined that day. *Breath. Breath.* Like a charm, she hoped it would work. She called the code—blue, like the color of the night sky just before dawn. "Code blue, code blue!"

The doctor on night duty rushed in. He was young and inexperienced.

A figure stood by Iseul's bedside. Perhaps it was the spirit of the bullets here to pay their last respect, or maybe even to finally call it a day on their travels through time and space and be laid to rest on familiar ears.

"Paddles... charge." The doctor's voice squeaked. He was shaking.

She didn't need the charge. Grandma Iseul swallowed a massive gulp of air, gasping for more. She was in a fit, her body flailing and grasping for something, anything... Where did all this energy come from?

Often, patients regain part of their bodily functions in their final days, but this isn't a sign of regeneration. The doctor was trained to say these exact words.

"Doctor," the nurse said. She could seriously hurt herself if she continued like this. He was thinking. "Doctor, Diazepam?" she said sternly. She needed the doctor's orders to administer medication.

"Yes…" he said, still dazed.

"0.3 mg of Diazepam, then." Her hands worked as he spoke, and almost instantly, Iseul leaned back, serene again as her breathing leveled out. Her eyes were ever so slightly dilated as she tilted her head towards the window.

It was protocol to call the patient's next of kin in case of a code-blue so she dialed the number on the registry again for the second time that day.

"I thought you said she was stable?" the lady on the other line said.

The nurse somehow felt responsible. She sat by Iseul for the rest of the night, nodding off.

The high-pitched note of the heart rate monitor lingered in Iseul's ears. It had been a while since the fireworks had died down, but the city still stood awake, blinking with colorful lights. Granny Iseul laid awake too, at first with a numb look on her face until she remembered something. With the same concerned and unnerved look she had been sporting all night, she thought, *strange… strange…*

The doctor, on the other hand, had been looking forward to a quiet night. He had been told when he took the job just three weeks ago that most cases could wait until the morning when the attending physician would make his rounds. High fever, chills, elevated blood pressure—these were quick fixes. Then there were others like code blue or pain. Those either meant a long sleepless night of patients complaining or a quick paper-work stint of signing a death certificate.

He rolled down the curtains of his on-call room to block out the night lights, cozying into his bed. *Adrenaline.* He knew he would lay awake for a while longer; it was a physiological certainty. Laying to one side towards the night lamp, the doctor opened a book to a random page. Surely, reading would take the edge off. He had barely read a page before his head burrowed into the pillow, burying his eyes away from the light.

A hand shook him. Fluorescent lights switched on and his room was as bright as day again.

"Doctor, code blue!" a nurse said.

In a haze, he jumped up, shaking the blurry grayness out of his vision. "Again?"

The nurse shook her head. "It's the grandpa next door."

The two made a left from his on-call room and paced down the same hall for the second time that evening. *Oh great, three code blues in one night.* Guilt struck him. Maybe tomorrow night, he would be up in his own room looking for a new job. Caught up in his own thoughts, he didn't notice that the elevator dinged open just as he passed by it.

My arrival marked no real significance to the night. Mother was with me and we were still in our pajamas.

Ahead in the hallway, voices trickled towards us. We followed close behind the doctor whose white coat whipped back and flapped around like a cape. Would this be the end? I had thought the same before. What's the difference now? Granny was a shell of the person she once used to be. And hadn't we all knocked on her frail frame long enough?

Flat line. It cried louder with each step. Mom tailed the doctor who made a sharp right into a room. She nearly collapsed right there out of sheer relief that he hadn't gone into granny's room. One door down, mother anxiously disappeared inside.

Mother had never met the old man next door—the one who woke granny up in the mornings, singing and dancing to his own tune. I wondered if granny would be sad if the grandpa died. Maybe she didn't remember the singing old man. Would granny miss what she doesn't remember?

The door to the old man's room was left ajar. The doctor was rocking his entire body in hopes to animate him. The old man's body shook, his arms dancing up and down in unison with the doctor's movements.

I stood between the two rooms in the hallway as I saw mother rattling granny as the doctor in the other room did. "Wake up," she said. Granny was probably just asleep or in some other catatonic state.

"Charge, 100. Clear," the doctor said in the other room. The old man's shell jumped in the bed. "Charge, 130... Clear!"

That would be the last time we'd see that man move. I didn't need to see what came next. I had seen it in movies and so, my feet passed through the doorway into granny's room. It was relatively quiet and tranquil, the man on the television reinforcing that everything was in fact, fine.

"Time of death," I heard a voice say, barely audible but assuredly drained. "Thursday, October 17, 03:05."

My mind wandered back into granny's room, watching mother take her spot on a small bed next to granny's bed. The heart rate monitor, often left on silent, would beep a steady signal to indicate granny was alive, at least until the day-doctor would arrive in the morning. It was standard practice, of which I was grateful for since it usually put mom right to sleep.

I was told to stay at home. And even now, past midnight, mom had given me money to take the taxi home. *You need a good night's rest to perform well tomorrow*, mom had said. She meant academic performance; it was the only type of performance that mattered.

I rolled myself into a ball on the couch. The lights outside were bright and the air conditioner blew on me. Granny liked it just that way but I'd need an extra blanket. I unraveled myself from the couch, tiptoeing to the cabinet where the extra pillows and blankets were kept.

A few hours ago, I had heard the brunt of it when I got home late from Yeoju. I tried to explain, but she didn't listen. '*Why now, when the exam is just around the corner?*' mom had asked. That was the only question she asked.

I had wanted to ask about grandpa, where he was from, and how he had died. I wanted to know more about the details of granny's life. *Yeong-Hoon. Jung-Soo.* Who were these mysterious men? I didn't get a word in. What was the point? She wouldn't listen anyway and I knew all she saw was a rebellious teenager.

A patch of cold air churned around me in eddies of thoughts and images. Yeong-Hoon, Jung-Soo—the two names rang familiar, yet I had never heard of them till a few weeks ago when my grandmother muttered the first and the white-haired grandfather seethed the second. *The war.* I'd have to check the online database. I had thought of that weeks ago, but with no family name, I wouldn't get far.

I could hear the sound of wheels on the marble hallway. They must be wheeling the old man's body away. It was such a pity since I liked the old man. My skin crawled, thinking the man was alive just minutes ago. I was sad for granny—who would be there to try to get her to smile now?

And then, the idea struck. Could it be that this old man was one of the two? I needed to check. I dropped the blanket and pillows that landed with a soft thud as I walked towards the door. In the hallway, the bed on wheels turned a corner and disappeared as the old man's room stood open, welcoming me with wide open arms.

Yes, it could very well be Jung-Soo! I paced faster into the room, looking for something...anything—a name tag or perhaps a letter addressed to him.

Surely, he must know my granny somehow, even if he wasn't Yeong-Hoon or Jung-Soo. No one was *that* nice. We were in one of the largest and most densely populated cities in the world where people pushed and shoved their way into the best spots on the subways and buses; this is where children are taught to fight for their place in the classroom, for places in universities and in the impossible job market. There must be some connection he had with my granny.

Perhaps the old man was from the countryside—from Yeoju even. They say half of the people living in hospice centers have been moved here because their children couldn't stand to make a trip outside of Seoul whenever one of their parents got sick. Yes, perhaps he was one of those.

There was nothing—no name tag, no prized possessions or mail from his family that revealed any inkling of who he was. The patch of cold air clung to me, as if it had followed me from granny's room. Perhaps I had been too hasty and cynical; maybe he was just some lonely man who wanted someone to keep him company...someone to talk to.

Perhaps the nurse would know his name and his story and I could catch her in the morning before her shift ends. My shoulders drooped in defeat as I walked a few steps towards the room where I belonged.

A piece of paper covered in plastic hung on the white walls of the entrance, almost camouflaged in the hospital setting. It was granny's chart. Her name headed the sheet in bold letters, "Ji Iseul," and next to it was the word, "Alzheimer's."

I took two steps back, and there it was, the old man's chart: *Ahn Byung Min. Pancreatic Cancer.*

That was all I needed to know. He was a man with a family, a genealogy, and a name to go with it. He was neither Yeong-Hoon nor Jung-Soo.

The monitor beeped on deep into the night. I recalled why I

had been so adamant to accompany mom to the hospice center. There was something I needed to return. Just above, where the guitar neck leaned against the bed stand, I opened the drawer to place the browned, aged slip of paper back into granny's care.

I watched my granny sleep, curled up on her spacious bed. Her head tilted towards that faithful guitar that kept her company while we were all away. It'd be there for her in the morning and perhaps she will even open the drawer and see that the note was back in her custody.

Another gush of wind met my flushed face. It seemed as if it came from a crack in the window. It must be the air-conditioned air bouncing back from the windows. I crawled next to granny, pulling up a second blanket over both of us as I wrapped my arms around her tiny frame.

"Granny," I whispered into her sleeping ear. I looked over to my mom who was fast asleep. "Don't worry, granny. That nice man next door wasn't Yeong-Hoon or Jung-Soo."

I wanted her to know too. I could imagine she would appreciate it. I slept with my hands next to her face. Mom had once told me I was just like granny when I slept. I guess I had the same sleeping habits.

She was so frail and almost cold to the touch; she didn't have much time left. I wrapped the blanket even tighter around us. If this were really granny, she would kick the blanket off of her even on a cold winter night. Who knows? She might have liked the chilly air, but she would have to make do with a warm bed tonight.

"Granny." I just wanted to call her. "Granny, do you remember when you used to come into my room and tuck me in? Everything was so simple back then. It was for me at least…"

I told her all about my trip to Yeoju and how her old home was exactly as she had left it. I told her how glad I was that she had left that place and asked if she missed it.

"Wake up, will you? Teach me how you did it…how you made it through all those tough years."

Mother's words pierced through the silence as if she were awake. *You know how they did it back then? They did not have the leisure to think, too hungry to question life. They just pushed forward and survived.*

If only I could be as strong as she is. Why can't I accept how wonderful life is now compared to the life granny lived? I wanted to tell her how much I missed her. Instead, I curled up next to her, and somehow, it didn't feel like my words would fall on deaf ears as if the words I thought would reach her one way or another.

Don't worry. I'll find your Yeong-Hoon. Just hang on a little bit longer.

The second hand of the clock ticked by, each one reaching the sound hole of the guitar, leaving it in larger echoes, urging me to sleep. But I couldn't. I'd never fall asleep with the clock so noisy and with so much on my mind!

In my dreams, granny tucked me into bed. I could feel her warm hands covering my eyes, telling me to sleep. I pretended to sleep with a grin on my face. With her other hand, she tapped a beat to a familiar tune.

"Like this granny?" my little-self said. "If I listen carefully and with all my heart, will my wish come true in the morning?" I would peek with one eye and quickly shut it close again. "Like this?" I could hear myself say before the night finally fell silent.

Lying next to granny on that hospice bed stirred something in me... something *strange*. They were like memories hidden deep within layers of dreams that came together in one thunderous jolt. They would fade away when I wake, but in that moment, they were so vivid, like déjà vu. They would leave me wondering if dreams were memories long forgotten, only to be revived in my sleep.

CHAPTER 14

The mind is a ruthless thing, wasting away quickly, but just slow enough to be aware that something is amiss. In the void, it fills itself with phantoms—ghosts of who we once were and figments of who we hope to be. It guides us, shields us, illuminates for us, and more often than we'd like to admit, it fails us.

There comes a point when the mind can no longer see what it wants to see. It starves to death until nothing but that which is, remains.

***

[Late Spring, 1950]

The Golden Palace was ablaze. The servants idled around the dusty road, while a few villagers, fearless enough to venture near the fire, joined the crowd of onlookers as the soldiers continued their hunt for communist traitors.

Byung-Guk's father hadn't left the site since he had seen Iseul dash and disappear into the hills. He wondered how she was, or whether she knew the hills wouldn't be so vacant that night. He stood behind the line the soldiers had made, unable to leave. He had seen someone enter, as the servants did, but he had his orders to stand down. He was grateful, but what would happen to his leader and his home?

Though Mr. Lim did not know the intricacies of the Palace, he had a vague idea of the treasures it held that was now burning to ashes. He must do as he was told. That had kept him alive and that will keep him alive.

"I'm sorry," he let out in a whisper.

Byung-Guk's father hadn't seen a tall figure that stood next to him, towering over his cowering self.

"What do you mean?" it said from above.

It was Byung-Guk who staggered back at his father's words. He had followed the commotion on the streets near his barn only to find his father, shivering and frozen in place in front of the inferno.

There was realization in both the father and son's eyes.

***

Iseul had hoped for the best, running towards the valley, anxious to see her loved ones safe. Maybe Jung-Soo had gone back for her family and had brought them here.

Iseul swung the cabin door open. Nothing but pitch darkness greeted her. Outside, a single gunshot reverberated in a multitude of echoes, and then another.

"No!" She heard a scream outside.

It could have been anything—a boulder falling, a soldier lost on the wrong side of the mountain. Iseul dashed out under the moon that reflected on the river that soaked up the echoes with each passing second.

"Jung-Soo?" she shouted, as the valley spoke his name back to her.

She heard voices from the other side of the river. Iseul dipped both feet in, wading through the icy waters that rose to her waist, stealing her breath until her muddied feet sprinted towards the dark patch of trees.

"Yeong-Hoon oppa?" Her voice died midair, muted by the surrounding trees.

Two bodies laid faced down. One was a large soldier and next to him was a more familiar figure. It could have either been Jung-Soo or Yeong-Hoon. She had never noticed how similar they looked.

He moved, shaking himself awake as he groaned and reached for his head where blood glistened with the sliver of moonlight that reached them.

"Iseul," Yeong-Hoon spoke, relieved. "You're alright!"

"Oppa!" she said, frantically. "Where's father? Where's Jung-Soo? Did the soldiers get to them? What happened?"

He rubbed his eyes, looking around just as Iseul was doing.

"He's not here?"

"Who?"

Yeong-Hoon spotted the soldier. "Oh no, the Captain." He rushed over to the broad-shouldered man as he flipped him over. Iseul gasped. His eyes were closed as blood oozed from his chest. Yeong-Hoon couldn't tell if the blood on his hands was from his own head or from the Captain's chest.

"Oppa, what about Jung-Soo?"

Yeong-Hoon ran to the bushes, towards the river and back again, still without any news. He tilted his head towards the moon. At first, he thought the clouds had come out to join the moon, then the fog began drifted towards them from the west.

"Oh no." He grasped Iseul's arm and pulled her away from the scene. She resisted, immobilized as the puddle of blood spread around the Captain and soaked into the ground.

"Father's been taken." He finally told Iseul. He looked towards the pillar of smoke.

That night, they would see red on the soil that quenched its thirst with blood. The night sky would burn in the gray dullness of smoke and ash that spewed with anger and righteous indignation of the souls taken—stolen from the land.

***

Charcoal is made when burning wood is deprived of oxygen.

There were enough people in the shed to drink up every last gasp of oxygen within, as the fire scorched their flesh and stole their last breaths away. The soldiers had come prepared. They put out the fire when the last of the cries died down, covering their deed with soil and rocks made from generations of their ancestors' remains.

They would smell the fresh scent of charred meat rising with the smoke as wails rose from the village the next morning. A young girl would mourn in silence in a valley between two mountains.

Ashes and charcoal. Ancestors and rocks. Those are usually the only things that remain.

… the only things that remain…

CHAPTER 15

Days of silence passed, days unaccounted for, and nights spent in utter darkness. Iseul scarcely remembered anything in those first few weeks after the fire that had massacred over fifty of their villagers. They were innocent, every last one of them! She was sure of it. But what if they weren't? Her thoughts teetered and tottered in a whirlwind of overwhelming guilt and numbness. Even if they were communists, did they deserve to be taken like cattle for slaughter as their families watched on? Ashes of her father's remains clung to her lungs and reminded her of that night whenever she breathed.

Iseul's spiral into madness scared Yeong-Hoon so much so that he startled awake in the middle of the night, hiked towards the cabin just to place a finger beneath her nose to check if she was still breathing. She did not know, nor did she care. She laid on the wooden floor for days on end, still—so very still.

Yeong-Hoon tailed her every move since that fateful night. Scarcely twenty-four hours had passed since the ashes rose towards the sky. Iseul had drifted like a ghost through the village, muttering something to herself and the occasional passerby.

"Traitor," they had all said.

He didn't need to hear what they were saying to understand what they meant. He knew some of them pitied her for the betrayal from a coward who had killed the girl's father. He was almost relieved that Iseul had that peculiar disability of having no sense of others' opinions of her.

Yeong-Hoon had become the man of the house that stood

desolate. The past few weeks had rendered a skillful carpenter to transform into a decent cook. He pushed aside the heavy lid that topped the rice cooker, steam pulling beads of sweat from his forehead. The bottom of the jar was barely covered with rice; it wasn't much but it would last him and Iseul for the next few days. Besides, he had been getting fat with all the rice Iseul wasn't eating and he couldn't let the precious grains go to waste.

He pressed the rice down in the lunch box, gently setting aside a small portion of kimchi as he also packed two pairs of chopsticks and headed towards the valley.

Iseul's body created a patch of gloss on the hardwood floor against the rest of the dusty ground. He could almost feel the layers of dust in her lungs that had accumulated over the past few weeks, sleeping where the wood still breathed. Any decent carpenter would know, as surely Iseul did too, that a newly carpentered item would shed dust and stray particles until years of use would finally settle it.

Footprints sprinkled here and there, leaving remnants of the few hours Iseul would wake and carve wood furiously before rolling back into a ball. In the hours of her slumber, they were back by the river on those long summer days, catching fish. Jung-Soo was there, and father had joined them too.

But dreams run out, like good wine wasted on the soil. The poor of rural Korea never knew that wine was made with grapes. Rice was all they knew; they toiled for it, ate it, and let it ferment into wine. It was white as a ghost that sank into the ground without leaving a trace.

Nightmares stooped in when Iseul slept and took her to the deepest, sorest places of her consciousness. When she wrestled in her sleep, Yeong-Hoon was sure to hear her across the hills. With his ears always wide open for Iseul, he heard the same two words: "Father... Jung-Soo..."

The next morning, Yeong-Hoon found her by the river, rolled up in a fetal position as she shivered. It was surely the aftermath of another nightmare. He looked down at her wet forehead and gently dabbed the sweat away with his sleeve. He picked her up to take her inside; she was lighter than he had expected.

He had dreamed of the day when Iseul would be in his arms when she became his. He had once been worried that she would be too heavy for his left leg to burden, but it seemed like a silly thought now that she was comfortably in his arms. It was a short trip back to her normal position on the hardwood floor as he gently laid her down. He pulled a blanket over her that he had brought weeks ago, but it had been left neglected most nights. She had always liked the room slightly cooler though Yeong-Hoon could never understand why and was nevertheless grateful it was nearly summer.

He took the lunch box out of his satchel, still warm to the touch as he placed it on the counter, opening the window to let the cool breeze in. The air would soon lose its crispness even in the mornings as a new season was being ushered in. The lunch box from the night before was still on the counter by the radio, half-eaten and the rice spread around to guise the fact. That would be his lunch.

He could tell Iseul had woken, though she pretended otherwise.

"Awake now?" he said, as he plopped down next to Iseul with the freshly steamed rice in his hands. A hint of steam reached Iseul's nose when he opened it. He scooped some out with his wooden spoon as Iseul prepared to refuse like all other days.

Much to Iseul's surprise, he ate the first bite himself.

Yeong-Hoon sat munching on rice and kimchi, looking up and out the window where green flourished in the valley. A bird stopped by the window to look in before fluttering away. If he listened carefully with his eyes closed, he could even hear the watermill churning.

"Oppa. I'm sorry." Her voice croaked from disuse. She stuffed her mouth with a heaping spoon of plain rice.

Yeong-Hoon's eyes drifted back towards her. She was a mess; she hadn't showered in a good while too. Tears and snot dribbled dangerously close to her mouth as she chewed with her mouth open. He took his chopsticks, picked up a slice of kimchi, and timed it with the rhythm of her chewing to place the piece in her mouth.

"Thank you," she mumbled through her chews.

He took another bite of rice, saving the rest of the kimchi slices for her.

She was crying now. She had always been a multi-tasker, juggling much more than she could handle at once, confused by the multitude of overwhelming feelings. She didn't need to say it; Yeong-Hoon knew what the cacophony of tears meant.

He smiled and gently brushed off the single grain of rice on her lips. "Couldn't you just pick one thing to do at a time?" Yeong-Hoon laughed.

Iseul shot a glare at him. "Really?" she said angrily, though the moment passed and she was left chuckling too. As their giggles drifted away, she thought of that other person who could make her laugh and frown at the same time. Something burst in her in that moment. What kind of absurdity was this?

He thought he heard her say another 'thank you' in the midst of her tears. When she finally swallowed her food, she quieted down as her eyes flickered, looking down. Yeong-Hoon had rarely seen this look before and it was one that preceded measured speech. The last time he had seen it was when she asked him whether or not he thought they would really get married.

"I'll be fine, you know," she started. "Oppa, you can leave now. I mean, you're welcome to be on your way."

She was trying to put together the right words and that had always fazed her. What she meant was, '*I know circumstances have changed. You have no reason to marry me, so you are free to leave.*'

Yeong-Hoon had been wondering when she would come to that conclusion. It was expected, yet sometimes, realized expectations can be just as difficult. He ruffled her hair and the strands seem to find their place.

"And leave all my inheritance?" Yeong-Hoon answered. "As soon as I marry you, I'd have your father's cabin and workshop to my name. I'll finally have my own carpentry shop. My place is here."

For a moment, she wondered if Yeong-Hoon had really stuck around for the inheritance, though that instant passed as nothing but gratitude filled her. Unexpected met overwhelming again as Iseul averted her eyes and ate another spoonful of rice. Tears dropped on the dusty floor and made splatter marks. Yeong-Hoon couldn't help but keep smiling. She had always been terrible at hiding her emotions.

Where Iseul's eyes met the wooden floor, Yeong-Hoon spelled out words on dust in bold simple letters.

"H-O-P-E."

When the cascade of tears finally stopped and she looked down, she saw the word masked by wet splotches.

"I remember a wise woman once told us," Yeong-Hoon began. "We are kings and queens, born and raised in a sacred place guarded by a wall that has been standing for thousands of years."

"Mother," Iseul murmured.

"Yes," Yeong-Hoon said. "She never said it would be easy."

"I guess so," Iseul said. Her mother was a distant dream now.

These days, she wished to be back in her arms again.

"She had faith, Iseul, that you and I would make a mark in this world, however small that may be."

Iseul slowly traced the mark Yeong-Hoon's fingers had made on the dusty ground.

"Hope," she read aloud.

***

Iseul laid still for most of the day, which was not so much a conscious decision, but one of unconscious stillness. I hope, my dear readers, that you'll never experience this kind of sorrow, but those who have gone through such loss can attest to the experience that every breakthrough often accompanies long dry spells of monotonous stillness—of *still missing.*

In those moments when her mind stirred awake, she would wonder, *'what happened to Jung-Soo?'* The villagers believed he had died in one of the two fires, yet there was no body. There were no bodies to be found, or recognized, she told herself.

She could only hope that he had escaped. And if he did, she hated Jung-Soo! How could he leave without saying goodbye? Maybe he was caught off guard like the rest of the villagers. No, that couldn't be. The Captain had come to get him, and the servants and Mr. Lim had told her the Golden Palace had been evacuated hours before the commotion had begun.

Even as she worried for him, missed him and swore that he was innocent, the nightmares would still come: *Jung-Soo faced her father with a gun pointed at him. A loud gunshot followed as Iseul stood immobilized, her father collapsing as his hand reached out for her.* The scene would dissolve before she ever got to hold that hand.

Iseul didn't want to believe the words she had heard in the village after the massacre. They said Jung-Soo and his father were responsible. They couldn't have been, could they? The harder she tried to push the thoughts away, the more intense her nightmares became.

Father's ashes laid with the rest of the villagers who perished in the fire. Once, Yeong-Hoon had come to the cabin holding a wooden box alongside the regular lunch box. It had been folded in a white sheet of ceremonial cloth. She knew what it was, though she couldn't bear to look at it. The box sat next to the radio and within the next few days, the wooden box disappeared amidst the comings and goings of other lunch boxes.

Iseul had managed to sweep the floors every once in a while to build up to the more arduous tasks. On a good day when the sun filtered through the paper windows, the sharp edges of Yeong-Hoon's word remained barely visible on the wooden floors. "Hope," she kept repeating it to herself.

And in the nights when nothing but the sound of the watermill kept Iseul company, she would rise with the moon and begin working again, each night longer than the one before. It was that darn haegeum she couldn't quite get right. The cry of the instrument wasn't quite long enough, nor the strings tight enough. Sometimes, it whined more than it cawed, and in her frustration, she would hack at the sound hole to widen it until it became so hollow that the pitch would sink a half note.

It was one of those frustrating nights. She leaned over the counter with strands of horse hairs to make the bow of the instrument. If the strands didn't break, it'd be the wood, and now, she was running short of horse hairs. *Pluck*. The strand snapped, and so did she.

"Arg!" she groaned, banging both of her fists on the counter.

A crackle. Something came alive in the room as Iseul's eyes darted here and there, her whole body tensing up. "Who's there?" she said.

Nothing but the sound of the watermill trickled into the room.

She sighed and returned to her bow. The lump of hairs was still too thin to play against the haegeum, but it'd have to do. She was getting hungry. Yeong-Hoon had always filled the lunch box to the brim, enough for her to have leftovers for dinner, and on the rare occasion, there would be a side dish other than kimchi. This time, there was rice, kimchi and some wild roots seasoned with salt. She ate another bite, savoring the bitterness of the roots that meshed well with the sour punch of the kimchi. It had been a while since she had actually tasted what she ate. She smirked, recalling the times when both boys had complained about how terrible her cooking was.

Guilt struck her as it did in calculable cycles. How had Yeong-Hoon been since that night? What about the paper and wood deliveries? How could they even afford food now? She imagined her fiancé next to the stove, waiting for the rice to cook. That was her job! She should have been stronger—done her duties better.

She had lost count of the days, though each day, she had thought about going home countless times. *Maybe today...* With the last bite of rice and kimchi gone, she felt she could have more. Rice coursed through her veins, fueling a new-found energy. She glanced at the door then back out the window she had kept open. The sun was setting now, and her counter was still a mess, her haegeum nowhere near finished. Perhaps today wasn't a good day; there was still much to be done right where she was.

She cleared the counter where Yeong-Hoon placed the lunch box each morning in front of the radio. She had neglected that space quite intentionally as she couldn't bear to look at the counter where she had shared her first intimate moment with Jung-Soo. Red flushed her face; she had been so unlike herself that day.

Bits and pieces of wood and sawdust strewn all around her work counter. With a quick look around the cabin, she could finally see how lopsided the place looked, all of her raw materials placed in the far corner away from the main counter top. Yes, today would be the day she deals with the counter. She would take on one demon at a time.

She placed the lid back on top of the lunchbox and set it on the windowsill. There wasn't any tidying to do. The radio was already in the corner, and all the counter top space needed was some wood to keep it company. She looked around and saw slabs of pine she was sure to use later that night. She took the slabs from the corner of the room and plopped them down on the main counter.

It came back again—the crack and buzz, like a summer mosquito that whizzes around the ears. She looked out the window again. Still nothing.

Perhaps the slabs of wood had made the sound. She picked them up and plopped them down. There it was again. The noise had come from the radio!

But how? She leaned over the counter and shook the radio, as the same static noise escaped its speakers. It seemed impossible. After months, the radio would be out of battery for one, and the thing almost looked skeletal. Jung-Soo had always been tinkering with it before he had so sudden disappeared and the half-constructed contraption was one clear sign that he wasn't ready to leave yet. Just when she thought she had forgotten about Jung-Soo, there he was again, rearing his annoying face back into her life.

She picked up the radio for a closer look, blowing the dust away from its surface. The radio snagged just inches away from the counter top where a black cord strung from its back and disappeared underneath the counter. She leaned under and saw that the cord ran out a small hole that led outside.

Curiosity overcame her as she jumped up, nearly hitting her head on the counter. *It must be electricity.* That's what had kept the radio alive. But from where?

She ran outside to the other side of the hole and saw that the black cord disappeared into the ground. She gently tugged at it, and traced the direction of the cord; it went straight to the watermill.

Of course! Jung-Soo couldn't have brought an endless supply of batteries to a remote valley. That must be why he built the watermill in the first place! An electrical source was probably one of the first things he created when he began constructing the cabin. She couldn't imagine Jung-Soo spending hours on end building a cabin without some music to keep him company.

She ran back inside, stood in front of the radio with her forefinger and thumb extended to turn the dial. It had been so long since she had turned the radio on. The music, the sounds of voices in stories—they all came back to her. And what about that one channel that played music in a foreign language? That had been Jung-Soo's favorite channel.

She switched it on, static noise emanating from it again. She flipped the channel. Again, nothing. Was the reception not good enough? The cabin was located in a valley, so that could explain it, but hadn't they heard music with such clarity the last time they were here?

She turned the channel, this time browsing more quickly. A single male voice rang clear. It was the same man that had always interrupted their regular program, his hoarse voice ringing with an urgency that wasn't there before:

"Earlier this morning on June 28 at 2:00 am, the Han River bridge was bombed and completely destroyed. Early reports believe this to be a preemptive effort to stop the North Korean troops from further advancing South. With thousands of civilians taking the bridge to evacuate Seoul, civilian casualties are reported to be in the hundreds, if not more."

What was happening? Iseul's eyes flickered, shocked as she soaked up the information. *War.* In the time she had been locked away in the cabin, the war had broken.

She did not think twice as her feet took off towards the door with a mind of their own. She didn't look back, her legs carrying her still hazy mind up the side of the hill and towards her home.

She busted through the doors of the workshop to find Yeong-Hoon heavily at work.

"Oppa! Did you hear?" Iseul said, out of breath. "Seoul is at war!"

Yeong-Hoon dropped the half-made buk-drum and walked past Iseul to close the workshop door. He took Iseul by the shoulder and scanned her from head to toe.

"How are you feeling? Are you okay? Why were you running?" Words spilled out of Yeong-Hoon.

"What do you mean? Of course, I'm okay. What's been happening?" Iseul said to him as if he were being absurd.

He looked around the workshop, full of suspicion as he lowered his voice.

"The war has begun," he almost whispered. "Our whole village is in an uproar now and all the men and boys who are of age are being conscripted into the army. Our rice is being ransacked and rationed too. Half the village is gone now; they're evacuating south."

She looked around at the workshop, her eyes still moving swiftly to process what she had just heard. The workspace was as busy as ever with planks of wood and wood trunks of various trees stacked near the entrance. They were all materials needed to make buk-drums.

Her brows furrowed as she looked towards Yeong-Hoon's crippled leg and up towards his sallow and skeletal face. He was drowning in work.

"How many?" Iseul said, restraining her anger. She couldn't believe it! Why didn't he tell her there was so much to do? She could have helped!

Yeong-Hoon hesitated. "Five by the end of this week."

Father always said there would be work when the war came. *Five.* She knew it was too much for one man to burden.

Yeong-Hoon had never seen that look before—anger, frustration and even hint of pity. But there were more pressing matters now than the number of drums he was ordered to make. He took Iseul by the hand and walked outside.

"There is something you need to see."

CHAPTER 16

How often had she gone down this route? Yet, it looked nothing like the Yeoju she had known for over seventeen years. Perhaps this was because she had skipped past spring cloistered away as the trees and bushes bloomed into a green shrubbery. She looked again; no, something was off.

Yeong-Hoon's hands still gripped hers as he limped down quicker than she had ever seen him. Tree trunks that had once covered the entire surface of the mountains were few and far between as the mountain seemed somewhat vacant. Someone had been cutting down a large number of trees near the base of the mountain.

They entered through the east gate and neared Mi-Jung's restaurant. Yeong-Hoon halted and ducked behind a tall line of bushes. Steam that usually emanated out of the kitchen shed no longer piped out of the chimney as the restaurant stood desolate with just two soldiers sitting in the yard.

"Where is everyone?" Iseul said a little too loudly.

Mi-Jung peeped her head out of her room and made eye contact with Iseul. Her eyes widened in shock as she quickly shut the door.

"Mi-Jung!" Iseul's voice trailed off, disappointed. They had never been the best of friends, but Mi-Jung had never shown her the cold shoulder before.

"Don't mind her," Yeong-Hoon consoled. "Byung-Guk's been conscripted last week so she's been feeling under the weather."

"Why would she feel sad about…" Realization glossed over her. "Really? Mi-Jung and Byung-Guk?"

Yeong-Hoon tugged at Iseul again. She could tell they were headed towards the village square, but why were they taking the long route?

She felt as though she had left a piece of her body somewhere else—at the cabin, or perhaps at a different time even. How did she end up here? The pine slabs…oh yes, the radio…the war. Her stomach wrestled uneasy with the rice she had eaten earlier. The sun was on its descent and it wouldn't be long till it would touch the tip of the hills and disappear again. She didn't want to be there for that.

"Oppa, why are we hiding?" Iseul asked.

He stopped, scanning the area before he felt comfortable enough to speak normally.

"Rice. That's what's they're after, not just to conscript men into the army. War is a game of outlasting the other side and so the South Korean military is collecting as much rice as they can before the North Koreans get to us."

"The North Koreans?" Iseul said, confused. "But the war, it's in Seoul. That's really far away. Surely the bombing of the bridge would keep them away."

Yeong-Hoon shook his head. How naïve was Iseul to think a single wooden bridge could keep the entire North Korean army from marching south? He paused, wondering how much he should tell her. It was no time for censorship, he knew. She must be prepared.

"Listen, Iseul. They're coming. That's one thing we can bet on. I say we bide our time here for a little longer, do our duties and make drums for the military. But sooner rather than later, we need to leave."

Iseul could not understand. She had seen just two soldiers passing their time at the restaurant. What happened to the ones she had seen weeks ago? Were they still here?

"The Golden Palace," Yeong-Hoon continued. Iseul's ears perked up. "They're using it as the headquarters to ration food and to conscript soldiers."

Not a day had gone by without Jung-Soo lingering in her mind, but it was the first time she heard his name out loud since that night.

"But I thought…" Iseul said with her brows still furrowed.

"The fire?" Yeong-Hoon completed her question. "Everyone

said it was a miracle, a demon or some curse. Somehow, only the garden and part of the house burned down. We might as well visit it since we've run out of our ration for the week."

There was no other place to hide now. They moved down the narrow street that led to the Golden Palace where more and more people walked by. It was busier than it had ever been. Mr. Chun stopped and stared at them in disgust as Yeong-Hoon quickly paced away to spare Iseul.

A taller man in uniform walked by. He stopped in his tracks and back-peddled to grab Yeong-Hoon's arm.

"Young man, what is your name?" he said with a grin on his face as he glanced towards Iseul from head to toe. "I knew it! I knew there would be more of you boys hiding out in the mountains."

Yeong-Hoon stood straight in front of Iseul in order to hide her behind him and gave a salute to the soldier.

"Sir, I am Yeong-Hoon, a proud carpenter for the Republic of Korea Armed Forces, sir! And this here is my sister."

The soldier peeked behind Yeong-Hoon to glance at Iseul. "Sister? And you a carpenter?" he guffawed in disbelief, rubbing his index finger against his chin, trying to figure out the situation. "Are you a cripple?"

"Sir, yes sir!" Yeong-Hoon responded and pulled out a necklace from under his shirt.

The soldier inspected the tag as he eyed him suspiciously, focusing on Yeong-Hoon's leg that contorted at the knee where his left foot stuck out a little too much to the wrong side.

"And what do you do as a carpenter?" he interrogated.

"I make buk-drums, sir!"

"How many?"

"Eight a week, sir!"

The soldier, unsure of what else to ask, spat on the ground. "Too many cripples these days." He had his eyes on Iseul as he gave Yeong-Hoon a rough pat on the shoulder before going on his way.

Yeong-Hoon watched as the man in uniform sauntered away towards the west side of the village, and when he was safely out of earshot, Iseul shot a glare at Yeong-Hoon.

"You liar! Five?" she said, recalling their previous conversation. "I'm sorry."

"What? You didn't want to worry me. It's none of my concern?"

Yeong-Hoon knew not to protest. He just kept walking as he

listened to the tirades that came from behind. She always knew how to shut him up.

"What were you thinking? You thought I couldn't handle it. That's what it is!" She continued until the village square came into focus as they walked on the road that led to Golden Palace.

"Oppa…" her voice trailed off as the Japanese building came into focus.

She was bewildered. It seemed as if the entire village congregated here. The villagers, including a number of unfamiliar faces lined up in front of the Golden Palace, each holding a wooden bowl in one hand and an identity card in another. Mothers stood with their children who whined, as grandmothers and grandfathers lined up with their children and grandchildren, stooped and hunched back while some remained collapsed on the dusty ground.

Yeong-Hoon tugged Iseul to the back of the line as he handed Iseul her identity card.

"It was about two weeks ago," Yeong-Hoon explained. "That's when the evacuation began. Since then, we've been seeing a large influx of refugees coming in. Most of them come to the village looking for food and a way to reach Busan."

"But there is no way south," Iseul added.

Yeong-Hoon nodded sympathetically. "They're forced to go back north to find another route, but at least they get a free meal. We've been hearing about a refugee camp down south in Busan and there's been a rush to get there before the North Koreans push further south."

Iseul scanned the line that twisted maze-like from the village square reaching the Golden Palace. So many people… so many hungry mouths…

"Impossible." Iseul sighed. "War or no war, we're going to starve to death first."

***

Many hours were spent each week standing in line to gather their meager rations. It was mostly rice and barley and nothing more than a small portion to stave off starvation. It kept the village alive and kept Iseul and Yeong-Hoon chopping, carving and sewing away at the buk-drums.

The villagers chattered about Iseul and how she had to nerve to show her face in the village, eating their rations. Yeong-Hoon was glad they only had to go into the village once a week, and as each week passed, the sneers and raucous rumors of Iseul and Jung-Soo eventually died down as the villagers continued to evacuate south.

Summer's sweltering heat was in full force the following week when Iseul and Yeong-Hoon were found scrambling to fill their quota. Ration day had come around again and Iseul had been starving since the night before, tossing and turning, making it difficult for the mosquitoes to feast on her.

Yeong-Hoon carved away at the edges of the drum, his hands trembling from hunger.

"Oppa, why don't I get the rice this time?" Iseul said as she noticed Yeong-Hoon's hands.

He thought for a moment and then shook his head. "It really is too dangerous for a girl to be walking around alone."

Iseul managed a forced laugh. "It seems to me that most of the people in the village think I'm a man." She looked down at her white work clothes.

"Even more reason not to go alone."

Iseul untied her long hair and let it flow down to her back. It was oily and tangled from weeks of leaving it unwashed. It took away Yeong-Hoon's breath; she was beautiful.

Iseul tossed her hair and tried to dust off her clothes. She wished she owned another dress other than her mother's dress that she treasured so much that she would dare not wear it. The hanbok she used to wear had ripped at a rather embarrassing place so she was forced to share Yeong-Hoon's work clothes.

"Don't worry, I'm the ugliest girl in the village." She smiled weakly. "I'll be back before you know it."

And just like that, she grabbed her identity card and bag as she carried her wobbly legs down the hill where the trees seemed to grow scanter by the day. Soon, the hunger pangs dissipated as the wind picked up around her. She felt free for the minutes she ran amongst the trees until soil turned to gravel.

She was attuned to the sounds of human activity. Soldiers would be patrolling the perimeter. She would need to make it into the village without anyone noticing so as to avoid the natural suspicion that came with living so far away from the village. She felt somewhat relieved when saw the Golden Palace appear before her, taking her place at the end of the snake-like line that still filled up the village square.

Iseul saw the butcher passed by with his ration. He held it against his thinning belly and walked away like a child with a new toy. He glimpsed Iseul as he passed by with a look of pity and then diverted his eyes. She sighed and remembered what Yeong-Hoon had said before. They were just afraid of being associated with her.

To the left of the food rationing station stood the conscription station, located where Jung-Soo's warehouse used to be. There, she saw Byung-Guk's father with his shoulders drooped.

If only Byung-Guk hadn't ratted Jung-Soo out. She had thought that before. At least Mr. Lim knew where his son was and she envied him for that. But there was no room for anger in Iseul's heart now. The last time she and Mr. Lim had met, they were standing right there in front of the Golden Palace, watching the flames engulf it. He had tried to help her; she would focus on the good that he did for her.

A large poster hung on both stations of the Golden Palace. She had never cared to read what it said as she was mostly too delirious in hunger to care, but she noticed Byung-Guk's father held smaller versions and was pinning them to nearby trees.

"Donate silver and gold. Save rice. Save our sons," she struggled to read the letters.

There was once a time when he would go around the village bragging about his wonderful son. But this was his job now—putting posters up, since all the rice had been collected and not a single grain was left to plant for the following season.

A soldier walked down the line, keeping it in check with his hands on his belt that displayed a hand gun in clear sight. Iseul looked away as he neared her. He was the same soldier Yeong-Hoon and Iseul had bumped into the other week and he was headed straight towards her.

"Hey, you! Sister of the cripple!" he shouted, drawing attention in her direction. "I see you've grown hair since we've last met." He sniggered, as he picked up a strand of her hair and dropped it.

Iseul flinched.

"Come now little girl, I won't hurt you," he said, grabbing Iseul by the wrist and tugging her close enough that she could smell his alcoholic breath. "Get out of the way! Out, I say!"

He waded through the villagers until they were in the front of the line. The soldier scooped two large bowls full of rice, yanked

Iseul's sack out of her hand, and filled it to the brim. "There you go. That'll last you a while," the soldier said, still holding onto her wrist tighter, waiting for her to respond.

"Thank you..." Iseul said, trying to wriggle out of his tight grasp. "I should be on my way now." She tried to turn her back.

"Where do you think you're going?" he said with a sinister grin as he pulled her closer. "It'd be rude not to return the favor."

Iseul was confused. What could she have that he could possibly want from her? His other hand reached behind as his fingers ran down her spine and brushed across her waist.

Moans and complaints began from the front of the line when Mr. Byun and his neighbor Mr. Park first noticed Iseul's plump rice sack.

"Hey, that's cheating!" Mr. Byun said.

The soldier realized the eyes on them and pulled ever so slightly away from Iseul, her wrist still tightly in his grasp.

"Isn't that Mr. Ji's daughter?" The others joined in the confusion.

"She's the one who ratted us out to the Commies!"

The line unraveled and pushed forward, even the refugees ignited with anger at the sound of communist traitors.

"She's still alive?" one woman said in disbelief, while the others jeered at her. "Get her!"

Iseul was forced into the soldier's arms as another group of soldiers filed in from the warehouse with guns to push the mob back.

In the commotion, the soldier lost grip of Iseul's wrist. She ducked down, covered her face with the rice sack and ran. Between her own breathless gasps and the blood pumping in her ears, she heard the distant sound of the soldier yelling, "Where do you think you're going?"

She dared not look back; she was sure he was on her heel. She could feel the pressure of the soldier's hand around her wrist and his fingers on her spine and waist again as she passed the threshold of the forest. She ran until her vision blurred and the world spun around her. Blood drained out of her face, and her fingers and toes tingled.

She tripped on a tree stump, the sack of rice tumbling from her grasp as a handful of grains scattered on the forest floor. *The rice.* There was no time; footsteps neared. She could picture Yeong-Hoon's skeletal figure, starving as he waited for her. *She couldn't lose the rice.* She clung onto the sack by the opening, gripping it so tight that her knuckles whitened.

"Come now, little girl. I won't hurt you." The soldier's voice tossed between the trees, her feet pushing harder and harder against the soil.

She could see her home now, smoke rising from the kitchen shed where Yeong-Hoon had started the fire, waiting for Iseul to return with the rice.

She was so close; she would soon be with Yeong-Hoon. And then what? Iseul pictured the gun holstered on the soldier's belt. Who was to say that he wouldn't kill them both? They would be helpless if she led the soldier home.

The gun, Iseul remembered. *"Turn the safety off when you're ready to shoot... you shoot to kill."* It was Jung-Soo's voice, echoing with the wind.

She turned around and scanned the forest. The soldier was nowhere to be found. Had she lost him? A twig snapped to her right in the direction of the village.

She needed to get to the cabin; she needed the gun from the secret compartment.

CHAPTER 17

He was a stubborn soldier. Iseul could hear the dry summer soil and rock rustling under her feet and from behind. The valley dipped in as the echoes intensified. She wasn't quite sure if these were the sounds of her own feet or of the soldier who followed close behind.

The door of the cabin flung open and then closed. She locked the door behind her and fumbled in a haze towards the compartment hidden along the right side of the wall. Where was it? Jung-Soo had hidden it well. Her fingers were the first to feel around the edges where it dipped in a ridge along the wall.

Suddenly, she heard three bangs on the door. Iseul jumped, her hands fumbling even faster against the hidden compartment.

"Iseul!" It was a familiar voice. "It's me, Yeong-Hoon! Open the door!" He banged the door again.

Relief flooded her as she leaped from the floor and opened the heavy oak doors. He came in and flung himself onto Iseul in a tight embrace.

"Are you okay? What happened?"

She wanted to say that she was fine, but her voice failed her. Yeong-Hoon knew and kept her tightly bound to him until her heart beat settled down and her breathing steadied.

She told him about the soldier who had given her the rice and about how he had touched her. The words crept up to the tip of his tongue, but he held it back: *I told you so.* He shouldn't have ever let her go into the village alone. He should have been more adamant.

Spending so much time in a peaceful farming village had made Yeong-Hoon weak. He had briefly forgotten about what the world was like on the outside and how men were rough and preyed on the weak. He had forgotten about his own journey to Yeoju and how the waves had tossed and turned him, dried him out and left him awash a solitary beach.

He would not let that happen to her again. He would make sure he was there for her the next time.

Iseul stood cradled for a long while until a sense of peace washed over her. What had become of her village? So much hatred, so much fear. The war. What was this beast called war that could wreak havoc without ever stepping foot in the village?

Her right hand was getting numb. Yeong-Hoon took the sack of rice from her as the blood rushed back in and left a prickly sensation. He gently took that hand and led Iseul outside.

They were both hungry and exhausted.

"So how was work today?" Iseul made small talk.

"Alright. Still one more to get done by tomorrow."

It was the height of summer as the cicadas sang their mating calls. It was their call to action. Iseul looked into the branches of trees overhead where the leaves grew plush and strong on their stems and branches, showcasing their greenery. How long will it be until they too would tire and drop to the ground?

They watched the steam escape from the top of the rice cooker, imagining how each grain would bloat into a tasty warm bowl of rice. They knew the rice needed at least another ten minutes under the heat, but it didn't matter. Their stomachs would pay the price later, but hunger drove them. It was only after they had eaten their last spoon that they realized how bland their meal had been. Iseul walked over to the jar planted underground and plucked a large leaf of kimchi straight from the jar and ate it whole, washing it down with a gulp of water.

They sat on the raised platform of their home, content enough to complain about the weather. They prayed for the breeze to pick up as they watched the light from the sunset scatter into a thousand rays between the leaves. It was just the kind of normal that they needed. Sitting there drowsy from the rice hitting their blood streams, they napped to the tune of the cicada calls.

***

Iseul made a habit of foraging the woods more often so as to avoid a desperate situation like the last. She would find the odd bitter root vegetable and when she was lucky, she would come across a sweet potato. But more often than not, she would mistake a rock for one and would come home slouched-back and forlorn with a mouth full of bitter roots to chew on. Even the once plentiful supply of wild berries was running low since more and more of the villagers braved the curfew to venture into restricted territory.

They had all been thoroughly warned by the posters that were on every corner of streets that read, "All villagers found wandering the woods will be in danger of being shot," which was understandable since it was becoming increasingly difficult to tell who was who with so many refugees funneling into the village. They came with rumors of rice only to be met with two insurmountable mountain ranges and no more food as most of them turned back to find another route south. For all the locals knew, any one of them could have been a spy.

She found a bush of wild blackberries. Some were still red, like poison berries, but Iseul knew which ones were edible. Her mother had taught her well. She bit into one that was still sour as her face contorted.

She had not completely neglected the cabin. Once in a while, she would visit to dust the floors and pick up her nearly completed haegeum for a quick play. She had first gone to forage and then realized the valley was no good for fruits or vegetables as the surroundings were too rocky. She would catch the odd fish in the stream now and then, but there weren't many and barely enough to stave off hunger between her and Yeong-Hoon.

She knew the path back home like the back of her hand. The most scenic route was also the most secretive one as well, though she was always wary of expending too much energy on the hike.

That day, she had caught two fish, dug up three baby yams and a handful of berries and was making her way home to help Yeong-Hoon with their quota of buk-drums.

Against every urge to wander the mountains, she took the quickest route back home. The path was well-shaped with tiny foot holes that popped up every so often, leading up to graves. Just weeks ago, the path had been well-trodden by the villagers who came to pay their respects, many of whom had relatives murdered in the massacre. Iseul was somewhat relieved to find that hunger and the immediate danger of being shot had halted the mass grave visits.

It was a thought she so rarely entertained. She was born here in Yeoju, just as her father and mother were, and just as her grandfather and his father before had been. They were all laid to rest on mounds of Yeoju soil. Yet, with the prospect of leaving Yeoju becoming more and more possible, Iseul wondered if she would ever make it back alive to her hometown. What would happen if she died on the road? Would she be left to rot on some foreign street down in a southern village where people spoke in a different tongue? For once, she envied her ancestors who knew where they came from and exactly where they would return to.

From the corner of her eye, she saw mounds of soil and grass that signified graves. A figure hobbled down in a faded hanbok, carrying plump sacks in both arms and balancing the third on the head. It was Mi-Jung coming down from her father's grave. It must be the anniversary of her father's death and Mi-Jung had braved the threats to pay her respects.

She stopped as if noticing Iseul's gaze and began precariously staggering down again. But with her sudden loss of concentration, Mi-Jung slipped on a loose rock as one of her sacks tumbled down the slope and plopped just ahead of Iseul's path.

In three swift hops, Iseul was in front of Mi-Jung, trying to help her up and gather her belongings. There was incense, bronze plates, and persimmons—valuables she hadn't seen in years. A sting of jealousy and guilt hit her; her father was lucky.

"Don't touch me!" Mi-Jung yanked the sack away from Iseul.

Iseul's hand recoiled. They stared at each other, wondering who would blink first. Iseul hopped back down to the main path and began collecting the items that had escaped the sack.

"I can do it myself, you know," Mi-Jung said.

"I know." Iseul lifted the full sack and headed towards the village. "Let me walk you to the east gate since it's getting late."

"Iseul," Mi-Jung called as she caught up with her. "Don't go telling people that you were with me."

"Alright," Iseul said, nonchalantly.

"You know what they say about you in the village, right?"

Iseul shrugged. "That I was involved in the massacre because I was close friends with Jung-Soo."

Mi-Jung saw her brazenness and wondered if she too could be

as strong if she were in Iseul's shoes.

The two walked silently down the hill, side-by-side. It seemed as if every other tree had been chopped down as more light filtered through the underbrush even with the sun setting just above it.

"Why are you helping me?"

Mi-Jung was the first to break the silence. Iseul paused. She had to think for a bit.

"It's not because I like you," Iseul said honestly. Mi-Jung eyes glazed over in surprise. "I don't know," she said, confused herself. "I guess I'm just paying it forward."

"Paying it forward?" Mi-Jung repeated.

"Yeah. Just like someone paid it forward to me."

Mi-Jung's arm was getting tired with the sack so she switched arms. "Was that someone Jung-Soo?" she said, nearly out of breath. Iseul stopped in her tracks. "Why? What's wrong?"

"I guess so," Iseul replied. Mi-Jung lugged her sack on her arm and moved a few steps up the hill to find Iseul in some profound moment of realization, her eyes glistening ever so slightly with the rays of the sunset directed towards them.

"Oh come on now, don't go all soft on me," Mi-Jung said. "You're supposed to be Iseul," she emphasized, "the girl who can do anything! The girl as strong as any man in the village with the grittiest personality."

Iseul cackled. "Is that what they say about me? It doesn't seem like it."

Mi-Jung began walking again. "Oh, don't let them bring you down like that," she said, taking on the maternal tone Iseul had so often heard from Mi-Jung's mother. "I'll let you in on a little secret," she said. "Not everyone in the village hates you."

Iseul's brows furrowed. "They don't?"

Mi-Jung nodded. "They're just afraid, you know, of your connections with Jung-Soo. But if you ask me, some of them even pity you. With your father dying in the massacre and you being a..." Mi-Jung hesitated.

"Oh, just say it. I already know. I'm an orphan now," Iseul said matter-of-factly.

The two walked like that for a little longer. There really wasn't much to be said. Everyone knew someone who had died in the massacre, and if they all went around pitying each other, they would have no energy left to continue living. They needed to be strong;

this was war.

"Sometimes I wake up in the morning relieved that we're at war," Mi-Jung said.

Iseul tried not to look too surprised.

"I hated the fact that I was born a daughter," Mi-Jung continued, scorn rising in her voice. "They pitied my mother for having me. You know what they used to say? *'It would have been worth being a single mother if I were a son.'* I'm glad there's a war. Now, everyone only seems to care about whose son would be conscripted next and pray for their safe return."

Iseul just listened, the silence dragging on a little longer.

"I envied you," Mi-Jung admitted. "You were as good as a son to your father. You were up in the hills with no one to care about whether or not you were born a son or daughter."

They could see the end of the road where the run-down east gate stood. Iseul idled for a little while longer before placing the sack back in Mi-Jung's arm. Mi-Jung took it with a disappointed look on her face, almost as if she didn't want the walk to end.

"You know where I live?" Iseul said. It was less a question than a statement. "You're always welcome there, my friend." Iseul beamed as she gave a lingering nod before turning around to head back up the hill.

Mi-Jung stood there, both arms heavy with the load of her father's ceremonial food, watching as Iseul disappeared behind a herd of trees. And when she had retired indoors, Mi-Jung's mother crawled out of bed to greet her daughter. The once boisterous woman had fallen ill in the past few months as the chronic pain in her back developed into something more sinister, rendering her bedridden.

"What are you so happy about?" Mi-Jung's mother said, pleasantly surprised.

It was only then that Mi-Jung realized she had been flaunting a smile. She blushed, realizing how it must look, coming back from the ceremony of her father's death. Mi-Jung's mother didn't pry, nor did she object; it had been too long—much too long since she had seen her daughter smile.

***

Iseul took the quickest route back home, wondering how much

Yeong-Hoon had managed to get done today and knew he would be waiting and possibly even worrying about her.

She was back on the road where mounds of graves popped up. A sting of guilt hit her again; it had been so long since she had visited her mother. It was small but she knew exactly where to look to see the tiny hill of her grave pop up. She saw a larger one next to it that was newer as the soil had yet to grow a full head of grass.

A song whispered in a wind, coming from her parents' graves. It had been a while since she had let herself hum that tune. It was strange, almost unfamiliar like a new song coming back from a long lost dream.

Yeong-Hoon. She must hurry. She mustn't worry him any longer. *Too late.* She caught a whiff of the evergreen thistles that had fully grown in from her favorite pine tree next to the family grave. She felt *nostalgic* deep within her bones. She glanced towards the path that led to her home and then back towards the lonesome pine tree.

The sun barely held onto its orange luster, shining rays on the twin mounds. *Mother had waited too long. Yeong-Hoon could wait just a little longer.* Iseul dug her feet against the familiar rocks to climb towards the tree.

When she reached the grave, she was surprised to find a familiar figure on top. Yeong-Hoon smiled as he stood next to her pine tree. *How?* Perhaps he had hoped Iseul would finally come to her senses and visit her father's grave so he had dropped by each day, hoping she would join him. Who knew? It was Yeong-Hoon, the mysterious boy who had appeared one day and had kept her company for all these years.

Yeong-Hoon reached down to help Iseul up the final bit of the hill. The tree swayed its evergreen branches and the thistles gave off its distinct incense-like scent in pungent doses with the rhythmic waves of the wind. She stood by her mother's grave, resisting the urge to lay back on the mound and have a little chat with her.

"Father, we're here. Iseul and I are finally here," Yeong-Hoon said, bowing in the formal ceremonial fashion. He poured rice wine on the fresh mound as if he had planned the ceremony all along.

Iseul couldn't bear to look. Her eyes filled up with tears and watered her mother's grave.

"Mom," she managed to say. "It's been a while."

"We're sorry it took so long," Yeong-Hoon addressed both of them.

He glanced at Iseul whose eyes were filling up again. He walked behind her and placed his hands on her shoulders, guiding her to the fresh mound. She meant to say something—anything. She meant to pay her respects to her father, yet no words came.

She was angry. It swelled in her like ocean waves in a storm. Her fists rolled up and shook her entire body.

"They say Jung-Soo killed you," Iseul spat out. "How could you die on me? You're all I had!"

She couldn't say any more. Yeong-Hoon stood by and watched as her body gently released her from shaking.

She turned her back against her father's grave. "Oppa," she let out. I just can't wrap my head around it. What exactly happened that night? What about father," she hesitated, "and Jung-Soo?"

Yeong-Hoon had been waiting for this question for weeks. He was beginning to think Iseul just wanted to forget about that night entirely. She looked intently at him as the realization struck him that this may be the last time she would look at him without blaming him for what had happened that night. He couldn't forgive himself. How could he expect her to?

He recounted the story with sorrow-filled eyes.

"The Captain and I reached the cabin thinking you and Jung-Soo would be waiting for us," Yeong-Hoon said.

"But I wasn't there..."

"We had to leave the cabin because we thought we may have led a few soldiers there. The last thing we wanted was to reveal its location, or wait to be raided."

Iseul's eyes flickered, processing the information.

Regret was all Yeong-Hoon felt. If only he knew the soldiers were leading Iseul's father into a trap, he would have never left him there to die. If only he could have saved the Captain. But Yeong-Hoon had lost consciousness and had woken up to the Captain's dead body.

"I'm sorry..." Yeong-Hoon said.

Iseul held back tears. "You were just trying to help. You were all just trying to find me."

It was more than she had bargained for that day as she felt the weight of that night return in shocking clarity. She held onto the same guilt Yeong-Hoon felt. Both stood there, counting the leaves of grass, as they watched the other become invisible with nightfall.

"So what exactly were you doing at Byung-Guk's barn that

night?" Yeong-Hoon said in the dark.

Iseul recalled Jung-Soo with a wig on. "Oh nothing much, just one of Jung-Soo's practical jokes," she said, grinning. It was the last memory he had of Jung-Soo and she would cherish it. Her smile faded as she remembered what had happened after. "You don't think he is somehow responsible for the massacre, do you?" She finally asked the question that had been plaguing her.

Yeong-Hoon shook his head. "Of course not. He seemed just as shocked that night. Why else would he have risked his life to look for you? He knew something would be happening, but there's no way..."

Iseul stopped him mid-sentence. Something didn't quite add up. Yeong-Hoon spoke as if he had actually met Jung-Soo that night. "How do you know he was looking for me? Did the Captain tell you? Did you see Jung-Soo that night?" Iseul's voice quickened.

Yeong-Hoon nodded. "Jung-Soo had a gun pointed at us when we arrived at the cabin. If only you had arrived a little bit sooner, you would have been able to meet him before he disappeared. He made us promise to keep you safe before he left."

The wheels of her mind were turning.

Jung-Soo. The gun. He had been at the cabin first, before any of them had arrived.

She was starting to feel dizzy. Perhaps it was the hunger setting in again. Could it be? Did he leave something for her?

She heard distant voices growing louder and louder by the second. She was sure it was Jung-Soo's voice that said, "I've got one last present for you. It's hidden somewhere in the cabin."

Iseul pulled herself out of her memories and saw Yeong-Hoon patiently waiting.

"What is it?" Yeong-Hoon asked. "What's wrong? Are you alright?"

Iseul swayed in dizziness. "Oppa, I'm sorry. There's something I need to check," she said, stumbling backwards then steadying herself.

She slid down the ramped hill and ran, letting the night air fill her lungs. She knew she could just be hoping, but the same voice kept echoing, *'You're close.... You're so close...'*

She had been here before, so close to opening the compartment the last time. Jung-Soo's voice lingered with Iseul's determination.

CHAPTER 18

Sleepy and restless, I lay by the river.
I cannot tell if it is my mind,
perhaps my spirit or even my soul that wanders.

To where? I ask. It did not know.
Where the wind or song takes it.

Away, away it goes…
I feel it longs,
or even hopes for a place to rest its weary soul.

Perhaps even a place to call home.

***

[Present Day]

I was seven again in my dream. Granny folded me in her arms that cold winter day when our family surrounded a fresh mound on the hilly graveyard.

Mother wailed and father stood helpless. Granny told me how wonderful he had been. *Grandfather.* Our family was small it seemed. I looked across to the other hills and it was full of grave mounds.

"That is your great grandmother, and your great grandfather," Granny spoke in my ear as she pointed to the two mounds further up the hill.

"And here," Grandmother Iseul pointed towards a flat terrain. "This is my spot." Her spot was closest to the tree that whistled against the light breeze. "When I finally go to sleep forever, this will be my bed," granny continued.

I smiled as I saw my younger self, so naïve and so full of imagination that granny had planted in me.

"That's impossible! How can you sleep here? There isn't even a bed!" my younger self exclaimed.

"Why not?" Granny said with that airy look as she closed her eyes, facing the tree. Taking in a breath with the wind blowing in her face, she said, "At night, I will come here to rest underneath this tree as I did when I was your age." She tapped my nose affectionately. "And in the day, I will go where the wind takes me, from shore to shore and house to house. I'll always be near you, watch you grow up and watch you grow old too."

My seven-year-old self plopped down on the ground and leaned against the tree trunk.

"Take me with you," the little girl said stubbornly. "I want to travel with the wind too! Teach me! Teach me…"

The shrill of the little girl echoed in the wind and died down as I found myself alone again, standing there by the tree, looking at a grave ready to be filled. My eyes welled up at the thought. My real granny was lying in a hospice bed getting ready to die while I visited her soon-to-be grave. Yet, I felt her presence here now more than when I sat by her empty shell.

It sickened me. How did I end up here? Yes, I had promised I would find out about the man in the letter—the man called Yeong-Hoon. I could only hope that it wouldn't be too late—that when I do find him, there would be enough of my grandmother left in her body.

I blinked to clear my eyes and turned around to head back. A gust of wind blew on my face and whisked the last bit of moisture away. Another gust came, this time, nearly toppling me on my bottom. I turned back around as I let the wind hit my back while it passed.

Where the sudden wind came from, to this day, I do not know. If I close my eyes to recall that day, I could have sworn the wind was warm, unlike the chilly October wind that time of year.

I am not superstitious, my dear readers, yet, if I am completely honest with myself, I can be quite certain that the wind had perfectly directed my attention to a patch of soil near the tree that caved in ever so slightly. It looked as if the soil had been tampered with quite recently.

Could it be my grandmother's doing? What had she been doing when she came to visit last year? Did she know she would soon die? She had long forsaken this little village, yet why did she feel the need to return?

In that little concave patch of soil beneath the tree, I was certain I would find the answers. A branch that had broken off was within grasp as I began to dig. I dug and dug some more as if I were digging a grave.

It was around the time I was certain I had finally driven myself crazy. *Exam stress*, they often diagnosed. *Heart palpitations, anxiety, hallucinations, and bouts of frenzy*. That is how my parents would rationalize the whole incident. At least I had an excuse; I flamed my madness.

The sun was in just the right spot as it shone through just the right branches to hit a glint. Something shiny laid within. I dug some more until I was ripping through plastic. My fingers brushed off the last bit of dirt, like an archeologist meticulously preserving the bones on site until I could see the brick of what looked like envelopes.

This was it. This had to be it! From the outside, the paper looked brown and aged. I was sure now. They had to be letters— more letters from Yeong-Hoon.

***

[Summer, 1950]

The bout of dizziness passed as Iseul's ears stopped ringing. It was just the sound of her feet now, running faster and stumbling as she zig-zagged through the hill towards her destination.

She was so close. She felt it in her bones and could wrap her fingers around the gun just as Jung-Soo had done before he had disappeared. She hoped it was still there, but then realized that perhaps it would be a good thing if the gun was gone. Jung-Soo might need it more than she did, wherever he was.

Iseul caught a whiff of the dusty air that whirled as she stammered into the cabin. She saw the invisible line on the wall. *The hidden compartment.*

She held her breath and tapped her foot against it. It popped open.

The gun. It was there, along with loose bullets that rolled

around. Beneath it, almost camouflaged against brown of the wood, was a wrinkled piece of paper.

She reached for it.

***

[Present Day]

My hand reached for the plastic that covered brown sheets of paper within. It was as if my arms were heavy. They moved slowly—reluctantly.

I wanted to rip open the plastic. I needed to know what was inside. Yet, something pulsated against my thigh. It was my phone, vibrating.

Strange...I didn't think there would be reception here. Still, I tried to ignore the vexing thing that kept beckoning and tried to focus on what was at hand.

The pages...the letters...

***

[Summer, 1950]

Iseul pushed the cold metal gun and bullets to one side as her fingers fumbled to clasp the wrinkled piece of paper. She unfolded it gently, yet hastily. The boxy letters revealed themselves first before the words on the page could be deciphered.

It was Jung-Soo's handwriting.

Iseul's heart skipped a beat as her eyes darted around on the page before slowly sinking into the message within.

"My dearest Ji Iseul, I am sorry. I wish I had something better to say. If this letter doesn't reach you, it saddens me to think that you'll remember me as a traitor."

Fog blinded her eyes, or perhaps they were tears. She was not sure. Even her ears seemed to have been affected. She heard things, my dear readers—things she couldn't have heard deep within a valley that bisected two mountains.

Jung-Soo's voice rang in the distance, strong and commanding. They were shouts of joy and pain, mingled with silent tears.

Yes! Jung-Soo was alive and he had not abandoned her! She

knew it. She felt it in her bones, and heard it in her soul. The entire village had been wrong about him; he had said it himself with his own words that attested to his innocence. The scribbles, the tilt in his handwriting—Jung-Soo had been in a hurry to escape with the Captain. He had at least left some message for her, even though it wasn't a proper goodbye.

Guilt came along with the ecstasy as she remembered the fresh mound atop a familiar hill, and the blood that spread from the Captain's chest. They had all been looking for her...

Gripping the page as tight as she could, she ran back out the door, sprinted across the hills and into the village. She didn't think to look around, watch for stray soldiers or even stop to take a break.

There was just one other person who knew something would happen that night—Mr. Lim. She needed to find him and ask if he knew anything about where Jung-Soo could have gone. Perhaps he knew if Jung-Soo was safe. Perhaps he even knew how to contact him! She knew just the place to look. When she finally stopped, she was in front of Jung-Soo's half-burnt Golden Palace, knocking over villagers and soldiers until she was face-to-face with Byung-Guk's father.

"You knew, didn't you?" Iseul said, still gleaming. "You knew Jung-Soo would be disappearing that night!"

Byung-Guk's father, who had been stacking newly printed propaganda posters, sprung up from his chair and grabbed Iseul by the arm to pull her aside. He had a look not unlike anxiety, yet Iseul was unsure and didn't seem particularly discerning in that moment.

"That day when this building burned down," Iseul said, still too loudly, "you were here, before anyone else saw the fire."

"Hush now!" Mr. Lim said in a serious tone. He looked around to find two soldiers glancing suspiciously at them.

Iseul handed him the letter. He skimmed through it and made Iseul hide it in her pocket.

"I wasn't sure how to tell you," he said, almost sighing, "With your father..."

Iseul cut him off. "Because his father killed mine?" she said, so sternly that it even caught her off guard. "I mean, you thought I blamed Jung-Soo for what happened that night."

Iseul glanced down at Mr. Lim's left hand. It was burned to the elbow. He quickly rolled down his sleeve to try and cover it.

"And what about you?" she asked, suspiciously. "Why did you

risk your life and jump in the fire?" she said with a tone of accusation.

Another two soldiers gathered together and were looking in their direction. Byung-Guk's father was getting more and more anxious, yet Iseul stood her ground; she no longer wanted to shy away from the truth.

"The Ham's saved my son. The Captain made sure Byung-Guk made it out alive when he went to the authorities with that letter. I owe him, no I owe them my life."

It made sense now—why Byung-Guk had showed up with the Captain that night at the barn, why the Captain rushed Jung-Soo out. Something had gone wrong. That's why Jung-Soo had disappeared so suddenly, and why he was rushed to write the letter.

"But that's not important now," Byung-Guk's father said, leaning in closer. He was eager to finish the conversation. "Listen, Jung-Soo is still alive! That's what I was going to tell you."

This was the news Iseul had been waiting for—wishing for.

"He's a soldier now, but not as Ham Jung-Soo."

"A soldier? Did he cross over to North Korea?" Iseul said.

Mr. Lim shook his head. "Mr. Ham disowned Jung-Soo. His name is Kim Jung-Soo now and he's in the South Korean army."

Iseul stood speechless, trying very hard to make sense of what Mr. Lim had said. She slowly began nodding. *Yes, a new name meant a new identity and a new start!*

"Kim Jung-Soo," Iseul whispered with a smile that creeped up her face.

The name was growing on her.

Part 2

CHAPTER 19

한
恨
Han

"A feeling of unresolved resentment against injustices suffered, a sense of helplessness because of the overwhelming odds against one, a feeling of acute pain in one's guts and bowels, making the whole body writhe and squirm, and an obstinate urge to take revenge and to right the wrong—all these combined.
- Suh Nam-Dong

***

[September 1950]

No one claims to have fired the first shot, though, at end of the day, victors always dictate who the heroes and villains are.

Over half of the soldiers from the South Korean military died that first week since the Han river bridge was blown to smithereens. Within two months, Jung-Soo had traveled the entire length of the Korean Peninsula, fighting hand-to-hand and shooting. Flies were everywhere, feeding and hovering around the dead that floated on Naktong River in the southeastern side of the Peninsula.

They sat on tanks and rode all the way up to the 38th parallel.

After that first bloodshed, battles were few and far between and the time between them stretched boundless into a million moments of fear and missing...*still missing.*

Jung-Soo rebelled against everything the Captain had taught him. What use was it now that he was in uniform? He recalled that newspaper clip that read, "Fire in Yeoju: Ham Young Nam, Influential Leader of the Communist Brigade burned alive in his own home." For all the stealth his father had, it hadn't saved him. Times have changed, and he had too; his changed name stood testament of that. The days when he sat around and tinkered with the radio dials, dreaming, scheming and wondering what his father's role was in the war seemed to be in the distant past, even childish for a man fit to serve his country with unrelenting devotion.

He didn't count. After that first week, everyone hoped for more soldiers, more guns, bullets, food, and more dead North Korean soldiers. They heard of men coming from distant lands— white saints sacrificing themselves for a civil feud they had no stake in.

He did not care. He killed, again and again, his hands steadier as the ringing of each shot reverberated into his bones. *One more kill and the missing would stop.* He would be a dutiful soldier and return to the only place he felt at home.

It was another summer day in the battlefield where grass and leaves turned crimson. Bullets flew past Jung-Soo, but he knew how to look out for them. He was meticulous. *Lay low; run in spurts with a destination in mind; find high ground.* If there was one useful thing the Captain had taught him, it was a sense of precision and a steady hand. *Breathe. Hold. Shoot.* Trenches were useful too. God knows they had spent enough time making them, so why not make the most of it?

He felt every resistance and tug of his rifle against his shoulder and hands. The enemy took cover in the distance. Sooner or later he could come out, and when he did, Jung-Soo would press just hard enough to lead the bullet straight into the man's head. Just like that—precise and humane.

There were soldiers on both sides who ran around like headless chickens. He would calculate how long some of them would last and more often than not he would be right, give or take a fortnight.

Jung-Soo heard the whizzing of the bomb, as he hit the ground. There was not much skill involved in avoiding bombs—it was all a cruel game of fate in which the ringing in his ears and the ever-increasing screams and shouts of anguish signaled he was still alive.

He saw a figure squirming in the mud long after the shell had dropped. The idiot laid face down and immobilized. Jung-Soo's shoes slopped against blood-kneaded mud as he ran towards him. Though the two were not particularly acquainted, Jung-Soo was not keen on seeing the boy die; Jung-Soo had other plans for him. The boy's chunky frame shrunk into a ball in the mud, hoping but failing outstandingly to sink in and disappear.

Jung-Soo surveyed the battlefield. The enemy drew closer, another plane flew by and dropped the next shell close enough that he could feel the debris blow in his face and knock the wind out of him. The idiot would die, as he had predicted weeks ago.

"Get up!" Jung-Soo yelled in his ear. The boy was startled, shaking and further curling up as if an enemy was about to put a hole in him. "Get up, you pig! I can't save you if you want to die!" he said, grabbing him by his thick arms and pulling him towards retreat. The idiot whimpered.

The calm eventually came, though not for the boy who shook in shock for a while longer.

The campsite of the 18th Infantry of the Republic of Korea Armed Forces was half-made, still growing and always ready to move at a moment's notice. Tents were set at the heart of the campsite and trenches made borders to it. Only the commander and those wounded were taken to the heart, where for the less fortunate, the triangular tip of the tent was the last thing they saw.

Soldiers on both the North and South Korean side retreated at nightfall as silence left a dull ring in every soldiers' ears. Fighting would commence when the conditions were more favorable. In the meantime, Jung-Soo dragged the boy half a mile towards the medical tent. The boy was merely scratched and bruised, yet the he did nothing but whine and groan and kept his eyes closed to prevent the blood from dribbling in. Jung-Soo bore the brunt of his weight as he felt his own blood congeal beneath his left shoulder.

The cover of night would mean the idiot wouldn't recognize him and he was glad for it; he did not need gratitude or any medal of honor, though a part of him knew the boy had earned his rescue. If it were anybody else, Jung-Soo wouldn't have cared if he lived or died.

Dinner was served, salty and bland at the same time. White rice.

He never quite liked the blandness. The kimchi was bland too, while the meager pieces of chicken meat were pumped with salt to preserve it. It was one of the few times in the day he felt alive. The headless chicken from Yeoju popped into his head, as did the bland food Iseul had often prepared.

He sighed and dug into his food, savoring the memories that came with it. He wondered if she had found the letter yet and whether she knew that he had no choice but to leave her. He imagined the note and wished he would have jotted something down about promising to return to her, though it seemed obvious to him that he would. Yet, he was half-glad he didn't; the war may reach Yeoju and he wanted Iseul alive and evacuating south, not stubbornly waiting for him to return. He would have to find a way to get through the war and back to Iseul in one piece, wherever she would be. He had no intentions of dying. Besides, no one knew where to send his body if he ever did.

The rice and salt hit his blood stream as he felt reinvigorated. He knew it wouldn't last long and would have to brace for impact. Soon, he would revert to his proverbial state of *missing*, though even in the stillness between battles, he dared to hope.

That last shell still rung in his ears that night as he kicked off the blanket from his sweaty chest. It was summer as the mosquito hovering around his ears helped drown out the dreams of the life he had left behind.

Amidst the whizzing of wings, questions about Iseul plagued him. Did she know where he had gone? He hoped there was enough food for her and Yeong-Hoon hyung and that they would gather enough before winter hit. Most of all, he hoped that it would remain silent in the quaint village of Yeoju.

***

The sirens woke Jung-Soo up the next morning. They were ordered to pack to head south, which was never a good sign; the North Koreans were closing in.

As the tents were being drawn up, guns and bullets loaded and the men in his company shuffled away, the sergeant walked up to Jung-Soo with orders from Commander Lee.

"Right now?" Jung-Soo asked.

"Leave your things," the sergeant said. "You won't be needing them."

The commander? Jung-Soo thought. What would someone so highly ranked want from a lowly private like him? For a moment, he wondered if he had been uncovered and his real identity disclosed.

He looked back for a second. He thought he might need something, a possession or a trinket. It was, afterall, what most soldiers carried with them. Then he remembered, he had become a new man, and such men had no past. There was only one way to go now, and that was forward.

The commander's tent would be the last to be put down and the first to be reassembled. As the camp slowly disintegrated back into barren land, he drew closer to the tent. The sergeant drew up the curtains in front of him. Inside, a wooden desk stood where the commander sat with spectacles and a pen, signing away at documents.

"Hey, it's you!" Jung-Soo heard a voice next to him. It was the idiot boy. Jung-Soo tried to keep a straight face.

The commander pushed the documents on his desk aside and rose.

"Kim Jung-Soo and Park Dae-Gun," he stated, as they saluted him. "At ease, soldiers. From this moment on, you are no longer soldiers of the 18th Infantry, but liaison officers. Make no mistake, your identity is no longer yours. You are to take your badges off and become nameless."

Did they know? Was this a test? Jung-Soo glanced towards the idiot and was relieved to find that he was not the only one who looked stunned.

"Our radio channels are being monitored more than ever. Our American friends have requested a secure form of communication to avoid the chaos of the past few months down south. That is where your task begins, Dae-Gun," the commander looked at the boy. "I hear you are an orphan." He waited for a response.

"Yes, sir!" the boy shouted. "Raised by Protestant missionaries from America, sir!"

"Good, good." The commander acknowledged. "And a fine young man they have raised!" He praised the boy. "Your task is simple: you are to be a translator during your stay at the U.N. base camp, currently stationed with the 5th Cavalry Regiment. You and Jung-Soo are to retrieve codes from Commander Rogers and bring them to me. If you fear capture, you are to burn the codes.

Remember, you live and die by the codes," the commander said with the conviction due to a man in charge.

"Yes, sir!" the two soldiers said in unison.

"If anyone asks, you are mailmen." He turned to Jung-Soo. "Do you read and write?"

Jung-Soo was startled. "Yes, sir." His voice shook.

"You are to filter through the letters and exclude the ones that are indecent." He handed Jung-Soo a leaflet and a quick glance revealed a short list of instructions for censorship.

The commander turned his back, ready to relieve them, but turned his head ever so slightly in Jung-Soo's direction. "I hear you are good with radios."

How did he know? "Yes, sir…" Jung-Soo said.

Jung-Soo had been tinkering with scrap electronics in his tent. Yes, that must be it. That's how he knew.

"Your task is to check in with our headquarters every day, assessable by a daily-renewed code. You are to relay information regarding the North's movements—where they are coming from, where they are headed, and report any other suspicious activities."

"Yes, sir!" he managed to say.

"We've just recaptured Seoul. We must keep the North out," he said with a tinge of weariness. "We cannot afford a loss like the last. This time, we must stand our ground, and we need all the help we can get from the Americans…" He didn't seem to want to admit the last part.

The commander's usual charm returned as he gave a confident nod and waved his hand for the two to leave as the colonel took over. Jung-Soo carried on right behind the colonel, trying his best to avoid eye contact with the idiot who stammered along. Once they had fully exited from the tent, Jung-Soo took a long overdue sigh of relief.

The colonel handed them their unmarked uniforms, devoid of the 18th Infantry badge as he also handed each a handgun and spare bullets. The colonel held out his hand as if to ask for something. The boy looked at Jung-Soo who likewise stood, clueless.

"Your tags," the colonel said. "We can't have you tracked back here, can we?" Jung-Soo pulled off his tiny metallic necklace and handed it to him. "Now, get changed."

With that, the two were left in a nearly empty campsite. He looked down at the uniform he was wearing, where the stitched badge indicated "18ᵗʰ Infantry ROK," and grazed his hand against his empty neck with some regret. It had been his sense of security, and the only thing that proved he had a definite place in the war. He sighed. It hadn't been more than a few months since he had put it on. He fell immobile, unnerved by the sudden change in duties. What other changes lay ahead?

The boy, Dae-Gun had been watching him like a hawk with a deep curiosity and even a little suspicion. When Jung-Soo stirred from his thoughts, he was startled by the piercing dark brown eyes on him.

"What are you looking at? Didn't you hear the Colonel?"

"Something real suspicious about you..." he said with eyes squinted. "Haven't I seen you before?"

Jung-Soo barely disguised his stutter. "Of course you did! I saved your ass from being blown up."

"No, not that, somewhere else," he said, curiously.

Jung-Soo kept his mouth shut; he would be damned if he were to admit to anything, not when he was stuck with this pig for the foreseeable future.

Jung-Soo began to undress, first unbuttoning his shirt and putting on the unmarked one the colonel had given him, hoping to divert his attention. The idiot looked on, eyeing Jung-Soo from head to toe with his finger laid on his chin. *Pigheaded.* That much was certain.

"Are you going to stand there and watch me take my trousers off too?" Jung-Soo said with his hands now ready to unzip them.

He snapped out of it. "Oh right," his face turned scarlet, fumbling through his new uniform. "Sorry. It's just, I'm certain I've seen you somewhere."

Jung-Soo went to a nearby fireplace and threw in his old uniform, holding out his hand for the boy's own uniform. "I'm glad you recognize the person who saved your sorry ass."

But just as Jung-Soo turned, Dae-Gun tossed his uniform into Jung-Soo's face.

He chuckled. "Thanks for saving me.'"

A pig with a sense of humor. At least he wasn't a complete idiot. Jung-Soo turned his face towards the growing flames and found himself grinning.

The last bit of the flame engulfed the uniform and there was no reason to stand there anymore. They had each been given a smaller sack that contained letters along with their normal supplies in their backpacks.

Jung-Soo went on one knee and unstrapped the top flap of his backpack. He saw the usual amenities: dried meat, uncooked rice, and salt. He found parts for a tent scattered here and there, and just by the look of it, it was much smaller than the one they had become used to. A radio stuck out of the side of the bag, like a massive growth that wasn't supposed to be there. He would have to rearrange everything once they find proper shelter. But in the meantime, they needed to follow orders and start heading east. He dug through his bag for a map and a compass and found them lodged deep within the side pocket of the bag.

"So, do you know how to read a map?" Jung-Soo said, looking behind. But the idiot was gone and in his spot, was his new backpack. Jung-Soo sighed, grabbed both backpacks as he began roaming the empty campsite. He knew it wouldn't take long to track him down, and sure enough, he found the boy as he followed the sound of grunts coming from a barren hillside.

"What do you think you're doing?" Jung-Soo said.

Dae-Gun jolted and banged the side of his head on a protruding rock.

"Just looking for something. It should be somewhere here," he said, rubbing his head.

"You shouldn't just disappear like that. For all I knew, you could have been taken prisoner."

He went two boulders to his left and began his search again. "Sorry about that. I thought you heard me when I said that I'd be back."

What could be so important? They had already been given everything they would need. Jung-Soo found himself digging his head into the crevices next to the boy.

"What does it look like?" Jung-Soo said, though as he spoke, he realized what it might be.

The boy yelled, "I found it!" as he dove between a bush and resurfaced with an object that looked very familiar. It was wrapped in linen cloth and in a distinct shape immediately recognizable to Jung-Soo.

"My guitar," Dae-Gun said, holding it up with one hand and dusting it with another. "I knew it! That Sam-Joon sure knows how to hide things well."

Astonished, Jung-Soo watched, tracing the outlines of the instrument as he soaked in every detail. He hadn't seen a guitar up close before. He had imagined holding one himself for so long and though he had seen other guitars when he lived in Seoul, somehow, having one of his own two hands had always eluded him.

"Musicians' code of honor." He laughed. "I knew he wasn't a heartless bastard! Do you know what this is?"

"No," Jung-Soo said rather abruptly.

"It's an instrument with six strings that you strum all at once. You must have seen me play it sometime."

In truth, Jung-Soo had seen the idiot with the guitar many times before. Just two nights ago, when the sound of bomb shells stopped for the evening, the band had played for the camp during dinner. It wasn't a large band, and at times, one or two of them did not return from battle, so it never quite sounded strictly uniform. They say they were lucky sons-of-bastards since a group of musicians were sent to the same squad and were allowed to bring their instruments with them. Jung-Soo had often idled around the band, mostly behind it, watching the boy play his tune as he tried to isolate the sound of the guitar amongst the other instruments. He hadn't quite been able to do that, still imagining and filling in the gaps of what it might actually sound like in person. He had set his mind to the task when just yesterday, the idiot cowered in his ditch, ready to be bombed to death. What was Jung-Soo supposed to do—just let him die?

"Anyway," Dae-Gun continued, "when one of us doesn't make it out alive, instead of fighting over who gets to keep the instrument, we all agreed to make a little grave for it at the nearest foot of the hills where our tent is set up. They must have thought I didn't make it when I didn't come back last night."

He looked at Jung-Soo who stood gazing at the guitar, unresponsive.

"You play with the band?" Jung-Soo said, attempting to sound disinterested.

"Yeah, at least I did," he said as a certain sadness spread across his face. "It was the best part about becoming a soldier."

Jung-Soo believed him. The whole band had lifted the spirit of the camp, and he had seen it up close—the look on the boy's face as he played.

"The past is in the past," Jung-Soo said, throwing one of the backpacks into his dreamy face. "There's only one way now, and that's moving forward."

"I guess so."

Jung-Soo held up the compass and took a few steps towards where the needle pointed east. Dae-Gun followed close behind. The sun was halfway past its pinnacle and it wouldn't be long before they would have to stop.

"You reckon the men in our platoon know what happened to us?"

"We're dead to them." Dead, as he was to everyone else he knew.

They walked in silence as the summer heat beat down on their heads, loosening the beads of sweat that clung to their eyebrows and dripped onto the dusty ground. The quiet did not last long as the boy began filling in the silence.

"What's your name?" he asked. "I'm Dae-Gun, Park Dae-Gun." He held out his hand waiting, then impatiently grabbing Jung-Soo's hand to shake it. "I'm from Jeongju, down south, or at least I think I am. I'm an orphan so no one really knows where I'm from. If you walk far enough from our orphanage, you can see the ocean. So, where are you from?"

The idiot could not shut up, and in a way, Jung-Soo was grateful, though he wasn't quite sure how to answer his questions. What was he to say? That he was a commie traitor who had been disinherited by his father and that he really should be fighting for the North instead?

"I'm Kim Jung-Soo from Seoul," he lied. "But what use is it now? We're spies, aren't we? We're not supposed to go around telling people our real identities."

Dae-Gun nodded as if he had just heard an enlightening proverb. "You're right!" he said, chirpy with a spring in his step. "We can be whoever we want to be!"

A *spy...just as his father had been,* Jung-Soo thought. One thing was certain—he was an orphan now. Two orphaned spies traveling together. It sounded pitiful.

They continued to walk with the sun running further and further away from them. They would chase it for a while—as long as it would last.

Jung-Soo found himself breathing deeper as his shoulders bloomed. It seemed, in the moments between the last battle and the one that was to come, there would be a lot of walking to do—days and days of walking and hiking. He liked the idea of that. Perhaps in those long hours of quiet contemplation, he just might be able to discover who he wanted to be.

CHAPTER 20

Jung-Soo and Dae-Gun headed southeast, hiking the edges of mountain ridges and avoiding the main routes shown on the map. Villages scattered here and there where ridges met streams and fields led to straw-thatched houses much like the ones in Yeoju. Every village they passed through seemed to be ghosts of what they used to be, as Jung-Soo wondered if the Wasteland of Yeoju would be transforming into one as well.

Spies were everywhere or so the villagers suspected. The number of dead bodies they had witnessed scattered at the edge of the village was more than enough proof as the swift South Korean victory with the arrival of U.N. troops stranded countless North Korean soldiers in the South. Children were huddled indoors, and those that roamed the village were newly orphaned, and left to fend for themselves.

Food was scarce so when Dae-Gun came across a piece of half-rotten persimmon or grains of rice still left to be harvested, he couldn't bear to take it. He would pick up the persimmon, recall a girl barely ten years of age they had just passed, and gently place it back on the ground.

Besides, their military rations seemed to suffice, and so the two completely avoided villages and the conveniences that came along with it, such as a private toilet and an abandoned kitchen shed to steam their rice in.

Dae-Gun was slow and loud, stepping on every twig, dawdling and swinging his backpack into every tree branch. It was no surprise that Jung-Soo began resenting his company when the cured meat began to dwindle, their hunger grew and their legs began weakening on a hike down from a particularly steep slope.

Dae-Gun grunted, holding his leg that had cramped up. "Sometimes I wonder if the gods cursed us by giving us too many mountains!" Dae-Gun said.

You'd think they'd stop fighting over a cursed land, Jung-Soo thought.

The mountainous ridges, though rough, had everything they needed if they looked in the right places. Legend has it that tigers once flourished in the deep crevices of the mountains, but not one had been seen in the better part of the century. When the occasional fighter jets roared by, Dae-Gun froze in place, petrified that either a tiger would swallow him whole, or a bomb would fall right on top of him. Black boars were fairly common and delicious when roasted, though unfortunately, Dae-Gun had the knack for scaring them away before they could even spot one.

As the sun dropped peacefully over the horizon, Dae-Gun heard the scuttling of tiny feet under the leaves. He carefully placed his heavy load down and began assembling twigs into what looked like a trap. Jung-Soo watched the little squirrel taunt Dae-Gun, scampering towards Dae-Gun's fingers tying the knot and then falling back again.

Jung-Soo had no patience to be made a fool by an animal. He shot a single blow to its head, to which Dae-Gun jumped and knocked his trap over into a pile of sticks.

Dae-Gun sighed. "I suppose that works too."

Jung-Soo blew the smoke at the end of the gun. He had seen it in one of those Western moving pictures that showed men in boots and large hats. He had always wanted to try that.

A natural hunter with a killer instinct, Jung-Soo didn't have a problem pulling the trigger, yet the other parts of hunting made his skin crawl. Somehow, Jung-Soo managed to convince the idiot that getting his hands bloody was part of his training, and so with much cajoling, skinning and cleaning the entrails became a dreaded part of Dae-Gun's routine.

Or so Jung-Soo believed.

But after that first night, Dae-Gun had gotten quite used to the task and even secretly enjoyed the fact that he would cook the meat and the rice to his liking, nearly charring the meat in the flames and making the rice into a porridge-like consistency. Jung-Soo didn't protest, and if he did, it only meant he would be eating a smaller portion, which Dae-Gun wasn't about to complain about.

The rabbit meat hung on the skewer that roasted on a fire they would soon have to put out. Around Dae-Gun's neck was a tin container he carefully opened, taking a large pinch of salt from it and sprinkling it on the meat. He glanced over at Jung-Soo, making sure he wasn't watching, since the last time he had done that, Jung-Soo had scolded him for using up their precious stash of salt.

"We'd better hurry," Jung-Soo said, as Dae-Gun froze in place with another pinch of salt between his fingers. "The North Koreans were here just yesterday. We wouldn't want to alert them by keeping the fire going for too long."

After dinner, Jung-Soo went about his usual routine, honing in the dials of the radio.

"Access code 901882, over," Jung-Soo spoke into the radio receiver.

"Standby…" the operator responded. "901882, what is the passcode?"

"Boars roam the mountains."

"Standby… Access granted. Report."

"We are nearing the southwestern border of Gyung-Buk. Enemies appear to have crossed the border less than twenty-four hours ago and appear to be headed east. We estimate approximately five hundred soldiers."

"Is that all soldier?"

"Roger that."

"Standby for the next passcode."

"Standing by…"

"We are running out of paper. Please repeat."

Jung-Soo repeated. "We are running out of paper."

"Encryption successful. Be on guard, Ham Jung-Soo."

Jung-Soo's ears perked up. He wasn't quite sure what he had heard. "What?" he said, but the familiar white noise of the radio was all that was left. How did the radio operator know his real name? He must be going mad. He looked back at Dae-Gun.

"Did you hear that?"

"What?" Dae-Gun said, sitting innocently on a stump of a tree trunk. "That we're running out of paper? Didn't you know? Everyone back at the Korean base had been complaining. Isn't that why you write in such small letters too?"

Jung-Soo went silent. He didn't realize Dae-Gun had noticed his note-taking habits. He watched as Dae-Gun rotated the meat on the skewer, swallowing his own saliva as his mouth kept watering. Jung-Soo must have heard it wrong. Yes, he must have heard Kim Jung-Soo. There is no way they could have known.

"You mind turning on some music?" Dae-Gun said, now dumping soil on the fire to put it out.

Jung-Soo turned the dials left and right. It seemed to take longer these days, as most of the channels had either been wiped out or were running outdated news cycles in between each song. He dug through his pockets to look for a scrap of paper and pencil to write down the next passcode. There was barely enough space left on the overcrowded page. He quickly jotted it down and sat to finally appease his stomach.

"Our orphanage used to have that one channel on all the time. You know, the one with American music," Dae-Gun said, taking another bite from the skewer.

Jung-Soo suppressed a smile. Of course, he knew! "I wouldn't know." Jung-Soo gulped down his hot porridge and took three bites of his meat at once. Out of habit, he held the pencil, ready to write down whatever stroke of inspiration that came to mind.

"That's a shame," Dae-Gun said. "It really was very good music. We all grew up on it. The kids at the orphanage I mean."

Jung-Soo scribbled on his page, completely focused on the task at hand. Soon, he would only have moonlight and he wanted to get out whatever he needed to write before then.

Dae-Gun ate as he tried not to savor the food as he was in a habit of doing. He wasn't used to having a lot, but he missed the little he used to have, like the sound of uninterrupted music, simple food that he could savor every note he tasted, and the company of little children following him around all day. He looked over at Jung-Soo's busy hands. He always seemed preoccupied, his eyes scouring the mountains and placing them on the map, his hands either holding a pencil or the dial of the radio. Even in his sleep, Dae-Gun noticed Jung-Soo was heavily preoccupied. In fact, he seemed to be doing all the talking he wasn't doing while he was awake. It had been weeks now and Dae-Gun had been shot down each time he had asked a question; yet, Jung-Soo's dreams revealed a jumbled cacaphany of words and haunting noises. Curiosity often struck as each day revealed an even more distant stranger by Dae-Gun's side.

Dae-Gun bided his time, waiting for the sun to completely disappear before he would try again. When the last embers of the flame barely glowed and they had adjusted to the moonlight, Dae-Gun mustered up the courage.

"Who are you writing to?" Dae-Gun asked as casually as he could. He had never been good that—sounding like something he wasn't.

Jung-Soo neatly folded the sheet of paper and tucked it in his front pocket. He then reached for his backpack and pulled out the map and placed in between them.

"We're here now," Jung-Soo said, ignoring Dae-Gun's question. "As we saw today, the North Koreans are headed east, just ahead of us. Their route is quite clear so we can assume we are safely out of their way, but it won't always be like this. We have to prepare. We won't always be able to light a fire and keep the radio running. Besides, the battery is running low, and so is our food supply. Do you know what I'm saying?" He looked at Dae-Gun intently.

He nodded his head, almost out of submission.

Jung-Soo sighed and rolled his eyes. If his projections were correct and the number of Chinese soldiers continued to head south, it wouldn't be long till a full-frontal attack will be at hand.

"You haven't got a clue, do you? Give me your backpack." Jung-Soo rummaged through it. There were just five portions of rice left and no more of the dried meat. He saw Dae-Gun guard his salt necklace with his fist around it.

"You must be kidding me! Where did all the food go?"

"We ate it," he said timidly.

"That's it!" Jung-Soo yelled. "I'm carrying all the food now! What were you thinking? What if..."

"Oh come off it! You're always going on about how much danger we're in! We're just a few days away from camp, and once we get there, we'll have more than enough to eat!"

Jung-Soo shook his head. What use was it to reason with a pig? He didn't want to admit it, but the pig was right. Starvation was the least of their concerns, and even now, in their meager state, they still ate like princes compared to the villagers they've come across. He felt a pang of guilt surge through his heavy stomach.

"Is food all you think about?"

The idiot chuckled. "Food, women and the guitar."

"What utter nonsense," Jung-Soo said.

It was instinctive how that phrase rolled off his tongue and caught him off guard. He pushed away the thoughts of his past life.

"Don't you think it kind of looks like one?" Dae-Gun said, raising up his guitar in the air. "A woman I mean?"

Jung-Soo gave him a stern look. "How do you know that's how a woman's figure looks like?" he said. "Have you gotten a closer look underneath the hanbok?"

Dae-Gun blushed. He remembered that one time near the river when a woman tied the rounded skirt of the hanbok up to keep it from getting wet. "No," he lied.

Jung-Soo smirked and looked away. "Since the radio isn't playing music, let's see how you charmed the women with that guitar of yours."

Dae-Gun jumped at the offer as he reached for his guitar that was tightly wound up in fabric. It had been too long and Jung-Soo had never let him play out of fear of being heard.

Dae-Gun sat at the edge of a tree stump and began playing a tune—one that Jung-Soo had heard the whole band play at the base camp. Yet, the same song that had once been so full of life seemed melancholy and lonesome. Oddly, it felt as though it was meant to be played that way. For the first time, Jung-Soo could picture Dae-Gun as a little boy at the orphanage, passing the time with just a single guitar in his arms. He could see himself in the little boy, except Jung-Soo had passed his time leaning over the lantern light, tinkering with the radio dials and electrical wires.

Each note lingered in the branches of trees and bounced back with the wind. The rice village and the cabin came to mind as Jung-Soo could imagine Iseul's heavy head on his lap when they were stuck in the school shed. It was the first time Iseul had heard the sound of a guitar over the radio. He had drawn a picture of it for her and Jung-Soo could picture Iseul busy in her workshop, making the guitar as she thought of him, thinking of her...

The embers were stubborn, like the both of them were in their own ways. They lit a soft glow on the two soldiers' faces as the moonlight eventually took over the evening. It was time to turn the lantern on.

There was still much to get done before they could call it a night. The flames must be quelled once and for all and the tent made. They even had to get through the mail for that night, or more accurately, Jung-Soo needed to get through them.

Dae-Gun was even slower at reading than he was at hiking. He huffed and puffed through each alphabet on the page and after pondering for a long while, became even more ambivalent as to which letters to burn and which to keep, mostly clueless as to which ones held communist propaganda, which Jung-Soo was surprisingly good at. It almost seemed as if Dae-Gun enjoyed a good read into other people's lives. He was nosy if you asked Jung-Soo.

"Why can't you just make a decision already," Jung-Soo said, flipping through the two-page letter in his own hands with such speed that Dae-Gun wondered if he was even reading the contents at all.

"Easy for you to say. I'm not as fast of a reader as you are!" Dae-Gun stopped and then began probing again. "Where did you learn to read and write so good anyway? You must have been an apprentice to a great scholar or something."

Jung-Soo no longer pretended to ignore him; he just went ahead and did it. After all, if it were true one's days were numbered and so were the number of the breaths one could take, Jung-Soo wasn't about to waste them answering the buffoon's questions.

"Listen, this one's good!" Dae-Gun said as he leaned in closer to the lantern. "He's telling his wife about where he put the plow in the stables, and then he asks her how to remove stains on fabric since blood stains won't come off easily."

Dae-Gun began reading verbatim: "Don't worry too much if the letters are delayed. It seems they are sent irregularly here in the military as supplies are always running low. Not a day goes by that I don't think of you. I miss you. Wait for me. I will soon be back home again, warm in bed with you."

Jung-Soo, doing the usual and skimming through the pages, jerked Dae-Gun's page from his hand and put in the dying embers. The fire fluttered with the pages that burned, engulfing them in a fleeting moment of brilliance before dying down again.

"What was that for!"

"For indecent content," Jung-Soo said, calmly reciting the guidelines: "Materials that display morbid scenes are not suitable for public consumption and must be discarded."

"What do you mean morbid scenes? There was nothing about the battlefield here!"

Throwing another letter into the fire, Jung-Soo responded, "blood on the uniform."

Dae-Gun threw his arms up. "You know what, I've had it with you! How can you be so cold-hearted? These people have families you know, wives waiting to hear from them!"

Jung-Soo did not respond, quietly flipping through the next letter and sorting through them with machine-like efficiency.

"Is that why you write all those letters and never send them out? Here I thought I was the coward, but you were the real one all along."

Dae-Gun waited. The silence dragged on and he was beginning to regret what he had just said. He didn't care; he meant every word of it. Jung-Soo acted as if he didn't hear, though he was noticeably slower.

"I sometimes wonder if it's worth making a promise you know you can't keep." Jung-Soo said, for the first time looking at Dae-Gun square in the face. "I mean, if I really love someone, how could I lie to her—give her false hope only to let her down?"

Could she ever forgive him? Jung-Soo thought to himself. That sting of hatred rushed through him. His own father had orchestrated it, or at least had some hand in the massacre plot. If only he had had more time...

A coward. That's what he was. He had believed the Captain when he said he would make sure Iseul was safe, but where was he now? Dead, most likely. Or else he would have made some sort of contact with him.

Iseul could be dead for all he knew. And what about Yeong-Hoon and Mr. Ji? Even if Iseul were still alive, he was certain she wouldn't want to hear from him.

The night filled with solemn reflection. A few long seconds passed as Jung-Soo searched Dae-Gun, perhaps even hoping for a response. He could see Dae-Gun's mind working in ways he had not deemed possible before that night. *The stubborn pig...that idiot.*

There was always more than what meets the eye, and that was what he was afraid of. There was always more—a deeper depth of sadness and loss waiting for him if he let it.

Jung-Soo averted his eyes. "I'll finish up with the letters. Why don't you start putting up the tent?"

***

That night, as Jung-Soo laid awake under his thin blanket, he imagined Iseul as he did each night before he would lose consciousness. Perhaps it was the light breeze that hit his nostrils or even Dae-Gun's snores that pierced his ear drums.

Dae-Gun seemed to be adamant about prying into his past life. That conversation had triggered a host of memories he had forced himself to ignore. The stars reminded him of the nights he would lay on the garden grass and look up. He smirked as he thought about the first time Iseul and Jung-Soo had held hands.

Jung-Soo glanced over at Dae-Gun's guitar that lay right next to his head. The lullaby of the guitar strums had always had to travel long and far through radio waves to reach Iseul and Jung-Soo. Iseul felt so far away, now that the guitar was so close, just out of reach.

He wished to hold it, see how it felt against his own hands just as he had imagined himself playing the guitar whenever he heard the instrument filter through the radio speakers. If only he could grab it without Dae-Gun waking up. If only he could start running with it, faster and faster underneath the cover of starlight until he reached Iseul's cabin. He would run through those oaken doors and find Iseul snoozing on the carpenter's stool. She would wake and say, "What took you so long?" and put him straight to work.

And then he could show her, finally give her the exact measurements she had asked for. Iseul turned her back as her figure faded... faded into a distant dream.

Dae-Gun's snores doubled, the guitar still situated next to his face. Jung-Soo reached for his pockets as he instinctively did in the middle of the night when he couldn't sleep. He saw the blackened pages and realized he was dangerously short of paper.

He still had that one page. He had been saving it for something more important—for someone more important, and he had been working on it for many weeks. But for now, it still remained empty.

It then struck him. *The guitar, the empty page, Iseul.* The guitar was in his reach. He would write down the measurements and send it to Iseul. Yes, it was a brilliant idea!

He crawled out of his place on the leaves and headed towards the snores. He was sure Dae-Gun wouldn't wake; he was a deep sleeper. He gently lifted the guitar from the ground and walked a safe distance away from ear shot where moonlight shined through scant branches of the meadow.

Jung-Soo squinted and drew as best as he could. He had the guitar in his hands. It wouldn't be like the last time when he had sketched the guitar from memory.

He used the page as a guide, drawing the outer dimensions of the guitar, and measuring the length the strings extended from the bridge to the neck. He colored in the sketch to indicate the darker patches of woods and made a rough estimate of the various angles and rounded edges on the guitar.

Something was missing—scale. How was anyone to know the exact length and width? He needed a ruler of some sort, units that could translate into something Iseul could work with.

Jung-Soo eased his grip on the pencil. He glanced back and forth from the drawing to the guitar. It seemed close enough, but he could still hear Iseul's distant voice scolding him for sketching yet another guitar without the exact measurements.

He would have to figure out a way. There must be something he could do. But for now, the moon had shifted ever so slightly as the night deepened. He felt his eyes fall heavy and his body ache from the day's hike. He wrapped the guitar back in its linen cloth and set it next to Dae-Gun's snoring face.

The idiot always looked so peaceful without a care in the world. He hoped Dae-Gun wouldn't notice he had borrowed his guitar. The snores grew loud in deep breaths and shallowed for a second before starting up again. There was no need to worry; Dae-Gun will never know.

Jung-Soo laid facing the idiot, and within the seconds of silence between Dae-Gun's snores, Jung-Soo had also fallen asleep.

CHAPTER 21

Smoke rose over the hill where Jung-Soo and Dae-Gun could hear distant battle cries. It was just past noon when they laid eyes on the enormity before them. The camp was larger than any other infantry Jung-Soo had ever seen, even larger than the training camp where swarms came in and left each day.

Dae-Gun eagerly trotted along, but Jung-Soo grabbed his sleeve. "Where do you think you're going?"

Dae-Gun looked at him as if he were crazy. *To the camp, of course,* his look said.

"They might mistake us for spies. We need to radio in before we set out."

They crouched around the radio on that clearing and began turning the dials. The usual operator signed him in with the passcode and asked him to wait. He was so near, yet so far. The radio waves would have to travel across mountain ranges, hitching on neighboring infantries along the way to reach the 18th Infantry, and then travel back towards the 5th Cavalry Regiment for approval before it would take the arduous trek through the same routes to eventually arrive in Jung-Soo and Dae-Gun's travel radio.

"Soldiers, you are clear to enter."

And with those orders, they edged towards the western bounds of the camp where tents rose endlessly in all directions and smoke billowed sporadically across the camp grounds. Soldiers marched in uniform groups to and from the various tents as a group huddled around a smaller fire and played what looked like giant black and red versions of a card game Jung-Soo's father used to play.

Occasionally, the odd Korean woman would appear from a tent and made a brisk walk towards the edge of the camp. *What are women doing on camp grounds?* Jung-Soo thought.

A shriek heard from the left. From the slip of fabric of the tent entrance, Jung-Soo saw nurses tending to the injured as another soldier, covered in dirt and blood with half of his right arm missing, entered screaming into the hospital tent. The sound of shells both distant and near seeped into the camp.

"This is really war, isn't it..." Dae-Gun said with all the strength dissipated from his voice.

Jung-Soo slapped him over the head. "Of course, you idiot! Or did you already forget I saved you from one of those just a few weeks ago?"

Dae-Gun shot a glare at him as he nursed the back of his head. "I suppose you're right." It seemed like a lifetime ago since he had been in battle.

"Of course, I'm right!" Jung-Soo said facetiously. "Let's find the commander's tent before we get ourselves shot. These ghosts are everywhere!"

"Ghosts?" Dae-Gun looked around to find soldiers watching their every move. "Oh," he realized Jung-Soo probably hadn't seen so many westerners in one place. Most of the soldiers were white, just like his grandfather missionary at the orphanage was, though many were dark as night and some in between. Others looked like them, though not entirely the same. They say these soldiers were from other parts of Asia. Dae-Gun gawked back at them. He had never seen so many young ones, wrinkle-free and tall. He was beaming, thinking back to a time when he believed all white people were tall, old and wrinkly because his orphanage grandfather had been.

"You'd think we were the foreign ones here," Jung-Soo said, as he turned his head to spot a rather large tent that could be none other than the commander's headquarters. He stooped down to reach deep into his backpack to pull out the commander's top-secret envelope. But just as Jung-Soo stood back up with the envelope in his hand, he felt a tug on the side of his trousers.

"Mister, mister," a soft voice spoke. It was a little boy, who barely reached Jung-Soo's hips.

"What's a little kid doing in the military base?" Dae-Gun said with a bright smile on his face. "You look just like my little brother!" He leaned forward to pat the boy on the head.

The boy shooed Dae-Gun's hand away and frowned. "Mister, I'm hungry! Give me some food!" the kid said with a straight face as if reciting a line to Jung-Soo.

"I don't have food," Jung-Soo said bluntly, nudging the kid away. "Go find your mother."

The kid, who had just been chirpy, crinkled his nose and mouth into a pout and began to wail. "I don't have a mother. I don't have a mother!"

Jung-Soo was frozen, unsure of what had just happened. He hated kids. They were so… well volatile and irrational.

"Bad soldier! Bad soldier!" Dae-Gun said, hitting Jung-Soo rather hard on the back. Dae-Gun swung his backpack around and dug for something, anything to appease the kid and found a piece of dried persimmon.

"Here you go!" he said, handing the fruit over to the child. A shadow towered over Dae-Gun.

"I'm sorry, is my boy bothering you?" the man said, in a language smooth and familiar.

Dae-Gun hadn't spoken English in a while and felt his throat constrict. "Not at all," he cleared his throat and looked up at the tall white figure. "Is he your boy?"

The white soldier had a smile on his face, friendly and inviting just as he remembered his grandfather.

"Oh no!" he said, waving his hands. "He's just my helper boy, aren't you, Zion?" the soldier said.

"Yes, I'm his helper boy!" the child said in perfect English.

"So," Jung-Soo said to Dae-Gun with a serious look, "What is the white man saying?" Jung-Soo didn't speak a lick of this foreign language and was rather perturbed that he found himself in a situation he wasn't in control of.

The child, who had gulped down the dried fruit in two bites, began looking for his next adventure. The curious little fellow, as all boys are at that age, ran in circles around Dae-Gun and banged his hand against the hollow body of the guitar that made a peculiar sound.

The boy stopped in his tracks and curiously watched Jung-Soo. More precisely, he was looking intently at the envelope in his hand. It was whiter and straighter on the edges than any other envelope he had seen before. The boy, Zion looked up at the white soldier who was deep in conversation with Dae-Gun and saw his chance. In one sweeping motion, the kid snatched the shiny envelope and ran with it.

"No!" Jung-Soo swatted at the envelope but the boy was much faster than he had imagined as Jung-Soo found himself stumbling to reach for the kid who zigzagged his way around tents and soldiers who seemed perfectly at home with a little Korean orphan boy.

Dae-Gun, who was sure Jung-Soo was just keeping the boy occupied in a game of chase, continued his conversation with the soldier, quite enthralled and keen to please the white man.

"Dae-Gun, my dear friend," the soldier guffawed. "I believe your friend might be in need of our assistance."

Dae-Gun swung around to find Jung-Soo making rounds around the nearby fireplace with a look of sheer defeat on his face.

"Alright, that's enough Zion!" the soldier said, calmly but with a force due to a disciplinary father. The boy immediately halted and Jung-Soo nearly bumped and knocked the kid over. "Be a good boy and give the man back his envelope."

It was only then that Dae-Gun realized what the boy had been holding—the commander's codes!

"What were you thinking giving that to a kid?" Dae-Gun said in a tone not unlike the way the soldier talked to the child.

The soldier placed both hands on the child's shoulders and gave an affectionate pat. "Why don't you say hello to our new friends," he said.

He bowed, like any Korean child would be taught to, but instead of saying "an-neong-ha-se-yo," he said "hello" in English.

Dae-Gun laughed. "Yes, hello indeed! I'm Dae-Gun, and this is Jung-Soo."

The soldier reached out his hand towards Jung-Soo. "And I'm James, Sergeant James Jones. Welcome to the 5th Cavalry Regiment."

***

The commander's tent was crowded as men stood around a table with the map of the Korean Peninsula on top as official documents crowded the edges. The commander sat broad shouldered with a patch of bald shining straight at them as he furiously examined a document in front of him. He finally noticed the two Korean soldiers and beckoned them with his right hand.

"Park Dae-Gun, Kim Jung-Soo?" The commander read from the page in his hand. "Soldiers from the 18th Infantry. Welcome!"

The commander took the envelope from Jung-Soo in grave fashion as he read each line of the contents within. He was engrossed in it, his brows somewhat furrowed and his lips tight. He glanced up at Jung-Soo and Dae-Gun with the same serious look and stared at them for a while longer than they were comfortable as if reading the soldiers with that single look.

"Soldiers, come back here at 19:00 tonight. I've got a message for you two."

Jung-Soo and Dae-Gun were excused and awaiting them just outside the commander's tent was Sergeant James Jones.

"I'll take that from you," the sergeant reached out and grabbed Jung-Soo's mail satchel. Jung-Soo instinctively clammed up to resist them being taken. "Many a soldier will be waiting for these letters," the sergeant added.

Jung-Soo didn't understand a word he said. He loosened his grip and allowed them to be taken from them.

"What will happen to the letters?" Jung-Soo asked Dae-Gun. He had grown rather attached to them, though he knew parting with them was an inevitability. Dae-Gun asked the sergeant.

"Moving on to the next leg of its journey, just like the rest of us," the sergeant answered with a guffaw. "This batch is bound east towards the 51st Regiment. This is just a checkpoint in between deliveries."

The boy came and held onto the sergeant's hand, looking up at Jung-Soo with an innocent smile.

"In any case, I've been assigned to take good care of you during your stay here," the sergeant said. "If you need anything, anything at all, let me know and we will make it happen for you."

Jung-Soo gritted his teeth and silently growled at the boy who had caused so much trouble. The boy responded likewise with his own subdued snarl. The sergeant seemed cheerful enough, though clearly, he was unaware of the little rascal he had under his care. The boy dared to imitate him.

"So when did you arrive in Korea?" Dae-Gun said, starting up the conversation again.

Jung-Soo listened closely, though the words were merely slurred sounds to him. Zion, who remained silent when the adults talked, came up to Jung-Soo and held his hand as they walked side-by-side as if they had not just come out of a fight. Jung-Soo gave in. The little boy skipped double time next to Jung-Soo's long legs until he held out a booklet to Jung-Soo.

"What's this?"

Zion just smiled and skipped along next to him. Jung-Soo flipped through the pages. It was a pocket-sized English-Korean dictionary.

He ruffled the boy's hair like Dae-Gun had done before. "*Gomawo*—thank you," Jung-Soo said.

"We were deployed a couple months ago from Japan," the sergeant answered, "fought in the battle of Osan, participated in the Inchon counteroffensive, before being deployed here." He fell silent, as if in reflection.

Jung-Soo noticed a word he had heard before. "*So-ool? So-ool...*" he whispered out loud as he looked up the English word in his dictionary.

"(소울)Soul- 영혼- the spiritual or immaterial part of a human being or animal, regarded as immortal," the page indicated. It made no sense. Why would the two strangers be talking about souls?

Dae-Gun nudged Jung-Soo and whispered, "Not soul, you dummy. Seoul!"

Jung-Soo realized his own stupidity and closed the booklet. The boy reached for his hand again as they walked behind Dae-Gun and the sergeant.

"Never mind when we arrived in Korea," the sergeant said, excitement growing in his voice. "The more important question is, when will the shipment arrive?"

"The shipment?" Dae-Gun asked as the sergeant nodded, pulling open the tent sleeve in front of them that revealed a much larger storage tent.

"It seems it finally arrived!"

Inside the massive garage were crates and boxes lined against the tent walls, each in segments and various sizes, some that had been cracked open and others still undergoing inspection. Soldiers with clipboards walked around them, peeping in as others stood guard over a section. Displayed on one long table, were dark brown bars the size of one's palms with the same curvy English letters on them.

"Chocolate!" Dae-Gun said, running up to the table.

They were massive bars, larger than any Jung-Soo had seen before. The soldier on guard tensed up as Dae-Gun moved rather rapidly towards him.

"At ease, soldier," the sergeant said to the guard. "These are our mailmen from the South Korean Regiment near Gyung-Gi-Do, here on R&R before they head back out."

Sunglasses were on the table next to the chocolate, more triangular and larger than the ones Jung-Soo had seen in the city.

"Soon, there will be enough chocolate and sunglasses for the entire South Korean Army!" the sergeant exclaimed.

"For the entire South Korean army?" Dae-Gun said in disbelief.

The sergeant nodded proudly. "Here, why don't you take some for your return journey." Sergeant Jones witnessed Zion nibbling on the side of a chocolate bar. "Not now, Zion," he warned. "No sweets till after dinner, remember?"

The boy sighed and put it away in his pockets.

Dae-Gun, on the other hand, grabbed as many chocolate bars as his back pocket could fill and placed a pair of sunglasses on the bridge of his nose, though it quickly slid down. Jung-Soo curiously mimicked Dae-Gun as he tore open a chocolate bar and raced it to his mouth, though he couldn't help but notice the stinging look of the little boy who pleaded with doe-eyes.

Jung-Soo made sure the sergeant was deep in conversation with Dae-Gun and then took another chocolate bar from the table. With the skills he had developed since he was a child, Jung-Soo passed an extra chocolate bar into Zion's hand without a single person witnessing the act. It was a real spy maneuver. Of course, the boy's beaming smile gave it all away.

"Captain Gonzales!" the sergeant beckoned a soldier. Zion jumped, startled by the sudden volume. "Why don't you take a snap of our new friends here!" Around the captain's neck was a square contraption he brought up to his eyes. "Why don't you put your backpacks down for a picture?"

Jung-Soo and Dae-Gun did not realize they had yet to put their heavy load down, doing as they were told. Dae-Gun, who was instinctively protective of his guitar, gently placed it between him and Jung-Soo as they managed an awkward smile before the flash blinded them.

"This here, is the Polaroid camera, specially developed for the military, along with the Polaroid goggles," the sergeant said as he handed Dae-Gun the picture that had immediately been printed out. "A present to commemorate your first day at our camp."

"Martin, Taylor!" the sergeant said to two soldiers, one white as a ghost, and the other as dark as night, carrying a box between them. "Why don't we give our guests a little taste?"

The two soldiers cracked the crate open to reveal rows of bottled beer.

"It's beer!" Dae-Gun exclaimed to Jung-Soo.

"Beer?" Jung-Soo said, peering into the box.

"American alcohol. I've heard all about it, and I've been dying to try it for myself!"

The soldier called Taylor popped open the bottle and handed it to Jung-Soo, who seemed more fascinated by the color of the man's skin. He popped open one for himself and clinked his bottle against Jung-Soo's with a stern smile and downed the bottle in one go. Jung-Soo copied the man, though he coughed at the first sip that seemed to burn his throat.

"Good, isn't it?" the sergeant said. Dae-Gun cringed with a sip just as Jung-Soo did, nodding politely. "You get used to the burn," he added.

By the time the sergeant was done showing Jung-Soo and Dae-Gun around the storage area, they had managed to each get a bottle of beer, two sunglasses, and a handful of chocolate bars—all that Dae-Gun adamantly claimed were necessary for the trip back to their base camp.

"Is there anything else that I can get for you? Supplies? Maps? Dictionaries?" He looked towards Jung-Soo.

"Supplies," Dae-Gun said to Jung-Soo in Korean.

Jung-Soo, who had been so enthralled by the American items, had forgotten all about the supplies they needed. He dug into his pockets until he pulled out a blackened piece of paper, filled to the brim with his own handwriting. "Batteries for the radio, dried food, blankets, perhaps even a winter coat."

The word stuck to the top of his roof. *A ruler,* he thought, but he bit his tongue. What was he to say if anyone asked why he needed one?

Dae-Gun hesitated for a moment before adding, "I was wondering sergeant, if you might have some guitar strings."

The sergeant scanned the warehouse for a while, quite intent on further impressing his guests, yet, the verdict was final: "I'm afraid we don't ship guitar strings…*yet*. You'll have to be resourceful with that one."

He watched as Jung-Soo ticked off the items on his list with the supplies he had been given.

"It looks like your friend there might need a bit more paper."

"Do we need more paper?" Dae-Gun asked.

"*Jong-e?*" Jung-Soo repeated in Korean. "Yes, definitely."

"It looks like it won't be easy to get our hands on them," the sergeant said. "Our stocks have nearly been depleted these past few weeks."

Jung-Soo could tell it wasn't good news. But out of all the things that they could be running low on, how could it be paper? He sighed. He would have to be careful about how often he picked up the pencil.

"Not to worry!" he said with his usual chirpy tone. "I'll make sure you get your stash before you leave! And if things proceed as they do, rumor has it that domestic production could potentially be overtaking imports soon."

"Domestic production?" Dae-Gun asked. "The government is making paper for soldiers?"

The sergeant shook his head. "Looks like it's a local movement. Some small farming village is doing the heavy lifting."

Dae-Gun had a curious look on his face. It felt oddly nice to know that they will still have jobs delivering letters if there was enough paper in circulation. At least that would mean he wouldn't be going back into the battlefield anytime soon.

"Dinner is in less than an hour," the sergeant said. "Rest up till then."

It wasn't a second after the sergeant disappeared that Jung-Soo pulled Dae-Gun by the sleeve and began marching to the other end of the tent.

"Let's go," Jung-Soo said.

"Huh?"

"Aren't you looking for guitar strings?"

Dae-Gun looked at Jung-Soo as if he had magically become fluent in English and had overheard his entire conversation with the sergeant. "How did you…?"

"You couldn't shut up about the 'E' string that's about to break for days."

"Oh, right."

Jung-Soo had noticed a pile of miscellaneous objects on the other side of the tent and was keen on exploring. He still had that one problem left to solve; he needed some sort of measurement device, units that Iseul would recognize in order to complete the final sketch as accurately as possible. He browsed the area, finding everything from batteries of all sizes to shoelaces, water canisters, lanterns, and gun parts.

Dae-Gun had already picked up half a dozen items, lifting them up to eye level, staring at them, until he woefully put the objects back down. He then picked up a spring, one that coiled above the barrel of the rifle and gave it a little tug. He smiled, grabbing a handful of different shapes and sizes, trying to work out how he would flatten the springs and place it on the guitar.

As for Jung-Soo, the only item flexible and long enough to measure the entire length of the guitar was the shoestring. He sighed, defeated. Unless he sends the shoestring with the guitar, it was useless, and if the soldiers going through the mail were even half as meticulous as he was, there wasn't a chance the letter would safely reach Iseul's hands.

But maybe...

Jung-Soo recalled the map that stood like an island in the middle of the commander's tent. Above it, he recalled a ruler, one of those universal lengths he had seen at his school in Seoul. Perhaps someone would have one just like it in the village! His heart beat quickened. He heard soldiers had set up camp in each village to conscript men and collect valuables. Perhaps the Wasteland of Yeoju would have a soldier who had a universal ruler Iseul could borrow.

Jung-Soo grabbed an extra set of shoelaces from the display table. It was now or never. They would be leaving at the break of dawn tomorrow morning, and the evening would be spent doing official business.

He grabbed Dae-Gun's arm again. "T minus 10 minutes. Proceed to secret mission. Code: ruler." Jung-Soo whispered.

CHAPTER 22

"What secret mission?" Dae-Gun said nervously. "I don't remember anyone telling us about a mission."

Dae-Gun dropped his collection of springs in one corner of the tent as Jung-Soo pulled him outside. Before Dae-Gun could resist any further, he and Jung-Soo were standing back in front of the commander's tent, both looking around anxiously, wondering if a stray soldier might be suspicious of two Koreans soldiers lurking around.

The campsite seemed rather empty and those they could see huddled on logs and chairs were sharing a card game or smoking the day away until the next battle.

"Today's mission is to find the ruler," Jung-Soo said.

"Ruler?" Dae-Gun said, utterly befuddled.

Jung-Soo held the slit of the tent open. "There!" He pointed towards the top of the map where a single metal stick lay. The room was nearly empty, though a soldier stood by the map and moved pieces around.

Dae-Gun sighed in relief. "Oh, that ruler." He rolled his eyes.

"Stand guard outside."

"What? Me?" Dae-Gun said, the panic returning.

But before he could grab a hold of Jung-Soo, he had slipped past the slit of the tent and disappeared within. Jung-Soo rolled in spy fashion, landing softly behind a stack of smaller boxes just next to the entrance.

The white soldier hadn't noticed a thing as he glanced back and forth from a document in his left hand to stray pieces on the map that signified troops. From afar, Jung-Soo could see that the pieces were placed northeast of where they were situated, just as he had seen the movements of the Chinese days before arriving at the 5th Cavalry Regiment. A solemn look flashed across the soldier's face before he laid the document down and ran straight past the boxes and out of the tent.

"Oww!" Jung-Soo heard Dae-Gun from the outside. The white man must have bumped into him on the way out. It sounded as if the soldier was scolding Dae-Gun as the voices dissipated.

It was his chance now. Jung-Soo was alone in the tent with the ruler just a small stretch away. He flung himself into another roll and landed behind the table, hiding from the entrance. 'Always plan an exit strategy or at least a safe place to hide,' the Captain had taught him.

Jung-Soo's head bobbed on the edge of the table, looking around while untangling the knotted shoelace into one long strand. He laid the shoelace next to the ruler, measuring the entire length of the ruler. He needed to mark the spot on the shoelace that extended longer than the ruler. Just next to the pieces that lay on the map, Jung-Soo spotted a marker. That'll do.

He squinted to make out the curvy letters on the ruler. The two edges of the ruler had two different units—one larger than the other. He was only used to seeing the smaller centimeter ruler and it seemed everything was bigger where the ghosts lived.

"One hundred units," he whispered to himself over and over again as he copied the English curvy letters "centimeter" as if he were drawing the alphabets that had no meaning to him.

That was the length of the shoelace to the marker. He wouldn't forget. He placed the ruler back to its original location and reached across the table to return the marker in its rightful place. His eyes followed the marker but landed on the map. Next to the pieces was the sheet of paper the white soldier had left behind with the number 50,000 next to it.

50,000 of what? Jung-Soo thought. Guns? Boxes? Soldiers? He glanced down at the individual pieces on the map and it became clear: the tiny miniature armies were the same ones he had seen lying around his father's warehouse, each one symbolizing a brigade of around 3000 soldiers. He counted the figures...*sixteen.*

It was simple math: sixteen divisions amounted to at least 50,000 soldiers.

"Impossible…"

One-hundred times more than Jung-Soo had witnessed, heading south from the northeastern front. There must have been at least twenty individual North Korean and Chinese regiments on the move towards a central location somewhere in the east. All routes indicated led to the east of Seoul, towards Gangwon province. They were close—far too close for his liking. It wouldn't be long till the enemy would gather force and march south. Just weeks ago, morale had been at an all-time low when they heard about the bloodbath near the Yalu that had gotten the Chinese involved in the war.

"Jung-Soo," Dae-Gun's head peeked through the tent entrance. "Are you almost done?"

"Yeah, just a minute," Jung-Soo woke from his trance.

"It's just, things are getting a little bit busier here. Oh no…" Dae-Gun disappeared back outside. "Commander, what a surprise to find you here! I mean, of course, this is your tent and all…"

Jung-Soo tumbled behind the boxes again, but he was trapped with the exit so close. The entire tent was closed off, except for that slit. He could wait there until the tent would be vacant again. That was his safest bet.

"Dae-Gun, was it?" the commander said. "I thought our meeting wasn't until later tonight."

"No, I mean yes…"

"So, what can I do for you?"

"Well, I was just wondering where Jung-Soo and I will be staying for the night."

Jung-Soo didn't need to speak English to know Dae-Gun was struggling. Surrender would be the safest route now that capture was inevitable. Perhaps the commander would understand. He looked down at the single strand of the shoelace that looked oddly suspicious. Perhaps not. He couldn't risk getting his makeshift ruler confiscated.

Just then, with a sudden stroke of luck, the sirens blared. Outside, footsteps grew louder and faster. The howling of the sirens matched the thunderous voices that commanded soldiers to move.

"He's gone!" Dae-Gun's head popped in again.

With his head kept low, Jung-Soo exited the crime scene. "What's happening?"

Soldiers ran in every direction in coordination with captains and sergeants who directed the crowd of marching soldiers. Men snatched helmets and clasped it on, while others grabbed a handful of rifles and rifle magazines on the way out from their tents.

"I don't know. The commander said to stay put. He said not to worry."

In the distance, two shells exploded simultaneously, cutting through the sound of the sirens as they came blaring back with greater intensity.

"We're under attack," Jung-Soo said. "The North Korean troops heading towards Gangwon province are already here." Impossible. No army could move that fast. Yet, his senses betrayed his logic, and the terrified look on the white soldier crossed his mind. Another blast sounded louder.

"We need to leave right now!" Jung-Soo said, frenzied. "Where's your guitar?"

"What?"

"I said where is your guitar?" Jung-Soo yelled. *The storage tent.* They had left all of their belongings there. How foolish they were! They should have been ready to leave at a moment's notice.

This time, Dae-Gun grasped Jung-Soo by the shoulder and shook him. "Wake up, Jung-Soo, we've been ordered to stay put! The commander said not to worry."

With a blank stare, Jung-Soo mumbled, "how can we know for sure?"

With a wrist twist and an elbow to the nose, Jung-Soo broke free and made a run towards the tent. What had he just done, attacking his own partner?

He couldn't think. The sirens broke through his thick skull and prodding him forward, his shoulders bumping into something— soldiers flooding in the opposite direction. His feet were as light as a feather; he felt the whiplash against his ankles where the Captain used to hit him to keep him on his toes.

The flap of the tent swished past him. Inside the warehouse tent, everything looked different—he saw a metal container that might survive a shell; weapons caught his eye, light and nimble to silently take out North Korean soldiers and sneak out of the camp. He still had time. Perhaps they could escape before the North Koreans infiltrated the camp. He scanned for the one thing he knew he must take: Dae-Gun's guitar.

He traced his steps. He had been in such a hurry to get out. Where had the idiot left the guitar? *There.* He found it leaning against a stack of boxes next to the display table.

Sirens seemed to shriek louder. He would go back for the idiot. Yes, right after he secured the guitar and found their backpacks; they wouldn't survive a week without them.

Jung-Soo grabbed the guitar by the neck and swung it around his left shoulder, just as he had seen Dae-Gun do countless times. Now their backpacks.

Just as quickly as the sirens began, it cut off mid-shriek, leaving an echo reverberating throughout the hollow tent. Footsteps outside filtered within the tent and no one was shouting anymore.

"Jung-Soo!" Dae-Gun shouted, running into the tent. "Are you okay? I thought you might have left the camp already. It was just a warning shot from the other side."

Dae-Gun let out a sigh of relief, holding on to his knees and catching his breath.

"What were you thinking disobeying a direct command like that!" Dae-Gun said with authority. It was a side Jung-Soo hadn't seen before.

"Sorry," he muttered. But as soon as Dae-Gun caught his breath and stood straight up, Jung-Soo couldn't help but chuckle. From both of Dae-Gun's nostrils, flowed a river of bright red blood, past his lips like a mustache and down the side of his cheeks.

"I'm serious! This is no joking matter, Kim Jung-Soo!"

"No, no, absolutely not."

Dae-Gun reached his hand out. "My guitar?"

Jung-Soo glanced at his left shoulder and hesitated. "Oh, right."

"Glad to know what your priorities are," Dae-Gun said, offended.

Jung-Soo handed over the guitar. He couldn't believe what had come over him! It was all because of that damn map, the letter, and the ruler. They had revived a paranoia he thought he had left behind in his past life.

"Here," Jung-Soo said, handing Dae-Gun an old shirt as he gestured to wipe his nose.

Dae-Gun's hand sprang to his nose and felt the moist stickiness before looking at his fingers. "Blood, blood! Jung-Soo, I'm bleeding!" Dae-Gun said.

Jung-Soo pat Dae-Gun in the back with a firm thud. "Oh, you'll be fine. It's just a double nose bleed."

Dae-Gun groaned. "You just wait! I'm going to get you for

this!"

"Yeah okay, I owe you one," Jung-Soo said, as he lugged his heavy backpack on his left shoulder.

Sergeant James Jones found them as they exited the warehouse tent.

"Ah, my friends. I was worried the sirens may have scared you off. Anyone hungry?

Jung-Soo and Dae-Gun were the only ones in full gear as they walked towards the center of the camp where a fire blazed into the night sky. They had missed seeing the sunset for the first time in a very long while.

Zion was strategically positioned near the fire as the occasional soldier ruffled the boy's black and oily head as they passed, some even sharing their food with the boy who had grown somewhat plump compared to the other orphans they had seen on the road.

The sergeant took the boy on his lap and laid out a plate of rice and grilled pork to share between the two. The boy had an appetite that matched Dae-Gun's and outpaced the sergeant. Dae-Gun and Jung-Soo were each given a plate as they took their place on a log near the sergeant.

The food was warm, though the rice wasn't quite what they were used to.

"Boiled, not steamed," Dae-Gun answered Jung-Soo's perplexed expression as he took his first bite. "The missionaries used to do that too. We had one of the old ladies in the village teach them how to properly steam rice."

A tin of white liquid boiled thick and creamy on the fringes of the fire. It was a staple at the orphanage—powdered formula.

"We call it hot ice cream," the sergeant said, who watched Dae-Gun mesmerized by the bubbling formula.

"Hot ice cream," Zion repeated, dipping his wooden spoon into it as he slowly slurped it like a popsicle.

"The boy probably doesn't even know what real ice cream is," the sergeant added.

Zion pouted. "Of course I do! It's this, but not hot?" The boy had managed to confuse himself.

"That's right, my boy! That's right!" the sergeant said, like a proud father. "It probably reminds him of his mother," he murmured to them.

Dae-Gun had already cleared his plate, resisting the urge to ask for seconds. He instead looked covetously at Jung-Soo's plate.

"It's a shame you'll be leaving us tomorrow. You haven't seen our make shift batting cages yet. And in a few weeks, the Canadians will be making ice rinks to play hockey on once it gets cold enough."

"Batting cages?" Dae-Gun said, wide-eyed. He had heard about baseball and football from his grandfather. He couldn't believe it! Batting cages right here in Korea?

"We'll be back in a couple of weeks," Dae-Gun said, excitedly.

A soldier walked up to Sergeant Jones. "Paper, sergeant," he said. "You have no idea how many people I've had to get permission from to get these."

Jung-Soo fixated on the pile of white sheets. Even from afar, they looked crisp, firm and white. Very white…

"Thank you," Dae-Gun said.

"Tank yoo…" Jung-Soo repeated, standing to bow in proper reverence.

The sergeant reached behind. "Don't think I've forgotten about your request, Dae-Gun." The light of the bonfire flickered, revealing what looked like coiled wires.

"I thought you didn't have any in stock!" Dae-Gun said in disbelief as his smile widened.

"I asked around for a favor. It seems one of our soldiers, Taylor, brought a few extras."

Dae-Gun's head moved side-to-side. "Where is this Taylor? I must thank him."

Dae-Gun spun around, looking for this soldier called Taylor as his gaze landed on Commander Gordon Rogers himself who appeared near the fire, the men surrounding him standing to salute.

"At ease soldiers."

Was it already 19:00? Jung-Soo looked down at his wrist where a watch used to be, though only a crease remained.

With the commander's appearance, the night was cut short. The two soldiers passed by as the sergeant whispered, "I'll relay the message to Taylor." He winked, smiling at Dae-Gun, who was unable to hide his disappointment that he hadn't been able to ask for seconds. He trailed behind Jung-Soo whose gaze lingered on the bubbling formula and the Korean boy who seemed right at home amidst ghostly soldiers. Jung-Soo looked forward to seeing them again in a few weeks.

He could only hope. In reality, this would be the last time he would see Sergeant James Jones and the Korean boy he had taken in as his own.

**

"Codes and code-breaking is the way of the future," Commander Rogers began as he looped behind his desk. "The Enigma," he gestured to a machine that looked no different from a typewriter. "Have you heard of it before?"

Dae-Gun shook his head.

"Alphabets are scrambled in this machine. No patterns, no formulas, purely arbitrary," the commander said.

He pushed a button on the side of the typewriter as the top popped open. "The South Koreans have one too. If these knobs aren't set up in exactly the same manner, the letters won't mean anything." The commander turned a few knobs to demonstrate. "It's a rather antiquated coding system that we managed to crack during the second world war. Do you follow what I am saying?"

"I think so, sir," Dae-Gun said.

"Translate," he commanded.

Jung-Soo nodded as Dae-Gun explained how the enigma machine worked.

"Do you know what I'm asking of you, soldiers?"

"You want us to carry the codes back to the 18th Infantry. Get rid of it if we are in caught, and by no means, transmit the codes over the radio," Jung-Soo said.

"Smart man, Jung-Soo was it?" the commander said, giving Jung-Soo a firm hand shake.

"Kim Jung-Soo, sir."

"A man smart enough to know that we are surrounded, but evenly matched with the enemy," the commander said with a quick glance towards the map and a look that seemed to pierce Jung-Soo's soul.

He knows. Jung-Soo held his breath as the silence lingered a little while longer.

"I put my complete trust in you, soldiers. We suspect the enemy will close in sooner than we've expected. You will have to hasten your journey."

Dae-Gun translated, his head held up high with the bravery the commander infused in them.

Jung-Soo bowed. "We will guard it with our lives," he said, as they were dismissed from the commander's tent, even as he wondered why the commander had gone to the trouble of explaining how the machine worked. Commander Lee, their own leader of the 18th Infantry, didn't seem particularly keen on letting them know any more than was necessary. There was something in the white commander's generosity and kindness that irked Jung-Soo. No one could be that nice, not in such matters of international espionage in the middle of a war zone, not unless the commander had ulterior motives.

They need not stay the night at the camp; that is what the commander meant by hastening, though Dae-Gun was quite certain that a warm sleeping bag would do the trick to keep them going longer the next morning.

There was no need to collect their belongings or stock up. Everything that they would need was strung on their shoulders that drooped just a little more with the supplies they had been given.

The further they went uphill and away from camp, the brighter the night sky shined. And the longer Jung-Soo breathed in the smokeless air with nothing but the smell of soil and trees to accompany them, the more he was certain the commander knew. There was no doubt.

"We'll have to take the hillside roads this time around," Jung-Soo said, picking up the pace.

"Why?" Dae-Gun groaned. "What's wrong with the route we took the last time?"

"Nothing. We just have to be extra cautious," Jung-Soo said, "and quick."

"But the last route is quicker!"

There was only one way he would regain the commander's trust and keep his cover. Almost all of the North Korean and Chinese troops would have gathered in Gangwon province by now. Time was of the essence.

If his hunch was correct, there would be others like them, soldiers with codes going to other military bases. He needed to deliver them before any of the other idiots got caught, or worse, handed the codes over to the North Koreans.

They hiked up the nearest rocky mountain and was half way down the other side. Every so often, when the complaints and huffing would quiet down, Jung-Soo would look back to check on

Dae-Gun and would be relieved to see the guitar still hanging on the boy's left shoulder.

Dae-Gun wondered when they would stop to rest. Surely, Jung-Soo didn't expect him to hike all night, and all of tomorrow without a wink of sleep! Perhaps, when they get to the next stream, or by that boulder or cave… Dae-Gun was certain each time, only to be disappointed.

When the moonlight hit its pinnacle, Jung-Soo stopped in the middle of the thick forest grounds to set up camp.

"No fire tonight," he stated.

Dae-Gun didn't care. He was thirsty. It seemed like it had been a week since they had left the camp, but the taste of boiled rice and roasted pork still lingered in his mouth. *Wishful thinking.* Somehow, food had never failed to disappoint him as his hunger grew even more pronounced with the aftertaste.

A nice flat surface was all Dae-Gun could ask for, but even that seemed to be too much. With a large gulp of water from his canister, Dae-Gun rolled over and began snoring.

It wasn't long before Jung-Soo fell asleep next to Dae-Gun. He was, after all, merely human. But the thought scratched the surface of his barely conscious mind—*tonight would be the perfect night to measure the guitar.* The moon was bright and Dae-Gun snored louder than ever. He felt the single strand of the shoelace press against his thigh and felt the sheets of crisp white paper clumped together in his breast pocket.

If only he could manage to lift his head from the ground…if only. Jung-Soo let sleep overcome him this time.

There will be another day, it enticed

CHAPTER 23

Somewhere south of where the two soldiers slept, peace still resided in the quaint rice-farming village of Yeoju. Dawn was still a while away, yet Iseul and Yeong-Hoon were awake, hungry and restless. There was nothing like idle hands to make hunger more pronounced, and so they woke to craft buk-drums as they had gotten in the habit of doing in the early hours.

The two marched to their own beat, carpentering in unison as the years of toiling had taught them. Dawn arrived and so did the twittering birds that made their daily rounds of foraging. The lower edges of the hills had been stripped bare as more and more birds seemed to migrate past the two carpenters' home, moving further up the mountain as if they too were aware of the bloodbath that would soon come.

Yeong-Hoon reached his hand out, waiting for Iseul to hand him the leather she had been softening. She sat on her stool, mindlessly turning the wheels of the stretcher. He gently reached for her hands and stopped her. She jerked, her right hand heading towards her ankle where a metal gun hung.

"Sorry," Iseul said, coming back to her senses as she quickly unclipped the edges of the leather and handed it to Yeong-Hoon.

The leather, a precious commodity of late, had been stretched thin in the middle, ready to rip.

"What's on your mind?" he gently asked.

"Nothing, really," she said, placing the next hide into the stretcher.

He waited, glancing down at her ankle and the gun that seemed too hefty for her thinning ankles.

"Oppa," she confessed. "If Jung-Soo is supposed to be alive, why hasn't he written yet? Everyone else in the village seems to be getting their mail with no problems."

She had seen the scholar the other day parading a smile she had never seen on his stoic face before. The letter was short and was more like a note, which disappointed him a bit, but the shortness was understandable; the villagers had been hearing complaints from their loved ones about the supply limitations they had been facing. And with the red army deep within the Southern territory, letters were few and far between as all those who wrote were careful not to upset the communists who were surely reading the letters and killing anyone suspected of being American sympathizers.

He gave her a warm smile and began working again. "If you're so worried, why don't you try writing to him first. I'm sure Byung-Guk's father would know where to send it."

Iseul thought for a moment. "Yeah, I guess so." Yet, somehow, she couldn't get herself to write anything. Besides, Jung-Soo knew where she was and he hadn't bothered to write so why should she? He probably wanted a new start, away from the people who accused him of being a communist, perhaps even away from her.

Yeong-Hoon got up and went outside. "I'll be back," he said, as he set off into the mountain to chop a fresh supply of wood.

"Why don't I help you?" Iseul said, though Yeong-Hoon shook his head and was already pacing quickly away.

She felt guilty. She wanted to be strong, but the events of the past few months had made her anxious and spooked by the most mundane daily occurrences. Yeong-Hoon knew this and thought it best that Iseul remained safe and sound at home.

Iseul watched the last of Yeong-Hoon's frame disappear between the trees as she was left standing alone in her dusty yard. She looked down at her browned work clothes and overgrown hair and sighed. Though she never cared for how she looked, she loathed the scratchy cloth of her trousers that showed how thin her legs had been getting and yearned to wear her hanbok again. She could imagine Jung-Soo's reaction if he saw her dressed like a man. She was sure he wouldn't even recognize her! She jumped up onto her raised porch and ran into the master bedroom where her father's masterfully handcrafted cabinet stood. She knew where father had kept mother's old clothes, though she never dared to open that drawer.

It was time.

The dress was long and worn, but the bright red and green remained in the most delicate hues. It was just as she had remembered it.

"It's perfect." Iseul let out a weak nostalgic smile.

The paper door to her parent's room slid open. It was Mi-Jung.

"Who are you talking to?" She said, bringing with her a box that was neatly folded in a colorful fabric. "Something's different about you," she said with a puzzled look.

Iseul gently pinched the side of the dress and spread it apart. "It's my mom's hanbok. Do you like it?"

Mi-Jung eyes widened in recognition. "I knew it! I knew something was different! It's beautiful."

It was hard to tell how much weight Mi-Jung had lost under her hanbok dress billowing near her ankles. She too had outgrown her hanbok, though not to the same extent Iseul had. Her gauntly face told the same story of hunger that many of the villagers shared, but the bruises near her eye sockets and cheekbone signaled a heavier hand.

Iseul knew but did not say anything. She was fuming inside; it was as if the Japanese were still here, taking young women from their families and doing unthinkable things to them. They were rumors, but everyone knew they were true.

"I just thought I'd come and drop off some food left over from the restaurant," Mi-Jung said. "I wouldn't want to disturb you or anything." Mi-Jung shifted in place, wondering if she had made the right decision to take up Iseul's offer and visit her.

"Of course not!" Iseul exclaimed. They made their way back to the workshop where she pulled out two stools by the window. "Here, come take a seat with me. Let's eat together."

Iseul knew it must not have been an easy task hiking up the mountain for someone who was not used to the trek. They sat by the window where the morning light filtered in at a sharp angle. The porridge that Mi-Jung brought was good. Iseul thought she tasted a hint of sesame oil, an ingredient she hadn't tasted since her mother passed. At least that's what she thought she tasted, but it could have been perilla oil. The silence was soothing, and even the thoughts on Iseul's mind seemed to calm in the moments they sat tending to their empty stomachs, like old friends catching up.

Mi-Jung began shifting again once the food was gone. She

wrapped the emptied lunch box in the fabric and got ready to leave. Iseul felt the heaviness of her stomach reach her chest, and though her noon-chi was never her strong-suit, she felt somehow sad to think that Mi-Jung would leave so soon.

"If you're not too busy, why don't you stay with me for a little bit. I could use some company."

Mi-Jung swung back towards Iseul. "Really? Could I do that? Why don't you teach me some carpentry so I can help you out?"

Iseul put her to work doing some of the easier tasks. Mi-Jung stacked the raw cow hide and handed Iseul the nails as she began hammering the hide onto the circular body of the drum.

"I heard you might be leaving next week," Iseul began.

"Oh, mother says we will, but I doubt it. She's been getting weaker lately," Mi-Jung said. "If it were up to me, we'd move closer to the U.N. military camp. They say there is work for someone like me and plenty of food there. I can earn a living until mother gets better."

Iseul thought Mi-Jung would be evacuating south, but it seemed she and her mother had differing ideas as to where they would be going.

Iseul could only imagine what Mi-Jung might be going through. No decent man, even Byung-Guk, would take her now that she was tainted goods. It was desperation that made her think that it wasn't such a bad idea to make a living out of it—out of selling her body.

"What about you?" Mi-Jung said.

"I can't imagine leaving this place."

Mi-Jung thought for a while. "I guess so."

Iseul was relieved to hear that and hoped she would decide to remain. She wondered if part of the reason Mi-Jung hesitated was because of Byung-Guk, despite all that had happened. Letters came sporadically, but at least she knew Byung-Guk would continue sending her letters as long as she stayed put. Iseul wished too, suppressing a hint of jealousy.

"Have you heard from Byung-Guk?" Iseul asked.

She nodded. "His unit is further down south so he should be safe."

Iseul could tell something was on her mind. She waited.

"Listen, Iseul. Byung-Guk feels terrible about that night."

She knew what Mi-Jung meant. Iseul held no grudges, at least tried not to.

"Honestly, it's my fault too." Mi-Jung added.

"That's ridiculous." Iseul tried to console.

"No, let me finish. Byung-Guk and I had been seeing each other for a while and then my mother found out. She said she'd lock me up in a cell before she'd sell me off to some farmer's boy."

"Oh…" Iseul said. She didn't quite know what to say to that. "But how is it your fault that Byung-Guk…"

"He was supposed to come and get me with an empty sack of rice. I made him believe we could go away together."

Mi-Jung was referring to an old marriage tradition that had its roots in a more savage past. A man would kidnap his woman-of-choice, wrapping her in a rice sack before riding away in the night. The next morning, they would be forcibly wed.

Memories of that night came flooding back in surprising clarity, almost as if Iseul could see Jung-Soo with that absurd wig on. Jung-Soo must have known about Byung-Guk and Mi-Jung's plans to go away. That must be why he thought to disguise himself as Mi-Jung that night. What else did he know that he hadn't told her? He had been acting suspiciously that entire day, following her and even holding his gaze longer than usual.

They worked in silence, letting the reality of their situation sink in. None of it mattered anymore. Iseul couldn't have imagined things getting worse after that night, but they had. They had seen their brothers and fathers taken into conscription as the number of soldiers dwindled in their village without any more men or rice to take.

She had heard it on the radio; they say the North Koreans have been making headway in the Southern half of the Peninsula. It would be wise to leave like most of the other villagers did. But where to? South? They all went south, killed on the road or if lucky, they would walk till they reached the ocean and either stayed or cross over to Japan—another enemy they had just gained independence from.

"Why are you still making your craft drums?" Mi-Jung broke the silence.

"I'm just doing it to pass the time. Maybe, our soldiers will come back and want some more."

Iseul was hammering the next round of nails when she heard whimpers turn into sobs.

"I don't know how you do it, Iseul!" she said through her tears.

"Just keep pressing on like that."

Iseul reached out towards her, wondering if she was supposed to tell her everything was going to be alright. That would be a lie. What had become of the proud and strong girl she had seen peering out of the restaurant's paper windows?

Her hands hesitated, unsure of what to do until the morning light came in at a certain angle and flashed a light against the white dust on her workshop table. It did not give off a luster, like a light on snow would, but it reinvigorated Iseul with an idea that slowly seeped through her. The sound of Mi-Jung's cries echoed stronger and stronger as Iseul's own will grew with it.

Iseul's right hand moved vigorously on the table as she shifted with uncontainable excitement that grew with the formation of her plans.

By the time Mi-Jung's sobs halted and she opened her eyes, a word was written on the dusty workshop counter.

"What does this say?" Mi-Jung said.

"Hope."

Mi-Jung mustered a weak smile. Iseul mimicked her, wondering why it had taken them so long to share a moment like this.

"A friend once did the same for me," Iseul said, remembering the time Yeong-Hoon had written 'hope' on the dusty cabin floor. She grabbed Mi-Jung and tugged her out of her stool to head towards one corner of the room.

"What are we doing?" Mi-Jung said, stumbling.

"We can't just sit around thinking about hope," Iseul said with a skip in her step.

She handed Mi-Jung a broom and took one herself as she pointed towards the pile of wood scraps and dust swept to one side of the workshop.

"We're making paper," Iseul said, out of breath.

"Paper?" Mi-Jung said, mimicking Iseul's sweeping motion.

"Just like I used to do before the war! It won't be much, but it can't hurt."

The workshop was nearly clear now, the wooden floors finally visible from the years of dust that had accumulated in the crevices. Iseul went outside to boil some water before dumping a pile of bark and sawdust into her the brass pot to soften the fibers.

"This way, you'll be able to write more letters to Byung-Guk and maybe we can share the rest of it with the others in the village." Iseul's excitement reached a pinnacle. "If we have enough, we just might be able to send paper to our men so that they'll have enough to write back with! Maybe, they'll even share with their friends too so the entire army will have paper!"

"The entire army?" Mi-Jung said. She was sure Iseul was beginning to lose her mind.

"Here, take this," Iseul said as she gave Mi-Jung a large wooden stick that looked a lot like the one she used to beat rice cakes with.

Iseul took one turn to beat the fibers as Mi-Jung followed suit.

"How are we ever going to make enough for everyone?" Mi-Jung said skeptically, carefully digging out another batch of hot fibers from the pot.

Iseul stopped to think. "Well…"

Mi-Jung felt rather embarrassed as if she had burst the bubble on the only optimistic plan they had since the beginning of the war.

"We'll figure it out," Mi-Jung said, grabbing the broom to sweep the floor a second time.

The sun was on its late summer descent when they realized they had spent the entire day sweeping, boiling, beating, molding and drying paper on the clothes line. It was summer and their day's work would dry before the morning. They just needed more bamboo frames, something bigger than the one they had if there were to even dream of making enough for everyone.

Iseul sighed in relief as she saw the clothes line filled with wet paper without an inch to spare. It stirred up the same contentment she felt when she used to hang clothes with her mother who had praised her for a job well done. It wasn't much—only about fifty pages or so—not nearly as many as they thought they would be able to make, but it was a start.

Iseul walked Mi-Jung back towards the restaurant, just as she had the last time. The two reached the foot of the hills just as they saw the last rays of sunlight fade. Mi-Jung grinned, though it was becoming increasingly hard to tell.

"Thank your mother for the porridge," Iseul said, making the most of the last moment with someone she could now call a friend.

"Thanks," Mi-Jung nodded and swiftly disappeared into a dimly lit room.

Though dark, Iseul thought she saw a slight spring in Mi-Jung's step as her silhouette met her mother who rose from the floor mattress to greet her.

Iseul strolled back up her hill, hungry though still running on the fumes of hope that the day had brought. Watered down rice porridge was all she had to eat that day and she was beginning to feel dizzy. She would need to graze for some food in the hills tomorrow. Perhaps she would find a few summer berries or even a young green persimmon that might stave off the hunger.

She returned home to find Yeong-Hoon already asleep in his room. With the thought of bitter persimmons and the metal gun hot against her skin, she fell asleep to the sound of her grumbling stomach.

On the other side of the village somewhere west of where Iseul slept, Mi-Jung walked purposefully, taking the back routes and rice-field detours to reach homes she had only seen from the outside. She was afraid, as was understandable considering what had happened earlier that week when two soldiers took her by force; but that night, she felt oddly brave, perhaps even brazen and careless as her mother would say if she knew.

She knocked on unsuspected homes she knew were still inhabited. Soon-Ja was still in the village, tending to her sick grandfather, as was Young-Soon and her mother. They too waited for her father and husband to come home from war. She waited by the plot of land in front of their homes, pacing back and forth from the stone-stacked fence to the raised wooden porch. They had all been customers at the restaurant at one point—ones she served because she had been born the daughter of restaurant keeper. They dared not approach her at work and used to stroll by with a bag full of books or a new dress her mother could never afford.

Mi-Jung swallowed her pride and knocked. She would go on to knock all night until she had no more doors to disturb.

It had been long since hunger and lack of sleep registered. By daybreak, Mi-Jung cooked another small portion of porridge, left it by her mother's bedside and kissed her goodbye.

"Don't wait up. I'll be back by dusk!" she said, as she was greeted by the orange sunrise.

The east gate of Yeoju's Wasteland was astir for the first time in the better part of the century. The wooden gate that rose high above their heads had lost its colorful decorations and had been infested by termites that feasted on the two pillars. It was a small miracle that it still stood upright, though no one paid attention to that minor detail.

Mi-Jung was the last to arrive as she took in the fruits of her labor. She had managed to convince two girls she knew well in the village, and they had accompanied her for the better part of the night, convincing the others to join in. Women gathered with small lunch boxes in their hands as some were joined by their mothers who refused to sit around any longer and watch more ruin befall their village.

"Follow me," Mi-Jung said. "Take a note of the route we're taking, because you're going to have to find your way back."

They promptly turned left from the gate, instinctively shying away from the misshapen road that led to the abyss of what they only knew as an abandoned road that led into a maze of mountain ranges towards the southern half of the Peninsula.

It was a long trek as they hiked on loose rocks and around freshly chopped tree stumps. They hiked stealthily, as was the way of all women who had been trained from a young age to walk discreetly on the creaky wooden floors of their homes in those early hours before the rest of the family rose.

"Listen for the sound of the river to your left," Mi-Jung said. "As soon as you near the river, you'll be able to see two houses. That's where Iseul's workshop is."

They all nodded and followed.

It was the look on Iseul's face that Mi-Jung looked forward to seeing and she was not disappointed.

Iseul's hunger woke her as she counted the seconds until the sun would rise to begin her daily scavenge for food. With a meager portion of young chestnuts and a handful of sour berries, she was met with over thirty women inside her workshop, roaming in utter chaos.

If Iseul weren't so hungry, she might have dropped everything she had picked, but instead, she placed them down on the counter where a line of small lunchboxes laid as the smell of food gently drifted into her nostrils.

"Good, you're here!" Mi-Jung said as she gathered the women around Iseul. "We weren't sure where to start so we began by gathering yesterday's paper from the line."

Iseul snapped back to her senses. "Mi-Jung, what is all this?" She looked to the side and saw Kyung-Hee, and Young-Soon, the butcher's wife and the rest of the farmers' wives.

With a smug smile, Mi-Jung said, "How else are we supposed to supply paper to the entire Korean army without any help?"

A girl gasped. "The entire army?"

Iseul took the scene in for a second as the women, old and young, watched and waited for her. Their audacious plan that had faded with a restless night of hunger came back in a flood of euphoria. She nodded and grabbed an axe that leaned against the wall and began to instruct.

"Yes. That's exactly what we're going to do," Iseul said with a confidence that dissipated any further doubt. "We're going to need more wood and mulberry bark."

Iseul put the crew to work. They were sturdier than they looked, their backs used to the hard work required to wash the linens and hanbok in the winter rivers, digging holes for underground jars that kept vegetables fermented, all the while lugging around their children on their backs. Most of the women chopped wood and roamed the nearby area for mulberry trees to harvest bark from. That was the first priority. They would need more lines and more flat stones, but that would come later.

That day, not a single sheet of paper was made. Instead, piles of logs were stacked by the large outdoor stove that once used to feed Iseul's large ancestral family. They lit a fire and poured water into the brass container, scrubbing it until steam emanated from it. The butcher's wife arrived soon after with an arm full of mulberry bark cut from a nearby tree. Iseul looked over to the tree and cringed. It was the one that Iseul's father had always cherished.

"Good, now follow me," Iseul said to the butcher's wife, as the other women gathered around to learn how to strip the outer layer of the bark. "Each of you bring an extra knife with you tomorrow."

They nodded. In the meantime, Iseul brought out every tool she could find in her house and the workshop—from axes to kitchen knives as half of the group began stripping and boiling the tender bark.

Iseul led the other half towards an area where a bamboo grove grew in hiding behind a small waterfall. They would need to build more frames for the next phrase and collect more mulberry bark. They needed much more! She then proceeded to follow the other half of the women who were in charge of collecting bark.

"Don't just harvest the young ones. We don't have enough on this hill so we're just going to have to make do with the older trees as well," Iseul added. Already, the hill she roamed as a child seemed barren with the white flesh of every mulberry tree in sight exposed to the elements. She ached for the trees and the hill but felt gratitude for their provisions.

By sundown, they had managed to create nearly fifty bamboo frames, which were surprisingly easy to construct since they were larger versions of the tofu trays the women had all been taught to create from their mothers. They began beating the softened bark and soaked them into the second brass container, the last phase of paper-crafting.

"Good!" Iseul said. "Who's hungry?"

At dusk, when the women realized they hadn't eaten all day, Kyung-Hee glanced over to the counter as the rest of them looked towards the unwrapped lunchboxes in a row. Sitting near the massive brass containers where steam rose, Iseul and her team of papermakers sat and shared their first meal together. Iseul nibbled on her chestnuts and berries, and when Young-Soon noticed, she dumped half of her rice into the lid of her lunchbox and handed it to Iseul. Mrs. Lee, the farmer's wife gave her some of her kimchi while Kyung-Hee scooped a large portion of steamed vegetables with her chopsticks and filled Iseul's lid to the brim. Iseul looked down at her lid and looked around. She had more than the rest of them had in their own lunchboxes.

Tears welled up. Halfway through her meal, Iseul stood up and went into her house to rummage for the ceremonial ingredients she kept safe in a box.

"Here it is!" she said, as she grabbed a kettle on the way out.

Though the unrelenting heat of the summer night made sweat seep unkempt through the layers of their hanboks, they sat to enjoy a cup of hot ceremonial tea that boiled on the remaining embers of the flame.

She breathed in the distinct concoction of that night—one she made a mental note to never forget. It was the dusky breeze mixed with the wisp of mulberry bark and the ceremonial black tea she used to drink each year next to her mother's grave.

Iseul sipped her tea and then stopped when she realized the women were watching and following her lead. A strange feeling washed over her, as a sense of friendship and community replaced what used to be eyes that looked at her with pity or hatred. Sure, she had grown up with these very people, but most of them had been customers and she had just been the girl who lived in the mountains to them. It seemed the tides were changing as they too found solace and refuge in their newfound mission; Iseul was glad she could share that with them.

For a moment, she wondered if her ancestors would frown on her for wasting the tea and the sacred mulberry trees near their home. But there was no divine retribution or even a slight tinge of remorse, deciding for herself that her ancestors' blessing was upon Yeoju's papermakers. She could picture her mother smiling at her by the evergreen tree, brighter than she had ever smiled before.

Yeong-Hoon was there too, of course. He had spent all day helping the women search for the right mulberry trees and bamboo. He came and sat closest to the boiling kettle. Iseul smiled at him and though it may have been too dark to see, Yeong-Hoon knew and smiled back, both in perfect contentment.

Mi-Jung was the first to stand. "Same time tomorrow by the east gate?"

Sluggish from the rice that weighed them down, they stood one-by-one and disappeared into the woods in groups of three or four.

Iseul doubted, like the night before when the excitement of the day wore off and hunger set in.

"You were great today." Iseul felt a hand on her back. Yeong-Hoon came and stood by her as they looked at the day's work.

Iseul's mind raced with all the things she must organize tonight to get ready for the next day, though a gust of wind blew in her face, taking away her worries with it. Fresh leaves rustled in their branches, hanging on with their natural summer poise. A single loose sheet of paper flew and slapped Yeong-Hoon's face. Iseul giggled.

"It must be a loose page that flew off the rope last night," she said, breathing in the air.

Yeong-Hoon bumped his shoulder into hers. "It's good to see you laughing again."

Iseul nudged Yeong-Hoon back. "Look who's talking, mister," she said. "I haven't seen a proper smile on your face for a long time!"

Yeong-Hoon did what Iseul did, the two closing their eyes to feel the invisible wind hit them in waves.

"I love the wind," Yeong-Hoon said. "When I was younger, I used to close my eyes and run across a field. It was almost like…like I was flying."

"Don't worry, oppa," Iseul said. "Our time will soon come!"

Yeong-Hoon opened his eyes to find Iseul gazing intently at him, piercing through the wind and darkness.

"Our time will come," Iseul said again.

***

Sure enough, as morning came, Mi-Jung and the women appeared in front of Iseul's workshop. They greeted her with a knife in one hand and a lunch box in another as they went straight to work.

Days passed and became weeks as the rim of their skirts grew shorter and muddier, eventually becoming shorts that their husbands and brothers had once worn. Once in a while, someone would announce that it would be their last day, as more and more trickled out of the Wasteland to find greener pastures, though most who remained had already decided that evacuating was not an option for them.

The radio brought news of the war as did the occasional refugee. They say the North Koreans had pushed past the 38th Parallel and had made it all the way down to Naktong river in the southern tip of Korea. Battles were being waged far away from them, and those that remained took solace in the fact that there was nothing the Wasteland could offer—neither food nor a safe passage south—a fact that would hopefully deter the enemy from infiltrating their village.

Every so often, a group of North Korean soldiers would appear unannounced to keep the village in line as they threatened to kill anyone suspected of going against the communist cause.

"It's not safe to be a woman in the village anymore," Kyung-Hee said one day with her hair up in a bun like the farmers' boys used to do before they were taken. She was in her brother's full work clothes.

Mi-Jung laughed. "It suits you!"

"It'll suit you too!" Kyung-Hee said seriously. "There are intruders in the village…and… and…"

"I know," Mi-Jung said. She had discovered a bruise on Kyung-Hee's left arm where she pulled up her sleeve to work. "Those savages…" she gritted her teeth. "It's better to die a man fighting than to die a woman in fear."

Kyung-Hee nodded. "We work as men do, even harder, and

we support our soldiers."

From then on, all the women, young and old, grandmothers and grandfathers, appeared in farmer's clothing, traveling in the cloak of darkness with knives to pull apart mulberry bark and to unsheathe in the presence of beasts that roamed the mountains.

Thousands of pages were made in Iseul's workshop those first few weeks. The papermakers feared bringing the pages home as wandering North Korean soldiers might shoot anyone involved in suspicious activities, causing the stacks of pages to grow and fill more than half of the entire workshop space. Nearly half of the pages had already been written on with words the villagers spilled onto the page that were too dangerous to send out.

But as the months passed, the news of American involvement and the successes they brought with them trickled into the remote village as many of the women braved bringing the letters home until they finally began sending them out. Despite their best efforts to bring home larger batches of letters and blank sheets, they were still producing much more than they could carry with them. The village grandfathers stepped in, moving the large stockpile of blank pages from Iseul's workshop to the Golden Palace that once again became the bustling headquarters for the distribution of paper to their own men across the Peninsula. They wrote letters to their hearts' content, and when there was nothing more to say than a string of "I miss yous," they began sending a bulk of blank pages in thick envelopes for their sons and husbands to write back on.

Some disappointment arose in the following weeks when fewer pages came back to the residents of Yeoju's rice village than they had sent out.

"Why doesn't he just save them for another day?" the butcher's wife complained.

"Can you imagine walking around with a pile of paper?"

"Where do you think all the other pages are going?" Kyung-Hee asked.

Iseul, who had been walking around the premises to check for any broken equipment, heard the conversation from a distance and came to chime in. "That must mean they're sharing the pages with other soldiers," she said in hopeful surmise.

"To our soldiers all over the Korean Peninsula," Mi-Jung said. "You reckon the mailman could handle all this?"

Yong-Soon smiled. "I saw him the other day. You should have

seen the look on his face when he saw the pile of letters in the Golden Palace headquarters. He had to come back the next day with at least five other mailmen."

"He's quite the determined fellow! He does seem exhausted, now that you mention it," another added.

They all joined in and laughed about the truck and the delivery men, some of whom were charming men who seemed to enjoy the fact that women waited to greet them every time they made their delivery run.

"Wait till they come back," Yong-Soon said, as she walked with freshly cut paper ready to be tied into another pile. Next to her stood rows and columns of piles just like it.

She was right. By the next week, the mailmen came ready with a larger truck and with more men to help load the paper. In fact, by the time Mi-Jung arrived at the Golden Palace to squeeze in her most recent letter, she found Byung-Guk's father furiously working to sift through the incoming and outgoing letters.

As much as Iseul loved it when Mi-Jung came back the next day with stories of the brave delivery men and the piles of letters and paper covering every inch of the Golden Palace, she took it with a grain of salt.

"Why don't you come and see for yourself?" Mi-Jung would say at the end their conversation.

But by the time the day came to an end, Iseul was too tired and busy to waste her energy on a hike to the village. Besides, someone had to finish up the tidying and begin preparing for the next day. Just like any other day, she sighed a deep breath of relief as she saw piles still left to be delivered as the remnants of their work day strewn all around her home. This is how it should be; it was how her father would have imagined the place. She did not allow herself to think of her parents; there was still too much to be done before she could properly grieve. She knew they would be proud; her goal of providing paper to the South Korean military seemed to be well on its way.

The night air was not nearly as hot and humid as those first few weeks. She had been meaning to pick up a pencil and put something down on the pages she made, but somehow, a whole season seemed to pass.

Mi-Jung always asked if she could take a letter down to the headquarters before she left, but Iseul shook her head each time.

Though Mi-Jung never pressured her to write, each day that went by without a letter from Jung-Soo was another day she postponed writing one herself. He could be dead, for all she knew. Maybe he just didn't want to hear from her anymore.

Or maybe he was waiting for her. The idea consumed her, as it had whenever she imagined writing and finally posting a letter to Jung-Soo. She sighed. Such optimism was childish. She must be realistic, now that she was…alone. She thought of father. She must forget about the past and march forward to fend for herself. That's what father would have wanted, and perhaps what Jung-Soo also wanted.

The page that had hit Yeong-Hoon in the face many nights before laid just as she had left it next to her thin mattress. She knew where the pencil was, next to the shelf where a handful of hand-woven books were.

It beckoned as she grunted and gave in.

The lantern still had a few minutes of life left as she pulled out the tiny sit-down table. It had been months since she had written anything, and she was already beginning to forget what few alphabets she knew. She might as well practice on the extra sheet, and test out the page with actual writing.

It felt rough, unlike the ones she had made before the war which were not snow white but was at least soft to the touch. She placed the end of the dull carbon tip onto the page as it stuck like glue and left a clear dark smear of black on it. The pencil flowed like it never had before, up in curves and round in loops in one sweeping motion.

Iseul couldn't help but let out a grin. The new paper made by the women of Yeoju's Wasteland was much more than she could have ever hoped for, the pencil on the page flowing like silk in bold markings on the rough page. She was finally beginning to understand why they had been so excited about writing letters. Some of them at least. She could imagine the village scholar, the grandfather who lived across the road from the butcher's, busily transcribing chatty women's words into letters.

She looked down at her page again. In the random squiggly line she had drawn, she saw a familiar figure. The curves on the page looked almost like one side of a guitar! She squinted and it was not unlike the one Jung-Soo had once drawn for her. She thought of the rough sketch that laid lonesome, tucked away in the secret compartment of the cabin.

But something was awry. She turned the page from side-to-side, and then up and down, hoping that moving it would reveal some misshapen aspect. And then it hit her. Iseul had never been good at drawing, but she did her best to complete the picture that was in her mind:

She smiled at her drawing. It was a stick figure of a man holding a guitar.

"JUNG-SOO," she wrote in bold letters and an arrow pointing at the stick figure. "Good," she said to herself as she folded it up into a neat square and set it on the corner of the table. It would sit there until she could think of something else to put on it, perhaps leave it as a scrap piece of paper if she needed to do some inventory.

Or so Iseul thought.

Call it a miracle or chance, but the very next day as Iseul rammed the paper doors open, panicking for having overslept, the very same page blew across the yard and lingered in a spot where Mi-Jung eventually found it.

"Summer wind. It is sometimes strong and unpredictable," Yeong-Hoon said to himself with a satisfied smile on his face.

Mi-Jung, who did not know how to read quite yet, could recognize that the alphabets looked like a name and a familiar one at that! She tucked it in her sleeve and forgot all about it until it fell out on the floor when she reached the Golden Palace with a shiny new letter to send to Byung-Guk.

Mr. Lim was quite busy that day. The mailmen and the mail truck was due to arrive sometime in the afternoon and he was still scrambling to sort through letters.

"Still more letters?" Mr. Lim said, flustered as he grabbed another pile. He sometimes wished he had more time, then perhaps he could open a few of the letters Mi-Jung was so obviously sending to his son. He resisted the urge.

Mi-Jung picked up the letter on the ground and suddenly remembered the strange page she had chanced upon earlier in the day. She handed it over to Mr. Lim who was somewhat irritated by Mi-Jung stopping his work flow.

"What is it?" Mr. Lim said.

"I found this letter on the ground and thought it might be a letter to or from someone," she said.

A quick glance and then a double take on the image was all it took for Mr. Lim to come to a standstill.

"I see," he said, as he took the page and inspected it closely. "Not to worry dear, I'll take care good care of it."

"Who is it for?" Mi-Jung asked.

"Oh, I think that's for the scholar's grandson," he blurted, preoccupied.

He was searching for something. He was sure he had left it on the table, perhaps near the radio. He traced his steps with his memory. *Yes, it must be here since I took the message by radio.* He unceremoniously swept the organized pile of letters to one corner of the desk and held up a slip of paper.

"Here it is!" Mr. Lim said, a little too exuberantly.

"What?" Mi-Jung said, just as excited.

Mr. Lim came to his senses. *How foolish of him? This was supposed to be a secret!* "Nothing," he said, rather quickly.

Mi-Jung turned around to leave, scratching her head at the whole endeavor. Why would the scholar draw a picture when he could write so well? And come to think of it, she was sure the handwriting looked too childish to be the scholar's.

As soon as Mi-Jung shut the door behind her, Byung-Guk's father scrambled to find an envelope for Iseul's drawing and wrote on it in clear bold letters:

KIM, JUNG-SOO
18th Regiment Infantry
The Republic of Korea Armed Forces

"It took her long enough," he said under his breath as he sealed it and placed it on top of the pile, nearest to the exit.

CHAPTER 24

The mailmen came and took the letters like clockwork as Mr. Lim anxiously watched that special letter disappear deep into the truck. He should have thought about it before he placed Iseul's letter first in line to be taken. Too late now.

The Post-Office division of the 40th Infantry had their work cut out for them. When the North Koreans had pushed the South all the way down to Naktong River, the men of the 40th Infantry had always found a road less traveled to reach Yeoju. Even when the South had managed to push the North past the 38th parallel, their task became a juggling act tracing the routes that each regiment took to send the appropriate mailmen into battlefields where soldiers fought hard, hoping to return to sweet words from their loved ones. The mailmen were soldiers too, like the rest of them, though they often took lonesome journeys at great lengths. They were often mistaken as spies or equipment suppliers, hence creating a sizable number of untimely deaths due to targeted attacks.

It was a pity for the men who died carrying but words on sheets of paper that were often left blank.

But the lucky soldier who had been assigned to the Wasteland of Yeoju had the nerve of steel and a stubbornness unmatched by anyone else in his division. This fool had made it out of enemy borders alive just to brave the same precarious border to deliver the next batch on time.

"He's going to get blown up one of these days," one soldier said at the post-office division headquarters, sucking in another mouthful of cigarette smoke.

"You think?" another soldier said, nervously.

"I bet you, he will." The mailmen stubbed out the cigarette bud on the sole of his boot. "I guess it's my turn."

The soldier headed towards the truck with an empty backpack to fill. He was happy to know his next round would be to deliver mail on foot to the 18th Infantry further south and away from the main battle fronts. The 18th Infantry was on the move, or so he heard. It was heading northeast, much to his dismay.

"The letters should already be organized by infantry. The man in the rice village does it well." the truck driver said as he let the designated mailmen for each infantry come and collect their respective loads.

"Double check so you're not grabbing from another pile."

"These darn envelopes are so thick, they're about to burst! Where are they getting all this paper from?"

"Idiot, they've been making paper for all of us!"

"Huh? Making paper?"

The soldier found his pile in the deepest end of the truck. "Go figure," he grunted and jumped in.

The load was heavier than the soldier was used to. He strapped his backpack on tighter, crawled out of the den of the truck and began walking. He would be walking for many days; there was no need to hurry about it.

"Wait, wait!" A voice grew louder from behind. The soldier looked back to find the truck driver running towards him, waving a single letter. "You forgot one! I told you to double check," he said, out of breath.

"Oh yeah, sorry. You could have just left it for the next round."

The truck driver frowned and whacked him with the letter. "There may never be another round!"

***

The 18th Infantry had been on the move the past few days, making the last leg of the trek back to home base all the more difficult. Jung-Soo and Dae-Gun had gone further northeast, moving further and further away from the 5th Cavalry Regiment, and closer to Gangwon Province.

It had been a difficult week. Torrential rains drenched them to the bone, forcing the two to dry their clothes against the heat of the fire. They stripped down to their underwear, trying not to look at each other while they were in such vulnerable states.

Jung-Soo wrung out his clothes a second time. It was risky to make a fire so close to the base; he wanted to put it out within the hour. They had been thoroughly warned of spies that roamed the outskirts of army bases, tracking its movement and looking for suspicious activities.

Jung-Soo had added the commander's code into his breast pocket collection with a box of matches in his right side pocket, just in case he needed to burn the codes.

Dae-Gun shook his tin case of salt that was nearly empty and let out a sigh.

"I told you to go easy on the salt."

"Yeah, yeah…" he said grumpily.

Ever since Jung-Soo had been in charge of the food supply, Dae-Gun seemed to have been losing a bit of weight, though his steps seemed to slow in contempt.

The tent was made and their clothes were nearly dry. They had long since read through all the mail allotted to them, and even Dae-Gun wouldn't dare pull out his guitar since the soldier on the other end of the radio had warned them of wandering spies. So these days, Dae-Gun twiddled his thumbs until his soft snores were the only tune that accompanied Jung-Soo's nightly ritual of writing.

That night, something kept Dae-Gun awake. It may have been the humid night air that clung to his bare chest or his stomach that seemed to stick closer and closer to his spine. And so, Dae-Gun watched Jung-Soo as his hand moved furiously on the page.

He was a curious fellow, this boy called Kim Jung-Soo. He had spent weeks alone with him, still, he knew nothing more than the fact of his daily writing rituals. Sure, he was a talented radio engineer and an excellent sniper. He wrote letters and whatever it was about, it seemed to have him consumed from the moment he put his spoon down to when he fell asleep.

Of course, there was that one habit only Dae-Gun knew— sleep-talking. Dae-Gun would wake in the night to hear two words on repeat: guitar and a two-syllable word that sounded a lot like a name—Iseul, a female name. Dae-Gun had imagined the entirety of Jung-Soo's past. He was a son of commander, taught to kill as soon as he was born. Of course, he would have had women flock to him.

That much, he was certain of. Iseul must be the one he loved, the one he wrote all those letters to—a beautiful woman who had managed to win Jung-Soo's rather cold heart.

"She must be real beautiful…"

"Huh?" Jung-Soo said, looking up from his page.

"What?" Dae-Gun didn't realize he had spoken out loud. "Oh, nothing," he said, averting his eyes to the damp forest floor.

Dae-Gun looked awkward, sitting there staring at the wet leaves under his foot. Jung-Soo always thought the boy seemed a bit lacking in intellect, of which he was somewhat grateful for. He swiftly glanced at Dae-Gun and back at his page again. Maybe Dae-Gun wanted some too.

"Do you want one?" Jung-Soo said, reluctantly reaching towards Dae-Gun with a single blank sheet of paper.

"That's alright. I have nothing to write anyway."

Jung-Soo took no for an answer and went back to his own page. When silence ensued longer than Jung-Soo thought was normal, peeking away from his page to find Dae-Gun still watching him with a curious stare. He felt exposed as if Dae-Gun's stares indicated he knew more than he should.

"Why don't you write back home to your orphanage?" Jung-Soo said, trying to divert the attention away from himself. "The white grandfather who gave you that guitar—why don't you write him a letter?"

"They're gone. They went back to America as soon as they heard rumors of war."

"And what about your brothers, I mean, the other kids at the orphanage?"

"All the boys who were old enough were conscripted, and the younger ones were left to fend for themselves. We were the lucky ones to be housed and fed by the army."

Jung-Soo averted his eyes back to his page again, tucking in that precious page back into his pocket. He couldn't have ever imagined that being conscripted into the army could be considered a fortune. After all that talk, Dae-Gun still seemed to be piercing through Jung-Soo.

"Remember when I called you coward for not sending all those letters?"

"Yeah," Jung-Soo said, as if wasn't a sore spot.

"I think I understand what you mean by giving someone false

hope."

Dae-Gun felt courage rising as he almost felt ready to appease the curiosity that had been nagging him from the moment they had embarked on their mission together. Who was this soldier called Kim Jung-Soo? So many secrets and words left unspoken. But most of all, he wanted to help—to reduce the burden that seemed to haunt Jung-Soo even as he slept.

"Who is Iseul and why are you so obsessed with my guitar?" Dae-Gun asked, quite assertively and certainly louder than he had anticipated. The question seemed to ring through the branches and thick trunks of the forest.

Jung-Soo froze, afraid to look up, and afraid to answer. Still, Dae-Gun waited. He worried about what Jung-Soo might do. He glanced towards their rifles that still leaned against the log, out of reach, then realized the rifle was the least of his worries. A small object protruded from Jung-Soo's belt: his handgun.

Dae-Gun took a deep breath, which broadened his shoulders. "You're lucky to have someone waiting for you, hoping and praying for you to safely return home. Home..." Dae-Gun muttered. It was a word that had always perplexed him. He did not have one, at least not in the traditional sense, and anyone who he considered family had always been flexible with so many people coming and in and out of his orphanage.

Dae-Gun began thinking aloud. "Mom. Dad. Did you know those weren't my first words? In fact, I wasn't even speaking my own language when I first spoke!" Dae-Gun could feel the fire in his chest of the truth that he had kept hidden for fear that it would eat him up alive. Somehow, this soldier—this boy who seemed to care more for his guitar than he cared for his own partner—had managed to open the floodgates.

"Who cares if a poor orphan boy dies in battle?" Dae-Gun continued. "No one will mourn for me when I die! But you... you still have hope. You still have someone waiting for you, someone you care for deeply. Write!" Dae-Gun stated. "Write when you can, when you're still alive and have the strength to do so. At least then, when this is all said and done, you will be able to go back to her with a clear conscience, knowing that you did everything you could."

When Dae-Gun finally stopped to take a breath, he came to his senses. The silence seemed to hang in the air, like the damp that clung to their clothes.

Jung-Soo wanted to scream at him, tell him that no one was waiting for him too…that he had blown it with Iseul and he was an orphan and a traitorous one at that! People would not even pity him; they would celebrate at the news of his death. Perhaps even the girl he loved would join in the celebrations if she were even still alive.

Dae-Gun's last words echoed in Jung-Soo's mind. '*You did everything you could…*' Did he do everything? He could beg and plead, grovel at the feet of those his father's people had burned to death in the village, make excuses to Iseul about how he never knew of his father's plans. That was a lie—he had always known something was amiss. He should have done something. He was a coward, just like his father, who would never own up to the pain that they caused to unsuspecting people.

"Alright." Jung-Soo cut through. He folded his sheets of paper like he always did, down the middle then sideways, sticking his stubby pencil into a crevice made by the folds.

Jung-Soo thought he had done a better job masking his strange fascination with the guitar. Dae-Gun was sharper than he gave him credit for. It was too late now to cover it up and bringing it up again would only entice more questions.

Sitting there with the summer night's wind on his back and a fire that was about to be snuffed out, Jung-Soo wondered if it was a good idea to be so secretive with his partner. Autumn would be upon them in just a few weeks, and then the wintry chills. Even worse, the North Koreans were coming. It would be weeks at most, perhaps even days till they would initiate a massive attack.

"Besides," Dae-Gun said awkwardly trying to continue the conversation. "It seems you won't have to worry about how much paper you're using so go ahead and write as many letters as you'd like."

Jung-Soo's ears perked up. "What do you mean?" It was insignificant news, compared to the scale of what loomed before them. But it was nevertheless news he welcomed.

"Sergeant Jones mentioned something about a local village producing paper, enough to overtake imports from America. Paper village. Have you heard of it?"

"No," Jung-Soo said, still fascinated. Paper village. The image of Iseul falling asleep on her workshop stool as she made paper crossed his mind.

"I overheard a few soldiers at the 5th Cavalry Regiment the

other night. Even the American soldiers were talking about it. Apparently, the women in this village have been sending letters to their loved ones."

Jung-Soo couldn't understand why this was news; of course loved ones would send letters.

Dae-Gun continued. "But the strange thing is, they're sending out mostly blank pages in thick envelopes, enough for most camps to share a page with every soldier."

Jung-Soo found himself nodding along with the story. It was ingenious now that he thought about it. A single village would have brothers and fathers stationed in countless infantries across the peninsula.

"But the most intriguing thing is, rumor has it that the entire operation is run by an orphan girl in some rice farming village in Yeoju."

Jung-Soo nodded along as if Dae-Gun had made a good conclusion to a great story. Then he felt a nudge—a familiarity in the story he heard. *Yeoju. Orphan girl.* No, it couldn't be, could it?

"Yeoju. Did you say?" His voice quickened.

"Yeah, didn't you hear me the first time?" Dae-Gun said, somewhat irritated.

It must be then... It very well could be...

"Iseul," he said out loud.

A sting of guilt shot through his body with every beat of his heart. He was glad, yes elated by the news; Iseul was alive and well! There was nothing more he wanted than for this news to be about Iseul. Yet, what was this weight he couldn't shake off? *An orphan girl.* The phrase rung with a sudden truth to it. All his fears and speculations of what had happened that night came rushing back.

He couldn't escape it, and there was no hiding from it now. The other side of this truth stung him with even greater force than the joy that first struck him: his father had killed hers.

"Jung-Soo, Jung-Soo! Are you alright?"

There was no way of knowing who this '*orphan girl from Yeoju*' was. It could be anyone. Somehow, Jung-Soo found comfort in that. He needed to find out, sooner or later. Perhaps, when they reach base camp again, he would find out more.

Jung-Soo and Dae-Gun snuffed out the fire and laid to sleep that night, as the thin remnant of smoke still wafted in the air. They tossed and turned, unable to find a comfortable position, the ground still soggy from the rain until finally, both soldiers drifted to sleep.

When Jung-Soo woke next, a hand clasped against his nose and mouth as a firm arm wrapped around his shoulders, pulling him backward.

"Shh, shh…" someone whispered. Jung-Soo gasped for air. "I think someone's coming," the same voice said.

It was Dae-Gun. Jung-Soo willed his mind to wake from his stupor. He patted his pockets and could feel the codes and the match.

"We have to go now!" Dae-Gun pulled Jung-Soo towards their left.

Jung-Soo took a second to listen; Dae-Gun was right. He heard footsteps and voices, at least two men, coming in fast from their right. Jung-Soo could smell the ashes of the fire; they had been foolish, making one so close to their base camp. He couldn't see much, but he knew where they had left their belongings. The guitar was to his left, the radio just behind and their two backpacks far to his left.

Dae-Gun was already making his way left when Jung-Soo broke loose. Dae-Gun groaned silently. Barely audible, Jung-Soo sauntered in leaps and reached for the guitar when he spotted the light coming from what looked like a lantern.

Jung-Soo could see Dae-Gun's shadowy figure gesture wildly. Jung-Soo shot a look at the radio and the two backpacks again. He sprung to his left, grabbed a single bag pack and broke into a sprint towards the flailing figure.

"What were you thinking?" Dae-Gun said, the anger and frustration evident even as he whispered.

"I couldn't. I just couldn't…"

The ground was wet, and the moon but a sliver behind a canopy of thick branches. Dae-Gun slipped on something slick, as his arms went flailing outwards, the side of the guitar hitting a tree trunk. A dull thud of hollow wood echoed in the dead of night.

"Who is that?" a voice shouted as three shots were fired in their direction.

"They're here!" another voice added. "Why would you shoot, you fool? You just gave away our location! We lost them, you idiot!"

Their voices drowned away as Jung-Soo and Dae-Gun ran and ran until they put a safe distance between them and the mysterious men.

231

***

The trees began to thin when Jung-Soo felt the lull of safety easing into his tense muscles. Dae-Gun's stomach growled as the crescent moon made way for the sun to inch into the horizon.

"I can't believe you managed to get the guitar and my backpack but forgot the two most important things."

"The radio and the backpack full of food?"

Dae-Gun huffed and puffed in revolt.

"I had to make a split-second decision."

"Exactly…"

Jung-Soo second-guessed his decision. They needed food, but they were close enough to base camp that they wouldn't die of starvation. If their home base had moved further away from their last known location, that would be problematic; but they could still catch something, anything with the tools they had in the backpack Jung-Soo had managed to grab.

He watched Dae-Gun sulk as he followed close behind. Food could wait, but who were those soldiers? They were North Koreans by the sound of their accents. But it almost felt as if they had been looking for someone specific, not just wandering the base perimeters.

They walked some more until the moon's skeletal edge was nearly invisible against the blue sky. The distant noise of a cascade trickled towards them, as did the rhythmic beating of bells.

"Do you hear that?" Dae-Gun said, breaking the silence between them.

"No." Jung-Soo listened carefully, though it took him another minute of walking towards it to recognize the distinct bells of the wooden fish. "Monks." He finally caught on. "We're near a temple."

They had passed many temples before, yet the war-stricken areas had forced even the bravest monks to retreat south, often leaving the temples nearly empty or at the very least, refraining from ringing their ritualistic gongs.

"Yes," Dae-Gun said with a sly smile. "It means it's past five in the morning, which can only mean…" Dae-Gun waited.

"What?" Jung-Soo said. He didn't like being made a fool.

"Wild boars, of course!"

Jung-Soo ignored Dae-Gun and walked towards the sound of

a waterfall; he was thirsty.

"You're a city boy, aren't you? That's what I suspected all along. How else would you not know this common fact about boars?" Dae-Gun was ecstatic. It hadn't occurred to him till then that there was something he knew that Jung-Soo didn't, other than English of course.

He continued to babble on. "Wild boars are most active in the early hours of the morning, and they tend to roam areas with a water source. Think about it, Jung-Soo!" Dae-Gun exclaimed. "We're near a waterfall and a Buddhist temple! These creatures are smarter than you realize. They know the monks here won't harm them. It's the perfect habitat for a wild boar."

Perfect habitat or not, it would be a miracle to find one, and he wondered if his tiny handgun would make a dent on such massive beasts, which probably meant that he would have to get close to such an unpredictable animal. He could imagine the men from last night feasting on their remaining food stock as his stomach rumbled even louder.

The cascade fell like mist into a small pond that trickled into a river down the mountainside. They drank to their hearts' content. Who knew when else they would chance on a water supply again, though Jung-Soo knew their chances weren't so terrible. It was still the rainy season and they roamed mountains where water would eventually trickle down.

They made their way east again, leaving behind the cascade and the temple as the sun began beating down on them. Dae-Gun's mouth seemed to shut close as the growling of his stomach grew louder. Still, there were no signs of wild boars.

"We should have gone hunting for the boar before we headed straight to camp," he said, resentfully. "How much longer do you think we can go without food?"

Jung-Soo scanned Dae-Gun's frame. "At least a month or two for you, and maybe around three weeks for me."

Dae-Gun groaned. "I'm serious, Jung-Soo!"

"I'm always serious."

Dae-Gun collapsed right then and there, careful not to bang his guitar on the ground as he landed with a soft thud. "I can't do this anymore," he said rather dramatically. "I need to rest, to replenish or else... or else!"

Jung-Soo obliged and sat next to him. He reached to his left for his water canister to find nothing; it was attached to the other bag. He let his saliva wet the roof of his mouth.

A disturbing sound erupted from Dae-Gun's stomach—a thunderous growl that pulsed three times. Why did Dae-Gun always have to be so glaringly obvious? He felt the sting of hunger in his own stomach.

It groaned again, this time, louder than before. A gust of wind hit the side of their faces as leaves rustled with it.

"I could just sleep right now, take a little nap until the sun sets," Dae-Gun said.

Jung-Soo heard another rumble and a misplaced growl. "Shhh!" he said, with a hint of realization on his face.

"I can't help it! My stomach just does that when I'm hungry."

The grunt and squeal rang even closer, as Dae-Gun's ears shot in that direction.

"A boar..." they whispered in unison.

Jung-Soo pulled out his hand gun on his belt. The wild boar, dark and hairy, dug with its two front legs into the side of a tree trunk. Jung-Soo sauntered towards it, his heart racing as the blood seem to drain out of his face. A single shot rang far and wide, and then two others, as the noise of a squealing pig overtook the sound of bullets with a loud thud of its body hitting the ground.

Jung-Soo leaped out of the way as he sucked in a breath of air as he almost collapsed right then and there. He couldn't believe it! The boar had appeared like an apparition in front of them. Jung-Soo dug into his bag and pulled out a knife with a glare towards Dae-Gun that said 'I told you so' as he handed the blade to Dae-Gun who penitently looked away.

"Okay, okay. You were right to grab this bag instead."

Dae-Gun slashed the neck of the boar, and cut its hind legs off, placing it to the side as Jung-Soo made a fire. It didn't take long before all four legs were skewered on a stick and roasted to crispy and chewy perfection.

"If only we had a bit of salt," Dae-Gun bemoaned.

Jung-Soo's incisors cut into the red-hot meat. He chewed contently though it burned the inside of his mouth. Dae-Gun, on the other hand, waited for the meat to cool before savoring the crispy skin and finally digging into the warm juicy flesh of the hind legs.

They would have to eat quickly and move away from the fire.

Jung-Soo kept his hand close to the gun as he watched the idiot meticulously devour the leg to the bone. When they were finished, they began packing the leftover meat.

"Such a waste..." Dae-Gun said as he looked longingly at the torso of the boar they would have to leave behind.

With a few found energy, they hiked with a spring in their steps as the two front legs of the roasted boar flung on Dae-Gun's right shoulder to counterbalance the weight of the guitar on his left shoulder.

CHAPTER 25

It was dawn the next morning when Iseul woke pleasantly from her sleep. It had been a while since she had slept through the night and it seemed the unbearably hot and stuffy summer nights were over.

"That's weird," she said, standing on her porch as she looked into her room. Something seemed out of place—something she seemed to have forgotten for quite a while. Iseul looked for the sheet of paper with the funny drawing of Jung-Soo holding that peculiar instrument he liked so much. "I'm sure I put it under the mattress." She scratched her head.

"Iseul! Iseul!" It was Mi-Jung, running towards her at full speed. "Come quick, Kyung-Hee is leaving with her grandmother."

"What, already?" She put on the upper layer of her hanbok and stumbled into her yard.

Mi-Jung nodded. "We're all saying goodbye to her by the west gate," she said, turning around to head back down the hill again.

A few other early risers huddled in a group around the two wooden pillars of the west gate that stood both high and wide in an array of colors.

"Kyung-Hee!" Mi-Jung waved at the young girl who carried sacks on her shoulder and head. "We're here! We're here to say goodbye!"

It was a tearful exchange, and the ones who would leave in mass in just a few weeks would not be so lucky to have such closure. Most of those who left had nothing in Yeoju to look forward to. A week before, a letter had been returned to its sender with an official document attached; Kyung-Hee's father had died in battle two weeks before.

The journey south would be treacherous. Even as Kyung-Hee exited the pillars, two mountains loomed ahead of them before they would reach the road that led south. The figures shrunk and completely disappeared.

"Do you think they will make it?" Iseul said to Yeong-Hoon, who had followed her into the village.

"I don't doubt it," Yeong-Hoon said. "They know the mountain roads well and Kyung-Hee is strong. She'll take good care of her mother."

Iseul stood in place a little longer, watching as she pictured the two further along than they really were. "I hope so. We'll meet again soon," Iseul concluded, as she turned back towards the village square.

She had been feeling quite strange that morning like something was missing. Strange how saying goodbye could do that to you. Of course, she had long forgotten about the stray piece of paper by then. Iseul looked around at the ghost of what her village used to be. She hadn't been down here in a long while, perhaps not once since they had begun their paper production.

A gust of wind lifted up the top layer of arid soil in a whirlwind of dust. It would be a hot day and the paper would dry faster. The group of women had already reached the eastern pillars with Mi-Jung leading the way, as they took a left up to the hillside roads.

"You know what could be a great idea?" Yeong-Hoon said.

"What?"

"You haven't been to see Mr. Lim in a while. You know he's been working hard to get all the letters out to the soldiers."

It struck her as an excellent idea. She was already in the village anyway and the women knew what to do; they were experts at their tasks by now.

The Golden Palace gleamed in the sunlight, the summer rainstorms washing away any remnant of ash and dust on the crevices of the building. It looked almost like it used to. Yeong-Hoon wandered away like he sometimes does. He was headed towards the food shed on the other end of the Golden Palace. The soldiers no longer occupied the space and had left the stores empty, not a single person standing in line for rations anymore.

Just beyond, the butcher's wife was bent over harvesting what little rice remained in the fields with a cloth over her head to block the sun.

Mr. Lim waved at her from behind the desk. "Iseul, Iseul! What a pleasant surprise!" He jumped out of his chair and ran to greet her.

"Hello, Mr. Lim," Iseul bowed to greet him, but when she stood upright again, Mr. Lim had disappeared behind towers of envelopes. She scanned left to right at the stacks that extended from wall to wall with her mouth agape. She knew they had been churning out pages daily for the past few weeks and months, but she had never stopped to imagine them in actual use. Pride swelled up in her as did her shoulders and then a sense of conviction. Surely there would be more soldiers than the number of pages in this room. It was a start, a very good start.

"How have you been?" he asked, as he picked up a pile and moved it aside. "You must be so busy lately. Are you getting enough food up there? Did I ever mention that you've been doing such a great job?"

Iseul chuckled at the frenetic Mr. Lim she was used to seeing. "Yes, I've been doing well, thank you."

He popped back out from behind the tower. "We've just got the mail yesterday, so I thought there might be one for you."

"For me?" she said, pointing an awkward finger at herself.

"But I'm afraid not. Next batch, I hope."

"I see," Iseul said, confused. Why would she be getting mail? Perhaps his son Byung-Guk wanted to write to her to make amends for what had happened. She sighed. It seemed like a lifetime ago, and she held no grudges.

"How is Byung-Guk doing?"

"Good! Excellent even. They seem to be feeding them well enough down south," he said, proud as ever.

Out of the corner of her eye, she could see Yeong-Hoon rummaging through the storehouse, picking up a hoe and a shovel and tossing it aside. Perhaps he found something to eat.

Iseul wondered how long they would last. None of them complained, but the village was already barren and barely anything was left to be scavenged in the forest and fields. Soon, winter will be upon them and the soil will freeze over. Where will they get water to make paper when the river freezes over? They were already struggling to bring in water from the nearby river with more and more people leaving every week.

Mr. Lim pulled the radio closer and began twisting the radio dials. His concentration accentuated the creases on his forehead and left sags that drooped beneath his eye. It didn't seem like he had been getting enough to eat either.

"I should get going now. Take care of yourself, Mr. Lim," Iseul said.

"Yes, of course! Please do visit me more often," he said with a fatherly tenderness. He seemed rather consumed by the task at hand. The radio gave out a weak hiss as he moved on to the next channel. Iseul bowed, though she didn't think Mr. Lim saw her.

"Did you find something in the food stores?" Iseul asked Yeong-Hoon as she joined him on the road that led back home.

Yeong-Hoon pulled out an apple from behind his back, hiding the rotten side so that it almost looked untarnished.

"Where did you find that?" Iseul exclaimed.

"I have my ways," he said, cheekily, like he always did. He hobbled in front of her and blocked her way. He split the apple straight in the middle with his bare hands.

Father. Iseul thought. It was something he used to do to make them share.

"Here," he said, handing her the good piece.

The sting of *missing* grew stronger. She took a bite when she felt her eyes burning, a cascade soon to fall. Iseul overtook Yeong-Hoon and paced ahead of him so her back was to him.

"Well, come along then," Iseul said with as much cheerfulness as she could muster.

That was all they could do now—move forward, full steam ahead.

***

"I wonder if we are closer to the east or the west sea," Dae-Gun mentioned one day as they hiked down the final mountain.

Jung-Soo held a map ahead of him, checking every so often at the coordinates he had written down for the camp's location. The 18th Infantry was sure to have moved in the past two days since they lost their radio, but an army that size couldn't have gone too far.

"East or west?" Dae-Gun repeated.

"Huh?" Jung-Soo hadn't been paying attention.

"I liked living near the East Sea, though I've never been to the West Sea," Dae-Gun continued.

Jung-Soo couldn't think of a single reason why the sea was on Dae-Gun's mind that day. In all honesty, if Dae-Gun continued blabbering on, Jung-Soo thought he would rather hike all the way down to the South Sea and back again than to take another day of his incessant talk. He glanced at the boar leg that swung and imagined tossing it into the sea for Dae-Gun to fetch.

"The women go out to fish there, diving into the water to catch all kinds of seafood with their bare hands! Can you believe it? With their bare hands! And when me and the other boys would visit the ocean, they would wave for us to come over and would gut the fish right then and there for us to eat. It's the freshest raw fish you'll ever taste!"

Jung-Soo liked raw fish too. He had had plenty of it when he lived in Seoul and when his father had hosted the Japanese. Yet, the ocean…it was not a place he had seen. He heard about the sound of the tide and seagulls near the shores. He heard there was sand uncountable and the air tasted like salt. Come to think of it, he wouldn't mind visiting such a place, though he wondered, for a brief moment, if he would feel trapped when he finally saw the edge of Korean soil meeting an infinite body of water with nowhere else to run from their enemies, just as he often felt trapped by the mountains that surrounded him.

"Jung-Soo, Jung-Soo are you listening?" Dae-Gun finally said, irritated.

"Yeah, I get it. You want to go to the ocean."

"No, not the ocean, I mean look!" Dae-Gun pointed straight ahead.

Smoke rose like it did when they reached the 5th Cavalry Regiment, as the two saw tips of tents poking into the sky. Soldiers, marched in groups all around the base.

"We're home!" Dae-Gun exclaimed.

Jung-Soo looked down on his map and the coordinates. They had arrived much sooner than they had anticipated. The 18th Infantry must have heard the news of North Koreans gathering towards Gangwon Province and must have been marching east towards them.

"What's the matter? Come on!" Dae-Gun skipped forward, leading the way for the first time since they had left camp.

Jung-Soo let his worries go, at least for the time being. He felt the weight of the pages that flopped in his pocket with every step he took. Yes, he was right where he belonged. Soon, the pages will not be his burden to carry and the codes will safely be delivered into the commander's hands.

Yet, the thought that had been festering in his mind, reared its impatient head again—the shoe string, the guitar, and the final piece of the puzzle to put together an accurate sketch for Iseul. He had put it off because of the hunger and the rain. Perhaps he didn't want to taint the delicate fibers of the page and smudge whatever he had already written. They were so close to camp anyway and perhaps he'd be able to find an actual ruler that would give a more precise measurement.

"Hey, Jung-Soo," Dae-Gun said in a dreamy nostalgic tone. He had been speaking for a while, but Jung-Soo had managed to block him out. "When this is over, you know, all this spy business and war, would you like to go see the west sea with me?" Dae-Gun spoke with sincerity.

"Sure," Jung-Soo answered nonchalantly.

The narrow dusty road they had been on expanded into a larger road where multiple tire tracks marked the comings and goings of trucks and tanks. The camp looked awfully large compared to how it was before, the roads wider and the camp fully equipped with tents that had previously been missing. It was almost as grand as the 5th Cavalry Regiment. It seemed supplies from America had also reached Korean infantries, just as Sergeant Jones had said.

So much had changed since they had last been at their own base camp. They had lost contact days ago and both commanders knew they carried the codes. There was no saying that they hadn't already been branded traitors in the meantime. Jung-Soo's pace slowed as he rolled his fist into a ball. Maybe Dae-Gun had an inkling of what was about to happen. Maybe that's why he was babbling on and on about the sea.

The soldier who guarded the entrance witnessed the arrival of two soldiers he did not recognize. He shot two warning fires and then shouted at them to hold their positions. Jung-Soo and Dae-Gun froze, afraid to even look at each other. It was another hour, sweating under the sweltering summer heat before another soldier came running towards the front gate.

"Kim Jung-Soo and Park Dae-Gun?" the soldier asked from

afar. Jung-Soo recognized the voice. It was the man on the radio.

"Yes!" Dae-Gun replied. "We're back. We're back from our mission!"

"Please verify your access code," the soldier asked sternly.

"Access code 901882," Jung-Soo said.

The two soldiers were escorted straight to the commander's tent. Outside, stood the colonel who had been the one to send them off. With a brisk hand gesture, soldiers surrounded both Jung-Soo and Dae-Gun as they patted the two soldiers, searching for weapons.

"Soldiers, welcome back!" the commander said with a certain unease. The escorts remained fixed next to the commander, as they heard footsteps that neared the tent. *More soldiers standing guard.*

Jung-Soo made certain not to make sudden movements, raising both hands ever so slightly as one dipped one into his front pocket to pull out a piece of paper no bigger than the back of his hand. Out of the corner of his eye, Jung-Soo saw the enigma machine, pulled out and dismantled.

"The codes from Commander Rogers, sir," he said, slowly handing it to the commander who took it in haste. He broke the seal and glanced down at it, puzzled and then looked in the direction of the enigma machine.

"Excellent work, soldiers," the commander said in a tone that verged on satisfaction. "You may all be excused." He placed his reading glasses on the bridge of his nose and took his seat, his eyes fixed on the page.

Jung-Soo sighed in relief, though the colonel still looked suspiciously at them.

"Kim Jung-Soo, was it?" the commander said as Jung-Soo was about to exit. "Why don't you take a seat here with me?"

The lump in his throat returned. Jung-Soo strode past the colonel who looked rather perplexed, loitering even after the last soldiers had exited.

"I'll be fine, Colonel." the commander waved him out.

With the codes still firm in his grasp, the commander unlocked a drawer and pulled out a second sheet.

"Do you know what this is?" he asked, holding out the second sheet.

It looked just like the ones he had carried. It wasn't time to play dumb.

"Sir, are they codes?" Jung-Soo asked.

The commander smirked as the side of his lips twisted upwards. "Good." He paused, still looking—examining him like a specimen. "Take another guess."

Why would the commander have a second set of codes? As far as he knew, the 18th Infantry was one the largest South Korean infantries with over ten others that followed its chain of command. The same went for the 5th Cavalry that acted as a command hub, coordinating twice as many infantries from various nations that came under the U.N. command. It seemed unlikely that a second set of codes would be sent between these two command posts unless multiple messages were being sent to the same post as a safety measure. It seemed unlikely, considering the risk of exposure.

Unless they were... "Sir, they are the real codes," Jung-Soo blurted as the thought came to him. Perhaps his intuition had been correct all along and the commander knew something of his past—something that made him suspicious of Jung-Soo's fealty, so had placed him on a trial mission.

"You're a smart one, you," the commander continued. "Reminds me of someone I used to know. It's a shame those smartest pledge their allegiance to none but their ideas."

Jung-Soo did not speak. He needed to be careful.

"Soldier, do you know why so many soldiers fell that first week when the North pushed past the 38th parallel?"

"No, sir," Jung-Soo said.

"Many fell in battle, that is true," the commander continued. "But the dead do not speak, nor do they harm our cause. The real threat is that many defected to the North when they saw the tides of this war turn." He paused to examine Jung-Soo. "Do you know what happened to the ones who were caught defecting, soldier?"

"Yes, sir. They were executed and rightfully so, sir," Jung-Soo said, poised.

"Do you know what I'm trying to say?" he said, rising from his seat and taking his time to walk towards Jung-Soo. "Kim Jung-Soo, your primary duty is to the Armed Forces of the Republic of Korea. Is that clear?"

"Yes, sir," Jung-Soo said, his face ever so slightly twitching.

"Strange..." the commander said. "You came highly recommended. It was a favor of sorts for an old friend. I have other specialists, radio technicians who would have been perfectly suited for this mission. Any idea who might have wanted you on the job?"

He seemed genuinely curious.

It came as a shock to Jung-Soo too. Recommended? By who? Jung-Soo never understood how the army found out about his radio tinkering habits, nor about why he had been chosen. Perhaps the Captain, or his father? But his father had died in the fire and he hadn't heard from the Captain since that night. Perhaps the Captain was still alive, he hoped, and was still orchestrating Jung-Soo's comings and goings. His hopeful thoughts turned sour. It didn't make sense. Even if the captain or his father were alive, which he doubted they were, why would they go through the trouble of placing him in such a place of scrutiny when he was perfectly disguised as an ordinary South Korean soldier? Something else was brewing.

"No, sir," Jung-Soo lied.

"Yes, of course. Commander Rogers at the 5th Cavalry Regiment seems to trust the both of you, which is always a necessity in such a delicate situation."

The white commander had been pleasant, but Jung-Soo was sure he had expressed some suspicions about him. Or was it his own paranoia that had projected onto the situation?

"Sir, if I may ask."

"Ask away, soldier," the commander said, enthusiastically.

"If those are the real codes. What did Commander Rogers give me?"

He waved the first codes at Jung-Soo. "Codes of other sorts, not for the Enigma, but a way of letting me know whether or not the two of you would be suitable as our liaison officers. He's let me know that you are fully aware of the North Korean movements in the east. As you know, we are dealing with something much bigger and potentially costlier than those first few weeks."

So it was true. It had been a test—a mission to see if they would be loyal, which he was certain they had been.

"Commander Lee," a voice interrupted. It was the colonel again.

"Come in."

The colonel entered and whispered news into the commander's ears and was excused again.

"I hear you're quite the writer," the commander said, eyeing the bulge in his front pocket. *Dae-Gun. He cracked.* The commander neared and plucked the folded sheets. For the first time, he was glad that he didn't have enough paper to write, making his writing barely legible.

"A poet, I see," the commander added.

There was nothing to hide in those scribbles, though Jung-Soo blushed. He waited for the commander to flip to the last page, which was the whitest of them all.

"An instrument, is it?" The commander squinted at the sketch, and then his eyes widened in realization.

"A guitar, sir," Jung-Soo answered. "It's the one that Dae-Gun carries around with him."

"Ah, yes. I remember. He used to play with the band here. It's a shame the band no longer exists."

"Dae-Gun would be sad to hear that, sir." He could imagine instruments scattered all across the Peninsula where the infantry had been, buried in the memories of the musicians who fell in battle.

"Any particular reason why you're so fascinated with the guitar?" he probed as if he had a new lead.

"I was just trying my hand at drawing, sir." He lied. He was glad he hadn't yet put down the measurement numbers on it. He could imagine how that might seem suspicious to the commander who now interrogated him as a spy.

The commander's forehead flattened again. "Perhaps your talents lie elsewhere," he added, before folding the pages and handing it back to Jung-Soo.

There was nothing more the commander could ask. Perhaps a word with the orphan was in order, but it seemed the colonel had him under control. That orphan boy was as harmless as they came, but the one sat in front of him with vacant eyes seemed to be more trouble than he's worth. *The guitar*, he thought. There must be some significance as to why the boy was surrounded by images and people with the instrument. A code perhaps? There was no way to know for sure. Perhaps he would confess with a little coaxing, though the image of his beloved mentor came to mind. He wouldn't be happy to hear that he had tortured some high-level official's son. He had still to wrap his head around why the boy had come so highly recommended, let alone whose precious son he was. He resolved to ask his mentor in a few weeks when they were due to meet.

Jung-Soo began to wonder what else the commander would want from him. Would he send them back out? Had they passed the test? If not, what would happen to them now? The commander turned around, as if to hide his face from him, and after some time looking at the inside fabric of the tent, he spoke.

"You are excused, Kim Jung-Soo. You and the orphan will resume your posts tomorrow." He paced around his tent for a while longer before handing Jung-Soo another envelope, just like the one he had given to the commander. "As per usual, they must be hand delivered no later than the first of December. This is no practice run. If you fail, one of our major lines of communication will be lost," he said in an official tone. "Do yourself a favor," the commander added as Jung-Soo tilted his head towards him. "Think less, and do as you're told. That's my advice to you, son."

Dae-Gun waited anxiously outside the commander's tent, standing between two soldiers and the colonel. The colonel still didn't seem fully satisfied with their interrogations as his stare lingered longer than was natural.

"You're lucky because we caught the spies responsible for handing over the codes to the Chinese last week," he said, watching their reaction like a hawk. The colonel stepped away as the soldiers followed him, leaving Jung-Soo and Dae-Gun alone for the first time since they had set foot on the 18th Infantry division base.

Dae-Gun sucked in a breath as if he had been holding it in for hours. "Spies! Can you believe it? Did the commander put you in a cell too? Torture information out of you? It was horrifying, just like the rooms we heard about when the Japanese were here!"

Dae-Gun was paler than usual, though a quick scan showed no physical damage.

"You'll be fine," Jung-Soo said. But with a hint of a glare, he couldn't help but ask, "Really? Did you have to tell them about... the letters?"

Dae-Gun broke down in a tirade. "I'm so sorry, I cracked. I really didn't want to, but they put me in one of those torture boxes! You know, the ones where your knees can't bend so you can't sit down. I had to! I'm claustrophobic and I thought I'd die!"

Jung-Soo had seen them before—coffin like structures that tapered slim near the knees so that it would lock in place. It would take hours, if not days before the muscles would constrict and the pain would set in.

Jung-Soo released his glare. "You're forgiven," he said. "Isn't that what your priests do at church if you confess?"

"No," he rolled his eyes. "That's at the Catholic churches. Our missionaries are Protestants."

"Oh," Jung-Soo said as if he should have known about the subtle differences in western religion. He hadn't a clue. He was born a Korean, raised by a communist, and was surrounded by Buddhists. "Well, it's a good thing we don't have anything to hide, or else we would not be speaking of confessions now."

A chill ran down Dae-Gun's spine. "Yeah," he said weakly, holding his guitar close to him.

"Tomorrow, we will be dispatched again," Jung-Soo stated their orders. He looked around the camp that seemed to bustle in unison. A soldier to his left was gathering his belongings to pack, as a few others were dismantling tents.

"What? Already?" Dae-Gun said.

"Yes, so we'd better stock up. Do what you have to do before we leave," Jung-Soo said. And all the better that they leave soon. The camp would soon be up in arms again, heading northeast, most likely to match the North Korean and Chinese forces pouring into the region.

His mind trailed to the single sheet of paper in his front pocket as he eyed Dae-Gun's guitar. "Do you mind if I see your guitar?"

Dae-Gun was speechless. Jung-Soo had made such an effort to guise his obsession for all those weeks, but he asked now with a sudden nonchalance that took Dae-Gun aback. What had happened in the commander's tent?

"Sure," Dae-Gun said, more than happy to entrust his guitar in Jung-Soo's care.

Jung-Soo didn't seem particularly interested in hiding the facts from Dae-Gun now that his obsession had already been found and even reported to the commander. His cheeks flushed again at the embarrassing thought. He found the nearest table and sat there, unfolding the piece of paper and unraveling the guitar from its fabric. Perhaps today will be the day he would finally send out the letter. He wondered how long it would take before the commander figures out whose son he is. Maybe he already knew. How much longer till his own execution?

Dae-Gun stood watching, wondering and imagining that special someone who would be on the receiving end of the letter. He sighed, as he could sense pride rising in him for having done his part in the exchange.

They had come a long way to get back to home base. He

scanned the camp. So much had changed and the base looked like a larger version of the one they had just come from, not the scrawny half-built camp in his memory. Perhaps the tide of this war was finally shifting in their favor.

The sound of men laughing filtered from within the tents as the distant sound of shells reached Dae-Gun. Soon, it will be dinner time and the boys in his band would begin their warm-up routine. Dae-Gun wandered east of the camp, searching for his old mates when a glint of a golden brass object caught his eye.

CHAPTER 26

Whatever notions Jung-Soo had about searching for another ruler was abandoned after his encounter with the commander as Jung-Soo reverted to his original idea. He dug deep into his pockets to feel for the strand of shoelace and unfolded the sketch of Dae-Gun's guitar. With a pencil, he marked the shoelace in increments, folding it in half, and then another half, taking the measurements of the guitar from the neck to the base.

Jung-Soo held the page out in front of him. It looked about right, though he was certain the measurements were not entirely accurate. He neatly rolled up the shoelace and placed it deep within his pocket again. From afar, he saw Dae-Gun approaching with what looked like a trumpet.

"I'm sorry," Jung-Soo said. He returned the guitar to its

rightful owner.

"I'm going to put it back," Dae-Gun said. "I just wanted to hold it for a while."

"I know. Take your time."

Dae-Gun slouched in a chair nearby, visibly forlorn. He looked over at Jung-Soo's picture and squinted. Dae-Gun was about to tell him how terrible of an artist he was when he realized he quite liked the picture—it had personality.

"Is that for me?" Dae-Gun said, attempting to divert his attention away from his fallen brother.

"No," Jung-Soo said too quickly. "I mean, I can draw one for you if you'd like, but…

"Don't worry. I know who it's for. She'll love it."

They watched as soldiers with both familiar and unfamiliar faces walked to and from various tents. Many of them had their pockets shoved full of what looked like wads of paper. Jung-Soo thought of the one girl who might be responsible for the skip in the soldiers' steps. He felt oddly close to Iseul, which may have had something to do with the completed sketch he held tight in one hand.

A new tent had emerged at the 18th Infantry base with a sign that read: "Administration." The post office would be here and maybe he would be able to figure out where to get supplies. Jung-Soo entered.

Inside, the tent bustled with soldiers who sat in front of desks with boxes and shelves behind them. A soldier entered behind him, knocking him by the shoulder. A single page fell from to the ground.
"

I'm sorry," he said with a cheeky smile on his face.

Jung-Soo picked the page from the ground as he noticed the soldier held multiple sheets of paper in his hand. A shot of envy flooded him. *Soon,* Jung-Soo hoped. He looked down at the page and rubbed it between his fingers. It felt awfully familiar. *Iseul.* He was almost certain it was Iseul those rumors of the paper village was about! He might even receive a large wad like the one the soldier held in the near future. He didn't read what was on the page, but he knew the soldier had written in large bold letters, filling at least five sheets of paper.

The soldier behind the desk impatiently waved at the one that had just come in. "Hurry now, the truck is about to leave. If you have something to send, you'd better do it quickly."

The soldier took the sheet back from Jung-Soo as he paced towards the desk and handed over his sheets of paper.

"Address?"

"129 Dalseo-gu, Daegu," he recited, and in a quick and efficient fashion, the pages were sealed in an envelope and dropped into a pile behind him.

"Next," the soldier said, directed at Jung-Soo.

It took a while for Jung-Soo to realize the soldier was talking to him. The man waited with his arms outstretched and his head fixed on the table, pushing papers. Jung-Soo fumbled through his front pocket and fished out that single piece of paper with the guitar sketch he had just completed.

"Addre...," the soldier stopped when he saw the sketch, sighed and shook his head. "Such a shame! And to think just last month, we were fighting each other for scraps of paper to write with. Now, this?"

He finally looked at Jung-Soo. "Name and address."

Jung-Soo was at a loss for words. "Kim, Jung-Soo, Yeoju, Gyung-Gi Do..."

The soldier's eyebrow edged up, his hand moving quickly to fold the page in half. "Kim Jung-Soo, Jung-Soo...that sounds familiar." He pulled an envelope from beneath a pile. "Ah, that's what I thought! Where have you been? We've been wondering if we should send the letter back since you haven't come to collect it."

The soldier handed him a thin envelope. On the front was a familiar name. *It can't be. Iseul.* He read her name on the envelope. But how did she know? He was supposed to be dead.

"You should thank the commander. He took one look at it and said to keep it around."

The commander? What had he seen inside? Jung-Soo flipped the envelope over to find the seal had already been broken as the flap hung loosely.

"Same address?" the soldier asked. Jung-Soo, so engrossed in the envelope, merely nodded. "You're a lucky man! The trucks are leaving in five minutes. Your letter will be first out the door."

"Thank you," he muttered, as he drifted away towards the exit.

A hand slapped Jung-Soo across his back.

"What you got there?" It was Dae-Gun, back to his usual chirpy self. He gasped. "Is that what I think it is?"

Jung-Soo nodded.

"Well," Dae-Gun said impatiently. "What are you waiting for?" He hovered over Jung-Soo's shoulder as they exited the administration tent.

"Don't you have something else to do?" Jung-Soo said, annoyed as he held the envelope close to his chest to hide it.

"Oh, right."

Jung-Soo could feel the disappointment from Dae-Gun as he waddled back towards the tent.

"I'll get the supplies for our trip," he said, deflated.

By the time Dae-Gun came back out of the tent, waddling again with a load of unfamiliar supplies, he witnessed Jung-Soo staring down at a piece of paper, looking rather puzzled. He couldn't help but look over his shoulder.

"A bit of a disappointment, isn't it?" Jung-Soo stated, matter-of-factly.

"Really? A guitar? Again?" Dae-Gun said, tilting his head to the side. "What's with you and the guitar?"

Jung-Soo finally realized why the commander had probed him about the guitar: two pictures, plus a boy who lugged a guitar around in a war zone. It was surprising that the commander hadn't pressed harder for an adequate response from him.

He hastily folded the paper. "Not everything has to be some code, you know," he said rather irritated. "Did you get everything?"

Dae-Gun dropped the weighted backpack to the ground and began unpacking.

"Hope you know you'll be carrying all that."

Dae-Gun glared at him. "Well, don't expect to be eating anything I carry."

Jung-Soo's mind wandered elsewhere, over the hills and south to the fields where rice grew. He was indeed happy—ecstatic even to have received a letter from Iseul. It was clear she lacked practice with writing by the looks of her childish bold letters. She needed someone like him to nag her, keep her writing and practicing. That was the way it used to be...

How long had she known he was alive? Who had told her? Why had it taken so long to write? For all he knew, she could have been dead all this time! They had been moving up and down the entire Peninsula. Perhaps, the mail service had been overloaded and disorganized till now. No, that couldn't be. Everyone else had gotten their mail on time.

"So now, all we need is water to get our food going. We won't even need a fire!"

Jung-Soo barely registered Dae-Gun's chatter. He was always going on about how fascinated he was about something. *Food without fire*, was it? Winter was coming, and now he was traveling with a lunatic.

"Are you listening, Jung-Soo?" Dae-Gun said, "Er—Jung-Soo…"

Jung-Soo felt an itch begin in his chest, one that he knew he could not stop once he began scratching it. He was angry. So angry, but why?

"What!" Jung-Soo said as he resurfaced from his thoughts.

"Sheesh, sorry for mentioning the obvious!" Dae-Gun was starting to get rather vexed by Jung-Soo's behavior. "I thought you wanted to check if we have everything so we can leave first thing tomorrow morning."

"Oh right," Jung-Soo said, barely apologetic. "Did you get everything? Food, water canisters, matches, extra bullets, blankets, coats…"

"Yes, I just showed all of them to you," Dae-Gun said, packing the last of tiny boxes into the bag.

"What's that?" Jung-Soo said, finally intrigued by the new addition.

Dae-Gun grunted. "Like I said, it's food."

"In boxes?"

"Food without fire, remember?"

"Oh right. Sounds crazy."

"Weren't you listening to anything I was saying?" he said, more agitated than usual.

He had had his fill of Jung-Soo's behavior! How could he be so insensitive and completely oblivious to how he was feeling? He had just lost his best friends and new brothers he had made in war. The trumpet he found belonged to Jong-Su, a boy who used to sleep in the bunker next to him and snored as loud as he blew his trumpet. Jong-Su, the boy who used to greet him in the morning no matter what had happened in the battlefield, was now dead! He didn't deserve it. No one did. He felt guilt-stricken that he had left without saying goodbye and that he had been the one to survive his brothers.

He imagined Jung-Soo would at least be in a better mood since he had gotten that stupid letter. That ungrateful prick! Dae-Gun was determined not to say another word to him. He packed his backpack and didn't even complain about how much heavier his looked compared to the one Jung-Soo carried.

All throughout the rather scrumptious meal they had of properly steamed rice, vegetables, pork seasoned to perfection with soy sauce and a hint of ginger and garlic, Dae-Gun made it point not to talk about how wonderful the food was, or even look in Jung-Soo's general direction. But on the rare occasion he did glance towards him, it infuriated him more that Jung-Soo didn't seem to notice his silence, or even enjoy the food that he stuffed in his mouth. *What a disgrace!* He thought.

The next morning, Dae-Gun woke first and had to clear his throat loud enough to wake half the tent before Jung-Soo stirred. Half-awake, they opened the flap of their temporary tent and took in the fresh dawn air that heralded autumn as they made their way out of the camp and towards their American allies.

Jung-Soo couldn't help but look back as if he were leaving something important behind. His feet kept on going, though his eyes wandered. He had snuck in a long glance of Iseul's letter the moment he woke and held in a grin. He tried to commit the lines of Iseul's handwriting to memory, promising that he would not wear down Iseul's delicate paper with excessive handling.

But even though he was grateful, he was in want for more, not just a stick figure and a badly drawn one at that. He wanted to hear her voice, how she had been all these months, and if she had enough food to eat. He wanted to know if he could ever be forgiven for what he had done—for what his father had done. His fists rolled in to contain the rage. She wouldn't have written to him if he were not forgiven. The hate he had for himself seemed to grow at that thought.

Past the edges of the camp, they neared the edge of the mountains where trees stacked side by side and hid the morning sun. That hatred flared up like a forest fire, uncontrollable; he would need to find a way to shut it in and enclose it in a safe place.

His feet felt heavy as he glanced back to find the base camp that had completely disappeared from view. He wanted to go back to the administration tent, take back that letter he had sent, and throw it into the pit of his burning rage.

There was no point now. The truck that took the letter would be miles and miles away from camp by now, going in the opposite direction. How could he? He realized too late that he would be doing the same thing to Iseul, giving her false hope—giving her more frustration. He should have said something, anything. He should have given an excuse for not writing, or at the very least, should have given an excuse for what had happened that night. If it were up to him, he would take it all back, including the letter he just sent her way.

He trudged forward, past Dae-Gun as he hastened to get off the well-trodden mountain-side road.

He had fallen for the naïve trap Dae-Gun had said about war—about writing to those he loved when he still had the chance. He blamed no one but himself. He should have stuck with his original plan: survive and return to Iseul a whole man, not as the son of a communist. He would beg her for her forgiveness then, and if she still hated him, or had moved on... The thought squeezed his already heavy heart. He would deal with it when it came to that. He didn't want her worrying, and most of all, he didn't want her implicated in the mess he found himself with the commander.

Dae-Gun didn't seem at all concerned about Jung-Soo's apparent distress. He did not ask what was wrong, nor did Dae-Gun care anymore. Just when he thought they had turned a new page in their friendship, Jung-Soo had proven himself otherwise—*a heartless corpse.*

***

Mr. Lim was jittery that day. He wondered if it was because of the piece of yellow melon he had eaten. The seeds were too small and the white flesh too bitter and too young to be picked and eaten. He listened for the sound of an engine approaching, and the doors being swung open. But each time the door opened, it was not the mailmen, but another villager asking if their letter had arrived yet, or another lost refugee looking for food and a way south.

Weeks had passed and the autumn leaves had fully turned golden, brown and red. Still, there were no signs of a response from Jung-Soo. Between the boredom that filled the gaps between meals that didn't come soon enough, it seemed everyone in the small village of Yeoju seemed agitated. They had all made their idle hands busy with the task of paper-making, but as the initial fascinating of the task wore off and food became scarcer by the day, it seemed as though those left in Yeoju were waiting for the war to end or to die waiting.

Mr. Lim became rather impatient even with the friendly truck driver, demanding that he check his truck again and again for a single letter that may or may not have even been sent. He had even been tempted to turn the dials of the radio and speak his mind to the one person he knew would be listening, until one day, the doors of the Golden Palace flung open and a truck driver came in with a huge grin. He flailed his hand up high in the air with a single slim envelope and ran towards Mr. Lim.

"It's here! It's finally here!"

"It took you long enough."

Mr. Lim knew he should wait for Iseul to come and collect it, but when had Iseul ever come to send or receive a letter? Besides, she did not expect one, since he had been the one to send Iseul's initial letter without her ever suspecting. Byung-Guk's father paced around the halls, looking quite worried and even bumping into the truck driver who was bringing in stacks of letters.

It was bad enough that Mr. Lim wasn't helping him unload the truck, but he was now getting in the way of his duties.

"Oh, just do it already. Go up to the hills and give the damn letter to her yourself," the truck driver said, frustrated.

"Such matters…" Mr. Lim cleared his throat, "matters of the heart, must be approached with the utmost care."

"What nonsense, you old fart," the truck driver said, plucking the letter he had just given to him back into his care. "This is war, not some folklore our mothers told us as children. If you won't, I will." The driver was ready to stomp out when the Mr. Lim beat him to the door and plucked the letter back again.

"Alright, alright. I'm going," he said. "The outgoing letters are in that…"

"I know where the outgoing letters are, old man," he cut him off, "just go already."

In the months leading up to this fateful day, Iseul had become increasingly shaky. Her hands shook and her stomach grumbled. Even in her sleep, she felt as if she were falling from the sky, shaking turbulently as she woke from her nightmares. Yeong-Hoon usually woke her up, rushing into her room and shaking her when she wasn't already shaking herself awake.

"I'm fine," she would say. "I think I may just be a little hungry."

There was never enough food, but some of the women left what they could for Iseul. Yeong-Hoon would scoop a spoonful of rice on the wooden spoon and let Iseul drift back to sleep with her stomach working on something.

Mr. Lim was so close. He could see the shapes of women moving around the yard between Iseul's home and her workshop. The letter fluttered in his hand as he made the final dash.

"Iseul, Iseul!" he exclaimed.

The women were the first to notice a mad figure running towards them. The old scholar, who had been napping by the porch, shuddered awake by the ruckus. Iseul stopped her task of collecting and examining the dried pages and ran towards Mr. Lim.

"What's wrong?" She was prepared for the worst. She felt the gun against her ankle. But the creases on Mr. Lim's forehead vanished and transformed into a wide grin.

"This is for you." He handed her the letter.

"Oh…" Iseul said with a sigh of relief, though one look at the envelope had left her looking even more distressed than she had before.

"A bit anticlimactic, if you ask me." The scholar looked smug and walked into the forest with his arms behind his back. "I must take a break from all this work! Especially now that you've nearly killed me with a heart attack," he strutted away, dramatically.

Mi-Jung took it as a cue to get the women and old men back to work as Iseul disappeared into her room.

"Is it from who I think it is?" Mi-Jung spoke quietly to Mr. Lim. He nodded. "But how?" Mi-Jung said. "I thought he was…"

"Dead?" he shook his head. "The Ham's are powerful and loyal. But most of all, they are as wise and equally cunning as a serpent. They always find a way."

Mi-Jung smiled and nodded. "I never did like that Jung-Soo boy, but I'm glad he's alive. Iseul deserves to be happy."

Iseul flopped down on the wooden floor as her hands trembled with the envelope in it. Yeong-Hoon had snuck into the room and sat with her.

"Is this real?" Iseul muttered. "After all this time, could this really be from him?"

Yeong-Hoon nodded. Iseul slid her index finger underneath the flap and pulled the folded page out. Nimbly, and even more carefully than she would handle her own paper, she used both hands to unfold the page.

"A guitar," she said, "with measurements." Yeong-Hoon smiled, as did Iseul. "He's alive! He's really alive, isn't he?"

"Seems to be the case," Yeong-Hoon said. "No one loved the sound of the guitar more than Jung-Soo did. It looks like he's found a real one."

"But a guitar, in the middle of a war zone?"

Yeong-Hoon shrugged. "You'd be surprised what men bring to war."

"How would you know?" Iseul nudged the side of Yeong-Hoon's shoulder as he toppled over his bad leg and nearly hit his head.

Yeong-Hoon gave her a silly glare. "Don't underestimate the cripple," he grinned and propped himself up again.

Iseul sighed. It was the silent kind, one that no one else by the two of them would hear, and one that signaled a deep and comforting relief.

The page was white, not like the ones she made. Good. It seemed Jung-Soo had been getting quality supplies. It gave her an added sense of ease. The address gave her nothing more than the name of the infantry he was in. For all Iseul knew, he could be far away, deep in the northern heart of the peninsula. But as Iseul delicately folded the page and held it up against her chest, Jung-Soo felt somehow closer, as if he were looking over her.

The guitar. She smiled at the thought. She recalled the first time she had heard the sound of a guitar in the school shed. She had promised she would make it for him. The memory floated as if it were a dream, drifting away like the blood that poured into the river Han and tainted the waters that reached them. It left a bitter taste, metallic, and sometimes even dyed their pages a subtle rusty brown.

Iseul had never once resented Jung-Soo. He was not his father, and though she hadn't known Mr. Ham personally, she wished to believe he had passed on some good traits she saw in Jung-Soo. Though she was relieved, she knew it was not over. The worrying would not stop until she would see him face-to-face. Yet, as she tasted the unexplainable bitterness that lingered, she couldn't help but feel a tinge of spite rise in her.

"Oppa," Iseul said, holding the envelope tight as it creased. "Of all the things he could have written, why this?" Yeong-Hoon just listened. "What's the point of all of this?" Iseul said, the pitch of her voice rising.

She could hear the bustle outside of another busy day making paper. This was her life now and between the hunger, lack of sleep and the strains of doing her duties for her country, she felt the weight of the entire village on her shoulders.

"After all this time, is this all that he has to say for himself?"

The page felt so slim and fragile. How had they come to this? She longed for days they had roamed the hills without a worry, when rice was still relatively plentiful and the only thing that rang in the hills were the sound of their own laughter and bickering, echoing through the branches and trees.

The hillsides were barren now. They had stripped down nearly every mulberry tree, as others trees were cut and stockpiled to prepare for winter. The days of laughter and daydreaming seemed to have permanently passed. Even the trees that had once stood, were no longer there to attest to how Jung-Soo and Iseul once used to be.

"I didn't ask for this," she said to herself. "I wish we could all go back to the way things were before the war." She felt like a shadow of who she used to be, hollow and haunted by the memories of her past self.

"And then what?" Yeong-Hoon said without the usual gentleness in his tone. "Before this war, the Japanese were here. Before the Japanese, the Chinese had always been on our doorstep. How far back should we go? Goryeo, Joseon Dynasties?"

Her head was down and the room was silent, just as the day they had held a moment of silence at the tomb of King Sejong. For all his might and wisdom, he laid dead underneath an elaborate pile of soil, as did her mother and father. The old mountain fortress of Pasaseong-Ji remained but a relic of their turbulent history where she was just a carpenter's daughter, biding her time until she too would become nothing more than a pile of soil.

Iseul's grip had tightened as Jung-Soo's drawing further bunched up. She wanted to rip it apart, burn it even. Outside, Mi-Jung was explaining to Su-Ji how thick the fibers of the mulberry tree should be and how they should be laid on the bamboo frames.

Yeong-Hoon raised Iseul's limp hand with the letter up towards her eyes. "At least you have this," he said.

A page. Another relic of bygone days to remind her of her

sorrows.

Yeong-Hoon shook his head. "No, Iseul, at least you have a past worth mourning for."

Mi-Jung slid open the door. "You okay there?"

"Yeah," Iseul turned around to hide the tears trickling down. "I'll be out in a minute." She put a smile back on her face. She must be brave for the women and men who had so much faith in her. These people were her family now, and this village her home.

"Actually, you'd better come out now," she said.

Iseul slid both her palms across her eyes and kicked up. "What is it?"

Outside, an unrecognizable woman and an old man stood surrounded by the papermakers who looked curiously at the two strangers.

"You'd better hear what they have to say," the scholar said, holding a gun at the strangers.

CHAPTER 27

[Present Day]

I never much liked ghost stories, though granny told me her mother once told her ghosts lived as specters somewhere between our present selves and the future selves we hope to be.

I once had a dream when I was around twelve or thirteen. I had no fear that day in the meadow as I saw a man approaching. I believe I felt sad if such a single word could explain the aching void I felt. Nothing really bad had happened to me to cause such a dream. Thinking back, I believe I had felt the depth of loss that a little girl my age was not yet capable of knowing. It was an aching void, birth pangs of sorts that would herald adulthood and the intense loneliness that was yet to come.

The loneliness yet to come...

I did not fear the man coming towards me in my dream, though I should have. Dreams seem to take on a separate logic of their own. The closer he came, the more intense I felt the aching. He came and placed his hand on my shoulder and the aching was replaced with a warmth that tingle then spread through every cell of my body. I woke up weeping, my pillow drenched in tears. I was both happy yet sad—happy to have known such perfect warmth and sad to see the man go.

They say loneliness is the longing for someone you will never get the chance to meet.

Grandpa passed when I was so young. He slipped in the bathtub while singing and dancing on a full stomach. Granny chuckled at his funeral and I caught her saying, "It was just the way he would have wanted to go."

When someone leaves you when you are that young, you believe that someone will return. After all, a child eventually grows to know that just because one can't see one's mother, it doesn't mean she's gone forever. But in time, you forget that you ever believed they would return and you grow into the reality of the finality of death.

I wish I had known him better.

***

My hand reached for the plastic that covered brown sheets of paper within. My eyes were heavy as was my head that seemed fixed in place.

Where was I? I seemed to have forgotten. Oh yes...I was in front of my grandmother's grave—the one where she would lay, and in my hands was a lump of something wrapped in plastic.

I wanted to rip open the plastic. I needed to know what was inside. Yet, something pulsated against my thigh. It was my phone, vibrating.

Strange. I didn't think there was reception here. Still I tried to ignore the vexing thing that kept calling, beckoning me again and again.

"Jia! Jia!" it said sternly. *Strange.* I hadn't answered the phone yet.

I was close. So very close. I unwrapped the plastic covering, my fingers heavy as if I were holding up a whole textbook. Envelopes, brown, rusty...old. This must be it! Letters. More letters from the man called Yeong-Hoon.

"Jia!" the voice said again. It was my mother. How? She was supposed to be back at home. My mind plunged into a haze. Still, I had to open the envelope. One. That's all I wanted to see. Just one more letter.

It felt endless; I was trapped in a body that did not seem to want to move. I lifted the flap of the old envelope and tugged on the paper inside. It was heavy. I just needed to unfold the page. Unfold the page...

"Jia! Wake up! You're talking in your sleep!"

My eyes shot open. It was mother.

"What?" I said. I was back at Sky Nursing Home, but how did I get here so fast? My fingers were still there, back at my grandmother's grave. I had unfolded the page; I was sure of it!

"Wipe that drool off your face. It's not something a young lady should be seen doing."

I see. It was as if I had woken from a deep sleep as the memories came flooding back. I had never left the nursing home. I had planned to, I really had!

The nurse came in to tell us that granny was still stable, though we should prepare ourselves for the worst. We had been preparing ourselves all year.

I calmed myself, reaching for the plastic cup left on granny's nightstand. It wasn't until ten in the morning when my two uncles filed in one-by-one to see grandmother. Their eyes seemed to sag a little lower than the last time they had come to see their mother. It seemed almost like a monthly ritual, each time being told to prepare for the worst and each time granny reviving again in a few days, as the uncles disappeared until the next round.

I wanted to tell them that she had unfinished business. That's why she was reluctant to go, but none of them seemed to care much about what I had to say.

I moved my textbook towards the window and let the sunlight shine on it. I had drooled a lot more than usual and it had seeped through more than a few pages.

"So unladylike," mom repeated.

The three siblings saw each other nearly every day at work. Mother was the product manager down at the guitar factory, while the two brothers jointly sat on the President's seat. There had been an ongoing feud of sorts, though mom never discussed the details with me.

My cousin Yoon-Sung seemed to know a lot more than I did. He had always been the bratty one, though the adults chalked it up to confidence, one that would come in handy as a leader. I'd say he was getting cocky with more air than substance in that mind of his. But the facts remained that he was the eldest son of granny's eldest son.

Business was not as it used to be. That's what the three siblings always said. *Ji Iseul Instruments. Co.* was not the only company that built guitars anymore. Competition had cropped up not just in Korea, but in other parts of Asia that could meet the global demand for quality products at an affordable price.

I saw my family situation just as it was, without frills or overwhelming anxiety. My mother was working ceaselessly for a dying company and my father was on the verge of being forced into retirement a decade too soon, working night shifts to help pay for my university tuition while his only daughter was likely to fail the national exam due to some unreasonable hunt for a nonexistent man. I could see our future right then and there. He would be working longer hours and taking on more night shifts. Perhaps I could help—earn a little bit of money once I got done with the national exam this November and maybe help pay for tuition come March. That is, if I got accepted to any. At this rate, it seemed unlikely.

At least we had the house. At least grandmother would leave us the house. We deserved it. Mother deserved it since we were the ones who took care of her ever since her diagnosis.

Mother always told me how lucky I was to be born in this generation, and not hers or my grandmother's. I could be whoever I wanted to be and the key to success was to study. '*Be smart, be pretty so you could marry into a good family, or at least earn enough to take care of yourself.*' It was the anthem of our household, one that my father could say nothing to refute.

I walked back towards the large windows where below, rush hour had kept the cars moving at a snail's pace. My textbook was dry now, wrinkled where the patch of saliva used to be. *Gross.* I could see why mom would say it was unladylike. The history book was turned to the page I had been stuck on for hours. I had forgotten what I was studying until I looked down and saw the iconic picture of King Sejong. Everyone knew who he was. He is the most famous King of Korea who created the Korean alphabet, Hangul and distinguished our language from that of the Chinese. I knew all that, but the details always seem to allude me.

Last week, our teacher had given us a test that asked, "What was King Sejong's childhood name?"

Needless to say, I got that question wrong. Only three others had gotten it wrong, meaning nearly everyone in the class, even that rascal Jong-Suk, had set aside his video gaming to get serious about the exam. Perhaps I was just not cut out for memorization, or studying in general for that matter.

"Be smart or be pretty." That phrase had always stuck out like a sore thumb.

It was a cloudy day outside and the windows reflected a faint figure of a girl slightly overweight, short and with disheveled hair. I sighed.

"Sejong the Great's childhood name is Won Jeong. Sejong the Great's childhood name is Won-Jeong." I recited to myself as I paced around the hospice room.

Mother seemed to be pleased when she looked over. I liked that. She already had a lot of her plate.

The room was silent but I could imagine the cars honking at each other, all trying to get to somewhere important. I never knew much about directions. The city stretched out endlessly like the sea. Somewhere out there was a place I needed to be, a place where I belonged, and where my life—my *real* life—would begin.

Yet, why was it that all I could think about was how granny felt this instance, trapped in her dying body? I tried pushed the thoughts away.

Yeoju. Perhaps you'll have to wait for me, at least a month until I finish the exam. The memory of that envelope still felt so real. I had been so close to opening it. I knew it was just a dream and I wouldn't find those envelopes underneath the grave. Yet, I felt it calling. Somewhere, those letters really did exist and they were taunting me.

I knew my uncles wouldn't stay long. As per usual, they entrusted the caregiving to my mother as they prepared to leave. Busywork would be waiting for them at the factory, something about defective products that fell apart in humid climates. Mother seemed to know all about it since she dealt with international sales and I began to wonder if my uncles knew quite as much. Dressed in leather shoes, a fancy suit, clean-shaven and relatively well-rested, my uncles rose from their seats and made their way out the door. Their hands that tucked their bellies into their belts looked soft to the touch. Granny used to hold my hand as I slept and I remember they were calloused like sandpaper.

Saturday. It used to be the day I didn't study, but those days were few and far between and it had increasingly been that way for the past few years.

"Hey mom," I called.

"Huh?" she said, barely acknowledging me.

"I'm going head to the library to study. I don't think I can concentrate here."

She nodded.

It was supposed to be a routine bus ride to the library, five stops and the first right on the corner of the street, but I was feeling like I could use a walk. My legs felt like they were getting weaker by the day and the extra bit of weight seemed to collect around my arms and thighs. I suppose all students in their final year gained a bit of weight, except for those few girls who would starve before they would grow out of their uniforms.

The subway station was a fifteen-minute walk so I decided I could manage that. The air was chillier than I remembered. Then again, I suppose it'd been weeks since I'd been outdoors for longer than a few minutes.

Seoul touted one of the largest and most efficient underground transport in the whole world with over nine lines. Or was it ten? There was always construction of a new line in the works somewhere in the city and another massive national train system that traveled across the entire southern half of the peninsula.

My railcard beeped twice against the register, indicating that I held the student card. It wouldn't be long before it would beep once, and I would have to pay an extra few hundred won each ride. The blinking lights over my head indicated which stop I was at. I remembered why I preferred the bus as the straps of my bag cut into my shoulder muscles. At least if I were lucky, I could sit on the bus and doze off.

Line two of the Seoul metro was a peculiar one. It ran in circles to the North and South of the Han river. In each intersection of the river on the east and west, the train emerges from deep underground onto outdoor bridges. For a brief moment, the train would meet the city of Seoul that shimmered as glass windows of tall skyscrapers reflected like diamonds on the Han river.

I've lived in Seoul since birth, yet I had barely ventured it. They say it is one of the most populated cities in the world—top five according to the most recent statistics. Mother told me I have the rest of my life to discover this city and the rest of the world. I suppose she was right. There will be lines 1-10 to roam, each stop telling me where to visit next, and likely even more lines and stops by the time the rest of my life begins.

"This stop is City Hall station. The doors are on your right. You can transfer to the blue line." A woman from a recording spoke pleasantly, reminding me that this was my stop.

The library would be another fifteen-minute walk from the subway station and my shoulders felt like rocks. I decided I'd take the bus.

It was early in the afternoon and the bus was nearly empty. I looked out the window as we passed by landmarks I knew like the back of my hand. First was the City Hall itself, built next to a large plaza that often makes an appearance on television when it is filled with peaceful protestors.

Deoksugung would be up next, the palace from the Joseon dynasty that stuck out, colorful and elaborate against the shiny square buildings that soared in the sky.

Once, I had seen an interview of a U.S. veteran coming to visit Korea where he had served as a medic during the Korean War. His words were long forgotten, but I memorized every line on his face as he entered Deoksugung Palace. They say it is one of the few landmarks that remains from before the war. I saw the old man look away so as to hide his tears from the camera that followed him around the palace. It was the only place that told him he was back in the war-torn Korea of his youth.

The war seemed so immediate as the American veteran came to mind. It was true; we were still at war with North Korea, yet no one really thought of the war in this day and age where skyscrapers soars high enough to block any view of the North.

The letter, the guitar, Yeong-Hoon, and the traitor Jung-Soo.

I hoped the author of the half-written letter wasn't Jung-Soo. Surely, grandmother would have thrown away a letter that implicated her with a communist. And if he really wanted to convince granny otherwise, he would have written more. The letter gave every indication that he had so much left unsaid.

My visit back to Yeoju had been almost entirely unhelpful as detailed records of the war had not been taken at all. There were names—Byung-Guk, Jung-Soo—ghosts of people who remained only in writing and in spiteful words of a bitter old man. Who were they and how did granny know them?

I could envision my fingers around the pages, replaying my dream again and again. Yet, the vision always ended before I could read any of the pages. Perhaps mother was right. There was no need to torture the old lady with memories of a past she likely wanted to forget. The war must have been brutal and there must be a reason why I had never heard stories from that time period from any of my grandparents.

But I couldn't help but feel granny had been searching for answers too. Why else would she have gone back to Yeoju last year without any of us knowing? If only I knew. I could have helped her navigate modern modes of tracking people and events down. I felt claustrophobic, as if I were the one trapped in years of unanswered questions.

Granny had always been boisterous. She used to comment over the dinner table, "I just can't wrap my head around why Yong-Nim is mad at me." We used to tell her it's because she shouts at everyone, to which she just shrugged and said, "I can't help it, I just have a loud voice, and Yong-Nim is losing her hearing." She would then proceed to take a whole kimchi radish and bite straight through it with her two good teeth.

We just shook our heads and laughed it off. We had all tried to get through to her but had failed miserably. That was just granny and we had no choice but to accept it. And now, somehow in the grind of daily life, we had lost her even before she had passed, even without the chance to properly say goodbye. I wonder if mother understood that, or even my uncles.

I nearly missed my stop.

"Mister! Mister! Open the door for me!" I yelled towards the bus driver at the front of the bus as I exited towards the rear.

The local library was open twenty-four hours a day, every day of the week, and every clerk who worked there knew me well enough not to ask for my identification card. The library was nearly empty on a Saturday, much to my dismay. I eyed the corner desk where I could glimpse the entire floor in one view without being at the center of attention. I liked that. I liked watching people go about their daily lives, though I much preferred cafes for that end.

My bag thumped hard against the wood-plastic composite desk. I took a deep breath and slowly let it out. I laid out my textbooks on my desk in order of how I would proceed—math first and history last. It was just the way I studied, a habit of sorts that was hard to break. In all honesty, I had been avoiding history for quite a while now. It had a way of numbing my senses and lulling me into drowsiness until I would have to break for a snack at the vending machine. It was not ideal for my weight. Two coins in the vending machine yielded a canned drink—royal milk tea, my favorite, and the pop of the can opening seemed to relieve some pressure off of my shoulders.

The resting area provided sofas and public computers that were usually quite full. Mother had gotten rid of the computer in our house, which was just another way to get rid of possible sources of distraction. I sat on the stool that was too high and too hard for comfortable use and opened the web browser for the first time in months.

A white screen loaded and for a split second, I felt a sense of freedom, knowing that for these few minutes, I could go anywhere, see anything, and indulge my curiosities. But that split second ended as the home screen filled with news articles, celebrity news, and the local weather. Fifteen degrees Celsius, it said.

The last thing I wanted was to be shoved more lies. A few years ago, the President of South Korea had been front and center of the headlines as she attempted to alter modern history by issuing her own textbooks, thereby making heroes of her dead parents. That same president was eventually impeached.

There was nothing I wanted to learn from the headlines, and more so the textbooks that awaited me. Perhaps, one day, I would like to find out more about the Korean War, the various Kings of Silla, Gaya, Goryeo and about our great King Sejong whose childhood name was Won-Jeong. But for now, my thoughts dwelled on my grandmother.

I was tempted to browse through the National Archives again, hoping to find something about granny's ancestors, but I already knew what I would find. Names and more names of fathers, and the father's father and so on. The line ended with granny since she was the only daughter to her father.

I reached for granny's picture of the two soldiers with a guitar between them. I hadn't asked for permission when I took it from granny's hospice room, though I'll make sure to ask for forgiveness when I give it back. I typed in "Korean War archival photos" in the search engine. It'd be a long shot but maybe I'd have better luck browsing through the photographs.

Most of the photos were taken outdoors of both civilians and soldiers, both Korean men and U.N. troops. I winced at the bodies and freshly dug graves. Oh god…the children… So many were emaciated with nothing but skin and bones, though a few managed to smile for the camera. My granny would be older than these children now, if they had survived.

Faces would be impossible to match. Maybe the setting might be helpful, but they all looked the same. Tents rose in the same fashion and men wore the same helmet and uniform. The hills and mountains were barren and all landmarks flattened. I clicked through a few more before exiting the browser.

I sighed. I've always wondered how much mother knew about granny. She had always shut me down, and though I knew it had more to do with my exam coming up, I had a feeling she wasn't fully being honest with me. I could ask her, though I knew she would just nag me for not studying again.

I was at a dead end. As time ticked by, my frustrations grew as my concentration waned. There was nothing more to do, no other avenues to inquire about my grandmother's past, unless perhaps...

I pulled out my phone from my pocket and called my dad. He picked up in two rings.

"Hey, dad, can I ask you a question?"

"Sure," he said. I heard the sound of him laying aside the newspaper he read every Saturday afternoon.

"It's about granny. I know, she's not your mother so you might not know all the answers, but just hear me out first."

"I'm all ears."

"Do you remember when we buried grandpa?"

"Yeah. You were just a toddler then."

"I'm quite sure I was older than that. I remember the day quite well. Anyway, I've been trying to look up grandpa's family history in Yeoju, but he doesn't seem to have one. I thought he had family there, but it seems he was actually buried with granny's side of the family. Isn't that strange? I thought once women married, she would be buried with her husband, not the other way around."

"Oh," he said.

"So..." I said as I waited.

"Didn't mom tell you?" dad said. "Your grandfather isn't from Yeoju. He's just buried there since he lost touch with his entire family during the war."

"Oh," I said. This was news to me. "What about the national cemetery? I thought soldiers who fought in the Korean War were all buried there."

"Apparently, your grandfather didn't want to be buried there."

Strange, I thought. It was an honor to have a spot there, why wouldn't grandpa want to?

"Any idea where his original home might be?" I asked.

"Not a clue. I don't think any of us had the fainted idea. The entire extended family was just scratching our heads when he passed. Your grandmother insisted there was no question where he would be buried. She made us promise she would be buried to the right of his plot, not on the left."

I chuckled. "Sounds like her," I said. "She wanted to be by that one evergreen tree."

"She's always been so superstitious about trees and spirits," he said. "Mom's cooking dinner now so you should think about coming home soon," he said, and then whispered, "Don't worry, I won't tell her that you asked about granny."

"For the record, I asked about grandpa," I said.

We chuckled and then hung up.

When the last ebbs of light banter wore off, the weight of disappointment fell like an anvil to my chest. Could grandpa have changed his name? Why else would they have no record of his lineage otherwise? He would at least have some record of his birth somewhere, even if he had lost contact with his family. It was a dead end again, or even worse. Perhaps my very own grandfather was indeed the traitor in the letter, perhaps even Jung-Soo, the communist. Grandpa had always been the jovial type if my memory served me right, and I couldn't imagine him as a communist somehow responsible for a massacre.

Perhaps it was better this way…for the past to remain in the dark. But for whose benefit? Granny had the instrument company to her name and that would remain for at least another generation or more, but for all the support grandpa had given her, his wouldn't even be remembered by his own family.

I wish I had gotten to know him while he was still alive. All I could recall was that laugh that would burst from his belly and shake the entire room to his tempo. That's how I would remember him.

I took one final look at the picture, fixating on the younger and grainy version of my grandpa. He looked so carefree. It was probably sometime earlier in the war. I remember someone told me how he had always loved foreigners, and for some reason, I felt I was looking at the origin of his interest.

I wished I had learnt to speak English more, rather than fixate on grammar. Maybe then, I would understand why grandpa was so intrigued by them. I allowed my eyes to wander towards the foreign soldiers in the background of the picture. What was grandpa doing in a foreign military base? The two soldiers held up what looked like bottles of beer in front of crates. I chuckled. I wondered if any of them were still alive.

It then dawned on me—the print on the boxes! They were grainy, but had a distinct symbol, square-like almost like a shield with two crosses, one over the other.

I opened another browser and typed in "U.N. army units in the Korean War" and translated it into English before typing that into a new browser. Perhaps they were Americans. Most of them looked white. It seemed likely, though I knew it had been an international war. I clicked through each one of the listed units, infantries, and regiments until I came across a single image. It was the coat of arms for the 5th Cavalry Regiment and it was a rough match to the one shown in the picture. I clicked through the listing, just to make sure there weren't others that looked similar; there wasn't.

My heart pounded in my chest as I read through its military history until I came across a short segment about the Korean War. It was in English, but I knew enough to manage.

"The 5th Cavalry Regiment was deployed to Korea with rest of the First Cavalry Division on 18 July 1950, twenty-three days after the North Korean forces crossed the 38th parallel, becoming one of the first American Regiments to set foot on the Korean Peninsula."

I felt pride rising for the regiment that my grandfather had some acquaintance with. I kept reading until I came across a familiar word.

"Following the Chinese entry into the war, the 5th Cavalry Regiment fought in a massive counteroffensive, meeting the Chinese forces on 24 November, just south of Cheolwon, coming to the aid of the 24th Infantry and 8th Regiment forced as far south as the southern mountains of Yeoju."

Yeoju. South of it. This was it! Granny's village is in the south of Yeoju. I continued reading:

"The brutal four-day battle in freezing weather soon followed with fewer than 5,000 soldiers fighting approximately 20,000 Chinese troops. The 5th Cavalry, alongside the troops of the 18th Infantry of the Republic of Korea Armed Forces were pushed into the mountain ranges of Southern Yeoju as fewer than 500 made it out alive."

I sat in front of the computer monitor, reading the same

paragraphs over and over again. I couldn't believe it. A battle in Yeoju? Only 500 survivors? And how many of them were still alive today? And would I be able to find them half way across the world?

I had to try. I translated the word 'veteran' into English and searched for the veterans' office phone number and saved it on my phone.

I glanced up at the monitor screen that showed the time. 5:40 pm. I calculated the time difference. It would be around midnight in many of the states in America. I'd have to wait till much later in the evening, or even wake up in the middle of the night to make the phone call.

I paced towards my desk and packed my bag. For the first time in a very long while, I was filled with such anticipation that I might have even called it hope.

CHAPTER 28

[Mid-November, 1950]

Back in the forests where leaves crackled against two soldiers' boots, early harbingers of winter hit Jung-Soo and Dae-Gun in winds that cut through their thick uniforms. It was only November and Jung-Soo couldn't recall a time when winter arrived so soon. One excessively chatty girl came to mind, explaining the necessity of firewood in the winter.

Teeth chattered and jaws seemed to fix in place, which was all well and good since Jung-Soo and Dae-Gun were both determined to remain reticent. It had gotten to the point where Dae-Gun was poking at Jung-Soo when he thought he heard footsteps, and nearly gouged Jung-Soo's eye out as he was turning around. Jung-Soo, who winced in pain, could not allow such a minor injury to break the silence he had been enjoying the past week so instead gave Dae-Gun the death stare.

There was no need to talk at that point. Dae-Gun knew how to put up a tent and gather firewood, as Jung-Soo knew the procedures of lighting a fire, filtering through letters and checking their guns and supplies at the end of each long day. He radioed home base every night with the information he had gathered and by the looks of it, the western part of the peninsula had largely been deserted for the time being. On one of those nights Jung-Soo became desperate to communicate to Dae-Gun, he spoke into the radio in a particularly loud voice.

"Tell me, sir, how is it that the U.N. issued military food can become hot without administering heat from a fire?" Jung-Soo asked the man on the other end of the radio.

"What?" The man was rather flustered. "I'm not sure. Actually, that's a good question," he said. "Is this related to your mission, soldier?"

"No, sir, not exactly," Jung-Soo cleared his throat. "Just curious, sir."

"Oh," he said, back to his usual form. "Stick to the mission, then."

Dae-Gun tried to explain through hand gestures how the new food in boxes became hot without a fire, but Jung-Soo's eyes exposed his mistrust of food that looked like it could last a century and still look exactly the same. He ate it, even enjoyed the taste of foreign food that reminded him of a life he had left behind. Dae-Gun had been watching, carefully examining Jung-Soo's expression, but Jung-Soo wouldn't dare give him the satisfaction of showing how much he liked the taste.

There was something strange about those footsteps they had been hearing, constantly hovering around them for the better part of the week. Jung-Soo first believed they were hooves of deer wandering the forest. *Good. Real food, not just the stuff that came in packages.* Dae-Gun, on the other hand, had noticed the footsteps far sooner than Jung-Soo, and had even identified the direction it was coming from, rotating from behind, left, and right, and always in that same pattern, always at dusk, and always when they had begun to light the fire.

The footsteps drew nearer as the last of their food disappeared. Whispers coincided.

"We shouldn't get too close. They might suspect someone is following them," one voice said.

Dae-Gun thought the voice sounded familiar, distinct with a northern accent. He looked at Jung-Soo, holding down the words as they nearly slipped out. Instead, he made an expression that said, *did you hear that?* He jumped from his log and began stomping on the ashes of their fire as he grabbed his backpack to run.

Jung-Soo flagged him down. "We're too late. Shut up."

Dae-Gun looked appalled. "I didn't say anything!"

"Shh, grab your gun."

Dae-Gun and Jung-Soo stood their ground, each with a loaded

rifle. Two footsteps approached from the northern direction, and just as Jung-Soo spotted two heads bopping between bushes, Jung-Soo shot a fire as the hills returned echoes.

"What are you doing?" Dae-Gun jumped towards Jung-Soo. "They might be on our side."

Jung-Soo reloaded his gun. "No, they're not." He shot again in the intruder's general direction. Feet shuffled as one of them yelled, "We surrender, we surrender!"

"You didn't hit them?" Dae-Gun said, confused. "You never miss."

"Some prey is better alive than dead," Jung-Soo said. Before Dae-Gun knew it, two soldiers appeared from behind the bushes with their hands up in the air.

"Who are you and why are you following us?" Jung-Soo commanded as he pointed his rifle at one soldier's heart. He was the one on the left, who shivered and lost his words with one look into the barrel of the gun. Good. Jung-Soo knew he had chosen the right one to break.

Dae-Gun patted them down and confiscated their rifles.

"Answer me, soldier!" Jung-Soo raised his voice. Perhaps he had thought wrong. The fool had lost his wits along with all his words.

"Ham Jung-Soo," the other one answered. "We were looking for you."

For a moment, Jung-Soo stood unsure of what he had just heard.

"Ham Jung-Soo? What are they talking about?" Dae-Gun said to Jung-Soo. "You two have it all wrong. You've got the wrong person. This here is Kim Jung-Soo, not Ham Jung-Soo."

So was true then, Jung-Soo hadn't misheard it.

The brazen one spoke. "We're here on your father's orders." He was older than the rest of them, perhaps a decade or so, though his long hair and a thick beard added years to his appearance.

"What's going on, Jung-Soo? Do you know these people?" Dae-Gun said.

Jung-Soo waved his gun again. "How do I know my father sent you. He's supposed to be dead."

"Your father is Ham Young-Nam, born in Mokpo, Jeollanamdo. He raised you and your three brothers in Seoul and eventually moved you to a small no-name village in Yeoju."

Jung-Soo lowered his gun ever so slightly. No one but those closest to his father knew about his true birthplace. He had suspected it for a while—the possibility that his father or the Captain may not be dead, but there was no denying that now. He was alive and these were his men. He felt anger rising. How dare he be alive, after all the misery he's caused at Yeoju! He deserved to be dead. And what the hell did he want from him now?

"Tell him I want no part in his schemes."

"Your father is dead," the soldier said.

"What?"

The North Korean soldier reached for something behind him.

"Stop right there!" Dae-Gun's gun raised towards him.

The soldier pulled out a radio, much like the one Jung-Soo carried with him. He tuned it until a familiar voice spoke through the speakers.

"Be on guard, Ham Jung-Soo soldier," it said.

Jung-Soo could recognize the voice now. It was the same one he had heard that one night on the way to the 5th Cavalry camp. He thought he had imagined the entire thing.

"We presume these were your father's final words," the North Korean soldier said. "It's been playing on a loop every thirty seconds on this channel since he recorded it."

"How?" Jung-Soo said, his voice trembling.

"We've been monitoring your radio communications, which helped us trace your location. Your father chose the closest channel to the one you've been using so it didn't take us too long to hone in on yours."

Of course, Jung-Soo thought. His fingers must have slipped when he turned the dial at the end of that night, which landed him on the channel his father had recorded on. He was never supposed to hear his father on the radio that night; it was meant for the two soldiers who stood in front of him. All they needed to do was crack the first code and they would have had access to all the other ones by eavesdropping on them. His father would have been more than capable of such a simple radio interception.

Yet, Jung-Soo couldn't help but feel something was amiss. His father, dead? After all the times he had evaded it? He had only been assigned to his radio frequency within the past two months, which meant he had been alive until quite recently.

"How?" Jung-Soo said again. "I mean how did he die?"

"Colonel Ham was deployed near the 38th Parallel to help with the peace talks. He had been attempting to eavesdrop on the South to determine their true intentions in order to gain an upper hand during the negotiations. We met him there. He hand-picked us because he knew we had family in the South. He promised us a new life, safe passage if we followed through on his orders. He promised there would be people in the South to ensure our survival, with or without him."

Jung-Soo had never understood how his father commanded such loyalty of the people around him. It was their fault they had believed his father. They had fallen for his trap and they were sure to be worse off for it.

"We crossed 38th parallel around a month ago, but General Shin found out and your father was shot on the run."

Jung-Soo's eyes faltered. He did not dare believe reports of his father anymore; he was the mastermind of such ruses.

"And you two?" Jung-Soo said, accusingly. "Where were you when all this happened?"

"On the run with your father that night. We crossed the border just ahead of him and we saw your father collapse. He was bleeding…it was a lot of blood."

"And so you left him there to die?" Jung-Soo said. The North Korean soldiers noticed the gun gripped tighter around Jung-Soo's trigger finger.

"We were following orders. He commanded us to leave him. Believe me, most nights I wish I had never crossed over. I shouldn't have ever believed a damn word he said, promising fortunes in such times. I'm the fool for it."

The soldier held a slip of paper towards Jung-Soo. "Here's to my fortune, Ham Jung-Soo. We've completed our mission so let us go."

Jung-Soo looked suspiciously at the wrinkly slip. Dae-Gun pointed the gun at them, while Jung-Soo yanked the sheet away from the soldier as he unfolded it. A series of scrambled Korean alphabets revealed themselves on the page:

ㅁ ㅑ ㅂ ㅇ ㅏ ㅊ ㄷ ㅋ ㄹ ㅂ ㅔ ㅋ ㅑ ㅂ ㅁ ㅐ ㅂ ㅐ

ㅣ ㅇ ㄷ ㅁ ㅍ ㄷ ㅁ ㅏ ㅑ ㄴ ㅛ ㅅ ㅑ ㅈ ㄷ

"What does it mean?" Jung-Soo said, glancing up at the older soldier.

"How are we supposed to know? We thought you'd know how

to decipher it."

"Me?"

Dae-Gun glanced over at the page. "It looks like a letter for an enigma machine, except it's in Korean." Jung-Soo shot him a glare for even mentioning it.

"Enigma machine?" the northern soldier said. "Beats me. I don't care how you decipher it. That's none of my business."

A letter encoded by the enigma machine. Surely it wasn't a coincidence that these soldiers held such a letter when he kept Commander Lee's enigma codes in his front pocket. Did they know he held the codes? Maybe he had mentioned something through the radio. He thought back. No, he hadn't. Not a single time.

"It looks like any one of you could have written this," Jung-Soo said, still suspicious.

"Look carefully," the soldier said. "Your father assured me that you would know it was from him."

He looked down again. The curvature of the consonants turned distinctly down and faded longer than most other calligraphy letters. This was his father's handwriting; that much was certain. But what did his father so desperately want to say to him that would merit sending two North Korean soldiers into enemy territory to find him? Perhaps it was a trap—get the son to decipher his father's last words. Even if he could, he would be a damned fool if he deciphered the code for the enemy.

"Jung-Soo," Dae-Gun whispered loudly. "They're spies. We should capture them and bring them back to camp with us. The commander won't be happy if he finds out we let them go."

Jung-Soo considered it.

The North Korean soldier sneered at Dae-Gun. "And who's to say your friend here isn't a double agent himself?"

Dae-Gun's gun had drooped towards the ground as he stood scratching his head. Could it be? He looked at Jung-Soo and the two others, bobbing his head back and forth. Even the quiet one seemed to know more about what was going on.

"Jung-Soo," Dae-Gun said. "That is your real name, right?"

Jung-Soo glared at him and smacked the back of his head. "Of course it is, you idiot!"

"Oww! What was that for?" Dae-Gun whined. "We've got to get the facts straight so we might as well start with the obvious. For all I know, you three are all on the same side, and you're here to kill me."

Jung-Soo rolled his eyes. "What a waste of a bullet," he said dismissively. "And you two," Jung-Soo said, shaking his gun at the northern soldiers. "You're not going anywhere until I figure out exactly who you are and what the hell you want from me. Tie them up, Dae-Gun."

They sat by the fire that had revived from Dae-Gun's stomping as Jung-Soo held his gun pointed at them. He must think… His father would know exactly what was wrong, but he wasn't his father. He'd have to apply himself. The entire conversation reeked of the stench of an elaborate plan that weaved delicately between truth and lies and Jung-Soo didn't where to start to unravel the tapestry these soldiers had brought with them.

Dae-Gun heard the hungry growls of two stomachs and glanced over to Jung-Soo, wondering what to do with the prisoners.

The quiet one looked solemnly at Dae-Gun. "You owe us at least one meal!"

Dae-Gun was surprised the boy could talk.

"What do you mean?" Dae-Gun said.

As if he had been waiting his turn to talk, the old soldier said, "Our friend bozo here isn't so useless when it comes to animals. We picked him up at a farm near the 38th parallel. Couldn't follow an order if his life depended on it, so your father thought he'd come in handy elsewhere."

"Good with animals?" Dae-Gun said curiously.

"Care to have a guess?" the older one said.

"The boar…" Jung-Soo's eyes widened.

The boy smiled and rubbed the back of his head.

"No way!" Dae-Gun yelped. "We would have starved to death without you."

"Don't be so dramatic," Jung-Soo spat out. "We would have been just fine."

"We got a few good meals out of the leftovers," the boy said.

All sense of logic eluded Dae-Gun as the sudden onslaught of gratitude led him to pull out two boxes of food for the prisoners. Doo-Hyung held his hand out to be untied, as Dae-Gun looked to Jung-Soo for permission. Jung-Soo reluctantly nodded. The North Korean soldiers ripped open the packet at the top, waiting for Dae-Gun to share his canister of water. Dae-Gun glanced over, stunned; they knew exactly what to do with the packaged food!

"So that's how close you've been to us?"

Dae-Gun remembered the first time he had acted out the instructions for Jung-Soo who couldn't read the English instructions on the back of the box. The two North Korean spies must have been watching all along!

"Oh don't be too surprised, you pig." The old one couldn't help but poke fun. "Just be glad we're one of the friendly sort of spies," he leered. "And if it wasn't for the domestic squabble you two have been having, you would have never known we were tailing you."

"Domestic squabble?" Dae-Gun asked.

"Usually, we have no problem hearing you talk, but once the silent treatment began, we couldn't quite gauge how far we were from you so we kind of stumbled into your camp."

The bozo reached for the tin with water, eager to get to the interesting part. He poured water into the packet and waited as it began to spontaneously heat up.

"I'm Gil-Dong," he said as he reached his hand out to Dae-Gun, who watched the boy like a circus animal.

Dae-Gun paused briefly before introducing himself, though he could imagine they already knew who he was.

"And what's your name?" Dae-Gun asked the older one.

"I'd rather not say."

"I'd rather you do," Jung-Soo interrupted. He looked intently, his gun raised slightly higher at him.

"The name's Shin Doo-Hyung."

"Any chance you're related to the same "Shin" that killed my father?"

"Yes, a distant relative, as all "Shins" are in that region."

Jung-Soo still couldn't quite grasp the situation. What did his father really want from him? And of all the people he could have sent, why did his father send this strange man?

There had been coincidences that had led him to believe his cover wasn't as deep as he would have liked. How had Iseul known where he was deployed and what his alias was? His father had resurfaced, only to be pronounced dead again. The two soldiers had appeared with a coded message when he himself held the commander's codes—that much couldn't just be a coincidence! And why had they waited weeks to relay the message to him?

He knew what this soldier called Doo-Hyung would say—

spewing more lies. He was not to be trusted. He saw the same glint of craftiness and guile that had always unnerved him about his own father.

It was clear then, that the only reason they were being followed, and not executed was for information. The commander's codes. No, not the codes. If they had wanted the codes, he and Dae-Gun would already be dead by now. They needed information that was still to come. But from where?

The soldiers must have been hungry since their food was gone before Jung-Soo could hone in the radio dial for the evening. He glanced back to make sure Dae-Gun's rifle was still pointed at the intruders. On the one hand, Jung-Soo needed to keep a safe distance away from them to minimize how much information they heard.

"No reason to be shy," Doo-Hyung said with a grin. "I've been falling asleep to your voice for the past few months. Please, do speak up."

Jung-Soo stifled a gag. He already hated him, but he was right; it would be a far greater risk to leave Dae-Gun by himself with the two soldiers.

"Access code 901882," Jung-Soo spoke into the radio receiver as he always did. The signal was weaker than normal. Jung-Soo extended the antenna upwards.

"Access code 901882," Jung-Soo said, enunciating each number.

"Standby…" The radio responded. "901882, what is the passcode?"

"Navigating winds."

"Standby… Access granted. Report."

Those who listened by the campfire seemed to tense up.

"We are still on the western face of the Yang-Pyeong Mountains. Enemy spies seem to be roaming the area, but no signs of Chinese infantries."

"Verify security risk," the operator said.

A long silence ensued. "Security risk: moderate," Jung-Soo answered.

The radio operator seemed to be deep in thought. "We advise taking an alternate route southeast."

"Roger that. We will be heading southeast for three kilometers before coming back on course."

"Roger that. Be advised. Chinese troops may be heading south in the same direction."

Chinese troops? This far west? He thought they had all reached the eastern side of the peninsula by now.

"Roger that," Jung-Soo said.

"Standby for the next passcode."

"Standing by…"

It wasn't until the hissing of the radio came to a halt that the soldiers could breathe again.

"Thanks for not selling us out," the old soldier said. "Detour. How convenient." He led his tied-up hand into his front pocket as he plucked out a single cigarette, poking it into the dying flames.

"Why's that?" Dae-Gun asked for all of them.

"I don't know about you, but winter has just begun and the further South we go, the warmer it will be." He sucked in a puff that inflated his chest and shoulders. "Frankly," he said, as he exhaled smoke, "you two should be glad we came along when we did. I don't know how you were planning to survive the blistering cold with such a tiny flame. Now, you won't have to worry about the other spies roaming the mountains with me by your side!" He roared in laughter.

Dae-Gun shot a look at him to which the old soldier gave a courteous nod.

"Dae-Gun, confiscate the prisoner's cigarette," Jung-Soo spited.

"With pleasure," Dae-Gun said. The old soldier obliged, though only after one last puff.

"What do you say, Dae-Gun?" Jung-Soo said, "Perhaps a shot in the thigh might force some humility into him."

The bozo tensed up. Dae-Gun's voice shook. "I'm not too sure about that, Jung-Soo." The prospect of shooting anything that moved gave him the chills. "I… I can't expect leaving a trail of blood would be the best idea."

It was the smartest thing Dae-Gun said since they've met. Besides, there was no point wounding a soldier who knew too much. They would have to die eventually, once Jung-Soo ascertained their full story.

"It's your lucky day," Jung-Soo said.

Doo-Hyung didn't even flinch. He reached into his inside pocket and pulled out a tiny tin can and took a swig out of it.

"What's that?" Dae-Gun asked. He couldn't help his curiosity.

"This, my boy, is my choice of poison," he said, gulping down another mouthful. "Rice wine from the deep underbelly of society," he gave a bellow that rumbled from his satiated belly.

"What do you mean, the deep underbelly of society?"

"He means he ransacked deserted homes. It's quite fascinating, actually."

Dae-Gun couldn't imagine how stealing from unoccupied homes could be fascinating.

"We raid the outskirts of villages from time to time. He has a knack for spotting the places old men hide their stash of wine from their wives."

"A real useful skill," Dae-Gun said, sardonically.

"And for your generosity, Dae-Gun, I'll be happy to give you your share of the rice wine on our next raid," Doo-Hyung said.

Dae-Gun watched as the man gulped down the last drop of his wine and cradled into fetal position just far enough from the fire. He didn't seem to have a care in the world and didn't seem to mind that two guns were pointed at him. Jung-Soo neared the old soldier and Gil-Dong to secure another rope around their torso for the night.

It was more than the howls of the wind that kept Jung-Soo awake that night. Dae-Gun's rifle had dropped from his arms more than a couple times as his snores carried in echoes that lulled the three soldiers to sleep. It was up to Jung-Soo to stand guard.

He had been enjoying the silence before the sudden intrusion of North Korean spies. And for the past twelve hours, he had oddly set aside his preoccupations about the guitar and the letter. Maybe that's what an immediate life-threatening event does to you—shut off all other non-essential functions.

He knew tomorrow would prove to be vital. He had willed his eyes to remain open and think, sift through the truth and lies that the spies had brought along with them. Perhaps it would be easier to kill them. Right here, right now. It would be a mercy to die in one's sleep. Somehow, Jung-Soo found himself feeling nostalgic. Perhaps the changing weather had brought on a bout of wistful thinking and yearning that was more than just the loss he felt when he thought of Iseul, the Captain, and even his father.

What would they say? What would they do in this situation? He didn't know his father well enough. His father had always been busy, and the man was never one to hit up a conversation. The

Captain would tell him to shoot the spies before they could shoot him. He would never forget that lesson upon a mountain in Yeoju when the Captain held a gun to him. "You're already dead... you're already dead..." Those words rung in his ears like the wind that howled in cycles.

The day's hike had taken a toll on Jung-Soo who felt his eyes heavy and droop to a close. *I must make a decision...decision...* He had fallen asleep only to be woken in the middle of the night to the sound of water. He jumped up and pointed his gun somewhere into the darkness.

Jung-Soo squinted and saw the silhouette of the old soldier standing with his back towards Jung-Soo as he pissed against the tree. With three shakes and a zip, he hobbled over to his original spot where he was nestled to find a comfortable position as he jostled the ropes around him. Jung-Soo rose from his spot and neared the man to check that the ropes had not gotten loose when he noticed two eyes gazing up at him.

"Hey kid, you're going to need to sleep tonight. We've got a long day ahead of us tomorrow. I'll take the next shift till the morning if you'd like," the old soldier offered.

Who did he think he was? Jung-Soo walked back towards his position.

"Dae-Gun! Dae-Gun!" Jung-Soo kicked the side of a figure that slept by the log. Gil-Dong woke.

"Oww! I'm not Dae-Gun."

"Oh sorry..." Jung-Soo said instinctively. He kicked the other body that snored.

"It's your shift."

Dae-Gun rubbed his eyes and sat where Jung-Soo had been sitting. Just in case, Jung-Soo laid right beside Dae-Gun with his foot directed towards him. Maybe a kick or two might do the trick and keep him awake.

CHAPTER 29

The first thing Dae-Gun saw that morning was the sight the old soldier gazing into the sunrise as he took a deep breath of that cigarette. His chest hairs stuck out from the two buttons left undone as his disheveled hair caught the occasional wind. Dae-Gun looked down at his shirt that seemed too constricting and unbuttoned the top one. He saw only skin, white and soft as a baby's bottom. He sighed, disappointed.

Jung-Soo was fast asleep, curled up in a ball next to the log that Dae-Gun had been sitting on for the better part of the night.

Doo-Hyung approached Dae-Gun. "Get ready, boy. We're running late," he said.

Dae-Gun looked at the disheveled campsite he would have to put together alone if Jung-Soo didn't wake up soon. He wondered if Jung-Soo heard Doo-Hyung, who also seemed to be wondering the same.

"He's a deep sleeper, isn't he?"

Dae-Gun shook his head. "No, not particularly, but his hearing isn't…"

Before he could finish his sentence, Doo-Hyung kicked Jung-Soo in the bottom as he toppled over until his face met the soil. Doo-Hyung proceeded to walk away and return to his previous poise, facing the sunrise.

"Oww! What was that for?" Jung-Soo's glare stuck with force on the first person he laid his eyes on.

Dae-Gun shuddered. "Sorry… it wasn't me…"

With a whiff of a grin, Doo-Hyung interrupted. "Serves you right kicking your comrade in the middle of the night." Jung-Soo groaned. "Get up, boy! Half a battalion has died while you snoozed."

The first thing Jung-Soo did was take up his rifle as he let Dae-Gun rest his arms.

"Half a battalion?" Dae-Gun's ears perked. "Why half?"

Doo-Hyung squinted at the sun. "First contact would have been at sunrise."

"What?" Dae-Gun said. "You mean to say, the North has begun their attack?"

Doo-Hyung shook his head. "No, the South did."

Jung-Soo scoffed. "What makes you so sure? There is no way you could have known that."

"Kid, just because your superiors don't tell you what's going on doesn't mean that I don't know either." He struggled to lug his backpack with the ropes around him as he proceeded to walk towards the sunrise. "We'd better walk while we talk."

Dae-Gun had already lifted his heavy load in sync with Doo-Hyung and secured his guitar on his left shoulder.

"Not so fast. I'm not going anywhere until I know exactly what's happening," Jung-Soo said. In fact, Jung-Soo hadn't done much packing yet.

Doo-Hyung looked at Dae-Gun. "Does he always act like he has a stick up his ass?" Dae-Gun chuckled, then felt Jung-Soo's gaze. "What would you like to know?"

"Well," Jung-Soo said, hesitantly. He was supposed to have done the thinking the night before and was regretting having fallen asleep. "For one, where are you taking us?

"You heard your guy on the radio. He told us to take a detour southeast."

"Oh," Jung-Soo said. It had been a while since he had felt so flustered by someone.

"Like I said, we should talk and walk at the same time. Your superiors aren't going to happy if we don't make headway today," he said.

"Yeah, Jung-Soo let's head out first." Dae-Gun nodded to reason.

Jung-Soo couldn't understand what had gotten into Dae-Gun and how he could so easily trust someone. The four soldier filed in a row and began their hike with Jung-Soo at the tail, ready to shoot someone if they veered off course.

The cold November wind dissipated the beads of sweat on their faces, leaving trails of salt-encrusted residue. There wasn't much Jung-Soo said as he hiked. He was cautious—perhaps overly so. He had hoped to get rid of the commander's codes soon, but he seemed to have collected a new set from his father. Jung-Soo felt somewhat relieved that the codes were useless without the proper enigma machine to decode any of them.

But if they did find a way to decipher his father's coded letter, what sort of information would it reveal? He couldn't imagine his father writing a personal letter to him. They had never had that kind of relationship. It must be related to the war. His father was just a lowly colonel in the North Korean army. How much could someone in his rank know that could alter the fate of this war? That too seemed unlikely.

Dae-Gun marched to the beat that Doo-Hyung set, moving relentlessly forward. It was only after four hours that Jung-Soo noticed a slight wobble in Dae-Gun's footsteps and breathing that sounded heavier. It seemed odd that Dae-Gun, who had never once been so silent for so long, did not care to whine about how quickly they were hiking.

"Let's take a break," Dae-Gun finally said, collapsing to the ground as he pulled out his water canister and drank without breathing.

"I was wondering when he would break." Doo-Hyung chuckled, moving back towards the ground and sitting next to the boy. "Not to worry, these things take time."

Dae-Gun reached into his backpack and pulled out two rations of food, and then another two.

"Do you mind?" Doo-Hyung said, raising his tied hands towards Dae-Gun to release. "Unless you want to feed me."

Jung-Soo shook his head as he made their prisoners watch them eat before he released their ropes and gave them one ration to share between the two of them.

The old soldier was on to his routine gulp of alcohol and a nice long inhale of his cigarette. It was a wonder how he didn't run out. Those two items could very well be the only things he carried on his back. Doo-Hyung stared into the woods, then intently at Jung-Soo, alternating as he would his two vices.

"Shall we get on with it then?" Doo-Hyung said first.

Jung-Soo did not answer.

"Let's let our two friends in on where we are," he said towards Gil-Dong and Dae-Gun. The two perked up from drinking water.

"Where are we? I thought we were headed Southeast?" Dae-Gun said.

Gil-Dong let out a subdued chuckle. "I think he means Jung-Soo has had enough time to think so they should probably begin talking about what's going to happen next."

"Oh," Dae-Gun said, yet again embarrassed.

"Let's start from the beginning, shall we?" Doo-Hyung said.

"Stick to facts, old man," Jung-Soo spat out, the old soldier acknowledging him with a nod.

"The bozo and I have been tailing you for the better part of two months. Isn't that right, bozo?" Gil-Dong nodded. "We clearly were close enough to shoot you and your friend down, but both of you are still alive." This time, Dae-Gun nodded. "And seeing that you haven't killed us yet, you're still making up your mind," Doo-Hyung added.

His gaze fixed on Jung-Soo who held his rifle to his chest.

"I'm sure you've figured out the discrepancies in my story," Doo-Hyung continued. "And you're wondering which are true and which are lies. Let me begin with one: Why didn't I hand over the letter months ago when I first tracked you?

Dae-Gun nodded curiously. "Yeah, why didn't you?"

Doo-Hyung continued. "Timing is of the essence, kid. And before you go thinking that I want your commander's enigma codes, let me make it clear: they're useless to me. We're too late now for those codes to be of any use anyway."

So he knew I had them. "And what are we too late for? Jung-Soo beckoned. He did not intend to speak, but the words just fell out.

"There is more than the two of us at stake. The truth is, in the span of our conversation our friends, both yours and mine, have spilled their blood on our soil."

"They are soldiers and this is war. Stick to the facts, not some naïve bullshit about restoring the Korean Peninsula under the Communist regime."

"Good," he smiled like a proud father. It looked oddly familiar, like the one the Captain used to give him. *How dare he?* "Communism. Democracy. All the same to folks like us. Is it not?"

"And what sort of folks are we?" Jung-Soo probed.

"Traitors."

Dae-Gun jerked at the word. "I won't have you accusing Jung-Soo, just because you're the traitor!" The stoic glint of truth in Jung-Soo startled Dae-Gun. "I know him. I'll vouch for Jung-Soo! He's followed every order and we've completed every mission. He even saved my life!"

Traitor. Jung-Soo let the word sink in. He resisted the word, denied it even. Hadn't he spent the better part of his life trying to distance himself from his father? Jung-Soo had picked a side; he would be a loyal South Korean soldier and return to the only place had felt at home, whatever it took.

Gil-Dong spoke. "It's alright, Dae-Gun," he said as if to calm him.

"No!" Dae-Gun jumped to Jung-Soo's side with his rifle. "You two are the traitors; we're not! I don't know what your intentions are with Jung-Soo, but leave him alone!"

The old soldier was intrigued, watching Jung-Soo's movement and gauging what the boy would do. "Has it occurred to you that we might be on the same side?" Doo-Hyung said.

"And which side would that be?"

"The side that is neither North nor South."

"So you are my father's man!" Jung-Soo accused. "A vagabond serving no one but his own interests."

He scoffed. "I am my own man. And we've both had to live with the decisions we've made."

He sounded oddly melancholy, as though tired of talking or even thinking back to his past. The old soldier sucked in a deep breath as if he were taking in a dose of his cigarette. He let it out before he began. *Measured speech.*

"Once, there were two boys who roamed the hillsides of Jeollanamdo," he began. "They were unstoppable, the two of them together. They made a fool of the entire village, if you asked them, stealing rice wine, drinking all night long as they dreamed up a grand future for themselves. They drove the servants mad, and they weren't just talkers like most boys their age. The older boy was a genius: numbers, construction, engineering—you name it, he could do it." He let out a little chuckle, nostalgic as he mused.

"One summer, the older one single-handedly constructed a pulley system that could transport fish from the shores to the warehouse. Needless to say, the villagers had the tendency to look the other way when the rice wine went missing. The younger one, well, let's just say he wasn't quite as talented, but he was always wondering what else they could do, and laid out grand plans for their future together."

"Are you one of them?" Gil-Dong asked.

"I sure was!" He smiled at him. "And I was determined to prove myself too!"

"What was a northerner doing all the way south in Mokpo?" Jung-Soo asked. Mokpo was on the south-western tip of the Peninsula where everything reeked of fish and salt, where a man of his breeding wouldn't be too comfortable. His measured speech, the way his back didn't hint of a slouch, and how he needed to bring along a boy who knew the elements of nature—they all pointed to high breeding Jung-Soo was not ignorant of himself.

"My maternal family lives there. It was an insurance policy of sorts to keep the General's youngest son safe. It's the same reason your father had you sent to Yeoju," Doo-Hyung answered.

"The General." Jung-Soo caught on.

"Yes, General Shin is my father," he said, almost regrettably.

Jung-Soo's rifle shot back up and aimed at his heart. *So Doo-Hyung's father had killed his.*

"I suppose there's no reason to hide the fact. You of all people would understand," Doo-Hyung said calmly despite the gun that was pointed to him.

Understand what? That both of their fathers were murderers? Jung-Soo could not deny it. He too was nothing more than an insurance policy for his father who had already lost two of his eldest sons.

"General Shin was never there when I was a child, but he had always sent toys to keep me company. Guns, animal traps, a thing called a light bulb and a box that stored the stuff to power it."

"Batteries," Jung-Soo said, completing the old soldier's thought.

The old soldier nodded. "The possibilities were endless. We were mesmerized. Your father and I were given guns to train with, shot bullets into trees and branches and made a game out of it. Though I must say, I was always the better shot between the two of us," he smiled, satisfied.

From the corner of Jung-Soo's eyes, he could see Dae-Gun's gun drooping to the ground as he was sucked into the spy's tale.

"Along with a set of the newest guns from the European mainland, General Shin sent battle textbooks that your father and I perused."

"Karl Marx," Jung-Soo said, already knowing what would come next.

Doo-Hyung nodded. "Communism had come knocking on two naïve boys' door and we were enthralled, no, brainwashed. It was as if the world we had always dreamt of was ready to be ushered into a changing Korea. And all the more since we hated the Japanese oppression more than your generation ever will."

Jung-Soo had gotten involved in the soldier's story more than he had anticipated. Stories of his father in his youth had never been discussed in the Ham household and it had never occurred to him before that his father was once young too.

"My father, General Shin was a decent father, though I am not naïve enough to believe he is a good man. He was training his sons to be generals and nothing short of it. One day, the General brought over old machines abandoned by the government due to defective construction or outdated modeling. That's when we came across our first enigma machine."

Enigma machine. Jung-Soo paid attention. He had a feeling that the spy's sudden appearance would soon make sense.

"It didn't look like much. It was just an old typewriter and we had plenty of it. In fact, it was a step down from the ones we already had, bulky and weighing at least twice as much as a normal typewriter. But eventually, your father figured out its true use. We tinkered with it—changed out the English alphabet for Korean ones and used our own code combinations to secretly communicate with each other."

Enigma machine in Korean. He pulled out the coded message from his father again. Doo-Hyung waited for Jung-Soo to come to his own conclusions.

"You think I know where the enigma machine is? Is that why you were tracking me?"

Doo-Hyung shook his head. "I already know where it is."

"Then why do you need me?"

Jung-Soo filtered through his memories. Had he ever seen one before? Perhaps when he was living in Seoul with his father? His father had been friendly with many shopkeepers. Maybe one of them sold typewriters.

"Tell me, Jung-Soo. Have you ever snuck into your father's warehouse—ever cared to see what your father was building next?"

His father's warehouse in Seoul had been a mansion in and of itself, a maze that had kept young Jung-Soo occupied. But it had been dismantled, most of the objects burned or sold and the small leftover collection sent to the smaller warehouse in Yeoju. That's it! The warehouse next to the Golden Palace! A typewriter. An enigma machine. He thought hard. Yes, he could vaguely remember a typewriter amongst his father's belongings!

"It's still in Yeoju," Jung-Soo said.

The old soldier nodded.

"And you need me to get it for you."

At that very moment, Doo-Hyung leaped into motion, pulling Dae-Gun's gun away from him in one swift dance as he pointed it at Jung-Soo.

"Correct." He smiled, ready to pull the trigger. "I knew you would eventually get there."

Impossible. Where were the ropes around his wrists? Jung-Soo saw them on the floor. He must have untangled himself while they were all distracted by his story.

"You wouldn't kill me," Jung-Soo said, his rifle cocked higher than it had been seconds ago. "You need me. You'd be dead within a day in Yeoju without me." The two stood head to head, looking into the barrel of the guns. "But I wouldn't think twice."

"Try me."

"Jung-Soo, are you sure about this?" Dae-Gun said hesitantly.

"You shot him, didn't you?" Jung-Soo said, his once stoic demeanor perturbed. "You're the one who shot my father!"

"Good," Doo-Hyung said. "But he had done it on his own volition. I was merely his weapon of choice."

"Stop! Stop the lies!" he said, frenetic.

"You are free to believe what you'd like. The bozo was there to witness the whole exchange."

"Speak!" Jung-Soo pointed the gun at Gil-Dong. "What did you see that night?"

Gil-Dong was shivering. "It's true. Your father was with us one minute, and then the next, he told us to go on without him. He kept saying 'do it... do it...' until Doo-Hyung shot him."

"Lies!" Jung-Soo said. "You told him to say that. You brought him all the way here to stand witness to lies! What's in this letter?"

Jung-Soo was yelling. "What is so important that you betrayed your childhood friend? Is it something to help your father—help the North win the war? I'll die before I give it to you!"

"You mean, you'll die before you become a traitor?" Doo-Hyung questioned. "And what will this great and mighty country do for you once you've sacrificed yourself? Will it even remember you? Honor you?" He raised his voice and taunted Jung-Soo. "Shoot me. You are a soldier and I'm the enemy, a traitor, a spy even, and your father's murderer. Your conscious is clear in every way and you'll even have Dae-Gun here to be your witness."

"Stop," Jung-Soo said, placing pressure on his temples to ease the throbbing. He couldn't think...

"Shoot me! Do what's right, don't hesitate!" Doo-Hyung shouted.

Jung-Soo's finger clasped harder around the gun, but the firmer he gripped it, his forefinger around the trigger seemed to loosen. "No..." Jung-Soo whimpered.

You're too late... You're already dead...Don't hesitate... Don't hesitate. A familiar voice rang in his ears. He looked at the spy's gun that was now pointed at Dae-Gun.

"Don't hesitate!" he kept saying.

Jung-Soo saw Dae-Gun shivering in fear. Why couldn't Jung-Soo be as cold-hearted as he had been on the battlefield? He had seen each man's face as it came to the realization that it was over and had looked away. He didn't count how many bullets he had placed in a man's heart... he hadn't felt anything.

"Don't hesitate. You're already dead," Doo-Hyung said. And with those words, he pointed the rifle back at Jung-Soo and shot a single bullet. The forest rang in interminable echoes, as though any living, breathing creature had stopped to hold its breath for the duration.

Jung-Soo's gun dropped with a thud on the crisp forest ground where autumn leaves had lost their luster. Dae-Gun watched as his friend dropped to his knees as he ran towards him. He looked for blood to seep through to make the forest floor crimson as he had witnessed weeks ago in the battlefield.

"The Captain..." Jung-Soo managed to say, his eyes painstakingly moving to meet Doo-Hyung's.

"I'm here to remind you of an old lesson," Doo-Hyung said. "There is always more than what meets the eye."

Of course, Jung-Soo thought, as his knees buckled against the soil. There was a second part to what the Captain had said that night; he had just forgotten about it. His ears rang again and again with the Captain's voice. All along, he had thought the lesson was about pulling the trigger first before his opponent could. He couldn't have been more wrong. Guilt stabbed him a hundred times over. He saw those faces—the ones he had shot down in the battlefield. And in each face, he saw the Captain's own.

His thighs felt weak and his knees wobbled, finding it difficult to stay upright on his knees. Sensation in his fingertips ceased as the trees and soil merged into one blurry vision.

"No!" Dae-Gun said as he patted Jung-Soo's body to feel for the hole, but could not find one.

"I'm okay," Jung-Soo said.

"What?" Dae-Gun said confused. "What happened to the bullet? You weren't shot?"

Jung-Soo caught his breath. "Apparently not," he said.

"You okay there, kid?" Doo-Hyung chuckled.

Dae-Gun fumed, stomping towards Doo-Hyung and seizing the collar of his shirt that flapped against his chest. "You asshole, you could have killed him! Give me that gun," he pointed his own rifle recklessly at Doo-Hyung. "One move and I'll shoot you myself, right between the eyes, you hear me!"

Doo-Hyung landed on his back foot with his hands above his head. "Alright, alright," he muttered. "I assure you, that thing is more dangerous in your hands than it ever was in mine! Put it down, before you hurt yourself."

"To hell, I'm putting this rifle down. Not after what you pulled on Jung-Soo!"

Jung-Soo managed a low grumbling command. "Do as he says, Dae-Gun."

Dae-Gun flung back around with his rifle, inadvertently pointing it at the bozo who flinched. He saw Jung-Soo had returned to his normal composure, and slowly lowered his rifle to the ground. "Are you going to be okay?" He asked Jung-Soo another time.

Dae-Gun collapsed next to Gil-Dong who hadn't moved an inch since the event conspired. They exchanged a look as if to wonder if they had both witnessed the same event. They tucked down to drink from their canisters, though Dae-Gun thought he might need something stronger than water. Gil-Dong twisted in his ropes to reach for his own water canister and handed it to Dae-Gun who caught a whiff of its contents. *Rice Wine*. Dae-Gun took it and drank a swig the same way Doo-Hyung would have.

"Sorry, kid, but you just weren't ready for what I had to say otherwise." Doo-Hyung pulled Jung-Soo back up on his feet. "I still need you to decipher the codes, and I think your father knew I couldn't do it on my own. But I'd rather you come on your own volition."

Jung-Soo was still between the present and the past as the image of his younger self standing in front of the Captain began to fade away. *There is always more than what meets the eye…* The Captain's words rang. Why had he forgotten this part of the Captain's lesson? He had been blind. No, he had intentionally turned a blind eye to his father, and even to the Captain. He had never really bothered to ask why they had chosen the path they were on, making his own judgments and filling in the spaces of who he thought they were. He had been young and too afraid, yes, that was the reason why; he had always feared what he would learn. He saw that now. The Captain wanted to teach him to keep an open mind and see the person in front of him as more than just an opponent. Even that lesson had evaded his already made-up mind.

"How do you know the Captain?" Jung-Soo asked, returning to his calm state.

"Is that what he likes to call himself these days?" Doo-Hyung said. "He was my bodyguard before he ever was your father's Captain. That old geezer pulled the same stunt on me when I was a kid."

Jung-Soo gave a weak chortle. "And so, did you shoot him first? I've always wondered if my gun was loaded."

"So you didn't pull the trigger," Doo-Hyung stated.

Jung-Soo shook his head. "How could I? I couldn't kill the man who had been a better father to me than my real father ever could be, even if he had a gun pointed at me."

"It's a shame he's dead now," Doo-Hyung said matter-of-factly, though his long silent gaze into the trees betrayed how he really felt.

Jung-Soo expected it, but the weight of guilt still hung heavily. The last he remembered of the Captain was his promise to keep Iseul safe as Jung-Soo vanished to save himself.

"So did you shoot first?" Jung-Soo asked, pushing his thoughts aside.

Doo-Hyung nodded. "And it was loaded. He had a limp for nearly half a year. Good thing I blinked at the last second or the bullet would have hit his heart. It was years before I shot at anyone after that—a good lesson for my trigger-friendly fingers," he chuckled, reminiscing.

"So I have you to thank for my childhood years then." Jung-Soo bantered along as if reunited with the Captain himself. After all, they had both learned that banter from the same source. "So," Jung-Soo continued, "my father still thinks that I can't take care of myself."

"He wouldn't have sent me if he wanted you safe," Doo-Hyung said. Jung-Soo made a confused face. "Trouble usually finds me. Can't remember how many times I've nearly lost a limb or two."

Doo-Hyung watched the skepticism spread across Jung-Soo's face. He sighed. "Kid, your father is a complicated man, as is my own father. It took me years before I could even begin to wrap my head around the challenges he faced trying to sift through people he could trust, and those who might betray him. We live in troubling times, Jung-Soo, but there's no denying the length they'll go to keep their sons safe." But even as he said it, Doo-Hyung wondered if what he said were true of General Shin.

Doo-Hyung waited as Jung-Soo processed the words of his father's close friend. Jung-Soo resisted the idea. He had always felt like a dispensable pawn piece, the last straw of his father's lineage to perpetuate his beliefs. Yet, he knew that the dose of truth in the man's words was what stung him.

"So, what really happened? Why are you here instead of my father?"

Jung-Soo raised his guards up again. He still wasn't quite sure if this old spy could be trusted, but he deserved to be heard at least once, if only out of respect for his late Captain.

"Your father and I had been trying to make amend for our past iniquities, if you will, by furthering the peace talks. Your father was tasked with fact-checking and eavesdropping on radio conversations, utilizing his extensive knowledge of devices, mechanics, and code-breaking. I was tasked with spying on your father," he said reluctantly.

"It was General Shin's test of allegiance of sorts, considering your father and I have history growing up together in Mokpo. When your father's projections of the extent of American involvement fell on deaf ears in the North, we decided that the peace talks would be furthered if the South Koreans had the information we had."

"So it's true then. My father is a spy," Jung-Soo said.

"Well, we like to call him an intelligence officer. Every country has them, and I'm willing to bet your father ranks among the best of them."

Intelligence officer. He kind of liked the sound of that. Jung-Soo reckoned he was one too.

"We had a plan. We were supposed cross the 38th parallel at midnight, hand over the information we have and return by daybreak. General Shin had been on to your father for a while now. Your father had that look on his face, you know, the way he twisted his bottom lip and frowned," Doo-Hyung said, imitating the look.

Jung-Soo knew this look.

"I never figured out what was troubling him, but it seemed he had come across something that might be crucial in bringing this war to an end. When I asked for details, he seemed to want to keep me at arms lengths, if you know what I mean."

Jung-Soo did.

Doo-Hyung continued. "That night, he was acting strange—stranger than usual I mean. We were supposed to stay at bozo's farmhouse near the 38th parallel when your father all of a sudden asked me to trust him. Your father, he really did push me to my limits," Doo-Hyung sighed. "We were to wait for him. He said he needed to go back for a message for his son."

Jung-Soo knew what would come next. His father would have come back, as promised, with the same message that was now tucked in his front pocket.

"I'm sorry, Jung-Soo, but he asked me to pull the trigger. There was a lot of blood."

Jung-Soo's lips tightened. "But there is still a chance..."

"I'm afraid not." Doo-Hyung looked to Gil-Dong who spoke with a firmness he had not seen before. "Blood volume by mammal size is fairly predictable. A man your father's size losing that much blood is fatal without a doubt."

Jung-Soo nodded, accepting the fact he already had months before, all over again. He felt resentment welling up. Doo-Hyung had a choice, hand is father did too... Why would he do this to him—make him bury his father twice? Jung-Soo wanted an explanation, even a semblance of an excuse from Doo-Young, but he made no such excuses.

"So what now?" Jung-Soo said, willing himself to move forward. "What did my father instruct us to do once you got the letter to me?"

Doo-Hyung shrugged. "He told me to wait to give you the letter until the North or South fires first on the 38th Parallel, and the South Korean side did this morning. It seemed fairly obvious after that."

His father probably meant for him to head straight to Yeoju. Jung-Soo was beginning to realize why he had been posted as a radio mechanic with the idiot boy. His father probably played some role in getting Jung-Soo on the road so that it would be easier for Doo-Hyung to find and convince him to leave to Yeoju with him. He wasn't about to play into his father's hands so easily.

"Any ideas why he wanted you to delay the delivery?" Jung-Soo said.

"He probably didn't want you to abandon your post and risk blowing your cover too soon."

Too soon for what? Perhaps Doo-Hyung really didn't know either.

"We go to Yeoju, find the Korean enigma machine and we decipher your father's letter, Doo-Hyung said.

He had the whole thing planned as if it were that easy.

"I can't go with you. I won't risk being caught and branded a traitor just for this." Jung-Soo looked at the coded message and he was sure it was no more than a sentence, succinct as was his father's usual style.

"Understandable," Doo-Hyung said, not in the slightest bit disappointed by his response. "So, you'll tell me where to find the enigma machine?"

Jung-Soo bit his lips. Could he trust this man with his father's codes? Doo-Hyung's forehead creased with heavy thought.

"Although, there is a peculiar discrepancy that I haven't yet been able to wrap my head around," he said, changing the subject to pique Jung-Soo's interest. "I've been trying to pinpoint when your father might have coded the message. Take a look at the page again."

Jung-Soo pulled the letter out and carefully unfolded it. He was looking but didn't see anything unusual.

"It isn't military grade paper. It's likely a locally-sourced page your father got a hold of, meaning he might have written the letter for you while he was still living in Yeoju. Do you remember anything—anything at all? Did he tell you anything about the upcoming war while you were still in Yeoju?"

"Ha!" Jung-Soo sneered. "Like he would tell me anything important. Honestly, we exchanged no more than a handful of sentences, let alone any meaningful conversations. In fact, back then, I wasn't even sure the war would occur, naïve like the rest of the villagers."

Jung-Soo thought about it for a while. "A locally sourced page, you say…" he said. "It makes sense, I guess. Father would have needed an enigma machine to code the message in the first place. But if he already had the coded letter written, he wouldn't have had to disappear to get the letter on the night he…died." Jung-Soo forced himself to say the word.

Jung-Soo let his fingers rub the page again. It felt oddly soothing, and even familiar. "It's Iseul's paper!" he muttered, realizing why the page had felt so familiar. It was certainly from Yeoju.

"Iseul?" Doo-Hyung asked.

Jung-Soo took out the letter Iseul had sent him. He was right; it was the same type of paper.

"She's the local carpenter's daughter. Rumor has it that she's taken over the paper production, working with the villagers to make enough paper to supply our soldiers to write letters with."

"It's quite fascinating, really!" Dae-Gun butted in. "The letters are sent in a bundle with blank pages so that the receiver will have enough paper to write back to the sender and share with other soldiers."

Doo-Hyung's fingers fidgeting around his temples to hasten his thoughts. He had assumed, up to that point, that the letter had been written in Yeoju before he had left.

"So either the letter was written while he was in Yeoju, or your father has been in contact with someone from Yeoju this whole time."

"It can't have been the Captain, could it?" Jung-Soo hoped, looking at Doo-Hyung for a confirmation.

"I'm quite certain he's dead. Your father would not lie to me about that. But whoever it is, he would have needed your father's enigma machine to code the message in the first place, and the only place your father and I know of the existence of a Korean-lettered enigma machine is in Yeoju."

"I don't understand," Dae-Gun said. "If Jung-Soo's father could make one when he was a kid, couldn't he just have built another one while he was in the North?"

"Yes, he could have," Doo-Hyung said. "But it wouldn't work with this letter. It has to be that exact model plugged in with the exact coding combination. He would have given me the new enigma machine with the letter if that were the case."

"So how do you know that the enigma machine in Yeoju is the one that would work with this message?" Jung-Soo asked.

"I don't. At least not for sure," Doo-Hyung said. "But your father and I have been reminiscing the past few months about growing up in Mokpo and how we had renovated this magnificent enigma machine."

"In any case, we'll have to wait and see what the message holds." Jung-Soo found himself saying. In the excitement of the new-found information about his father and the message, he had managed to imagine decoding the message himself.

Doo-Hyung was ready to lead the pack, adjusting the straps on his backpack as he went ahead and untied the ropes around Gil-Dong.

Here's the plan," Doo-Hyung said. "We head straight to the 5th Cavalry base, hand over the codes and then we head due south. It won't take more than a day or two to reach Yeoju."

Jung-Soo's heart leaped at the thought of heading back home. He wondered if there were any villagers left in that remote place. He knew the ones who remembered him may possibly be the first to shoot him, but surely there would be at least one person who would welcome him with open arms.

"And if we're going to get there on time, we'd better hurry," Doo-Hyung said as if Jung-Soo had already agreed to the mission.

"What's the rush?" Dae-Gun said with a look of grave concern. "Yeoju…that seems awfully close to the eastern front."

"You forget a second army is tailing us from behind," Doo-Hyung said.

"A second army, tailing us?" Jung-Soo said, his interest piqued. "No, I'm sure the last of the Chinese troops have made it to the eastern front by now."

"Didn't you hear?" Gil-Dong said.

"Hear what?" Dae-Gun said, panic rising.

"Oh boy…" Doo-Hyung said as he strutted next to Jung-Soo

to help lead the way. "Today is your lucky day then, I reckon as good as any to gamble with our fates."

Dae-Gun gulped, his mouth drying out.

"Spit it out then, will you?" Jung-Soo said.

"A second Chinese army has been marching past the Yalu, lying in wait in the mountains on the western side of the 38th parallel. They're just about ready to mount a surprise attack."

"Waiting for what?" Dae-Gun managed to say.

"For the South to attack first, of course. They'll be marching east to meet the troops already there. The South Koreans won't know what hit them. And if all goes as planned, all South Korean troops will be surrounded from both the Eastern and Western fronts, forced to the center of the Peninsula and then all the way south from there."

"That's why the man on the radio was advising us to head southeast to avoid the second army coming in from the northwest," Gil-Dong added.

Dae-Gun's knees wobbled as he tried to keep up with the group.

"Impossible..." Jung-Soo said, as his mouth fell ajar.

"The Americans have mounted the 'Home by Christmas' campaign. Rather brash if you ask me. They want to be gone before winter hits."

"How about we head south to Yeoju first?" Dae-Gun found himself saying. It suddenly seemed like the better choice.

"Damn it, those Chinese," Jung-Soo spat out. "They've been planning a two-frontal attack all along."

"I'm afraid the Americans have sorely underestimated their position in this war, and the peace talks your father and I have been advocating is in complete ruin."

Jung-Soo's eyes flickered. He stopped in his track and turned around, looking far into the trees they had just passed by. The momentary bliss he had experienced at the thought of going back to Yeoju crashed with a fatal realization: If the North Koreans and Chinese were forcing the allied forces to the center of the Peninsula and south from that position, the battles would eventually reach Yeoju. There was that possibility that they would bypass Yeoju and take a different route, but with armies of that magnitude, more than a few infantries will reach Yeoju where they would wreak havoc on anything and anyone they came across.

There was no question about it now. Time was of the essence. They needed to warn the people of Yeoju before that would happen. All Jung-Soo could think of was the Wasteland, the village trapped in by two insurmountable mountain ranges. It'll take them an extra day or two to evacuate to the northwestern road before they can safely head south.

"What's wrong, Jung-Soo?" Dae-Gun asked.

"We're going to Yeoju first," Jung-Soo stated, almost as if he were commanding the soldiers.

"Jung-Soo, I know I suggested that but I didn't mean it," Dae-Gun said. "That's against protocol. What about the codes? Commander Rogers is counting on us!"

"To hell with protocol!" Jung-Soo said.

"Jung-Soo, wait!"

Doo-Hyung read the concern so prominent in Jung-Soo's face and wondered if Young-Nam knew it would be so easy to convince the boy to risk his post. There was a girl, he was sure of it. No man would lose all his wits unless there was a woman involved. He pictured Yeoju on the Korean map, central in the Peninsula, recalling that preposterous rumor he thought might be the cause of all this. He hoped not, yet his footsteps followed close behind Jung-Soo's.

Even as Doo-Hyung paced next to Jung-Soo, he wondered if they were doing the right thing. Jung-Soo would be branded a traitor yet again, and the boy's hopes of leading a normal life after the war would come to ruin. It wasn't just Jung-Soo's hopes; he knew his mentor wanted that for his son too.

Doo-Hyung marched on, quelling his reservations. After all, there was more at stake here than the possibility of being caught disobeying orders. If all went well, Jung-Soo would return the hero, not the traitor. He would make sure of it!

"Jung-Soo, don't be stupid," Dae-Gun said, as the gravity of their situation set in. "We can't just abandon our post and think all will be forgiven. We'll be executed for it!"

But what other choice did Jung-Soo have? The words of Commander Lee echoed in his ear, *get there before the first of December.* They had at least another week, but the villagers couldn't wait; they needed to evacuate now. What if he is too late? *The slaughtering, rampaging…raping…*

Perhaps they could split up, leave Dae-Gun to pass the code

along to the commander, while he heads to Yeoju first. No. That was not an option. Dae-Gun would be questioned and he would never be able to leave the 5th Cavalry base alive.

If only there was a way to warn the villagers. By radio? No, that wouldn't work. They were too far, with too many mountains between them. He needed to get closer.

He stared into Dae-Gun's desperate face. This is exactly why he didn't plan on making friends.

"Fine," Jung-Soo said begrudgingly. "We deliver the codes to Commander Rogers first." Jung-Soo changed their course again, this time due northeast, on the same path the incoming Chinese troops were on.

They must hasten…

Jung-Soo initial curiosity of his father's last words dissipated as his thoughts dominated with the villagers of the Wasteland and that one girl who he hoped would have evacuated Yeoju by now.

Yet, in the back of his mind, he couldn't shake off the feeling that somehow, these surreptitious events were all connected—his father's death, the surprise Chinese attack, these strange North Koreans and the timing of their arrival, even Iseul and her handcrafted paper his father's last words were written on.

He'd get to the bottom of it.

Part 3

CHAPTER 30

He hadn't fallen asleep at all. No, the scholar had been daydreaming on Iseul's porch—as was his usual pose, dreaming of pork and chicken and the spicy red chili paste that seasoned them in an exquisite concoction of mouth-watering deliciousness. His wife's cooking was undoubtedly the best, and he knew just how to compliment the woman so she wouldn't skimp on the red chilli paste. If it weren't for Mr. Lim intruding on his perfect afternoon with something as insignificant as another letter, he would have surely finished the entire chicken!

His arms extended back and balanced on the base of his spine as he trotted away from the commotion, trying to hold on to the taste before it disappeared from his memory. *A letter for Iseul,* he thought. He couldn't recall the last time a letter had arrived for her. He had always assumed she went into the village just like all the other women to send and receive her letters. Come to think of it, Iseul was an orphan. It had always felt as if her father was at war, like the rest of the younger fathers in the village. *Poor kid...* He didn't feel quite so bad about the last bit of chicken he hadn't gotten to.

The wind blew in his direction; surely a sign. The wind gods were blowing their approval on their paper production, making them dry faster. He nodded, content. The chatter of the women had died down when he realized how far he had ventured out. He might as well do his routine perimeter check.

The wind blew again. It wasn't until he felt cold metal against his left cheek that he realized something might not be quite right.

"Don't move," a woman's voice said.

The scholar froze. Surely, it wasn't a gun on his head...was it?

"I don't mean to hurt you. I just need to talk to her."

"Who?" The scholar said, confused. He reached for his gun, patting his back pocket to find it empty.

"Looking for this?" an old man croaked. He raised the scholar's handgun then looked to the woman. "Dear, you're going to have to be more specific if you're going to persuade this nice young man."

"Father," the woman sighed. "For once, can you let me handle this?"

"Young man?" the scholar roared, brushing his hand against his long white beard. "Who are you calling young?"

The old man seemed to want to say something when the woman gave him a look. It was not unlike the one the scholar's wife shot at him quite regularly. And then it hit him—a woman with a gun, and one that talked back to her father! He shook his head. What was the world coming to?

The woman spoke. "I need to speak to the orphan girl. The one in charge of the paper production."

"Iseul?" the scholar said, though in the moment her name slipped out, he thought perhaps it wasn't such a good idea to mention it.

"Yes, her," she said. "We promise, we're not here to hurt anyone. We're from the village in northern Yeoju and we have some news for her."

The woman's father cleared his throat. "You know, dear, it isn't proper etiquette to have a gun pointed at a man's head when we're trying to convince him we're friendly folks," the old man said. "Here." He gave the scholar back his gun and held out his hand for his daughter's gun. She obliged.

"Right then, show us the way." The old man walked in the direction the scholar had come from.

The scholar began to think—ponder, if you will, on the situation. "Who's to say you're not spies from the North? Maybe you're here to kill us, murder Iseul so the paper production halts."

"Precisely," the woman said. "No, I mean, we're not here to kill her. We're just here with news." She seemed to be digging herself into a hole.

"Here, take my gun too," the old man said, giving him his rifle that seemed to magically appear from behind his short frame.

"Oh, that simplifies things," the scholar said, relieved.

It wasn't until they were nearing Iseul's workshop that he realized the old man's eyes were covered in a thick layer of white. *Cataract.* He was blind, at least partially.

"Don't underestimate the old man," the woman said with a grin. "He's stronger than he looks, and an excellent shot if it comes to it."

"Right," the scholar said, doubtfully.

The women welcomed the newcomer. Her name was Kim Su-Jung who lived just on the northern border of Yeoju near the wall of Pasaseong-ji. She came with stories of horror, of soldiers strewn on the ground and tanks rolling over dead bodies. None of them doubted her stories and Mi-Jung, who had been trying to motivate the hungry women, welcomed the fire she saw in this woman. They could use some of that.

A gun shot rang through the hills. The old man had shot towards the forest, his gun and his eyes pointed in different directions.

"Anyone hungry?" Su-Jung said with a cheeky smile.

In the distance, a thud heard on the dried leaves of autumn. They couldn't believe it! He had shot a fawn from further away than their eyes could see. The scholar stood scratching his head, wondering how the old man could have had another gun hidden on him.

"The chatter might be problematic, but I think I can manage." The old man chuckled.

The women guffawed in unison. Mr. Lim stood wide-eyed at the old man.

"You mean to say, you're planning to stay?" Mr. Lim said to the woman.

"Yes, no, well... maybe. It depends," she said, flustered again.

"We could definitely use any kind of help we can get," Mi-Jung said as she looked to Mr. Lim for approval, disappearing into the house to fetch Iseul.

"Please?" another middle-aged woman added.

It was clear that they needed help. They were getting thinner by the day, and what about Iseul? The strain on her was evident in her gaunt look.

Iseul appeared from her room.

"You'd better hear what they have to say," the scholar said, holding the old man's rifle at the strangers. "They're from a village on the northern border of Yeoju."

Why was he holding a gun to them? Iseul broke from the thoughts of the letter that had arrived just moments ago with the sudden appearance of suspicious visitors. She must not forget, spies were everywhere.

"How can we trust what you say?" Iseul said, with a tone of authority that she herself was surprised by.

"Spies…" Mi-Jung whispered.

"But surely not! Not with that accent," the scholar's wife said.

"You never know," Mi-Jung added.

"We need to know exactly why they are here before we let them in," Iseul said to the women.

Su-Jung did not seem the slightest fazed, directing her gaze only at Iseul. "We are descended from the Ansan Kim clan, west of Seoul. My great grandfather relocated to Yeoju and I'm certain we have distant relatives who are residing here, even in this village."

"My husband is an Ansan-Kim too!" one farmer's wife said.

Iseul stood in contemplation.

"It's really quite intriguing," the woman began. "I heard about the papermakers of Yeoju from my uncle who is all the way on the north eastern side of the peninsula. He asked if I was part of it."

"Get to the point," Iseul said.

Su-Jung nodded. She dug into her pockets and brought up a page and unfolded it. She seemed to be looking for something on the ground, and when she spotted a thin branch collected for firewood, she grabbed it and began drawing something on the dusty yard, referencing the page to replicate what was on it. It vaguely resembled the map of the Korean Peninsula.

"We are here," she said, pointing at the middle of the peninsula where Yeoju is situated. "Just a few weeks ago, our distant relatives of the Ansan-Kim clan came here to Yeoju, fleeing from the occasional bomb, but mostly from rumors."

"Rumors?" Iseul asked, intrigued. The women circled around and listened intently.

"Rumors of Chinese soldiers. Hordes of them, more than the number of U.N. soldiers who have come to help us. They are coming into the western mountain ridges, using the mountains as camouflage, lying in wait north of the 38th." She marked the edge of the mountain ridge.

"What does that have to do with us?" Mr. Lim said. "We're so far away from the rest of Yeoju and everyone knows the path south is blocked here. Surely, the troops would stay up in the northern area of Yeoju and march down a different path," Mr. Lim said, certain he had worked it all out. "We are safe here."

Su-Jung shook her head. "You are sitting ducks here," she said as she circled the end point of the "V" where the eastern and western mountain ridges came together, right there in the Wasteland of Yeoju. "The North Koreans and Chinese have begun their two-frontal attack from the East and West, ready to push our soldiers South again. Our soldiers won't know what hit them, and I'm willing to bet some of them will be pushed into our village."

"Sounds improbable," Mrs. Park, the farmer's wife said, though her eyes betrayed her.

"We hope so, but this letter warns of that possibility. Even if our troops aren't inadvertently pushed into the Wasteland, anyone who knows anything about Yeoju will come here looking for rice. These new Chinese armies are starving. They don't have the same supply lines as the U.N. folks do."

A silent terror rose in the group of women as the scholar snorted in disbelief.

"But we don't have any rice," Mi-Jung said. "Surely they must know! No one took interest in our village the last time the North Koreans marched south. Why should it be any different this time?"

"Who's to say the old man drew the map himself. It's all a ruse of a man making up conspiracy theories!" Another woman added.

Su-Jung butted in. "This old man used to be one of the nation's leading military strategist," she said, proudly. "And we're here to meet the person who sent us the letter. It's clearly one of your pages," she said, looking at Iseul.

Iseul took the page from Su-Jung. It's tinted brown hue left nothing to doubt; it was certainly one made right there. But who could have sent it? She examined the handwriting but didn't recognize it, other than the formalized lettering of the consonants that disclosed the writer was likely an older man.

"The page has been made here, but other than that, I haven't got a clue." She handed the page to the others as they all examined the handwriting, drawing the same conclusion.

"What are we doing still here?" Mrs. Park said, almost

muttering to herself. She was looking for her daughter who sat on the porch and played with a straw doll.

"We should leave when we still have the chance," another one said.

"There, there…" the old man said, "Settle down now. We still have some time and there are certain measures we can take to protect the village. But you're right. Flee from this place when you still can because once the North Koreans start marching south, you may not be able to make it to the northern roads in time."

The scholar's wife seemed to waver, looking forwards her husband to gauge his stance.

"What about our husbands, brothers, and fathers?" Mi-Jung said. "They'll be coming home. We should be here, guarding our village. That's the least we can do for them."

"I agree! We stand our ground," another woman said. "We wait for our families to return to us."

"Don't be foolish," the newcomer Su-Jung said. "Don't think you'll survive an attack of this scale, if it does occur. And even if the Chinese come just for food, we women of all people should know they come with more than an appetite for food. Leave when you can. You can always come back once the war ends."

Panic and murmurs erupted again from the crowd who gathered in Iseul's front yard. Mrs. Park was already gathering her belonging, ready to hike down to the village.

"What will happen to our paper production? Our men are always waiting for the next batch," a woman said.

"It's such a morale booster for the men who are serving our country. We can't just abandon them now!"

"The old man's right!" Iseul said as the chatter died down. "The paper production can wait. If we're all dead, what use is paper to our loved ones?"

Iseul still had her eyes fixed on Su-Jung, gauging the truthfulness of what she had said. Can she be trusted? What harm would she want from a group of powerless women? After all, she had come to warn them, not pilfer them of what little they had left.

"But for those of you who are willing to stay," the old man said, "there will be help coming. There are quite a few of us in northern Yeoju who are willing to forfeit our chance to head south."

"A few from northern Yeoju?" Iseul said. "Why would they?"

Su-Jung's old man knew the whole operation was a secret, but he was rather surprised not one person had a clue.

"Rice," the old man said, "at least rumors of it."

Mr. Lim, who had been examining a corner of the map Su-Jung had brought, pulled his gaze away from the sheet and stared at the old man, stunned. *Could it be? That this old man knew too?*

"We don't have…"

"I know," the old man interrupted. "We're not talking about rice harvested in this village. We're talking about a massive store of rice, collected for decades and hidden somewhere in these very mountains."

He knew, Mr. Lim thought. How many others knew about it too? He had known the rice store existed, but he had always thought it was a myth that the rice was stored right in the very mountains that surrounded them.

The old man reached for the map from Mr. Lim and pointed at the bottom right corner where there was a tiny signature, recognizable only now that the old man pointed it out.

"Ham Young-Nam," Mr. Lim said, as he too recognized his leader's signature he had been eyeing for a while.

"He's a traitor, responsible for the massacre that killed over fifty of our villagers!" Mi-Jung yelped.

"He's been hoarding all the rice for himself? Is that why we're all starving?" another woman added. Iseul's yard erupted in an uproar of venomous tirades at the sound of the name.

The secret was out at last. Mr. Lim knew the day would come, but not this soon, and not this public. Mr. Lim shifted in place, his eyes flickering with doubt. "I guess it's as good a time as any to fess up…" he said. He didn't intend to speak so loud, but all the attention focused on him.

Fess up? Iseul thought. Could it be, that he knew about this rice store? She remembered the burn that ran up his arm and how he had known much more than Iseul thought was possible. Was this related to how he knew about Jung-Soo's whereabouts?

"I think I know why the North Koreans are marching to Yeoju," Mr. Lim said. "I've been in contact with Mr. Ham both over the radio and through coded letters. That's how he got Iseul's paper. He must have sent you the spares I had given him as a sign, hoping you'll know what to do," he said, looking at the old man.

"You've got to believe me!" Mr. Lim looked hopelessly at the women and old men, ready to hang Mr. Lim. "He didn't do it for himself! He had been siphoning rice from the Japanese tax collectors for years. It was supposed to be for peace and for an independent future for Korea!"

"He's right!" the old man joined in. "Ham Young-Nam convinced many of the yangban leaders in each district and their farmers in northern Yeoju to contribute to the rice stores. We all believed in his vision and trusted him. We swore that we'd never lose our precious rice to another foreign bully again. You can hear for yourselves when those very farmers arrive. They're all coming to protect their rice and make sure it doesn't get taken again!"

The women began mumbling and whispering amongst themselves again.

"Surely, Young-Nam wouldn't have sent people to help us save the rice if he really were a communist!"

"I'm not sure. How do we even know if the rice stores are here? No one has even suspected that much rice was being transferred to our mountains. We would know if it were here!"

Mrs. Park had already collected her children and made her descent down the hills, as others joined in the mass exodus.

"We can't risk our lives for some mythical rice stores," they exclaimed. Fiery contempt bubbled beneath the surface of the women filled with terror. They couldn't believe that yet again, they were being forced out of their own homes. As if it weren't enough that they were forced to give up their lifeline to the Japanese, they would now lose the supposed rice-stores to the Chinese and the North Koreans! The promise of survival and a better future were nothing but lies.

"What's the point?" the village grandmother said, her deep sigh attesting to her experiences of horror in bygone days. "They're just going to take it from us again. Best to just stay still and die in my own home." She retreated, pacing slower than the others who raced towards the village.

Iseul retreated into her room as Mr. Lim beckoned the old man and her daughter to come inside with them. She fought the urge to collect her belongings and leave right that moment, aware that there might be others watching her, waiting for her to make her decision so they could make theirs.

"I knew him back in the day," the old man said, starting the smaller meeting within closed doors. "Ham Young-Nam. He was one of my brightest students in the military academy and was poached by the most powerful because of it. I retired before the situation became volatile with the rise of the Communists, but Young-Nam got into some nasty squabbles and spy business before I left. It's a shame really." He shook his head. "How do you know him?"

"I'm just another farmer who happens to still be here in Yeoju," Mr. Lim said. He could sense that Iseul was deeply flustered. He turned towards Iseul and asked, "Have you ever wondered why only half of the Golden Palace burned down?"

She broke from her thoughts and shook her head. "We thought the soldiers put the fire out."

"They did, but they had no reason to until they found out what was in the warehouse of the Golden Palace."

"What was inside?"

"Rice," the old man guessed.

Mr. Lim nodded. "Jung-Soo's father went into the fire and he came out with a truck full of rice. He burned one side of his body in the process. A rash thing to do, but it caught the soldiers' attention. They knew there would be more rice inside the warehouse. And all that rice went straight to the South Korean military and fueled the first few weeks of the war. Even the Americans would have starved without it since their U.N. supply lines were scant back then."

"So, we're supposed to guard this fictional rice store and wait for the Chinese to come fetch it?" Iseul was incredulous.

"It exists," Mr. Lim stated. "You have to understand, rice is our blood line and our future. Our children's livelihood, the future of our country depends on it. That's why so many of us are willing to risk our lives to guard it."

"This is a fight for our future," the old man added.

Mr. Lim nodded and continued. "The massacre—the fire that killed our villagers was not meant to target communists. In fact, the communists were behind it, working covertly within the South Korean military. When they found out about possible rice stores, they made up a fictional list of communists, labeling our innocent farmers to justify a raid so they could interrogate us and go into the mountains themselves to look for the rice."

"Despite what had happened that day, it seems Young-Nam still outsmarted them before he disappeared, making me a proud teacher all these years later." The old man chuckled.

"Yes. When the soldiers found rice in the Golden Palace, they had no choice but to report it to the South Korean military. And that was just the most recent collection, ready to be transported into the mountains."

Iseul found herself nodding as the pieces began to fall into place. That's why there were so many soldiers in the mountains that night—they weren't just there to capture communists; they were scouring the mountains for the rice store.

Mr. Lim continued. "But Jung-Soo's father knew about the raid beforehand. That's why he intentionally left a large store of rice in his own warehouse in plain sight, making it impossible for the communists working undercover in the South Korean government to covertly take it. Mr. Ham probably hoped the soldiers would leave the villagers alone once they found the rice, but instead they had gone ahead and burned them alive."

Iseul felt guilty for ever doubting the men who perished in the fire—for doubting her father.

"So, where's the rest of the rice?" Iseul asked.

Mr. Lim shrugged. "Not many know that such a large supply exists and those us who contributed did so knowing that it was better to keep the location unknown. He never told me over the radio or through the coded letters he sent me. He never trusted anything but face-to-face intelligence and unfortunately, I lost contact with him weeks ago."

Iseul thought of Jung-Soo. How much did he know about his father? About the rice? He had always assumed Jung-Soo's father was the mastermind and Jung-Soo always seemed quite certain that his father was a traitor. Yet, hearing what Mr. Lim and the old man had to say, she couldn't say for sure; nothing seemed to be as black and white as she had once believed. She knew the village would nearly be empty by tomorrow and she didn't know how much time she had left to decide.

She had just gotten in touch with Jung-Soo. What would happen if she just left without notice? Would they ever meet again? She hadn't even made up her mind about what she thought of the letter, nor about the scolding she would give him for writing so little.

She looked side to side as if looking for something—someone. Where was Yeong-Hoon oppa when she needed him? Outside perhaps?

CHAPTER 31

It didn't take long for the northern citizens of Yeoju to make their way to the Wasteland. Old men, women, and children flooded into the western gate, marching with guns, farming hoes, and anything sharp enough to help with the manual labor that could even double as a weapon.

The farmer's wife, Mrs. Lee had gathered her belongings and kept her daughter holding on to the front of her skirt. The little girl's eyes widened in excitement as children her age came with their mothers, holding dolls made of straw and pebbles rounder than she had ever seen in her village.

"Why can't we stay like them?" she whined.

Just two weeks ago, she had received a return letter with an official statement of decease. She no longer had a husband to wait for. She must be strong; she must keep her daughter alive. The farmer's wife seemed more hesitant than she had been when the news first came of Chinese troops just a day ago. The trek down south would be treacherous, deadly even, as they would likely starve to death if they didn't freeze to death first. But everyone knew the odds were better. Only the weak and sickly remained in the Wasteland—those who could not physically make their way down south. She renewed her resolve.

She had filled her sack with as much food as she had gathered though she knew it wouldn't be enough. She leaned forward to double check. She was beginning to wonder if she should have brought extra clothing instead of food. It was mid-November and her daughter always complained about the cold. She should probably go back and pack a little more, maybe just wear an extra layer. By the time she looked up from her supplies, her daughter was laughing with a little girl holding pebbles in their hands.

"Young-Hee, dear!" Her mother called for her.

Her head turned with a beaming smile. "Just a second!" She had somehow convinced the little girl that the rocky pebbles tinged with red spots (ones that littered the Wasteland mountains), were worth trading with the smooth pebbles of the north. With two round pebbles tight in her grasp, she came running back to her mother.

"Look! Look!" she said to her mother.

"I see, dear." For a moment, she was about to tell her daughter to put them down—that the pebbles were dead weight and couldn't come along with them. She was a smart one. Her daughter would grow up to be someone special, and perhaps become more than just another farmer's wife. The child took after her father, and she was grateful for it.

"Let's go, mommy," her daughter said, resigned to her mother's stubbornness. She held out her tiny hands and waited for her mother to hold them.

The farmer's wife seemed to be deep in thought. And with a massive smile, she took her daughter's hand and said, "Let's go home, dear."

Still, many more decided to leave Yeoju than those who remained. It didn't take long before news of work and potential food stores spread to the other villages in northern Yeoju as the ones who had the guts to remain or too weak to travel, trickled down to the village they knew only as the Wasteland.

Mr. Lim had become even busier as he took it upon himself to do a lineage check of each new resident with the help of Su-Jung who could already identify many of them. There were countless people with the family name "Kim," distant relatives of the scholar; a few Lees and Parks trickled down too, all claiming to be related to the ones who lived in the village.

Mr. Lim was meticulous. He had managed to get involved in a flurry of debates with Su-Jung about the possibility of spies coming in with the influx, arguing that many of them were probably after the rumored rice. But eventually, the task was completed as he put each of them to work. In a matter of days, distant relatives were reunited and new friendships forged as the Wasteland came alive with laughter heard in every corner of the village, seeming to resemble the village it once used to be.

Iseul had the task of training the newcomers in the art of paper-making. Many seemed to have some idea about how it was made, considering each village had paper artisans and apprentices, all pitied by their villagers for having to do the grunt work. A few had the touch, but on the rare occasion, Iseul was forced to shoo away blubbering old men and women who would inadvertently rip nearly every page they touched.

Su-Jung took it upon herself to arm these outcasts, equipping the ones who could aim with the rare gun, and others with hoes and swords. Together, they stood guard at either the Golden Palace or in the vicinity of Iseul's workshop, using gingko trees as targets and their swords to cut branches to use for firewood. And so, a week passed in a bustle of excitement and looming doom, as the women and old men of Yeoju's Wasteland continued to churn out browned pages.

The scholar sat by the porch with the old man, dozing off to the chatter of women and children as they went about their business. Little boys, charged with the excitement of guns and swords, begged mothers to let them accompany the men to target practice only to be met with more chores. Instead, the little ones carved swords out of the branches used as firewood and poked each other to pass the time.

Yeong-Hoon had been kindling the fire to boil the day's mulberry bark when he discovered two heads poking out an empty underground jar meant to ferment kimchi. The kids turned and laughed at each other, strategizing ways to get to the bowls of berries and chestnuts hidden too high for their reach. Yeong-Hoon couldn't help but smile as he began limping towards the children.

"Did you see him coming?" the little boy said, his knees against his chest inside the kimchi jar, hiding from Yeong-Hoon.

"He's just passing by, I'm sure," the girl patted the boy on the back as she giggled.

"Psst…" Yeong-Hoon opened the lid as the boy and the girl screamed and jumped out, running towards their respective mothers in the paper drying area.

Yeong-Hoon scratched his head. "I was just going to help you get to the berries…" He sighed and limped back towards the fire. He loved children, but they didn't seem to like him much.

Mr. Lim huffed and puffed his way towards the workshop, looking gaunter than ever, though his high spirits more than made up for the disconcerting look.

"Mr. Lim!" Iseul emerged from the workshop. The half-blind old man joined Mr. Lim and Iseul inside her home as she pulled out a small table between them. The scholar slipped past the paper doors and decided he would be welcome in the group.

"The mailman thinks he can make it one more time in a few days before it'll be too dangerous for him to come back," Mr. Lim said.

"Alright, we'll coordinate our production so that we can get as much paper made before then. Have we heard back from the men surveying northern Yeoju for any military movement?"

Mr. Lim nodded. "They came back yesterday with a sack full of rice and a few bags of chestnuts. No signs of soldiers yet." He turned his attention to the scholar and the old man. "What's the progress on the food storage operation?"

The scholar cleared his throat in a deep grumble, but before he could respond, the old man spoke. "We're having to send old men and children further away from the village."

"What he said…" the scholar said, disappointed that he wasn't the one to report the news.

"We need to allocate more people to scavenging. Winter is coming and our stores are still abominable."

The scholar nodded in agreement.

"I'll take volunteers from the women making paper," Iseul said. "And once the mailman comes to take the last batch, we'll all switch tasks."

Mr. Lim and the scholar acknowledged with a nod.

"I've done the math. We have a total of eighty new members of our community, all allocated to various tasks," Mr. Lim added with a sigh of relief.

Su-Jung abruptly slid open the paper doors and plopped down next to her father. "We're going to need to train snipers and place them around the western gate, maybe get a few of the old men with swords to tag along to trim the branches so the snipers will have a good enough view."

The village needed someone like Su-Jung. She was a no-nonsense kind of woman and Iseul looked up to her for that. The way she was so calm about the possibility of a battle right there in such a peaceful village was a mystery to Iseul who was glad her tasks were solely limited to papermaking.

"We should also begin to think about finding an alternate route out of this Wasteland," Su-Jung added, as the group looked towards Iseul.

"There is no other way out," Iseul said, definitively.

Su-Jung rolled her eyes. "I know, I know. That's what everyone's been telling me but just think about it for a second. Why would the village have the east gate if there wasn't some way in and out?"

The scholar nodded rather noticeably.

"I've been asking that myself for years," Iseul said. "But I've been living near the east gate my entire life and all I see past this mountain are two other larger ones in the way."

"We still have to try," Mr. Lim said.

"I'll help," the half-blind old man said.

The scholar snorted. "You? You're a blind old fart! You wouldn't be able to see a wide-open road, let alone some hidden path. I shall offer my services," he said, tilting his head as if to formalize his offer with a bow.

"Iseul," Su-Jung said. "We need you. We're more likely to find a new route with someone who knows the area well to begin with."

Iseul had been thinking about leaving when the last paper shipment left the village, but if she were to take on another responsibility, she would be committing to staying. She looked around and saw so many who seemed to be counting on her. If they didn't find a route south, how many of these people would survive?

"Any ideas where we should start?" Mr. Lim said.

For some reason, Jung-Soo's cabin came to mind. She had almost forgotten all about it if it were not for the small handgun strapped on her ankle and the letter from Jung-Soo with the guitar measurements in her pocket. If she stayed, questions would have to be answered and the cabin's whereabouts made public. She didn't mind so much. It could yield some results, but as far as she knew, there was nothing in that valley except for that idyllic cabin and the watermill churning the river water. She had promised herself that once all such petty matters of war and survival was over, she would return to the cabin. Perhaps that day might come sooner than expected.

"I think I might have an idea," Iseul said.

Su-Jung nodded, pleased to have Iseul's cooperation. She reached into her satchel and pulled out what looked like small radios.

"I'll keep one at the western entrance where the snipers are, and the search party to the eastern gate can take the other."

"What is it?" The scholar asked.

"Short-range radios. They won't work well past this village, but it'll have to do." She handed Iseul the radio and an extra set of batteries. "I assume you know how it works?"

Iseul nodded. Mr. Lim dug into his rice sack and pulled out a familiar square object. It was the old village radio Iseul and Jung-Soo had 'borrowed' countless time. "It's old and clunky and one of the speakers seems to be broken, but I'm sure it will come in handy. I'll leave it with Mi-Jung and the women here at the workshop."

"We meet at sunrise tomorrow at the east gate. We'll start there," Iseul said.

They looked at each other, waiting to hear someone raise an argument against their plans. None came. The scholar rose as the others followed suit. There was much to be done in preparation for their journey.

Iseul was beginning to realize that it might be days before she would return home. She began packing an extra change of clothes, picked up her mother's hairbrush and a few scraps of paper that had been too ripped or browned to be sent out. She sighed and laid them back down. They were all dead weight now.

Her hands began trembling. *Why?* She held on to her right hand with her left, waiting for the shaking to stop. She trembled all night until dawn filtered through the paper-thin walls of her door and signaled for her to wake.

This was it then. She picked up the small lump of her belongings she had wrapped in white cloth and began her way downhill towards the eastern gate.

"Wait! Wait!" A voice grew louder. It was Yeong-Hoon, running with a limp out of his room holding a lunchbox. For a moment, Iseul saw mother as a warmth tingled throughout her body. She smiled as she gave him a lingering hug, longer than siblings or mere friends would do.

"Thank you," she said.

"It's not too late," Yeong-Hoon whispered in her ears. "Let's get out of this place and start a new life. Just you and me."

Iseul knew Yeong-Hoon might say this. Even she could not

understand the overwhelming weight she felt when she thought about leaving. A part of her wanted to; it was the most logical thing to do. She could feel mother and father urging her to leave, even Jung-Soo. But with Yeong-Hoon's leg... It would be an ordeal.

Iseul's hands trembled again, her heart palpitating as beads of sweat rolled down her back. Yeong-Hoon held her close, his hands caressing the back of her head against his shoulders.

She had never noticed his warmth and was beginning to think she could get used to it. "See you soon," she said, as she wriggled free from his embrace. Her steady hand squeezed Yeong-Hoon's with as hopeful a smile as she could muster, before turning her back.

But Yeong-Hoon kept a hold of her hand. With his free hand, he reached into his satchel as he pulled out a carving knife neatly tucked into a leather strap. It was the one father had given Yeong-Hoon as dowry for their future wedding.

"For when the bullets run out," Yeong-Hoon said he gripped her hands around the freshly carved handle.

"I can't," Iseul said, trying to let go.

"And to keep your hands busy when get bored out there," he said.

Iseul looked curiously at the carving knife that had been in her family for generations. It was meant to carve wood to make cabinets and instruments, not for violence. Yeong-Hoon had given it to her as a reminder of just that.

Teary-eyed, she grasped the knife and said, "I'll bring it back to you. I promise."

CHAPTER 32

As autumn turned to winter, gingko trees turned yellow and its fruits ripened to a bright orange and fell to the ground like marbles, firm and round.

The ginkgo fruit serves as an excellent snack for those who seek refuge underneath the tree's wide branches. But as the days grew colder and the fruits were trampled on, the gingko fruit rotted, repelling even the hungriest animal from its stench-ridden path as vultures and crows circled the tree as if it were a dead carcass.

In the early winter months of 1950, it was hard to tell the difference between the stench of a rotting corpse that once belonged to a brother and the rotting fruits that heralded the coming of the deep freeze.

***

[Present Day]

It was nearly 3 AM in Seoul as I stared down at my notepad. I had scribbled English phrases and questions I thought might be relevant to my phone call with the veterans' office. I checked the time in Virginia where the U.S. Office of Veterans Affairs was located. 1 pm. They would be back from their lunch break by now.

My hands were sweaty. I could hear dad snore through the walls. Good. I'd have approximately two weeks before my phone bill will show that I made an international call. I'll think of some excuse between now and then.

"Hello," I said, my voice shaky. I looked down at my notepad. "I'm call from Seoul, South Korea. I look for veterans who fighting in Korean War." I knew my English wasn't perfect, but I was sure she could understand.

"One moment please," the lady on the other end said. She put me on hold as I waited to the tune of some patriotic American song.

"Veterans Office of Survivors Assistance. I hear you are calling from Seoul. How can I help you?"

I cleared my throat and read from my notes again. "My grandfather, Baek Sung-Man, look for friend in Korean War from 5th Cavalry Regiment. You know survivor from battle November 27, 1950 in mountains south Yeoju?"

"Let me look at the records," she said. I could hear her typing away at her desk. "Umm… I'm looking through records of those who were deployed on that date. It seems there weren't many survivors and of the survivors, only two are still alive today. Do you understand?" she said, enunciating every word.

"Yes, yes. Can I have phone number?" I said rather enthusiastically.

"I'm sorry, but we cannot give out that information. But if you give me your contact information and some details about your grandfather, we can contact the survivors for you and ask if they would be willing to speak with you."

"I understand," I said, trying to find the right phrase on my notepad. "Also, I look for American soldier who know Korean man name Jung-Soo or Yeong-Hoon."

"It's a long shot, but I'll ask about them too," she said.

"What? Long time?"

"I mean I will contact you when I know more information. Maybe in one week."

"Yes, yes," I said and gave her my email address.

The following week was the most excruciatingly long week. I checked my emails every five minutes and even woke in the middle of the night, thinking the time difference would have yielded some incoming message at that ungodly hour. No doubt, my best friend Mi-Na noticed and probed me when a teacher walked past us during class.

"What's gotten into you?" Mi-Na said during lunch.

I shrugged. "I know I shouldn't get my hopes up, but if this doesn't work, it's a dead end again."

I had been thinking of every probable outcome to pass the time. I wish I knew family names for Yeong-Hoon or Jung-Soo, which were fairly common Korean names. Somehow, I had a feeling American soldiers would have had a hard time remembering foreign names, and that's if the two remaining survivors had met the Korean soldiers in the picture. My grandfather seemed out of place in the U.N. camp and may have just been passing through. How many of the soldiers in the 5th Cavalry Regiment would remember two stray Korean soldiers?

Perhaps the old grandfather from Yeoju was correct and Jung-Soo was indeed the son of the man who used to live in that old Japanese building. Maybe the records were all jumbled up. Ham Jung-Soo would have been his full name.

I grunted and facepalmed.

"What? What is it?" Mi-Na said as she took a bite of her pork cutlet.

"I should have prepared more notes before I made the phone call. I probably should have spelled out the names for her too."

I was already thinking of calling the nice lady back and had written down a phrase on my notepad again when my notification alert went off. It was an email in English.

Math class had just begun but I didn't care. I slid my phone under my desk and began skimming through the email, looking for the English vocabulary words I knew.

"Contact…5th Cavalry Regiment…"

I needed to focus. I began at the beginning of the email again.

"We are happy to inform you that we were able to contact one veteran who fits your description. Mr. Richard L. Martin served with the 5th Cavalry Regiment and is currently in Alabama. He is willing to talk to you about the events of 27 November during the Korean War."

At the end of the email was a phone number. I couldn't believe it! I re-read it, making sure that I had understood the entire message. All throughout the rest of class, I pulled out a scrap piece of paper, hiding it between my textbook and notebook as I began thinking about what I would ask him. *Mr. Richard L. Martin.* He already seemed like a nice man. I wondered which of the names he recognized. Maybe he even knew my grandfather!

That night, I counted the seconds before I could hear my dad snore and crept out of my bed to dial the number.

"Alabama State Veterans Nursing Home. How may I help you?"

"Hello, may I speak to Mr. Richard L. Martin, please?" I said. I hoped she would understand despite my accent.

It took longer than expected and the lady hadn't put me on hold. While I waited, I looked up the word 'nursing home' as I listened to the sound of chairs squeaking, a television that spoke in English and old people talking to nurses about various ailments. I felt as if granny could be on the other side of the phone, somewhere in the crowd of old people.

"Hello," an old man spoke in a hoarse voice. "This is Richard speaking."

I choked, collecting my thoughts again. "Hello. I am Jia Kim from South Korea."

"Hello, Jia!" Mr. Martin said. "I hear you are looking for me."

"Yes."

A long pause proceeded. I hadn't quite learned English conversational skills and the old man's words were mumbled and barely understandable. I wanted to exchange pleasantries, ask how he was doing, and if he had been to Korea since the War. Or maybe he just wanted to forget about it all, as the rest of the world seemed to have.

Perhaps I even wanted to thank him. I knew Korea in no other light than the one I was born into, but looking at those archival photos and reading about the details of war had given me some appreciation of how close we came to a completely different Korea.

"Can I help you, Jia? What would you like to know?" he said, speaking slowly, almost as if he had done it before—enunciating to foreigners who didn't speak a word of English.

I stuttered. "You know Korean soldier, Baek Sung-Man, Jung-Soo...Ham Jung-Soo, or Yeong-Hoon? Fighting November 1950 Yeoju in mountain?"

"Yes," the old man said. "I knew a man called Jung-Soo. We fought together."

My words were stuck in my throat. I felt almost giddy. "Good! Good!" I said, over-enthusiastically. "What happen Jung-Soo after November 1950?" I asked.

"I'm sorry, I don't know. I went back to Yeoju in the summer of 1953. I met his friend, Park Dae-Gun who fought with us, but Jung-Soo was not there."

Park Dae Gun? I didn't recognize the name, though I made a

mental note of it. "Yeoju 1953?" I asked. Why would he go back to Yeoju three years later?

"Korean soldiers and American soldiers. We were fighting together as a team and we became good friends. I went to say goodbye before I returned to America," he said, almost as if he knew what I was asking.

"Yes, I understand, thank you." I couldn't hide the disappointment in my voice.

The old American soldier seemed to want to say more, but allowed time to pass and questions to stir. I wondered if he knew how much has changed since he was last here. I imagine South Korea was a pile of rubble and bare hills back then.

"You visit Korea after war?" I asked.

"No, I have not visited, though I'd love to. I've seen pictures. It is very… different now," he said.

I understood what he was saying, though I could feel he meant much more.

"Yes, very different now. Thank you."

"You're welcome," he said. "If you have any more questions, you can call me back."

I had meant to thank him for his service, despite the deep scorn I felt about war and politics, and my dubious feelings about the current American military presence in South Korea. Yet, one thing was clear: this man had sacrificed so much for a country he had no reason to fight for, and that sacrifice, whether I liked it or not, had become the backbone of a place I now call home.

"Thank you for fighting in Korean War," I said.

"You're welcome." He understood.

We hung up. I fully intended to call him back at some point, but I'm sad to say that over ten years has passed since then, and I am quite certain he has passed on. Thinking back, I believe I knew that would be the last I would hear from that old American soldier, and in that realization, I had a glimpse of the true price of war. Excuse my sudden intrusion, my dear readers.

I had said my goodbye to the old American soldier only to be filled with the frustration of having met another dead end. I had at least confirmed the suspicions I wanted to deny—there had been a person called Jung-Soo and the old man from Yeoju may have been correct about him. But how could a man who had befriended an allied American soldier also be a communist traitor?

Perhaps he had a change of heart. I would have liked that. But the other more sinister possibility took a hold of my attention by storm: perhaps he had played some role in the demise of so many that day. How was my grandmother implicated? I feared the worst.

CHAPTER 33

[November 24, 1950]

"Iseul, Iseul, can you hear me?" Jung-Soo spoke into the radio microphone.

"Give it a break," Dae-Gun said. "You've been at it for days."

The four Korean soldiers made camp for the night as Gil-Dong cooked up a stew of boiled barley rice and whatever ingredients they had left over from the packaged meals. Hunger took precedence over flavor, and even Dae-Gun had accepted his salt-less state, pulling his guitar out to ease his dull palate instead.

Jung-Soo's finger trembled as it nudged a bit too hard on the ridge of the radio's antennae.

"You're just going to break it," Doo-Hyung said, as he forced the radio out of Jung-Soo's hands.

Jung-Soo grunted. "I nearly had it. We just have to get a little closer to Yeoju."

"You've said that at least twenty times," Dae-Gun added.

Every time they had stopped to take a break, Jung-Soo fiddled with some dial or wire on the radio. December was nearing and Jung-Soo felt increasingly helpless as the days went by.

"Tomorrow we reach the 5th Cavalry Regiment. And then we make a dash for Yeoju. It's as simple as that," Dae-Gun said as he would to his little brothers.

Doo-Hyung took a sip of his wine to wash down the bland

barley porridge. "You can learn a thing or two from your friend there. All that worrying isn't going to get you there any faster. Look around, enjoy what you already have, savor the flavors," he grabbed a hold of Jung-Soo's head and forced rice wine down his throat. "Don't be so selfish now," he said as he chugged a gulp himself.

Everyone except Jung-Soo chuckled. Instead, he coughed, nearly vomiting the barley rice he had inhaled. "The only thing I'll enjoy is when we get rid of you tomorrow."

"Speaking of getting rid of them, what's the plan once we arrive at the base?" Dae-Gun asked.

"We wait," Doo-Hyung said.

"No, you go," Jung-Soo said.

The topic of what Doo-Hyung and Gil-Dong would do had been a sore point of contention the past few days.

"This is not a request," Jung-Soo said. "Get to Yeoju as fast as possible and wait bt the western entrance. Go in and warn the villagers if you have to. You'll do as I say or I'll shoot your useless North Korean asses right here."

"Look, it is possible that the entire village has already been evacuated. Who's to say your beloved girl isn't long gone from that god-forbidden place?" Doo-Hyung paused, wondering if was a good idea to say what was really on his mind. "The truth of the matter is, women are replaceable."

Before Doo-Hyung knew it, Jung-Soo landed a punch square on his jaw.

Dae-Gun winced for him. "You deserved that." Gil-Dong nodded in agreement.

"Enough!" Jung-Soo said. They did not have any more time to spare. "If the South Korean military didn't know about this attack, I'm certain the villagers are completely unaware too. They're just waiting to die, can't you see?"

"The South Korean military probably knows but couldn't care less about what happens to a tiny rice farming village." Doo-Hyung spoke the harsh truth. "We're no martyrs. Might I remind you that you are the one who said we wouldn't last a day in Yeoju? It doesn't matter if these villagers are just peaceful papermakers and farmers. As soon as they see me and hear my accent, they'll shoot me or drive whatever sharp object they have lying around in me and bozo here."

Dae-Gun took a good look at Doo-Hyung from head to toe. "He's right. He reeks of the North. And it doesn't seem like you'll be so welcome there either, considering what happened before you left."

Jung-Soo knew Dae-Gun spoke the truth. He just felt so helpless. "What are you saying? You want to wait around at the edge of the 5th Cavalry base for a patrolling soldier to find two idling North Koreans?"

"They won't find us," Doo-Hyung said with pompous certainty.

"What makes you so sure? All camps are on high alert now." He looked to Dae-Gun for support. "Tell me you haven't forgotten about how Commander Lee tortured you. He's already suspicious enough of us without spies lurking around!"

Dae-Gun furrowed his brows. "But I thought we cleared our names and they caught the spies responsible for the leak?"

Jung-Soo kept quiet.

Even Doo-Hyung managed a look of concern. "Does he know? About who you are?"

"I don't know," Jung-Soo admitted. "Commander Lee seemed to wonder why his superiors had been so adamant to appoint me as the radio operator when there were others who could do the job."

"He knows something is awry," Doo-Hyung said. "Damn it, we've just wasted days trying to prove your loyalty by delivering those meaningless codes to a commander who already mistrusts you."

Jung-Soo knew it was partially true, though his decision to perform his duties had more to do with the idiot than anything else. And a part of him hoped that he could still choose a side and get back to Iseul once it was all over.

"We're here anyway and I'm delivering these codes," Jung-Soo said, justifying the decision he had made.

"Then it's decided. We'll stay a good distance away from camp, but we're waiting," Doo-Hyung said. They knew he wouldn't budge.

"Alright," Jung-Soo agreed. "But if we don't return by nightfall, you leave and head straight to Yeoju."

Doo-Hyung eyes flickered, still dubious of the plan. Jung-Soo waited. He didn't need them to be martyrs, but if there was one thing Jung-Soo could bank on, it was the fact that Doo-Hyung, for one reason or another, had gone through a lot of trouble to get his father's letter deciphered. Jung-Soo wondered if he was willing to go deeper into enemy territory to decipher the message alone if he had to.

"You've got a deal," Doo-Hyung said, confirming Jung-Soo's suspicions.

The two men shook on it. Jung-Soo planned to make it out on time. If Doo-Hyung had something up his sleeve, he would be there to stop him. They had become allies in the past few weeks, but he knew better than to trust a spy with intelligence.

"I don't suppose you'll tell me where the enigma machine is hidden," Doo-Hyung said.

Jung-Soo ignored him.

The four Korean men shared nods as Jung-Soo and Dae-Gun turned their backs and headed towards the 5th Cavalry camp, hiking downhill towards the perimeter.

Smoke rose where green tents poked out of the ground, yet, where were all the soldiers? Even from a distance, they could usually see tiny men walking around the campsite, yet the camp stood still, almost as if it were deserted. Jung-Soo honed in the radio dial to report that they wished to enter. Even his home base didn't seem to know why they would not answer.

"I'm sure they're just inside their tents because it's cold. They know we're coming," Dae-Gun said.

"They're not expecting us till next week," Jung-Soo corrected.

The closer they moved, smoke stacks rose higher and thicker, perhaps even darker for so early in the afternoon. Jung-Soo swung his rifle from his shoulder and kept it abreast. Dae-Gun followed. Jung-Soo tilted his head, examining the footprints and breathing in the smoky air.

"This is fresh."

Dae-Gun shuddered. "The Chinese army tailing us must have come through here at some point."

The camp stood at an eerie standstill and the closer they approached, the clearer it became; the camp had been hit hard from the northern side, attacked with crude weapons, torching tents and setting off grenades as they stampeded across the camp. Soldiers who had once been playing cards lay dead with red and black cards strewn all around them, trampled on by what looked like a charge of men in vehicle and on foot.

"An ambush," Jung-Soo said.

"But from where?" Dae-Gun shivered while hugging his rifle. "We should go. I don't think Commander Rogers is here."

Dae-Gun was right, though Jung-Soo wondered what had happened to all the troops. There had been at least three thousand men here, and many more Chinese soldiers to account for the bodies left on camp. Where had they all gone? The mountains surrounded them in silence. They must have gone south, past the mountains.

"Let's get out of here," Dae-Gun said.

And then Jung-Soo saw it—two familiar figures of a boy and a soldier amongst the sea of bodies. It was Sergeant James Jones huddled over none other than his little boy, Zion. Jung-Soo intended to spare Dae-Gun, pulling his arm in the other direction, but it was too late.

Dae-Gun stopped in his track, deadweight against Jung-Soo's nudges.

"I'm sorry, Dae-Gun."

Dae-Gun could not hear, no he refused to hear. He set one foot ahead of the other until he reached the boy, Zion and then collapsed onto his knees on the rocky gravel ground. He seemed unsure of what to do. He wanted to hug the boy but he was laying so peacefully in the sergeant's arms. A single bullet had pierced the two of them and so they had landed in such a position.

Jung-Soo watched on, feeling anguish for the first time for his friend who was still and calm. To his left was the southern bounds of camp at the foot of a mountain. The sergeant and boy had been so close to escaping into the trees.

He squinted and saw figures moving about in the trees. It then struck Jung-Soo. That's where they had gone, retreating into the mountains! But they were so quiet. On the opposite hill facing the one immediately next to the camp, he saw men sitting still, almost perfectly camouflaged. Those must be the Chinese troops. In the small valley between the two mountains, Jung-Soo could see what looked like bodies. It wouldn't be long before the troops would break stalemate again.

"Dae-Gun, we have to go," Jung-Soo attempted to pull him away from the soldier and his boy.

"I have to bury them first. Please just let me bury my brother," Dae-Gun said, his voice crackling under the pressure of holding down sobs.

"We don't have time. Look," Jung-Soo directed Dae-Gun's attention towards the mountains where soldiers hid like well-guised insects.

Dae-Gun had not completely lost his sense, seeing that a battle would soon wage. But he still couldn't bring himself to leave.

"Why don't you on ahead. I'll be just behind you," Dae-Gun said. He released the sergeant's tight grip on the boy and carried the little one to the foot of a small ridge.

Jung-Soo glanced back and forth at the stalemate and Dae-Gun who went back into camp and returned with a shovel. He wanted to yell at Dae-Gun and tell him their lives were in danger, and they didn't have time to make graves when real people would die if they didn't get to Yeoju in time. But he bit his tongue. He had come back to the 5th Cavalry to spare Dae-Gun from treason; he could spare him a few minutes to say his goodbyes.

Dae-Gun clunked the shovel into the wintry soil. It was no use; the ground had frozen solid.

"But it isn't even December yet," Dae-Gun protested weakly. He let a few tears loose.

Jung-Soo knew Dae-Gun was thinking of his brothers. He could see now. There wasn't a day that went by that Dae-Gun hadn't thought of his brothers at an orphanage. It no longer existed and the only place that had taken them in had abandoned them too. Many of them would have been met with fates much worse than what they witnessed before them.

Dae-Gun carefully held the boy's body and walked back to where the sergeant lay, placing them together just as they had found them. Dae-Gun lowered his head and closed his eyes for a moment of silence and when he was done, he took his guitar, still wrapped neatly in cloth, and laid it next to Zion.

"Are you sure?"

Dae-Gun nodded. "It belongs here."

Jung-Soo thought he witnessed a semblance of a smile, though it disappeared into a look of dogged stoicism unlike Jung-Soo had ever seen in him.

"What are we waiting for?" Dae-Gun said as he walked past Jung-Soo. "The commander is waiting for the codes."

Jung-Soo's nerves edged, suspicious of the eyes in the mountains that were sure to be watching their every move. He looked into the mountain ahead, hoping they were headed towards the ally and not the enemy.

***

"Commander," Lieutenant Smith spoke as he neared the battle-worn commander. "We're seeing movement in the camp. Two stray soldiers, sir."

The commander seemed preoccupied. "Shoot them," he said as he waved the lieutenant away.

"Sir, I don't think they're from the North."

This piqued the commander's interest. "What makes you say that? Every South Korean soldier is on the eastern front. Civilians perhaps?"

"Sir, they were in uniform, trying to bury some of our soldiers."

The commander grabbed the binoculars from the lieutenant and paced towards the edge of the cliff and looked through them.

"Impossible. They're not supposed to be here for at least another week," the commander said. "Escort them in, and make it quick before the Chinese shoot them down first."

Jung-Soo and Dae-Gun heard them coming before they saw them, blinded by the stray rays of the sun that poked above the hills. They held their rifles close by, inching step-by-step towards the towering figures.

"Kim Jung-Soo and Park Dae-Gun?" a familiar voice said. It was Sergeant Martin, the American soldier who had given them beer the last time. The escorts hasten them into the safety of the brushes.

"Remember, we give the codes and we leave," Jung-Soo whispered to Dae-Gun.

The Chinese fired a few stray bullets in their direction.

Dae-Gun remained unfazed. He nodded. "I know what's at stake."

They paced until they were deep within the hillsides, standing in front of the commander. Dae-Gun and Jung-Soo saluted.

"Good work, soldiers. I knew you wouldn't let us down."

"Sir, the codes," Dae-Gun said as Jung-Soo handed them over.

The commander quickened his steps toward the typewriter contraption, unfolding the page and turning the wheels above the keys to match the codes. It didn't take long for the commander to decipher the short scrambled letter he had in his other hand.

"Gentlemen, if only you had arrived twelve hours earlier," the commander said, disappointed as he handed the deciphered letter to Dae-Gun.

It read, "Chinese troops heading due south from Cheolwon. Retreat."

"Cheolwon?" Jung-Soo heard a familiar word amidst the foreign language. "What do you mean?" he nudged Dae-Gun.

Dae-Gun whispered a translation to Jung-Soo. "The Chinese troops having been waiting in Cheolwon to attack."

"Due north of here. I can't believe it! So, our suspicions had been correct, perhaps even worse." Jung-Soo spoke to Dae-Gun in Korean. "They're planning push our troop South from all fronts, including from the North. The retreating troops on the Eastern front wouldn't know what hit them."

The commander spoke again. "Men, we've been ordered to retreat and join forces with the incoming Korean infantries from the east. Dae-Gun, Jung-Soo, thank you for your service. You are dismissed to join your home infantry. We will escort you until we rendezvous with the 18th Infantry due south of here."

Jung-Soo shifted in place, unsure of what to do next. They had gotten their orders and he was glad of it. But the commander had no idea they would be headed towards another ambush. The commander was about leave.

"Sir," Jung-Soo grabbed on to his sleeve.

The commander stopped, shooting a glare in Jung-Soo's direction.

"Tell him," Jung-Soo said to Dae-Gun.

"Huh?" Dae-Gun looked hesitant. "I thought you wanted to leave as soon as possible?" he whispered.

"Spit it out, soldier," the commander said to Dae-Gun.

Dae-Gun looked around the make-shift tent and found a rolled up map. He explained all they had suspected about the movements of the North Korean and Chinese troops.

The commander was engrossed. "Mountains south of Yeoju, you say? And how is it that you know all this? I can't imagine General Kim not knowing about the landscape of his own country to lead us into a trap."

Jung-Soo measured his speech. How was he to convince the commander without revealing his own background and that of his father?

"I grew up in the southern-most part of Yeoju where the village meets two insurmountable mountain ridges." Jung-Soo began as he pointed to his village on the map. "During the Japanese occupation, I saw trucks moving towards the eastern gate, since that is the obvious route south. But the drivers would always come back up. It is a well-known fact in our village that the route south has been blocked for at least a century; the northwest gate is the only way in and out."

"And what makes you so sure that the North Koreans know about the peculiarities of Yeoju, a southern territory?"

"You must understand, commander, not everyone in the South were supporters of democracy. Communism had been in the works even during the Japanese occupation and many in the South went North when the war began."

The commander listened to Dae-Gun's translation, his hands gripping his hips as he processed the information. He stared intently at Jung-Soo, wondering if he should probe into his story—wondering if he should ask if he knew of such people who defaulted North with such information. Jung-Soo would tell the truth if he had to.

"Does the commander of the 18th Infantry know?" the commander said.

"No, sir. I don't believe so," Jung-Soo said, relieved. "We can't be sure if the North Korean movements are intentional in funneling our troops towards Yeoju, but at this rate, I am certain more than a few of our infantries are at risk of being trapped. We've only just realized this may be a possibility when we heard about the Chinese troops lying in wait at the western border of the 38th parallel."

The commander nodded as he moved the pieces on the map that symbolized Chinese troops. "The timing is impeccable—a more obvious eastern troop marches first, followed by the western troops and then the final northern forces to push the entire South Korean and U.N. forces South, directly on route towards Yeoju. Retreating directly south would mean certain death to a significant number of our troops."

Those who stood by the map knew defeat was imminent. Losing this battle may even be a fatal blow to the outcome of the entire war with winter so near. The war had waged longer than anyone had expected. The Chinese were desperate and ill-equip for long-term fighting, though their sheer numbers could run down the entire allied forces in due time. The Americans were restless to go home. Both sides needed an outright victory, and the current tide of the war pushed heavily against the South Korean side, as their prospects of returning home by the end of the year looked bleaker by the second.

Jung-Soo waited for the commander to come to his own conclusions.

"We've been ordered to retreat, but considering the sheer number of Chinese forces, we won't go far anyway," the commander said, disconcerted. "We stand and fight. Ask for reinforcements to keep the northern forces at bay. We allow our troops retreating from the east to have a fighting chance of making it west, across the peninsula to find an alternate route south."

That was the answer Jung-Soo was hoping for—a difficult decision that would leave most of the commander's own men dead if reinforcements didn't arrive soon. If they were lucky, the Chinese and North Korean troops would chase the South Korean soldiers down this alternative route and Yeoju would be spared.

Perhaps he wouldn't have to abandon his post to go to Yeoju after all. Iseul would be safe and as for father's encrypted letter— that could wait till after the war. Even as he said it, he glanced at the hill where countless expendable Chinese soldiers lay hidden and began to feel the panic rising in him again. He needed to get to Yeoju as soon as possible.

"We'll have to inform the troops in the east to push on west," the commander said.

"Will they believe us?" Dae-Gun said, apprehensively.

The commander spoke to his lieutenant. "Bring me Martin and Taylor. Get the marines ready to move."

"Sir," the lieutenant saluted and left.

The commander faced Dae-Gun, inches away from his face. "Make them believe. That's an order," the commander said. "The incoming troops know they'll be met with Chinese troops on the west, but they'll be glad to find out about an ambush from the north. We're out of radio range here, but Martin and his marines will get you to the next mountain south. You'll be able to intercept the infantries retreating from the eastern front."

Dae-Gun translated their orders.

"Marines?" Jung-Soo said. He understood why they must come. If the Chinese were vigilant and broke through the 5th Cavalry's line of defense, they would catch up with Jung-Soo and prevent the message from being relayed. They needed time and the marines would help them buy as much of it as possible.

"What about Doo-Hyung and Gil-Dong?" Dae-Gun whispered in Korean as the marines assembled around them.

"Let's hope they've caught on to what's happened here and leave sooner rather than later."

Jung-Soo hoped they were already on their way to Yeoju, warning somebody—anybody—near the entrance about the incoming armies. It was now a certainty. With three massive North Korean and Chinese armies pushing southward, at least some of them would end up in Yeoju.

Jung-Soo looked towards the hill beyond. *South.* Just a day's hike and he would be in Yeoju. He wished to run there right then, but he knew he had a better chance of reaching them faster by radio. Perhaps it might reach the village sooner than Doo-Hyung and Gil-Dong could.

Gun shots were heard near and far, the high-pitched voices of the Chinese coinciding with the men who spoke the slurred English language.

"Godspeed," the commander said as he hastened away to lead his men into a battle he was sure to lose.

CHAPTER 34

It hadn't been more than two hours since the search party left the eastern gate and made their way towards the side of the hill where Jung-Soo's cabin stood. Iseul had forgotten how peaceful the birds sounded as they too had abandoned their usual abode near the village and hid deeper and higher up in the mountains.

Su-Jung's father turned a few dials of the radio as Su-Jung's voice burst from the speakers.

"I've been heading further north. I've managed to talk to a few refugees and they've seen bodies scattered east to southeast of Gangwondo. They're near." Her voice was lively, as though she were doing exactly what she was born to do.

"Copy that, over," Su-Jung's father said. "I suspect we have three days at most." He turned the radio off as he breathed in the chilly valley air around them.

Three days. Iseul had heard the sound of bombs and gunfire from afar. She couldn't believe it will soon be her village under fire. Everyone kept saying it would be much worse than the last time the fire massacred their villagers. She didn't doubt it.

The scholar had become restless the past hour. "Are you sure we're on the right track? There isn't a single sign of trees thinning or water flowing."

"You old buffoon! That's the whole point of a hidden location," the old man said.

Iseul nodded. "We're near now."

After taking a sharp turn and hiking down the steep face of the mountain, the scholar pointed at the tiny cabin in the distance, and next to it flowed a river where a watermill churned on.

"Just like his father," Mr. Lim said, gleaming at the sight.

Iseul turned to him. "Who is?"

"Jung-Soo, of course, always making provisions," Mr. Lim said, grinning at Iseul.

Iseul reciprocated. She was glad someone else thought of Jung-Soo fondly. "We set up camp at the cabin for lunch and venture around the area." She raised her head high to the top of the mountain that seemed insurmountable. She remembered the day Jung-Soo had first taken her to the cabin. They had seen green eyes that peered down like tiger's eyes.

Iseul led them inside. It looked exactly the way she had left it—disheveled with wood chips and dust collected on every work surface.

The old man whistled as it reverberated inside the cabin. The scholar jumped. "What was that for?"

"Just checking how big the place," he said. "It's not big, but it can shelter the women and children if it comes to that."

Mr. Lim had already gravitated towards the radio, turning the dials as it awoke from its stupor. "It's still working, after all this time?"

"It's connected to the watermill outside," Iseul said, proudly.

"Very impressive."

"I doubt it'll catch much of a signal though," the old man said. "We're straddled between mountains in what looks like the lowest valley for miles."

Mr. Lim turned up the volume. It blared music from the only channel that still functioned on national radio.

The old man nodded, yet again impressed. "But does it have a transmitter?" Mr. Lim held up the radio and tugged at the wires until something resembling a microphone toppled onto the wooden counter. "Excellent!"

After a quick meal of bland rice and a few berries, the old man rose with his gun and radio, stretching his arms and legs before exited the cabin.

"So," Mr. Lim addressed those remaining in the cabin, "We're going to need someone to stay here to check the radio range." Mr. Lim directed a stare towards Iseul and then towards the scholar and back to her.

"Oh, right." Iseul cleared her throat. "I can do it." She could see Mr. Lim shaking his head furiously, and then she realized what Mr. Lim wanted her to do. "But, I think it would be a great honor if the scholar would oblige us with the task," Iseul said.

"If you insist, I must oblige!" the scholar said with his nose poking towards the ceiling of the cabin. "For the good of this mission, and the whole village for that matter."

"Excellent!" Mr. Lim said. "We thank you for your service."

With the scholar left to monitor the radio, a savory nap and static noise to accompany him, the search party headed towards the mountain facing southeast. The climb was steep and rocky, like most of the mountains in the Korean Peninsula.

"Watch your step," the half-blind old man said.

The sun was bright against their eyes, making it difficult to have a clear view of the top, but something shiny caught Iseul's attention. It was poking out of the top of the mountain, darker and slimmer than the tree trunk of an evergreen.

"Do you see that?" Iseul said to Mr. Lim as she pointed.

He squinted. "I think so. If it is what I think it is…"

The rays of sunlight hid behind the brush of an evergreen, and then Iseul finally saw them—two towers near the top of the mountain.

"They're radio towers," Mr. Lim said, astonished.

"That explains why there is reception at the cabin," the old man said.

"Someone's been here," Iseul said, mouth agape and shoulders wide as hope began to rise.

"Like father, like son," Mr. Lim said again, unsurprised.

"You really think Jung-Soo or his father did this?" Iseul said.

"Mr. Ham, no doubt about it," Mr. Lim said, as they all began wondering what else awaited them.

The old man turned the radio back on. "Su-Jung, Su-Jung, do you read me? You old hag, wake up! We've got full radio signaling for miles on end!" he said, calling to both his daughter and the scholar in the cabin.

"Hello?" a voice responded. It wasn't a voice of a woman. Iseul and Mr. Lim looked at each other. "Retreat! North Korean forces headed to Yeoju. Retreat!"

Iseul grabbed the transmitter from the old man.

"Is that who I think it is?" Mr. Lim mumbled.

"Jung-Soo, is that you?" Iseul said.

Nothing but static returned. She tried again. Still static.

"Is it on the same channel?" Iseul asked frantically. The old man nodded.

"Hello?" a voice responded. Iseul held her breath. "I just woke up. I hear you loud and clear, over." This time, it was the scholar.

Iseul collapsed in place as they let the scholar talk freely for a while.

"Good range. Standby at the cabin, over," the old man finally said, as he turned the radio off.

"Was that really him?" she recalled the anxious voice in shrilling clarity. He was worried. Iseul hoped Jung-Soo wasn't in any trouble...that he wasn't going to try anything brash.

Mr. Lim nodded, reassuring her that he too heard it too.

"How much do you think Jung-Soo knows?" Iseul said to Mr. Lim.

Mr. Lim stared inquisitively. "He must know something, or else he wouldn't be contacting us."

Mr. Lim reached down to Iseul as he helped her stand back up. They directed their attention back towards the top of the mountain at the two steel structures.

"Hopefully, we'll be able to see much further into the mountain ranges from the top," the old man said. "Keep an eye out for infrastructure or anything that might look flat enough to be a road."

A look of dread came over Iseul. They had embarked on their journey to look for a possible route south, yet, it never occurred to her that they may end up stumbling on the rice store instead.

"Perhaps it was a bad idea to bring your two here," Iseul murmured.

The three of them were minutes away from the top, the two radio towers soaring above them as imposing eyes that signaled something was just beyond the ridge. She clenched her stomach just thinking about a massive storehouse of rice. How many of these newcomers flooded into the Wasteland because of the rumors of this storehouse? And should they find it, what would come next? Without a way to escape south, they would just be fattening up for slaughter. Perhaps the rice store was better left undiscovered. She couldn't bear to imagine that she would be the one to lead the North Korean and Chinese straight to the rice.

Mr. Lim gave Iseul a reassuring look. "I'm sure Mr. Ham is

wise enough not to place the rice stores next to two gigantic radio towers."

Iseul gave a weak smile. She hoped so too.

***

"Retreat, North Korean forces are headed to Yeoju. Retreat." Jung-Soo spoke into the radio transmitter. He had been flipping through each channel, waiting for a response for about ten seconds before moving on to the next. It was a futile attempt, none of which reached the remote village of Yeoju, let alone an incoming infantry thus far.

"Stick to the known channels," Sergeant Richard Martin spoke intimidatingly. "Besides, we shouldn't be giving out classified information over open radio."

"Tell him he can shove classified information up his ass. And then we'll see if he can keep quiet!"

Dae-Gun didn't translate as he smiled and nodded at Sergeant Martin.

Richard Martin wasn't a huge fan of the Korean boys. The taller one was arrogant and the fatter one was useless as a soldier. He was particularly annoyed by the fact that the Koreans could understand everything they said, while he didn't have a clue what the arrogant one was saying. Richard did what he could, hovering over the two Koreans, deciphering their body language as they secured their moving perimeter every thirty minutes.

"I can't, for the life of me, understand what the commander saw in those two scrawny kids," Sergeant Martin said to Corporal George Taylor. The corporal shrugged. Richard signaled his men and they were on the move again. "We've been ordered to protect these Koreans with our lives, while our own flesh and blood are dying in the front lines as we speak." He cursed the half-frozen mud as he pushed further south.

Jung-Soo had gone through all the channels and was back again to the top of the list, dialing closest known South Korean infantries. His frustration was about to boil over. He was supposed to be on his way to Yeoju by now, yet, here he was, on yet another mission.

Duty. He felt the word shackle around his ankles, forcing him in place.

He was sorely aware of his father's coded letter that beckoned him to run away. Maybe he even knew a way out of this mess Jung-Soo found himself in. *Duty*—he was only slightly grateful to it for giving him a reason not to play into his father's plans to return to Yeoju. What kind of a father would send his son into a trap and to the front lines of a battle he was sure to lose? Yet, he felt time slipping through his fingers with each chilly November wind that trickled past the surrounding trees.

"This is Kim Jung-Soo from the 18th Infantry, reporting to the 12th Infantry. Requesting immediate backup on behalf of Commander Rogers from the 5th Cavalry Regiment."

A crackling noise exuded from the speakers, and then came to life. "I read you, over. Where is the backup needed?"

Jung-Soo looked over to Dae-Gun in disbelief; they had finally reached an incoming infantry. "Chinese are southbound from Cheolwon. The 5th Cavalry Regiment is holding them back, but they need help."

The speakers hissed on and off with the noise of worried men coming through. "We are confused about the situation. We've been ordered to retreat south immediately. Why hasn't the 5th Cavalry Regiment retreated?"

Jung-Soo proceeded to explain the situation. The surprise attack on all fronts was met with utter disbelief, and they regurgitated their orders to retreat south promptly.

"It's a trap. I'm telling you, it's a trap! If you must retreat, head west, past the Gyeonggi province. I repeat, do *not* head towards Yeoju."

Jung-Soo could sense apprehension on the other end.

"Alright," the man on the radio said. "I'll report to the commander. Over."

Jung-Soo felt like a failure. How many more infantries would dismiss his warning? He kept flipping the channel and when he chanced upon the next, he proceeded to relay the same message, only to be met with the same stubborn disbelief.

"Still no luck?" Dae-Gun asked. Jung-Soo shook his head and kept trying. In between dialing military channels, he continued to hitch on civilian channels with warnings to retreat from Yeoju. He blatantly disregarded Sergeant Martin who directed a scornful look at him every few minutes.

"Jung-Soo," the radio spoke to him this time.

"That's our commander!" Dae-Gun said.

"Sir," Jung-Soo responded promptly.

"I've been on the radio with the other commanders in the vicinity. I hear you've been confusing our troops with your theories. Explain yourself."

The commander was calm, though Jung-Soo could sense his patience was wearing thin. He explained the situation as best he could.

"Sir, the 5th Cavalry needs our support. Our window of opportunity is closing. You've got to convince them, commander, you've got to!" Jung-Soo realized he was yelling.

"Alright," the commander said. "I believe you. We just received eye-witness testimony of Chinese soldiers marching to the northern front."

Jung-Soo couldn't believe it. "Sir, I'm awaiting your orders," Jung-Soo said, hopeful as Dae-Gun gripped Jung-Soo's arm.

"Standby," the commander went offline.

Dae-Gun shuffled to Sergeant Martin, trying to convince him that they needed to hold their position until the commander of the 18th Infantry responded.

Jung-Soo renewed his resolve. He had already made a mental map of how he would reach the Wasteland of Yeoju, just as soon as he removed these shackles of duty and stalled the Chinese. Dae-Gun would have to stay; he didn't deserve to be branded a traitor. He knew that once he left, he would never be able to live under his new identity again. *Once a traitor, always a traitor,* he heard the voices say. But for now, it seemed like such a small price to pay.

"Jung-Soo," the commander spoke again, this time out of breath. "I'll be leading my infantry north to meet the 5th Cavalry. I've managed to convince the others to join forces to push past the Chinese troops in the west."

Jung-Soo felt his heart leaping as he paced in place. "But sir, will it be enough?"

"It'll have to do. No other infantry is willing to march north with us and we are still standing by for General MacArthur to answer our call. Good work, soldier. I need you to stay in position and get in contact with the infantries behind us. They'll be tired from fighting on the eastern front, but you have to convince them to keep pushing west."

"Yes, sir," Jung-Soo said as he walked towards Dae-Gun who

was still in conversation with Sergeant Martin.

"Dae-Gun!" Jung-Soo yelled from afar.

Sergeant Martin and the men raised their arms and surveyed their surroundings. "Tell your friend to shut the hell up," Martin said.

"What's wrong?" Dae-Gun said.

Frantically, Jung-Soo walked up to Sergeant Martin and held his hand out towards him, as if to ask for something.

"What is it?" Dae-Gun asked.

"Tell the American to get his radio out," Jung-Soo said in Korean. Dae-Gun translated, and the sergeant obeyed, curious as to what had brought on the sudden request.

"What is it? Is his radio broken? What happened?" the sergeant said.

As soon as Jung-Soo saw the massive square object poking out of the sergeant's backpack, he yanked it out himself and set it on the ground.

"I'm going to need you to do something," he said to Dae-Gun as he turned the radio on. "You see this dial here. You turn it to the channels we still haven't reached yet. You relay the same message I've been telling them. Talk to the commanders, not just the radio operators. Tell them that the 18th Infantry has joined the American Regiment on the northern front and the others are joining forces to meet the western line."

"You did it?" Dae-Gun said, pulling Jung-Soo in a tight embrace. "I can't believe it! You actually convinced them!" Dae-Gun rose from the ground and translated to Sergeant Martin and the few other marines around them. They laughed and shook hands with each other. Jung-Soo even thought he saw a gracious smile directed towards him from the sergeant himself.

"Listen, Dae-Gun. I need to ask you a favor," Jung-Soo began. This was his opportunity. The Americans wouldn't shoot him now; he was sure. Not when they were so euphoric and he had done his duty. "I need you to take charge of the radio. You've been around me long enough to know how to operate one, and you can speak both English and Korean so it won't be a problem communicating with both the U.N. and the South Korean forces."

Dae-Gun noticed Jung-Soo's backpack was fully packed with the radio and his gun slung over his shoulder, ready to run at a moment's notice.

"Don't do this," he pleaded. "We have our orders. You'll be committing treason."

"I know," Jung-Soo whispered, though he knew no one else could understand. "But I have to. Iseul. My father's letter. I've been thinking, Dae-Gun, maybe my father knew a way out, and it might just be written on here."

"Get a hold of yourself!" Dae-Gun said, trying to suppress his tone of voice amidst the curious stares directed towards them.

"I know it's a long shot, but it's the only shot we have," Jung-Soo said.

"Don't you see it's already too late? You're running straight to your own death. This is your second chance. We'll get through this together, and once this war is over, we'll get to start a new life, a better one—on the same side."

Jung-Soo wavered, though only for Dae-Gun. He hadn't expected to become friends with the idiot pig who had proven himself to be a far better and loyal man than he could ever be. Jung-Soo glanced towards the sergeant who began frowning at them.

"You can do this, Dae-Gun," Jung-Soo reassured.

Dae-Gun's face betrayed a momentary look of an anxious boy. "What if I can't?"

"Think of Zion. Your brothers," he said.

Dae-Gun nodded, suppressing the emotions that bubbled just beneath the surface.

"Thank you," Jung-Soo managed to say. "I want you to know that I'm glad I got the chance to meet you."

Dae-Gun could see there was nothing he could say that would change his mind. "Who else would have sung you a lullaby and played the guitar for you every night before bed?" He grinned. "Wait, don't answer that…"

Jung-Soo chuckled. "Here," he held out a single sheet of paper folded into two halves. "I remember you said you wanted one too."

"What is it?" Dae-Gun took it and unfolded the page. It was a sketch of his guitar he had left with Zion, complete with measurements and identical to the one Jung-Soo had mailed to Iseul. Tears welled, though Dae-Gun was afraid a drop might ruin the only thoughtful gift Jung-Soo had ever given him. "Thanks," he managed to say.

Dae-Gun nodded to signal his approval as he turned his back on his friend and walked towards Sergeant Martin. "Sergeant, can you do me a favor and locate our position on the map for me again?' Dae-Gun asked.

It was Jung-Soo's cue as he darted into the icy cold forest, one foot ahead of the other, heading straight towards Yeoju.

"Hey! Hey! Where do you think you're going?" Corporal Taylor shouted at the disappearing figure. He raised his gun up, but Sergeant Martin pushed it down as the bullets skidded on the soil.

"Let him go," he said. "Let him say goodbye to whoever he needs to."

Dae-Gun's eyes widened. "You knew?"

"I don't need to speak Korean to put two and two together."

CHAPTER 35

Jung-Soo sprinted until he felt like his lungs would freeze from the midnight air. He would stop only for food and when he did, he would broadcast again, hoping Iseul or someone in Yeoju would be listening, but no one answered. He would then flip through the radio channels and eavesdrop on the progress of the battles on all fronts. The radio operators were cautious; they neither gave too much or too little information over open radio, and the information they gave out was immediately actionable with minimal consequences should the North Koreans be listening. They were listening; that much was certain.

It appeared the 18th Infantry reached the 5th Cavalry. That was a relief to hear. The eastern North Korean forces were slowing down and the western Chinese ones were not as large as the one they had been fighting in the east. Good.

After hiking two hills, crossing a river, listening to a barrage of ever-nearing bombs, Jung-Soo reached the Northern border of Yeoju. He passed the mountain fortress of Pasaseong-ji and into the village centers, where nothing but empty thatched homes and rampaged rice fields greeted him. It was a good sign. Perhaps they had all escaped. Maybe Dae-Gun was right and they had evacuated a long time ago. He pushed further south until he could see the west gate of the Wasteland, still standing tall in colorful hues.

"Psst!" A voice heard in a bush. Jung-Soo shot a glance towards it. It was Gil-Dong, looking petrified and pointing towards the tree to his left. Jung-Soo saw it—a figure holding a gun pointed towards him.

A sniper. He dove and rolled into the bush as a shot skidded somewhere near his right ear.

Doo-Hyung lunged forward and pulled Jung-Soo by the heel towards the safety of a denser tree trunk.

"That was a close call," Gil-Dong said.

"I swear that woman is crazy," Doo-Hyung said, agitated. "Couldn't she have found a different hobby than shooting at moving targets?"

"Wait, the person with the gun is a woman?" Jung-Soo said, doubtfully.

"Don't remind me," Doo-Hyung said rolling his eyes. And then pulled Jung-Soo in a tight fatherly embrace. "Welcome back, kid!"

Jung-Soo was rather surprised as he awkwardly reciprocated the embrace with two sturdy pats on the back. "Oh, right. Thanks."

"Where's Dae-Gun?" Gil-Dong said.

Jung-Soo explained what had happened in the past two days they had been away.

"So we have hope," Gil-Dong said. "If they hold back the Chinese troops long enough, maybe, we can find a way out of here."

"Arg! I can strangle that woman! We've risked everything to come all this way, only to be thwarted by a woman playing sniper," Doo-Hyung said.

"You've got to hand it to her," Gil-Dong said. "She's good."

"Yeah, yeah..." Doo-Hyung said rather morosely. He knew that he had evaded death more than a few times in the past few days, and somehow, he felt he had been spared a few times too. "Don't go telling her that. She's got more arrogance than the General I know."

"So, you've talked to her?" Jung-Soo said. "Have you tried explaining to her that we're not the enemy?"

"I did," Doo-Hyung said.

Gil-Dong shook his head. "Not a chance."

"Who is she anyway?" Jung-Soo said, scratching his head. He couldn't think of a single woman in the village who was trained as a sniper.

"Her name is Su-Jung. Apparently, she's not from here."

"Oh great. I barely had a chance convincing someone I knew from the village that we're here to help," Jung-Soo said. "Seems you've had an entire conversation with her," Jung-Soo added, eyeing him suspiciously. "What did you say to her?"

"Just the usual stuff I say to women. It usually works."

Gil-Dong's eyes widened, and Jung-Soo could imagine why.

"I think that might be the problem," Jung-Soo said. "Let me give it a try. How much have you told her about us?"

"Not much," Doo-Hyung said. "I told her armies were on the way and that we're here to help them find a way out of the village."

"What did she say?"

"She told us to piss off," Gil-Dong said, a little too loudly.

A bullet skidded and hit the tree truck they were behind. "I heard that!" a woman's voice yelped. "If you're going to talk about me, why don't you try talking to my face, you cowards!"

"Why is she here?" Jung-Soo was whispering.

Doo-Hyung pointed to the other side of the west gate. Behind the thatched homes, stood men in hordes with guns and hoes, ready to attack. The whole situation reeked of an operation in progress. But who would be interested in saving a small farming village doomed to be raided by North Korean troops?

"Something's not right," Jung-Soo said, as he began to move towards the sniper, hiding behind tree trunks for cover. Gil-Dong and Doo-Hyung followed close by.

"Su-Jung." Jung-Soo called out in the direction of the sniper. "That is your name, right?"

"You got that right, mister. What the hell do you want from us?"

"I know you don't trust me, but I'm from this village. I grew up here. That Japanese construction at the foot of the western hills—that used to be my home. People call it the Golden Palace."

"Alright. You've got me interested. At least you don't have a funny accent. What are you doing, colluding with a bunch of northerners?"

"It's a long story. I'll explain later, but we're running out of time. There is a girl here. Her name is Ji Iseul. Do you know her?"

"Who doesn't?"

"She's a friend of mine. I want you to do me a favor and bring her here. Tell her Jung-Soo is here. Ham Jung-Soo."

"I can do better," she said.

Jung-Soo could hear the sizzle of the radio and the sound of a muffled conversation. His heart began to race. Could it be Iseul on the other line? He was so close… He could imagine her in front of him with a smile that welcomed him home.

***

"It was a miracle that we found those two radio towers. What more could we expect?" Mr. Lim said.

Iseul was glad there was nothing but valleys and mountains when they reached the top. It meant whoever else made it to the top would see the same—not the roof of a warehouse full of rice.

"So, what now?" the old man asked.

"We keep moving," Mr. Lim said. He laid out a frayed piece of aged leather with a detailed map and crouched over it. "We're here." He pointed to a faded spot on the map's edge. "The map doesn't have all the intricacies of the mountain ridges ahead," he said concerned.

"I say we turn back," Iseul said. "As far as we know, these mountains are endless and if they are similar to the mountains we know, most will be too steep to hike on foot, let alone with a group of children and elderly. It'll take months to scout out a path that is feasible."

Mr. Lim seemed to waver. "We have to keep going. What other choice do we have?"

He was right; there was no other way but forward. Iseul looked due south where the mountains rose insurmountable and rockier than any of the others in the eastern direction. She was beginning to realize they had sorely underestimated the search expedition.

The old man sighed. "We'll freeze to death and die of starvation in less than a week while the villagers die waiting for our return. If only we only had a better map. There must be one somewhere. Someone must have a marked route out of the village."

Mr. Lim and Iseul sighed too. He was thinking about his father, and his grandfather. Had they ever said anything about a way out? The land had been occupied by their ancestors for thousands of years. Surely someone must have ventured out.

"We know. The east gate is there for a reason. But we've asked everyone and all we've been getting are stories and legends," Iseul said, frustrated.

Perhaps Mr. Ham knew a thing or two about the mountains since he hid the rice there, but that was exactly the premise of their rice warehouse—hidden. They needed more supplies if they were to take on the mountains ahead. The three turned back towards the two radio towers that taunted them. Iseul couldn't help but feel disappointed. The villagers were counting on them, and their own soldiers would die by the thousands, just because they were too cautious.

Despite Mr. Lim's decision to stall their hiking expedition for the time being, plans were well on their way in the Wasteland. The group of food scavengers had collected and stored as much food as they could as Mi-Jung and the papermakers made and delivered their last supply of paper, as the brave mailman drove out the western gate, and hopefully south.

"He said he heard bombs on the way here," Mi-Jung said to Iseul.

Iseul took one last look at her home as she evacuated the papermakers of Yeoju. She decided she wouldn't cry, or even feel nostalgic about leaving. It had served its purpose for many generations, and should she survive the war, she decided she would not return. Those were the thoughts of clarity that emerged as she stood beneath the two radio towers, scanning the horizon into the mountains that seemed to have no end.

"Go on ahead," Iseul said to Mi-Jung who hiked at the tail end of the group of the last papermakers. "I'll meet you there."

Iseul made what might be her final journey to the cabin. She knew what else she would be leaving behind—Jung-Soo. It was hard to admit, but she had been hoping he would return to her. She was fighting for her village, as Mi-Jung and the rest of the villagers did so that their men would have a home to return to.

It seemed that dream had faded long before she was forced to let go. Jung-Soo would return; he was strong. Once all was said and done, and once this thing called war was over, he would return. And if she was lucky enough to make it out alive, she would come back to Yeoju, perhaps help rebuild the village, and find another plot of land to start over.

Yeong-Hoon appeared next to her; it was as if they had never left each other.

"I thought you were walking the children over to the cabin," Iseul said, pleasantly surprised.

"I thought I might be of better use here," Yeong-Hoon grasped her hand, like Jung-Soo once used to. It was still shaking but a lot less with something to grab onto. "Besides, the kids are still scared of me."

"No, they're not," Iseul said. "They're just not used to your…leg."

"It's not every day they come across a cripple," Yeong-Hoon joked.

"So, they should be honored."

"That little girl skipping stones is a force to be reckoned with. She reminds me of you."

"Young-Hee?"

"Yeah. She'll be great…bossing everyone around."

Iseul knocked into Yeong-Hoon on the shoulder as she usually did. They chuckled softly. They enjoyed their quiet banter, as if the past few months hadn't happened, just as they used to be, sitting next to each other in father's workshop making buk drums or the odd cabinet and table.

Yeong-Hoon picked up a thicker branch of wood that laid in their path, and handed it to her.

"Pine," Iseul said.

"Your favorite."

She reached for her carving knife and began working with the wood out of habit. She stripped the bark and was about to discard the wood beneath when she realized she didn't need the bark anymore; her paper-making days were over. She tossed the bark into the forest floor and began cutting into the wood. She didn't quite know what she was making, but it felt good to be slicing away at something, just as she used to when she lay beneath that pine tree beside her mother's grave—beside her parents' grave. She liked the idea of being buried there, below that pine tree, joining the family in the afterlife.

"So why do you think Mr. Lim went into the village again?" Iseul said as she flipped the pine wood over to its end and began slicing there. She remembered Mr. Lim hurrying against the tide of people heading towards the cabin and thought it was strange.

Yeong-Hoon shrugged. "Unfinished business, I suppose."

They strode quietly, even peacefully through the chilly mountain, enjoying the sensation of cold against their faces, and the birds that still chirped and sung of long lost times. They stood at the ridge of the hill they called home, wind blowing in all directions as they looked into the valleys and mountains that stretched ahead.

"So, this is it," Yeong-Hoon said. "Somewhere, on one of those mountains, there is rice and lots of it."

Iseul nodded. She could barely make out the tip of the two radio towers on the hill adjacent. She had noticed Yeong-Hoon had changed his attire. He was out of his white and brown-stained work clothes and had changed into an outfit she hadn't seen before. It was a light blue linen hanbok paired with a top hat made with black silk—the humble attire of a groom-to-be. Iseul hadn't noticed his beard that had set, thick and black, covering his usual sharp jawline.

"It suits you," Iseul said. It almost seemed like father was alive again, heading into the village for a drink with the butcher. She knew she couldn't stop him from going. He had wanted to fight for a long time, though the military had denied him. The situation had changed, and no one cared that he was a cripple in the front lines.

Iseul sheathed her carving knife, the family heirloom her father had given to Yeong-Hoon, and handed it back to him.

"I can't take that," Yeong-Hoon said.

"You can. It's rightfully yours."

He pushed it back into her hands and wrapped his hands over her fingers that clasped the knife's handle. That was that, and Iseul did not push the matter any further.

They heard the chatter of little children as they neared the cabin.

"Iseul!" It was Mr. Lim running towards them.

Iseul and Yeong-Hoon were startled, looking at each other as they ran to meet him. "What's wrong? Did something happen at the west gate?" Iseul said.

"What took you so long?" he said, out of breath. "Never mind. It's about Su-Jung. Three men appeared at the western gate a few hours ago."

"Are they North Koreans? Some of our forces?" Iseul asked, impatient.

He shook his head, out of breath. "One of them claims to be Jung-Soo. Ham Jung-Soo."

***

Shots fired in succession towards Jung-Soo, Doo-Hyung and Gil-Dong.

"I told you she's insane!" Doo-Hyung yelled out as he led the way towards another tree closer to the village. Other snipers joined in, shooting at anything that moved.

Why were so many of them shooting at the same time? Gil-Dong heard it first, as he directed their attention to the incoming stampede.

"They're here," Jung-Soo said. He felt his knees buckle, as his legs toppled over each other. "She must think they're with us. Are the troops even on our side?" Jung-Soo said, squinting into the line of men marching towards them at an alarming pace.

"It doesn't matter anymore." Doo-Hyung led the way. "A hundred, one-fifty at most. It'll keep the snipers busy while we sneak in."

Jung-Soo didn't like the idea of betraying whatever trust they had built, but soon, there would be more forces coming, and more fighting will ensue. He hoped the ones that were coming were South Korean soldiers. At least then, the snipers here would have a chance to group together and hold off the incoming North Korean army.

The three men dashed towards the next largest tree trunk and scattered, each passing the bounds of the Wasteland in various points a good distance away from the west gate where men stood guard.

Jung-Soo waved at them to follow him. They were headed towards the Golden Palace and into the warehouse where he last saw the enigma machine.

"Su-Jung?" Iseul said, as she shouted into the microphone of the radio.

"We lost the men. They breached our perimeter." Su-Jung said, seething.

"Is it true? Is Ham Jung-Soo here?"

"Yes, he's here with two North Korean soldiers."

Iseul faltered. What was Jung-Soo doing with North Koreans? Were they Mr. Ham's men? "I'll take care of it," she said.

"Alright. We've got bigger fish to fry anyway. An infantry of over a hundred is just about to breach our perimeter. We think it might be an American one," Su-Jung reported.

"Copy that," Iseul said, pushing the radio aside.

"He's here, Iseul," Mr. Lim said with hope.

"I can't believe it," Iseul stood stunned. "He must know something, right? That must be why he's here."

"I believe so," Mr. Lim said. "But we can't be sure he's not under duress. Those North Korean soldiers might have him at gun point, here to find the location of the hidden rice."

Iseul nodded, pacing in place. "What do we do? I have to find him. Figure out what's happening." She began racing down the hill.

"Wait! Wait!" Mr. Lim followed after her. He had managed to pluck the smaller short-range radio and handed it to Iseul. "Take this with you. Radio in with any information you have."

Iseul nodded and clutched the radio under her arm as she dashed off.

Where to? Her mind raced. She did not let her legs falter, though she knew it would be minutes before she would have to make a decision. This must be about the rice. *The Golden Palace?* But there was nothing left there, no clues, and every room had been rampaged and thoroughly examined. Did he know about the radio towers? Maybe she should have stayed put. Maybe he was headed towards the cabin. No, that was always meant to be a hideout. He wouldn't bring the North Koreans there, unless...

Maybe he had gone over to the other side. No. Iseul denied the thoughts. Her feet quickened. She couldn't let them find out any more about the rice, about the radio towers or allow them to endanger the people at the cabin. She was determined she would find them first.

Iseul made a sharp turn. She would catch them in the center of the village. If she ran fast enough, she would make it before Jung-Soo ever reached the eastern gate.

The Golden Palace. Her heart skipped a beat.

***

"Where is it? Where the hell is it?" Jung-Soo said as he kicked aside a piece of a metal propeller in his father's warehouse. It was empty, except for broken pieces of wood, metal and unwanted luxury furniture sprawled across in patches on the floor.

"Are you sure this was the last place you saw it?" Doo-Hyung pushed.

Jung-Soo paced, closing his eyes to picture the strange looking typewriter. "Yes, of course. But who else might have known... think Jung-Soo, you idiot, think!" He shouted at himself.

Doo-Hyung and Gil-Dong watched on as they tossed over a few stray batteries and broken propellers. Doo-Hyung was impressed at the remnants of the collection his friend Young-Nam had managed to keep. He knew his friend had always been a collector and it was good to see his tastes haven't changed much since their childhood years. He still seems to have the same infatuation with batteries and all sorts of automotive vehicles. Despite the situation they were in, Doo-Hyung couldn't help but reminiscence. *What better time than just before your death?* He thought.

"Someone else. Who would my father give an old typewriter to?" Jung-Soo kept repeating. "The scholar? Mr. Lim?" No, Jung-Soo couldn't imagine the scholar capable of working with a machine when he was always so adamant about reading only traditional manuscripts. Mr. Lim? Did his father trust him enough to hand over the typewriter? He never truly trusted anyone other than the Captain. But perhaps his father had changed. He scoffed at himself just thinking about it; he knew nothing about his father.

He thought about his own correspondence with those connected with his father. These two North Koreans. Iseul. But how did Iseul know where to send the letter? That had been a mystery he was still working on when the tides of the war changed so suddenly.

"Did I ever tell you about a girl called Iseul?" Jung-Soo thought out loud.

"Boy, this is no time for romance and reminiscing!" Doo-Hyung scolded as he broke from his own thoughts of childhood. "It's not over. At least not yet!"

"No, just listen to me!" Jung-Soo said. "I was trying to work up the courage to write to her. Months had passed since I had left the village, and one day, I received a letter from her."

"So, what?" Gil-Dong halted his silent streak. "She wrote to you."

"But I never told her where I was. The plan was for her to think I was dead. It was supposed to be easier for everyone that way."

"Someone must have told her," Gil-Dong said matter-of-factly.

"Exactly! I enlisted in another province so no one would know my identity which means no one was supposed to know where I was posted. The Captain died that night. My father disappeared across the border. Yet, someone knew where I was posted."

"Your father," Doo-Hyung said with certainty. "He has eyes everywhere. He would have known where you eventually ended up. He knew where to send me so he must have known."

"So, someone here must have been corresponding with my

father after the night of the massacre, and must have told Iseul about my alias and where I was posted."

Doo-Hyung knew what this might mean—Young-Nam had indeed someone here who might have sent him the coded message. He had thought the message would be a map Young-Nam had written down before he had left Yeoju, but it seemed it had been written more recently. Perhaps something had transpired during his time as colonel under General Shin. Perhaps it was a way out of this god-forsaken village to save his son who would have gone into a losing battle for a woman. This complicated the matter.

Jung-Soo continued. "That someone must have told Iseul where to send the letter. Iseul. We have to find Iseul."

In that moment, the doors of the warehouse flung open and there stood none other than Iseul, holding a gun towards him.

CHAPTER 36

Iseul heard the voices in the warehouse and pulled her gun out from her right ankle. The voices seemed cordial enough, though the intonation was certainly northern. And then she heard it. *Jung-Soo.*

She couldn't believe it! What in the world was Jung-Soo doing, colluding with North Koreans? She released the safety and cocked the gun, just as Jung-Soo taught her to.

She stumbled into the warehouse, her arms shaking as she pointed the gun at the first figure she saw. It was Jung-Soo. Flustered, she pointed it towards the older soldier.

"Iseul?" Jung-Soo said. His face flashed with confusion, relief, then beamed. "You're still here!" The words began to take on a different meaning as he flung into a state of panic. "What were you thinking? Why didn't you evacuate?" He was verging on anger.

"Well," Iseul said annoyed. "Look who's talking. You're here too."

"Hello, I'm Doo-Hyung and that's Gil-Dong," the older soldier held out his hand towards Iseul. "We've heard a lot about you."

It was only then that Iseul realized there was a third person in the warehouse, sitting in the corner. For a moment, Iseul was confused and then poked the gun back at the North Korean soldier. "Get back! Are you crazy? I have a fully loaded gun and I'll shoot if you take another step."

"Feisty," Doo-Hyung said to Jung-Soo with a semblance of a wink.

Jung-Soo rolled his eyes. "Alright, everyone, let's just put the gun down and talk this through." He gestured back and forth between Iseul and Doo-Hyung.

"I'm not putting my gun down until I know exactly what's going on," Iseul demanded.

Doo-Hyung lit his cigarette and moved towards the corner, plopping down next to Gil-Dong.

"Technically, that's my gun, but suit yourself," Jung-Soo said.

Iseul fumed, though her eyes rested momentarily on Jung-Soo's. He smiled warmly. He was glad to see her, she could see that. But she couldn't let her eyes deceive her. This was not the Jung-Soo she remembered—the Jung-Soo she knew would never openly work with the enemy.

"Spill it," Iseul demanded.

"We're here to help you find a way out of this village," Jung-Soo began. He explained how his father sent Doo-Hyung with a coded message and the circumstances under which they had met.

"Your partner, Dae-Gun, was it?" Iseul said, clarifying the story. "Where is he now?"

"He's with the American marines, trying to warn the incoming South Korean soldiers about the attack."

"What? American soldiers?" Iseul said, utterly confused. "I thought you were with the 18th Infantry of the South Korean army?"

"Yes, I am, but I am a radio technician and Dae-Gun could speak English so they paired and sent us off." Jung-Soo seemed to want to explain everything at once. "It's a long story," he said.

"I get the idea," Iseul said. She had been thinking about that coded message Jung-Soo mentioned. She had to stop herself from blurting out that Mr. Lim had been receiving similarly coded messages too, and that Mr. Ham had reached out to an old military strategist from Northern Yeoju.

"Any idea what the message might be?" she said, though she feared what it might hold.

"We don't know. That's what we're here to find out. We're hoping it'll help us find a way out. Which is why we were looking for you."

"Me?" Iseul said, although seeing how difficult Jung-Soo found it to hide his enthusiasm, it wasn't a surprise. She missed him too—

a lot, and much more than she was willing to admit with a gun pointed at the North Koreans.

Jung-Soo grinned at her expression. He seemed to have seen a blush. "I thought my father might be in contact with someone here, and maybe that someone told you where to send that letter you sent me."

Iseul's blush deepened. "Mr. Lim sent the letter without my knowing." It was a small blow to him; Iseul hadn't intended to write to him. But Jung-Soo's conjecture had been right. It was Mr. Lim who had been in contact with his father.

She glanced back and forth between the North Koreans and Jung-Soo, debating whether or not they already knew about the rice store. Jung-Soo hadn't yet mentioned it, and it seemed wise to keep it that way.

"What is it? Is there something you're not telling me?" Jung-Soo said, as a look of both concern and suspicion glossed over him. "Does this have something to do with why our village has snipers stationed at the west gate?" Silence echoed in the empty halls of the Golden Palace warehouse.

"Alright, alright I admit. I wasn't telling the whole truth." It was Doo-Hyung who broke the silence. Even Gil-Dong was taken aback.

"What?" Jung-Soo seethed and reached for his rifle. "I knew it! I knew there must be some other reason you would agree to come all the way down here!"

"Rice," Doo-Hyung spoke, looking straight into Iseul's eyes. "You know too." Iseul did not give any indication she did. "I thought you wouldn't come if I told you the letter wasn't really for you, but about another one of your father's elaborate plans." Jung-Soo positioned himself next to Iseul as they both held their guns toward the North Koreans.

"They're only rumors," Doo-Hyung began again, "myths even, that the mountains in the southern bounds of Yeoju held stores of rice able to sustain a large army for years."

"That's preposterous!" Jung-Soo interrupted. "Everyone in the village has been verging on starvation for years."

"Exactly," Doo-Hyung stated. "This is a farming region. Where did all that rice go? The Japanese have been gone for over five years, but the village is still starving. From what I hear, Young-Nam had been taking rice due to the Japanese for years so that's at least a decade worth of rice collections."

Jung-Soo turned his head to Iseul. "Is it true?" he asked, "Wait, no. Don't say another word." He glared at Doo-Hyung, "You think the coded message from my father will lead to the rice stores. You're here on your father's bidding!"

It was beginning to make sense. His father had known the army was headed to Yeoju for the rice and wanted Jung-Soo to secure it and make sure it doesn't fall into the hands of the Chinese. Doo-Hyung had betrayed him. He had kept the message until it was too late for Jung-Soo to do anything but hand over the rice. And to think they all believed the North Koreans were planning on trapping their armies in Yeoju! No, their plans were much more sinister—plans to secure an outright victory with enough rice to keep the massive Chinese army alive throughout the winter.

"No, I'm not." Doo-Hyung flatly dismissed the charge. "But I can't be certain if the letter is about the rice or a way out of this village."

Jung-Soo scoffed as he aimed his gun at him. He couldn't imagine a scenario in which his father would send someone to save the villagers; the only people he would raise a finger to save were his own flesh and blood, and ones he could use later for his own purposes. Jung-Soo had fallen into his father's trap, knowing he would go back to the village if only to save Iseul. Hot anger coursed through his veins and stung him somewhere in his chest. *Betrayal.*

"Don't jump to conclusions," Doo-Hyung commanded. "I wouldn't have given the letter to you if my motive was to find the rice stores for my father."

"Don't patronize me," Jung-Soo roared back. "You knew you would never get here alone, let alone find the enigma machine without my help—without Iseul's help. And you certainly took your time to get the message to me so your father's army could take it before we could secure the rice store." He instinctively drew closer to Iseul and stood in front of her so as to mask her frame from the traitors.

"Jung-Soo," Iseul spoke. "Maybe we should give him the chance to explain."

"I've heard enough."

"No!" Iseul pulled away from Jung-Soo. "You're just as stubborn and bullheaded as I remember!"

"Thanks." Doo-Hyung sent a smile towards Iseul.

"Shut up." Iseul scowled at him. "Listen, Jung-Soo. If your father sent them, maybe there is a reason."

"What reason? Isn't it obvious? He's the son of the North Korean General and he's here to find the rice stores to win the war for his father."

"North Korean General?" Iseul was surprised.

"And you're the son of a North Korean spy. How do you think that looks?" Doo-Hyung said.

Iseul frowned at both of them. "He's right, Jung-Soo. Honestly, it looks bad either way."

The pang in Jung-Soo's chest deepened. "You don't trust me?"

"I do," Iseul said. "I want to…"

Jung-Soo's gun drooped and slung on his shoulder at resting position again. He was tired and confused. The weight of the letter pressed against his already heavy chest. He didn't care who found the rice anymore. Hadn't he come here to find a way out to save Iseul? He looked into her face that had thinned and hardened along the edges. How long had his nights been, imagining—dreaming of this reunion?

Yet, he saw the face of a woman filled with disappointment. How would Iseul think of him? How would the villagers look at him if he handed the rice over to the enemy? The enemy was already at their doorstep; it was too late to evacuate through the west gate and likewise too late to scramble to find another exit. He should just burn the letter and then figure out an alternative plan, buy enough time to save the villagers somehow.

In the silence that ensued, Jung-Soo's footsteps reverberated against the warehouse floor as he paced towards Doo-Hyung. He dug his hand into Doo-Hyung's front pocket and took his match out, reaching for his father's letter as he walked back to Iseul.

"We burn it," Jung-Soo said, lighting a match as he neared the flame to the edge of the letter.

In an instant, Doo-Hyung and Iseul jumped toward Jung-Soo. "No!" they said in unison as Jung-Soo lurched back.

He groaned and blew the light out. "You've got a better idea?"

"Actually, yes," Iseul began. The soldiers listened skeptically. "I've been playing out the possible scenarios and it doesn't matter what we do. Chances are, we've already lost the rice with or without the directions to get there."

"What do you mean?" Jung-Soo said, though he quickly

realized Iseul was right. With the sheer number of soldiers scouring the mountains, it was only a matter of time. He had hoped that burning the message would stop them from finding the rice altogether, but he had been rash to conclude.

"Jung-Soo, there's something you have to know about your father on the night of the massacre."

Iseul told Jung-Soo about how the Golden Palace was only half burnt down and how Mr. Ham had risked his life to save the rice that was in the warehouse.

"Do you remember when we saw those two green lights near the cabin?"

"Yes…" Jung-Soo was confused. "You said they looked like a tiger's eyes."

"It wasn't a tiger. They were two radio towers with green lights attached to the top."

Jung-Soo still looked at her as if she were spewing random facts. "Don't you get it?" Iseul exclaimed. "Those trucks full of rice in the warehouse were meant to drive towards the rice stores, and the radio tower built to aid communications between the rice store and the village."

"You mean to say the rice was never meant to be hidden?" Jung-Soo said.

"All I'm saying is, it's highly likely that there are roads that lead straight to the stores."

Jung-Soo let the idea sink in a little longer. "Years ago, I saw trucks coming back from the east gate. I always thought the drivers hit a dead end and drove back, but it seems they had gone down that road to place more rice into the store." He came to the same conclusion they all had. "Dammit! It's over," he said, completely deflated.

"If the Chinese and North Korean troops get here and they know about the existence of a rice store, it won't be long till they find the road that leads to it. There is a slim chance that they won't find it in time and starve out during the winter, or the South Korean and Americans gather up enough strength to strike back."

"Unlikely," Doo-Hyung said. He too seemed disappointed by the news.

Gil-Dong cleared his throat. "What if there is a way…"

Iseul didn't realize the boy could speak. Doo-Hyung and Jung-Soo didn't seem to take him seriously.

"What if this is a blessing in disguise for us?"

Doo-Hyung pat him firmly on the back, almost as if comforting the boy who realized his end would come in some remote South Korean village, far from home.

"No, listen," he shrugged off Doo-Hyung's hand. "What if the rice store is identical to our way out of this village?" Gil-Dong said with a flash of quiet vision in his eyes. "If your father paved a road big enough for trucks to reach the rice stores, he may have also paved a road through the mountain ridge that connected to a road south."

It was simple—too simple. "He wouldn't be so obvious..." Doo-Hyung said, though his own words deceived him. The longer he thought about it, the more probable it seemed. His friend Young-Nam always had a contingency plan; Doo-Hyung couldn't imagine him sitting around, hoping a large remote store would not be found.

"So, we find the rice stores," Gil-Dong said.

"Look around for a road south and take as much rice as we can," Iseul added.

Jung-Soo concurred though he had his reservations. There was still the possibility that they would lead the Chinese straight to the rice on their way out. He could not imagine a small village hand-carrying decades-worth of rice stored away. The thought didn't bother him too much; he had decided long ago that he did not care if the Chinese took the rice. All that mattered now was to get the villagers out. He'll think about the rest later.

"Let's decipher this damn letter," Jung-Soo said.

Iseul plucked the letter from his hand with a smirk. "Leave that to me." The three soldiers were stunned.

"You knew where the enigma machine was this whole time?" Jung-Soo said.

"Enigma machine? Is that what the old typewriter contraption is called? Well, I couldn't just blurt that out, could I? Not with these two North Koreans in earshot," Iseul retorted.

Jung-Soo couldn't believe it. "Noon-chi. It doesn't seem like that's a problem for you anymore."

Iseul scoffed. "I've got more noon-chi than all three of you combined. And I'm doing everyone a favor since I'm the only one here who can be objective about the outcome of this letter. Any objections?"

Jung-Soo's fingers felt oddly empty as the weight on his chest lifted. He shook his head. Doo-Hyung anxiously shook his head too.

Iseul turned the radio on. She didn't know what to expect, but she hadn't expected the raucous string of gunshots and screams blaring from the other end. "It's Iseul. What's happening? Who's on the other line?"

"The west gate is under heavy fire!" It was undoubtedly Su-Jung's voice. "Where have you been Iseul? We thought something might have happened to you. Luckily, the 13th Infantry joined the fight, but there are at least twice as many Chinese…" Her voice cut off, then the signal died, coming back on with more gun shots as Su-Jung shouted commands at her men.

Iseul went pale. "They're here."

"Quickly," Doo-Hyung helped Iseul along towards the door. "We're counting on you."

Jung-Soo noticed Iseul's hands shaking. He placed them in his and squeezed it tight, whispering in her ear, "I trust you, Ji-Iseul. With my life."

Iseul snapped out of her dazed state and gave him a reassuring nod. "Wait at my house. I'll be back, I promise." She grabbed the radio that stuck out of Jung-Soo's backpack and turned the dial to the channel she and the rest of the village were on, handing it back to him. And with a quick peck on Jung-Soo's lips, she raced out the door of the warehouse.

Jung-Soo's face flushed red. Doo-Hyung stared at the poor boy who could have hidden under a rock as Gil-Dong chuckled. But before any of them could comment on Iseul's blatant display of affection, Jung-Soo's radio came alive.

"Mr. Lim." It was Iseul. "Are you there Mr. Lim?"

"Iseul, are you alright? What took you so long?"

"I'm fine. About that typewriter," Iseul said. "If I'm not mistaken, did you go into the village earlier this morning to retrieve it from the Golden Palace?"

The line went silent. "Why don't you get back here. It's best we talk in person."

Jung-Soo's hunch had been correct. Someone had been using the enigma machine to communicate with his father. But of all people, Mr. Lim? He didn't realize his father put so much faith in him. The father Jung-Soo thought he knew didn't seem to exist, and it didn't bother him. No, not one bit.

"Batteries," Jung-Soo thought out loud as he scanned the

warehouse for spares. He found a few and bagged them before exiting the warehouse. With guns held close, they crept out the front gate of the Golden Palace where guns fired and the screams of men filled the once peaceful air.

Jung-Soo led the way to the east gate and up the hillside road to the left. He was surprised to find it was a relatively quick hike compared to the mammoth journey they had been on, gallivanting across the entire Peninsula.

It seemed every other tree had been either chopped down or shaved of its bark, much worse than any other mountain by a village; it was a sacrifice that had made such a difference in the battlefield all across the Peninsula.

Iseul's home and workshop came into view, looking more worn and abandoned than it was before he had left. They set up camp in Iseul's workshop. Memories haunted every corner of the room. He perched the radio on a counter in the middle of the workshop and blasted the volume. Still, no news came other than Su-Jung, fighting for her life.

Gil-Dong appeared with thicker coats he had found in Iseul's closet and hung it on Jung-Soo's shoulders. It was Mr. Ji's old coat. A smile clung to the corner of his lips. Iseul's closet may be the only one that hadn't yet been raided by someone else in need. That was the sort of respect she commanded as clearly, she had achieved so much since they had last met. Stacks of paper, bamboo frames, flat stones, brass pots and a large pile of wood stood testament to the mass-scale paper production that had taken place in the very ground he stood. He was proud. So very proud.

"You're going to break the dial." Doo-Hyung slapped Jung-Soo's hand away from the radio. He glowered at Doo-Hyung who had also helped himself to one of Mr. Ji's old coats, though it was a tight fit for him.

Jung-Soo paced around the radio, trying to convince himself that he was doing his best to help win this battle by hiding out in an abandoned paper mill.

Doo-Hyung noticed. "Look, kid, I'm not one to back down from a fight, but we did the right thing." Jung-Soo nodded, still pacing. "General Shin always told me we are fighting for something much bigger than ourselves." Doo-Hyung filled the silence. "I believed him. Your father and I both did."

"Don't sell your communist bullshit to me," Jung-Soo said,

almost in passing. Commander Lee had once said the same to him, before proceeding to tell him to do as he was told. In any case, he was in no mood to debate politics.

"The problem is, the other side believes their cause is just as worthy—enough to die for."

"Some world we live in," Jung-Soo said, sardonically. "Do you have something to say about that, Gil-Dong?"

Gil-Dong shrugged and picked up a gayageom and strummed its fibrous strings, moving on to the buk-drum as he gave it a curious thump.

"Yeah, that's what I thought," Jung-Soo said. For a brief moment, as Gil-Dong stood fascinated by the workshop and all that it held, he wondered what really went on in this boy's head. There was certainly something bubbling beneath the silence he so naturally held. A boy who lived on the border—it sounded familiar, almost as if he were looking into a distorted mirror.

Jung-Soo squinted at the boy, sighed, then collected his focus back on the radio. He was beginning to wonder if he should just take the road from the east gate and wait till a large store of rice appears. What then? Wait for the Chinese to arrive?

"That rice was never ours to begin with," Jung-Soo said. "It was for the Japanese, and the next invader will happily force it out of our hands again."

"That's it then? Just roll over and die?" Doo-Hyung probed. Jung-Soo knew what the old soldier meant. *What about us? What about our birthright to the land and all that it yields?*

In the quiet of a run-down paper mill, Jung-Soo felt the rising sense of injustice. If the people of Yeoju couldn't eat their own rice, maybe it wasn't such a bad idea that no one gets to have it. He could imagine blowing rice up with the most powerful explosives as the grains of rice would scatter across the mountains. At least then, the Chinese will have to work for the rice and gather it one grain at a time, like these farmers had to when they harvested the rice.

"What happens if the Chinese find the rice? Do you think the villagers will leave without a fight?"

Jung-Soo shrugged. He didn't want to think about it, but somehow, he could see Iseul with a gun in one hand and a knife in another, fighting to guard her rice.

Doo-Hyung hesitated. "Would it be such a bad thing if they did find it?"

The idea didn't sit well with Jung-Soo, but he knew Doo-Hyung wasn't wrong. If his brothers were still alive… his father… then perhaps he would have sided with the North Koreans and Chinese and would have happily given the rice over to them. The Chinese had manpower behind them, though not the artillery and supply chain the Korean and U.N. forces had. With rice and manpower on the North Korean's side, the war might come to an end sooner rather than later. How many lives would be saved because of this? Wouldn't this be a victory in and of itself? The Korean Peninsula would be reunited under Kim Ill-Sung and the Communist realm. Kim Ill-Sung seemed competent enough. It wasn't ideal, he knew. But even if the war dragged on and the South Koreans eventually won, wouldn't Korea still be under western democratic colonization? What had happened to their resolve to find Korea's independence—their own voice and future governed by their own people?

Jung-Soo sighed heavily. This war was never meant for that end; it should have never happened to begin with. He knew it wouldn't be so simple. History would not change so easily and their nation, fraught with foreign agenda for thousands of years, would not suddenly become independent. China was waiting to impose as was the Soviet Union. The Americans wouldn't sit around and wait for such a strategic location to be taken by their enemies.

"The Chinese don't deserve the rice," Gil-Dong said, breaking Jung-Soo from his thoughts.

Jung-Soo and Doo-Hyung were intrigued. "And why's that, kid? Don't you want your own side to win?"

"Of course, I want to go home and be on the winning side. But we didn't farm that rice; the people of Yeoju did. They deserve it."

Doo-Hyung bellowed. "Good on you, kid! You're the most sensible one here!"

Jung-Soo felt a well of gratitude rush over him. Gil-Dong hadn't a clue about the minutia of war, nor did he learn a single lesson on international politics, yet he seemed to know what the right thing was to do. The North Korean side didn't deserve the rice, and neither did the South Korean army. It was for the people of Yeoju to decide what they wanted to do with it.

Jung-Soo's mind churned. How? He paced from one side of the workshop to the other end. "How do we make sure the rice isn't taken by either side? How do we keep it hidden in Yeoju?"

"One step at a time, Jung-Soo," Doo-Hyung said. "We wait first. See if your father's message is what we think it is."

Time was ticking. There must be something—anything he could do.

Jung-Soo halted. "The radio towers." Doo-Hyung stared at him, as if crazed. "We just might be able to reach…" He dialed the radio to another channel and pulled the microphone close. "Dae-Gun, Dae-Gun. Do you read me?"

***

Mr. Lim plopped the old typewriter on the wooden counter top of the cabin where children gathered around to view the spectacle. They began pushing the buttons as their eyes lit up with the corresponding alphabets that protruded on the top portion of the enigma machine.

"This isn't a toy," Mr. Lim said, as he shooed the children away who left in dismay until another boy picked up the nearest piece of wood to begin their routine swordplay.

Iseul had been replaying that peck on Jung-Soo's lips over and over again as she pushed her burning thighs forward. By the time she arrived at the cabin, she was relieved that the flush on her cheeks appeared to be from running the entire distance there.

When she flung open the door to the cabin, she found Mr. Lim looking down at a sheet of paper. "You're here!" he said, surprised by Iseul's sudden appearance. He wiped away what appeared to be tears and sloppily hid the page beneath the typewriter.

Iseul sensed something was wrong as she walked up to Mr. Lim and the typewriter. The edges of the crumpled page revealed words on the heading. Reading every alphabet was painstaking and slow but it undoubtedly read, "Notice of Death."

"I'm so sorry…" Iseul said. Byung-Guk must have died in battle.

Mr. Lim tried to remain lighthearted. "I've known for weeks now. I shouldn't bother you with such things." He pulled the enigma typewriter closer. "What was it about the typewriter you said?"

"Does Mi-Jung know?"

Mr. Lim nodded. "I told her soon after."

Iseul gently slid the page from under the typewriter and flatten it, though the wrinkles were stubborn.

"Why didn't you leave?" Iseul peered out of the window and saw Mi-Jung with a fishing rod in the stream. She knew why Mi-Jung couldn't. Crouched in the far end of the cabin was her mother, lying with the thickest blanket over her.

"I was going to." Mr. Lim voice was muffled. "I had all my things packed, but the paper kept coming from your workshop and the truck driver kept promising he would be back. Before I knew it, another day had passed. Tomorrow… maybe tomorrow," he said, dolefully.

She understood. Somehow, she too had stayed one day longer and found herself standing there with Mr. Lim. They had made their decision, just as the rest of the villagers did and just as Su-Jung and the northern residents of Yeoju did.

One of the little orphan girls had found Iseul's haegeum. She raised the bow of the instrument and placed it against the instrument string. A screeching noise added to the already rambunctious atmosphere. She could use a bit of practice. The instrument was light enough to carry and it'll be a great companion for the little girl on the road south.

Iseul broke from her thoughts. There wasn't much time for any of them. She tried to summarize her encounter with Jung-Soo as quickly as she could, though she left out the part about North Korean soldiers hiding in her home. Mr. Lim dusted off the typewriter and pressed on a few keys.

Iseul attention fixed on Jung-Soo's letter—on Mr. Ham's last coded message to his son, as Mr. Lim took a stubby pencil, ready to write down the deciphered words.

CHAPTER 37

"Dae-Gun, do you read me?" Jung-Soo said as he checked the dials. It was on the same channel he had been using to communicate with the 18th Infantry. Surely, Dae-Gun and the marines would be on the move by now, and all incoming infantries warned. Perhaps he could find a way to get more troops into Yeoju again and convince the General there is really rice here to be fought for.

The radio finally came alive. "Jung-Soo, is that you?" It was the welcoming voice of none other than the idiot, Dae-Gun.

"Yes, yes, I read you! Are you okay? How about the marines and the retreating forces?"

"We're all fine, well, most of us." He chuckled. "Glad to hear from you too!"

Doo-Hyung yanked the microphone from Jung-Soo. "Report your status, soldier."

"Doo-Hyung?"

"Yes, now report," he said, restless.

"We've managed to convince most of the infantries to avoid taking the route to Yeoju under the order of the General himself. Those too late to push west have been briefed about the situation in Yeoju. The commander of the 18th Infantry has agreed to hold the northern front with our American friends from the 5th Cavalry."

"So?" Jung-Soo poked his head towards the microphone. "What happened at the northern front?"

A pause ensued. Jung-Soo held his breath.

Dae-Gun continued. "When the 18ᵗʰ Infantry arrived, the Chinese were retreating back north. We did it, Jung-Soo, we saved them! Our infantry helped save them!"

Doo-Hyung cast a concerned look towards Jung-Soo. He shut the radio off. "Something's not right."

"What are you doing?" Jung-Soo tried to reach for the switch. "This is great news!"

Doo-Hyung spat. "Don't be stupid, Jung-Soo. Think, Jung-Soo, think! Why would the Chinese retreat when they were winning? When the 18ᵗʰ Infantry had barely begun fighting them?"

Doo-Hyung was right. But couldn't they just accept a bit of good news? Jung-Soo breathed deeply. "What are you trying to say?"

"By now the North Koreans know that the South Koreans are unaware of the rice hidden in Yeoju because all the South Korean troops are avoiding Yeoju."

Jung-Soo felt guilty; he had been the cause of that. If only he hadn't helped divert the troops away, they would have had more time at least, and a fighting chance to defend their rice.

"The Chinese are pulling back so our forces won't be driven into Yeoju. They don't want any more troops here, so they're giving our forces a chance to retreat southwest."

Something akin to suspicion had been surging in Jung-Soo—the notion that Doo-Hyung, despite all that he had said, was not to be trusted. How many lives had they saved by diverting them west, only to be massacred once the North Korean and Chinese got their hands on the rice? If only Doo-Hyung had been honest with him from the beginning.

"Perhaps it wasn't a good idea to meddle like this," Jung-Soo said, tinged with scorn. He knew what Doo-Hyung would say. He lied because Jung-Soo wouldn't have ever believed him, and he would have killed Doo-Hyung before they even made it to Yeoju. Why was Doo-Hyung so desperate to follow him into an ambush? If it were just to decipher the letter, he wouldn't have yielded it to Iseul without some resistance. It was time for answers and not the half-told ones that had kept Jung-Soo satiated for the time being.

"Why did you really follow me all the way here?" Jung-Soo asked. He tried not to sound too accusing.

"Your father ordered me to," Doo-Hyung answered. It was done with a straight face that commanded belief without a shadow of a doubt.

"I thought you said you were your own man."

"I owe him," he said, somewhat confused himself. "Listen, I'm not one to question your father's intentions. He needed me here next to you, so I'm here."

"Liar. What did he do to convince you to march to your death?" Jung-Soo still couldn't wrap his head around why his father would have asked Doo-Hyung to wait so long to give him the codes. If only they had time, they might have been able to get the rice out of Yeoju and into friendly hands.

"He didn't do anything. I did," Doo-Hyung whispered, like a man at a loss for words and full of guilt. "That night the fire killed over fifty villagers, it was my job to keep the communist spies in the South Korean military from raiding the village until after midnight. They were on my heel, following me."

"Who were?" Jung-Soo pressed.

"I don't know. Someone from the military—from the South. Not one of our men. I choked. I was drunk. I don't know which, but I ran without telling our inside man the exact time. I didn't think it would matter so much."

"Chaos is not usually a part of my father's plans. That explains why the Captain was so rushed when he came to evacuate me." Jung-Soo believed it had been Byung-Guk's letter that had been the impetus for the early attack that night, but it seemed the string of events that led to the tragic outcome that night, ran much deeper than he was aware of.

Guilt spread across Doo-Hyung's face.

"So, you're here because you felt responsible for the Captain's death?"

He didn't need to respond. *Truth.* He saw the man with his father's eyes. Loyal, but incompetent. And certainly not bright enough to fully understand or execute his father's plans the way he needed him to. He was a bona fide bodyguard to his father's only remaining bloodline.

Jung-Soo let it go. Doo-Hyung was not the only one to blame for what had happened that night. He took the radio from Doo-Hyung who yielded it without too much resistance.

"Dae-Gun, I'm back," Jung-Soo said.

"Jung-Soo, is something wrong? What's happening there? How much time do you have?"

"Not much," Jung-Soo said, truthfully. He was relieved to

know his friend would survive, at least this battle. He would live to fight another day, perhaps receive a medal for his services. "But listen Dae-Gun, maybe there is a way to let the General know what is happening. Maybe he can send help."

"Commander Lee has been on the line with the General. They know our troops are trapped there."

"I see." Jung-Soo bit his tongue, wanting to yell that the Chinese are after the rice and that he needs to find a way to convince General MacArthur, but he couldn't. For now, he could only hope the General would consider a few hundred of his men worth saving.

"Standby." Jung-Soo got off the radio. Unless he had something concrete, there wasn't much Dae-Gun could do but worry. He turned the radio back to the local channel that buzzed with the monotonous white noise.

Jung-Soo slouched against the counter top, sitting on the stool just as he had so often seen Iseul in that position. All he could think of was Iseul back on the radio with news of his father's letter, decoded.

"We've retreated to the Golden Palace. I repeat, we've retreated to the Golden Palace. Another South Korean infantry has joined us, at least what's left of it." Su-Jung seemed out of breath as the clanking of steel against steel and bullets firing accompanied her report.

"Copy that." It was Iseul.

Jung-Soo sat up straight and leaned in. "Copy that."

"Who the hell is on the line?" Su-Jung responded. "Iseul, are they your North Korean friends?"

"I'll explain later," Iseul answered. "How long have we got, Su-Jung?"

"Guard the door, you good for nothing farmers!" Su-Jung kept the microphone running as she yelled at her soldiers. "You have till sundown," she said. The line went silent.

"Jung-Soo, I'm on my way. I have it," Iseul said.

"Copy that. Standing ground."

Had he sensed a tone of unease in her voice? Perhaps he was overreaching. He knew he would have to wait, twenty minutes at most.

Jung-Soo was thinking out loud, hoping it would help him plan a course of action while they waited. "What if... what if..."

Doo-Hyung and Gil-Dong watched on, rather concerned

Jung-Soo might be losing his mind.

"How is it possible that the North Koreans knew about the rice while the South didn't?"

"I'm sure your father wasn't the one to tell them," Doo-Hyung said with too much certainty.

"But their plan of attack, their movements," Jung-Soo said. "They're too calculated as if they know for certain the rice is here. They're not acting on rumors; they must have some proof. But how?"

"You said it yourself, spies are everywhere. Maybe the rumors spread amongst them until it reached General Shin's ears."

Jung-Soo listened incredulously. "Perhaps the villagers have seen suspicious men roaming the area." Jung-Soo grabbed the microphone again.

"Hello, is anybody listening? Hello?"

The radio sizzled alive. "Hello?" It was another girl.

"Mi-Jung? Is that you?"

"Jung-Soo!" she exclaimed.

"Listen, I need to know if you've seen anyone suspicious in the area since the war began. Any communist spies?"

"So, it's true! You're really back!" Mi-Jung said.

She seemed welcoming and it surprised Jung-Soo.

Mi-Jung continued, "Suspicious people? No, not really. We've been warned that spies are everywhere, but for the most part, we've only had refugees stumble into our village. I don't remember anyone suspicious, other than you, of course."

He could hear the others discussing in the background. They must be in the cabin.

"There were patrolling North Korean officers, but that was months ago when the North Koreans first invaded the South. They left as soon as the South pushed them back north," someone else said.

"Thank you," Jung-Soo said, warmer than he anticipated as he got off the radio.

"Strange, isn't it?" Doo-Hyung said.

Jung-Soo had been thinking the same. "Every other village we've passed through knew of at least a few spies coming down from the mountains to raid the village in the cover of night."

They were surrounded by mountains, which would serve as the perfect cover for spies. Yet, not a single spy had raided the Wasteland for food. Jung-Soo's mind drew its conclusion.

Almost simultaneously, Doo-Hyung and Jung-Soo spoke. "They found the rice."

"What reason do they have to raid the village when they have enough rice to last a lifetime? The radio tower. They must have found a way to contact the North," Jung-Soo said.

Iseul ran into the workshop, pale as a ghost with a single sheet of paper in her hand. "I've got it," she said out of breath.

Jung-Soo sat her down on the stool and barked orders at Gil-Dong. "Get her some water. There's a river outside."

Jung-Soo thought his head might burst. Doo-Hyung looked over his shoulder as Jung-Soo unfolded the page. This was it; they had finally deciphered his father's last words.

He read them out loud:

THE TIGER GUARDS HIS CAVE AS IT GUARDS ITS CUBS

They looked at each other, wondering if the others knew what it might mean. Jung-Soo scoffed. He hated it—all the codes and metaphors his father lived by. His knuckled wrapped white against the fragile fibers of the page. Doo-Hyung's hunch had been correct. The letter wasn't addressed to him. His father's letter had brought them to the most dangerous place in the Korean Peninsula without an apparent way out.

"Great," Jung-Soo said sardonically. "Another pointless metaphor to decipher."

"It's not pointless. Enigma codes are not necessarily foolproof. The British broke the codes years ago during the second world war," Doo-Hyung said, as he recalled a text he had read during his battle studies.

Doo-Hyung felt an unsettling weight drop to the pit of his stomach. Was the message what he thought it meant? He was here, wasn't he, guarding Young-Nam's cub, just as he asked of him? This must be some cruel joke, or just another ominous reminder of his duties to protect Jung-Soo. How was he supposed to do that? He felt something akin to anger directed at his dead friend. There must be more to his plan, Young-Nam always had another plan!

But all Doo-Hyung could think of was the life oozing out of his mentor's body, as blood pooled around him. Young-Nam was dead, and the dead can no longer scheme.

Gil-Dong rushed in with a bowl of water as Iseul drank.

"The tiger," Iseul said, catching her breath. "I think I know where the tiger's cave is."

All focus centered on Iseul.

"I don't know how I could have been so stupid!" she said. "We were discussing it in the cabin and the older women reminded me of an old wives' tale mother used to tell me. The east gate has been closed for centuries. They say there used to be a tiger that inhabited a cave on that road, devouring the flesh of those who traveled on its path. Some say it is the tiger from none other than the Legend of Tangun, bitterly roaming the cave in which he failed to transform into a human. No one dared to kill such a divine creature, so they closed off the gate and the road that led to it."

"A legend?" Jung-Soo said in disbelief. "We're hedging our bets on a folklore? Besides, your mother wasn't exactly..." He bit his tongue.

"What?" Iseul said.

"Well, you've always described your mother as... superstitious. I don't think she's the most reliable source of information," Jung-Soo said.

Iseul didn't like what she heard, but couldn't deny it.

Yet, the more Jung-Soo reflected on it, the more it seemed like a possibility. "The Captain drove us on the road that led to the east gate that night he passed. Maybe, there is a way out of this village down that road after all..."

"So, what are we waiting for?" Iseul jumped up, wobbling. "I told everyone to get packing before I left."

"We can't," Jung-Soo said.

"The tiger is guarding the cave," Doo-Hyung recited.

"What utter nonsense!" Iseul said. "Weren't you the one who said a tiger hasn't been seen for over a century!"

"The North Korean spies found it first."

Iseul was confused. "But how? There's no way. There are no spies in the Wasteland at least not since the Americans have arrived and drove the North Koreans back up."

"Exactly," Jung-Soo said. "The Battle of Inchon. When General MacArthur mounted his counteroffensive on the western shores of the 38th parallel, many of the North Koreans who were fighting near the southeastern tip of South Korea didn't made it back North in time. They've been hiding in the southern mountains ever since."

"You think they're here, in our mountains?" Iseul said, still skeptical.

Jung-Soo nodded. "Every other village we've traveled through has been raided by spies at some point. Why do you think our village has been spared? We believe they've been using the radio towers to communicate directly with North Korea."

Slowly, Iseul fit the pieces together. "What do we do?" she said, defeated. Not only did they have the rice, they were blocking potentially their only feasible route south. "We fight. We go armed and kill those North Koreans! We fight our way out!"

Doo-Hyung shook his head. "That's suicide. They're men and well-fed soldiers at that. What are we but a group of sickly old people and young women without weapons?"

"We can't just sit here and wait to be raped and killed!" Iseul fumed. "Not when they're also taking our rice—our future away from us too!"

The soldiers were taken aback by the indelicate terms Iseul used, but it was the truth they all knew was coming. Jung-Soo leaned against the counter with his hand caressing his throbbing forehead. His father must have known about the spies lying in wait. All doubt of Doo-Hyung dissipated; Jung-Soo believed Doo-Hyung now. He would have gone straight into an ambush if he had gotten the message earlier. His father had always meant for there to be more soldiers to fight alongside them, to secure the rice, fight past the spies in the mountains and flee south. That's why his father sent for the villagers of northern Yeoju and instructed Doo-Hyung to wait for a massive attack so their own troops would be funneled into Yeoju so that they too, could join in the fight. But he had inadvertently thwarted his own chances of escaping when he had diverted the armies away from Yeoju.

"We blow it up," he said, sober and serious as he looked up at the group.

They were sure he had finally gone insane.

Jung-Soo continued with fiery eyes. "We give the coordinates to Dae-Gun and he can convince our commander or even General MacArthur to get a fighter jet to fly over and bomb the cave."

"That way, no one gets the rice." Iseul was on the same page.

"But we might also be sabotaging our only potential route south," Doo-Hyung added.

"We're already sitting ducks here," Iseul said, fearless.

"Or maybe, the General can send more troops to get us out of here," Gil-Dong said.

"Either way, we'll need to be sure if we're going to convince the General. I'll go," Jung-Soo said. He took on Iseul's audacity. "Someone has to check if those spies are really there and if they're really sitting on a treasure trove of rice."

Iseul spoke into the radio. "Mi-Jung."

"Yes, we're ready, on your cue."

"You're going to have to hold tight for a little bit longer."

"What do I tell the others?"

Jung-Soo had taken the radio and switched the dials before Iseul could respond. "Dae-Gun, Dae-Gun!"

"Jung-Soo. What happened? We thought we lost you!" Dae-Gun said, relieved.

Jung-Soo sneered. "Can't get rid of me that easily. Listen, I need to talk to the commander. Have you rendezvous with him yet?"

"Yeah, which one?"

"Any, no actually both, if possible." This was good. He would need more than just the commander of one infantry to back him.

"This is Commander Lee. Dae-Gun to translate for Commander Rogers. Speak, Jung-Soo, and you'd better be convincing because as far as we know, you're a deserter and I'll personally shoot you if we find you."

"Sir," Jung-Soo said. Threats of death were moot considering the situation they were in. "What if I told you I know why the Chinese retreated at certain victory in the northern front," he began.

"Shut up boy," his commander said in Korean. "Be very careful what you say."

"Then I assume you already know," Jung-Soo said, mimicking the surprised look that spread across everyone's faces.

"You mean to say you found it?" Commander Rogers said.

"No, sir. But say I have a way of finding out. Say, we also found a way in and out of the village…"

"I thought no such route existed?"

"It does. Are you willing to take all measures necessary?" Jung-Soo pushed.

"That is not for me to decide. Not for either of us."

"Sir, you are convincing when you need to be."

"How many of our souls left in your village?" Commander Rogers said.

"At least a hundred of our villagers and nearly two whole

infantries that made it alive into the village."

The line was muted with white noise. Jung-Soo knew they were considering their options on the other end. Bombing would be a simple fix that would slow down the Chinese access to rice, but would they be willing to march to Yeoju and risk more lives? The Chinese were hungrier and more desperate with victory so close and with infantries just north of Yeoju, ready to jump in should they need to.

"Get me the coordinates and then we'll talk," Commander Rogers said as the radio fell silent.

"Good..." Jung-Soo was thinking out loud again. "This way, they'll have enough time to convince General MacArthur." He checked to see that his rifle was loaded and began pulling out supplies from his bag until he held a map, compass, a few scraps of paper and extra ammunition.

"What are you doing?" Iseul said, concerned.

"Stay here." He barked an order. He proceeded to shove the items back into the bag and reached for the radio and extra batteries.

Iseul got to it first. Eye-to-eye, they were at a standstill. "You're not going anywhere, not without some backup."

He sniggered. "You're just a girl. What would you know about soldiers at war?"

She couldn't believe her ears. *Pompous asshole.* Why she ever thought kissing him was a good idea, she did not know! "I know the terrain a hell of a lot better than you do."

Doo-Hyung stepped in. "There there, boys and girls. No need to fight about it..."

"Stay out of it!" Jung-Soo said, as Iseul simultaneously responded, "Shut up!"

"Dammit, you can't just leave us here!" Doo-Hyung wasn't about to back down. "How the hell are we supposed to communicate with the others if you go ahead and die all alone?" He shouted at Jung-Soo, though his head turned toward Iseul too, "And that goes for you too, young lady."

Gil-Dong chuckled in the background. He had been enjoying the view the entire trip. Such were the perks of a boy who had lost both parents, and whose home straddled between two feuding brother nations. He didn't care about the outcome, nor did he care to go back to a home that had been left in ruin.

"It's settled then," Gil-Dong said. "We all go."

CHAPTER 38

"The first thing is to figure out the coordinates," Jung-Soo said, his mind racing as they approached the run down east gate. "Even if we convince General MacArthur, it'll take time for the planes to dispatch and the troops to get here."

The horizon illuminated with a tinge of orange; there wasn't much time left. Not only had they not found rice store yet, they hadn't a clue where they would find a route south from there.

They walked and talked, knees buckling against the frozen soil. Iseul noticed a tear in her rubber shoes that seeped cold from her toes and spread to her heels.

"Yes, we get the point," Doo-Hyung said, wearily. His whole arm trembled as he reached for the bottle and took a drink. "The next right?"

"Oh…" Iseul said as she realized Doo-Hyung was asking her. "Not for a while longer."

They had already been on the main road from the east gate for over thirty minutes. The road was overgrown with thickets and trees that blended into the mountainous rocks as it narrowed and naturally curved right.

"Have you ever been here before?" Jung-Soo asked.

"To the tiger's cave, or down this road?" Iseul said.

Jung-Soo shrugged. "Either."

"When I was little."

"You're still little." Jung-Soo ruffled her hair like he used to.

She managed a grin. "When I was little, I ran down a hill and sprained my ankle. Yeong-Hoon oppa put me on his back and began walking this road, even with his bad leg. He told me the tiger is our village guardian and it would heal me."

Jung-Soo chuckled. "Did you believe him?"

"He scared the living daylights out of me! He made me promise not to run in the mountains again before we turned back."

"Serves you right, scaring him like that. Imagine having two cripples under one roof."

Iseul frowned. "Don't say that! He's not a cripple. He's just..."

"Slow," Doo-Hyung butt in.

"Yeah, I guess so," Iseul said.

A hand grabbed onto her arm. "I mean, slow down," Doo-Hyung whispered.

They came upon an enormous dark patch on the side of the mountain.

"We're here..." Iseul said, gazing into the gaping hole of the cave.

The group shuffled into the thicket and began unpacking and setting up their guns.

"I wish we had binoculars," Jung-Soo groaned.

Gil-Dong pulled one out of his pocket as Doo-Hyung peered through them into the dark hole. Light tapered inside until the center of cave plunged into pitch darkness.

"Any movements?" he asked.

Doo-Hyung shook his head. "No. It's getting cold so if anyone is around, they'll have to light a fire soon."

"We don't have that kind of time," Jung-Soo pressed. He took his turn with the binoculars. "They're probably in the mountains." It made sense. Smoke emanating from a dark cave would be too conspicuous.

"So, what now? We just wait here and hope they make a fire?" Jung-Soo said.

"They can't be far." Doo-Hyung spread the military-grade map and compass, determining their exact coordinates. "Dammit, this place isn't on the map. At least not accurately."

Iseul took a glance. "Here, let me help." She traced the hills surrounding them—the one she lived on and the other two mountains that the cabin was straddled between. "The radio towers are here, the east gate here, so we should be just around here." Her finger landed on a single spot on the map.

Doo-Hyung nodded and glanced between the compass and the map.

"Someone needs to go into the cave and check the surrounding area to see if the road south really does exist." Jung-Soo was ready to leap into the open road again to race within.

"We can't just do that!" Iseul said. "If the spies are really guarding the area, we'll just be shot before we can figure out anything."

He was rash, beads of sweat rolling down his forehead despite the frigid weather, full of nervous energy. Iseul brushed her hand against his, but he jerked away. He couldn't bear to look at her. He hadn't come all this way just to lose courage when it counted. Not like this. Not when the only option was to await death.

Jung-Soo felt so helpless. If he gave the coordinates to the rice store, the flyby strike might be possible. But the General still wouldn't be able to send troops to save them unless they knew exactly where the road into village began on the other side of those mountains.

"They're using our radio towers," Gil-Dong said. "So, we try to listen in on their conversation. You can do that right?" He spoke to Jung-Soo.

It took a moment for Jung-Soo to take in what Gil-Dong said. "Yeah, I think we can."

The radio blared on as Jung-Soo turned down the volume. It wouldn't take too long to find, that is if the channel was being occupied. With the North Koreans and Chinese troops so close, there must be some ongoing communication. He hoped. It went both ways. If the spies were really here, they would be listening too. All they had was time, so it was safe to assume they would have heard every conversation they've had till now. He turned the knobs of the radio through each channel, only to be met with a series of white noise and battle cries.

"Got it!" Doo-Hyung said, thrilled with his work. "I never thought a lesson in mapping coordinates would come in so handy."

Numbers were written in disarray across a tattered page. Jung-Soo paused to think. So far, the North Koreans seemed to be avoiding the radio. Perhaps there was a way to get them back on. He grabbed the coordinates from Doo-Hyung and brought the radio close.

"So, we're going to announce the coordinates, just like that?"

Doo-Hyung said, hesitantly. "What if the incoming armies don't quite know the exact location of the rice store yet? We'd just be leading them straight here."

"He's right, we should think about it first," Iseul added.

"I have a plan," Jung-Soo said. "Iseul do you have that letter I gave you?"

"Huh?" Iseul said, confused. There was only one letter he had sent her. She took out the neatly folded page from inside her hanbok sleeve and handed it to Jung-Soo. He took the page as well as Doo-Hyung's coordinates as he began scribbling furiously beneath the coordinates.

"What are you doing?" Doo-Hyung said, apprehensively.

"Coding the coordinates."

"How?"

Jung-Soo brought the microphone close. "Dae-Gun."

"I'm here. Do you have it?"

"Yeah. How's the convincing coming along?"

"Negative. We've been trying to get the General to sign off on a rescue mission, but it's impossible at this point to march back north. He's not willing to put more lives on the line. Listen, we might be able to convince him if there is another way we could get in."

"We're working on that," Jung-Soo said. The path was here somewhere; it felt so near. "What about that fly by strike?"

"The General needs the exact coordinates and proof of...you know, before he can order the planes to take off. Do you have a visual?"

"Yes. We're here and we have a visual," Jung-Soo lied.

"Alright. Standing by for the coordinates."

"Dae-Gun, do you still have the drawing I gave you?"

"What drawing?" Dae-Gun said, confused, just as Iseul had been. "The guitar drawing? What are you getting at?"

"Take it out in front of you."

Dae-Gun did as he was told, as Commander Lee's eyes widened. "That sketch..." the commander said in the background.

"It's out," Dae-Gun spoke into the receiver.

"Reorder the numbers on there from smallest to largest."

"Alright, got it."

"Subtract the number on your page from the one that I'm about to give you."

"Roger that. Standing by."

"1-0-2-7-0-0-3-1-7-8-5-3. I repeat 102700317853. Did you get it?"

"Got it," Dae-Gun said, as he got off the line.

Doo-Hyung flashed a look of utter bewilderment. "I'm telling you, kid, you're just like your father."

Jung-Soo had already gone back to turning the dials of the radio until voices with northern accents emerged. He smirked. "Nothing like giving away coordinates to provoke a response," Jung-Soo said.

Whoever was on the other end was scrambling to make sense of the numbers.

"Are those the right coordinates?" A senior officer barked.

"We don't know sir," someone said, baffled.

"Dammit. Don't confirm. Not over the radio."

Jung-Soo's hunch had been right—the North Koreans didn't know the exact location. The North Korean spies were lower ranked foot soldiers without the necessary military training to do what Doo-Hyung had done.

Iseul and Gil-Dong looked to Jung-Soo for an explanation. "What's going on?" Iseul said.

"That idiot boy Dae-Gun was jealous of the guitar drawing I had sent you so I drew one for him before I left, complete with all the measurements. You and Dae-Gun are the only two people who know those numbers so I coded the coordinates using them. It isn't too different from how the enigma machine works, actually."

Both Iseul and Gil-Dong didn't seem to completely understand, but it didn't stop a smile from creeping up their faces.

Jung-Soo continued. "From the look of things, it seems the plan is to wait until the Chinese are past the east gate before someone shows them into the cave."

"The old-fashioned way," Doo-Hyung added.

Iseul thought she saw movements in the mountains. "There." She pointed.

"They're moving. They think there will be fly-by strike soon," Jung-Soo confirmed.

"Maybe they're running away," she hoped.

"They won't," Doo-Hyung said. "Not if they want to live. Winter is coming and they won't last long in the mountains, not without the rice. And if they run and are caught, they'll be executed."

Iseul had been thinking about ways to get past the spies in the mountains. If they knew how many, perhaps they could mount an attack. She knew the women were strong. They would fight to the death, especially the ones with children. If only they could get past those spies, they might find a way to get Jung-Soo's friends to come and save them. They seemed willing enough.

She knew what the others would say. They were military experts; they would be shot before they ever reached the cave entrance and had the time to find a way out, let alone lead their allies in.

Amidst the chatter of northern accents on the radio, an older, calmer voice came through.

"Enough," he commanded.

Doo-Hyung's jerked his head towards the speaker. "It's him," he said, ominously.

The older man continued. "Stand your ground, or I will personally shoot you and your entire families for desertion. Commander, I order you to push forward. I don't care how tired or hungry you are. Tell the Chinese rice is awaiting our victory."

Gil-Dong aired a look of concern.

"Who was that?" Jung-Soo said anxiously, darting his gaze between the two North Koreans. How could Doo-Hyung possibly recognize the man just by his voice? Jung-Soo's eyes widened. It must be...

"General Shin," Doo-Hyung announced.

"Who?" Iseul said.

"His father," Jung-Soo answered for him. "He's close enough for the radio to pick up."

"Of course," Doo-Hyung said, dazed. "He wouldn't trust anyone else to get the job done."

The suspicion Jung-Soo had been nursing surfaced, full-fledged and roaring. He had to stay calm, collected, just as the man on the other line. Could Doo-Hyung have known? The blood-drained look on his face said otherwise, but sight often had a way of deceiving reality.

"Did you know about this?" This time it was Gil-Dong who spoke. "How could you? We trusted you!" His usual serene demeanor dissipated.

"I didn't know," Doo-Hyung said weakly. Gil-Dong shook him, though his smaller frame barely made a dent. "I told you I didn't know!" Doo-Hyung's slight shove jolted Gil-Dong back. "He must have found out somehow."

"He found out from you!" Gil-Dong's accusations grew. "You betrayed your friend and tricked all of us to come here to find the rice for you, just so you can go back to your father and prove your worth. Can't you see? Your father never trusted you to get the job done, you incompetent bastard!"

"Calm down!" Jung-Soo placed Gil-Dong in a headlock with his arms braced behind his back. He wasn't quite sure where the rage from this quiet boy was coming from. He was from the North, was he not?

"Your father," Doo-Hyung said to Jung-Soo. "He must have known about this. Did my father kill him? Was it because of General Shin that Young-Nam decided to bleed out on the 38th parallel?" Doo-Hyung grew paler, breathing heavily with his hands pressed against his temples. "Your father must have a plan for us. He must have known…" He sauntered towards Jung-Soo and took the deciphered letter from his front pocket. His hands trembled as he inadvertently tore the sheet in half. "No!" he screamed, putting the page back together as delicate as his trembling hands could manage. "The tiger guards his cave, as it guards its cubs." He repeated the words over and over again, is if those same words would take on another meaning they hadn't yet determined.

The man looked pitiful. Iseul went on her knees and tightly grasped his arm. He eased.

"I believe you," she said.

A mixture of emotions spread across his face that was not unlike a child asking *how* and *why* she would believe him. She did not know. Perhaps she saw the end and she could not muster the energy for hatred.

"What can we do now?" Iseul spoke towards the three men who mulled in fear.

Hatred. Hopelessness. Iseul felt anger rising, a sense of injustice at the situation she found herself in. "Wake up! Can't you see, there are people counting on us. Mi-Jung and the women and children in the cabin. What about Su-Jung risking her life in the front lines and all the other soldiers stranded in this god-forsaken Wasteland? What about them?"

Like a chant, Doo-Hyung mouthed the deciphered words of his dead friend.

"Fine, I'll go." Iseul headed towards the clearing that led to the cave.

"No!" Jung-Soo leaped to pull her back.

Iseul sighed. "Someone has to go and check if the road is viable, and confirm if the spies are really out there guarding the rice, and guarding the road south."

"You go," Gil-Dong said to Doo-Hyung in disgust. "You're his son. They won't shoot and even if they do…" *he deserved it,* he thought.

"A tiger guards its cubs," Doo-Hyung kept saying. "Guard its cubs…"

In that instance, the words began making sense, first to Doo-Hyung and then Iseul as she spun her head towards Jung-Soo who stared back with the same epiphany.

Surely the General, even if he wouldn't guard his cub, wouldn't shoot him!

They moved in one swift motion, Jung-Soo turning the dials as Doo-Hyung took his rifle abreast.

"Convince your father," Jung-Soo began.

Doo-Hyung nodded. "I must tell him I'm here to secure the rice stores myself. I'll get in, and figure out which route they took to get into the mountains."

"We might not be able to stop the General from getting to the rice store altogether, but maybe you can stall him."

"Just until the bombs drop," Doo-Hyung added. He knew what that meant. He would have to stay there too until the bombs took them all out.

Iseul had been thinking, indulging the thoughts she had been mulling over for the past hour. Perhaps there was another way—a way to get everyone out safely before the flying machine came.

"Take me hostage," she said.

CHAPTER 39

"No!" Jung-Soo put his foot down.

"You're crazier than I thought," Gil-Dong said. He had grown to like this girl called Iseul, brazen and just insane enough to give this last ditch effort a try.

"It might work." Doo-Hyung shrugged. "In any case, we have to move fast."

Jung-Soo pulled her aside. "Iseul, you can't do this—put your life on the line for such a far-fetched idea. Please…" Jung-Soo was begging.

"You have a better plan?" she goaded. "I didn't think so."

He knew what the alternative was. They would have a little bit more time together, but the Chinese army under General's Shin command was coming; nothing would change that.

"It's not your decision to make," Iseul said sternly, trying to avoid his eyes. She had told herself she would leave no room for discussion. She knew Jung-Soo; he would be bull-headed to his dying breath. But the real reason she avoided his gaze was that she couldn't quell the guilt that kept welling up. She knew he had come for her and she couldn't, no wouldn't accept that today would be their last day together.

Iseul loosened her hair and shook it out. She looked beautiful, even in her tattered hanbok dress. Jung-Soo only just noticed it wasn't the same one she had been wearing for years. This one actually fit her. When had she grown up? She took soil from a patch of muddy soil still somewhat unfrozen and rubbed it on her face.

"How do I look?"

"Perfect for the part." Doo-Hyung stepped in.

"Make it believable," she ordered Doo-Hyung.

Jung-Soo glowered at him. "Don't you dare let her die!" His trust had worn thin, but what choice did he have? He was smitten with a stubborn mule.

Doo-Hyung pulled on the radio microphone and took a deep breath. "Father, it's me, Shin Doo-Hyung." The three tensed as they waited.

"Son, where's your position?" General Shin responded. He wasn't even surprised, nor did he scold him for venturing south. He hated that more—the indifference.

"General, permission to approach the rice stores," Doo-Hyung said, masking the venom within.

"Granted. Private Yoon, come in," General Shin said.

"Yes, sir." The same North Korean accent came on. "Waiting, sir."

"Doo-Hyung, you are to do as Private Yoon says. Stand your ground, men," the General said as he disappeared.

Doo-Hyung sighed. He was to follow the command of a mere private. His father must really be angry at him.

"That was easy enough," Iseul commented, as she took the radio. "Mi-Jung."

"Yeah."

Iseul couldn't bear to leave without some sort of a goodbye and hear an update on how the battle was commencing—how Yeong-Hoon was doing if he were even still alive. "What about the others?" she said.

"The old man, Mr. Lim, and the scholar left the cabin to help fight in the village. They said something about stretching their legs and getting in on the action."

Iseul knew they must be losing ground quickly. Yeong-Hoon had gone to the front lines hours ago without a single weapon in his possession. Even the scholar, who spooked at the common house mouse, had gone to fight. She felt the knife under her dress; she shouldn't have taken it from Yeong-Hoon... She let go of the guilt with the rising awareness that the fates of the women and children in the cabin would be far worse if she did not succeed.

Iseul lifted her dress to hide the radio beneath as the three men momentarily looked away.

"Ready?" Doo-Hyung said.

Iseul's hands began to shake again. She angled her body just enough towards Jung-Soo that he knew she wanted to say something to him. The others turned away.

Iseul sifted through the mountain of questions and conversations she thought she would have with Jung-Soo once he got back to Yeoju. But why wasn't a single one coming to mind? She hoped he would know how much he meant to her, how much she appreciated all the memories, but it felt too…final.

"Don't you dare say goodbye," Jung-Soo said, looking away from her.

She laughed. "Don't presume," she said wryly. "I have just one question for you. What's all this I hear about your prolific writing?" She held her hand out as if demanding something from him. "How about you hand over all those letters you wrote to me?"

Jung-Soo was shocked, turning bright red. "They weren't for you," he said, stammering. It was not the right answer, he knew. "I mean, they're just scribbles really…"

Iseul loved watching him sweat, the way he used to watch her. Oh, how the tables have turned! It gave her a smug smile that would keep her hopes up for a while longer. "Well, you'd better have a fat stack of letters by the time we see each other again."

Jung-Soo reluctantly nodded. "And you'll hand over the guitar when I give you the letters?"

Iseul nodded. They grinned at each other, as Doo-Hyung finally pulled Iseul away.

***

Dae-Gun couldn't keep his eyes away from the map as he trudged along the dusty road south. They were so close, yet so far. He looked left where the mountain ridge rose tall and at a steep incline.

"Let it go." It was Sergeant Richard Martin who was walking next to him as if to fill the empty spot Jung-Soo had left behind. He knew the sergeant meant well.

"Yeah," Dae-Gun said defeated, though he held on to an inkling of hope. "You'd think there would be a way through those mountains. He pointed. "Apparently not."

It wouldn't be long till the mountain ridges separating their southwestern road with the one that led to Yeoju would be completely behind them. He saw the troops ahead of him, battered but strong and couldn't help but think of the possibilities. Of course, they couldn't fathom the number of spies at the cave, but surely, the joint effort of the 5th Cavalry and the 18th Infantry would put up a good fight. He sighed. Who was he kidding? Their numbers dwindled to less than half of what it used to be at the beginning of this war, spilling their fresh youthful blood on the greedy Korean soil.

He made his way to the radio operator who seemed to be weary. He thought he glimpsed a slight eye roll.

"You know you're putting us at risk too. What if another Chinese army is on our tail and they're listening in on your conversation?"

Dae-Gun didn't register a word he said. Honestly, he wanted to shove the radio down his throat. "At least keep the radio running, just in case." Dae-Gun knew the radio operator would soon complain about the battery, but if he did, he would seriously consider hurting him; he could imagine the act with appalling ease.

The radio came on. "Dae-Gun." It was Jung-Soo again. He sounded wired.

He yanked the radio away from the operator. "Yeah, I'm here."

"I thought a proper goodbye might be in order, all things considered…"

Dae-Gun was ready to hit someone over the head. "Don't you go down without a fight, you hear?"

He chuckled weakly. "Thanks for the reminder."

A solemn silence overtook them. Dae-Gun's mind began to drift past those mountains and he was standing right next to Jung-Soo, facing the North Koreans together. He wondered if they were listening. Probably.

"Dae-Gun."

"Yeah."

"I wish you would play me that one song on the guitar. You know the one that used to play on the radio," Jung-Soo said. He sounded oddly punctuated when he spoke.

"Huh?" Dae-Gun's brows furrowed; it had been forever since a song had played on the radio. And when he did pick up his guitar, he had mostly been playing his own songs. He had played a song or two he had picked up from his American grandfather at the orphanage, but he never a song from the radio.

Still, Dae-Gun tried to play along. "That song on the radio was sure nice."

"Don't you miss it? How it used to play on that one channel?"

That one channel. It hit him. It was a message for him. He recalled the channel that played American music they both used to listen to before the war. His heart raced; he wanted to sit down to listen carefully—to confirm what he had heard.

"Dae-Gun, it's going to get ugly here. I don't want you to be listening to this channel anymore," Jung-Soo said. It felt awfully like a goodbye again. Perhaps it was too. He knew what Jung-Soo wanted him to do: turn the channel and start listening to the other one. He had no idea why but that much was clear.

"Alright, I understand."

He hoped to hear more, but the line went silent. Jung-Soo wouldn't come on again, not unless he thought Dae-Gun didn't get the message and that would be easy to check; there was no way in hell Dae-Gun would abandon Jung-Soo, even if it meant listening to him die over the radio.

When he looked over, the radio operator seemed pleased, as if the constant monitoring would stop now.

"Did you hear that?" Dae-Gun said, elated. "You heard him, right?" He could hug that man, but his hands instead when to the dials as it turned to the old American channel. It only blared the familiar white noise of a radio signal gone dead.

Dae-Gun could see the pity in the operator's face as he shook his head and walked away. He knew he looked crazy, but he didn't care.

***

"Keep your eyes open," Doo-Hyung said, as he pointed his rifle at Iseul and tugged hard on her shoulder, almost dragging her along.

The sun had dropped from its pinnacle, shining at an angle that lit the gaping black entrance of the cave.

"Do you see anything?" Iseul whispered back.

"It's hard to tell, you?"

Iseul grunted. "No."

Brushes lined the road to the cave to the right and left, without a single indication of a path that led up the hill where they had seen movements earlier. The entire mountain looked untouched and it seemed improbable that there would be a road large enough for trucks to move south.

"We'll have to ask our spy friends."

"Look!" Iseul said. Doo-Hyung followed her gaze towards the cave as light brown sacks of what must be rice rested as shadows within the cavity.

Leaves rustled and two men came into focus.

"Sir," a North Korean soldier said, as he looked apprehensively at Doo-Hyung and the disheveled young girl who had come along.

"Shin Doo-Hyung, Sergeant Major, and son of the General. Get that thing out of my face," he spoke with scorn as he flicked the barrel of the gun away.

"Apologies." He bowed with his back straight at ninety-degrees. "Shall I shoot the girl, sir?"

Doo-Hyung showcased the most sinister grin. "Wouldn't want to treat my guide with such disrespect, at least not until we've shown her a good time." He pulled her close, grabbing on to her hind before shoving her till she tumbled to the ground.

Iseul groaned and whimpered. It was a side of Doo-Hyung that was alarming, as the pain sunk deep into her skeletal frame.

"Sir," the North Korean soldier said, fear lingering behind his composed façade.

"Show me to the camp, and brief me on the current situation," he commanded.

The camp was well hidden behind a boulder in a clearing in the middle of dense trees that surrounded them. Doo-Hyung nodded in approval. The men, nearing a hundred, were thin though clearly not starved as they rose from their logs and makeshift tents to greet their new leader.

"Who's in charge here?" Doo-Hyung said. The man in front stepped forward and saluted. He must be Private Yoon. He had the flicker of intelligence that the others did not have. He glanced at his worn uniform that showed a simple badge—a foot soldier and another body count at best. But rank did not matter so much outside the bounds of the military; brute strength and wit did.

"I apologize for not greeting you myself." Private Yoon spoke with the finesse of a man who was well-versed in politics.

He knew he had been placed in charge of the General's son,

yet, the private kept his tail between his legs, erring on the side of caution.

"And how is it that you've managed to find the rice stores that the villagers themselves weren't able to?" Even as he asked, his eyes wandered into the thick forestry. He knew he was asking the wrong question, but such formalities and patience were necessary.

The soldier betrayed a momentary hesitation. "We heard rumors of rice in Yeoju." Doo-Hyung waited for further explanations. "Truth be told, I was an intelligence officer before I was sent to the front lines, sir."

An intelligence officer in the front lines? Unusual. Was he one that worked with Young-Nam?

"Front lines? What did you do to get yourself in that position?" Doo-Hyung said.

Private Yoon looked away, hesitating. "I was serving in the Pyongyang when I first heard the rumors. I saw a file on our colonel's desk. I figured it must be true if our best intelligence officer was on it."

So, it was true. It must be Young-Nam who sent the boy away when he found out. But an official file on the secret rice store on Young-Nam's desk? General Shin must have known about the rice for a while and had Young-Nam in charge of the operation to extract it. Doo-Hyung felt sick; had his friend finally yielded his knowledge to the Communists? He thought he knew his friend better. Young-Nam didn't seem the type to just give the rice away as military supply. And why hadn't he confided in him? It seemed not even his father, or his best friend trusted him.

The soldier continued. "I found a few northern comrades on the road, and the word got out. They came here looking for rice, and a way back home, sir."

"Smart man." He laughed jovially as he gave a reassuring pat on the soldier's back. "Never mind how you found the rice. You've done your country a great service! Tell me, have you discussed plans to get the rice out with the General?"

"Not yet, sir. Waiting to have that conversation face-to-face."

"Not over the radio. Again wise. We have plenty of men to carry the rice back out the way we came in," Doo-Hyung said, as he waited for any other options.

"Yes, sir," he said, falling silent.

"But just in case," he nudged. "Is there an alternate route out of this god-forsaken village. Perhaps there might be a faster, easier path."

Private Yoon hesitated. "There is, sir. The path we took to get here. I was surprised to find a road at all and one without a single person walking it. Due southeast." He pointed. "But if I may add..." he paused.

"Go ahead, son!" Doo-Hyung encouraged.

"I suspect the South Korean armies might be at the end of that road, still retreating south."

Doo-Hyung drifted his gaze towards where the private pointed. It seemed no different from the rest of their surroundings. It was then that something red caught his eye. It was Iseul in her red hanbok, tied to the tree with North Korean soldiers gawking at her like a piece of meat.

He paced and then slowed, heading towards the tent nearest to Iseul. He snapped his fingers at Private Yoon. "Clear this tent and bring the girl here, untouched. And get me a radio."

"Sir," he said, as he promptly ran towards the men who were ready to pounce, shouting and shooing them away. They might have had food to fill their stomachs, but that also meant hunger wasn't there to douse the desires of young men. They flinched, just wise enough not to touch the leader's woman, even if she were just his plaything. The soldiers scattered, wondering if they too would get their chance once he was done.

From a distance, Iseul saw the soldier who had been talking to Doo-Hyung storm towards her. He grabbed her by the arm. She couldn't understand why they always preferred her right arm; the bruising had set in and became tender even with the slightest graze. Even still, she was relieved none of the soldiers had lifted up her dress far enough to reveal the objects underneath.

The tent flap opened and closed behind her. She felt spite for Doo-Hyung who stood composed, even relishing in the aggression that seemed so natural for him. He towered over the boys, older and more battle-worn. For a moment, she wondered what he would do to her now that they were alone, without Jung-Soo there. He turned around and sat on the ground covered in straw, still silent and ignoring her.

"So..." she said cautiously.

Doo-Hyung shook his head and held his finger to his lips. "Not yet," he mouthed.

The soldier came back in with a larger radio, bowed and then left them alone.

He rose and neared her. "Iseul," he said, leaning in closer than she felt comfortable. "It's our lucky day. There seems to be a road south!"

She beamed. "Which way is it?" She was ready to bolt out of the tent.

"Right behind the tent."

"Good, what's the plan?"

"I'll pretend to take a nap. The men are mostly grouped together in the middle of camp, but who knows who else might be lurking around that side of camp. You have to be careful."

Iseul was restless. She fumbled with her carving knife that bulged out from her dress and clutched it, almost praying to it—to Yeong-Hoon who would do anything to keep her safe.

Precious time ticked by until finally, Doo-Hyung gave the nod. She slid the knife down the side of the tent, cutting through the fabric as if it were a piece of paper. She poked her head out, looked left and right before she extended the incision large enough for her whole body to fit through. She sheathed the knife and pulled out her gun.

"Wait," Doo-Hyung said. He grasped her right arm, though this time gently, handing her two large mounds of cooked barley rice. She gladly took it and repaid him with a gentle smile. That is how she would remember him—the kind-hearted man who did the right thing when no one was watching.

She ran as fast as her skinny legs would take her, with her heels off the ground as the cold seeped through her torn rubber shoes. The autumn leaves still crunched beneath her as she tried not to bump into the trees that stacked side-by-side. The trees provided a good cover, though she worried that her red hanbok would catch someone's eye in the middle of camp.

It did. Bullets flew in her direction, shouts coinciding. She didn't look back until both faded and the trees began to thin, becoming bushes, and then a clearing of soil and wild weeds that poked from the ground.

She peered ahead and there stretched a road that curved around the valleys of the mountainous region ahead.

***

Dae-Gun's nerves were as thin as the layer of ice that formed above a roaring river. He stared at the radio, hoping something other than white noise would appear. Just as he was fed up, he would briefly turn the channel back to the one Jung-Soo was on, before dialing it back to the remote channel that once used to sound American music.

He wondered if he should say something. Maybe someone on the other end was waiting, just like he was.

"Hello? Is anybody there?" Dae-Gun said. Martin gave him a strange look as the others sniggered. He checked the battery. The dials were still responsive and the volume loud enough.

As he was checking it, he heard a voice. "Park Dae-Gun." He jerked his head up, certain that his commander had spoken to him. *Odd,* he thought. Martin, with a look of sheer shock, came running towards him.

"What's wrong?" Dae-Gun panicked and ran in the other direction. He knew if bombs were falling, he didn't have time to see from which direction. He ran and ran, as fast as his chunky legs would take him, until he felt a weight from behind as he tumbled over. The bomb had fallen on him, or a piece of debris. Surely, he would die now!

"Get up, you fool!" a voice said in English. His stomach was sore. He looked down to find that he had fallen onto the radio.

"Oh no, oh no..." he kept repeating. He fumbled with the dials. It was still working, thanks to the extra layer of stubborn fat on his stomach even war could not completely eliminate. He came to his senses, realizing the commander had not called him nor were there bombs falling.

"Well, turn that thing up," Richard Martin said.

"Huh?" Dae-Gun looked down at the radio with the faintest realization that the voice that had called his name had come from it.

"Park Dae-Gun, I'm here. I'm here. Can you hear me?"

Martin looked at Dae-Gun, then back at the radio.

"Dae-Gun, is that you?" It was that girl who had been speaking to Jung-Soo over the radio.

"Yeah. Are you with Jung-Soo?" Dae-Gun finally said.

"No." She seemed out of breath, though it was quiet around her.

"What happened? Is everything alright?"

"I'm out," she said, catching her breath. "I'm on the road south. I found a way to escape. Dae-Gun, where are you? I need to speak with you—in person."

Iseul was worried someone might be listening in on their conversation. She tried her best to keep the conversation short, but between the chatter of a weird language surrounding the boy called Dae-Gun and the confusion around figuring out her location, it was a drawn out talk.

"What do you see around you?" Dae-Gun said. The American next to him seemed to disapprove of the question.

"Trees and mountains," she said. "That's a terrible question. How about the coordinates of the rice stores? I'm just south of that place," Iseul said.

"That's a little vague. Is it due south? Southwest?"

"Don't know." She wished she had brought a compass with her. Maybe Jung-Soo could have taught her how to use that.

Voices were in deliberation. "Which direction is the sun facing?"

"Behind me, to the left."

"Alright, that's good." The voices seemed optimistic.

"How long have you been walking?"

"I don't know. Maybe around thirty minutes? Maybe more. But I'm fast."

"Alright, hold on. And keep walking."

Dae-Gun watched as Martin and a group of Korean and American soldiers huddled together.

Martin spread his map on the ground. "I suspect that she's around here." He pointed to area in a valley surrounded by mountains and thick forestry.

"The sun sets southeast in the winter," another soldier added. "I suspect we're walking parallel to the road she's on, just west of it. As you can see, our road veers east in about two kilometers."

Dae-Gun felt giddy. "The roads might converge," he said what the other saw on the map, "in about fifteen minutes." He got back on the radio.

"Are you there? Hello?" Dae-Gun was impatient.

"Iseul's the name," she said. "I'm still walking."

"Good. Keep walking for about ten more minutes. Stop when you see a larger road converging. It's best to keep hidden, just in case someone else is on that road."

"Alright," she said.

"Did you get that?"

"Don't worry, I got it. Ten minutes and stop at the main road."

"Good."

"Good," Iseul said.

She got off the radio feeling giddy. Maybe, just maybe, there might be hope for the Wasteland. She paced faster, counting the seconds, wondering if she was counting too fast, worried that her ten minutes would not be accurate. Even as she counted each step, she wondered if the voices in her head would stop whining for her to come back.

Don't worry. I'll be back. I'll be back...

The soldiers of the 5th Cavalry Regiment and the 18th Infantry had become brothers, even reverting to their child-like states as they spoke past their language barrier with their hands and bodies, sharing cigarettes and pieces of chocolate amongst themselves. Mostly, they had all been trying to figure out why both commanders looked so serious and what had really been said on the radio. Ahead of the troops, their only translator fervently spoke between the two commanders.

"Sir, we have to be ready for the possibility that the girl has been sent to call for help," Dae-Gun said in one language after another. They nodded.

"We don't know how many Chinese forces we're dealing with here," Commander Lee said.

"I agree, we can't just assume the rest of the Chinese from the east and western fronts retreated just because the ones we fought did."

"We've been through this already. We understand that if there is a rice store, they wouldn't send a massive army to attract attention, but that secret is out of the box now."

Dae-Gun was reluctant to translate. "So, we check with the other troops ahead of us—figure out the approximate number of forces we are dealing with."

The commanders nodded. It was perhaps pity or a sense of indebtedness that drove them to oblige the boy who had come to their rescue just a day before. The boy had, after all, saved thousands of their own men. The commanders called on their radio operators who checked with their respective Korean and U.N. forces in the vicinity.

"How long till they get planes in the air?" Commander Rogers asked.

"Sir, they're still awaiting clearance to leave the Japanese base," the operator said.

"We might have a window here," the commander spoke to Dae-Gun and Commander Lee.

Dae-Gun translated, then added his own pleas. "Sir, please. We might not be able to push the Chinese back, but what about our soldiers stuck there? What about the civilians? We can buy them enough time to rescue them before the bombs drop."

"Do we know how many North Korean spies are guarding the rice stores?" Commander Lee asked.

"No, sir," he said reluctantly. "But once we meet Iseul, she might have more information for us."

They nodded. "Then we wait."

"Sir, but…"

Dae-Gun's own commander gave him a stern look. "Listen, if we do this, we're going directly against General MacArthur's order to retreat. You must understand the implications."

"I do, sir," Dae-Gun said, still adamant. Commander Rogers stood curiously watching the two.

"Don't be too hard on the boy," Commander Rogers said. "After all, we owe him our lives." Dae-Gun translated word-for-word, though his own commander seemed suspicious of what Commander Rogers had said.

"Thank you, sir," he addressed Commander Rogers. "Sir, if I may add," he said in both languages so as not to further anger his own commander. "Don't forget what Yeoju did for us those first few weeks of the war." He looked towards Commander Rogers. "With all due respect, even the Americans were starving before U.N. supplies came through."

Dae-Gun knew it would be risky, but he knew which spot to hit, and it was their sense of honor and responsibility. Wasn't that the reason the 5th Cavalry stood their ground and fought on the northern front and why the 18th Infantry risked their own safety to stand with them? They were all indebted, in one way or another.

Commander Rogers smirked. "I never did like that stuff. Rice. Too sticky if you ask me."

Commander Lee seemed somewhat irked, though Dae-Gun knew it might be a good sign.

"But I was there," Commander Rogers continued, "in the

battle of Osan and the weeks after. He's right. We have the civilians of Yeoju to thank in some part for our survival."

Dae-Gun beamed and was not shy to show them. *Jung-Soo*. He thought of his friend, and the two other unexpected ones he had made along the way. They would remain nameless, like those who had farmed the rice and those they had left behind on the battlefield, their bodies soon to be covered in a blanket of white snow.

Just then, Dae-Gun thought he saw something red flash behind the trees to his left.

CHAPTER 40

Jung-Soo hated sitting idly by. It reminded him of all those years he had spent waiting for something to happen—for his brothers to die, for his father's plans to go awry, for someone else he loved to die.

He had been feeling his mother's presence of late, though it wasn't always the warmth he remembered; he could feel the blood oozing out of her where the Japanese sword had pierced.

Trust did not come easy. Perhaps it did with Iseul who seemed so simple-minded. He loved that about her. He smirked at the thought of Iseul. She had come into her own, much to his dismay. *Reckless, loudmouthed and stubborn.*

How could Iseul trust a man she had just met? Perhaps he should have tried harder to convince her to stay. He winced at the thought of what those men could do to her. Then again, if she got out with Doo-Hyung's help, and stayed out... His thoughts trailed, even wished. But he knew Iseul would be back; she would never abandon them.

It was Doo-Hyung who concerned him most, especially now that his father was involved. He knew not to underestimate a son's need for his father's approval, as much as he wanted to deny it. He never knew the man and how he was with his father. He worried about the one unassailable truth: blood runs thicker than water.

A piece of him wanted to believe his father had been looking out for him. He had welcomed the radio loop his father had made, even accepted Doo-Hyung sooner than he should have. This trust and loyalty he saw in his father's men always fazed him, but he knew the truth—that everyone was a pawn in his great scheme. He taunted the skies, wanting to yell for his dead father to watch him. *Are you happy? I'm here waiting to die, doing your bidding.*

Jung-Soo flipped the dial to that remote American channel and waited. Perhaps Dae-Gun didn't get the message; perhaps he had really meant to say goodbye and shut the radio off completely. He fidgeted with the bullets next to him as he kept his view fixed on the patch of ground Doo-Hyung and Iseul had disappeared into. He was nervous to stay on the American channel for too long as he flipped back.

"Mi-Jung, are you there?" Jung-Soo spoke into the microphone.

"Yeah, Jung-Soo. How are things going over there?"

"Still trying to find a way out."

"That's good," Mi-Jung said, wondering if Jung-Soo had anything else to say to her.

"Tell me about the village. How has everyone been?" Jung-Soo said. He didn't quite know what to say, though he knew he needed to keep the village radio channel occupied so as not to draw attention to the American channel he had told Iseul and Dae-Gun to use.

Mi-Jung seemed overwhelmed by the question. "Well, a lot has happened since you left," she said, still confused as to why Jung-Soo was on the line with her.

They talked about the conscription, the rationing system that completely collapsed once the North Koreans marched deep into southern territory. She talked about the day Iseul had befriended her and how the two of them were elated when they first came up with the idea of making paper for both the villagers and the soldiers.

"It seems like a lifetime ago." Her voice trailed.

"I knew Iseul was stingy, but seriously a single sheet of paper with doodles when everyone else was sending thick packets of long letters and blank pages?"

Mi-Jung chuckled. "You should thank me. You wouldn't have gotten a single sheet if I hadn't stumbled on her doodling with your name on it." She told him about how she had inadvertently given that sheet of paper to Mr. Lim.

"Oh great. She didn't even mean to send it to me."

The soft laughs quieted down to a silence.

"What about Byung-Guk?" Jung-Soo asked. He sifted through

his memory to that one day he found Byung-Guk loitering around Mi-Jung's restaurant. Jung-Soo wondered if she knew how much he liked her.

"He's dead," she said as a matter-of-fact.

"I'm sorry to hear that. I really am."

"I know. He was really sorry about everything that happened. He wanted me to tell you if I had the chance."

"He doesn't have to. I know." His mind wandered to that night of the great fire. "Hey, Mi-Jung?"

"Yeah."

"You know, he really liked you."

She didn't speak for a while. Mi-Jung seemed different too and she wasn't just taller. There was a sense of responsibility—of a warmth he hadn't seen before. They had all grown up, he supposed.

***

Doo-Hyung knew he would be branded an incompetent soldier after he let Iseul escape from his tent. He heard the first shots and then the yelling before waiting another few seconds to head out of his tent.

"What the hell is happening here?" Doo-Hyung stormed out of his tent, scratching his head as if he had just woken up.

"Dammit," Private Yoon said, as he shot another stray bullet in the direction of the red hanbok. "Sir," he said apologetically, "She got away. What happened, sir?"

"I'll tell you what happened," he yelled inches from the private's face. "I tied her up, but you fools forgot to check her for weapons before you brought her to me." He waved for the private to follow him to the tent where he pointed at the gaping hole on the other side. "She had a knife, that's what happened! Wait till I report this to the General, he'll have your head."

The private fell on his knees. "Sir, I deserve to die. Please have mercy." He shouted back at his men who inanely watched on. "What are you doing just standing there! Go after her, you morons!"

The men scattered, some running with their guns as others jogged directionless.

"Stop," Doo-Hyung ordered, his command ringing until every man stood still. "Men, stand your ground. Did you not hear the General's orders?" They seem to be coming to their senses as they shuffled back into the center of camp. Doo-Hyung sneered at the private before making his way into the tent again.

He collapsed on the straw mattress and exhaled. Their plan was working so far. It was up to Iseul now. He felt around his pockets where his flask usually was, only to remember he had already had that last sip of rice wine a while back. His fingers fumbled with the flask before he noticed the radio. He turned it on. It was Jung-Soo talking with a girl from the village.

Some soppy story.

He was tempted to switch the radio channel, though it probably wasn't a good idea just in case the sound filtered outside his tent. The men were still outside, idling so as not to seem lazy in front of the General's son. He should at least wait a bit before switching—give Iseul enough time on the road. Besides, Jung-Soo's story was just getting interesting.

Minutes ticked by and the clearing still rang with the voices of men. He gazed out of the hole Iseul had ripped on the side of his tent and saw the shadow of his own tent cast on the side of the hill. The sun was dangerously low.

Even if he listened in on Iseul's channel, he knew his own instructions he had given her: don't discuss exact battle plans until you meet face-to-face. There would be a real possibility that he would be caught in the ambush if Iseul succeeded in coming back with reinforcements. How much longer did they have till the planes would bomb this very location?

Enough time had passed for Iseul and boy Dae-Gun to have convinced his commander. They should be on their way back, he hoped. He peeped out of the tent. The men poked at each other and quieted down, staring nervously at their new commander.

Doo-Hyung coughed as he exited the tent. "Private Yoon," he said.

"Sir," he saluted, still somewhat shaken from Doo-Hyung's threats.

"Why don't you take me around a bit. Show me the rice stores and how you've rationed the food with your men."

"Straight away, sir."

They marched away from camp and back towards the cave. The shadowy hole quickly came into view, though the walk over took a while longer. The silence put the private on edge as he lit the lantern long before they reached the opening.

They stood at the mouth of the cave, looking into the abyss as a shiver ran down Doo-Hyung's spine. "How far back does it go?" He asked as he took the lantern from the boy. Already, the temperature rise was noticeable. Where was the heat coming from?

"We haven't seen the end yet."

"Is it a tunnel?"

"Doesn't seem like it, sir."

Sacks of rice near the entrance had been poked and prodded as precious grains of rice spilled on the stone floor. The sacks towered above their heads in rows that filed deeper than the lantern's light could reach. Young-Nam must have found a way to siphon a significant amount of rice from the Japanese; the amount that stood in front of him could not have been collected in the past five years since the Japanese had left.

And soon it would be General Shin's stolen legacy. Perhaps it was a good thing, a blessing in disguise that would bring this war to an end. Peace—that's what Young-Nam wanted most of all.

But what of their plans for an independent Korea? Doo-Hyung could almost be certain that was the reason the rice store had been made in the first place.

The sound of their footsteps echoed, each step creating the illusion that a hundred men were in the cave. He could imagine how a tiger's roar would have sounded.

"Sir, we should probably head back," Private Yoon said hesitantly. He did not wish to press the General's son, but in the few times he had gone in this far, he had heard more than footsteps echoing back at him. He was shaking, but he had decided a long time ago that he would rather die of a bullet than disappear into the abyss of the cave.

"That would be wise...yes," Doo-Hyung said. He turned around slowly, wondering if they had gone far enough into the cave. He pitied the boy. He had done nothing wrong; he was a capable soldier who had just been unlucky being in the wrong place at the wrong time, dealing with the wrong people.

Doo-Hyung slid his revolver down his sleeve and pointed it at the boy's head. For a moment, he witnessed the terror of the gods in the boy's face then quickly put the boy out of his misery.

The cave rang in screeching echoes, reverberating off the walls as it rang louder with each rebound. Doo-Hyung promised he would remember the boy as a valiant soldier. Though in the moment those phantom bullets ricocheted all around him and the life quickly faded from the boy, he wondered if the boy could hear them too—hear that he wasn't the only one shot—that Doo-Hyung was right there with him.

The echoes faded and the lantern flickered with the cold draft that wafted from the entrance. He faced the light that shone in. The echoes continued, some louder than others, some accompanied by screams—delayed responses bouncing back from behind him as if the private had so quickly become a ghost to haunt his killer. Or was it the soul of a mountain god chasing him away? He wondered if they were real or if the ringing had singed themselves into his eardrums.

He blew out his lantern and ran towards the light, the air around him thawing the delusion from within the belly of the cave. Another shot heard, or was it a bomb? It grew louder and more pronounced. Had the fighter jet finally come?

The bright orange light of the setting sun engulfed him now. He looked up, blinded by the rays, hoping to glimpse a flying figure in the sky. His eyes adjusted, but there was no plane.

To his right, shots fired again.

**

The girl in the red hanbok had been ushered towards the commanders upon her arrival as Dae-Gun followed the trail of men who gawked at the sight of a woman. He had had high hopes for this girl called Iseul and her beauty, considering the months he had spent with Jung-Soo's obsessive fixation on the girl.

Dae-Gun was close enough to hear her as he waded through the soldiers, weaving in and out of the taller ones.

"Park Dae-Gun," she seemed to be calling.

"I'm here!" he waved his hand and yelled above the chatter and excitement.

She turned towards the voice and in that instant, Dae-Gun's hand stuck in the air, midway waving as he froze in place. She was, in every sense, an average-looking girl. There was some rationalizing that ensued. Yes, Jung-Soo had been fixated on his guitar too and no one had called that clunky thing a beauty.

"Finally," she said, relieved. "Is that really Dae-Gun?" she turned to Commander Lee, pointing at the rather stumpy-looking boy who waddled over.

"Yes," he said, punctually.

She knew the tides of the discussion had already swayed in her favor as soon as the questioning began. She looked to the boy called Dae-Gun, grateful beyond any words could express.

"As far as we know from the radio interceptions, the North Koreans have not infiltrated the rice stores yet and do not know the exact coordinates. Is this true?"

"Yes," Iseul responded, with a brief nod of confidence.

"We've been attempting to convince the General to issue a fly-by strike, but with the current intelligence, he cannot risk revealing the rice stores and cutting off the only feasible way out of there." Commander Lee explained to Iseul as Dae-Gun translated the conversation to Commander Rogers.

The conversation felt surreal to Iseul as she slowly began to realize she had somehow become part of the discussion that would decide the fates of so many. She tried to focus.

"We have a short window of opportunity here. If we know the approximate number of North Koreans standing guard of the rice stores, we might be able to take them out before any of them can lead General Shin to the location. We have a duty to our own men to get them out safely if we have the chance."

Iseul glanced around her. The soldiers were bruised and worn, yet they far outnumbered the North Korean soldiers she had escaped from.

"It's possible, sir," Iseul said, as sternly as she could. "The North Koreans are a hundred at best."

A concerned frown came across the white leader. He spoke in a strange slurred language to Dae-Gun who mimicked the commander's own concern. Dae-Gun was sorely aware of his own commander who waited intently.

Dae-Gun looked to Iseul. "He wants to know how you managed to find the road south and evade a hundred soldiers. He wonders why you didn't come sooner and bring anyone else with you."

Dae-Gun and Iseul stared at each other, wondering what the other might say, wondering if it was a good idea to reveal that the son of the North Korean General had helped her get away. Surely, Dae-Gun could also vouch for the North Korean too, if it came to that.

"Speak, girl," the commander ordered her in her own tongue.

"Sir, I know what your concern is," Iseul began as Dae-Gun tensed up. "You think I'm colluding with the North Koreans."

Panic rose in Dae-Gun. The implications were serious—how else would Iseul have gotten out without the permission, or at least the help of a North Korean who guarded the rice stores. What would happen if they found out about Doo-Hyung? They would never march to Yeoju, not when they suspected Iseul might be on the North Korean side, planning an ambush.

He was always so slow. Why couldn't his mind work like Jung-Soo's? He stared at Iseul. She was a stranger to him, to all of them. Better the news came from someone the commanders trusted. He had at least earned that much in the past few days.

But then, a thought struck. The day he was tortured and Jung-Soo interrogated, Commander Lee had let them go despite intense suspicions. Hadn't Commander Lee so quickly trusted Jung-Soo when he called on the 18th Infantry to aid the 5th Cavalry? Something about Commander Lee didn't quite add up.

Iseul was about to speak when Dae-Gun halted her. "Sir, Jung-Soo's father has connections higher up in the North Korean military," he said, in both languages.

Commander Rogers could not mask his shock, though Commander Lee was surprisingly calm. Dae-Gun's hunch might be correct though knew he was walking on very thin ice. He turned to Commander Lee.

"Sir, I believe you had some idea about Jung-Soo's involvement with the communists long before tonight."

Commander Lee instantly looked away, his accusing demeanor now shifty and defensive as Commander Rogers' look demanded an explanation.

"That is a serious accusation, Dae-Gun." Commander Rogers managed to find his words. "Do you have proof, son?"

Dae-Gun nodded as he directed his question at Commander Lee again. "Sir, how is it that you were the only one to know about the northern troops awaiting us? You told us about eyewitness accounts of soldiers in the northern front, but clearly, no one else was convinced enough to march north with the 18th Infantry. Jung-Soo wouldn't shut up about the first of December. That was our deadline to deliver the codes. If I'm not mistaken, commander, Jung-Soo and I were at least a week early when we delivered the codes to General Rogers, and that was the first known evidence of troops lying in wait in the northern front."

"Commander, please answer the question," Commander Rogers pressed. Commander Lee did not appear to be the same jovial man who had marched north to come to the aid of the 5th Cavalry when all others had abandoned them. What wasn't this yellow man telling him? Commander Rogers had come into this war certain about America's involvement, yet he was beginning to realize he had sorely underestimated the vagaries and gray areas a civil war between brother nations would yield.

The sun had touched the horizon, ready to disappear and engulf the peninsula in darkness. They were running out of time.

"May I ask why you suspected Jung-Soo and I were spies on that first mission back from the 5th Cavalry?" Dae-Gun pressed again.

"If you had such strong suspicions, why did you let them proceed on the mission?" Commander Rogers spoke sternly.

Commander Lee sighed. He was ready to give in, though he paused for a moment as if collecting his thoughts. "Jung-Soo came strongly recommended by a senior officer who is also my mentor. I have been suspicious of my mentor's allegiance for a while now so thought it best to keep an eye on Jung-Soo. I've personally been monitoring his radio logs," Commander Lee said, though his tone betrayed that even he thought keeping Jung-Soo on his mission was a liability. It was clear that his loyalty to his mentor had clouded his judgment.

Commander Lee continued. "My mentor was found and executed a week ago by the North Koreans, but he had given me intelligence about a potential full frontal attack, including the northern front, the night before his execution. I was skeptical at first, but I was inclined to believe a man facing death and Jung-Soo confirmed my mentor's intel."

"He's not a communist!" Dae-Gun declared, though for a moment they wondered who he meant—Commander Lee's mentor or Jung-Soo.

Iseul echoed Dae-Gun's response. The skepticism in Commander Rogers seemed to ease ever so slightly. "We can't be certain, but are you saying that intelligence coming through Jung-Soo might be from the same source as your mentor?"

Commander Lee nodded. "I believe it is reliable."

Commander Rogers paused to think about it. He remembered the scrawny boy called Jung-Soo loitering in his tent with a shoelace and a ruler. He had witnessed the moment the boy shifted his gaze to the map as fear filled his eyes when he saw that a North Korean attack was imminent. It was perhaps that moment that had convinced him about Jung-Soo. He was just a boy—a smart one, but still full of adventure and naïveté. It was clear he hadn't known about the attack beforehand. And hadn't he just saved thousands of their own troops by rerouting them? If he had meant to divert the attention away from Yeoju to retrieve the rice for the North Korean side, why would he ask for reinforcements now?

Commander Rogers tilted his head, amused at the thought of Jung-Soo measuring a guitar with a shoelace. "So, he went through all that trouble to measure a shoelace." He was thinking out loud.

"Sir?" Dae-Gun said, confused.

Commander Rogers realized his thoughts had gone on a tangent. "He was measuring a shoelace with my ruler when you two were at our camp."

"Oh, that sir!" Dae-Gun said as he pulled out the sketch of the guitar again. "He was trying to measure the dimensions of my guitar." Dae-Gun translated to Iseul who also pulled out a worn piece of paper carefully tucked away in the sleeve of her hanbok. It was nearly identical.

"It was for her. She's the village carpenter's daughter, sir," Dae-Gun said.

"I promised I would make a guitar for him," she added. "And it's a promise I intend to keep."

The commander's doubt seemed to ease at the sight. He had been right about the boy, Jung-Soo after all—rash and adventurous, but most of all, loyal to the ones he loved as it was clear they too were loyal to him. This boy Dae-Gun and the girl were proof enough of that.

Dae-Gun, Iseul and Commander Lee could sense Commander Rogers' shifting demeanor as they waited for him to speak.

"First signs of an ambush and we're out." Commander Rogers looked down at his watch. "If we don't move fast, General Shin might make it to the rice stores before we do and we would be headed towards an ambush after all."

Dae-Gun pumped his fists in silence, unable to control the overwhelming sense of victory.

Commander Rogers summoned Sergeant Martin. "Do we have news of the fighter jet from General MacArthur?"

He shook his head. "Negative sir, he says the priority is to save our men. He won't send the fighter jets until they're all out, or you're certain there is no other way to extract our men."

Commander Rogers nodded.

Iseul was unsure what all the chatter meant, though Dae-Gun certainly seemed overjoyed.

"So, they're coming?" she asked.

Dae-Gun nodded. "They're coming to save us!"

The men were halted from their retreat, called on by their sergeants to begin the march back north. Iseul and Dae-Gun watched as the men, who had been in high spirits, turned into a sea of concerned faces, some stoic as others looked to the ground to hide their rage. Iseul felt the weight on her shoulders. She knew it was a debt she, nor anyone else in the village could repay.

The commanders had dispersed in the midst of their men as their deep and arresting voices crescendoed. They called on their men with a speech that urged each soldier to be courageous because they were going back to save their own men—men who had not been lucky enough to escape the initial attack, men who were not from their own infantries, or even the same country, but who fought together as brothers.

Iseul and Dae-Gun were ordered to tail the troops, straddled between the commanding officers of the 5th Cavalry and the 18th Infantry. Dae-Gun could sense the concern in Iseul's expression, and echoed the same sentiment. Both knew that Jung-Soo and Gil-Dong would be near the cave, and Doo-Hyung in the heart of enemy territory. How could they be sure that they wouldn't be caught in the crossfire?

CHAPTER 41

The Legend of Tangun, as narrated by Yeong-Hoon

This is the story of how this great nation of Han (Korea) came to be. As the story goes, there was once a prince of heaven who begged his father for a kingdom and was granted his rule over the mountain of Taebaek and all the land it overlooked.

Upon hearing about this anointed prince, a bear and a tiger traveled far and wide to put in a request of their own. They too wanted to be humans. As ordered by the Prince, the bear and the tiger began their journey of transformation, eating a sacred food made with garlic and mugwort and was ordered to hide in a cave for a hundred days.

The tiger's patience waned as his hunger grew, venturing into the world before his hundred days were over, failing to transform. On the other hand, the bear succeeded as it transformed into the most beautiful woman. Yet, the greed of humankind infested the woman's heart. Instead of living out her days as granted by the gods, the bear-woman proceeded to pray for a son. After making offerings to the prince of heaven, her wish was granted, and so was the next. Her son went on to become the King of the Kochoson Kingdom.

Is there no end to a man's ambition? The king prayed yet again, his prayers accompanying offerings of great riches and fortune. Upon his death, the King went on to become a mountain god, as was his final wish.

The mountain god knew of no higher peaks nor of grander

valleys, except for Mount Tae-baek upon which the prince of heaven himself reigned. The mountain god lived out his eternity in contemplation and awe, but centuries of viewing the skies and the people below rendered the mountain god a bitter old man. He began cursing the land on which he stood. How could he have been so blind? How did he not see the pain of his own people?

Oh, cursed is the day he was born! Curse the day the bear transformed into a weak woman! He cursed the prince who had granted the bear's request, for he had caused his mother to grovel at the feet of her oppressors, his men to die fighting for his own seat as king and the villages surrounding his mountain to starve for he had taken up the land that could have been used to farm rice.

He wept and wallowed until it became unbearable, swallowing his soul in the deepest hollowed cave of the mountain's heart so he could feel no more.

***

Doo-Hyung stood at the mouth of the tiger's cave, wondering if the bullet that had killed Private Yoon still rang in his ears. More shots rang from his right. He took in a breath of fresh air from the world outside the cave, clearing his head from echoes and voices that emanated from within. Just when he was beginning to realize something strange had happened in the cave, he heard multiple shots, now louder, accompanying shouts of men in multiple languages.

Iseul. She had finally come and had begun infiltrating the North Korean camp.

"Doo-Hyung." He thought he heard his name, echoing from the two mountains facing each other. "Doo-Hyung," it called again.

He woke from his stupor and spun left. It was Jung-Soo and Gil-Dong, waving their arms frantically, beckoning for him to come.

"What were you doing just standing in front of the cave?" Jung-Soo said.

Doo-Hyung couldn't say.

"Never mind." Jung-Soo knew what had happened: two men had gone in, a single gunshot followed and only one man had come out. "Looks like Iseul's back," he changed the subject.

"And good timing at that," Gil-Dong added. Jung-Soo and Gil-Dong had been worried when they heard the gunshot, wondering if the other men at the hidden camp had heard it and would begin searching for a missing soldier.

Heavy artillery fired.

"How far is the camp, anyway?" Jung-Soo said curiously as he took the binoculars to his eyes.

"It's quite near," Doo-Hyung added. Noise was deceptive, especially with the tight rows of trees surrounding the camp. He could see why the camp had been undetected for so long. He began gathering the objects strewn on the ground, snatching the binoculars from Jung-Soo's face. "We've got to move," he stated. Gil-Dong followed without question.

"Where?" Jung-Soo asked.

"Not you, boy."

"Why not?" Jung-Soo realized as he said those words. He looked down at his uniform that had been worn but marked distinctively as a South Korean uniform. "Oh…" He had forgotten how it may look to an army of South Korean and American soldiers if they witnessed him with the two men from the North.

"Not to worry, I'll take my father and his men on a merry chase around the other mountains before I bring them over." Doo-Hyung nodded, and that was his goodbye.

Jung-Soo nodded too. "Take them to the eastern-most mountain," he said. "That's where the radio towers are."

He would hear from Doo-Hyung again; he was sure of it. If not by radio, he would hunt the man down himself and get the answers Jung-Soo hadn't yet gotten. There was so much more he didn't know about his father, about their time together in Mokpo and how they had gotten to be the men they were.

When the two northerners disappeared towards the east gate, Jung-Soo had nothing but his radio and his naked eye. Su-Jung was a trooper. She had taken the incoming Chinese troops towards the southern-most tip of the village where the largest mountain towered over the battle that waged below.

Jung-Soo took the radio. "Mi-Jung."

"Yeah," she said. He could sense the tension in the cabin.

"It's time."

They would need to move towards the east gate before the troops would completely block off the gate. The women and children were likely celebrating—a road south had finally been found and they were on their way there! But he knew it was far too early to celebrate.

Silence fell once again on the hills where the spy camp stood. Men marched towards Jung-Soo in neat files that told him they were his own men, marching unfazed, still ready for more. The American men filed behind, just as doggedly as the Koreans. He squinted, looking for a red figure that would emerge from the dreary brown and green camouflaged uniforms, and then he saw it—a figure of a woman in a red hanbok, billowing down from the mountain behind the army of soldiers.

Jung-Soo beamed. *Iseul.* But what was she doing? Her arms seemed to be flailing around. He squinted, wishing he hadn't let Doo-Hyung take the binoculars. Was she…bickering with someone?

"How could you forget to translate the most important part?" Iseul complained. She had been running towards dead bodies strewn on the mountain, flipping over and prodding any one that looked like Doo-Hyung.

"When was I supposed to mention, 'By the way, look out for an older North Korean soldier. Don't shoot him because he's on our side.' That would have taken till next year to explain how we got ourselves into that predicament!"

Soldiers stirred in front of them, startled by what seemed like an incoming soldier, sprinting towards them from the foot of the mountain. The men held their rifles up, as others shouted, "Hold your fire! Hold your fire!"

"Dae-Gun, Iseul!" It was Jung-Soo, yelling at the top of his lungs.

"What is he thinking, running head first into an army just out of battle?" Dae-Gun said.

"Jung-Soo, what happened to Doo-Hyung and Gil-Dong?"

"They're safe," Jung-Soo said. Iseul sighed in relief.

Commander Lee and Commander Rogers joined them.

"Sir," Jung-Soo saluted.

"At ease, soldier," Commander Lee said. "Report status."

"Sir, Su-Jung and her men have been pushed back to the southern-most part of the village. She's dealing with about half a battalion, while the other soldiers are taking on the other half near the east gate. They're running out of time." He pointed at their respective locations.

Dae-Gun translated, as the two commanders coordinated and began sending men off in tactical groups led by the marines.

"Sir, when is the fighter jet arriving?" Jung-Soo asked.

"They're not. We're on our own. Our orders are to make sure everyone retreats safely. Jung-Soo, you're in charge here. I'll leave a few soldiers behind. You make sure all of the civilians make it out of this god-forsaken village alive," he said, as he walked away to his colonel.

Dae-Gun and Iseul fell silent, as did Jung-Soo whose eyes flickered confused and frustrated.

"He's not taking the news well, is he?" Dae-Gun commented to Iseul who shook her head in response.

It was what Jung-Soo had wanted, wasn't it? All this time, he had hoped his father's letter would yield a way south and it had done just that. Then why did he feel like he had failed—that the message his father had left him had only partially been deciphered? He took the tattered letter back out again as he noticed that only the latter half of the page remained. Doo-Hyung must have taken the first half when he had ripped it.

"...as it guards its cubs," the half-note read.

If the rice inside the cave were his father's cubs, he had failed to guard them because in less than an hour the Chinese and North Koreans would take it all—years of toiling, of being beaten by the Japanese, of his father risking his and his family's safety to ensure that the rice stores continued to grow.

What had he done? He had found it only to hand it over to the Chinese. He will have single-handedly sabotaged his father's legacy. The thought gave him a sense of sick pleasure. How much had his family suffered for that legacy of his? *What about me? When will my time come?*

"So that's it, isn't it?" Jung-Soo said in disbelief. "We just walk away from it, as if it never existed."

"Technically it…" Dae-Gun began saying when Iseul shushed him.

"Don't you want to eat the rice that you've toiled for? Don't you think you deserve to eat the rice that you farmed?" Jung-Soo said.

"Technically, she's a carpenter so she wasn't farming…"

"Shh!" Iseul cut Dae-Gun off again. "You're right. It's our rice and no one will know that it was ours to begin with. Those starving Chinese soldiers will be happy to have their bellies filled for another day, and will march the next day to die fighting in a country they have no business being in to begin with," Iseul said. She was surprised by the words that came out of her mouth. The bodies of men on the mountain she had just come from had hit a nerve in her—they were brothers who were killed for wearing a different uniform.

She couldn't understand, no refused to understand. What was so important about this war that would make brothers kill one another. Hadn't they all seen enough sorrow? Hadn't she seen her fair share of toil, sacrificed enough to have a claim to that rice too, not just the men in uniform? She had lost her father in the crossfires for that rice, her mother to sickness and hunger as she wasted away, making sure everyone else in the family had had enough to eat. *How much more? How much more?*

"So, what do we do now?" Iseul said, looking at Jung-Soo who stood helplessly stoic.

Jung-Soo shrugged. "We live to fight another day, just as we've been ordered." He watched the soldiers disappear into the village as four soldiers paced towards him, ready to start the evacuations. Iseul saw the line of villagers slowly making their way towards them, dressed in colorful hanboks and white work clothes in stark contrast against the brown and grey of the mountainside.

Jung-Soo ordered his men to come. "Collect small sacks from the villagers and fill them with rice from the cave." They nodded and went off, though they didn't seem too keen on the idea of entering the eerie cave. Even from afar, the place looked as if it might eat them alive. But the journey south will be harsh for all of them, and not one seemed to be dressed warm enough for the coming bitter winter weeks. At least they would have enough food for the journey with rice to fill their stomachs, however bland that may be.

Mi-Jung had come over to reunite with friendly faces. "You did it, Iseul. I can't believe it!"

Iseul gave a weak smile and hugged her friend. "How is everybody?"

"Good. They're ready to do whatever it takes."

"Perfect. They'll need all that energy to march south."

Mi-Jung looked around the deserted scene. "Where are all the soldiers?"

"They're went into the village to buy us some more time. Come, we'd better hurry now." Iseul tugged at Mi-Jung's hanbok sleeve.

Yet she resisted. "I thought they were here to take the rice with us." Their attention went to the gaping hole on the side of the mountain. Sunlight had diminished, but soldiers holding torches at the entrance was enough for Mi-Jung to see piles of rice stacked as far back as the light reached. How deep did it go?

"We don't have enough man power to get it out in time."

"Impossible…" her voice trailed. "We can't just leave it here! Especially not for those greedy Chinese to steal. That's our rice in there! That's our bloodline!"

The group from the cabin muttered amongst themselves, watching Mi-Jung come to the inevitable conclusion as they themselves did too.

Despite his best efforts, Jung-Soo's couldn't stop himself from thinking of a possible way to salvage the situation. "If only there was a way to bury the rice, so deep that no one would ever find it but us."

"So, we bury it," Mi-Jung said, matter-of-factly.

"It's not that simple." Jung-Soo explained. "If we blow it up, it might block the road south and risk all our lives. And we don't have time to move it somewhere else."

"Well…well then, we build a wall in front of the cave."

She already knew the answer. "We don't have time," Jung-Soo confirmed.

Mi-Jung grunted. "Why didn't they send us more troops to fight them off? Don't they know the war is as good as lost if the Chinese get their hands on it?"

A pang of guilt hit Jung-Soo. Hadn't he been the one to convince the troops to retreat? What would have happened if he had let nature take its course—let the U.N. and South Korean forces take on the Chinese? Wasn't that what his father planned all along?

There was nothing natural about war, he sighed. It would only mean more men would have died. Besides, the only reason the North Koreans weren't sending more troops into Yeoju was because they didn't need a larger army to collect the rice. They ventured to divide and conquer; they were holding Seoul siege and the entire region of Gangwondo had fallen into their control.

Mi-Jung's mother, slouched-backed and breathing heavily, beckoned for her daughter to come. Jung-Soo had seen the expression on her face when she had first glanced towards the rice store; she barely flinched, hardened by the fact of life that she was once again being looted of her birthright. They were lucky just to get out of the Wasteland alive.

"The tiger guards his cave, as it guards its cubs." Jung-Soo kept repeating. Small sacks of rice were being filled by soldiers, all their meager belonging packed for the long haul.

"You still think your father has a plan?" Iseul asked.

Jung-Soo sighed. "For all I know, he's been guarding the rice long enough to deliver it to the North Koreans to finish off the war."

"I don't think so," Iseul said with certainty.

"Oh yeah? What makes you so sure?" His tone gave way for bitterness. "Sorry…" Iseul didn't deserve his spite. She had done nothing but sacrifice herself and that was long before the war had begun.

"He saved the rice for you, for all of us so that we could build a future for ourselves. I'm sure of it! The rice isn't the tiger's cub, you are!"

"Yeah…" he didn't believe her. "On the bright side, at least in a few days, we might wake in Busan with news of a reunified Korea."

Iseul glared at him. "That's not funny."

The radio buzzed on. "Jung-Soo, what's the progress wtih the evacuation?" Commander Lee said. His surroundings resounded with artillery and a distinct female voice. It was Su-Jung, still going at it with her men.

"Sir, we're leaving the location now.

"Good."

"What about the progress over there, sir?"

"As good as can be, except this woman thinks she's the one in command. You'd better hurry before I accidentally shoot her."

Iseul and Mi-Jung burst out in teary laughter, though Jung-Soo held in a chuckle. It was nice to hear that his commander was still hopeful. They suppressed their urge to ask how the old man was doing, or if the scholar had managed to stay alive with Mr. Lim. Iseul bit her tongue, wondering if Yeong-Hoon was still alive. Instead, their gaze approached the cave where it swallowed the last rays of sunlight as darkness enveloped it, erasing all signs that rice filled it. If only it would stay dark in the mountains of Yeoju till the war ended…

"Jung-Soo," Commander Lee wasn't quite finished.

"Sir."

"The North Korean General seems to know exactly what he's

doing. He's been trying to split us up and according to the woman, she thinks some of the Chinese are splitting off into groups to venture into the mountains."

"Sir, we'll be on guard."

"Alright, report any movements."

The night had turned shifty as the surroundings bred an ominous air with each branch of a tree that rustled in the wind.

"You think they're here yet?" Dae-Gun said over Jung-Soo's shoulder. His gaze sprinted towards one side of the mountain and then the other, echoes of the wind bouncing around the mouth of cave. Jung-Soo joined the soldiers who were gathering rice.

"Finish up now. You, you," Jung-Soo pointed at two soldiers. "Set up on the eastern side, you two on the west. Dae-Gun and I will take the southern point. We're taking high ground to look for Chinese soldiers scouting the land for the store. We shoot to kill, soldiers, and preferably before they confirm our location to the General."

Dae-Gun had heard it first—a slight buzz ringing from the skies that seemed to be looming closer.

"Jung-Soo…" he said, nervously. "Do you hear that?"

After months of second guessing Dae-Gun's sense of hearing, Jung-Soo knew not to ignore it. It was dull, but it was certainly there—an indistinct buzz that came from afar, getting louder by the second.

"Planes," the soldiers said in unison, as they looked at each other in panic.

"Everyone, get moving as fast as you can," one soldier said, as he herded the women and children up towards the mountain where the obscure road began. The once calm group burst into a frenzy towards the road.

"Careful now," a soldier took an old granny on his back and began the trek up.

Iseul joined Jung-Soo and Dae-Gun. "What's going on? Have the Chinese arrived?" Just as she spoke, she heard the whizzing above.

"No, much worse. Fighter jets."

In the quaint village of Yeoju where the loudest noise came from drunk men returning home late at night, Iseul was startled by the foreign noise.

"The question is, is it ours?" Dae-Gun said as he looked into the darkness where the sound came from.

The tail end of the group had made it far enough that it would soon become impossible to spot them.

Jung-Soo held the microphone close. "Sir, are you hearing what I'm hearing?"

Commander Lee responded. "I am. It's not ours. Do you recognize it?"

Jung-Soo's heart sank. "No sir, we haven't been able to see it yet."

"Status of the refugees?"

"They've just started on the road."

"Stand your ground. Let's give them a head start. Standby." The line went silent.

"You should go," Jung-Soo pushed Iseul away towards the disappearing group.

She didn't budge. "I have a gun too." Jung-Soo was beginning to regret giving her that tiny handgun. It had made her brash, fearless even, when the logical thing to do was just to run. "Besides, an extra set of eyes won't hurt. I don't reckon any of you have the kind of experience I have in the mountains at night."

Jung-Soo grunted. "Don't you know what that sound means?" He looked into the crescent moon.

"Of course, I do. I'm not stupid."

"Then you'll know it's best to leave before it starts dropping bombs on us."

Iseul watched as the soldiers found their patch of earth as they laid low and positioned their rifles. The next pair of soldiers were headed west as the road south was again deserted, the last of the villagers gone. Iseul shifted in position, looking towards the road South and towards Jung-Soo again.

"Come with me," she said with her hands extended towards him.

Jung-Soo watched as the same hand that had reached for him on the first day of school had grown even more calloused. He was supposed to take it. It had been the way he had planned this moment, though he thought he'd be the one to hold his hand out this time to beckon her to run away with him. What happens then? How many times can his commander excuse his insolence? The words lingered on the tip of his tongue, '*Let's run away, just you and I, atop a mountain where no one can find us.*'

How ignorant had he been? What mountain had not been unearthed a thousandfolds before where tigers had come and had already left more than a century ago? What betrayal hadn't gone unpunished, if not in one's own life, but through the suffering of those who would come after?

"I can't," he said. "I have my orders." He pushed her towards the road, though she was anchored in place. She was angry; her silence attested to that. She stomped off towards the soldiers who had reached their location in the west.

Jung-Soo boiled inside. How could she be so stubborn? How could she not know the reason he was pushing her away—that this was the only way he could return to her, a whole man?

He grabbed the back of her hanbok, as she stumbled back. "Not that way, stick close," he eyed her from head to toe with a disapproving look. "If you're going to stay, you'd better do something about that red hanbok. You're a walking bulls eye."

She looked down at her dress, self-conscious, though her head popped up with a beaming smile; it meant she could stay!

Dae-Gun and Jung-Soo took their places, facing north, right above the cave, as Iseul sat between them and began taking the top layer of her hanbok off. She bunched the outer red and green layer together, ready to throw it out, but couldn't bear to; this was her mother's dress.

She sighed. Then she had a better idea. "Don't look." She stood up and took a few steps back, stripping herself of the hanbok, flipping it inside out before putting it back on. "There, that's perfect." Besides, it was getting colder so she would need that extra layer.

Jung-Soo glanced over to a woman completely dressed in white with her pitch black hair flowing down her shoulders to her waist. "You look like a ghost," he said curtly.

Dae-Gun seemed to have blushed though only the moonlight witnessed his flushed face. Iseul took her place again, looking down at her white hanbok, wondering if red might have been a better camouflage than white.

"Strange isn't it? What's the plane doing? Why hasn't it started bombing?" Dae-Gun commented. The sound of the plane waned and then grew louder in cycles.

"Is it just me or does the plane sound odd?" Jung-Soo added.

"I don't think it's a fighter jet."

"Maybe it's just not as close as we think it is."

"Umm…" Dae-Gun said, honing in on the sound again. "I don't think so. It's definitely not the same type of plane that flew past us a few weeks ago."

"What's a fighter jet supposed to sound like?" Iseul said.

"I don't know," Jung-Soo said. "Just louder I guess."

"Like the roar of a tiger," Dae-Gun added with a self-satisfied smile.

Jung-Soo rolled his eyes. "Like any of us have ever heard one before."

"Geez, a little imagination won't hurt anybody," Dae-Gun retorted.

Iseul gazed into the moon, hoping the plane would fly directly beneath it so she could see what this elusive flying object looked like. She shivered, though it wasn't just because of the cold. A lot had happened in the past few days and her legs had taken a toll from runner faster and longer than she had ever run before. She remembered the lump of rice Doo-Hyung had given her and grabbed it from a small satchel around her. She sighed. The ball had been flattened to an unrecognizable blob. She could only be grateful that it was not filled with kimchi as she had mistakenly done that day she had brought lunch to share with Jung-Soo.

"Again?" Jung-Soo seemed to remember too as he stole one mound from Iseul and stuffed a huge bite into his mouth. She waited to dump the blame on Doo-Hyung, but he didn't complain. He broke it in half and shared with Dae-Gun, leaving her with a whole blob to herself. Her mouth watered though she knew her stomach could no longer handle more than a few bites before it would lurch. It was bland but oddly rich with the flavors that are usually masked by the pungent spices in kimchi.

The sliver of moon now held its head high in the night sky as the plane droned softer then louder in succession. The night had caused the condensation of the ground to freeze in crystals that glimmered underneath the soft moonlight, as a warm, but humid air seemed to waft up from the cave where the three laid in wait. They drifted in and out of sleep, wiggling their numb toes to keep the blood flowing and to keep their mind off of how sleepy they felt.

Dae-Gun turned to his right where Iseul was nearly snoring. He wanted to laugh, make a joke of it, but he couldn't seem to make the words form in his mind as his tongue twisted before he could even open his mouth. *Strange,* he thought. It must be terribly cold, yet, he wasn't shivering.

Strange, Jung-Soo also thought as voices emanated from the radio speakers that seemed to have come alive on its own. Had he accidentally changed the radio station? He kept his eyes fixed on the unmarked road that led to the cave. A tree rustled but nothing was there, another twig broke but it was just a hedgehog, rising from its slumber to feed.

The white noise of the radio grew louder. Perhaps he was too tired to tell if it was actually the noise of plane overhead. He couldn't be sure so he pulled the speakers to his ears, leaning against them like a pillow until the weight of his head fell completely on it.

"Bear," someone said out of the speaker.

"Tiger," another voice responded.

Tiger? Jung-Soo thought. He'd better listen. If only he could keep his eyes open…

"Took you long enough."

"Yeah? What took you so long?"

He chuckled. "We're getting old, my friend."

"No, my friend, you are. I'm still in my prime."

It was so quiet. What happened to the gun shots and the shouts of men? Where had they all gone?

"Do you ever wonder if we're doing the right thing?"

"Wondering if maybe we took a wrong turn? All the time."

"What if we had it all wrong?" he said.

Jung-Soo tried to listen closely. Did he know the voices? It did sound familiar. Where was Dae-Gun? Why wasn't he saying anything about this weird conversation?

"We were so happy weren't we, fishing by the ocean and planning our next adventure."

"We really were."

"But we grew up and did what we had to do to survive. We couldn't stay young forever."

"Umm…" the voice pondered. "We were just…born before our time."

"I like that," the tiger chuckled. "Born before our time…" he seemed to question.

"Ah, my friend, I see now. I did my sons no favors. I should have lived as an honest man, teach them there is no such thing as a means to an end, *teach* them, no, *show* them how to live as the same man today and tomorrow," he spoke regretfully. "In any case, we are here, aren't we? At this crossroad..."

Crossroad? Jung-Soo thought. Fishing... all of it sounded so familiar.

"Have you done everything I've asked?" the bear asked, firm in his resolve.

"I tried."

"Then that's enough. I couldn't ask for more. Where is my son?"

"Guarding the tiger's cave, just as you've asked. You should be proud."

"I am. How is it with your father?"

He bellowed. "Not to worry, my father is taking good care of me and we're finally going on that father-son hike I've always wanted to go on with the old General."

The man on the other line paused. "Listen," he said. "I'm running out of fuel."

The line fell silent for a moment. "I understand. I wouldn't blame you if you choose your son over a friend."

"If I don't make it out alive..."

"I'm the one who's the living target here," he chuckled, awkwardly.

"I know, but you'll make it out alive. And maybe somehow, if someone else is listening... I want my son to know, it wasn't for the rice... it wasn't for the rice..."

"He knows."

"You'll tell him, won't you?"

"I'm sorry I wasn't able to tell him sooner. We weren't sure about your plans for the rice—about you. I should have known. I shouldn't have ever doubted you!"

The bear listened. He did not resent the tiger. No, not one bit. Hadn't he been there for him—for his son when he couldn't himself?

"I saw the two radio towers," the tiger continued. "I saw the road you paved with my own two eyes. How could I have been so blind?"

"You noticed?" the bear said, proudly.

"Of course!" he said, tinged with regretful recollection. "After hearing you all those nights, yammering on and on about the future of our country, and how we must be connected...You were certain that the fishermen in Mokpo would surely become brothers with the farmers of Yeoju when they finally got to taste their grilled fish paired with freshly harvested rice from Yeoju. How much more could we have done if the road leads North, connecting our brothers by sharing food and our rich resources, all joined together by trade routes? And to think we all thought the rice store was your legacy. There is more than what meets the eyes. I should have realized sooner. If only I had seen the radio towers sooner!"

"My legacy..." the bear said, nostalgically, almost as if he had given up on the notion. "A legacy that stored rice for the enemy and paved a way for them to invade our land." The words hovered in the sky like a vulture circling a carcass. "It's time, my friend, time to set things right."

Iseul had woken from her nap in a haze of drowsiness, almost drunk as if she had mistaken her father's rice wine for water. She could see two figures, slouched over their rifles and completely incapacitated. What had happened? She poked them with her elbow, tried to rise but swooned and fell on Dae-Gun.

"Ouch," Dae-Gun said, as he rose from his stupor. "What's happening? I don't understand..."

It must be the cave, Iseul thought. "We need to move away from here. The cave... something's in the air, it's making us..."

Iseul kicked Jung-Soo on the side, but he didn't budge. "Come help me," she said, as she grabbed onto Jung-Soo's left leg and beckoned Dae-Gun to help with the other.

But just as soon as they managed to inch him across the frigid forest earth, the eastern sky lit up in a cacophony of fire and light, the sound hitting them a second later with a force that stunned them in place.

Jung-Soo jumped up from the ground and pointed his rifle towards the light. He felt dizzy...so very dizzy... Why couldn't he focus? Where was that blinding light coming from?

"The bomb," Dae-Gun said. "It finally fell."

Right as Dae-Gun said those words, heavy artillery fired from below, directed at them from behind the bushes where the enemy laid hidden.

"Iseul, stay low!" Dae-Gun said as he jumped to tackle her to the ground. "Your white hanbok! You've just given them our location!"

Something other than Iseul and Dae-Gun's bodies fell to the ground. It was Jung-Soo with his rifle still held tightly in his embrace, blood oozing from somewhere.

"Owwww..." Jung-Soo whispered in a delayed response.

Iseul couldn't see where the blood was coming from. "Wake up, Jung-Soo, you can't just die on me!" She let her hands touch the blood on the ground, trying to trace it back to its origins. "Wake up, you fool, you promised…you promised you'd write me those letters. It's not your time yet, you hear?"

A voice was crying, but he couldn't quite recall whose it was or for what reason she was crying. He wanted to console her, tell her nobody is going to die today, but why couldn't he speak? Why couldn't he think?

In the darkness, Jung-Soo saw the first snow flake fall from the sky. The days and nights had been freezing; it was about time. The sky illuminated with a great ball of fire, or perhaps it was moonlight…yes, it must be the moon. The flake was soft, not cold to the touch as snow should be. Was this the way it all started—the first stages of death? It was too sweet, too alluring… No, he mustn't give in. The faint scent of someone he knew floated in the air around him—someone who would be so sad if he gave into the sweetness. Who?

"Jung-Soo," a familiar voice spoke in his ear. It was soft, almost warm like the snow that fell on his face. "Don't worry," it said, too kindly. "Leave Iseul to me. I'll take good care of her." *No*, he wanted to say. He would not give in so easily. He pried his eyes open and saw Yeong-Hoon with his arms wrapped around a girl in a white dress, dancing to the tune of death. The ghost of his mother joined in; she had come to take him home.

"But…but…" he managed to say with all his might. "I'm not done yet…"

"Shh, shh…" the voice hushed him, as it would a fussy child.

"No, listen! I'm not ready." He dug deep into his fast-fading memories, hoping to find anything, everything that would remind him of what he had been living for, as he painstakingly searched for something to hold on to.

And then it struck him. "I haven't even lived yet!"

The rice, Iseul. The memories came rushing back with the roar of pain. They were at war. Yes, he remembered now. Soldiers were dying all around him. The next second, a pain in his left leg seared as the terrifying screams of his own dying voice pierced his ears. "Take her away, you hear? Keep her safe!" he heard himself saying.

Where was Yeong-Hoon? He was just here, promising Jung-Soo he would take care of Iseul. Where was he? He tore his head from the ground and searched all around. Iseul was gone... That was a good sign, yes, he remembered. Yeong-Hoon had come to take Iseul away... far far away from this god-forsaken place where a bomb would soon take the rice and his pain away.

He was at peace now. The screams had stopped as he let the blood drain his consciousness away. He held onto a faint memory of a story—a legend perhaps of a bear and a tiger. What was it again? It was a good one, maybe just good enough to fall asleep to.

"My legacy...my legacy..." Jung-Soo kept saying, before giving into the sweet lull of sleep, like taking a nap under a pine tree on a bright summer day with no one to bother him or to wake him from his slumber.

CHAPTER 42

[Present Day]

"My legacy," Iseul said, drifting in and out of consciousness. She was by the ocean, praying to the waves as she threw her worries into the vast ocean to receive a token of peace that would wash in with the next wave.

Strange, she thought. This time, the ocean was calling for her. She had always known that when her time came, the ocean would call her home. Was this it?

"My legacy. It hasn't been written yet...I'm not ready." Somewhere in the deep crevices of her mind, she knew these words by heart. She had heard these words spoken to her once, but that was a lifetime ago.

Yeong-Hoon was a man of the sea. Those too were words that lingered somewhere, sometime. He had come for a brief moment, lured by the sound waves that reverberated from instruments and the radio, and by trees that whispered secrets the ocean did not hold. He had meant to leave but had stuck around for another decade, and then another, keeping his promise to an old friend about taking care of a young girl who had grown into her own and was now ready to come back into his embrace.

He was proud, so very proud.

The guitar sat lonesome by the bedside of an old lady. It had served its time, kept its owner company in the space between the high and low tides of life, heralding enough hope to endure both.

Iseul woke from her long nap, confused for a moment before setting her eyes on a familiar face. It was Yeong-Hoon, who squeezed her hand just hard enough to let her know he was there. With his other hand, he caressed her head and smiled the most welcoming smile meant to reunite long-lost friends.

She recognized that smile, but somehow it made her sad.

"I'm not ready yet," the words rolled off her tongue. She had said these words by the ocean, and by the tree where her parents were buried as her husband beckoned for her to come join him.

She was a child once again, running among the pine trees of the mountain where the scent of spring ushered new life and reinvigorated the mind. All at once, she was underneath the grandfather tree of the school yard, pacing towards the Golden Palace with the sun in her eyes, listening to the trickling water that turned the mill by the cabin.

What happened? She did not understand. Outside her window, dusk had filtered in the bright lights of skeletal buildings. There was once a man named Jung-Soo. He had made her so happy. But why did the bright lights make her feel so...guilty?

That's right, her eyes widened. They were supposed to grow old together in the cabin, making radios and guitars. They were supposed to write letters, make paper, rebuild...

Rebuild what? What was there to rebuild? Life had been perfect, just the way she had always imagined it.

An incense-like scent wafted into the room, a mixture of medicine, antiseptic and dying flowers. She knew where she was; the bright lights outside reminded her. She gazed at the hand that held hers and squinted at the face that looked into hers. Who was this man?

"It's me," the man said.

Who?

"Yeong-Hoon."

"Oh yes..." she said, looking into his face. But why did another name come to mind?

"It's me, Jung-Soo," the man said again.

Her brows furrowed. She knew the name—both names, but it did not seem to matter anymore.

"Have you come to take me away?"

He nodded.

"But I'm not ready. There is something I have to do… I just can't seem to remember…" Her eyes flickered, now more awake than she had been in a long while. "I've said this before, haven't I?" *That smell*, she thought. Where was she when she last breathed in this air? Where was she last before she had passed out?

She closed her eyes and she was in her mother's red hanbok. A little girl was on the back of an older boy, crying as they neared a cave.

"Oh yes, I remember," her eyes drifted. "I was that little girl." She was big and little at the same time, yes, that's why she fit into her mother's red hanbok. A ghost had appeared and bright lights blinded them, and then she was crying and running. Running…

"I remember," she said, breaking into slow sobs. "You were shot. The ghost shot you by the tiger's cave, and I ran. I ran to save myself!"

The man looked on with pity. How many times had he heard her say those same words? How much longer would she have to suffer?

"You promised me you'd send me all those letters, and I promised to make you that guitar," she said, regretfully. "There was rice. So much of it. Oh yes! We were supposed to rebuild our village, feed our neighbors, our children and grow old together. What happened, Jung-Soo?"

"Don't you remember?" the man said.

***

[December 1, 1950]

Iseul thought she heard the plane coming closer. Her hands were moist with Jung-Soo's blood, drying against the wind as she ran towards the soldiers. Where were they? Had they deserted them? *Please god…*

In an instant, the night plunged into pitch darkness as the roar of an engine was just above her head, blocking the crescent moon. She hit the ground and closed her eyes, certain that the bomb would drop directly above her. But when she opened her eyes again, the noise subsided as she saw the thing—a monstrous metal bird flying right past her. *Why didn't it bomb the cave?*

She didn't care. She leaped up and began running again. Jung-Soo was losing so much blood and they needed help carrying his limp body. *Please god*, she pleaded…

The plane was approaching again and Iseul thought she saw figures moving in the forest. But just as she was about to call for them, the ground shook below her, the night sky crashing into momentary daylight, brighter than the brightest day she had ever seen. A blast followed that blew her to the ground, the thundering crash of the bomb tearing into her eardrums. No…

***

Doo-Hyung replayed the look on his father's face when he saw him for the first time in over a year. *Not even a hello, or what are you doing in Yeoju?* The General had set up his headquarters at the Golden Palace where just hours ago, Jung-Soo had been reunited with Iseul. He didn't expect that sort of a reunion with his father, but this?

He knew his father well enough to know his military strategy: divide and conquer. He was exiled once again, away from where he could get in the General's way, assigned to lead a task force to find the rice store. His father had always underestimated him. He smirked; he knew just where to take his men.

Doo-Hyung and Gil-Dong reached the top of the mountain where two towers stood side-by-side, just as Jung-Soo had described. With a clay jar filled with rice wine he had found in an abandoned home, he plopped down and leaned against one of the towers. His men looked at him, astonished.

"What are you looking at?" he spited them. "Get a move on it!" He waved the Chinese soldiers away. The order was self-explanatory: venture the valleys surrounding the tower to find the rice store. The soldiers scurried away like scared mice.

Even in the dark, Doo-Hyung could see the hand of his deceased friend written all over the architecture of the towers. It was placed just below the pinnacle on the highest mountain in the vicinity, guising it within the pine trees that pointed upwards. He saw green lights blinking at the tip of the tower. Young-Nam used to say this would be the way of the future, where so many planes would fly overhead that they would have to avoid crashing into tall infrastructure. Blinking lights on top of mountains would be modern lighthouses that kept planes safe. He had always thought it was all farcical—the product of an imagination of a teenager who had been cooped up in a small fishing village for far too long. But

Young-Nam's intuition had been spot on, and even now, over a decade since they had left the fishing village, Doo-Hyung lived each day surprised by the next prediction that came true.

The radio tower was just one of the many ideas he had shared with him about the future: instant communication, roads that connected every village in the peninsula and funneled in and out like blood would to and from the heart in Seoul. Roads, trains, planes, trade routes, international trade and cooperation…

He finally opened his eyes and saw the village as his friend had meant for it to be. Doo-Hyung had always thought Young-Nam had exiled himself to Yeoju. On the contrary, he had great plans for this region that stood at the center of the peninsula—plans that were greater than the vast rice stores he had collected and plans that would outlive both of them, meant to create a better future for his last living son.

He sighed. Such a shame he died before his time. He missed his friend and mentor, but he had no time to grieve; others were counting on him. Jung-Soo needed more time, and soldiers deflected away from the cave.

With one last look around him, he turned the radio back on, hoping to eavesdrop on the battle that raged below. In a few minutes, his men would find the cabin in the valley and he would report to his father that he had found something that might be the rice store. Maybe the General would send another search party towards him. He took a gulp of wine and let it hit his stomach like an old friend as he sighed in satisfaction.

And then he heard it—the one voice he could never forget.

"Tiger," it said. It came from the radio.

Ham Young-Nam. He's alive? Impossible. He looked towards Gil-Dong who was staring back at him, wide-eyed.

"Tiger," it said again.

Doo-Hyung turned the volume up, and as surely as he had heard it the first time, he heard it again. "Tiger," He checked the channel. It was still to set the one Iseul had dialed for him. What was Young-Nam doing, hijacking the village channel?

He spoke into the microphone, "Bear."

"Tiger."

It really was him! But there had been so much blood. How did he survive? Doo-Hyung had so much to say—so much to ask, but over open radio? He was exhilarated; he was little kid again, and they were back in Mokpo, roaming the shorelines and stealing fish.

"Took you long enough."

"Yeah? What took you so long?"

He chuckled. "We're getting old, my friend."

"No, my friend, you are. I'm still in my prime."

He saw the shadow of the plane cast on the valley ahead of him. He looked up and saw the machine, small but sturdy-looking. It was exactly how they had imagined it, except he was supposed to be up there with Young-Nam, piloting the plane with lightning bolt yellow and black stripes painted on it. *Tiger.* He remembered the day they had argued about how the plane would look. Young-Nam had wanted it to be an obscured brown and green, like their military uniforms, but Doo-Hyung was adamant that mud brown would be the least threatening way to present the plane. Young-Nam liked the stealth; Doo-Hyung wanted to put the fear of god in anyone who saw the plane.

"But we grew up and did what we had to do to survive. We couldn't stay young forever," Doo-Hyung said.

"Umm..." Young-Nam pondered. "We were just...born before our time."

"I like that," he concurred. "Born before our time."

"In any case," Young-Nam said. "We are here, aren't we? At this crossroad."

The plane had flown overhead at least four times since he had first heard its engine roar. Doo-Hyung could guess what Young-Nam was planning. If Young-Nam had refurbished the plane as they had discussed in their youth, it would likely hold two small compartments just large enough to hold a few bombs at most.

They both knew what must be done. It was ingenious, living up to the grand schemes Young-Nam had always orchestrated—a plan to bomb multiple locations so as to disguise the real whereabouts of the rice. If it worked, it would require weeks of digging past heavy mountain rocks to attempt to find the correct store and would completely block off the entrance to the cave.

There was some guesswork to be done on Doo-Hyung's part. He could see the cabin in the valley from where he stood beneath the two radio towers. That would likely be hit. He was near—far too near for his liking, but it was a risk he was willing to take. The General knew Doo-Hyung was roaming the eastern mountains. He could only hope the bomb would send his father's troops here first.

The tiger guards his cave, as it guards its cubs.

Perhaps there was a heart in the old General that would be inclined to send his troops to save his son. He did not bank on it, though if the General himself came, he would be more than happy to take that hike with his old man.

He hoped Jung-Soo was listening in on them. If not, the first bomb would be a signal for Jung-Soo to run away from the cave.

"Listen," Young-Nam said. "I'm running out of fuel."

"I understand. I wouldn't blame you if you choose your son over a friend."

They spoke for a while longer, hoping Jung-Soo would come on at some point, but he didn't. It was only the bear and the tiger, scheming together as they once used to. Yet, the excitement of their youth had long since faded as they were left with the solemn reminder that perhaps, they had dreamed too big, and thought too far ahead for anyone else to follow.

"My legacy," the bear said. "A legacy that stored rice for the enemy and paved a way for them to invade our land… It's time, my friend. Time to set things right."

He hardly had time to respond. Before he knew it, a single bomb hit the lonesome cabin in the valley. Chinese soldiers screamed in agony, some set on fire as they ran towards the stream of water while others blindly ran into the trees. A small blaze took hold at the edge of the valley and began spreading into both mountains. The forest fire was headed straight towards Doo-Hyung and Gil-Dong.

"Come on, we've got to go!" Gil-Dong tugged hard on Doo-Hyung's sleeve as he stood half-drunk and immobilized by the chaos that unfolded beneath them. Doo-Hyung dropped the clay jar of wine and began running, the night air against his face clearing his mind. A few moments later, he heard the bang of the second bomb to his left.

The cave. Jung-Soo.

Half a minute later, a third bomb exploded less than a kilometer ahead of them. It was the west gate, completely obliterated. There was no way out in and out of the village now, not unless they knew about the hidden eastern road or hiked mountain routes back North.

He tilted his head towards the moon to see where the plane was headed next. Yet, nothing but the sliver of the crescent moon painted the night sky.

His heart plunged deep into his gut. That last explosion wasn't a bomb—it was the Young-Nam going down with his plane.

***

Sleep was so sweet, yet the warm soft snow had stopped falling from the sky.

"Jung-Soo, wake up!" It was a familiar voice that called.

His eyes seemed to weigh a ton as he forced them open. Blinding lights. But from where? To the east, it seemed. There was a plane; that much he could remember. He tried to sit up, blood pumping faster and harder as his sight momentarily blurred. Where was he?

Dae-Gun supported Jung-Soo's back, but a pang struck below his waist.

"Oww!" Jung-Soo said as he looked down. His left leg was on fire.

"Easy, easy, you've been shot in the leg. Don't be so dramatic, you'll live. Iseul went to get help," Dae-Gun said eagerly. The plane flew overhead again.

"Why isn't it bombing the cave?" Jung-Soo managed to say.

"I don't know, but we should be grateful," he said, as he inched Jung-Soo's dead weight away from the cave.

"We'd better hurry. The North Koreans are on our heels," Dae-Gun said, lifting Jung-Soo up by the shoulders. Jung-Soo breathed, holding in the pain as he clenched his jaw.

"Wait," he said. His voice was weaker than he thought. "The radio."

Dae-Gun grunted, placing Jung-Soo back on the ground before reaching to the ground where the radio had been by Jung-Soo's head.

"What happened?"

"I don't quite know. I heard voices and then Iseul got up and you were shot. We must have been breathing in something from the cave. It's a good thing we heard the first blast, or else we would have been goners."

The first blast. Yes, he could recall that. Jung-Soo looked to the east where a fire blazed into the night sky as smoke began to canvass the entire village. The plane. Where was it now? Who was on it?

"The voices," Jung-Soo said. "Who were they? What were they talking about?"

Dae-Gun tilted his head back and forth as they continued deeper into the southern mountains towards the road south. "I don't know. Something about a bear and a tiger. I thought it was a dream."

"No," Jung-Soo wracked his brain. He knew the voices. It was Doo-Hyung and...*impossible*. His father?

'My legacy... It's not about the rice... you'll tell him, won't you?... It's time to set things straight...'

The voices rang clearer. His father was alive and was here in Yeoju, overlooking the entire village on his plane! Hadn't he seen that same plane before in parts and pieces in the warehouse: a propeller here, a battery there, an oversized engine underneath a tarp?

He forced Dae-Gun to stop as he looked into the smoky night sky. Where was the plane now? He dialed the radio. Where was his voice? The plane came out of nowhere and flew close to the tip of the trees, as Jung-Soo and Dae-Gun hit the ground. The plane made a U-turn and flew away from them.

"Why didn't it bomb the cave?" Jung-Soo said.

"Come on! We don't have time to sit around and think." Dae-Gun pushed his weight on Jung-Soo, forcing him forward. Just as they made it to the nearest valley, the plane returned, this time landing a blow in the cave that sent shock waves down the mountain as Dae-Gun tumbled over Jung-Soo.

The plane flew out of the smoke and into the west skies.

"I can't believe it! That was my father!" He was suddenly gaining new strength.

"In the plane?"

Jung-Soo nodded. But why was the plane losing altitude? He squinted into the cockpit, but nothing but glass reflected off the window. Why wasn't he flying North? Jung-Soo knew why. Who would take him back in the North now that he had committed treason?

No... The stripped tiger flew straight towards the west gate, diving until it disappeared into the night horizon with a third blast, echoing throughout the Wasteland, ringing then ringing again.

"No!" The word was stuck in his throat as he groaned in an agony that immobilized him. A force kept pushing him forward, forcing him to turn his back on the plane that held his father. Who would be so cruel as to split a son from his father? Who?

"We have to keep moving," the voice said, firmly. "We have to find Iseul."

Jung-Soo could not hear anything but the ringing of the third explosion that kept his head turned towards the smoke that rose from west, another warmth spouting from eyes and spilling like hot blood against his face.

'Born before our time... I should have lived as an honest man...show them there is no such thing as a means to an end...'

His father's words rang with the echoes of the explosion—his father's last words.

What do you mean, father? There is no means to an end? I know father, I understand... Come back and tell me yourself. You can't just leave me, again...

'Live as the same man today and tomorrow...

I will, father. I will.

Jung-Soo's neck strained to watch as pillars of smoke canvassed his home.

But what was that falling from the sky? A body? Pieces of a house or a straw-thatched roof blown into the sky? He blinked, letting the warm tears follow the trails that had already been made.

The figure fell slowly, gracefully into the pillar of smoke in the west skies. *Father?*

Fly, yes, fly far away, Jung-Soo hoped. There was no place for his father in this Peninsula where mountains and sea trapped them in a cursed land. There was no place for him past the shores of his southern hometown that led to the shores of another enemy.

Fly far away, father. Past the west gate and then further, until the sea meets shore again, where you can live as the same man today, until you die an old man, warm in your own bed.

He felt light, as if he were walking on top of the pillar, waving his father goodbye.

Yet, he still hoped. He took the radio in a tight embrace. One day, he would hear his father's voice from a faraway land, and this time, he would recognize it. Yes, one day, they will be reunited.

***

Standing by the towers, watching the cabin burn, Doo-Hyung

knew what he must do. "Father," he spoke into the radio, "We found it."

It did not take long for him to respond. "Stand your ground."

General Shin knew what the final bomb in the west gate meant—the South Koreans wouldn't yield the rice without a fight. It didn't matter if he couldn't bring any more soldiers in; he had more than enough troops in his command to kill every last one of his enemies. He would carry the rice on his own back if it came to that.

A wall of Chinese soldiers followed behind Doo-Hyung as they faced another wall of South Korean soldiers ahead of them.

"Men, we stand our ground," Doo-Hyung said, as his father commanded, even as he hoped that the South Koreans would retreat to save themselves. They had done everything they could, and they could only hope Young-Nam had done enough to keep the rice stores undiscovered.

The fire encroached the mountain where the two towers stood testimony. His men were anxious, yelling something in Chinese he did not need to know the language to understand. A group of Chinese broke rank, running down the mountain and back into the frigid winter night, only to be met with the guns and scythes of the villagers at the east gate.

This is madness. Gil-Dong turned to Doo-Hyung. "Hyung," he said. "You're condemning your own men."

The old General had finally lost his mind! There was still time for their own troops to fight against the wall of American soldiers ahead of them, but no one could beat the inferno gaining on them from behind. The blaze left Doo-Hyung's back in a pool of sweat as he looked at his men standing in a long thin line horizontally, hoping their commander would soon come to his senses.

Doo-Hyung waved his hand forward. "Push forward men!" They gladly marched away from the fire. He could imagine the South Korean troops pooling towards the east gate to head to the road south so he marched his men North. That's where they all belonged.

"Father, we must retreat," he said.

"Stand your ground."

Did he not know that all that remained of the rice were ashes and a fire that will not stop until it consumed every last grain? He felt so helpless. His men paced north into the hills, as far as they could away from the fire while still holding ground.

There was no stopping the General; someone must convince him of his folly.

'It's time, my friend. Time to set things right.'

He heard the final words of his friend, echoing—insisting.

"Commander Ryu, take your troops North to the 38th parallel." Doo-Hyung shouted his command to the North Korean commander who looked hesitant, glancing west to see if the General would appear to give opposing orders. Doo-Hyung's words fell on deaf ears as the commander and his men stood ground with the roaring fire now close enough to singe their hairs.

***

Su-Jung could barely think straight, yet she heard the beating of the buk-drum that urged her forward. ONE, she marched. TWO, she raised her heavy arm to aim, THREE, she fired, a spark to light the cold night air. FOUR, she reloaded to begin again. The drums did what her voice failed to do—command her men to march forward.

Little did she know, it was Yeong-Hoon's drum that carried her men forward, hit at an offbeat by the scholar who knew little about how to hold a beat, let alone aim and fire.

Su-Jung's old man died with a smile on a face and a bullet in his heart. The scholar noted where he laid. He promised he would be back to bury him and the others.

"It's time! It's time!" A voice repeated amongst their own men until it reached the weary ears of Su-Jung and the scholar. "It's time… finally time."

***

[Present Day]

"Time for what?" Iseul asked, her voice failing.

"It was time to leave the village. Su-Jung, the villagers and the soldiers stranded in the village had fought so hard and for so long. The 18th Infantry and the 5th Cavalry had done all they could to give the women, children and the grandparents enough of a head start on their way south and it was their time to leave."

Iseul was confused, squinting hard to see the edges of the

man's face. Who was this man again, who so gently caressed her face and held her hand?

"Jung-Soo, remember? I'm Yeong-Hoon," the man said.

Oh yes, she had heard this before. Yes, she was sure.

"It's time to leave," the man said.

She knew this too. It was the call of a man who was there to take her away from all that she knew and loved. She resisted, turning her head away. "I'm not ready…"

The man did not force his way. "Don't you remember?"

"Don't leave me," Iseul said towards the window where the bright lights of Seoul kept her company.

She remembered…

Guilt struck the man as if no time had passed.

***

[December 1, 1950]

The shock waves of the bomb knocked Iseul over, though only for a second. She pushed herself back up and ran towards the light of the flame that guided her. Where are you, Jung-Soo? Please, please…

"Iseul," a voice called from behind. It grabbed her by the arm and pulled her away from the flame. It was Dae-Gun, but where was Jung-Soo?

"Don't worry. We managed to get out before the bomb dropped."

Iseul sighed as Dae-Gun led the way to where Jung-Soo laid.

She saw him lying on the cold floor, blood still oozing out of his left leg as he held the radio tight in his embrace. She ran and collapsed next to him.

"You idiot, you scared the living daylights out of me!" she said, beating her hand into his chest a little too hard. Jung-Soo clenched his jaw.

"I'm fine, you see! As good as new!" Jung-Soo said. He was glad the night was deep and they were far away from the fire. But it was getting so cold; he couldn't stop the shivering.

"You'd better be." Iseul choked on her own tears.

Dae-Gun raised Jung-Soo by his arm. "Help me lift him." Jung-Soo winced as Iseul took the weight off of his legs. How did Dae-Gun manage to carry him this far by himself?

"Listen, they're coming. Our troops and the rest of our villagers will be here before long and we need to make sure they can find the road back."

Jung-Soo was right. The fire was gaining on them from the cave and into the hillside road. The cave would be unrecognizable, and so would any landmarks that led up to the road. The radio fumbled against his shaky hands.

"Commander Lee, Commander Rogers, come in. Anyone?"

"Jung-Soo?"

"Yes, sir," he spoke in a bare whisper. "You've got to hurry sir. The roads are closing up because of the fire."

"Roger that. We're about twenty minutes out."

Jung-Soo was wheezing, his breaths short and weary. "We've got to find a way to signal which way the road is. Take Iseul with you," he said to Dae-Gun. "Find a path that hasn't been taken by the fire, but promise me you'll leave before the fire gets too close."

"I'm not going anywhere," Iseul insisted.

"She's right. We need to take you away from the fire first."

"No, we don't have time for that."

"We will have to make time." Iseul pulled him towards the main road faster as Dae-Gun followed her lead. Twenty minutes had come and gone as the three reached the path where the road began.

"Here. I'll wait for you here," Jung-Soo said. Iseul leaned him against a tree, making a rough patch of autumn leaves under him to keep him warm.

Dae-Gun took his coat off and blanketed Jung-Soo. "I won't be needing it where I'm going," he chuckled.

"Don't get too close to the fire."

"Let's go," Iseul said, not even glancing at Jung-Soo who searched in the darkness to see her face.

"Iseul…" Dae-Gun said, hoping she would oblige Jung-Soo, but she turned her back completely and marched back towards the path that lead to the burning village.

"Hang tight, Jung-Soo," Dae-Gun squeezed his shoulder one last time before jogging to catch up with Iseul.

***

"Sir, they're retreating!" The North Korean commander said to General Shin. "We did it, sir!"

"We did nothing," the General seethed as he climbed the mountain. "Don't be hasty." He waved his hand as the commander flinched and walked away.

The General's patience was wearing thin. He turned around as he recognized a face—one that had too much of his mother in him.

Doo-Hyung looked intently at the commander who nodded and turned back, the footsteps of thousands of soldiers guised by the roaring flames that crackled in loud bursts in trees that fell left and right.

Doo-Hyung pulled Gil-Dong next to him as if he were his little brother. Hadn't they become brothers by now?

"The commander will take the troops past the northern mountain ridges of Yeoju. Make sure he doesn't turn back," Doo-Hyung said as he tried to pull away, back towards the fire but Gil-Dong didn't let go of him. His stubborn silence had always found words for the boy. Doo-Hyung did not look back as he released himself from the boy's grip.

"Father," he called as he neared the unrelenting General. "Come, let me show you to the rice store."

It was the first time his son had shown him he was not a coward. Where had this son been his entire life?

"Soldiers, march with me. March to our victory and our survival!" The General spoke into the haze of smog and scorching fire to the phantom army. Here was a man who had never seen failure. Up toward the tower they marched where the fires had begun consuming the evergreen pine thistles, burning like incense that welcomed the coming death. It was the hike Doo-Hyung had been waiting for as a child in a fishing village of Mokpo, waiting for his father to visit him, to guide and share his life with his son.

"There." Doo-Hyung led his father towards the towers that were still visible. Reaching the pinnacle, they looked down into the valley below where half of the lonesome cabin stood, blown away by the bomb.

The General did not question his son; all he saw were the endless possibilities that were burning inside the cabin—of the war that could be won if they could manage to salvage the rice within. The longer they waited, the more they would lose. No matter—his men could take on the fiery army if he commanded them.

"Men, we go and retrieve the rice!" the General commanded, as he turned his gaze away from the cabin. Fire and smoke rose everywhere he looked, but where were his men?

"Traitors," the General growled into a shrill that echoed louder than the sound of falling trees. It stung in that secret place deep within Doo-Hyung—a sore he had been nursing his entire life. Knowing his father's disappointment would come did nothing to ease the pain.

"Father, we must retreat. There is nothing left for us here," Doo-Hyung said. It was the last duty he owed his father. He had not been the most dutiful son, he knew, but it was all he could muster.

Doo-Hyung knew his father wouldn't come, no, couldn't come. Whether it was his father's own pride, or the execution that awaited anyone who failed, Doo-Hyung could not be sure. He pictured his estranged brothers still in the North whose lives would be spared because of the General's honorable death in battle.

"No…no…no…" The General ran towards the abyss of the fiery den, though his body resisted against the heat. "Traitor!" he shrieked towards his son again as he reached for his holster. There was no gun there. Doo-Hyung had taken care of it while the General had been preoccupied on the hike up.

"Father, have you no pity on your son?"

He scoffed. "I'll have you hanged and stick your head on a spike as a lesson to all those who defy General Shin."

There was nothing more to be said, though Doo-Hyung hoped that he would see remorse or even a semblance of regret in the man through the fire that illuminated the night sky like day.

The last of General Shin's words fell on deaf ears as the crackling of wood had done just enough to ease the pain of having to listen any further.

I should have tried harder, Doo-Hyung would later regret.

He turned his back and began his trek down, the heat beating on him on all sides. He did not seem to care too much, though the thought that it was winter and the world below was frozen solid did occur to him. It wasn't until he saw a figure hovering in the smoke and moving towards him that he was startled back to his predicament.

"Hyung! Hyung!" the ghost-like figure yelled. It was Gil-Dong. At least it was his voice.

"What are you doing here? It's dangerous." Doo-Hyung paced, then broke into a sprint down the mountain.

"I came to check, just in case you did something…stupid."

The boy had been right. He ruffled his hair. "Why would I? Let's get out of here. What about the others?"

Gil-Dong had the biggest grin Doo-Hyung had even seen on the boy. "Not to worry! The commander is taking the Chinese troops into the northern hills. It'll take a few more days but they'll be back in North Korea safe and sound!"

"Good," Doo-Hyung said, though he let his eyes briefly drift back up the mountain, hoping to see his father, but that is not how history records that day. The General burned to ashes, consumed by the *han* of generations of men and women who had died long before their time, fighting for their land—fighting for what is rightfully theirs.

***

Jung-Soo drifted in and out of consciousness, his head tilted towards that narrow path, hoping to see or hear anything that might resemble a young girl in a white dress. He chuckled at the thought of the girl who had turned her hanbok inside out. Only Iseul would believe such a ludicrous idea would help, and he had been shot because of it.

He reached into his inner layer of clothing and ripped a piece to wrap around his left leg. He winced with the pressure, wondering if he would ever walk again. Maybe he wouldn't even survive the night, which meant becoming a cripple would be the least of his worries. Was it midnight yet? Had he made it to the next day?

And then he witnessed it, an army of angels in white who rose from the smoke and walked towards him. Could it be? No, it did not seem possible. Yet, he could hear the cheerful chatter of men, and the smell of smoked pine thistles coming his way.

"Jung-Soo!" A white figure ran towards him.

"Iseul?" Jung-Soo whispered.

"No, boy. I'm your commander." Jung-Soo blinked once more and he saw Commander Lee, joined promptly by Commander Rogers and a group of familiar faces—Mr. Lim, Mr. Seo, the farmer, and even Dae-Gun, who stood in front of him, all dressed in white.

"The boy mistakes me as a girl!" he bellowed. The others joined in the laughter, though Jung-Soo blinked again and again to find that one familiar face he had been waiting to see.

"Looking for me?" Iseul said, as she appeared from behind

Dae-Gun's large frame, dressed again in her red and green hanbok, her hair raised in a bun as if she hadn't just emerged from a village in flames, except for—

"Your face," Jung-Soo said, cringing.

"What? What about my face?" Iseul said as she rubbed her cheeks. It was covered in soot, her ash covered hands coating her face in another layer of grey and black.

"It's fine," Jung-Soo said.

"When did she get changed?" Dae-Gun said, scratching his head. "We all had to take a few layers off to cover our faces when we went through the fire."

"The flames singed half my hair off!" Iseul whined.

The sun seemed to be rising upon the road they were about to take. Jung-Soo had lost track of time and thought dawn wouldn't come for a while. He was glad. It seemed the worst was over.

***

[Present Day]

"Was it?" Iseul asked.

"Was what?" the man said, confused.

"Was the worst over?

"Impatient as always," the man by Iseul's bed chuckled. "I'm getting to that part." For a moment, the man saw the look of innocent realization in the old lady. "Are you ready?"

Iseul nodded, like a child waiting for the next part of the story.

***

[December 2, 1950]

"One more day," Jung-Soo muttered to himself.

"Huh?" Iseul said. She had insisted that she would be the one to carry Jung-Soo, but it was Dae-Gun who caved first, saying he was too tired to carry him, and they'd better let the others help out. They walked together on the path that Jung-Soo's father had paved.

It had worked out, hadn't it, father? The road you meant to unite Korea had united us, Jung-Soo thought. He looked around and saw men and women, American and Korean, speaking in two tongues as they joined together in one spirit. Even as he scanned the crowd, he knew that many more had not made it out alive. There was still one thing left to do.

Hours had passed and the sun had given the travelers enough warmth to keep at a decent pace. They eventually came at the crossroad that connected Young-Nam's road with the west road the 18th Infantry and 5th Cavalry had been on.

Shouts were heard from afar, stirring the soldiers into panic, before realizing they came from the villagers who had left earlier. A few had been waiting at the fork in the road, hoping the rest of the villagers would emerge from Young-Nam's road.

"Mr. Lim!" Mi-Jung yelled. "You made it!"

Her mother hushed her daughter, likely telling her that a lady mustn't be so loud and crude and that she must think of the others.

Tears of joy accompanied the mourning of those who had lost their fathers and husbands. The scholar—where was he? His wife stood by the road, waiting, still hoping that her husband would emerge from the crowd of unfamiliar faces.

Jung-Soo and Iseul watched on, their minds wandering back to the village where the scholar, the old man and her daughter Su-Jung had fallen. Soldiers and villagers alike assembled in the fork, gathering leaves and wood to build a fire, cooking rice to celebrate their survival.

Dae-Gun came to share his portion, though Jung-Soo shooed his friend away as he was happily spoon-fed by Iseul instead.

"I can't wait to be old so you can feed me every day," Jung-Soo joked.

Iseul shoved the spoon a little too aggressively. "Just shut up and eat, will you?" she said. Even through her soot-covered face, a blush came through. "Seems you've been faking how sick you are, considering how lively your mouth still is!"

In truth, Iseul's noon-chi had kicked in as she sensed the dreaded conversation was looming. She fed Jung-Soo another spoonful even before he had swallowed, until the bowl of rice porridge was empty and Iseul's stomach still growled. She had barely had any herself.

"Let me get another bowl," Iseul said, getting up as quickly as she could.

But Jung-Soo grabbed a hold of her. "Iseul."

She breathed deeply, knowing the time had come. "I know, you need to leave. You don't want to, I mean, who in their right minds would want to leave someone like me, right? But I understand.

You've got to finish what you've started, make your father proud and start fresh as a new man."

He waited until the tidal wave of her words stopped. "We'll meet again," Jung-Soo promised. "We'll come back to our village, rebuild it again, get married and grow old together."

Iseul nodded. "We'll plant the entire mountain with pine trees and build the most spacious workshop I could ever dream of, with all the special tools to make instruments. You'll be there, right next to me."

Jung-Soo smiled. The conversation they had had in the school shed came to mind. They were so young and full of hope. "I'll be there next to you," he promised.

"Remember what you said in the school shed?" Iseul asked.

Jung-Soo remembered fondly as Iseul quoted his words back to him.

"Iseul, that day is coming! The world is changing as we speak, and you and I can soon dream all we want!"

The words rang like a long lost dream, recalled by sheer force of will.

"Not yet," Jung-Soo said. "But soon."

Iseul nodded. "Soon."

There were no tears or any show of emotion. So much had been lost that day that Jung-Soo and Iseul's temporary goodbye felt full of hope. In that fork in the road, they waved, not to each other, but each to the soldiers and villagers who had made their hopeful farewell possible.

Iseul left Jung-Soo's side and walked up to Dae-Gun, whispering something in his ear before taking her place next to Mi-Jung and the other villagers.

"What did she say?" Jung-Soo asked Dae-Gun who walked towards him with a huge grin that hung from ear to ear.

He shook his head. "I can't tell you! That's between me and Iseul," he said.

"No fair, she's my girl!"

"You sure about that?" Dae-Gun joked to a gravely serious Jung-Soo. He gave Jung-Soo an apologetic smile. "She told me to make sure I remind you every day about how lucky you are to have a friend like me."

From afar, Jung-Soo saw Iseul giggle at his expression. Jung-Soo wasn't quite sure if those were the exact words Iseul had whispered in his friend's ear, but it was enough to whet his curiosity.

You just wait! When I get back, I'll ask you myself and we'll see who's laughing then.

Eyes lingered on the unknown road that led to a small rice-farming village only known as the Wasteland. Mr. Lim knew there was nothing left for him there. His son was dead, his house gone, and his friends scattered across the Peninsula. It would be another three decades before he would bury his son in his heart and begin to find happiness elsewhere.

Jung-Soo, Iseul, and Dae-Gun looked down the road, past the village towards the northern mountains. Doo-Hyung and Gil-Dong were brothers in a different uniform and no outcome of the war would change that. In those final moments as they looked down that road, they did not doubt that they would meet again, once all was said and done.

Yet, moments of hope rarely come to pass. Decades later, on those long nights they would shudder awake from nightmares of a war long past, they would lay still in bed, wondering if the others were still alive and if they still remembered their brothers and sisters across the border of the 38th parallel.

CHAPTER 43

[Present Day]

It was mid-November when I woke from an oddly fresh night of sleep as I stood in front of my bedroom window, fully awake and ready. I blinked twice and got into my uniform. My skirt had seen better days, as did my button-up shirt, but so did everyone else's. We had all outgrown it, much to the satisfaction and distraction of teenage boys who took a slight to the raised skirts and shirts that wore tighter than it had earlier in the year.

Throughout the years, I noticed a strange trend in the weather in the week before and after the National Exam. Every year, during this time, the temperature would drop at least five degrees, enough to warrant the changed title from autumn to winter. Never mind the uniform; I had set aside a thicker coat for the day of the exam and it had finally come without a hitch, along with the colder weather I had predicted.

The past month had been spent in a haze of revision and lack of sleep. Even the sharp edges of stress had completely disappeared in the past week when all seemed to be lost. Perhaps the only other change that could account for my rather chirpy disposition was the fact that I had gotten eight hours of sleep last night, still an hour less than the total number of hours I would spend in the exam halls.

I am happy to report that I survived the national exam. It was not fun; no, it was intoxicating. In fact, I don't remember much of the day except for filling in way too many answer bubbles. Mi-Na and I had spent the evening on the phone, exchanging answers to tricky questions and inhaling a large spread of pork-belly barbeque and my favorite kimchi-stew. It didn't taste quite right, not like the way granny used to cook it, but my taste buds were shot with euphoria to know the difference.

There would be three weeks of blissful waiting until the results would be in. I knew I was a lost cause even before I had gone in to take the exam, perhaps even earlier in the year when I allowed my preoccupations with my granny's past to get in the way. It all seemed like a lifetime ago. I knew my results would get me into a university somewhere in the country; in fact, my grades usually split the class in the middle. And as statistics show, if you're not in the top five of your entire class of hundreds, you couldn't dream of getting into a school within Seoul. Really, there was no point in trying so hard once I realized I wouldn't be going to a university worth mentioning.

A week had passed and a few students didn't show up to class. Rumor has it that Seok-Jun had to miss class for a psychiatric evaluation, while another student dropped out of high school just weeks before graduation to enter into mandatory military service. It was a shame. I had liked that boy and for a while, I wondered why he would do such a thing, but eventually shrugged it off.

Mi-Na and I went on a shopping spree, spending every last crisp bill we had been given from our elders last Chuseok on winter coats that looked slimming, but would soon be obsolete once the temperature reached below zero. I shrugged that off too, spending our last few bills on a fancy dinner of king crab I had always wanted to try.

It was the first of December, marking the final month of an excruciatingly straining year. Aunts and uncles began calling mom, prying to see how I had done and with no more money to spend, I was forced to lie in bed, overhearing her trying to make up another excuse as to why the results might not be so promising.

What had happened to my resolve to earn what I could to help with tuition? Gone—down the pipe with the last meal I had. I sighed. What was the use? Tuition would be a waste of money. I wanted to try to convince mom, but I already knew she would hear no such thing. Mother seemed to have evaded the topic of my exam marks and moved on to my father's forced retirement. That day would come before the year is out, and then mother would again fixate on my university admissions, reminding me of how lucky I would be to get a job that was half as good as the one father used to have.

My mind wandered to the soldier from America, Richard Martin, if anything just to keep my mind away from the phone conversation in the other room. There were questions left unanswered, and perhaps they were better left that way. *Jung-Soo*, I whispered to myself, hoping it might churn something in me. It did and I did not like the feeling. With just a week before my exam results would be announced and with just a few more weeks to apply for university, the idea that someone in my family was implicated in a communist massacre of so many civilians and soldiers felt like an omen of misfortune that would make me second guess myself every wrong turn I took.

So, with the last few bits of change I had left in my savings, I jumped out of bed and snuck out of the apartment, heading straight towards the subway station. I put the rest of my money into topping up my transit t-money card and hopped on the next train headed east.

Had I known granny would be dead in a few hours, I probably would have taken the bus to the nursing home to read the letter to her one last time; but like most things in life, hindsight is 20-20.

Transferring onto line four, I got off at Dongjak station just twenty minutes since I had first boarded. I knew where the National Cemetery stood but hadn't gotten to visit it yet. Somehow, I had missed that field trip every Korean took as an elementary student and never thought to visit it on my own time. Typical Seoulite.

It was probably the first place I should have visited, but I had decided to go to Yeoju and scour the internet first. Maybe I just didn't want to see dead people.

The subway burst into the outdoors and we were on the bridge crossing the Han River. The sunset splashed yellow and orange on every inch of the water, along with the windows of high rise buildings casting their spectrum of light. It was a typical view of Seoul. I was still drunk with the scene when the subway door opened. It was my stop.

The cemetery was just a quick five-minute walk from the station. It was a weekday so not many people roamed the premises other than a few older women, most of whom looked like my grandmother. There were rows and rows of identical tombstones; it was a wonder that these old women could find the right one. But they did, and they placed flowers by their loved ones and picked weeds off of the surrounding grass.

There was no reason for me to be there. Grandpa's lot had been forfeited since granny decided she would take his body to Yeoju instead. I wondered which one might have been his.

With the sun in my face, I slowly drifted towards the Memorial Tower I had seen on television each year. It seemed oddly barren without the flowers and flags of countries that had fought alongside South Korea. Apparently, flags and flowers were only erected every year on the 25th of June to commemorate the Korean War as a flood of foreign veterans would visit Korea for what might be their second and last time on the peninsula. Even to this day, every year in June, I'd watch the ceremony on television, imagining Mr. Richard Martin amongst the crowd of foreign veterans.

When I got bored of the tower, I walked back to the tombstones, wandering between and around each, whispering the names etched on the marble just loud enough to avoid people looking at me and thinking I had gone insane. Nothing really changed; they still remained a sea of faceless names of a time that seemed to have no relevance to my life.

I wandered towards the Memorial gate, my feet taking me where my subconscious told me to go. I took one last look at the place. I decided I liked it without the frills they attached to it to make it look presentable on television. This would be the cemetery I would remember, not the colorful one I would see each year in June.

The road quickly turned to asphalt as I was on the pedestrian walkway next to the highway under another highway bridge on one of the busiest four-way intersections in Seoul. The subway entrance was just visible to my left. It was close, but I had to cross two intersections to get to it and it seemed my feet were not willing to wait for the stoplight to turn green. Instead, I continued where they led me, straight on without rest until the same burst of yellow and orange lights hit me. I was standing on the bridge of the Han River.

The Han River was glorious throughout the year, but more so in the summer when water sports were visible on every river bed, as couples and friends alike laid picnic blankets to eat the national snack of spicy fried chicken and beer. December did not allow such scenic luxuries other than the occasional cruise ship filled with tourists that drifted on the waters.

As surely as summer turned to winter, the day turned to night and the light that reflected off the water became a subdued yellow that spoke of regrets, failing to live up to the blinding lights of the day. I saw the river as it was—a greedy bowel, ready to swallow the bodies of men and women alike.

I felt a hand lay on my shoulder. It was a woman around my mother's age. "Are you alright, my dear?" she said with a deep and concerning look.

I smiled. "Yes, isn't it a beautiful day?"

She seemed to be satisfied with my answer. She reached for my hand and gave it a tight squeeze before she went on her way.

I can only recall a handful of times a stranger came up to talk to me. I saw myself through the woman's eyes: here was a teenager in a school uniform, looking over the side of the bridge. She must have thought I was going to jump. It was so common that it happened every year across many of the bridges of the Han River. I remembered the story of a boy five years my senior who had jumped from our school rooftop to his death. He was my age when he had jumped.

I had thought about it in the year leading up to the exam. *Suicide.* It certainly seemed alluring, until I began thinking about how my parents would take the news. Mom and dad never seemed to talk much to each other; it was clear that I was the glue that kept them together. They say marriages don't last when a child dies and I liked seeing them together. They were all they had in the world, and I would be lucky if I could find someone who would weather the years with me when my time came.

I began walking again. The last thing I wanted was for some stranger to call the police on me. I looked further out into the water as I walked, viewing the other bridges on the Han. One of them was called the 'suicide bridge' where over a hundred souls in a span of five years attempted to ease their pain by jumping. One of the companies owning a skyscraper overlooking the bridge decided it might help the cause by putting up signs of encouragement.

"You're tired, aren't you?" One sign read.

"Do you have a secret?"

"Look into the blue sky."

"What kind of father will your child remember?"

Our parents held the weight of the world on their shoulders. Knowing that, there was no way I could do such a selfish thing as suicide. I know some kids did it to spite their parents for being so overbearing. Compared to that, I knew I had it a lot better. Perhaps

I wouldn't go to the best university compared to these kids whose parents pushed them, but at least I didn't hate them for it.

At the end of the day, we grew up with the realization that they did it for our own good. They do it so we will not have to—my dad worked twelve-hour shifts so I would not have to when I grew up, my mother took on extra responsibilities so that I wouldn't grow up to become a tired working mom like she was. They were all sacrifices made so we could have a better life they couldn't ever dream of having themselves.

I wonder if they knew this is how their lives would turn out to be. They were once young too, full of hopes and dreams of a better future. My mind's eye returned to the tombstones of faceless soldiers who had died fighting, but for what? For this future? For the future that was set before me?

It was not a reassuring thought. The glass orb of my childhood was breaking already and I was afraid. There was no place for me in this world. Best case scenario, I would find a job like my father and I'd tell my boss that I'd be happy to work weekends and twelve-hour shifts, cleaning the company halls and shuffling coffee to my superiors. I'd be lucky if I snagged a guy—any guy who could hold down a job for the family and for the future of the children.

A train whizzed past me. It was the one I had taken on the way to the cemetery. My legs were getting tired and my eyes wandered back to Dongjak station. It was quite far away now and I probably would be closer to the next stop. I looked for a bus stop but realized more cars were on the road now. Rush hour would soon come and no bus could take me home faster than the subway. I pushed forward.

Trains and subways. They were the jewels that marked South Korea as a first world nation, cheaper, faster and cleaner than any other city in the world. But as cheap as they were, mother always seemed to walk to work or avoid taking the subway too often. Bullet trains are oddly expensive, considering how cheap the subway trains are. That was the reason I took the bus to Yeoju, instead of Korail. I knew a bullet train existed that could take me from Seoul, through the tunnels in the mountains of Yeoju all the way down to Busan and Mokpo, the two major southern cities to the east and west, in just about four hours. Four hours! What my ancestors would give to travel so quickly! I remember hearing some old folks complain about how they used to walk for weeks, just to make it to their hometown in time for the annual chuseok and seolnal celebrations.

My dad had once said if South Korea were reunited with North Korea, one of the perks would be that we would finally be able to put down railway tracks so that we would be connected to the Eurasian Continent by land. Of course, none of us really wanted reunification; the logistics alone were daunting and the ones who had family in the North had mostly died off.

I remember when I had a streak of enthusiasm to learn English. The plan was to read one news article a day and that was when my anxiety kicked in. It seemed every other week, North Korea hit the headlines and then it dawned on me—we lived just an hour away by car from North Korea! I told my dad we had more important things to worry about than putting railway tracks down in North Korea. They were building missiles for god's sakes and nuclear ones at that!

"One of these days, they will launch one successfully," I'd say to my dad.

Sometime after that, I got busy and stopped reading western news and realized I no longer cared about North Korean missiles. To be honest, until a missile flies over Seoul and fell on one of our buildings, I don't think any of us would bat an eye. Besides, we'll all be dead if they were nuclear ones, so we wouldn't even know what hit us.

I finally reached the next subway station: Ichon. Who was I kidding thinking about reunification, nuclear missiles, and bullet trains? Such idle thinking was for the rich who had all the time and money in the world to think and ponder about what ifs.

Panic. All this thinking…it was no good.

On the platform, a tune rang, informing me that the train was approaching. Twenty minutes. That's all I had before I'd be home. But I wasn't ready. I wasn't ready to feel the overbearing look of my mother.

It then hit me—I was done with the exam! I didn't need to study anymore! Mother didn't need to give me that disappointed look anymore.

But then the same realization bulldozed over me as would a bullet train that came out of nowhere: I was done with the exam. My life would soon begin. I had but a few years before I really had to worry about holding down a guy or a job but right now, what I really needed was a time turner to go back a few months and tell myself study. I would scream at my past self that my grandmother's mysterious past could wait, but university and the future of my well-being couldn't!

I wasn't ready…not yet…

The train halted and opened its doors, ready to swallow me whole.

***

The man still held granny Iseul's hand.

"I'm not ready," she said again.

He nodded. He knew, but after years of asking and telling her the story of her life time and time again, he had yet to figure out what would make her ready. He missed her; he yearned to hold her in his arms again.

"What happened to the rice?" she said, still avoiding eye contact as she looked into the bright lights outside.

The man wanted to talk about something else. "Iseul," he whispered in her ear. "Why do you like the night lights?"

She turned back and looked at him, confused. "What do you mean? Of course, I like the lights."

"Of course, you do," he said. He didn't push.

"Why do I like the lights?" she muttered to herself. "Do you know why I like bright lights?"

He shrugged. "I have my theories."

"And…" She was looking at him again and that made him happy.

"I used to lay in my garden at night, sleeping under the stars. You caught me in the act a few times. I think the buildings remind you of the stars."

"Oh yes," Iseul said as if recalling something vaguely important. "I think I used to do that too. It was a summer night and I was waiting for you to come home."

"Yes, you were waiting for me that night."

But Iseul couldn't piece together what had happened next. Her brows furrowed as she waited for the next part of the story. They had come full circle, and the man knew the time had come once again to tell that part of the story.

"So, did you? Did you come back?" Iseul said, impatiently. "Of course, you did. You're here with me now," she concluded.

***

[July 27, 1953]

There was no place Iseul went without the radio by her side, and it was all well and good since an important announcement had come on as the women and children gathered around.

"Stop calling us women and children," Mr. Lim protested. "We're old but we're still men!" The grandfathers of Busan's Refugee Shelter had also joined in the gathering.

"The Armistice Agreement has finally been signed in Panmunjom. U.S. Army Lieutenant General William Harrison, Jr. did the honors in representing the United Nations Command as the North Korean General, Nam Ill represented the Korean People's Army and the Chinese People's Volunteer Army. The Armistice signifies that all parties will ensure a complete ceasefire of all hostilities until a more permanent settlement of peace can be agreed upon in the coming days."

My dear readers, as history records, a permanent settlement of peace has yet to be achieved.

"All that fighting and bloodshed for nothing!" Mi-Jung said. "They've drawn the line at the 38th parallel again. We haven't won an inch more land in three years of madness!" She had lost her home, the man she was betrothed to and her mother on the road south from the evacuation.

Mr. Lim couldn't agree more. Hadn't he lost his son? Yet, he was still eager for the days of violence to be over—eager for the days when people would leave the refugee camp, instead of flooding in. Young-Nam used to talk about retirement, somewhere in one of the southern islands where the ocean can be seen from every angle. Fishing. That's what he'll do. He'll die an old man, fishing.

"What are you going do now?" Mi-Jung turned to Iseul who was already packing her rucksack with the few bits of clothing she had, turning the radio off and packing that too.

She smiled. "Going home," she said. "I have a promise to keep." She began a brisk walk towards the northern entrance of the refugee camp.

"Wait," Mi-Jung said as she too began gathering her belongings. "So soon? What about all the others? What about our paper production?"

Iseul took one last look at the makeshift paper factory she had set up at the refugee camp. The production in Busan had been at least twice the size of the one she had set up in her family workshop, creating an output far greater than they could have managed in Yeoju. Pages of hanji paper were strewn all around the tent, along with bamboo filters, clay pots, and bark barely lifted from their mulberry trees.

She was grateful. Making paper had given her something to do to keep her mind off of the hunger and late nights lying awake, worrying for the men at war—worrying about Jung-Soo. But it was time. Two and a half years of making paper in Busan was more than enough for a lifetime. And Yeoju was beckoning her home.

Besides, she had been itching to get back to the workshop to get her hands on some good quality wood to begin Jung-Soo's guitar. She was ashamed to say that she had put it off, though it had been because wood was precious and old women were dying left and right because of the lack of firewood.

"We won't be needing paper anymore," Iseul answered Mi-Jung's question. "The war's over." She strapped her father's carving knife on her right ankle and the gun on the other.

"Then why do you need that for?" Mi-Jung pointed at the gun.

Iseul shrugged. "Force of habit."

The little ones were the first to hear the news of Iseul's departure as they ran towards the North Entrance to bid her goodbye. She waved to her heart's content, each wave a blessing on the orphans and fatherless children as she wished them a long, healthy and peaceful life.

"Wait!" Mi-Jung ran towards the sea of children, trying not run them over. "I'm going with you."

"Took you long enough!" Iseul put her arms around Mi-Jung's shoulder and squeezed tight.

"Only because you were in such a hurry. Forgetting something?" Mi-Jung said, holding up a packet of what looked like fat envelopes held together by string.

"Jung-Soo's letters!" Iseul said, grabbing them and holding it in her embrace. "I can't believe I almost forgot about them!"

Iseul and Mi-Jung walked for two weeks, stopping by rivers and taking the hillside roads as hungry men and newly discharged soldiers roamed the villages. The two women changed into farmers' clothes and had cut their hair to disguise themselves as boys. Iseul imagined what it might have been like for the two Korean soldiers delivering letters through mountainous routes in the dead of winter. It was hard enough in the summer.

"Hungry?" Iseul asked as she held out a sock filled with rice.

"Where did you get that?"

"Rice from the tiger's cave. I saved some, just in case."

They ate as much as their stomachs could handle, perhaps a little bit more, but only because the stars were bright and hopes were high.

"I still imagine our village as it used to be before the war."

"I do too," Iseul said. Although in her nightmares, it was always blazing in a fire that would never cease. Best case scenario, the village would be intact, but there would still be bodies rotting where they fell on that night they had escaped. They were going to rebuild it, make it better than it had been before. That much was certain.

"You reckon we can find the same road that leads to the east gate?"

Iseul had to think about it. "Probably not. It was fairly dark when we left and I don't think the same landmarks will be there." She could tell Mi-Jung was a bit disappointed, if only for the extra day of hiking they would have to do.

They pushed harder that final day, hiking all day and all throughout the evening, urged on by the rice paddies of Yeoju that welcomed them home. It was nearly midnight when the west gate appeared before them underneath the light of the full moon. Iseul couldn't believe it. They were finally home!

Mi-Jung broke into a sprint. "We're here!" she said.

Iseul wanted to tell her to be quiet—that they didn't know who lived in the village anymore or whether it was even safe. But as she entered the rugged west gate, the village stood at a peaceful stillness. It was as if the farmer, Mr. Kim were still living in that house closest to the gate—as if he and his son were sleeping in there and hadn't gone off to war.

But where were all the bodies? Hadn't the battles begun right where they were standing?

"Come on!" Mi-Jung waved her over.

"Where are we going?" Iseul said, dazed.

"The Golden Palace, of course."

The Golden Palace? "Why?"

Mi-Jung shook her head, frustrated. "Aren't you seeing what I'm seeing? There are obviously people who live here since the place has been cleaned up. I'd bet you, we'd find the person responsible in the Golden Palace."

Of course! She paced to keep up. But what were they to do? Barge into the halls of the Golden Palace and wake whoever was inside? Who knew who was occupying the place, or if they were even friend or foe? And even if the occupant intended no harm, she couldn't imagine anyone responding peacefully to an intruder in the middle of the night.

But before she could voice her concerns to Mi-Jung, they were standing in front of the steel gates of the Golden Palace. She had forgotten how small her village was. Memories flooded of the first day she had met Jung-Soo. It was also the day he had held her hand in a lingering handshake. She blushed. *That sly Jung-Soo! I'll have a stern word with him once he gets back.*

Yet, it didn't occur to Iseul until that moment that the person occupying the Golden Palace may be the very person who owned it. Jung-Soo? Perhaps. The war had been over for two weeks and Jung-Soo had been stationed closer to Yeoju than she was. And who would take the time and effort to clean the village up if he wasn't once a villager himself? Her heart seemed to beat out of her chest.

"You don't think maybe…" Iseul wanted Mi-Jung's reassurance, but she just gave a blank stare.

"We should probably wait till morning," Mi-Jung answered.

"Yes…" her voice already drifted into the halls against her better judgment. "We probably should."

Mi-Jung led the way back out of the Golden Palace and entered into one of the abandoned homes. It was Mr. Park's old home where he raised two daughters. Iseul and Mi-Jung wondered whatever happened to them, or whether they would be coming home anytime soon.

All night, Mi-Jung's gaze drifted east until she fell asleep, no doubt thinking of her old home that also doubled as the village's only restaurant. She would soon be home, but not tonight. Iseul could tell she wasn't ready yet, not when she had left her mother's body by a tree, unable to bury her.

It wasn't long before Mi-Jung's heavy breathing filled the small room. Yet, Iseul was restless, just lying there, turning on the mattress far thicker than the floor she had gotten used to over the years. She kicked the blanket aside and reached for the letters in the rucksack that leaned against the thin wall.

She began with the first, as she always did.

"My dearest Ji Iseul, I am sorry. I wish I had something better to say. If this letter doesn't reach you, it saddens me to think that you'll remember me as a traitor."

It was written on the night Jung-Soo had disappeared to become a soldier. It was also the night she had lost her father. Her mind wandered to her ancestral grave where her parents were buried. It was so near, yet so far. She wasn't ready yet. Just like Mi-Jung, she wasn't ready to meet her parents yet.

Iseul sighed. What was she doing in the middle of the night, reading letters underneath the moonlight when the person who wrote it might be sleeping in the house next door? Hadn't they been apart long enough?

Iseul crawled from the mattress towards the sliding doors, careful not to let the old wooden floors creak. Mi-Jung tossed but eased into her sleep again as Iseul took in that silent midnight air of her hometown. It was as if she were back at home, waking in the middle of the night to go to the workshop to craft her instruments. That time may soon be returning.

She paced down the road she had walked on hundreds of times before as she neared the gates of the Golden Palace. Her breathing quickened. This was a bad idea; she was sure of it. She needed to wait a bit longer, at least until the sun rose, or at least think about what she was about to do.

A patch of enticing green grass called for her. It was the same patch of grass Jung-Soo would often lay on as he gazed into the night sky. Iseul took her place, digging her back into the soft grass that pulled her close into its embrace as if welcoming her home. She heard herself humming a tune she had forgotten in the years she had been away as peace was taken from her. It was as if her mother was singing to her from her grave and the song traveled through the fresh summer night's breeze, lulling her to sleep. She slept with a heart so content and hopeful that for the first time since the war had begun, she felt as if all would be alright.

Iseul squinted as a shadow hit her eyelids. When she woke, she saw the cause of her rude awakening—a large head had cast a shadow on Iseul who had gotten used to the sunlight on her face.

"Ah!" she yelled.

"Ah!" The man was also startled, as he echoed her screams. "Who are you, woman? Or man?" He squinted at her.

Iseul jumped up till her head started spinning and her vision blurred. Her hand reached for the gun until she realized she was in the garden of the Golden Palace and she must have fallen asleep. *Oh no,* she thought. Mi-Jung must be so worried. Taking one quick glance at the man, she decided he did not look like a threat and began pacing towards the gates to find Mi-Jung.

"Iseul?" the man said. "Is that you?"

She had heard that voice before, but who was this man? Jung-Soo? She certainly didn't hope so! She turned slowly towards him and found a man, a little more rotund than she remembered Jung-Soo being, with a beard that hadn't been shaved for weeks and in a muddied attire of a farm boy.

"It's me!" the man said, "Dae-Gun!"

Iseul squinted. "Dae-Gun!" Sure enough, it was him, just fatter and jollier. Three years had passed after all, and she had seen him just that once in the night when the village was under siege.

"I can't believe it! You're here! Jung-Soo said you'd be back, but I didn't think this soon! How have you been? Tell me, how is everybody from the village?"

"I'm fine," she said, even as she glanced to the left and right of Dae-Gun to look for another familiar face.

The idle search for their mutual friend didn't go unnoticed as Dae-Gun shifted and fidgeted with his fingers, unsure of what to say, and how to break the news.

Iseul tried to be polite, though she kept looking past Dae-Gun's heavy frame towards the door that led inside the Golden Palace. Why wasn't anyone else coming out? Surely, all this ruckus would have woken someone inside, if there was anyone else.

Was there anyone else? She searched for the answer in Dae-Gun's face but found nothing but anguish, perhaps even remorse.

No, Iseul thought. Hadn't she just received a letter from Jung-Soo less than a month ago?

"I'm so sorry," Dae-Gun managed to find the words.

***

[Three weeks earlier]

"A medal of honor upon discharge!" Dae-Gun read from his

dismissal papers. "Can you believe it?"

Jung-Soo held the same pearly white page with his name written on it. "Kim Jung-Soo." It was not his birth name, but he had earned it—one that was not tainted by his father's communist past and one that he could proudly return to Iseul with. He pulled out that tattered sheet his father's code had been written on. "As it guards its cubs," it read. Only the latter half of the sheet remained as the first half had been ripped by Doo-Hyung that night by the tiger's cave.

"I can believe it," Jung-Soo said as he held Dae-Gun in a headlock. "You'd better believe it because if anyone deserves it, you do!"

Dae-Gun was blushing, though he was glad the headlock made blood rush to his head. They had been stationed near the 38th parallel since the Yeoju ambush and had the honor of working with the highest military officials in the negotiation process. Needless to say, they had been highly recommended by Commander Lee for their extraordinary translating and negotiating skills.

It was early summer, hot, but still manageable. There would be some last-minute negotiations and meetings, but there was an air of optimism and a spring in every soldier's step, including the commanders' and the general's. Jung-Soo even thought the North Koreans seemed perkier during the meetings than their usually gloomy selves and that was always a good sign.

Of course, the 38th parallel was still a very volatile place, perhaps even more so in the past few weeks leading up to the final negotiations, if only to show the other side that they would not yield under unfavorable terms of ceasefire. It had been the same for the past two years when turmoil erupted in the border when a treaty was imminent.

Yet, most of the time, Jung-Soo and Dae-Gun sat on their asses, waiting for their orders as they traded in one packaged food for another, tasting the whole assortment of semi-bland but filling meals over the past few years.

Dae-Gun even managed to track down a guitar that used to belong to an American soldier who had died in battle, though he needed Jung-Soo's help to get it in his possession. It required great tact and finesse to convince the house band of the 65th Infantry Regiment to "lend" Dae-Gun their dead friend's guitar. In the end, Jung-Soo convinced them that Dae-Gun would solemnly trade his services as a guitar player in the house band for the guitar. That was the way negotiations usually worked with Jung-Soo—convincing the subject that he was doing himself a favor for doing him a favor. And so Dae-Gun found himself in a win-win situation with a new guitar as he resumed his post as a military performer every Tuesday night.

And on those lonesome nights Dae-Gun was called away to play guitar or to translate an important exchange between the Korean and U.N. forces, Jung-Soo wrote long letters to Iseul and tinkered with the radio dials, hoping another new station would have found its way onto the radio waves again. And when he had done all this and laid in bed in those early summer nights, he thought about that ordinary conversation he had had with Iseul, stuck in the school shed.

'Have you thought about what you want in life?' Those were his own words to Iseul—foolish words of a boy who thought his whole life was set before him even before it had started.

He looked all around and saw men and boys who dreamed of the end of war, and of returning to a home that would welcome them back to the life that they had left behind. Iseul will go on to be an excellent instrument craftsman—that much he was certain of. Dae-Gun would become a musician and a translator. He saw the world as a much smaller place now that he had gone through war. The ties they had made with brothers who spoke a different tongue, the roads and radio towers his father had imagined for the Korean Peninsula—Jung-Soo was certain all these would come to pass and more.

Yet, in those early-summer nights, Jung-Soo couldn't help but wonder, what about him? What would he do and what would he become once the war was over? He hadn't thought past getting back to Yeoju and reuniting with Iseul. And then what?

He would think of something; he always did. He imagined the world after the war and he was in it, doing his part to make it a better place. He loved the radio. Maybe he would go to school to become a proper mechanic or an engineer even. He had no money so he'd have to work for a while. He didn't know how or when, but he knew he liked wires and batteries—lots and lots of batteries. Hadn't such simple parts come together to create the one object that had defined his childhood? He would have gone mad if it weren't for that tiny device that connected him to the world outside that helped him envision life beyond his tiny village. He wanted to share the same experience with others—create a window that brought people outside their current realities. That, and instant communication. His hands were getting tired of writing, but most of all, he worried that not much would be left of Iseul's hands making all that paper for so many people. If only he could pick up the radio and talk to Iseul as they had in Yeoju. That would be the way of the future. He would talk to Doo-Hyung and Gil-Dong in North Korea and call up his friend Richard Martin in America. Every man would be entitled to such a life.

He let a smile creep up his face, wondering how he ever thought he was so different from his father. He finally saw the vision his father had of Korea—a nation strategically connected to the rest of the world by both land and sea, not trapped in by their enemies as he had originally thought. He did not know what he was fighting for while he was fighting, but he found himself nodding as he thought of such a Korea.

Jung-Soo had once promised he would be different from his father and he still held on to that promise; he would not die as his father did, full of regret—full of plans for the future that he forgot to see what was right in front of him. Jung-Soo knew that's what his father would have wanted.

It was a Tuesday evening as Dae-Gun strapped his upgraded leather guitar case on his left shoulder to hike down a small hill for his routine performance. He raised his hand and gave one wave as he exited their tent. It meant, 'see you in a few hours.'

Had Jung-Soo known it would be the last time he would see Dae-Gun, he would have—well, he wasn't sure what he would have done differently.

The light from the setting sun shined on the side of the tent, making the inside almost unbearably hot. They had spent the last two summers in a tent much like the one he was in as he remembered to thank the gods for summer because winter had been twice, no thrice as unbearable.

He leaped out of his tent mattress and made his way outside, taking in the last remnants of the spring freshness. It was a new season, and a new chapter of his life would soon begin. He took out his dismissal papers and placed it against the sunlight, but the bleached white fibers of the page did not do much to block the sun from his eyes. He favored Iseul's browned paper; though it wasn't quite as white, it had character.

The smaller hills of the Korean Peninsula surrounded him as tents upon tents did too. The Panmunjom building where peace talks were well on their way stood in bright blue contrast against the grass of the hills that had begun to grow in. Next year, they'd grow all the way out, without soldiers trotting them and men dying on them.

Just ahead of him was a patch of land that looked like it had once been a rice paddy. It had been taken over by a field of dandelions, whose circular fuzzy seeds had caused the entire camp grounds to lay awake at night, sneezing and coughing when they had first bloomed in the spring. It seemed like just last week the entire field was covered in yellow; now the green stems of the flower made it seem as if rice were growing instead.

He found a stray stem, still covered in white fur as if frozen in time. *Strange*, he thought. He felt an odd sense of camaraderie with the little flower that had failed to bloom. He walked towards the field with a limp he had gotten as a little souvenir from the battle at the tiger's cave. His left leg hurt for a while, but when the pain had subsided, he had grown quite attached to the limp that he figured he'd just keep it.

The dandelion yet-to-bloom called for him and Jung-Soo heeded.

A thought came to him, as accidental as his discovery of that single flower in a bed of dying ones. What if? His thoughts trailed on. What if he hadn't been born to his father? What if he hadn't met Iseul? Would he still be standing there in front of the little unborn flower? He plucked the fluffy dandelion from its stem and gazed intensely into its guised center.

Probably not. He would have still been a soldier, but one with a family waiting to hear from him. He would have still written on Iseul's paper, though he wouldn't have thought twice about where it had come from. There probably would have been a girl too, at least one or two he could imagine himself marrying once the war was over. All these could have been his life, like the lives of a million other soldiers he had fought with and against, and the other millions who had lost their lives in this thing called war.

In the past weeks as he saw the end near, he had been toiling with the question of where he truly belonged. If he really had the choice, where would he go: North or South?

He didn't know the answer to that, and frankly, it was a futile thought now that a series of chance events had brought him exactly where he stood. He blew into the dandelion as the individual cottony seeds burst into a hundred separate ones. He made a wish, just as it was customary and just as he had done weeks ago when the entire field was covered in a bed of white. They flew upwards and in swirls, following the indecisive current of the wind before disappearing somewhere south, he thought. He couldn't be sure because the sun was in his eyes.

It was not the sun that shined in his eyes in that moment. Only as he laid there in a pool of his own blood did the thought occur to him—*snipers*. The sniper's scope should have been his clue, if only he hadn't been so preoccupied—if only he had looked into the hills as he usually does when he exits his tent.

It did not matter anymore. He wondered if his wish would change now that it had become his dying wish. No, it didn't.

Jung-Soo died with his eyes open and his head tilted slightly south, his soul easing out of his body as it followed the seeds of the unborn dandelion, going where the wind led him.

He was going home.

CHAPTER 44

영혼: Spirit/Soul*

- * Pronounced 'Yeong-Hon'
- * Not to be confused with the common Korean name, Yeong-Hoon
- * Not be phonetically confused with the capital of the Republic of Korea, Seoul

***

[Present Day]

"I'm not ready," Iseul stated, adamantly. She turned her head away from the man who claimed to be Yeong-Hoon and Jung-Soo alike. "And even if I were, I won't be going anywhere with you."

She was sulking; it was understandable. The man leaned back to enjoy the view of the modern stars that reflected on the surface of the river Han. It was as if he were young again, lying by the stream next to the unfinished cabin, dreaming of a future with Iseul. He looked past the bright lights and into the northern darkness, wondering if anyone else thought about the people who lived across the border.

"Why should I go away with a man who abandoned me over sixty years ago!" Iseul seemed to be fuming inside. It was endearing. "I kept every promise, didn't I? You told me to wait for you; I did. You told me to make you that damn guitar, and I did. What did you ever do to keep your promise?"

The man knew when to be silent when the woman talked. He listened with his head down, ever so slightly nodding to indicate he was listening.

"Don't you start telling me how hard it was to write those letters and that you're a man of few words!" Iseul began again.

"Say, whatever happened to those letters?"

Iseul blinked, unsure. "That's none of your business!" she retorted. "I mean, isn't it a bit too late for you to prance back into my life and act as if you've never left?"

"I didn't just 'prance' back into your life, thank you very much!" the man protested.

"No?"

"No."

"Why should I believe a single word you say? For all I know, you've been lying to me this whole time."

"And you're an old lady who's lost her mind."

Iseul crossed her arms and turned in her bed so her back was to him.

The man wasn't too worried. In a minute, she'd forget about the whole conversation. Oh god! He'd have to start all over again! He didn't mind, he told himself, just as long as his sweet Iseul came back to him. He sighed. Who was he kidding? This was the real Iseul he knew and loved—the one who had always tested his patience.

"So," Iseul said, pouting. "If you didn't just prance back into my life, how did you come back? Tell me, if you really are who you say you are, what did you write about in all those letters you sent me?"

Jung-Soo shrugged. "Nothing really important." She still looked cross. "A hundred ways to say the same thing. You know, you've read them all, and I'm certain you haven't forgotten."

"Remind me," Iseul said with a taunting look. "You're the one who said I am an old lady who's lost her mind!"

He rolled his eyes. "You want me to say it? Right now?"

"I must be certain you are who you say you are. You wouldn't want to dupe a dying woman, do you?"

He blushed as he leaned over to her right ear and whispered the words.

"I believe you...mostly," she said with a grin that highlighted every wrinkle on her face.

But as quickly as her lucid moment came, it left as she eased into that perpetual look of confusion. "Where am I?" She looked around and found comfort in the bright lights outside. "My children, I remember… I had children, didn't I?"

"You did. Two boys and a girl," he said with a somber smile. "You met a very nice young man who took good care of you."

"Did I?" she said, trying to dig through her mind. A feeling was all she could grasp and it was good. Somehow, she knew he wasn't alive anymore and she could sense that it used to make her sad, but it hadn't in a while. He was in a better place. "I can't imagine you were very happy when I married this nice young man," she teased.

"It was fine," he said, mechanically. It clearly wasn't.

She chuckled. "Alright, I believe you."

"It's fine because that nice young man was my best friend."

"Your best friend?" A figure popped into her mind and made her cringe. She saw a chunky boy with a beard, wearing dirty farmer's clothes. "Him? He doesn't seem like he can take care of himself!"

Jung-Soo guffawed. "Don't worry. He shaped up quite well after the war. And you're right. You two took good care of each other."

"That sounds more like it," she said, content as she closed her eyes for a brief moment. She heard the sound of waves crashing on the shore as the song of her mother rang as a wordless tune in the space between life and death. Was it really time?

"What happened?" she said, anxious and uncertain. "Oh god…' she said, remembering pieces. "You really died, didn't you? The rice…they took it…they took the rice from us. Those bastards! How could they? It was meant for us…for our children, for our future together. Come back, you thieves!" She grappled towards something in the air.

The man took a hold of the hand that flailed. There was nothing to be done; it was all in the past, irrevocable and unchangeable.

"What have we done?" Iseul said, exhausted. "This is not how it was supposed to end." She saw the trucks and massive machines come into her beloved village as they pulled away boulders and rocks from the tiger's cave, taking every last sack of rice within. The villagers stood watching as their legacy was ushered away.

"It is for the future of our country; it is for us all. We will all be prosperous or none at all." Those were the words echoed to them that day—false hope and meaningless promises.

She saw the birth of her three children, the long days of working and the death of her husband flash before her eyes. All the while, the lights had gotten brighter and reached higher towards the stars with each year that had passed. Where had she been? She did not remember much of the time between...

"I was wrong...I did it all wrong..." She wept in remorse. For the first time, she saw the empty room where a single hospital bed filled the empty space, bought with the money she had earned from all those years of toiling... toiling... with nothing to show but furniture. She spited every last one, including the guitar that stood lonesome by her side.

She saw herself as she truly was—a bitter old woman, dying alone as her children toiled and toiled out there in the bright lights for their own children to one day toil some more.

She blinked and the man was there again, holding her hand. Who was he again?

"I am Yeong-Hoon," he answered. "I am here to remind you that you are not alone and that you have lived a beautiful life."

It was he who stood by her side when her only living parent was killed, and when Jung-Soo had fled the village, standing by her in those lonely first few years after her husband had passed. He filled the space between missing, the space between grief and pain, even accompanying the old lady in those long pauses when nothing ever happened as she sat by the phone, waiting for one of her children to call.

"Oh yes...Yeong-Hoon," she whimpered. "I know that name. I've heard it before."

It was her daughter. What was her name again? She had always stayed up waiting for Iseul to come home. She had the talent her father had with the guitar—self-taught, or had her father stayed up late with their daughter to teach her? She could not quite recall the details. Yes, that name, Yeong-Hoon! Her daughter had named the guitar on one of those long nights as she stayed awake practicing.

"Your daughter, Baek Ji-Sun," the man said. "She has a beautiful daughter too."

"That's good..." she yearned to see them again, one last time. But she had had her chance with her children, and she knew that time had already passed. "They'll understand, won't they? That I did it all for them, for their future..."

The man nodded. "They do."

"That is all we ever knew. We did not have parents, never both living at the same time, orphaned, starving, looking for the next meal. They must understand…"

The man kept nodding.

"You understand, don't you? I didn't want to forget you!" she said.

It was ten years after the birth of her first son when she first traveled back to Yeoju with a stack of letters neatly wrapped in a clear plastic tarp, kneeling beneath that pine tree to bury Jung-Soo's letters. Even decades later, after her diagnosis, she knew exactly where to kneel to dig up those letters again as she read through each one as if to commit them to memory. She had pulled just one dirtied sheet, tucked it into her pocket as she wrapped the rest of the letters and placed them back where they belonged. She felt guilty—she had never once forgotten about the boy called Jung-Soo even as her husband had stood by her for decades and laid dead in the soil adjacent. *Traitor,* the note said, but she willed herself to remember the Jung-Soo she knew, not the one on the page.

"You understand, don't you?" she said like a broken record. But Iseul did not believe a single word that came out of her own mouth; how could she expect anyone else to? She saw the lights outside, but it dimmed in comparison to the ones she had seen with Jung-Soo all those years ago. "At least the rice had gone to good use," she said in melancholy.

Iseul was struck with *missing*, remembering the day when father and mother took her to the tomb of King Sejong and pointed to the great wall of Pasaseong-ji. Her parents had never gone outside the bounds of Yeoju let alone the bounds of the Korean Peninsula. They did not know that cherry blossoms bloomed brighter and larger in Japan, nor did they know that the rose of sharon in Korea grew more plump and red in the middle than anywhere else in the world, attesting to the blood shed by its people as the *han* of the nation raised voices to push the Japanese out for good. She wished to go with them to the ends of the earth. She wished to reunite with them and tell them all that they had missed and take them to places they've never seen before.

"Soon," the man said.

"Soon…" Iseul repeated. "Remember that day in the school shed?"

"Like it was yesterday."

"Remember you promised me that the world is changing and we'd soon live in a world where we can dream all we want?"

"Soon, Iseul," the man reassured her. "Weren't we just young kids roaming the mountains and fields of Yeoju? Look where we are now."

"Old and wrinkly, about to die," she sighed.

"We are but waves that wash up on shore for a brief moment until we are called back to make way for new waves."

Iseul nodded. "Yeong-Hoon, the man of the sea—the funny man inside the radio, taken here and there by the wind and ocean waves, wandering until you briefly found a home and then wandered off again," Iseul chuckled, repeating the words she had said to Jung-Soo that day in the shed.

The man laughed. "You've always had an overactive imagination."

"I did, didn't I?" Iseul said as the realization washed over her. Yeong-Hoon oppa—the man she was betrothed to, the man who had a limp and was her father's apprentice, the man who had spoon-fed her in those weeks after her father was murdered and Jung-Soo disappeared—was never there.

"I was there," he corrected. "I witnessed every second of it. But you did it all by yourself; you are stronger than you remember. You got back on your own two feet, buried your father's ashes by your mother, started making drums for war, and started the paper-making movement in your village."

A wet trail made its way onto the pillow where her head lay. She saw herself shoving a note into the sound hole of the guitar, thinking she were underneath the pine tree, burying that single letter with the others. She had meant to keep it safe. She knew it was a recent memory.

"I just really wanted you to come back. I prayed every night to Buddha, to the gods of the mountains and sea, and even to the western god to bring you home to me."

The tears cleared her eyes as she saw the man for who he really was—Jung-Soo, standing in uniform with blood on his left leg. It was just as she recalled on that final day she had seen him alive. She should have hugged him tight, made sure he knew that she loved him. If only she had known how things would end...

"I know," Jung-Soo said. "I really wanted to come back, come home to you, and build the life that we've always dreamed of. But there is more than what meets the eye."

"More than what meets the eye?" Iseul repeated.

He nodded. "I was there with you all along. I am here now and I certainly didn't just prance back into your life, did I?"

She giggled like she was thirteen again. Iseul could see now. Yeong-Hoon had always been there, and he was more than Jung-Soo's specter, passing on from life to death.

He was more...

***

[Present Day]

I let at least five trains pass me by on the way home from the cemetery, and I probably would have let the next one pass by too were it not for the crowd of men and women shoving to get in on their way home from work.

I hate closed spaces, and I tried to imagine I was back in Yeoju where rice paddies and mountains stretched on and on. Instead, I closed my eyes and I was a sardine in a very tight can. I sighed and breathed in the musky air. Twenty minutes and I'd be home.

Breathing in the sweaty scent of dress shirts and caked makeup, I wondered if I'd ever be as lucky as any of them in the future. It was only six in the evening and these were the lucky ones who actually got to go home on time. I wondered if things would change in my time, or if it will get progressively more difficult since couples didn't have as many children, and the weight of the dying generation rested on the young working class.

I thought of granny Iseul all alone in her hospice bed. I decided after dinner I'd ask mom if we could stop by to see her.

"Jia, is that you?"

"Yeah, mom. I'm home." I walked into the kitchen where my mom was in the heat of cooking. Dinner had always magically appeared on time and if food wasn't on the table, there was always money left there for me to deliver in. I watched as she tossed the fresh vegetables into a bowl and sprinkled sesame seed and oil onto it. It smelled amazing.

"What's for dinner?" I asked.

She opened the top of the boiling pot. "Kimchi stew." She dipped a spoon in and placed it against my mouth for me to taste.

"Good," I nodded. "I love granny's recipe. You should teach it to me sometime."

"Now that you have time, you can learn while helping around the kitchen," she said. For some reason, I felt like she had already moved on from the idea of making her daughter into a diligent student to preparing me to become a good wife. I looked away.

"Did you know that this isn't granny's recipe?" mom said. It was the first time she had mentioned granny without first being asked.

"It isn't?"

"Oh god no!" She shook her head. "She was terrible in the kitchen. Your grandfather taught it to her."

A man in the kitchen? I thought. That was almost unheard of, even today. But somehow, it didn't surprise me.

Mom chuckled. "He made sure your grandmother got all the credit. Your grandmother wasn't known as the best wife in town, and your grandpa did his best to keep up appearances."

I remembered that conversation I had with dad about grandpa's burial. It was something I said I'd get around to asking mom about.

"A few months ago, I was talking to dad about grandpa and why he was buried in Yeoju."

"You talked to him about my dad?" It was strange to hear mom talk about grandpa in such informal terms. It was uncommon in that generation to say anything other than 'father.'

"Yeah, he told me he lost contact with his own family during the war, so he was buried with granny's side of the family. He also mentioned something about grandpa refusing to be buried in the national cemetery. Any ideas why?"

"Oh Jia, your grandpa never had a family to begin with. He was an orphan and your grandma was his only family. I think he was just so enthralled with the idea of having a family of his own that there was no question where he'd be buried."

"An orphan? How come I never knew?"

"There is a lot that you don't know, dear," my mom said.

It certainly seemed to be the case. I never once questioned why I was in Seoul; I was born here, and this was my home, but that hadn't really been the case for my parents and certainly not for my grandparents.

"I don't understand," I said. "Why did they leave Yeoju if they both felt at home there?"

"Simple. They needed work. Your granny was a carpenter, your grandpa a musician. After they helped reconstruct their village, they left Yeoju and moved to Seoul where the reconstruction was at a much larger scale and people were willing to pay for carpenters."

"Carpenter? I thought she was a luthier."

Mom shook her head. "Who would buy instruments when they couldn't put food on the table or a roof over their heads?"

I nodded. "It makes sense." I can imagine it would have been hard work. Seoul was completely decimated by the war, unlike some of the smaller villages that still remained mostly intact. "It must have been a blow to grandpa. I imagine he had big plans when they moved to Seoul," I said.

She shook her head again. "Your grandpa had a way of taking life in his own stride. It was your grandmother who had a difficult time; she was the dreamer between the two. Even when their carpentry business was suffering, she was adamant that they begin selling instruments alongside their cabinets, tables, and chairs. Your grandfather put up with a lot. You know your grandmother can be a handful."

A tinge of resentment tainted her words. Mom had always disapproved of granny's stubbornness and loud voice. I can still recall her saying that if granny weren't rich or successful, no one would have stood for her behavior. If you ask me, they were two sides of the same coin, my mom's stubbornness manifesting in the stern belief that women should be homemakers and are happiest when they do what they are genetically inclined to do.

"Did you know your grandfather changed his name sometime after the war too?

Mom seemed to be in a talkative mood. Perhaps she too had a lot she wanted to say, but we had always been too busy, afraid to bother the other.

"Apparently, your grandfather went back to the orphanage where he was raised and found a document with his given name on it. He used to be called Park Dae-Gun."

"Park Dae-Gun," I repeated. It sounded awfully familiar. "Park Dae-Gun! I know that name! He fought with a man called Jung-Soo and Richard Martin in the battle of Yeoju. Do you know if he ever mentioned a man called Jung-Soo?"

The stew was ready to boil over and mom jumped towards it

to turn the flame off. She waved her hand for me to lay a cloth on the table to place the hot pot on.

"Jung-Soo? No, it doesn't ring a bell," she said, moving the boiling hot kimchi-stew from the stove to the table. "It doesn't sound like a name from that era. Doesn't it sound like a common name someone your age would have?"

My shoulders slouched again. "Oh, I guess it does."

Maybe they were all friends during the war or at least acquaintances. Still, here was yet another piece of evidence that a man named Jung-Soo really did exist and he had fought in the war. Whether or not he was the man who wrote the letter to granny, or whether he was one of the communists responsible for the death of the villagers in Yeoju seemed to be a question that may never be answered.

I sighed and changed the topic. "Is dad going to be back home soon?"

"He's running late."

We sat at the table, just the two of us, as we dug into granny and grandpa's kimchi-stew. The picture seemed to come in focus, though many of the pieces were still missing. It made sense that granny wasn't a good cook; she had spent her entire life at the workshop and later, the factory. Wasn't her old room proof enough that creating instruments was her life's obsession?

All I remembered of grandpa was his unrelenting smile and a rotund belly that I had sat on top of as a child to watch TV. He was there one day and gone the next. I was young and thought he would come back, but he had vanished from my memory before I had the chance to miss him.

And what about dad's side of the family? They lived so far away from Seoul that we rarely got to visit. The past few years had been more difficult with the pressure of the exam mounting. Dad's side of the family was from Busan. It was the second largest city in Korea, and though the city life didn't particularly excite me, perhaps another trip was in order.

"I'm glad we talked," I said after a long pause. "At least I found out grandpa was an orphan who had two aliases. It makes me feel less ordinary."

Mom chuckled. "Then we should have told you earlier! Back in the day, we never spoke of such things because it was a disgrace to the family. You know what else? Your grandpa was also a fluent

English speaker who translated for the highest officials at Panmunjom when they signed the peace treaty! Of course, he lost most of his English in his later years, much in the same way the previous generation forgot how to speak Japanese once the occupation ended."

"A fluent English speaker? How come he never taught you a single word of English?" I said, jokingly.

She gave a sly grin. "Who knew English would be so important today?"

"You could have helped me with my exam preparations!"

"Hindsight is 20-20."

We giggled as friends would for a while.

"By the way, Jia, I noticed one of the framed pictures is missing from your grandmother's room," mom said as if granny were still living with us.

"A picture?" I said. "Oh, you mean the old page that has the company name printed on it?

Mom chuckled. "I'd forgotten all about that old thing."

Her response intrigued me.

"I've always hated that tattered page. Your grandmother and grandfather had one of their biggest fights about it."

"A fight? Over a piece of a paper?"

Mom nodded. "Your grandma wanted to throw that thing away and print a new one on a nicer, thicker sheet of paper, but your grandfather snatched it from your grandmother, framed it and gave it back to her as a birthday present."

I laughed. "Grandpa has some sense of humor."

"It drove your grandma crazy. Your granddad wanted to 'preserve history,' as he used to say, but it seemed granny was all about the new."

Granny all about the new? I doubted that. Weren't the framed pictures of celebrities with traditional Korean instruments proof of the contrary? The page probably reminded her of a time she wanted to forget.

"Well, I'm glad grandpa kept that page framed," I said, though she would never know the extent of how much I meant what I said. She would have probably disapproved if she knew it was one of the clues that had kept me digging into granny's past and was one reason I hadn't done so well on the national exam.

"What about you, mom?"

"What about me?"

"Do you have any secrets I don't know about? Or will I have to wait until I have children of my own who want to pry into your life?"

"Umm…" she said deep in thought. "I have two names as well."

My jaw dropped. "No way!"

She proudly nodded. "It was quite common back then. I have one official name and another nickname my friends and family knew me by."

"What is it?" I sat at the edge of my seat.

"Yong-Sun."

"Yong-Sun…" I repeated. It rolled off my tongue awkwardly. "The question is, did dad know about it before he married you?"

She shook her head with a mischievous grin. "And you know what else he didn't know about me?"

"What?"

"That my parents registered my birth certificate two years after I was born. I am actually a year older than your father!"

She laughed so hard it sounded like a roar.

"Can you imagine the look on your father's face when he found out he had married an older woman?"

Utter shock, just as I was in. "You're joking, aren't you?"

"No, I completely duped your father! And there you have it—secrets you can pass on to your children about their grandmother!"

It was the first time we cried laughing until a lull of diminishing euphoria settled.

"Hey mom," I said. "Sometimes I wish you would have fought harder for yourself, you know?"

She was thinking. "In our generation, we believed obedience was the way to happiness."

I could tell she still believed it, though she had grown to understand that she was reciting words spoken to her from a time she could no longer vividly picture.

"I know," I said. "But times are changing." It was all I could say to express what I felt, though I knew it was not enough.

Years later, as I waited in front of a vending machine to pull coffee for my superiors while my male colleagues sat comfortably in their desks, I would come to realize what I had meant to say to my mom that day. I wished she would have fought harder to make the world a better place for her daughter.

I am happy to report that we had many such nights together, sharing the same stories, each time adding a few other details here and there, some more exaggerated than others. Not to worry, we included my dad in the conversations and what a glorious sight it was to see his expression as he retold the story of my mother's less than truthful identity.

My grandmother Ji-Iseul died that night with nothing but Seoul's vast night lights to lull her into that deep and infinite sleep. We mourned for her, regretted the time not spent with her, and swore we would make time for the family we had left. We cried and laughed together at her funeral.

Granny left mom that old guitar and I made sure the letter was placed back into the sound hole of the guitar where granny intended it to be. She was buried to the right of grandpa's plot, underneath the pine tree that overlooked the family burial grounds. For a moment, as we laid her body to rest, I thought we might find a pile of letters wrapped in plastic as I had seen in my dreams, but no such letters were found.

We did not know from where, but birds came that day and sang us a tune, a homecoming for a woman they somehow fondly remembered.

We stayed at the burial site for hours and hours, talking and reuniting with the odd cousin, uncle, and aunt. The songbirds eventually returned to their nests as relatives drove off one-by-one in their cars, back to the city.

"Jia, we'll wait in the car okay? Hurry up!" My mom called me as she began packing up the car.

"Alright," I said.

There was something that had been in the back of my mind the entire day sitting by the grave—something that one of the villagers had said at the burial. It was, in fact, the man eating ice cream at the bus ticket booth who said, "It's a shame that they'll be bulldozing the old paper and instrument factory next month."

I recalled the workshop next to granny's humble home that had been covered in dust as if not one person had stepped foot in it for decades. Yet, to think that it would no longer exist!

I watched as mom and dad filled the car trunk with ceremonial trinkets and attire they had bought from the hospice store. There was still some time and granny's old house was not too far away. I ran as quickly as I could against the dying light, taking the large route past the east gate, hiking around two hundred meters until I saw the faint outline of the two buildings side-by-side.

I knew what I was there for. I barged into the old workshop and saw my own footprints made just a few months ago with pages and pages strewn all around as it had been left more than six decades ago. The paper windows had been left open as the sunset angled itself into the room, lighting the place as if it were mid-day. One-by-one, I gathered the pages on the ground, on the countertops, and under rocks. It wasn't much, but it was enough to make a small notebook.

Years later, as I sat in a windowless office, waiting for the time to tick by on the electronic clock on the corner of my computer, I wondered if granny ever loved the job she had, regardless of whether or not she was successful. I could imagine it made her forget time ticked by so relentlessly. I willed myself to be grateful that day because I had zapped through my work and had the leisure to even be bored that the work day wasn't over yet. In those few minutes of exhaustion-induced madness, I would pull out the browned notebook and ponder, mourn even for a life-never-lived—nostalgic for something I had never known.

I wasn't sure what I'd do with the notebook and it would be years before I'd begin digging into the art of papermaking, and the rich history and heritage of the hanji. Another few years would pass before I would realize the impact my granny's handmade paper made during the war and how it had brought families, strangers, and even foreigners together.

There is good in the world, I'd like to believe. But my grandmother's story was so far in the past that it felt no more real than a legend. If time flowed then as it does now, I am certain there would have been more in between the momentary successes that amount to a heart-warming story—that there is a reality in which these moments came between long stretches of *missing*, in which time would turn anger into resentment, which would then churn into the sweetest wine of bitter *han*.

Everyone remembers the tiger in the *Legend of Tangun* as a failure. After all, he had failed to follow the simple dietary and lifestyle instructions laid out by the Prince of Heaven and consequently had not turned into a human. But what if the tiger did not fail, but had refused to grovel at the feet of those who dictated who should and should not be considered human? It is he who roams the cave, not out of regret for having failed to become human, but to declare his defiance and to remind others that he was once a tiger who decided he would become human on his own terms.

Still to this day, the bright lights blind me. I often forget that there had once been a time when the only bright lights in this beautiful city came from bombs that blanketed the stars with ash and decimated the very ground I stand on. I rarely ever think of our brother land still plunged in darkness just beyond the lights.

There are no landmarks to tell us what had happened other than a cemetery and museums that come in vogue once a year—a true testament of how our people tried our very best to forget the problems we cannot fix, as if the war isn't still ongoing, marching to the rhythm of progress made in the past sixty years to eradicate all memories of our most recent trauma.

Make no mistake; the *han* still burns within us. We are reminded every so often of this unique brand of injustice by the rise in international tension from our non-compliant North Korean neighbors, only to momentarily reflect upon our past and relinquish our reflections as phantoms of a past that we hope will never return.

I miss my grandmother Iseul; I miss my grandfather with a deeper longing of never having known. Still, the bright lights taunt me; they command that I march forward, remember what must not be forgotten, lay to rest that which haunts us, and invent—imagine even—the world we must fight to create.

I promise I will not forget.

***

[Last day of summer, 1953]

There was much to be done in the little Wasteland of Yeoju, where land, fields, and mountains alike were naked and ashy from three years of war and desolation.

Iseul volunteered to plant trees as her extensive knowledge of how the trees had once been came in handy for the task. Occasionally, she would put down the seed of a pine tree a few more times than was necessary, but in the scope of the massive mountains they roamed, it was negligible.

A visitor had stopped by in Yeoju in those first few weeks after the war—a man named Richard Martin. Iseul figured it was one of the American men who had helped during the battle of Yeoju. He wore the clothes of a Korean farmer, tied a headband to soak up the beads of sweat and plowed the land with Dae-Gun. The young girls giggled at the gangly man who swung the plow all wrong, but some were nice enough to offer the occasional slice of watermelon that had sprung in a hidden patch.

"Thank you," he said, as he bowed to receive the lukewarm and soggy slice.

The children joined in the rebuilding of the village, skipping stones on the dusty road just as they had done before the war. They were not helpful in the traditional sense, but the laughter and occasional fights of who would get to play with which rock was a reminder of the once-lively village, as it cultivated the drive to dig deeper into the ground and place pillars stronger and higher to ensure the laughter will never cease.

And when the foundations of the Wasteland were set, the villagers traveled to the northern regions of Yeoju to help their distant cousins in their own reconstruction efforts, just as they had come to aid the Wasteland in their time of need. The west gate was enlarged to make transportation easier and so began a small-scale trading cooperation within the region.

The east gate remained somewhat deserted other than the two mammoth tanks that rolled past its gate and rolled out with truckloads of rice. The villagers watched as men with crisp white paper came with official documents from President Rhee himself, promising to make the country better than it had ever been before, richer and brighter than in all of Korea's history. He had come in and made promises as all men in power do, and as swiftly as they came, they left with the rice that their sons, daughters, mothers, and fathers had toiled years for and had given their lives for.

"Stay with us," Dae-Gun said to Richard Martin as he pulled the headband off his forehead for the last time.

"Thanks for the offer kid, but the last plane home is leaving in a few days."

"Home…" Dae-Gun said those bitter-sweet words, thinking of his lost brothers. He was thinking a trip back to the orphanage was in order. "Anyone waiting for you?"

"Sweet Home Alabama. My sweetheart's waiting for me," Richard winked. "She just doesn't know it yet."

Dae-Gun always thought the man had a funny accent. Maybe

everyone in Alabama had it too; he couldn't be sure.

"You're welcome to visit anytime, my friend," Richard said, patting the chunky boy on the back.

"As you are too, my friend. Hold on just a few minutes, will you?" Dae-Gun ran as fast as he could to the Golden Palace and into the oversized warehouse. He took his rubber shoes off and then his left sock. With a smelly old sock in one hand, he poured rice into it from the small store of rice they had managed to extract from the cave before the tanks had arrived.

Dae-Gun ran back and handed the sock to Richard.

He looked in. "Rice?" He smiled crookedly and thanked him. In that moment, he was certain he had had enough rice for a lifetime, but he knew what the gesture meant. Hadn't he come to visit Yeoju because he had nothing to take home but memories of dead bodies, and years of resenting these yellow people because he longed to go home? It took three years of war to even open his eyes to the people he and his countrymen had come to fight and die for. He was certain there was more to see and more to learn; he had barely picked up a few words during his years in Korea!

Richard looked down at the rice-filled sock and swore he would be back again. "Gam-sa-hap-ni-da," he thanked him. "But between you and me, I've really been missing freshly baked bread, maybe even some biscuits and gravy to go with it. You must come to Alabama and try our family recipe!"

"Bread?" Dae-Gun said with a subdued sense of aversion. He knew what it was, but it was not widely available and frankly, it tasted a bit...stale and bland. "Yes, bread is certainly lovely, but there is something incredibly appetizing about the steam coming off of freshly steamed rice. The grains that are stuck together just melts apart in your mouth."

Richard Martin thought about all the times he had eaten rice and could vaguely remember something that matched Dae-Gun's description. "I suppose so. I'll have to remember that when I cook this up."

"Good! It's settled then," Dae-Gun said. "Rice for old time's sake so you won't forget us." Even though the soldier hadn't been the keenest, Dae-Gun knew Richard would cherish that smelly sock as he held it close in his embrace, twirling the top of the sock so that every single grain would be preserved within.

Summer had reached its peak and was on a decline that humid

night when Dae-Gun came back to the Golden Palace to rest. He walked past the iron gates and in the corner of his eye, saw a figure laying on the garden grass.

Dae-Gun jumped. "Good god! What are you doing there?"

"Haven't you ever seen a lady star-gazing before?" Iseul said from the patch of grass. She had gotten back into her hanbok, though at night, she took off the colorful front layer to cool off as she once again transformed into a ghost-like figure.

"No, I don't suppose I have."

Iseul patted at the grass next to her, beckoning him to come join her. He gladly did, only hesitating for a moment as his mind drifted to his fallen friend.

You see, my dear readers, Dae-Gun had slowly been falling for this country girl, much in the same way Jung-Soo had. But if Dae-Gun was superstitious before he came to Yeoju, he certainly became superstitious in those first few weeks with Iseul.

Every night, when the villagers returned home to rest, Iseul hiked to her father's workshop, chopping and sanding away at planks of pine and cedar wood. She had begun making Jung-Soo's guitar.

Dae-Gun once followed the girl back, and though his intentions were to remain hidden in the shadows, he quickly tripped and fell on a root that protruded from the ground. Iseul giggled. His poor attempts at spying on her did not go unnoticed, though she held her breath and let him believe she didn't notice for a while longer until he tripped again and tumbled into the workshop.

He scratched the back of his head and tried to laugh off the pain. "I thought I might help you, just in case you needed it," the boy said shyly.

Iseul put Dae-Gun to work, though every piece of wood he touched seemed to either chip away at the wrong place or cause the most painful splinter on his hands, even puncturing his boots to stab him in the feet.

"I swear this workshop is haunted," Dae-Gun yelled as he held his bleeding hand again.

Iseul laughed. "Don't blame the workshop for your utter lack of talent!"

"I have talent! I swear!"

In the years to come, Iseul would find this out for herself. He was not a half-bad carpenter, just as she was not half bad in the kitchen.

From the second night onwards, Dae-Gun brought his guitar over to be measured, inspected and act as a supplement to Jung-Soo's handwritten measurements. But it was an ongoing process that required the guitar to be present at all times. Dae-Gun didn't mind. He sometimes even played for her, and it had the odd effect of keeping Iseul awake, which was unlike her usually drowsy self.

They were back at the Golden Palace again, lying side by side as they breathed in the slight chill that had set upon that summer night, gazing into the sky. Dae-Gun wanted to touch her hand and feel it for himself. He wanted their shoulders to touch as they laid there together, but it was fear that hindered him—fear of divine retribution.

Dae-Gun never mentioned it, but he could swear his friend was watching him…very closely. Or perhaps he was watching her. It was hard to tell since Dae-Gun and Iseul spent so much time together. He breathed deeply and contented himself to be lying next to her.

Iseul revived a time when life was simpler, easy even. She was a simple girl thrust into a complex world. She watched the sky, mostly wondering what Jung-Soo had seen in the stars, but she would never know for sure. Who knows? Maybe that's why he liked them.

What was next? She hadn't a clue. When had she ever? *One step after another…* Those were the words of her father that came to her in an epiphany laying underneath the bright stars.

Jung-Soo. It ached to even think of him. He had come by storm and left with it, leaving her with memories and half-forgotten dreams that were left in pieces in a valley somewhere in the mountains.

But that cabin had been Jung-Soo's dream; he had always been the one to think and plan for the both of them, but he was gone now. She glanced over to the bearded boy who laid in utter peace. It seemed she would have to do the thinking from now on.

It was about time. There was something she had kept in the back of her mind, dismissed as a foolish dream of a young girl who didn't know any better. She still didn't know any better, nor was she even much older, but she figured now was as good a time as any to begin.

One step after another…

Dae-Gun's superstitions eventually eased as the weeks became months and even the fateful year, 1953 ended. He could not pinpoint the exact moment Iseul decided she was ready for someone else. It might have been when she leaned in ever so slightly as their shoulders finally met. He reckons it had something to do with the chilly wind that arrived later that night, but who could be sure?

All he knew was that she slept so peacefully, her snores accompanying the sound of hooting owls that were probably telling her to be quiet. But Dae-Gun didn't mind, not one bit at all.

Iseul fell asleep under the bright lights of the night sky, at peace—finally ready. She slept like a child as she once used to when her mother sang her into the most delightful sleep. She hummed to her mother's singing, complete with her angelic voice and lyrics just as Iseul had always imagined it.

The End

Author's Closing Remarks

Why is the Korean War called the Forgotten War? It's not that we forgot the war happened all together, nor did we forget it because not as many people died in the most gruesome and fashionable way possible in modern warfare.

Perhaps it is aptly named the Forgotten War because Korea had very little to do with why the war was fought in the first place. We were just caught in the middle of a story that is not our own, in an international dispute of those who deemed it more convenient that death and suffering is better contained outside their own borders.

Then again, that is an apt summation of our entire war history.

I've always thought the name of our country had some relevance to the topic at hand:

한국 (Hanguk): the nation of Han, or Korea

The Chinese root of the word "Han" has nothing to do with the phonetically identical words Han (one), or Han, the sorrow and suffering brought on by centuries of injustice that leaves our spirits aching. Yet, I wonder if Han (Korea), Han (one), and Han (such sense of injustice) are not one and the same, or at the very least, inextricably intertwined.

We are not a nation of heroes. We are a nation of survivors who somehow made it out the other end and kept going, just waiting for the next bomb to drop. For a while, I wondered if we had all given up, stopped thinking about what we had fought for, or if we had fought for anything at all. We are all struggling and squirming towards an end that we have yet to figure out for ourselves. Sometimes, I fear we are a nation who has lost the ability to define ourselves.

In the two years it took to write this novel, I kept asking myself: what happens to a nation still fighting the same war three generations later—still fighting for the same reason for centuries on end? What does independence mean to a nation that has never known what it means to be its own nation?

I look at my grandmother and wonder what her generation would have to say to us before they all pass into history. All the more so because the Korea of my grandmother's youth is nothing like the one I know, with barely any landmarks to show for her time in this world as *The Miracle on the Han* catapulted South Korea from a third world to a first world nation in less than four decades.

Once, I asked her what she thought about the American military presence in South Korea. She was neither thrilled nor hateful. "It is what it is,' granny would say. They gave us democracy, but they too came and made us into their own image, like the rest of them. I guess that is what we do—morph so much that we don't even realize this was never us to begin with.

This is just a story—one that imagines the world as I wish it were, or perhaps as I wish it weren't.

I have two grannies, one who is just as opinionated, stubborn and loud-mouthed as Iseul. My other granny died a cripple, smiling because she had been beaten if she displayed any other emotion. I never knew this granny and I only know this by rumors whispered by my aunts and uncles. Sometimes, I feel the loss of something I never had in the first place. Perhaps the greater tragedy is never having known.

Our whole family moved away from Korea when I was just a one-year old in the early 90s. I had come back to Korea for university seventeen years later and was utterly shocked! It was not the Korea my mother had always romanticized and certainly not the one shown on television!

I asked my mom one day, "What do you think went wrong in Korea?" She said Korea used to have "jeong" and a sense of community when she was growing up. Like the word "han," "jeong" is another cultural significant word that is difficult to translate. It signifies love that comes from time spent with one another, and from years of toiling together. Mother said all our "jeong" was gone, and we have become so selfish and individualistic. She said these words as if resenting the Americans for coming and destroying our one redeeming cultural glue that had been so flippantly discarded as we decided to put on our western masks.

We used to actually spend time with our families and our extended families. Now, I see children go to academies and come home to sleep before being herded out of the home again at dawn. Fathers don't come home until the children have all gone to sleep, and a mother who decides she too wants to be career women, is forced to come home just as late.

Children are left alone and placed in the care of people who want nothing but money from their parents. I spent a year working for a company that promised a parent to send an 11-year old child to Harvard for a fee of 8000 dollars a month. We stuck the kid in a windowless room for six hours after school as we forced her to look down at a textbook the entire time. We tell our children it is a small price to pay for one's future. We tell them everyone else is doing it.

Is it really such a small price? Would you trade your childhood for Harvard?

We have lost our *jeong* and have replaced it with an underdeveloped sense of individuality. No one really knows when to say stop to the immensity of a trend that has snowballed out of control.

It is high time that we begin questioning who we are.

"We sacrifice the *now* for the *future*," we say it as if it is our national anthem. But don't we know that who we are now is a map to who we will be tomorrow?

When my younger cousin turned eighteen, she came to me for advice. I told her that our mothers aren't wrong when they tell us to stop eating so we'll be skinny like those girls on TV. That way, we'll find a decent husband. I told her that's just their way of telling us that they love us and want the best for us. It is, after all, the only reality they know.

Times have changed, and the reality we know is fluid. I told her that reality becomes reality because it is perpetuated or changed. If we believe in another reality and make that happen, *that* can be our new reality. We are not doomed to live a life pre-planned by our parents, by a man who claims to be in charge, nor by some sadistic god-figure who condemns us from birth to tragic death.

Fact: South Korea has the second-highest suicide rate in the world and the highest suicide rate for a member of the OECD.

I recall the famous words of encouragement written on Mapo bridge ("suicide bridge"): "What kind of father will your child remember?" I understand the motivation behind this message. Surely, a father who kills himself is implying that he doesn't love the child enough to continue living—continue providing for. It is meant to deter a father from abandoning his child through suicide. But wasn't it the crushing expectations that we place on our fathers that caused him to look over the railings of the bridge and find comfort in falling to his death? Didn't society tell him that he is unworthy because he failed to live up to its impossible standards of what it means to provide for one's family?

They say a collective society is one that isn't lonely. Perhaps it may not be 'every man for himself,' but it is 'every family for themselves,' where crushing another man's child is acceptable so long as my own child is able to rise to the top. Isn't that the very pressure we place on our children in the current education system that places friends at odds against one another, giving children the impression that love and acceptance is given upon fulfilling the condition of success? Isn't that the pressure we place on parents who must fend for their children at all costs because the world outside the home is against them?

Solution: Leave the country, but that too requires money. Either that or stop having babies. At least that's the solution our generation of newly married couples talk about.

I understand I am overreaching and overanalyzing comments and anecdotal evidence of rumors heard in confidence. Nevertheless, these are the stories that have stayed with me over the years, and continue to stir up the *han* in me.

Tragedy is the language of my ancestors. We are born into it, grow into it, and eventually breath it till it is our last dying breath. It is so cliché that is almost sickens me to repeat it: *we do it so the next generation will not have to*. It is noble, self-sacrificial, and undoubtedly the reason why so many bright lights shine upon this city that is the true "city that never sleeps" in this part of the world.

Yet, I wonder, if tragedy is all that is shown to us—if a life of sorrow is the only one exemplified, how can we expect ourselves to become anything else? God knows, reaching that elusive goal of success isn't the answer—a temporary fix as cosmetic surgery is to happiness in this country. How much more rice do we need to store to be happy?

It is a symptom of a democracy that Tocqueville foretold almost two centuries ago, before all modern forms of democracy hailed money as god, prevalent in America and spreading like wildfire to the rest of the world. Nothing wrong with that. But it is my observation that such a symptom of democracy is acutely intensified in a nation like Korea whose turbulent history makes us more vulnerable to the lures of comfort and security that money brings. But is more money the answer to reclaim our sense of security stolen from us from centuries of foreign invasions? Money to escape the misery of living as a powerless commoner who are treated less than human because of their status, and more to ensure our children do not have to live such demeaning lives?

*Rice and more rice...*We are sucked into the lies of our leaders telling us how to define ourselves—telling us how they can help us reclaim our forgotten lands and dreams. We buy into their false promises, all the while, forfeiting our own claim to define ourselves, to push ourselves to achieve our own versions of success, and to make promises to ourselves that we will amount to more than just bigger and brighter lights.

And what do we have to show for it but a string of Presidents who usurped more power and more money than they were given by the people. We are a nation of dead Presidents, assassinated, killed by suicide, and impeached.

We go to the ocean for inspiration and respite from our hard lives. Yet, we peer in and are met with the souls of nearly three hundred victims, mostly children, lost at sea due to the greed and insolence of men who deemed their bottom line more valuable than the safety of those of us who put our trust in them (I am referring to the Sewol ferry accident).

Where were our leaders when tragedy struck? What had they been doing all this time—obeying orders with unquestioning loyalty? Apparently, our chief of state was busy beautifying herself in her chambers. Either that or doing some voodoo religious shit while the President ordered her men that she was not to be bothered until she was done—not to be bothered while our children drowned.

Children are strong; they are intuitive, and they have the will to live just like the rest of us. It's a tragedy to see all sense of the innate humanity quelled by men "older and wiser," telling us it is best to sit still and let the water wash over you. Did we not train one child to think about the orders he or she is given, to question it and choose what one's fate will be? Instead we are busy drowning the disobedience, and crushing the defiance out of our youth.

We are a nation running on the fumes of men who think their status, age and money is wisdom incarnate.

I guess I'm just tired of excuses, of shortcuts and burying reality under a guise of bright, shiny lights. Sometimes, I wonder if all we've become is a skeleton of what we used to be, encased in a steel infrastructure of a heartless country who seeks nothing but one's own share of high-rise metal.

"We lay down our own dignity so the next generation will not have to." But how can we teach our children dignity when we ourselves do not live such a life?

I can't help but believe King Sejong the Great created the Korean alphabet to distinguish Korea as a proud nation amidst the frightening immensity of China and the powerful forces surrounding our Peninsula. Is it not time to do ourselves a favor and give ourselves the chance to find out who we are as individuals?

Remember that dream I had about bombs falling as Seoul's vast infrastructure crumbled around me? I really had that dream while writing this book. My grandmother really had given me a tip of war: Don't go running about when the bombs fall; it's better to die comfortably in your own bed.

With all due respect, I say we run the hell away, figure out what we are running away from and what we are running towards. We are worth more than a string of forgotten wars and faceless names. We too have the right to question if the world as we see it is the world that we fought so many wars for.

I began looking—really looking into my mother's life. I memorized the way she looked when she put away the dishes, gently snored in her sleep and went on her knees to mop the last bit of dust off the floor that already appeared to be clean. She peeled the orange all the way down to the core so my dad and I wouldn't have to. All the while, her wrists were slowly degenerating from some form of osteoporosis. I asked her about feminism, abortion, cultural incompatibilities, religion, and gay rights.

My mother is a product of her environment and from a generation that was told that a woman's sense of self-worth is tied to a man and her children. She doesn't know any better, though she has a vague idea that her life could have been better. Still, we talk and talk and talk. I've stopped trying to change her mind, and she grew tired of trying to change mine too. We cherish the hours spent explaining and eventually learnt not to be offended by disagreement.

I cannot help but think there is only so much the previous generation can imagine about what a better future looks like. All the while, I wonder if we are doing the right thing, just adopting the American mask as if it were our own.

And to those who look at Korea's skeletal bright lights and mourn for our lost history and culture, I plead you do not. This story is not meant to romanticize a past that will never return. Certainly not! It is to ask: how can we move forward mindfully without forgetting the past or becoming lost in it.

This is our brief interlude of freedom before the bright lights come raining down on us again to destroy then rebuild us in their own image. In this brief idyll of freedom and peace, between generations before and after us that will wage war, what will we do?

We do it so the next generation will not have to. This is the cry of men and women who have already died for our freedom, for our right to choose our own path and to define what happiness is to us.

Sometimes I wonder if the *han* of our nation is what defines us so much that each generation brews its own unique concoction of *han* to suit our current tragic needs and to wallow in our repeated history. It is certainly a sobering thought.

But I see hope outside my window in the form of candlelight, overlooking a mass of men and women, old and young, children of all ages, participating in our innate right to protest against our current government. I am proud that such a young democratic nation is able to come together to protest in peace. We are a people who will not stand for anything less than the democracy promised to us. That, I am proud of.

I hope that in our generation, our *han* will manifest in more than bouts of rage or the occasional protest, but perhaps in the somewhat counter-intuitive form of curiosity. I hope that it will spurn us to question who we are as individuals and cultivate that same sense of curiosity and self-love in the next generation.

Here's to us, who understand that we must usurp our right to discover who we are in the here and now, so help us god, we raise another generation who know nothing but the tragic existence of bleak hopefulness, imagining a future that might never come.

Till the day the *han* of our nation rests in peace.

Disclaimer of A Personal Nature:

As is self-evident with the topic I have chosen, I write this piece of fiction to reflect on my own internal struggles of ethnic, cultural and family identity I have been harboring for much of my adolescent and adult years. I am *not* a Korean in the traditional sense, nor will I ever claim to be anything more or less than the unique and often confusing concoction of cultures I've been exposed to.

It is *not* my intention to present Korea as if I completely understand it as a native Korean.

In fact, because I have struggled with the idea of a one-size-fits-all type of identity, I feel it strange that such a thing as "a native Korean identity" should exist at all. Yet, in all the places I have lived, I have never found a place quite so fiercely adamant that such a thing does, in fact, exist.

I have no doubt that a collective mentality was a crucial part in the evolution of our nation whose survival hinged upon fighting off the constant infiltration of the "other." It is then understandable that a strong "us" must form to fight against "them."

But as an individual whose identity remains a question mark, I have come to resent the words often spoken to me: "You are *not* Korean, so how would you understand?" It is as if I have no right to imagine or pry into the dirty family matter that is present in every culture. But as often as I have heard this phrase, I have been told the complete opposite: "You are Korean, so you must know." If I had listened to any of these voices, there would only be one character in this story and this person would live somewhere in the clouds, waiting to fall into a non-existent country where he will be accepted in a truly colorblind, and culture-blind utopic society.

Like my earlier disclaimer states, this is not a story about Korea, though I understand I am contradicting myself to a certain extent. I do not necessarily write for some political agenda or social issue, but from a place of feeling misunderstood. I am certain this is a universal experience to an extent, manifesting in far worse than being an expat Korean.

I hope that this particular exploration of the topic of identity will be a source of enlightenment and curiosity for all those looking from inside of Korea, outside or somewhere in between.

Inspiration and Acknowledgments

This story is inspired by an actual event in my grandmother's life. At around the age of seven, my grandmother stumbled on an underground bunker at her school where she found a particularly white sheet of paper. Without knowing the contents of the page, she had taken that peculiar sheet home. Her brother later discovered it to be a communist pamphlet and contacted the authorities, leading to the arrest and execution of over thirty communists, including my grandmother's own teacher. For years after, my grandmother's brother was on the run from family members of those executed that day.

From this story, I began piecing together a plot that centered around paper, contemplating on its various forms (trees that are cut down to make paper, household items to instruments that seem to give voice to inanimate pieces of wood). It was my way of creating an allegory of South Korea's development as a country, rising from the ashes of war to become the modern and highly developed nation we are today.

But most of all, I wanted to show South Korea in a more realistic light, not just in another rags to riches story, and certainly not as merely the country next door to North Korea. This is a study of national and personal identity, wrapped up in a coming-of-age adventure. It is a warning, but also a call to action to begin to search for our own personal voices thereby our national voice despite our long history of foreign invasions.

Pieces of the plot have also been taken from my experience translating for U.S. and Filipino veterans of the Korean War who were visiting South Korea at the time. The little boy "Zion" in the story is dedicated to one Filipino soldier who had come back to Korea in search of a Korean boy who had been his "errand boy." At the time, not a single journalist was interested in an interview with a Filipino soldier. I am indebted to these nameless soldiers.

I also want to take the time to thank my dad who patiently answered every question I had about what it was like living as a country boy, farming rice and whatever else that grew on land. Likewise, I thank my grandmother for sharing her experiences of war and my mom for obliging my endless tirades with a loving and non-judgmental ear. They have been invaluable sources of inspiration.

Likewise, I thank those who took the time to comment on my work to help make it as unobstructed as possible.

Last but certainly not the least, this is dedicated to both of my grandmothers, Oh Hak-Sun and Lee Young-Im.

Works Consulted

Chae, Han Kook; Chung, Suk Kyun; Yang, Yong Cho (2001), Yang, Hee Wan; Lim, Won Hyok; Sims, Thomas Lee; Sims, Laura Marie; Kim, Chong Gu; Millett, Allan R., eds., *The Korean War*, Volume II, Lincoln, NE: University of Nebraska Press.

Hopkins, William B. (1986). One Bugle No Drums: The Marines at Chosin Reservoir. Chapel Hill, N.C: Algonquin.

The Korean War in Colour Documentary. [online] Available at: https://www.youtube.com/watch?v=cPsqKzRvujs [Accessed 14 Sep. 2017].

Yoo, Boo-wong (1988). *Korean Pentecostalism: Its History and Theology.* New York: Verlag Peter Lang. p. 221.

"5th Cavalry Regiment- Korean War." First-team.us. http://www.first-team.us/assigned/subunits/5th_cr/5crndx03.html.

"The United States, South Korea, and "Comfort Women". Stanford University. *January 22, 2009.*

About the Author

Young-Im Lee was born in Mokpo, South Korea and relocated to Manila, Philippines at the age of one where she grew up in an international setting. She graduated with a BA in English Language and Literature from Seoul National University and an MA in English Literary Studies from the University of York(UK). She currently resides in Seoul, South Korea.

Connect with Young-Im

Goodreads
https://www.goodreads.com/goodreadscomyoungimlee

Facebook
https://www.facebook.com/youngimleeauthor/

Website
youngimleeauthor.wordpress.com

If you enjoyed *Forgotten Reflections: A War Story*, please leave a review on Amazon, Goodreads, Barnes and Noble or your preferred store. Reviews help books reach a wider audience.

www.ingramcontent.com/pod-product-compliance
Lightning Source LLC
Chambersburg PA
CBHW050101120726
47904CB00004B/1171